READER'S DIGEST CONDENSED BOOKS

OPPOSITE: TOY HORSE-DRAWN PUMPER (c. 1874)

READER'S DIGEST
CONDENSED BOOKS

Volume 5 • 1977

THE READER'S DIGEST ASSOCIATION

Pleasantville, New York

Reader's Digest Condensed Books are published every two to three months at Pleasantville, N. Y.

CONTENTS

The Melodeon

In the memorable last Christmas of childhood
a boy becomes a man

A condensation of the novel by

Glendon Swarthout

Illustrated by Brinton Turkle

During the Great Depression thirteen-year-old James is sent to live with his grandparents on their Michigan homestead. Here he begins to understand the real meaning of love and pride when his grandfather embarks on a project involving the family's melodeon, counterpoint to the lives of four generations. Then, on a hard-times Christmas Eve, in the midst of a howling blizzard, James is faced with the most important challenge of his young life: to find a way to restore a father to his son and to assure the son that his father has not forgotten him, even in death.

ONE

I WRITE these lines in the fifty-fourth year of my life. They begin a tale I might long ago have told, but an intuition stayed my pen. And so I waited. The years passed. Now, this autumn, as the days wither and the stars recede and another Christmas nears, I am old enough at last to tell it truly, and young enough at last to know what it means.

When I was thirteen years of age I was literally farmed out by my parents—put on a train in Philadelphia and sent west to Michigan, to live with my grandparents on their farm a few miles south of Howell. It was the 1930s, the decade of an unexampled American depression. My father had lost his job, for months had walked the streets seeking another, and his relief checks of ten dollars a week did not suffice to pay rent and raise a growing youngster. I was fortunate to have a farm to go to, for farmers, everyone said, were luckier than most. No matter how hard the times, they always had enough to eat.

Will and Ella Chubb were my mother's parents. Their farm was half a section homesteaded and cleared by Will's grandfather, a man named Major Chubb, who came west in a covered wagon in 1836. The land had been kind to Major, and his son Ephraim, and Ephraim's son, Will, good farmers as their Yorkshire forebears had been before them. There were twenty-acre fields now, and

9

fox-squirrel woods and green pastures for the sheep and a huckleberry marsh and a lake, deep and blue and troubled with pickerel.
There was a barn, with haymow above and sheepshed and horse
stalls and cowshed underneath. A large granary stored the harvests
and a treasury of machinery—thresher, tractor, hayrake, tedder,
mowing machine, plows, ensilage cutter, cornhusker, stoneboat,
reaper, cultivator, and several wagons. The house itself was white
frame, with a bathroom, a screened porch, a parlor with a pump
organ, and a feather-tick bed in my very own room. If one had to, I
soon decided, this was a good place to be an orphan.

I wore overalls. I walked three miles to the one-room schoolhouse next to the church at Chubb's Corners, where another boy
and I constituted the seventh grade. After school I helped Will,
my grandfather. I learned to hitch and unhitch the team, to fork
shocks into the ensilage cutter at silo-filling time, to pick sheepnose
and Baldwin apples in the orchard, and assist at the cider press.
I tried milking but simply couldn't get the grip of it. I was thirteen,
all arms and legs and thumbs, and a city boy, and much less a
menace to the cows when I did domestic chores for Ella, my
grandmother.

I dried dishes, split kindling, fetched wood—and I separated.

In the woodshed, behind the kitchen, stood a cylinder of steel
with two spouts and a wooden handle. You poured pails of fresh
milk into the open top, placed a milk can under one spout and a
cream bucket under the other, bent your back, braced your feet,
laid both hands on the handle, and began to crank. I had no idea
what went on inside the separator, but considerable did, for a
growl commenced to emanate from the rig, which, as you revolved
the handle faster and faster, increased in pitch and volume to a
howl, then to a scream. Milk streamed from one spout, cream from
the other, and a deafening music, appropriate to any number of
swashbuckling scenes, assailed the ears.

You could crank and crank and close your eyes and be at sea
in a typhoon, masts toppling as you fought the wheel to keep your
schooner's bow into the wind. You could be a fearless cowboy
galloping to the rescue, spurred by the heroine's shrieking as she

clung to the edge of a cliff. My favorite fantasy, though, while cranking and puffing, was that I was spinning the prop of my silver monoplane, *Spirit of St. Louis*, taking off from Long Island, then clutching the controls as the engine droned over the dark Atlantic until we landed, the eyes of the world upon us, at Le Bourget.

And always, always, there were eggs. Ella kept two hundred chickens. Good layers, she called them—a characteristically rural understatement. Those leghorns were veritable volcanoes of eggs. Evidently they never left the nest long enough to cackle, scratch, or cluck, for I gathered, washed, and crated hen fruit till I couldn't face it boiled, fried, or scrambled on my breakfast plate. Ella sent two crates to a grocer in Howell each week. They brought eight to twelve cents a dozen, and her egg money she divided evenly—half for staples and half to be hoarded for an automobile.

It was a source of shame and bitterness to her that the Chubbs were the only family thereabouts without one. The Cadwells, down the road, trucked her crates to town in a Model A, the Stackables had a Nash, even Joe and Abby Henshaw strutted a Model T. While drying dishes I learned from Ella that three years previously, when she had her husband almost at the point of investing in a car, a smooth-talking salesman had persuaded him instead to trade in his old tractor for an expensive new Rumely Oil Pull. That was the beginning of payments and the end of the automobile. Will was pitifully "soft on farm machinery," she confided. This tragic flaw had kept them machinery-poor throughout their married life, and though she had put her foot down about indoor plumbing, they still made do with a gas lighting system, the only one in a neighborhood elegant with electricity.

And so she saved her money for a Studebaker. When I asked what was wrong with a Ford, she said nothing. However, an advertised feature of the Studebaker was "Free Wheeling," and she believed it implied that you could get up speed, turn off the ignition, and coast for miles, thereby using little gasoline. But when I argued that you could buy a lot of gas for the difference in price between a Ford and a Studie, Ella dismissed the matter. She would not admit to inconsistency. She was a woman.

That was my problem. She was not supposed to be. She was supposed to be a grandmother. I didn't know Will and Ella well when I arrived at the farm, for I had visited them only twice as a child. It took me till Christmas to comprehend that they were human beings and to love them deeply as such. "Grandparents," meanwhile, was an easier category to handle. A boy could easily separate "grandparents" from "people." Grandparents were a little unreal, like actors in a play. They might have been young once, have loved and hated and grieved, been weak and stubborn and inconsistent, might have known fear and passion, rage and wonder, but these feelings they had long ago forgotten.

Yes, I was convinced at the start that grandparents were gray and kind and frail and soon to die, and that was all.

IT WAS an eventful autumn. The church at Chubb's Corners burned down in October. Electricity had just been installed, and faulty wiring was probably responsible. The men of the congregation, farmers every one, set to work on Sundays and in rainy weather, and by the first of December a new church was built. Money for materials was hard to come by, and while the structure was unpainted on the outside and unfinished on the in, and lacked lighting, it had a pulpit and a wood stove and benches for pews. The Lord, the Reverend Leon Ledwidge assured his small flock at the first service, would be pleased.

The second event was Will's coming in from the barn Thanksgiving eve and informing us that one of his old ewes was pregnant. "Don't believe me," he added. "I don't believe it myself, but she is. Four months along, I calculate."

"What's so impossible?" I inquired.

"Sheep," he said, "never lamb in winter. I know. I've kept sheep for forty years. Lambs are dropped in April, May, or June."

"If I was a ewe," said I with urban impudence, "I'd drop a lamb any old time I wanted to."

He looked at me and tugged an end of his drooping mustache. Will called it his tea strainer, because when he drank green tea from a saucer he could strain the leaves through it. "No," said he, "if you were a ewe, you'd get around to lovering when you and the ram were ready. Would you like me to explain?"

My grandmother hopped over that indelicate puddle quickly. "Maybe we'll have a lamb born for Christmas—wouldn't that be nice?" she said, putting the morning oatmeal on the stove so as not to waste the overnight heat. "Now that I think of it, Will, I've seen pictures on calendars, of the Christ Child in the manger, with Mary and Joseph, and there's usually a lamb nearby, and that was Christmas. So lambs must have been born in the winter back then."

"Those pictures were painted by painters," stated her husband. "Painters do not keep sheep."

The third event was something which didn't happen. It didn't snow. The days were gray, November had turned cold, skim ice appeared on the lake, and Will put a barrel of cider in the back-yard, but there was no snow. The neighbors mentioned it at every meeting and over the party line. The winter wheat would suffer.

But it was winter now, unmistakably, and Christmas neared. A time or two, walking home from school, I shed a tear. I wrote my father and mother every other day rather than every week. The barrel of cider froze over. Will chunked out the ice and let it re-freeze again and again. When there were but a few inches of clear liquid at the bottom, he clasped the barrel fondly to his chest and carried it into the basement. Meanwhile he studied the old ewe from every angle, he felt her woolly sides, he shook a skeptical head, but she was irrefutably pregnant.

Then, on the day before Christmas, we woke to a world of snow. A real blinger of a blizzard whirled down upon us from Canada. I gathered the eggs in the afternoon, but the day was so dark and the flakes so thick that, stumbling knee-deep in snow already, I located the house only by its lights. I wore a corduroy cap, with the flaps down over my ears, yet the wind almost tore it off. Will declared he had never seen such a storm.

At supper, Ella said her customary grace. "Dear Lord, bless this food to our use and us to Thy service," she murmured, then added a postscript: "And let the storm pass so that we may worship Thee tomorrow. Amen." Christmas fell on Sunday that year, and my grandmother never missed church. For dessert she served a short-cake filled and topped with black raspberries she had picked in August and canned. The Lord may have blessed the food to our use, but I am sure He envied us that shortcake.

Will went to the barn again after supper to see to his expectant ewe. Usually I dried the dishes and Ella washed, but tonight I volunteered to do them all while she prepared a hen for tomorrow's dinner, scalding the bird and plucking and drawing it, then setting it to cool overnight in the woodshed. In the morning she would pinfeather, stuff, and truss it, and let it roast while we were at church.

"As long as I live," said my grandmother out of a clear blue sky, "I'll never understand your grandfather."

I accepted that. If you had been married to a man forty-six years and still didn't understand him, you probably never would.

"I told you," she went on, "he's soft on machinery."

"Yes." I paid her only partial attention. Using the pump beside the sink, I had filled a dishpan and teakettle and put them on the stove, and both were boiling now.

"He can't even bring himself to kill a hen."

"He can't?"

"I have to do it myself, always have. And he's certainly soft on the neighbors."

"How come?" I lugged the dishpan to the sink and set to work, dispirited by a tower of baking pans in addition to the dishes.

"Why, everyone around here owes him for the summer threshing, and last summer's, too," she said. "That's how he justified buying a new tractor. 'I'll do the threshing for the whole township,' he told me, 'so much a bushel, and that way we'll pay off the tractor and you can have a car to boot.' And I let him. And what happened? They didn't pay a penny last summer or this and they don't intend to." She plucked fiercely.

"Why not?" I asked.

"Because wheat's down to twenty-eight cents a bushel, so they're all storing it in hopes of a better price. If he'd only ask them to pay something, I know they could, most of them. But he won't.

'Times are hard,' he'll say, 'and they're my friends.' That's what I mean—soft."

"Oh," I said.

"But he can be as stubborn as a mule, too. When that ewe drops her lamb, you watch. He'll insist it isn't a lamb at all, because it's the wrong time of year." She put the heart, gizzard, and liver away in a bowl for eventual gravy. "I'll give you another example. Did you know that when he was six years old he could play the organ beautifully?"

"He could?"

"But when he heard his father was dead he never played another note?"

That stopped me. "He didn't? Why not?"

"Stubborn," she replied. "His mother begged him, she told me so, but he never would. That's what I mean—hard and soft at the same time. I'll never understand him if I live to be a hundred."

I rinsed from the teakettle and stood there drying. Some of the family history my mother had told me. Ephraim Chubb went away to war with the 10th Michigan Cavalry from this very farm in 1863. His young wife, my great-grandmother Sarah, received a letter in 1864 saying that he was missing in action. Sarah waited, as did her small son, Willy, who had never seen his father. Five years later, in 1869, she got a second letter from the War Department. Ephraim's remains had been plowed up near Strawberry Plains, Tennessee. He had been killed on a raid and interred hastily by his comrades. He was shipped home to Sarah, who buried him in the Putnam Township ground near the church at Chubb's Corners.

"Maybe that's why Will never played the organ again," I speculated. "I mean, after he found out his father was dead. Maybe his heart was broken."

"Fiddlesticks," she said. It was her only expletive.

In a few minutes we heard Will enter the woodshed and stomp the snow from his boots. I finished the dishes, Ella the hen. Will came into the kitchen and warmed himself at the stove and said he'd never seen such a storm and the ewe was about due. Then Ella said there would be just time to have the tree before my telephone call. That was to be my Christmas present from my parents. They had given up their telephone, but would go to a friend's house and call me at eight o'clock, and we could talk precisely three minutes. So Will and Ella and I went into the living room.

The tree was a tall one that Will and I had cut in the huckleberry marsh, and while it lacked the ornaments I was accustomed to at home, Ella and I had strung about a mile of popcorn. And when she lighted the candles, the tree was lovely. There were only two presents, both for me. My grandfather's was a walnut-handled pocketknife, my grandmother's a scarf she had knitted, long enough to wind round and round.

"Gee, thanks a lot," I said. "They're really swell. I don't have anything for you, though. I don't know how to make anything and I didn't have any money."

"Why, you're our gift, James," said Ella, and kissed my cheek.

Will put a hand on my shoulder. "We haven't had a pup around here for a dog's age."

We wished each other Merry Christmas, then pinched the candles out and returned to the kitchen, for it was nearly eight o'clock.

They sat at the table and I stood by the wall phone. After five minutes I decided someone must be on the line, so I lifted the receiver. Universal sin absolves individuals, and since everyone did it, listening in on a party line was not considered sinful. But the receiver hummed and I hung it up.

Wood hissed in the stove. Over the table the clock ticked. Wind boxed the house. Under us the joists creaked with cold.

"Just imagine," said Ella, crocheting a potholder and making conversation, "a body speaking to someone in Michigan all the way from Philadelphia. Whatever will they think of next?"

"A night like this, maybe the lines are down," Will suggested. His wife frowned at him.

"Now when they call," he said to me, making amends, "don't fritter your time away having us talk to them. We can write. It's your present and you use every blamed second of it."

"Thank you," I said. My palms were damp. I was developing a lump in my throat.

When the phone finally did ring, and we held our breath counting three long and one short, I seized the receiver and could scarcely say hello. The lump in my throat was as big as an egg with a double yolk. Then the sound of my mother's voice broke the egg and me with it. She warned me that she was watching the clock and three minutes was all they could manage, and that rendered me even more inarticulate. I determined that she and my father were well. She ascertained from me that I was well and so were Will and Ella. The weather in Philadelphia was clear. We were having a blizzard. My father, to whom I next talked, had not found a job. One of Will's sheep was about to have a lamb. I had a dandy new jackknife and scarf. There was an excruciating pause, after which we wished each other a Merry Christmas and they were saying good-by and I heard a click and hung up the receiver and couldn't turn around because my eyes were swimming.

"I have an idea," said my grandmother briskly. "Why don't we go into the parlor and I'll play the melodeon and we'll sing a carol or two?"

I swallowed hard, still facing the phone. "I didn't know you could play."

"I can't very well anymore," she confessed. "My fingers, the arthritis, you know. That's why I never do. But I used to. Sarah taught me, Will's mother. Anyway, I'm game if you are."

She nodded at her husband and I tagged after them through the living room, where they opened the sliding doors, and on into the parlor. Will turned up the gas, struck a match, and we had light. I looked at the melodeon as though for the first time.

It was a handsome instrument of cherry wood, thirty-three inches high, forty inches wide, and twenty-one inches deep. The hinged top folded up and back and became a music rack, revealing a five-octave keyboard and above it, in gilt lettering on the fall board, the name of the manufacturer: MASON & HAMLIN. At the base were two ten-inch-wide pedals, which were pumped to fill the bellows, and they were covered with frayed needlepoint in a floral design. At the left of the pedals a small wooden treadle protruded. It was called a swell, or a loud and soft damper. To adjust

17

the volume, one depressed it with the left foot while double-pedaling with the right. There was a bench, covered with needle-point, too. Ella told me later that the coverings had been done by Sarah, my great-grandmother, in 1911, the year of her death.

Ella folded back the top, sat down, and played several carols, singing along with Will and me. We sang "Silent Night" and "We Three Kings of Orient Are." She hit a few black keys when she should have white, and when I glanced at her fingers I saw that they were gnarled by arthritis. She pumped with vigor, though, and we sang with zeal. The tones of the melodeon sounded true and faintly elegiac. The union of their two old voices with my soprano, which would not change to tenor for another year, was not unharmonious. But something gave me gooseflesh. Other presences seemed to join us in the parlor on that Christmas Eve. Other voices, quavery and distant, seemed to swell our choir. It had never occurred to me that ghosts could sing.

We started "It Came Upon the Midnight Clear." Suddenly my grandmother stopped. "Oh, Will!" she whispered. "I've just had the most wonderful notion!"

We waited, mouths open.

"The melodeon—let's give it to the church for Christmas!" She rose from the bench. Behind her spectacles her eyes were wide. "They haven't even a piano—it would help the singing so much. I never play it—and you won't. Why don't we give it to the church?"

Will tugged his mustache. "No harm in it, I expect."

"Tomorrow's Sunday and Christmas both—we'll surprise them—when they come in, there it will be!"

"Tomorrow?" He shook his head. "Ella, you forget. This blizzard. I couldn't haul it there tonight."

"Can't you take the team? With a wagon?"

"There'll soon be drifts three feet deep. No team could—"

"Fiddlesticks!"

"Girl," he said, "I hate to disappoint you, but there won't even be a service tomorrow. The roads will be drifted full."

She turned away and lowered the top of the melodeon over the keyboard. "If only we had an automobile," she muttered.

That angered him. "No damned automobile would get there either! Not even a damned Studebaker!"

"How would you know, Will Chubb?" she demanded. "You've never owned one!"

I held my tongue. I was embarrassed and incredulous. In my four months on the farm I had never heard them say a cross word to each other. Old men were not supposed to call old ladies "girl." Even more shocking, grandparents were not supposed to quarrel, ever, and especially on Christmas Eve.

Will glared at his wife's intractable back, then glared at me, then nodded at the doors. "I'm going to the barn," he said gruffly. "Have you ever seen anything born?"

"No. No, I haven't."

"Do you want to?"

"Gee, I don't know."

"Make up your mind. I don't know what in Hades that old ewe will have—fish or fowl or a two-headed Hottentot from Timbuktu—but she can't have a lamb. Not this time of year. Well?"

"I guess so," I said. "Okay."

"Then get a move on."

I took my new scarf and we stepped into the woodshed and pulled on our galoshes, and stuffed pant legs inside, and put on heavy jackets and caps. We lighted two kerosene lanterns and got them burning clean and each of us carried one.

"Females." He scowled.

Since I did not know whether he referred to wives or ewes, I let my silence concur.

We went out into the storm.

TWO

I WOUND my scarf round and round my head, binding my face to the eyes, but even then a net of wind-thrown snow tangled my eyelashes. Without the scarf over my nose I doubted if I could draw breath. Without his lantern to guide on, I could never have followed my grandfather to the barn.

We slid the door open wide enough to pass through, entered, and slapped snow off each other with our mittens. At the far end of the barn we went halfway down a flight of steps and sat down to overlook the sheepshed. Below us a hundred sheep, wearing heavy winter gray, lounged about on yellow straw and considered us calmly.

"Which one?" I asked, unwinding my scarf.

"There." Will pointed at a ewe who lay near the steps. She got up, then lay down again. She was restless.

"How'll we know when she's going to have it?"

"We'll know."

"Well, what do we do now?"

"Meditate."

We raised the earflaps of our caps. It was warmer in the shed than outside, but our breathing still made little fogs before our faces. I peered until I found the horns of Calvin, the ram. They had a beautiful curl, and he knew it. He was a registered rambouillet and had a long, complicated name on his papers, but for short Will called him Calvin in honor of Mr. Coolidge. Neither the ram nor the former President spoke very often, he explained, but when they did, they were worth heeding.

"I wonder what sheep think about," I said.

"Females," Will answered. "The contrariness of the critters. Isn't it just like a female to drop a lamb on a winter night when a man might better be in bed? And isn't it just like a female to expect a man to haul a pump organ three miles through a snowstorm? Any automobile ever invented would founder in those drifts."

I held my face with my hands. After a time Will said, "I intended to buy one in '28, but traded for the Oil Pull instead. Then I intended to buy one in '29, with the threshing money, and you know what happened in '29."

The old ewe stood up, then lay down again.

Will said, "She hasn't played that organ in three years."

I concentrated on Calvin. He was chewing and being very nonchalant about the drama that was about to unfold, a theatrical for which he bore in large part the responsibility of authorship.

"You can't get blood out of a turnip," my grandfather said. "You can't ask friends and neighbors for money when they don't have it. They're fine people. They'll pay when they can."

"I'm sorry you had an argument," I said. "It was my fault, I guess. If I hadn't been here, she wouldn't have played the melodeon, and if she hadn't played, she might not have got the idea."

"Oh, we spat," he said.

"You do?"

"Don't your ma and pa go at it now and again?"

"Well, sure, but they're younger. I didn't think—"

"Old folks fight? Well, they do, sonny. Scratch and bite as much as ever, and love as much as ever. You have to take the vinegar with the honey. That's marriage for you."

The old ewe stood up and lay down again. She was making me restless. "Guess I'll go give the team some extra hay," I said. "It's Christmas Eve."

As the delivery drew nigh, I grew less and less inclined to witness it. I hadn't a glimmering what to expect, but I was convinced I was too young to be exposed to the barn-based facts of life.

Taking a lantern, I went upstairs and took a look at Tom and Dolly in their stalls below. Both were standing, sound asleep. I pitched three forkfuls of hay down the chute for each of them, which woke them up, and I could hear them munching gratefully. I wished them both a Merry Christmas and went back to the sheepshed. "My gosh," I said, "hasn't she had it yet?"

"She will when she's a mind to," my grandfather replied.

I took my post on the steps again. The old ewe moved restlessly. I had to think about something else, so I asked Will where the melodeon had come from, and I got another helping of family history.

One day in April, in the year 1863, my great-grandmother Sarah was standing at her kitchen window watching her husband, Ephraim, plowing in a nearby field. Suddenly he stopped, dropped the reins, left the team, and walked toward the house. He had never done that before—once he started a furrow he finished it— and although she was a very young wife, married only two years,

Sarah knew what her husband was going to tell her. But she didn't cry or faint, she merely held on hard to a pot in which she was soaking beans when he entered the kitchen.

They were forming a cavalry regiment around Howell, he said without preliminary, and if she were willing, he wanted to enlist. It would tear him in two to leave her, he said, but he wouldn't be gone long, the Johnnies would soon be whipped, he would get her a hired man to work the place, and if she could manage the separation, he could manage the war. It had been on his conscience, he told her. He loved her, but he loved the Union, too, and he revered Mr. Lincoln. He was young and able-bodied, and he believed it was his duty to get in a lick for his country while he could.

"What did she say?" I asked.

"She said yes. Of course he ought to go. A man should do what he believed in. It was what she didn't say that cost her."

"What was that?"

"That she was carrying me."

"You?"

"She was two months along with me. If she'd told him that, he'd never have left her. But she didn't tell, and let him go, and that must have cost her plenty. She was a brave woman."

Outside, the storm cried like an animal seeking shelter.

"But what about the melodeon?" I asked.

"Oh. Yes," he said. "Well, he joined up in the cavalry. A week later they brought that organ down from the store in Howell in a wagon. He'd bought it on his way to the war. It was his thank-you to her for letting him go. Not knowing about me, I expect he thought it would keep her company. Sarah could play the piano, so she picked up the organ in no time."

"And later she taught you how," I added.

"Yes. I wanted to play for him when he came home."

"But he never did. I know that part of it. How come, after you found out he was dead, you never played it again?"

He looked at me with such intensity that I wished I hadn't pried. "Because my pa would never hear me," he said. "Nor would he ever see me, nor I him. Reason enough?"

"Sure," I said, turning away from his look. I had not realized that loss could be so long-lived. I tried to imagine how I would feel if I had never seen my father. But I couldn't think about it. Boys were not supposed to be morbid. Grandparents were not supposed to grieve.

So I concentrated on the ewe and did not want to do that either. Suddenly she let out a bleat of distress.

"Holy Toledo!" I jumped to my feet. "What's the matter now?"

"She's due."

I grabbed my lantern. "Guess I'll check the chickens."

"Afraid they'll lay snowballs tomorrow?"

"Just call me Chicken Inspector!" was my retort. I walked across the sheepshed and into the chicken house next door. It was quite a sight to see two hundred hens and several roosters perched on poles, dead to the world. Facing me row upon row, they resembled an impolite audience, and it seemed appropriate to shake them up. I put down the lantern and struck an elocutionary pose.

"Ahem," I began. "Ladies and gentlemen, it gives me great pleasure to address you tonight. But since the hour is late, I will be brief. You have a reputation as good layers. Well, I have a word to the wise." I drew a deep breath. "Lay off!" I roared.

Not an eye opened, not a feather turned.

"Slow down," I advised. "Rome wasn't built in a day. A Studebaker isn't bought in a week. Cut your output. Enjoy life. Appreciate nature. And let's try to be artists, not machines. Take a crack at some Easter eggs, nicely decorated. Because I warn you. No matter how hard you strain, someday for your reward my grandmother will take you to the chopping block and *pow!*"

I paused for effect, but I might as well have been addressing Congress for all I achieved. Nary a rooster squawked, nary a hen went pale. These were really dumb chickens.

"That concludes my remarks, ladies and gents," I said. "I wish you a Merry Christmas and I now depart." I bowed low and took up the lantern.

But before I reached the sheepshed I heard the old ewe over the storm. There was no mistaking it. She was in serious trouble.

23

WILL KNELT BESIDE her in the straw. She was lying on her side with her hind legs stretched out, and bawling her head off. Every animal in the flock, even Calvin, was standing now, concerned.

"What's wrong?" I asked.

"I don't know. She's trying, but she can't." He laid hands on her side, pressing, examining. "Maybe there's a leg tucked up. Or maybe it's a breech."

"What's that?"

"Lamb the wrong way to. The hind end first. Should be head first." My grandfather sat back on his haunches. "I can't tell. I wish I could."

He bit on a knuckle. I had never seen him so upset. Cold as it was, there were beads of sweat on his forehead. Finally he removed his jacket and rolled up his right shirt sleeve and the underwear beneath it to the elbow.

"What're you going to do?"

"Reach into her."

I went weak. "Oh jeepers no," I blurted.

"Have to. Or we'll lose her and the lamb both."

"Oh my gosh," I said. "But what can you do?"

"If it's a leg, untuck it. If it's a breech, turn the lamb around. I've done it before."

I gritted my teeth. "Any way I can help?"

"Yes. Comfort her. Sit down and take her head in your lap. She's in bad pain."

"Okay," I said. "If I have to."

I had never wanted to do anything less. I was sorry for her, but I didn't know what she might do in her suffering—bite me or kick me or what. Cautiously I sat down close to the ewe and put an arm around her neck and pulled her head into my lap.

"Now old girl," my grandfather said. He came to his knees between her hind legs. "Now let's see."

The scene in the shed made me think of a picture on a calendar—the halos of the lanterns, the beaten gold of the straw, the flock standing silent, an old man kneeling by one of the animals as though in prayer. Then I thought of the predicament the three of

us were in, and it was too much for me. I squinched my eyes shut. Suddenly the ewe bawled louder than ever, and reared her head, and I had to throw both arms around her neck and hug her against my face to hold her.

"Please, old girl, hold still," I begged, my nose full of the waxen smell of her fleece. "There, old girl, we can do it."

An hour passed, or a minute. Then, just as suddenly, she relaxed, and I was sure she must be dead.

"There, by Jehu," I heard my grandfather say.

I could not open my eyes. "What happened?" I choked.

"She had a lamb, that's what."

"Is it all right?"

"Fine and dandy."

I peeked. He was cutting the cord with a loop of binder twine and swabbing red off something small with a fistful of straw. I squinched my eyes shut again.

"A Christmas lamb," Will said. "I will be damned."

"I'll be damned," I echoed.

"You can let go of her now," he said. "She wants her kidlet."

I released her head and stood up and opened my eyes. Will laid the lamb on the straw by its mother, and she stretched her neck and commenced at once to lick it. I took one look and wobbled to the stairs and sat down, limp as a dishrag. With a forearm I wiped the sweat from my own forehead. I had a general grasp of the theory of birth, but I had been vague, and glad to be, about the reality. Now I knew how a lamb was born, and therefore how Ephraim, Sarah, Will, Ella, my father, my mother, and even I were born. We had come into the world in agony and struggle and bright blood, and something else, something akin to exaltation. For when I looked at my grandfather he was grinning ear to ear. I stood up and grinned back and felt enormously mature and alive.

Without warning, Will cracked a palm with a fist. "The Oil Pull!" He yanked on his jacket, clapped on his cap, and faced me with eyes blazing. "James, my boy, do you think we could get it started?"

"The tractor? Why?"

"To haul the organ to the church!"

"Oh," I said. "Oh! Why not?"

"Because I've never seen or heard of one being run in the winter, that's why. But if we could start it, boy—drifts be damned! We could haul anything in Christendom anywhere!"

"Sure we can!" I cried, catching his excitement. "We can do anything!"

"Hold your horses," he cautioned. "It's three long miles and a fearful night. Think we're up to it?"

"Sure we are," I asserted.

"I'm no spring chicken anymore."

"I'll help you."

"That's a mighty valuable piece of wood, that organ."

"We'll be careful."

"It tells in the manual how to start the Oil Pull in cold weather. But reading's a damn sight different from doing."

"We'll learn as we go along."

"And then there's Ella. It's got to be a surprise or it isn't worth a pinch of dried owl dung."

"We won't tell her."

"But she's a light sleeper. And you can hear that tractor from here to Dee-troit."

I had no way around that.

"We'd better sit a spell and meditate," he said.

We sat down on the steps. I chewed on a straw. Will tugged his mustache. The question was, could an old man and his thirteen-year-old grandson start a tractor on a below-zero Christmas Eve and then, unbeknown to wife and grandmother, transport a melodeon three miles through a blizzard to a church in time for Sunday morning service?

"She may not play it, but she loves that pumper," Will reflected. "It'll cost her to give it away."

This question involved another. I knew Will had the sand, but did he have the stamina? He must be in his late sixties, I reckoned, and men that age had at least one foot in the grave. What if something terrible overtook him en route? What could I do?

"She's a brave woman," he said. "Just like Sarah, my ma."

And he had already told her there wouldn't be a service tomorrow morning anyway. So what was the use of getting the organ there by then?

"This blow might last all night," my grandfather said to himself. "And then again, it might not. You never know."

What if Ella heard the tractor and that spoiled the surprise? What if we bogged down and both of us froze to death?

"First Christmas I haven't given her anything," Will mused. "This would be a corker, though."

He touched my arm. He was grinning again, and his eyes snapped with schoolboy delight. "Can't you see her face in the morning when she sashays into that church, and there it is?"

"Can I ever." I grinned.

He beamed, then put out a hand. "Well, partner, shall we give it a try?"

"You bet!"

We stood up, shook on it, and forgot immediately the baying of the storm outside and the three impossible miles. We planned and plotted. Gradually, as the idea evolved, it took on elements of gallantry and heroism which warmed our backsides, plus bonuses of danger and rascality which shivered us to our boots. And the longer we conspired, the greater the challenge, the bigger the adventure became.

"All right," Will said, dropping his earflaps. He nodded at the ewe and her lamb. "If that old lady can have a baby on Christmas Eve, the age of miracles isn't past by a long shot."

"Absolootle, positivle," I agreed, treating him to a little of the latest Philadelphia lingo.

He snorted. "Let's get a move on."

We plodded toward the house. If our minds conceded that what our hearts had bade us do was beyond our powers, we kept mum. In the woodshed, we unbuttoned and unbuckled. Will took a lantern down into the basement and I entered the kitchen.

"Well, have we a lamb?" my grandmother asked.

"Not yet," I lied. "We might have to be up half the night with that darn ewe."

28

"You poor dears. Where's Will?"

"Oh, in the basement. He'll be right up."

She was putting the soapstones on the stove, a winter ritual. Progress, so-called, had already invented the hot-water bottle and would eventually bestow upon us the electric blanket, but I am not persuaded that these gadgets have been as salubrious as soapstones used to be. They were smooth-edged rectangles some sixteen inches long and three inches through and weighed approximately ten pounds. You put them on the stove in the evening to absorb heat. At bedtime you wrapped one in a length of worn flannel, toted it upstairs, and shoved it between the sheets. You got into an arctic bed and slowly, with your bare feet, eased it to the bottom. There it burned the night through, blessing only its own locality. If you were weak, and bunched up your legs, you lost the good of it. If you were incautious, you could practically fracture a toe. But if you were strong, and disciplined yourself to lie full length and wed your warmth to that of the soapstone, your reward was a sleep as virtuous as it was blissful.

Will came into the kitchen carrying two tin cups. "Thought we ought to try the cider," he said.

"Won't it be hard by now?" asked his wife.

"Shouldn't be. Takes a warm day or two to turn it."

She pursed her lips. My grandmother abhorred alcohol in any form. I never knew her to accept so much as a glass of wine. But rather than pursue the subject, she went to a drawer, took out a large ball of string and a tangle of loose lengths, sat down at the table, and began to unravel the separate bits and pieces. This provided Will with the diversion he required. Getting three small glasses from the cupboard, he poured the contents of one tin cup into two of them and emptied the other cup into the third glass. He winked at me, then offered the third glass to Ella and one of the others to me.

"A toast," he said. "Here's to an end of the blamed storm, and a Merry Christmas tomorrow."

"Peace on earth, goodwill toward men," added his spouse.

Will and I drank our sweet cider. She sipped.

"You're right, Will," she granted. "It isn't hard yet. It's quite tasty." She smiled. He smiled. I smiled.

We seated ourselves with Ella while she balled string. She would tie a loose piece onto the ball, roll it up, tie on another, and so on. "Idle hands do the devil's work," she would say in defense of her industry, but another reason why her hands were never idle, I now understood, was the arthritis. Crocheting and balling string kept her fingers as supple as she could hope.

She had more "cider." Then she said to me, "Let me tell you a little story, James. It has to do with pride." She glanced at her husband and continued. "I've been thinking. Perhaps it was pride that made me want to give the melodeon to the church on Christmas morning and make a spectacle of myself. I don't know. But the story is about your mother, and what pride can do."

We watched her intently.

"When your mother was young, sixteen or so, she was invited to a grand party in Howell, at the banker's house. Oranges were a great treat in those days. If you had one a year, you were lucky, and one in your Christmas stocking made the day."

She sipped a little more "cider." "My, that's good." She tried to knot two bits of string together and couldn't seem to. She frowned and brought the string close to her glasses. "Gaslight," she sniffed. "If only we had electric. Well, as I was saying, your mother was invited to the party, and we knew that sometime in the evening a bowl of oranges would be passed. So I told her to be a lady of taste and refinement. Not to take an orange when the bowl came round. Be proud, I told her, as though you have an orange every day at home. Let everyone else snatch and grab. Then when the bowl is passed again, hesitate, and finally take one. That's being ladylike— Fiddlesticks."

She was trying in vain to tie another knot. Will winked at me. She sipped again, then began to ball the string without tying it.

"Where was I?" she asked.

What she was imbibing, of course, was not sweet cider but applejack, a tonic Will had turned out by freezing and refreezing the barrel in the backyard, thus distilling the juice of the apple down to its essence. Taken in moderation, he had informed me in the sheepshed, applejack was "as fine as the fuzz on a butterfly's behind." Taken in excess, it had the "strike of a massasauga rattlesnake." He intended only to get her a little tiddly, just enough to induce a sleep so sound we could fire a cannon without waking her.

"Where was I?" she repeated.

"The party," I reminded her.

"Yes, the party." Her speech was slurred. "Well, the oranges were passed, and your mother refused. Everyone was impressed."

Ella put down her glass. The ball of string dropped to her lap and rolled across the floor.

"The party," I said.

"What party?"

"Mother refused the oranges."

"Oh, yes. She wanted one so much, but she said no, thank you. The perfect lady." She stared down at the ball of string.

"What happened after she refused the orange?" I asked.

"Oh. The orange. Well, the bowl wasn't passed a second time— I declare..."

"Declare what?" Will asked.

His wife rose, putting a hand on the table to steady herself. "I declare. I'm dizzy. I don't know what's come over me. Will, I'm so sleepy."

He was on his feet in a flash. "Let me help you to bed, dear."

He put an arm around her waist and assisted her to their bedroom, off the kitchen. While he was putting her to bed, I wrapped a soapstone in flannel and gave it to him through the door. I returned the ball of string to the drawer. Next I sampled the applejack left in her glass. It descended equably enough, but when it hit bottom it went off in the manner of a firecracker under a tin can, with a bang and a clang. I had to sit down.

Ella sang several bars of "We Three Kings of Orient Are" rather loudly. Then she giggled, which was another thing grandparents were not supposed to do.

Will came out and sat at the table with me. We looked at the clock. It was almost ten. We waited. It wasn't long. In a minute

31

or two we heard a soft, reassuring snore. Whispering, he told me
to go upstairs and put on a second set of long johns and another
pair of socks.

I did so. After I rejoined him, we turned the gaslight low,
bundled up in the woodshed, lighted the lanterns, stared into each
other's faces for a moment, searching, making sure of each other,
then opened the door and stepped again into the storm.

THREE

WE WENT directly to the granary. It was open-ended, fortunately,
at the south, for the wind raved from the north. First we filled the
lanterns. They must not fail us. Then, while I held them, Will filled
a ten-gallon can from the kerosene tank, and as I lighted his way
through a hodgepodge of implements, he went back and forth to
the tractor, fueling it to capacity.

I wish to describe the tractor in as much detail as I have the
Mason & Hamlin melodeon, for if one is the end of my story, the
other is the means. Let the reader erase from his mind any image
of the modern tractor—a pampered darling packed with horsepower and with every luxury from self-starter to headlights to
seat cushions to radio. What I present in its stead is a 1928 Rumely
Oil Pull, Model 20-40, a monstrosity which has not been seen on
American acreage for forty years or more.

The front end was surmounted by a four-sided smokestack the
size of a ship's, which, according to the engine's mood, emitted
stinks of black smoke. On its side was lettered OIL PULL, ADVANCE-
RUMELY COMPANY, LA PORTE, INDIANA. The engine was an 8 by
10, horizontal, two cylinder, kerosene burning, and oil-cooled, with
magneto ignition and a spur gear transmission with two speeds
forward and one reverse. Low speed was 2 mph, and shifting into
high would hurtle you down the road at 3.2 mph. This engine
pulled 20 horsepower on the drawbar and 40 on the belt wheel,
turning it at 450 rpm. The wheels were spoked cast iron, and the
rear wheels were almost six feet high. Over the drive wheels and
transmission was an open cab with a four-post corrugated roof

covering an iron driver's seat, steering wheel, and the controls. The Model 20-40 was sixteen feet long and ten feet high, counting the cab, and the whole awesome shebang weighed almost six and a half tons. Given some armor plate, and a gun or two, and a rotation rig for the cab, it might have competed on fairly equal combat terms with any tank in the First World War. There was certainly nothing like it elsewhere in Putnam Township.

To my grandmother the Oil Pull was an abomination of great price—the price being many times that of the automobile she coveted. To my grandfather the Oil Pull was the symbol of power and glory. It must have been, however, a love-hate relationship between farmer and tractor. Love it he assuredly did, for the Rumely had powered the threshing of every bushel of wheat in the neighborhood for several summers. But hate it he must have, too, for though he had had no pay for the harvest, and in those cruel years lacked the cruelty to demand it, Advance-Rumely demanded its pound of flesh every month. To me, at this hour, on this weather-wild Christmas Eve, the Oil Pull was but a mighty contraption we had to command in order to move a small pump organ to a church, a process rather like firing up a mountain to move a mouse.

The catch, of course, was starting it. It was probably ten below zero, and the engine was cold clear through. Tractors of that magnitude were never started in winter—there was nothing for them to do.

Will first filled the two priming cups, one for each cylinder, with gasoline.

"But I thought it runs on kerosene," I said.

"Well, it does. But gas burns hotter. So we'll start 'er on gas and run 'er on gas till the block gets hot enough to gasify the kerosene. Then she'll purr on that."

He stepped to the flywheel, took off his mittens, extended the handle, which retracted automatically, bent to it, and turned the wheel once, twice, three times, but nothing happened. He spit on his palms and whirled the flywheel perhaps a dozen times, but nothing happened.

"Thunderation," he said.

Motioning me to provide light, he rummaged in a corner of the granary and located a blowtorch. Filling it with gas, he pumped up the pressure, lighted the flame with a match, trimmed it down to a blue cone, returned to the Rumely, and handing over the torch, told me to heat the glow plug. This was a dingus extending from the head. Its function was to transfer heat from outside the engine to the inside, and to concentrate it, thereby vaporizing the gas inside a cylinder so that it would fire more easily. I directed the flame until I got a good glow, whereupon Will seized the handle and whirled the very dickens out of the flywheel, completely in vain.

Breathing hard, he stopped and stood for a moment in thought. "I'm not going to cuss on Christmas Eve," he resolved. "That might put the kibosh on the whole damned thing. But we have one more string to our fiddle. Come around here."

He led me to the other side of the tractor and told me to heat the manifold, which would heat the air taken into the cylinders and thereby vaporize the gas more thoroughly. So I used the torch on the manifold until he grabbed the handle again and rotated the flywheel so fast and so long that if the engine had been a separator, he'd have had whipped cream.

When my grandfather let go, I could hear him wheeze even over the keening of the wind outside the granary. I had heard him before, whenever he did anything strenuous. He had what was known as hay lung, a respiratory ailment common among farmers. Years of cutting and raking and mowing hay lined the lungs with its dust, it was then believed, leading to shortness of breath and susceptibility to infection. Medicine now knows that the cause is not dust but rather the inhalation of microscopic spores from a mold which breeds in warm, moist hay. There was no cure for hay lung then, nor is there now, except to quit farming.

"We're whipsawed," he declared. "Heat the manifold and the plug cools. Heat the plug and the manifold cools." He stood for another moment, thinking and wheezing.

"We're not giving up, are we?" I demanded.

He scowled. "What would you recommend?"

"Want me to try it?"

"Help yourself."

Full of optimism, I strode to the wheel, removed my mittens, and took hold. By dint of spunk, determination, two grunts, and a groan, I gave it one grudging half-turn.

I was flabbergasted. It was incredible that a grandfather should be strong enough to spin that wheel like a top when a clean-living young man of my muscle could barely budge it.

"Thank you," he said.

"For what?" I was prepared to be offended.

"You gave me another idea. Your arm won't do, but maybe we can use your legs. Here now."

He placed a lantern on each side of the tractor, midway. "Now you heat the plug," he directed, "and when she's red hot, skedaddle around to the other side and heat up the manifold, and when it's toasty, skedaddle back here and go at the plug again, and meanwhile I'll turn away slow and maybe, just maybe, if you run fast enough and keep 'em both hot enough, maybe we'll do it."

It was worth a try, and for perhaps three minutes try we did—Will rotating the flywheel slowly while I heated and ran, heated and ran—but all we got for our efforts was exhaustion.

We surrendered. He sat down on a front wheel and I leaned against the smokestack. We were both wringing wet. His faith in the machine had been shaken. My faith in him had been taken down a peg. I had believed him a first-class engineer, but he was apparently much better at obstetrics.

And then, in the depths of that iron beast upon which we rested, we heard a sound. It was not a sigh of apology, but a protest of discomfort from its very guts. Will put a finger to his lips, tiptoed to the flywheel, and gave it one tender, almost seductive, turn.

Huff! Combustion! *Huff! Huff!*

Huff-huff-huff-huff! Huff-huff-huff-huff!

The Oil Pull shook, shimmied, and belched black smoke. We had won!

Hands on hips, we grinned at each other like idiots, exulting in sound and smell and achievement. He had to shout in my ear, because the uproar of the tractor was reverberating from the roof. "We'll leave 'er here to warm up! Let's get a move on!"

He had evidently mapped out tactics earlier. Communicating with gestures, we first wheeled the tedder and a spring-tooth drag from the granary by their tow bars. That made way for the stoneboat, a crude sledlike vehicle used originally to clear the fields of stone. About eight feet long, it had two small logs for runners, across which rough boards were nailed into a solid floor. Attached to each log up front was one end of a rusty chain. We pulled the stoneboat outdoors, too, then piled onto it two four-foot lengths of two-by-four, two moldy horse blankets, a coil of rope, and a lantern. We started for the house.

We put heads down and closed our eyes and tugged at the stoneboat's chain. By the time we reached the house we were snowmen. We pulled alongside the steps of the screened porch, ran the rope twice under the stoneboat's flooring, endwise, left the ends loose, set the lantern aside, and laid the two lengths of two-by-four to serve as skids from the porch down to the stoneboat.

We padded across the porch and entered the living room. Sliding the doors like burglars, we edged into the parlor. With each of us at one end, we rolled the melodeon through the living room and onto the porch on its casters. So far, so fancy.

We draped the instrument with the horse blankets. Then, together, we hoisted one end onto the skids and let it roll down far enough to raise the other end and place it. I held on to the high end for dear life while Will went to the low and inched the organ slowly down the skids. Then he braked it until I joined him and we warped the thing off the skids and onto the floor of the stoneboat. We passed the two ends of rope over it and tied it down. I brought out the bench and set it under a skirt of blanket. Then we swung the skids and lantern aboard and started out for the granary.

Had there not been a slight grade in our favor, I doubt we could have done it. The stoneboat sank under the organ's weight of two hundred and fifty pounds, and we labored knee-deep in the snow. Will wheezed. I panted. The tow chain hurt our hands, even through mittens, and eventually we harnessed it around our waists and leaned into it like a team of horses. It required ten minutes to cover the hundred yards to the granary.

We rested there. The 20-40 huffed away, running on kerosene and readying itself. I could have kissed any part of that cast-iron monster. When we had caught our breath, Will got the bench from under the blanket, mounted the step, stowed the bench beside him in the cab, backed the tractor out and up to the stoneboat. "You ride the boat and steady that pumper!" he yelled at me. "Sit on 'er if you have to!"

I looped the tow chain over the tractor's tow bar, gave Will a lantern, and set the other on top of the blankets. He pushed the hand throttle forward, the two cylinders quickened tempo, he shifted into low gear, the drive wheels dug in, and we were off.

It was a false start. He stopped within ten feet and jumped from the cab with his lantern. "Can't see your hand before your face! Wait a minute!"

He disappeared into the granary, emerging presently with two S hooks he'd made by bending pieces of fence wire. Taking both lanterns into the cab, he hung the hooks from the cross struts under the cab roof, then hung the lanterns from the hooks, one on each side, to serve as headlights.

He throttled up, shifted into low, the great wheels revolved, and we were off again, hurtling down the road at 2 mph. The worst was over. We had only three miles to go now, and an Oil Pull and gumption and Divine Providence to take us.

Huff-huff-huff-huff! Huff-huff-huff-huff!

The black breathing of the tractor was borne back to me upon the gale. The Oil Pull loomed above me like a tramp steamer towing a dinghy. I had glimpses of the lanterns swaying in the wind like masthead lights and of my grandfather seated at the helm, hunched forward, squinting into an ocean of white. The next moment vessel, lights, and captain were swallowed up, for the spume of snow blinded me.

I did not need to see in any case. My duty was to keep the

melodeon in place, protected by blankets and tied down by ropes. It was no easy assignment. The stoneboat rolled and pitched on the drifted township road. Remember, too, that the instrument stood on casters, giving it an agility which belied its bulk. The only way I could be fairly sure of it was to stand behind, plant my boots solidly, bend my knees, and embrace the organ with both arms. The position was awkward. My arms turned numb, my teeth chattered, the two sets of damp long johns iced my skin.

The Oil Pull battered into a drift deeper than most. It slowed. When it crunched ahead again it took up slack in the tow chain, and the stoneboat shuddered. The melodeon trembled in my arms. I hugged it to me as I had the old ewe's head. Only then, there, staying the melodeon in night and storm, did revelation of how precious it was, how beloved it had been, come to me. We were removing it from the only home it had ever known. It had been freighted seventy years ago from the factory in Boston to the village of Howell, and from there had been transported by wagon seven miles to a young wife alone on a farm, her soldier husband gone, on a day in April, 1863. She had played it and taught her small son. It was the only tangible link between a boy who had never seen his father and a father who had never seen his son.

The son had grown to manhood, and married, and his widowed mother taught his wife in turn to play it. My own mother's childish fingers must have strayed the keyboard, her tiny feet must once have tried the pedals. Surely, as a young woman, she became aware of the instrument's human and historic value. Ephraim and Sarah, Will and Ella, my mother, and now me—the melodeon had been counterpoint to the lives of four generations. And now my grandmother, with my grandfather's aid and acquiescence, was offering it to her Maker.

I cannot recall whether at age thirteen I believed or not. At that late hour, on that uncharitable eve of Christmas, it did not matter. I prayed that we might get the melodeon safely to the church. And I tacked on a warning—if He were really real, He had better appreciate a gift like this.

No deity, however, takes kindly to an admonition. We came to the one hill between us and the county road—and couldn't climb it. The Oil Pull did its level best, but the grade was steep and the drift across it four feet deep. The engine did not stall, the drive wheels turned, the V lugs bit into gravel. Sparks struck from iron, and clods of dirt and a hail of stones were hurled at the organ and me. Will set the hand brake and got down from the cab.

"I can do it if I get a start! Let's pull this rig to one side and give us room!"

We unhitched the chain and pushed the stoneboat downhill perhaps ten feet. Then we hauled it to one side of the road. He mounted the cab and put the tractor into reverse, then backed to the foot of the hill and thirty yards or so beyond. He shifted into second, throttled up as high as he could, and let 'er rip. The 20-40 went up the hill like a locomotive, roaring and scratching. They hit the drift with a terrible thud. They hesitated. Sparks flashed and dirt flew. Then they broke through to the crest, and I cheered like free beer and the Fourth of July.

Will backed down and set the hand brake, and we harnessed ourselves with the chain and panting and wheezing pulled the stoneboat into the track and made it fast to the tow bar. This time we made the hill as easy as pie and plowed down the far side.

Through a chink in the dark I saw a light wink on at the right of the road. That would be from a window at the Henshaw place, and of course we could be heard coming. A sound as implausible as a Rumely's, at night and at this time of year, would have Joe and Abby out of bed as fast as the jingle of sleigh bells on their roof.

We ground to a halt in front of the house and Will descended.

"We better warm up! They're awake now, so they won't mind!"

I made no objection. I was as cold as he. We left the tractor puffing away in the road and trudged to the house. But no sooner were we on the porch than the light went out in the window. Will knocked, but the door did not open. He took my arm and led me off the porch where we could speak freely.

I was outraged. "What's the matter with 'em?"

"Ashamed! Because they haven't paid me for the threshing!"

"You haven't asked!"

"Makes no difference! Old Joe believes in paying his debts, and when he can't, it binds him."

"Let us freeze out here?"

"Poor as church mice. They're the hardest hit folks around."

I knew that. Everyone was sorry for the Henshaws. They had neither chick nor child nor assets, excepting one emaciated cow and eighty acres of the poorest land in the area. It was remarkable they found money enough to buy gasoline to drive their Model T to church every Sunday.

"I don't care! You have to let people in on Christmas Eve!"

"Hurts them more than it does us. We can't let 'em do it. They'd never forgive themselves!" He took my arm. "Come along."

We returned to the porch and Will knocked on the door again, and after the fourth knock the light went on and the door opened. Joe Henshaw admitted us, apologizing he hadn't known who we were—a barefaced tergiversation if I had ever heard one.

It was practically as cold inside the house as out. The fire in the potbellied stove was low, and though Will said we had just stopped by to thaw, neither of our hosts made a move to poke it up, much less add wood. We were seated in the kitchen, on the only two chairs. Three things damped my own heat at the Henshaws: they were even older than Will and Ella; they were small and wrinkled as prunes; and they had no Christmas tree, which proved they were really scraping bottom. Joe wore long johns, evidently his sleeping attire, and Abby had put on over her nightgown a mangy muskrat coat. While my grandfather explained what we were doing out on a night like this with the tractor, husband and wife stared as though we must be crazier than bedbugs.

"I didn't give Ella anything this year," Will added lamely. "So James here and I thought this would be our surprise in the morning."

He realized at once he had put his foot in his mouth, that the Henshaws had been unable to give each other anything either, and said no more. The four of us stood or sat shivering and twiddled our thumbs till the shortage of conversation became, despite the wind outside, almost audible.

Abby Henshaw broke the ice. "When I was a girl," she said, "my mother would tell me how she used to trade for berries with the Indians hereabouts."

Will pretended he hadn't heard. "Joe," he said, "there's something I want to say to you. We've been good neighbors thirty years. Nobody's paid me a nickel for the threshing, and I don't expect 'em to, not now."

"Money makes the mare go," replied Joe.

"Well, mine'll go awhile yet. I want you to forget about it till times are better."

"I'm a man pays what I owe."

"I know that."

"When I was a girl," said Abby, "we used to pop popcorn over the fire in a skillet. We had all the popcorn we could eat."

"Everybody's hard up," Will said.

"Hoover," said Joe.

"If you're in a pinch, Mr. Henshaw," I piped up helpfully, "why don't you ask the county for relief?"

The Henshaws were horrified. "Relief!"

"Sure," I said, rushing in where good Republicans feared to tread. "I'm from Philadelphia, and my father's on relief and we're not ashamed."

Joe bared his three front teeth at me. "We'll starve before we slop at the public trough."

"When I was a girl," said Abby, "I had a dress of taffeta and lace." Her eyes watered. "Mercy, but it was beautiful."

"But there's nothing wrong with relief," I contended.

"Ahem." My grandfather cleared his throat and rose. "We'd best be going," he said to me. "We've got a long row to hoe tonight." He smiled at the Henshaws. "Much obliged for taking us travelers in. See you at service. And a Merry Christmas to you."

"I was married in that dress," said Abby.

We took our leave. When we reached the Rumely, I hollered at Will. "What's wrong with her? Bats in her belfry?"

"Folks get that way sometimes!"

"I'm as cold as ever!"

41

"Wood costs. I offered him a cord this fall, but he wouldn't take it. Pride!"

I thought of Ella's story about my mother. "Oranges!"

He shook his head and climbed into the cab, I posted myself on the stoneboat at the rear end of the melodeon, and we were off again. It was snowing and blowing more relentlessly than it had been when we stopped.

FOUR

WE HAD clear sailing to the county road now, barring an invulnerable drift, and we chugged away at a good hickory, Will steering, lanterns waving, stoneboat sluing, organ secure in my embrace. After a quarter of a mile, lights blinked on like beacons to the right of the road, three of them, upstairs and down. That would be the Stackable place, and our phenomenal passage in the night would rouse Clyde and Kate as surely as it had the Henshaws.

To my surprise, the Oil Pull stopped. I went forward at once. My grandfather stepped down from the cab very slowly.

"What's the matter now?"

"I'm tuckered, boy!" He wrapped his arms around himself. "We'd better meditate a spell! They're all up anyway!"

I was impatient. Dillydally along the way and we'd never get there. And I especially didn't care to drop in on the Stackables. I wasn't tired and did not see why he should be. But then, as we headed for the house through knee-deep snow, he staggered, and I had to put my arm through his. He was exhausted.

This time we were welcomed. In bathrobe and hairnet, Kate Stackable opened the door and bustled us in, insisting we sit on the davenport, plugging in their Christmas tree to cheer us, and putting water on to boil for my grandfather's green tea.

"Sorry to get you out of bed," said Will, removing his cap and mittens. "Where's Clyde?"

"Down with chills and fever and a chest cough, poor man. I'm keeping mustard plasters on him—you should hear him yell when I take one off. A pity to be laid up over Christmas."

"A pity," Will agreed. "You keep him in bed and well plastered and let him yell." Politely he acknowledged the row of tousle-haired girls in nightgowns seated on the stairs. "Good evening, young ladies. You know my grandson, James, here, don't you?"

They giggled. I warmed up immediately. They were the four reasons why I hadn't cared to drop in on the Stackables. Clyde and Kate had been unfortunate enough to beget girls rather than boys, and four of them—Agnes, Frances, Delores, and Gertrude, or "Toody," ages fourteen, eleven, nine, and six in that order, and arrayed down the stairsteps in that order. I went to school with them. I had no alternative.

If I evinced little or no regard for her daughters, who were as pestiferous as most girls their ages, I liked Mrs. Stackable very much. She reminded me of a stove. She was short and stout and reddened up quickly and radiated a hospitable warmth. She put hands where her hips were supposed to be and addressed my grandfather.

"Now tell me. What in heaven's name are you doing out on a night like this with that tractor?"

He told her.

Her cheeks flamed with pleasure. "Will Chubb, that's one of the nicest things I ever heard of in my life! Giving an organ to a church! On Christmas Eve! I can just see Ella's face tomorrow morning! Girls, isn't that wonderful?"

Agnes, Frances, Delores, and Toody nodded like metronomes.

"Oh, I think that's the nicest, sweetest, most loving thing," their mother carried on. "Will, I'll make you green tea till it comes out your ears!"

She slippered into the kitchen, which left us alone with the girls. I decided to let Will carry the burden of dialogue and began assiduously to study my knuckles, the Christmas tree, the pattern in the carpet, and the ceiling, conscious that they were simulta-neously studying me. It wasn't that I was a snob, or a connoisseur for that matter, but when I contrasted Philadelphia girls with the Stackable progeny, the former, as I recalled them, were paragons of beauty, charm, fashion, intellect, and every classifiable virtue.

43

The fact was, Agnes, Delores, Frances, and Toody were hicks. Moreover, they were mean. They had once persuaded me that dragonflies, which they called darning needles, would sew up male lips if opened, so for a full two weeks that autumn I walked to and from school with lips sealed.

"Here's that tea, Will." Mrs. Stackable came in with cup and saucer. "Will?"

We looked at him. My grandfather had fallen fast asleep on the davenport. His head was back, his mouth open, his breathing so labored that the hairs of his mustache oscillated like reeds.

Kate Stackable put a finger to her lips and motioned us to follow her into the kitchen. When we had, she closed the door. "Here, James, you have his tea. We mustn't wake him."

She gave me the cup and offered me a chair at the kitchen table. Green tea was vile, in my opinion, but no more distasteful than Agnes, Frances, Delores, and Toody, who sat down, put elbows on the table, chins in hands, and observed me imbibe as though they'd never seen anyone take tea without saucering it.

For warmth, Mrs. Stackable turned on the oven in her electric stove and opened the oven door. Then she stood at the counter watching me, too. I sipped tea. Occasionally I could hear Mr. Stackable hack and cough in the bedroom, and over the wind the panting of the Oil Pull out in front.

"Your granddad's worn to a frazzle," Mrs. Stackable said at length. "He ought to get his sleep out."

"Yes, ma'am."

She frowned. "It's dangerous for a man his age to be out on such a night. What you're up to is the sweetest, kindest thing I ever heard of—but his health is more important. James, do something for me?"

"Ma'am?"

"Let him sleep, and when he wakes up, talk him into going home and bringing the organ to service in the morning."

"Oh, no," I said. "Gosh, no."

"Why not?"

"Because that's half of it, the surprise," I protested. "You don't realize how much trouble we've gone to getting this far. We can't quit now."

"I see. If Clyde was well, he'd go with you. And I can't leave him. Do you know how to drive that tractor?"

"I never have," I admitted, "but I've watched Will a lot."

"Then let me do this. Let me phone the Dunnings—they're just half a mile past Chubb's Corners. I'll ask Otis to meet you at the church—he'll be glad to—and you let your granddad sleep and go on and meet Otis. Is that all right?"

She had me over a barrel. I couldn't chance anything happening to Will, but on the other hand it would be a prodigal waste of elbow grease to forsake the mission now, when we were so close to success. He had his stubborn heart set on having that melodeon in church tomorrow morning, and so did I, and so had Ella, really.

Still I hesitated. I couldn't handle the organ alone. Otis Dunning wasn't Will Chubb, but in the end it didn't matter who did the job as long as it was done.

"I guess so," I said.

She beamed. "Thank you, James. I'll go call."

She went to the phone in the dining room. I set the tea aside.

"Don't like it, do you," said Frances.

"Sure I do."

"Liar-liar-big-fat-tire," said Delores.

"What a sheik," said Agnes.

"Bet he plays a uke," said Delores.

"It's not polite to stare at people while they're eating or drinking," I instructed.

"It's not polite to go visiting on Christmas Eve and keep Santy Claus away," Toody instructed.

"Banana oil," I rejoined.

"There isn't any Santa Claus," said Frances.

"You shut up," Delores told her. "You know Toody's not old enough to—"

Kate Stackable returned. "Oh, dear. I can't even get the operator. The lines must be down. Now what're we going to do?"

I was about to say, Mrs. Stackable, it's not what we're going

45

to do, it's what I'm going to do, and I'm going on. To say it with
more authority, I stood up and squared my shoulders.

"Mrs. Stackable—" I began.

"I'm going with him," Agnes announced.

I might as well have been flattened by Jack Dempsey in the
first round.

"Oh, no, you're not," said her mother.

"Oh, no, you're not," said I.

"He can't lift that organ by himself," said Agnes. "He's too
puny."

"I'm going, too!" cried Frances.

"Me, too!" cried Delores.

"I wanna go!" cried Toody.

"Now hold on here!" I cried, springing from my corner like the
Manassa Mauler. "I can do this by myself! I'm not taking any
doggone bunch of—"

"James." It was Kate Stackable. She had slipped off her hairnet,
revealing the sausage curls she had set with an electric curler. She
had also changed her mind. "James, maybe it's not such a bad idea
after all. The girls are strong, and you're really not big enough
yet for that organ. It's only a mile or so to the church from here."
She looked at the clock. "It's twenty past eleven. I can bundle them
up, and you can be back here by midnight and take your grandfather home."

"We're going." Agnes smiled, recognizing the signs.

"We're going! We're going!" squealed her sisters, jumping up
and down.

I experienced a sinking sensation, that lassitude familiar not
only to Samson but to men in all times when hornswoggled by the
weaker sex. "But, but Mrs. Stackable," I stammered.

"Sssh—don't wake Mr. Chubb," she warned her daughters.
"James, if it wasn't such a wonderful thing you're doing, I'd never
consider it. But I love your grandma, and if this is what she wants,
why, you should let us do our part, shouldn't you?"

"I guess so," I groaned. Will falling asleep, a gang of insufferable
girls barging in on the adventure—events were taking too dire a

46

turn for me. I threw in the towel and sat down again at the table.

She sent her four upstairs to dress and, when they were gone, went to a crockery jar and gave me a handful of sugar cookies. "I'll bet you're starved. I shoo the girls away from these, I don't want them as heavy as I am. But you could use some pick on your bones." She seated herself across from me. "Helping out will put some starch in their spines—they're much too flighty. You keep a tight rein on them. Just tell them what to do and see they do it."

Her cookies were excellent, but the taste on my tongue was that of despair.

"I'll bet you miss your folks something fierce, being it's Christmas. Don't you?"

My mouth was full. I nodded.

"That was real nice you could talk to them tonight, though."

My mouth was still full. I stared.

She smiled. "Oh, don't worry, we didn't listen in. But everybody knew they were calling you. Long distance from Philadelphia is news around here."

She tilted her head to check on the girls thumping and clump-ing upstairs. "James, sometime soon, when you get a chance, you tell your granddad we feel awful about not paying him for the threshing. Clyde stews about it. But we just don't have anything to spare right now. Will you?"

I finished the cookies. "Yes, ma'am."

"That's another reason I decided to send the girls. Money may be tight, but being neighborly doesn't need to be."

"Thank you," I said.

The girls pushed in, swaddled in overalls and sweaters. "All right," approved their mother. "Now go get your presents from under the tree and bring them here and be quick about it."

"Our presents? How could Santy get here already?" a skeptical Toody wanted to know.

Kate Stackable glanced at her older daughters. "Why, he must have come earlier, while we were asleep."

Toody's doubts were not easily dispelled. "I wasn't asleep, and I didn't hear anything."

"Don't fret about it. Get your presents—and sssh."

Agnes, Frances, Delores, and Toody tiptoed into the living room and returned, their expressions something less than anticipatory, holding four identical packages wrapped in white paper decorated with green leaves and red holly berries.

"Well, open them," ordered their mother.

They did. Each girl's gift was a new pair of rubber galoshes.

"Well, well, old Santa really knew what you needed this year," said Mrs. Stackable. "Your old ones are just about gone."

"Galoshes," said Agnes.

"Galoshes," said Frances.

"Goody goody," said Delores.

"I asked for a doll," pouted Toody.

Their mother frowned. "You be glad for them. Millions of kids won't have anything at all under the tree this Christmas—I expect times are just as hard for Santa as they are for everybody. Now into the woodshed and put them on and your coats and caps, and hurry. It's getting late and James is anxious."

They left us. "You're a dandy, James," she said to me. "I wish we'd had a boy. I love my girls, but they need a big brother sometimes, to set an example."

Her brood entered, new galoshes buckled up, stocking caps pulled down over their ears, and scarves up to their eyes. I was about as glad to see them as I would have been to enjoy a second cup of green tea.

Kate Stackable inspected her troops. "Got your mittens?"

They bobbed heads.

"James is in charge. You do what he tells you or I'll tan your hides—d'you hear?"

They bobbed heads.

"And you listen. Maybe tonight will teach you something about the meaning of Christmas. Christmas isn't just getting, whether it's galoshes or dolls or what. Christmas is giving. That's the joy of it. So for once in your young lives you behave, and help, and give—d'you understand?"

They bobbed heads vigorously. She stooped, swooped arms

48

around them, bumped their heads together, then stood back, biting a lip.

"Off you go. Don't wake Mr. Chubb. I won't tell your father what I've done till you're back safe and sound—I wouldn't dare. Take care of them, James."

"I will," I said, meaning one way or another.

She cat-footed us through the living room. My grandfather was snoring. I'd have given my new pocketknife to wake him and explain my predicament and beg forgiveness for this treachery.

Mrs. Stackable opened the front door and came with us onto the porch and into the snow and wind. She took both my arms in her hands and gripped them tightly. "Oh, James," she said into my ear. "May the Lord be your shepherd!"

"Yes, ma'am," I said.

FIVE

TAKEN huff for huff, pound for pound, splash lubrication for magneto ignition, the Rumely Oil Pull 20-40, I believed that Christmas Eve and do to this day, was the most steadfast, dauntless, radiant tractor then in existence and since invented. What it was asked to do it did, asking in return only a pittance of kerosene and a tithe of faith. An ignoramus could have driven it. I set the throttle up, shoved the shift lever into low. The drive wheels turned and it was on its way once more, smoking and grinding through the malevolent night.

In the rear, riding the stoneboat and hugging the melodeon, were Frances, Delores, and Toody. I had ordered Agnes there as well, but she refused, which got us off to a good, insubordinate start. Instead, she climbed up into the cab and sat on the organ bench beside me. If she had been a boy, I'd have beaten her into pulpy submission, but she was a girl, and taller and huskier than I, and in the eighth grade, too. So I let her get away with it, consoling myself I did so out of pity. That she was obnoxious by nature she couldn't help. That she had warts on her hands was not her fault. And that she had to carry a name like Agnes Stackable to the grave—she would certainly never marry—rendered her automatically an object of compassion. Most pitiful, perhaps, was the evidence that she had developed a crush on me. It was a hopeless cause, of course. I intended to leave a litter of broken hearts behind me for a long, long time.

We reached the county road. We turned right and the stoneboat followed our lead obediently. The road was wide, there were no hills, and we had just over a mile to go.

The two cylinders settled into a soporific beat. I must have dozed. It seemed to me I was astride a great black horse cantering down a road in Tennessee, saber clanking at a thigh, Colt revolver snug against the other hip. We were on our way to Strawberry Plains. I wore blue. I was young and strong and knightly. The Union must be saved, the slaves freed, and my comrades and I would do these things for Mr. Lincoln and our loved ones. And so I dreamed. Of Sarah, my sweet wife. Of the letters from her underneath my tunic. Of her silent courage when she let me go, and of the boy she'd given birth to. His name was William, she had written, and we would call him Willy. Of the melodeon she played, and would teach our newborn how to play. I longed to see her, and my son, and hear the music he would make for me. I could not know a sniper's bullet waited for my breast this very day. And so I rode my great black steed, and soon it seemed to me that someone's arms had taken me, and someone's voice was bugling in my ear.

"Dummy! You're going off the road, you dummy!"

I woke with such velocity I almost hit the roof of the cab. Agnes Stackable's amorous arms enfolded me, the tractor was tilting to the right—we were indeed rumbling off the shoulder!

I spun the wheel. We lurched left and regained the level. I breathed again, free of Agnes' clutch, but another peril impended. I couldn't see. It was snowing harder than ever, and the light from the lanterns was insufficient. I pulled the throttle back, let the Rumely come to a halt, and set the hand brake.

"Whatcha waiting for?" Agnes caterwauled. "A streetcar?"

I unhooked the lanterns and handed them to her. "Get down!"

I yelled through my scarf. "You and Frances take these and walk in front so I can see where the road is."

"And have you run over us? Not on your life!"

"Remember what your mother told you."

"Ma's not here."

"What about the meaning of Christmas?"

"Banana oil!"

I grew desperate. Appeals to law and sentiment were unavailing, as would be resort to brute force. That left guile.

"Agnes! You like me, I know you do. And I like you. But I'd like you a lot more if you'd cooperate."

"How much more?"

I knew then that Adam had not tried the forbidden fruit to indulge his appetite. It was to save his sanity.

"Lots!" I proclaimed. "Pecks! Bushels! Loads!"

To my masculine gratification, she jumped down from the cab and slogged back to the stoneboat. In a moment Agnes and Frances, each carrying a lantern, spaced themselves ahead of the tractor and began to serve as living headlights. I released the brake, throttled up, shouted "Hang on!" to Delores and Toody, and put the Oil Pull into motion.

That was how we traversed the last half mile. The youngest Stackables guarded our cargo, I crouched in the cab, while a few yards out front the eldest Stackables guided me down that howling, inconstant path. Much as I disliked to, I had to give credit where it was due. If it was one degree below zero it was ten, and permitted little or no movement on the stoneboat; Delores and Toody must have been frozen stiff as boards. Now and then the drifts were so deep that Agnes and Frances struggled, slowed, and stopped, and I had to halt the Rumely until they could trample through and wave me onward with the yellow beacons of their lanterns. Kate Stackable would have been proud of her girls. In cold and dark and travail, at a top speed of 2 mph, they were learning the true meaning of Christmas—although the fuel that motivated Agnes might have been romantic rather than altruistic.

It was a road we walked every school day, and we knew when

we reached Chubb's Corners. Behind the new church was the Putnam Township cemetery, and beyond that the one-room schoolhouse. Following the lanterns, spinning the wheel, I turned the Oil Pull off the road and transcribed a wide half circle, aiming between two large maple trees and the church in order to come up alongside the stoop. We hit it on the nose. I swung about in the seat and, shifting in and out of low, nudging forward, brought the stoneboat within a foot of the steps.

I bowed my head for a moment. It was done. Hallelujah. I set the hand brake, left the engine running, cramped down from the cab, took the bench, and placed it under the stoop roof.

I turned to the stoneboat. Delores and Toody unhugged the organ and got off as Agnes and Frances came back with the lanterns. Telling them to stand clear, I untied the ropes and dropped

them. Then I pulled the ends of the two-by-fours off the floor of the stoneboat onto the floor of the stoop and spaced them to accommodate the casters. I shouted at the girls to listen.

"Nice going, you guys! Now here's what we've got to do. This thing rolls on casters. So we've got to lift one end up on these skids and push it up, then raise the other end onto the skids, then push the whole thing up the skids onto the stoop."

"I'm sleepy!" This was Delores.

"I'm frozen!" This was Frances.

"We can't do it!" This was Agnes.

"I wanna go home!" This was Toody.

"You can in a minute!" I stepped to the instrument, its protective blankets mounded with snow. "Come on now, everybody take hold and lift till the casters are on the skids."

I bent, got mittens under one corner, and waited till they assembled at the other corner.

"Now, lift!"

I heaved. The organ swayed. Then I felt their answering pressure. I pulled and heaved and they must have, too, for with a thud, casters settled onto skids.

I straightened up. "Now we've got to pull the other end around straight. Toody, you watch and see the casters don't roll off the skids. You other guys get hold of our end and roll it around."

Agnes, Frances, and Delores joined me, and after I pushed snow off the flooring with a galosh, we had no difficulty rolling the melodeon around to line up with the skids.

"Now—help me push till we get it up the skids. Push!"

We strained. We rolled the instrument up the skids till the rear casters stubbed the lower ends of the two-by-fours.

"Now—lift!"

We heaved. "Lift!"

We couldn't do it. The angle of incline from stoneboat to stoop was steep, so that we had both to lift and push two hundred and fifty pounds at the same time.

I got down on my knees. "Lift!"

We couldn't do it. I tried to rise. But the enormity of our failure kept me on my knees. My grandfather and I and Kate Stackable's daughters had brought the melodeon three miles through thick and thin. The bulk of it rested on skids not six feet from the door of the temple to which it was to be my grandmother's offering. Lift the low end two inches and the merest fraction and the deed would be wholly, magnificently done. And three stout girls and I simply could not do it.

I was sweating again, and my back hurt, and kneeling in snow and cold I lost control. Tears came. I felt them hot upon my cheeks. And that made me mad enough to bite nails. I reared up and threw my weight against that of the organ.

"Girls!" I raged. "Damn girls! If I had another man here we'd do it, but all I've got is weakling good-for-nothing girls!"

Agnes Stackable began to cry, which set Frances to crying, and after her Delores, and after her Toody. There we were, children of the storm, on that handmade, hard-times Christmas Eve, weeping with such abandon that at least a minute elapsed before we woke up to what had happened.

It had ceased, suddenly, to snow.

The wind had ceased, suddenly, to blow.

We stood there on a midnight clear, in lantern light, except for the respiration of the Oil Pull, at the crystal center of a silence.

We ceased, suddenly, to cry. For in the wake of the wind we heard them, far away at first and muffled in snow, coming up the road from the south. They were not the slow *clip-clop* that precedes a wagon or sleigh. They had the rhythm of a canter.

They were the hoofbeats of a horseman.

IN THE dark he was upon us suddenly. He rode a black horse. He was hidden by a greatcoat, and on his head was a pillbox cap. He dismounted at one of the maple trees, looped reins over a limb, and laid his coat on the saddle. He strode to the tractor and reached in under the hood. The engine gasped and died. Then, with the squeaking of boots in snow, he marched in our direction.

He entered the yellow light, a tall young man with a brown spade beard which gave him an ancestral expression. His frayed uniform was blue, with a stripe down the cavalry breeches. Hanging from his belt on the left side was a saber, while on the right a Colt revolver was snug against his hip.

He towered over the five of us. The Stackable sisters stared up at him, eyes over their scarves as big as buttons.

He touched the visor of his cap. "Good evening, misses."

He inspected me in an almost military manner, and I squirmed. "Well, well," he said.

I did not know whether I passed muster or not, but I had to set a bold example for my staff. "You shouldn't have turned off the tractor," I said. "I might not be able to start it again."

"We'll see about that, sonny." He rubbed his hands. "Now let's leave off cussing the ladies and get this old pumper inside. You stand guard up there and keep a sharp eye on those casters."

It was an order. I moved to the skids, elbowing Toody away.

The cavalryman bent to the low end of the melodeon, hoisted, set the casters on the skids as slick as a whistle, put a shoulder to the instrument, and with one powerful lunge shoved it up and over the skids and onto the stoop.

"Open the door," he directed me. "And you, misses, fetch the lanterns."

I opened the door. Agnes, Frances, Delores, and Toody had turned to stone. I got the lanterns and waited by the door.

He lifted the organ over the doorsill, then rolled it into the church and down the aisle between the benches. I lighted his way.

"Whereabouts?" he asked.

"There, I guess." I indicated a place near the pulpit.

I went outside, picked up the organ bench, and hissed at the girls. "You get in there and help!"

But all they could do was shiver and hold on to each other.

"Oooooh!" moaned Toody.

"Ohhhhh!" groaned Delores.

"Eeeeee!" squealed Frances.

"A ghost!" quavered Agnes.

"He is not," I snapped.

"Then who is he?"

"Never you mind. Come on, shake a leg!"

Finally they crept into the church. I closed the door and herded them down the aisle. But they would not go near the stranger, huddling down on a bench as close together as they could squeeze.

He had removed the horse blankets from the melodeon. I brought the organ bench and placed it.

"There," he said. "There." He stepped back and feasted eyes on the instrument. "Good as new, big as life, and twice as natural. Ain't it a beauty, though, boy?"

"Yes, sir," I said.

"Hmmm," he mused. "You don't reckon my note's still there? Let's have a look."

He folded back the keyboard top, raised a lantern, and bending, peered inside the cabinet. "I'll be dogged. It is."

"What note?" I asked.

"Why, the one I wrote and stuck inside for her. Lookee here."

I went to him and, while he held the lantern, squinted into the cabinet. Sure enough, at one side, pasted to the wood, was a slip of yellowed paper with a faded brown inscription: "for my Sarah, to keep her company."

"Don't know if she ever found it," he said. "D'you?"

"No, sir."

He set his lantern down and seated himself on the needlepoint bench, taking care to put his saber aside. "Oh, I recollect that day. Traded a cow and two hogs for it, and what cash money I had, and would've given my right arm if need be," he said. "I won't so much as touch it, but I'd enjoy to set a spell and meditate."

We were quiet, the girls and I. The cavalryman sat motionless at the melodeon, his long back to us. The lanterns uncovered a rude mural of raw walls, bare floor, rows of unbacked benches, a white-pine pulpit, and beside that, the gift of my grandparents. The new wood smelled of sacrifice, the old wood of remembrance. In the lanterns' glow the cherry cabinet was enriched, and the scrollwork of the music rack possessed the symmetry of art. What we had come to was a small, poor place, as houses of worship go, but I understood then what the Mason & Hamlin would mean. It would do much more than keep the hymns on key and accompany the passing of the plate. The love and loss and resurrection of which it was a symbol would consecrate the little church.

"Have you got a real beard?" Toody's voice gave us a start.

The man on the bench turned around. "I have. Why don't you sit on my knee and give it a pull?"

Toody was reluctant. "Are you Santy Claus?"

"I might be."

Toody was dubious. "Santy Claus rides in a sleigh with reindeers and wears a red suit."

"Sometimes."

"And he's fat and jolly and you're not."

"That's so. But then, I expect Santa comes in many a shape and suit and disposition."

57

"Anyway," said Toody, getting down to brass tacks, "I wanted a doll, and you gave me darn old galoshes."

"I see. I'm sorry. But let me tell you, missy, I know a regiment would trade their boots for yours and be glad of it."

Toody was unappeased. "Well, I have to have a new doll next Christmas. A Bye-Lo Baby that opens and shuts her eyes."

"Will you be a good girl?"

"I'm always good."

"Then I'll think on it," he promised.

Turning back to the instrument, he lowered the folding top and covered the keyboard. "How I wish I'd been there, to hear my Sarah play," he sighed. "And little Willy, too."

He sat for a moment, then sprang up with a jangle of his saber chain and smote a palm violently. "Criminy, I've got an idee!"

He reached and grasped my chin in his hand. "James, tomorrow morning, when you come to meeting, you get Willy to play. The song he was agoing to when I came home. So's I can hear him!"

My chin might as well have been in a vise. "He won't," I managed between my teeth.

He released me. "Won't? Why not?"

"He never would. Not after you didn't come home."

"I know that, boy. But why?"

It was difficult to express. I tried to recall Will's words earlier that night in the sheepshed. "I asked him why, and he said, 'Because my pa would never hear me. Or see me, nor I him.'"

The cavalryman's eyes clouded with pain. Only now I noted how ashen was his color, how drawn and weary was his face.

"Oh," he said. "He couldn't know, but I would have heard him. And if he will play tomorrow morning, I can hear. You've got to get him to, James."

He was asking the impossible. "I don't know how. He's too stubborn. Can I just tell him you said to?"

"Oh, no." He shook his head. He swept the girls and me with a glower. "That's the one thing you mustn't do, none of you—tell a soul I was here. They won't believe you anyhow, because they're grown up and past believing. No, you mustn't tell."

"I can if I want to," said Toody.

He looked pins and needles at her, then at her sisters, then at me. He drew himself to full parade-ground height. "You let out one peep," he said evenly, "and I'll be around someday when you're not looking and fetch you a swat on the behind with the flat of my saber'll make your teeth rattle and your ears fall off."

We knew he meant it, and even Toody did not dare sass him again. But when he saw that his threat had sunk in, his face softened. "Time you spalpeens were in bed. James," he said wistfully, "you'll mind now about tomorrow? I lend you a hand tonight, you give me a song in the morning—turnabout's fair play."

"I'll try," I said. "I really will."

"Good lad. Oh, you're a Chubb, I'll vouch for that. Time to go, young ones. Bring the lanterns."

I took one and handed Agnes Stackable the other, and we went down the aisle before him and outdoors onto the stoop. He closed the church door behind us.

The night was still as it had been. No wind gusted, not a single snowflake fell. Over by a maple tree a horse nickered.

The cavalryman dropped to one knee. "Come near now, all of you." He spread his long arms and drew us into a circle. "It don't take a soldier to be brave. You've done a fine thing tonight, as brave as ever I saw. And I thank you every one."

"You're welcome," said Toody.

Since he was leaving, I thought I'd better ask while I had the opportunity. "The war," I said. "Was it awful as they say?"

He nodded. "It was."

"Well, was it worth it?"

"Worth it? What do you say, boy?" he demanded proudly. "Good times or bad, ain't it a grand and glorious Union?"

"Yes, sir," I said.

"And don't you forget it." He smiled. "And now good night, young misses, good night, James. And a Merry Christmas to you."

Before we could wish him one, too, he rose and marched to the Oil Pull. Seizing the handle, he gave the flywheel a mighty whirl, and instantly the engine banged into smoky life.

The cavalryman tipped his cap to us, strode jangling and squeaking through the snow to his black horse, hauled on his greatcoat, unlooped the reins, mounted, gigged the animal about, and rode off beyond the trees, heading south.

Agnes, Frances, Delores, Toody, and I stood where we were until the sound of hoofbeats became the canter of the tractor cylinders and was gone.

SIX

WE WERE homeward bound, and through the commotion of the 20-40 the odious Agnes shrieked in my ear. "Who was that?"

I shook my head.

"He knew your name! You knew him!"

I pretended not to hear.

"I'll tell my pa!"

I heard that. "Agnes, you better not. Remember what he said about a swat of his saber."

"Banana oil!"

"He said don't tell a soul!" I roared. "You tell anybody and I'll hate you!"

That sewed up her lips as effectively as a darning needle, so I could steer the Oil Pull in peace, and down the county road we rumbled, lanterns swinging as we turned onto the township road. It was easy going, following the tracks we had previously cut through the drifts, the stoneboat dragging submissively after us. The four girls perched on the fenders over the drive wheels, Agnes and Frances on one side, Delores and Toody on the other, facing me, while I maintained a captain's composure on the bridge and allowed them to admire my seamanship.

Lights blazed from practically every window at the Stackable place, and when we halted, and the girls hopped off the fenders, Kate Stackable and Will were standing by the road. Kate hugged her darlings as though she had never expected to see them again.

"Bless you, James! See you in the morning," she called. "Merry Christmas!"

I waved a modest mitten.

Will climbed into the cab, but I sat where I was, in the driver's seat; throttled up, shoved the lever into high, and took off with such a jerk that he had to grab an upright. He seated himself on a fender, and the rest of the way home superintended me with a mixture of amusement and apprehension.

It was a straight run. I thought about my grandmother and what she would say and do when she walked into church in the morning. I thought about the cavalryman, and how the Sam Hill I could ever persuade his son, my grandfather, to try the keys of the melodeon in public when he hadn't touched them in private for sixty years or more. I thought about my father and mother for the first time since they had telephoned me, and preened myself on how proud I would be when they heard what I had accomplished tonight. Then I remembered Ella's fable, and made up my mind to decline pride and settle instead for a big, fat orange of contentment.

When we reached the granary I turned left, facing the open end, and using the expertise I had acquired at the church, piloted the Oil Pull into its berth. Will descended, shut the engine off, and the Rumely breathed its triumphant last.

We unhitched the stoneboat and dragged it where it belonged. We put away the ropes and horse blankets. Everything had to seem undisturbed to Ella in the morning. Then we stood for a minute outside the granary and listened to the tinking of iron and steel as the Oil Pull cooled to rest again till spring.

"Storm's over," said my grandfather.

"Yup."

"I'll wager it's ten below."

"At least."

I glanced up at the stars. They twinkled in the cold and black, but they were remote.

"I'm sorry I went to sleep at the switch," he apologized. "I was just tuckered out."

"That's okay," I said affably.

"You made it to the church all right then."

"In a breeze."

61

"And you and those girls got that organ inside by yourselves?"

"Sure."

"How?"

I had to be careful. "Same way you and I got it out of the house onto the stoneboat. On the skids."

"Bosh. That's too damned big a load for kids to heft."

"Oh, those girls are strong."

"Boy, I don't believe you."

"You wait. You'll see in the morning."

He was looking at me, but I was looking at the distant, secret stars of Christmas.

"Well, if you did," he said, "I'll be eternally grateful."

"My pleasure, Gramp," I assured him with an adult insouciance. We started for the house.

"Hey," I said. "Hadn't we better take a look at the lamb?"

"All right, if you're a mind to."

We took the lanterns to the barn and walked halfway down the steps to the sheepshed. Most of the flock were lying asleep, possibly dreaming about green grass and the pleasures of shearing and the mating season. Calvin, the ram, was awake, however, and so was the old ewe. She was standing. Her lamb knelt at her side having a midnight supper, its tail alive with delight.

My grandfather tugged at an end of his mustache. I noticed how gray and weary was his face, and how much, if he had worn a spade beard, he'd have resembled someone else.

"I still don't believe it," he harped. "Unless you had help."

"You didn't believe that lamb either," I said.

We headed for the house again, plodding through snow. We were sleepy and numb and our soapstones would be cold by now, but we didn't give a whoop.

I was wakened early by a hullabaloo of cackling in the backyard. Then I realized it was Christmas morning and we'd be on our way to church soon and somehow I had to figure out PDQ how to get Will to play the melodeon.

I dressed, shivering, in my best bib and tucker and went downstairs. It was a dashing winter day, colder than a dogcatcher's heart, but bright and sunny. I washed and combed my hair and searched my upper lip as usual for omens and stepped into the kitchen. Ella was simultaneously getting breakfast and plucking another chicken.

"Merry Christmas," I said.

"He did it," she said.

"Did what?"

"Your grandfather killed a hen—the first time ever. I'll never understand him as long as I live."

"Where is he?"

"Doing the chores."

"How did you sleep?" I inquired.

"Like a log. I declare, I don't know what came over me last night. Oh, Merry Christmas, James."

Will entered and said he thought we could get to service after all, provided the Cadwells put on chains, because it appeared to him—with a wink at me—that the county equipment had been down our road during the night and broken the drifts.

The next two hours were busy ones, which was ideal, for Ella had neither opportunity nor excuse to stray into the parlor and discover anything missing. We breakfasted on eggs, about which I wasn't particularly thrilled, and on johnnycake, about which I was. Then I did the dishes while Ella stuffed our chicken and put it in the oven to roast while we were gone, and dressed the second hen, Will's victim, and packed it in a basket.

By the time Mr. and Mrs. Cadwell came by for us in their Model A sedan we were ready and waiting—Will in suit and shirt, although he eschewed a necktie, and Ella gussied up in a cloth coat and crepe dress and green hat pinned modishly at the side of her gray head. We climbed aboard, me in back with the ladies, and Will up front with the basket, and found the snow no obstacle, thanks to chains and the indefatigability of the Ford.

At Will's request Reuel Cadwell stopped at the Henshaw place. Joe and Abby had already gone to church, and Will deposited the basket on the front porch. No one made any comment. Charity in those days, unlike that of the present, was for the most part individual and spontaneous rather than impersonal and systematic. It had nothing to do with taxes. It was an act of addition rather than deduction.

We passed the Stackable place and soon turned onto the county road. I had only minutes now to come to a decision. The cavalryman had me over a barrel. Oh, I could tell myself he hadn't really ridden to our rescue last night, that the girls and I had wrestled the melodeon from stoneboat to church stoop by ourselves—a lie is often the nearest exit from an adolescent dilemma. But the truth is a better way to maturity, and the truth was, what was to happen in a few minutes the Chubb family—four generations of it—owed almost entirely to the man on the black horse. He had asked for a song from his son, the son he had never seen, the song the boy had planned to play for him on his return from war, and I had said, "I'll try." Try I must, then, and chance the anger and embarrassment and laughter and the psychic damage I might do.

We were late arriving at church, and it was apparent from the number of cars that there would be a full house. Reuel Cadwell parked the Ford, and we got out and tramped through the snow. Will delayed the three of us and let the Cadwells go in first. It was a ruse, I knew, to be certain his wife would have the full, undistracted impact of our surprise.

"What else did you put in the basket?" he inquired of her.

"Peach preserves, some hickory nutmeats, a mince pie—for goodness' sake, why would you ask now?"

"I just wondered."

"Fiddlesticks." And she adjusted her hat and preceded us to the door with a spry, impatient step. She opened it and entered, Will and I behind her.

I will not attempt to describe the look on my grandmother's face as exactly as I have described the Mason & Hamlin melodeon and the Rumely Oil Pull. She must have seen the rows of benches crowded with friends and neighbors, their every eye upon her. She must have seen the iron wood stove in a corner, roaring with religious ardor. She must have seen the Reverend Leon Ledwidge,

64

white-haired and benign, standing by his pulpit smiling at her. She saw them, but perceived them not. The organ transfixed her. She looked at it, then at Will, then at me, then at the organ again. And the long-awaited look on her face was—language is too often imprecise, but I shall do my best—beatific. Her face itself, for a moment, was young as that of the girl she once had been. And after that moment, Will took one elbow, I the other, and together we escorted her to a bench.

A little overwhelmed, we heard Reverend Ledwidge say he wished, before beginning service, to acknowledge the generous gift of Mr. and Mrs. Will Chubb to the church—a melodeon which, so he understood, had belonged to the family since 1863. Such a gift, he said, would be appreciated by the members, he was sure, to the same degree it had been cherished by its donors. He understood also that special thanks were due Will Chubb and his grandson, since it was only through their efforts that the instrument had been delivered, by tractor and stoneboat and despite last night's storm, to the church in time for Christmas devotions.

"Reverend?" It was my grandfather.

"Yes, Mr. Chubb?"

"I'm afraid I can't take much credit," said Will. "We got as far as the Stackables', and I couldn't go on. We had a miserable time trying to start that tractor, and then, earlier, we'd had a lamb born. And so I—"

"A lamb?" Charley Greeve was startled into asking.

"This time of year?" scoffed Emmett Roach.

"Yes sirree, we did," Will maintained. "I know, I know, but we did. And so I plumb tuckered out. And I think folks should know Kate Stackable sent her girls on with James here, and the youngsters did the rest."

Everyone smiled at Agnes, Frances, Delores, and Toody, who wiggled on their bench and produced demure blushes.

"Then we thank them, too," said the minister. "And now, I think it would be fitting if Mrs. Chubb did us the honor of playing the first selection on the organ."

"I'm sorry, Reverend." This was my grandmother from her seat.

"I simply can't. I wish I could, but I'm troubled with arthritis in my fingers, and I'd be ashamed of my mistakes. So I hope you'll forgive me if I ask to be excused."

There were murmurs of sympathy.

"Of course, Mrs. Chubb," said the parson. "Then I'm afraid we must—"

"My grandfather can play." I was on my feet. "My grandfather can play it. Ephraim wants Will to play the song he planned to when he came home from the war."

Except for the ebullience of the stove, the silence was as absolute as it had been last midnight, when the cavalryman appeared. But I could not turn tail now. I had already decided to tell the truth, no matter how it hurt. It was the only way to close the mortal circle, to restore a father to his son, and to assure that son his

66

father had not forgotten him even in death. And it was also time I grew up and ceased to treat two people near and dear to me as grandparents rather than the human beings they so stubbornly, inconsistently, passionately were. So speak I must, and trust in Christmas.

Reverend Ledwidge frowned. "Who is Ephraim?"

"My great-grandfather, sir. Ephraim Chubb. He was a cavalry-man in the Civil War, and he gave Sarah the melodeon when he went away."

"Sarah?"

"My great-grandmother. And she taught Will to play when he was a little boy. But when Ephraim, his father, was killed, he never did again. His father wants him to, this morning."

"How do you know this, James?"

"Because he told me."

"When?"

"Last night, sir. Right here."

"Here?"

I fixed upon the eyes of the minister. If I had caught even a glimpse of Will's or Ella's face, I might have collapsed.

"Yes, sir. The truth is, the girls and I couldn't get the organ up the skids onto the stoop—it was too heavy. Then the cavalryman came along and helped us. And afterward he asked me to get Will to play the song he learned for when his father came home. And I said I'd try. He told us not to tell anybody he'd been here, because they wouldn't believe us. But I don't know any other way to get my grandfather to play. I'm sorry."

To this day I wonder that I got it all out. But I stood stiff as a ramrod and tried to make sense, because I had a bone-deep conviction that someone else besides those present was watching.

"Maybe you don't believe me," I said. "But the girls will tell you. He was here last night, wasn't he, Agnes?" I appealed.

Perfidious creature—she pretended I didn't exist.

"Wasn't he, Frances?" I implored. "Wasn't he, Delores?"

The loobies sat like bumps on a log.

"Toody!" I cried. "You've got to tell!"

The youngest Stackable stood up on cue. "Yup, Santy Claus was here," she said. "I think," she said. "He had a beard all right, but he wore a blue suit, not a red one, and he rode a horse, not a sleigh, and he had a sword, not a bag of presents, and he wasn't fat and jolly, he was sad and skinny. That's all I'm telling. Oh, and he promised to bring me a doll next Christmas, because all I got last night was darn old galoshes." She might have taken a bow had Kate Stackable not pulled her down. She had not helped. The congregational disbelief could have been cut with a knife.

"I can prove it!" I cried, and my voice cracked in a new and interesting way. I entreated the minister. "Sir, if you'll just look inside the top of the organ, you'll see the note Ephraim pasted in there for Sarah to find—he showed me last night. It says, 'for my Sarah, to keep her company.' Honest it does."

Reverend Ledwidge stared at me, then stepped cautiously to the melodeon, lifted the top, peered inside the cabinet, adjusted his spectacles, and peered again.

He straightened. He pinched the bridge of his nose. "There is a note," he announced. "And those are the words—'for my Sarah, to keep her company.'" He cleared his throat. "Mrs. Chubb, were you aware of this note?"

Everyone strained to hear. "No," she said, almost whispering. "Sarah wasn't either. None of us were." She shook her head. "I don't understand it."

Nor did anyone else. Men studied their hands. Women looked in other women's faces for confirmation or dissent. Children scuffed their shoes. The yarn I had spun about a cavalryman on a black horse could be safely discounted. I was a boy, and it was a fact that boys were prone to whistle in the dark. And the jabber of a six-year-old like Toody could be attributed to candy, excitement, and an upset stomach. But the note was also a fact, and two hundred and fifty pounds deadweight was a fact, and it was clear to practical farmers and their wives that one feckless boy and four girls could not, unaided, have transferred these facts from stoneboat to stoop.

I could stand no longer. I sat down.

The Reverend Leon Ledwidge removed his spectacles and polished the lenses with a handkerchief. He put them on again, stepped to the pulpit, and folded hands upon it. He closed his eyes for an interminable minute.

"Friends," he said finally, "I don't know that it will profit us to vex our hearts over what we have seen and heard here. It may be that we have been witness to a miracle. Children have eyes to see things we cannot. And who among us is to say it is not possible? It is a miracle, is it not, that in these times, and on the ashes of the old church, we have built a new? Is it not miraculous that we have an organ today, an offering from the very bosom of a family, and brought to us by children? Last night, let us remember, was Christmas Eve, which has always been a time of mystery and magic. And if a child could be born long ago upon that holy night, a child our Lord and Saviour, which of us shall doubt the mystery and magic of this morning?"

He paused. "Dear friends, let us pray."

We bowed our heads.

"O Lord, we thank Thee for the miracle of the melodeon. We thank Thee for the courage of these children, who have brought to Thy sanctuary not gold or frankincense or myrrh but the gift of music. Bless this good woman, Ella Chubb, and her husband, Will, Thy faithful servants, for the generosity and love they have manifested to us and to Thee. Lift up Thy countenance, dear Lord, and make Thy face to shine upon them. And finally, our Heavenly Father, we ask of Thee another miracle. We ask that one of us be generous of his spirit as he has been of his strength and worldly goods. We ask that he play the song his father never heard, and give him peace. We ask it in the name of Thy son, in Christ's name. Amen."

The old man raised his head and looked at the three of us. "Will?" he asked.

My grandmother took my hand in hers, tightly.

Slowly my grandfather rose, moved down the aisle. He stood before the melodeon as though before a bar of judgment, then slowly seated himself upon the bench. He put his feet upon the pedals. He pumped. The bellows of the organ filled with air. He lifted hands above the keyboard, hands trained to plow and sow and play the iron scales of his machinery, hands which had the night before brought forth a lamb. He closed his eyes.

We held our breath. Time seemed to tick backward over the seasons. And as we waited, the man at the melodeon, withered now upon the tree of life, seemed to alter visibly, to sit erect, to ripen into prime, then green into a boy, a boy who slumped in sorrow, fatherless and lost. Would memory fail him? Could fingers do the bidding of his brain, turn the anguish of a lifetime into melody?

He touched the keys. There, in a shaft of sunlight through a window, tears trickling down his cheeks, he filled the church with music haunting and lovely, a song familiar only to the elders in the congregation. One by one they rose, those like him whose wounds had never healed, those who had not forgotten sacrifices made, loved ones lost in fratricidal conflict to save a nation. Their voices were quavery but brave:

> *"We're tenting tonight on the old camp ground,*
> *Give us a song to cheer*
> *Our weary hearts, a song of home,*
> *And friends we love so dear.*
>
> *Many are the hearts that are weary tonight,*
> *Wishing for the war to cease;*
> *Many are the hearts, looking for the right,*
> *To see the dawn of peace.*
> *Tenting tonight, tenting tonight,*
> *Tenting on the old camp ground."*

SEVEN

I STAYED at my grandparents' farm till the next summer. My father found employment then and the means to bring me home.

Two years after my sojourn on the farm the half section of land which had been the family's for a century was sold. I never saw it again. I do not know if the barn and granary still stand, or the church at Chubb's Corners. I do not know what became of the Stackable girls—if Toody got her doll, for example, if Agnes ever lost her warts or found a husband. I hope they did.

It has been forty-one years. I have not encountered the cavalry-man a second time. For many years I disbelieved in his appearance on that Christmas Eve, but I am young enough at last to know better, to accept the minister's assertion that children have eyes to see things we cannot. I trust that in the meantime my forebear has forgiven me for telling on him and that I may never feel, on my mature backside, the flat of his terrible swift sword. Now and then in cold and dark of night I hear the *huff-huff* of the Oil Pull on its invincible way, just as I sometimes hear, on a winter morning, the antique strains of a pump organ.

I will never forget the gifts of that Christmas. If my grandfather gave the melodeon to his wife, in one sense, together they gave it to their God. I received a jackknife, which remains in my possession, and a hand-knit scarf, and better yet, the beginning of awareness that no matter what its failings, ours is indeed a grand and glorious Union. Born in struggle and exaltation like the lamb, it has been made from the faith and blood and devotion of those who have gone before us. To it, as to them and their example, we must be true. Best of all, however, storm and Christmas and self-lessness and a horseman out of the past gave me two beloved human beings, not grandparents, but a man and woman I could esteem and learn from and remember.

Will Chubb died the last week of that April. He was afflicted with hay lung, the reader will recall, and caught a cold while plowing. The cold developed into pneumonia. The doctor drove down from Howell several times—Will was too ill to be moved to the hospital. Everything that could be done for him was done, to no avail. He worsened rapidly.

It happened in midmorning. Clyde and Kate Stackable and Joe Henshaw and Mrs. Cadwell had come by with a cake and a pie and a loaf of new-baked bread, expressed their sorrow, and departed. Ella emerged from the bedroom off the kitchen and said that Will had regained consciousness and asked for me. I went in, to stand tentatively by the bed. I was frightened. I did not know Death then, that he is no more to be feared than the man on the black horse. He can be kind, time teaches us. Grace is his comrade, memory his foe. In the end he prevails, but triumphs not, so long as we remember. And so, thirteen and afraid, I knelt beside my grandfather. His color was gray, the eyes sunken, and his mustache drooped, bereft of luster. His lips moved. I leaned forward, placed my ear above his open mouth.

"Go for a walk," he whispered.

I shook my head.

"Go find the flock. Find our lamb."

"No. I won't."

"Go!"

The word came out of him like a command. I had hopped to that kind of authority before, outside the church on Christmas Eve. Startled, I raised my head to look at him. His eyes reminded me of my great-grandfather's. They were soldierly.

I stumbled through the kitchen and out the door, marched between barn and granary and down the road, more lorn than I had ever been in my life. I hiked through the huckleberry marsh, then climbed a fence into a green pasture, and there, at the far end, was the flock. I walked toward them. I knew now that Will had ordered me away so that I would be somewhere else, doing something, when he died. I knew that when I returned to the house Ella would be waiting and that she would say, "He's gone, James."

It was a lucent morning. The sun was warm, the grass rich, a few clouds like puffs of tractor smoke floated under a blue sky, and the air was sweet with birdsong and fertilizer and innocence.

I approached the grazing flock. They were white now, having just been sheared of their winter gray. Some of the ewes were fat and would be lambing soon. Calvin, the ram, scratched his hindquarters against the fence and cast, occasionally, a benevolent glance in their direction. I tried but could not identify our lamb. And the reason was, I couldn't see the animals clearly, my eyes were too full, and when I addressed them, it was with considerable difficulty.

"You stop!" I shouted. "You stop eating and standing around acting like nothing's happening!"

They were impervious. I began to sob.

"You damn sheep! Don't you know what's happening to the man who's fed you and dipped you and sheared you and helped bring your babies into the world? Well, you better know! He's dying!" I bawled between sobs. "Will Chubb is dying right now! My grandfather! Your friend! He's going away and never coming back! Do you hear? Or don't you care?"

It was evident they did not, and I turned from them and began to run. I ran across the pasture and over the fence and down the road and between the barn and granary and slowed down and swiped away the tears with a sleeve, because my grandmother stood in front of the house, waiting for me. I walked toward her endlessly, just as Ephraim had left the team and walked endlessly over the field toward his wife in another April.

I came to her, and she put her arms around me, and I put mine around her. I thought of Sarah, and of Strawberry Plains.

"Oh, James, he's gone," she said.

Services for my grandfather were held in the church. My mother could not afford to come, but all of Will's friends and neighbors were in attendance, and the Reverend Leon Ledwidge officiated. Ella played a hymn on the melodeon, because she thought Will would want her to:

> *Abide with me!*
> *Fast falls the eventide,*
> *The darkness deepens—*
> *Lord, with me abide!*
>
> *When other helpers fail,*
> *And comforts flee,*
> *Help of the helpless,*
> *Oh, abide with me!*

She never got her automobile. She herself passed away two years later, of loneliness, I have surmised, but she is no longer alone. She was laid to rest beside Will and his parents in the township ground.

So my Christmas story ends in springtime. They have long been reunited now, Ephraim and Will, father and son, and their dear wives, Sarah and Ella, gathered unto each other beneath the oak trees near the church. May the music of the melodeon attend their dreams forever.

There is much in *The Melodeon* that is real: the names of the people, the midwestern farm setting, the Oil Pull tractor, and the melodeon itself. In fact, the author explains, the novel is "a sort of memorial to my grandparents and great-grandparents, a labor of love, you might say." And although it was conceived over the years, it was written in haste, so that three or four of Glendon Swarthout's closest relatives, now in their eighties, would see the book in print. It is but one example of the strong sense of continuity that runs in the family.

Mr. Swarthout, who once earned a Ph.D. in English literature, began as a teacher, writing fiction on the side. That changed in 1958 when, with the success of his novel *They Came to Cordura*, he became a full-time writer. Since then he has published a number of books, including *Bless the Beasts and Children* (a Reader's Digest Condensed Books selection) and most recently *The Shootist*, which was adapted for Paramount Pictures by Mr. Swarthout's son, Miles.

Although he grew up in Michigan, as did four generations before him, Mr. Swarthout now lives at the edge of the Arizona desert. The nearest he comes to the academic life nowadays is to present the annual creative-writing prizes he and his wife have set up at Arizona State University.

Glendon Swarthout

From the windows of his study he exults in a flock of Gambel quail that he feeds. So familiar has he become with their habits that he knows when to put out water for the newly hatched chicks. Without it, he comments, those "gray feathery little golf balls" would perish within twenty-four hours.

Above Mr. Swarthout's writing desk is a Colt revolver, a family heirloom he was given when he became twenty-one. The pistol belonged to his great-grandfather, the cavalryman who left his plowshare to go off to war.

PHOTO BY NYLE LEATHAM

A President's
well-kept secret
may force him
out of office

Full
Disclosure

A CONDENSATION OF THE NOVEL BY

WILLIAM SAFIRE

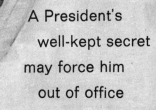

ILLUSTRATED BY GEORGE JONES

It is the mid-1980s. America is faced with a shocking crisis: after a bizarre assassination attempt on Russian soil, Sven Ericson, the Lincolnesque, immensely popular forty-first President, is blind!

Can a sightless President carry out his awesome powers and duties? The Twenty-fifth Amendment of the Constitution should provide the answer, but never before has its "disability" clause been invoked. As powerful forces demand his resignation, Ericson, behind dark glasses, morally certain of his competence, fights the political battle of his life.

Former White House staff member William Safire writes knowledgeably about the explosive secrets, love affairs, and cover-ups of people in power, while posing an absorbing, believable dilemma.

"The shrewdest Washington novel since *Advise and Consent*."
                                        —*Kirkus Reviews*
"Fascinating in its insight into the highest echelons of power . . ."
                                        —*Publishers Weekly*

I: AMBUSH AND AFTERMATH

Harry Bok looked out the window of *Air Force One*. The brown Russian countryside gained contour as the aircraft descended toward the Black Sea resort. All these years—he had joined the Secret Service when he turned twenty-one—he had been stuck in presidential protection. A bodyguard.

Counterfeiting, that was for him. Meticulous work, satisfying results. He took his souvenir phony hundred-dollar bill out of his wallet and crinkled it in his hand; the paper was a touch too heavy. He felt sorry for the engraver, to work so painstakingly and then lose out on the failure of his paper supplier.

Sitting next to Harry was a Russian guard detailed to the Soviet Foreign Minister, who was up in President Sven Ericson's cabin, meeting with the President and the Secretary of State.

"I never met an agent as old as you," said the Russian.

"I'm only twenty-six, but I drink a lot," Harry replied.

The Russian was right, of course: Harry Bok, forty-six, was no longer sure he was ready to put his body between a President and a bullet. He was ready to face the fact that he was an aging agent, but nobody else was. He was a presidential favorite, and Presidents kept passing him along to their successors. They thought he was easy to talk to. Probably it was the sympathetic expression on his face. The furrows and the jowls and the soft brown eyes seemed to assure the speaker that Harry was a safe and understanding repository of top secrets.

The ground was getting closer. Harry grunted out of his seat and went to the washroom. When he emerged, Buffie Masterson was waiting for him. Strawberry-blond hair, no makeup, athletic young body in a green jumpsuit, and, as usual, insistent: "I want a ride in the chopper, Harry. Can you get me on?"

She was the forty-first President's official photographer, the best picture taker to hold the job in years, and part of her talent was a likable pushiness.

"Come up to the Boss's cabin about five minutes after I do," Harry told her, "and ask him yourself."

Harry did not know if President Ericson wanted her to go with him on the Russian chopper or to ride with the press corps. The plan called for the President, accompanied by Secretary of State George Curtice and Soviet Foreign Minister Vasily Nikolayev, to arrive in Simferopol Airport in a few minutes to be greeted by General Secretary Kolkov. Ericson and Kolkov had met earlier, in Moscow; then, while Ericson was touring Leningrad, Kiev, and Minsk, Kolkov had gone to his dacha at Yalta, on the Black Sea, to await the American President for the final weekend of the visit. At the Soviets' suggestion, the two leaders—accompanied only by guards and an interpreter—were to be helicoptered from the airport to the dacha, followed by a guard chopper. The rest of the party—about two hundred correspondents and a hundred staffers— would meet and be briefed at the airport hangar, then driven to Yalta's Oreanda Hotel. That would give Ericson and Kolkov some unofficial hours together, with no press pool.

Harry stood in the aisle, not worried about security. Electronic surveillance around the dacha would be intense. Also, the President had been permitted to fly around the Soviet Union in *Air Force One*. But Harry was not happy about the forthcoming chopper ride, for a personal reason: choppers made his stomach queasy. He would have preferred that they all take the two-hour motorcade trip, but Foreign Minister Nikolayev was anxious to show off the new Soviet equipment, so the White House advance men had agreed. Just as well, Harry conceded. The chopper ride would only be twenty minutes.

Harry told himself he was more concerned about the trip home. First to Lajes Field, in the Azores—which had just become American territory—then to Andrews Air Force Base, in Washington, D.C. Big crowds, always a problem. Harry took an empty seat next to Lucas Cartwright, the President's chief of staff.

"Are you having a pleasant voyage, Mr. Bok?" White-haired Cartwright was the last courtly gentleman left around the White House, where he dated back to service under Truman—"as a lad, a mere stripling," he liked to add. The Tennessee gentleman farmer was the consummate presidential adviser, the unflappable man who was self-assured, always dependable and cool. Harry liked him because he added a note of formality to a new administration that tended to be too lazily with-it. The President liked Cartwright because he felt a President should have a chief of staff who had useful memories, Washington connective tissue, and a low personal center of gravity.

"I get the feeling that this summit is a big, flat flop," Harry said. "Why? Ericson's supposed to be smart as hell on the foreign economic stuff. He was a professor."

"According to the Secretary of State," Cartwright answered carefully, "the purpose of President Ericson's visit was, first, to get acquainted with Comrade Kolkov, which he has done brilliantly. Second, the President was determined to find out if the Soviets were putting out feelers to the Far Eastern powers. The President is troubled. Not even Nikolayev, who is supposed to be Kolkov's protégé, can assure us of the old man's tendencies."

"Our boy Curtice is pretty chummy with Nikolayev."

"Harry, the nation's first black Secretary of State is never referred to as 'boy.'" Cartwright smiled, then became serious. "Friendship has nothing to do with these dealings; the national interest always comes first."

Cartwright continued: "You know the President better than I do. You, and Dr. Abelson, and Hennessy, and Melinda McPhee—what does the inner circle think?"

81

"The President's physician never gets his nose out of his black bag. Hennessy's sore because he didn't get to go on the trip. After all, he *is* special counsel. Melinda thinks the President is a little cocky."

"Melinda has good instincts," Cartwright said obliquely. "The President is fortunate to have a secretary like her."

The Page Boy alarm on Harry's hip went off, sending vibrations into his body. He left his seat and checked in at the command post ahead of the President's cabin. The deputy chief of detail went over the assignments for each of the agents on the plane. Harry was to be the only one with The Man on the chopper.

"Go AHEAD, push the button," the President said, smiling. "It doesn't blow up the world."

Vasily Nikolayev pushed the button. The desk in the working cabin of *Air Force One* lowered to coffee-table height, and a panel slid back to reveal nuts and dried fruit. The Soviet Foreign Minister permitted himself to look impressed.

"I think the summit meetings have gone well so far," Secretary of State Curtice remarked. Nikolayev gave a polite nod, as if he agreed.

In fact, the talks had gone badly. Not just for the Americans, but from Nikolayev's point of view as well. Kolkov, now in his late seventies and getting more paranoid every day, had tried to lull the Americans with promises of further strategic arms limitation. Ordinarily that would have pleased Nikolayev, but he thought about what Kolkov had told him only two weeks before: "Vasily, ever since the Far Eastern powers have joined together, American efforts to split the Communist world have become intolerable. We cannot afford to have a billion Chinese, with Japanese technology, in opposition to us. We must work with the Chijaps. I have begun the rapprochement."

Nikolayev had guessed that Kolkov had lost touch with reality. If Moscow tried to ally itself with Peking-Tokyo, it would find itself the junior partner in a Communist world, not the leader.

Now, as if reading his mind, the American President said to him,

"We hear the Soviet trade mission in Canton is about to make a deal to exchange your computers for their oil."

Nikolayev assured the President that the deal was only a counter to the trade openings of the Western consortium.

"Tell that to the marines," President Ericson said easily. "You're trying to get something going over there."

To change the subject, Nikolayev asked what the President's reference to the marines meant. Ericson explained the ordinary seaman's opinion of gullible marines—soldier-sailors who helped man ships in the early 1800s. Nikolayev liked the new American President. Ericson was tall—six feet three inches—and angular, sitting far back in his chair and talking over his jutting knees. "Lincolnesque" was the word admirers used about him. Interesting face, Nikolayev thought. A genuine tragedy that Ericson would be killed in approximately one hour.

Nikolayev felt he had much in common with Ericson: both were nearly fifty, coming into the prime of life and peak of power, stimulated rather than intimidated by the possibility of great failure. Unlike Ericson, Nikolayev had not yet taken command, but that was only a matter of a few hours.

Nikolayev decided yes, he was definitely saddened by the requirements of the plot he had conceived—Kolkov had lived too long and richly earned his execution for his intention to realign the Soviet Union with the Oriental powers. But Nikolayev would have liked to deal with Ericson on the world scene.

The assassination of Kolkov would split the Politburo; Nikolayev could not be certain of getting the upper hand. But the deaths of the two leaders together—blamed on the Far Eastern powers—would be a blood tie that would unite the U.S.S.R. and the United States against the Chinese and Japanese for decades.

The ambush, presumably by the Chinese, would take place when the Soviet helicopter was conveying the two leaders to the Kolkov dacha. Only Ericson, an interpreter, Kolkov, two Soviet guards, one American guard, two pilots, and a woman steward would be on the helicopter. After five minutes in the air, at a scenic spot near the Black Sea shore, the backup helicopter, supposedly accompanying Kolkov's party as a safety precaution, would shoot down the other craft with a single rocket. The assassins—four trusted airmen, all Mongolians, acting on orders from the chief of the Soviet air force, who was Nikolayev's closest ally in this enterprise—would then land near the shore, embark in a small speedboat for what they thought would be a waiting submarine. There would be no submarine, of course; the speedboat would be destroyed by Soviet pursuit aircraft, to avenge the deaths of the U.S.S.R.'s martyred leader and his American guest.

Nikolayev wished President Ericson could know he was to die in his country's best interest. There was no better way for a leader to lose his life. The Russian suppressed a sigh.

A burly man in a cheap-looking gray suit with holster bulges put his head in the doorway. "Mind if I join you for the landing?" That was Harry Bok, Nikolayev knew. The Secret Service agent was required to be seated next to the President on landings.

"You've met Harry," Ericson said, waving him in.

"We know all about him," Nikolayev replied pleasantly.

"You have a file on me at Dzerzhinski Square," Harry Bok said, buckling his seat belt.

"Dzerzhinski Square . . ." said Secretary Curtice slowly. "That's where the headquarters of the KGB is. Lubyanka Prison."

"Who was Dzerzhinski?" the President wanted to know.

"The first head of the Soviet secret police," Nikolayev replied. "'Iron Felix.' Hateful man, a pioneer of torture and murder."

"And you haven't renamed the square?" Curtice asked.

"An oversight." Nikolayev could not relax with Curtice, as he could with Ericson. Curtice was formal, inexperienced, and black, without the sangfroid of President Ericson. He was not flatterable, possibly not even bluffable. It was unfortunate, thought Nikolayev, that he could not replace Bok with Curtice on the helicopter.

A white light flashed on the telephone and the President picked it up. "Sure, send her in." A striking young woman appeared in the doorway, draped in cameras. "Here is our official photographer," Ericson said. "She's going to record this historic meeting." The photographer leaned against the doorjamb. At that moment,

Ericson's deep-set eyes registered amused pleasure; over the past week Nikolayev had seen those intelligent, Nordic blue eyes flash in anger, become intimidatingly cold, drill into negotiators across a table, and adopt a detached-observer cast.

As was known in intelligence circles but discreetly held to a small group in the White House, the official photographer was President Ericson's girl friend. He had much to be proud of, Nikolayev noted. The young woman radiated excitement, and her smile was difficult not to return. One reason there was so little gossip was that her talents as a photographer were recognized. Another was the fact that the President was divorced.

After taking shots at different angles, Buffie said to the President, "Any chance of me coming along for the chopper ride?"

Ericson's eyes turned that question to Nikolayev. Nikolayev shook his head regretfully and pretended not to hear the girl mutter "Hell" as she bounced up and slipped out the door.

Nikolayev looked at Ericson and sadly saluted this good man and the man of Polish descent who was his bodyguard. But he felt no shame at what he had set in motion.

"NOT even you got to go along on the chopper, Buffie?"

The President's official photographer, who had been grumpy for ten minutes after landing at Simferopol Airport, now grinned and shook her head. "I shot most of the area stuff already, Charley, with the advance party." Buffie called every member of the press corps Charley, except other photographers. She had had some difficulty, however, figuring out what to call Sven Ericson in private. She had settled on the acronym on his Call Director: POTUS, for President of the United States.

James Smith, the President's press secretary, was at a lectern in an empty hangar for the day's press briefing. Blowing into a microphone for a sound check, he called to Buffie, "How do you spell Vorontsov Palace?" The President's guest quarters were at the palace, near General Secretary Kolkov's dacha.

"P-a-l-a-c-e," she called back helpfully, and when no laugh was forthcoming, added the spelling of the Russian name. Another

85

voice asked her who she was rooming with at the Oreanda Hotel.

"Three Secret Service guys and they're terrified." Actually she had been assigned to a room with Marilee Pinckney, Smitty's deputy press secretary. Marilee was an aristocrat, a willowy beauty who, unlike Buffie, was a feminist. Buffie appreciated the way Marilee demolished anyone who suggested Buffie had gained her position by anything but professional talent. That perversely brought to mind Melinda McPhee, the President's secretary. Possessive, protective, thinking—in Buffie's eyes—that her loyalty was so fierce and her memory of political favors and slights so good that she could afford to mother-hen Ericson. Melinda and Ericson had started working together at the university. She was attractive, with jet-black hair, good bosom. Buffie looked around for the White House staffer she liked least and spotted Melinda against the wall, waiting for Smitty to start the briefing.

"This will be short," Smitty said now. Reporters and White House staffers, burdened with souvenir fur hats and balalaikas from Kiev, settled down in the corner of the hangar. "The President and General Secretary Kolkov," Smitty went on, "will be arriving at their quarters by chopper in about fifteen minutes. They will be joined by Secretary of State Curtice, Foreign Minister Nikolayev, and two interpreters for an informal lunch."

Why not the official photographer? Buffie wondered. If Potus didn't want photographers, she could do sketches. The sketches belonged to her, and someday she would make a killing on a book.

"Why no press pool, Smitty?" a voice asked angrily.

"There's no pool because the General Secretary and the President wanted to be alone together," Smitty replied. "And I'm in touch with Harry Bok at all times," he added, slapping the radio on his hip. "If anything develops, I'll get word around the hotel, but there's a lid on till four thirty."

ERICSON and Kolkov faced each other on swivel seats in the noisy chopper. Harry and the Soviet interpreter faced each other alongside. Kolkov's guards were seated in back. Harry looked out the window and saw that they were getting away from the housing around the airport and coming up on the Crimean Game Preserve. The trailing helicopter was about a thousand feet back and a hundred feet higher, as called for in the flight plan. Two of the agents of the White House detail were aboard it, plus an American medical technician and a group of Russian guards.

The Russian stewardess came along with a vodka bottle embedded in ice. While Kolkov and Ericson each took up a shot glass and knocked it back in fine style, Harry fixed his eyes on the following chopper, and frowned. The guard chopper was now only a few hundred feet back and maybe fifty feet higher.

Worse, someone was opening the side door. What Harry saw next made him bring out his gun. A man's body was being pushed out. It drifted downward in the air. A second body followed. Harry motioned to the Soviet guards to look out the rear window.

A third body, clothed in white, rolled out. The American medical technician, Harry thought. The other two bodies had been the White House agents. A long metal tube, which could be a gun barrel or rocket launcher, appeared in the doorway of the guard chopper, with a couple of men behind it.

Harry forced the President to the floor. Then he lurched forward, reached over the pilot's shoulder, and jammed the control stick, plunging the chopper downward just before the explosion.

The aircraft careened. The Russian pilot, who must have thought Harry was the danger, began wrestling with him, and Harry silenced him with a chop of his pistol. He felt a rush of cold air; behind him, the copilot was hanging out of the aircraft through the shattered glass bubble that housed the flight deck; the body of the stewardess was underfoot.

Harry assumed the rocket had hit the high rear tail, not amidships as intended. He grabbed the pilot's headset and yelled, "Mayday! Mayday!" into the speaker and pulled his way back to the main cabin, where the President and Kolkov were on the floor. The chopper was sinking toward the treetops.

One of the Russian agents was firing his pistol through a shot-out window, while the other was bringing out a submachine gun that had been stowed under his seat. Harry squatted down, jamming seat cushions around the President's head. He heard tearing sounds and the blade thrashing and the crash.

He was conscious, his elbows braced on both sides of the President's head, which was bleeding. He smelled gasoline and felt the heat of flames, and dragged Ericson out of the wreckage and into the forest shadows before collapsing. He put a hand on the President's chest and could feel the heartbeat. He saw one of the Russian guards carrying Kolkov, and the other guard, with the submachine gun, following behind.

The second chopper was coming down for a final assault. Harry staggered to his feet. The Russian with the submachine gun seemed to be picking out a small ravine in which to set up a defense perimeter. Harry hated to move the President, whose scalp wound was running blood down his face, but he got under him and followed the others down into a little crater.

The other chopper landed in a clearing and cut its engine. Harry could hear men's voices and crashing about in the bushes, coming their way. Four or five, he figured. A Chinese face was the first surprise. He shot at it and the face came apart. Carbine gunfire began to chatter in from three sides. One Russian guard took a chance and rose to his knees, and was cut down.

The other Russian guard took up his mate's weapon and began shooting bursts at sounds. Hand grenades exploded around them. The guard dropped. Kolkov was dead or dying. Harry dragged Kolkov's body over Ericson's, making a shield for the President, and picked up the submachine gun to await the last assault.

There was the blast of another grenade, raking Harry's back and side with shrapnel. An instant later, from his left came a great crashing sound. An animal scream ripped the forest and three men rose, to run away from the source of the noise. Harry killed the group with one burst.

Harry waited, conscious now of his own bleeding back and his inability to move his legs. Where did wild animals come from? The Crimean Game Preserve. The realization that he was surrounded by unknown dangers was too much for him to cope with. He passed out over his gun.

"**B**UT WHY ME?"

Dr. Perry Lilith had never been routed out of bed on an emergency call in his government medical career. He was a specialist in diseases of the eye at Bethesda Naval Hospital, on the outskirts of Washington. The commandant of the hospital, waking him by telephone, had used Lilith's naval rank to remind him he was not a civilian. "To be truthful with you, Commander, the two ophthalmologists senior to you are unavailable."

"But what's it all about? I don't know what to bring."

"Doctor, I am ordering you to pack a bag containing what you need for emergency eye treatment. A White House vehicle will pick you up in front of your home in twenty minutes and transport you to Andrews Air Force Base, where you will learn your destination. Tell nobody of your assignment. It's top secret."

"Aye aye, sir," Lilith said sarcastically.

Now, at four a.m., he hurried out of his suburban home to the waiting black Mercury. There was another passenger, a civilian.

The car headed for the airfield at a lawbreaking speed. The man slumped in the back seat was a small, pugnacious-looking fellow, smoking incessantly. When he lit his flame-throwing lighter, he showed curly red hair and a freckled, mottled skin. He stuck out his hand. "I'm Mark Hennessy, special counsel to the President."

"Do you know what this is all about?" asked the startled Lilith.

"No," Hennessy stated firmly, and Lilith knew he was lying.

"You'd think the President would tell his own lawyer," Lilith needled the White House aide.

The needle got to Hennessy. "All I know is, I was told to get on a plane and make sure I was with the eye doctor."

Lilith began to remember what he had read about Hennessy: a New York lawyer who had met Ericson five or six years ago, when he was governor, handled his divorce, and then became his confidant and hatchet man. Supposed to have made many enemies in the presidential campaign—mercurial, hot-tempered.

The White House car pulled to a stop in front of the VIP lounge at Andrews. Inside, Lilith was introduced to six other physicians, including the leading heart specialist and the best-known brain surgeon in the area; an X-ray technician, an anesthetist, and several nurses. Outside, a jet was warming up—blue and silver, with black lettering that said: THE UNITED STATES OF AMERICA.

NURSE Inge Kellgren, First Lieutenant, USAF, did not like the idea of the three visitors coming to talk to Harry Bok. But one of them was her superior, Dr. Herbert Abelson. Dr. Abelson, the President's longtime friend, made no claim to being much of a doctor. That was why the M.D. nearest the President had been Abelson's assistant, a doctor listed as a medical technician, who was trained in emergency procedures. Unfortunately he had been killed in the ambush.

Dr. Abelson was accompanied by Secretary of State Curtice and Chief of Staff Cartwright. The doctor dismissed Nurse Kellgren with a nod, and she walked to the end of the long ward that had been cleared for the American. This was no modern hospital, but an old czar's palace in Yalta converted to a sanatorium. To her surprise she could hear the whispered conversation at the patient's bedside. Some trick of the domed ceiling, she guessed.

"You're going to live, Harry," she heard Dr. Abelson say. "You have some metal chunks in your spinal column that will have to come out, but you'll be all right."

She could not see Harry's face, but she could hear his croaked question: "President?"

"The President has his problems," Cartwright said. "But he's alive. General Secretary Kolkov was killed."

"Mr. Bok," the Secretary of State said in his deep voice, "it is now eleven thirty in the morning. The helicopter was shot down a little over two hours ago. In Washington it is four thirty a.m. Foreign Minister Nikolayev has placed a blanket of secrecy on the event, on the ground of protecting the President, but actually to inform the members of the Politburo first."

"We've objected strenuously," said Cartwright.

"We need to know from you exactly what happened in the ambush. There are no other witnesses," said Curtice.

Harry began to tell the story. The men leaned forward to hear his whispering. "I dragged him out of the wreck . . . set up a perimeter . . . Chinese face, right between the eyes . . . grenades got me, killed Kolkov. I dragged his body over the President's. . . ."

Nurse Kellgren, listening, used a Kleenex on her eyes. Harry Bok was a kind man. She had told him about Dr. Abelson's order not to sedate him completely until he could be debriefed. She had not told him what she had heard from one of the Russian nurses—that the Soviet doctors did not think he would walk again.

"Might it not have been possible," asked Curtice, "that Kolkov, while still alive, tried to protect the President with his own body?"

"Dead, I think. Dragged him over—"

Cartwright interrupted Harry to say, "The Secretary isn't asking you to be sure about anything, Harry. It's just that everybody is terribly nervous after the assassination of Kolkov. The Russians are not letting us get out of here as quick as we want, and not telling the press is going to cause trouble. The Secretary is looking for something that might lessen anti-Soviet reaction at home. Like some heroism on the part of Kolkov."

"Okay," Nurse Kellgren heard Harry say. "Coulda been that Kolkov crawled over."

"Then it is possible," said Curtice, "that Kolkov saved the President's life?"

"Wouldn't swear to it. Coulda been."

Nurse Kellgren began walking across the room. Cartwright was saying, "Priority is to get the President the best American attention. On American soil. Herb, is he fit to travel?"

"We're okay once we get to *Air Force One*," Abelson said. "But we need a specialist."

"Is Harry here fit to go along?"

"No," said the doctor. "Harry can't be moved right now."

"Mr. Secretary," Cartwright said formally, "you are the ranking American on the scene. It's up to you to spring us immediately. And now you have a card to play."

"Want a sawbones from home," Harry said.

"We got a communication through to Bethesda hospital," Cartwright assured him. "We rendezvous with a medical team at the

Azores. An eye doctor and one or two others come back with us to the States, the rest come here to you."

"Eye doctor?"

Dr. Abelson put in, "The President has a problem there, Harry."

After a silence, the agent said something that seemed curious to Nurse Kellgren: "Better get Hennessy."

"Odd you should say that," said Cartwright. "Those were the very words the President spoke after he regained consciousness. Mark Hennessy will be with the medical men."

Outside the ward, Nurse Kellgren told Dr. Abelson that he should not be sure that their conversation went unheard by the Russians, since the acoustics in the ward were unusual. The doctor, distracted, said he would pass the information along.

"WE ARE leaving right now, Vasily."

"Not right away," said Nikolayev, seated behind the desk.

The Secretary of State felt a wave of fury surge in him. They were in the hospital administrator's office, on the ground floor of the czar's palace, which the Foreign Minister had taken over as his command post. Upstairs lay the President of the United States, unable to see, attended by unknown Soviet doctors and his half-competent personal physician. An impossible situation.

George Curtice looked at his watch: twelve thirty p.m., Yalta time, three hours since the ambush. A mile or so away, members of the world's press corps were sunning themselves on the beach. As far as they knew, the two leaders had gone off to lunch.

Curtice said, his voice under control, "This delay is endangering the life of the President."

Nikolayev rose. "I have ordered the helicopter. But I must make certain that its pilots are not allied with the assassins."

Curtice knew exactly what Nikolayev was doing: freezing the situation, blacking out all news reports, until his fellow leaders in the Politburo could decide upon a policy. Nikolayev was under enormous pressure.

"How long will that take?" Curtice asked calmly.

"The logistics require at least four hours," Nikolayev said.

Curtice smashed his fist on the desk in frustration. He came around to Nikolayev's side, opened a couple of drawers, took out a sheet of paper. "You want an official note?" As the Russian watched, he wrote, "To the Government of the U.S.S.R.: At this moment, 12:35 p.m., Yalta time, over three hours since the attack upon General Secretary Kolkov and President Ericson, the United States protests the deliberate delay by Soviet Foreign Minister—"

Nikolayev stopped his hand. "Tear it up. Three hours."

Curtice left the note unfinished. Lying on the table in that state, it was a threat. Three hours would not satisfy Cartwright or the President. Curtice played his hole card.

"I have just come from the bedside of the Secret Service agent, Bok," Curtice said. "Bok is not sure of his memory. He was bleeding from grenade wounds, and everything happened so fast."

"Go on." Nikolayev betrayed an uncharacteristic nervousness.

"He thinks he remembers General Secretary Kolkov lying on top of the President, shielding him with his body. The agent is in pain, partly sedated. When he's better, it could be he will remember that General Secretary Kolkov died a heroic death saving President Ericson's life. Or"—Curtice shrugged—"he will remember that the General Secretary just died."

He let the Russian think it over. Curtice knew that if Kolkov died a hero, then Nikolayev, Kolkov's chosen successor, would be strengthened inside the Soviet Union.

"Two hours," said Nikolayev.

"Immediately," snapped Curtice. He had won.

"Thirty minutes."

"Done."

"Tell your President," Nikolayev said, "that a helicopter will be on the front lawn to take him to *Air Force One* in exactly one half hour."

"And the press?"

"Have your press man talk to mine."

Curtice hurried to the staircase. His footsteps echoed in the silent halls as he went to the President's room. The head of the White House Secret Service detail stopped him at the door.

"Can I go in?"

"I'll ask, sir."

Cartwright came out. "Did you spring us, Mr. Secretary?"

"I'd like to tell the President, Mr. Cartwright."

"He—um—I know he wants to see you, but he asked me to find out from you . . ." Awkward.

The Secretary of State took that to mean he was an appendage of power, with no place at the center. "It's not a good time for visitors," he conceded. "Lucas, the ploy worked. Tell the Secret Service to move the President down to the front lawn at one fifteen."

"Great work, George. Can you wait here a moment?"

Curtice paced the hall, going over the reasons why he had been shut out. Because he was black? No—he had been appointed to the job because Ericson wanted a black at State, so he would be tougher in his dealings with the demands of the African nations. Most likely, Curtice thought, Ericson was lying there, blinded and confused, and did not want any other presence to deal with.

It occurred to the Secretary of State that he could be most useful at the U.S. embassy in Moscow. Remaining behind during Niko-layev's most delicate time of trial might cement a relationship that could be useful. And—after the initial press briefing here—he would be out of the flow of news. The first press reaction would be wild, to file the story; the second reaction he would just as soon miss. The reporters would turn on those who had kept the story from them for so long.

Cartwright returned. "The President is personally very grateful, Mr. Secretary. By the way," he added, "I didn't think this was the time to go into the business of Bok's story."

Curtice would have preferred to have presidential approval of his idea to encourage Bok's memory along lines that would make Kolkov heroic, but he could not really insist on a decision from an injured and distraught President. He told Cartwright of his plan to remain in Russia during the postassassination crisis.

"Good idea," said the chief of staff.

"What about the press?"

95

"Let's call Smitty," said the white-haired Cartwright.

They trotted down the stairs and received permission from an aide of the Soviet Foreign Minister's to telephone James Smith, the press secretary.

"Smitty? Listen carefully." Cartwright was crisp. "Call a press conference at the hotel immediately. The Secretary of State will brief. And have some buses there. As a private note, Smitty, I hope you have not unpacked. Sorry, you'll find out why at the briefing. Wait." He covered the phone and turned to Curtice. "Should he tell his Russian counterpart that Nikolayev will be there?"

The Secretary of State motioned him to wait, went into the inner office, where the Foreign Minister was speaking into an ancient telephone, and interrupted with: "You want to join me in the briefing?" Nikolayev, still talking, nodded yes.

Curtice went back to Cartwright and nodded his head.

"The Soviet Foreign Minister will join the Secretary in the briefing," Cartwright said into the phone. "Look, Smitty—get set for something. Okay? Good-by."

He turned to Curtice. "You mustn't allude to this in your press conference, but if the President should have to step aside, temporarily, I'll try to get word to you first."

The thought of the government in the hands of Arnold Nichols, the Vice-President, dismayed Curtice. "God save the President," he said, and meant it fervently.

As *Air Force One* BEGAN its descent toward Lajes Field, in the Azores, Dr. Herbert Abelson gave a nervous start. He had promised Sven Ericson he would wake him a half hour before arrival.

He had been wrong to take this job. "C'mon, Herb," Ericson had said, "it's just for the campaign. You'll see the play of power from the inside, and it's fascinating."

An editor of a successful medical monthly should never let himself be put in a position of having to deal with flesh-and-blood human bodies, especially—Abelson shook his head slowly—the eyes. Now the President of the United States is in trouble, Abelson accused himself, because he has had inadequate medical attention. But what made the situation intolerable was that only he, of the people around the President, knew of the worst part of the problem—the political part. At Lajes he would share that part with Hennessy and the responsibility would be out of his hands. Then he would give the medical secret to the Bethesda team.

The doctor went forward to the President's sleeping quarters to find Ericson sitting up. "You're awake," Abelson said.

Ericson was in pain, brow furrowed, eyes staring, his fingers lightly touching the bandages around his head. "I feel sick and my head hurts," he reported.

"You're lucky to be alive, Sven," the doctor replied.

"How long was the first time?" the President asked.

"Forty-one hours."

"The second time lasts longer?"

"Sven, I wish I knew," said the doctor. "It was such a big secret, I was afraid to ask around."

"This eye doctor coming aboard, can he be trusted?"

"Who knows? I suppose we could shut him up for a while, but when we fly an eye doctor all the way out here to see you, word gets around. I had to do that. I still lose sleep over the first time."

"That's not what I meant," the President said. "We'll have to tell the truth about my condition. In a calm way, just the temporary effect of the concussion. And in a couple of days I'll be out of it."

"You mean you don't want to tell the eye doctor about the other time, during the campaign?" Abelson knew the value of a patient's history. "It could affect his treatment."

Ericson started to shake his head, which made him wince. "Not a word, Herb. Let's go over who else knows."

"Buffie was in the compartment with you. She's been very good. Harry Bok knows. And Arthur Leigh knew. That's all." Then he went over the people from whom the secret had been kept. "Not even an eye doctor was told. Cartwright, Hennessy, Smitty, Melinda—not one of them knows. I haven't said a word."

"How much does the press know?"

"Not a hell of a lot. You have a concussion and a problem with your eyes—maybe a problem focusing. We left it vague."

97

"Good. Less the better."

"They're teed off, Smitty says, at not having a pool on this plane right now. He's here with us. The press planes will follow in about a half hour."

"When Hennessy comes aboard, you tell him about the last time." The President took a deep breath to fight back his nausea. "Nobody knows I'm blind yet." The first time he had used the word. "Otherwise, Herb, keep the last time quiet."

Abelson nodded. "I will, Sven," he said aloud.

MARK Hennessy, special counsel to the President, bounded up the steps of the ramp ahead of the medical team and spotted Melinda McPhee, the President's secretary.

"The Boss?"

"He can't see." Her voice was rigidly controlled.

Hennessy's chest contracted. "Blind?"

Hennessy was the man who carried the Letter. All Presidents had written agreements with their Vice-Presidents about the transfer of power in emergencies, to be used before the Twenty-fifth Amendment was even examined.

Herb Abelson came up and led Hennessy toward the conference room in the jet. "First I talk to the doctors," Abelson said. "Then I have to see you alone." He was on the edge of hysteria.

Hennessy let himself be guided up into the room where the medical team was assembling. Abelson looked around at the dozen doctors and nurses crammed into the room, and appeared to get hold of himself. "The President suffered a blow on the upper right temple a half inch from the hairline, and began to bleed profusely from a three-and-a-half-inch scalp wound...."

Finally, at the end of Abelson's briefing, the eye doctor from Bethesda asked, "Any previous history of concussions?"

Abelson answered carefully. "We never had a blind President before, that's for sure. You want to see him now?"

The group followed Abelson down the spiral staircase to the President's quarters. Hennessy, lagging behind, heard the eye doctor say, "Known this, would've brought a neurosurgeon."

Abelson, coming back from the President's bedroom, pulled Hennessy into the galley. "The President has a problem," he began. "Remember the campaign train back in September?"

Hennessy remembered it well. Arthur Leigh, the campaign manager, had chosen Ohio, a swing state with good communications facilities, for the Ericson whistle-stopping.

Hennessy thought back to that period, less than a year before. Ericson, Leigh said, was presenting too detached an image. "We've got a hoity-toity professor of economics," Leigh would growl, "a divorcé, a governor who got in by a fluke and looks like he's riding his luck. We've got to show he's not a jet-setter. When he rides on an old-fashioned train, it's sorta democratic."

When the campaign was over, Hennessy had made certain Ericson knew that his campaign manager had had some questionable dealings that might embarrass an Ericson administration. He had shot Leigh out of the saddle, expecting to slip into the chief of staff spot himself, but Ericson wanted someone with Washington Establishment savvy, like Lucas Cartwright.

"Remember how we canceled the last tour stop?" Abelson asked.

Hennessy nodded. "Well, it wasn't laryngitis," the doctor said, "the way I told the press because Leigh made me. Ericson was in his compartment with Buffie. When the engineer slammed on the brakes, Sven's head smashed into the doorframe. He was unconscious for about an hour, and Leigh and Harry Bok wouldn't let me call a hospital. Finally the spirits of ammonia got some results and Ericson came to. But he couldn't see."

"Did he get his sight back gradually, or all at once?"

"The second day—the pressure came off the nerve when the swelling went down, and he could see as well as ever. But when these things happen more than once, it's not good. This time I got an eye doctor before anybody stopped me. Cartwright passed the message on to Bethesda without knowing the background. Now we're going to have to tell the world that the President is blind and that this is the second time it's happened."

"We have to look at this thing with a detached retina," said the lawyer. The doctor shook his head in frustration. "No," Hennessy continued, "there's no problem about making full disclosure concerning the current state of the President's health when we arrive in the U.S. The President is in complete possession of all but one of his faculties, and you and the specialist will be able to suggest that his loss of sight is probably temporary. Not from any past history," he added carefully, "but from your general knowledge of optic nerves and concussions."

"Why can't we just tell the whole thing?"

"I don't think you quite understand," Hennessy went on. "The fact that the President did not volunteer the nature of his ailment during the campaign could cause unfavorable reaction now."

Abelson nodded dubiously. "Mark, I'm in over my head."

Hennessy squeezed the doctor's shoulder and went down the corridor to meet with the President's chief of staff.

Moving down the aisle, Hennessy felt the enormity of the President's problem beginning to grip him. The threat of upheaval in the Soviet Union as a result of the assassination must be foremost in the mind of the man elected to protect his own nation's survival. And the President was blinded. Even if the condition were temporary, he would have to grope around, physically as well as mentally, at a time when the situation cried out for the appearance of supreme ability.

And then the concealment of the previous blindness could invite the charge that Ericson had failed to fully disclose the state of his health before the election.

That reminded the lawyer of Roy Bannerman, the Treasury Secretary, who had been Ericson's rival for power in the party. If Bannerman were to learn of the previous blindness, he would challenge the President, invoking the Twenty-fifth Amendment.

Hennessy felt the thrill of being needed. Ericson trusted him. Just as Ericson needed power to be a whole man, so Hennessy needed to be wholly trusted. He was certain he would prove to be the most important support to Ericson.

Hennessy ran his stubby fingers through his short red hair and, keeping in mind that Cartwright was not to know of the previous blindness, he made his way to the cabin of the chief of staff.

"Make the desk turn into a coffee table," Hennessy told the chief of staff. "I like to see the play of power."

"I never play with presidential buttons, Brother Hennessy," Cartwright replied. Lucas Cartwright was a White House person, a relic from the mellow past, nobody's competitor, nobody's friend. Cartwright suited Ericson's needs when the new President wanted experienced judgment, restraint. The chief of staff did not mind in the least being called courtly, and his style—excessively polite, circumlocutious—was a good mask for deliberation.

He knew that Hennessy wanted his job; it did not bother him. Hennessy might get it one day—if he learned to control his temper.

The lawyer laid the Letter on the table. Cartwright picked it up, noted the admonition: "For the Vice-President's Eyes Only," and read it through slowly.

"The President wanted you and the Letter here because he cannot see," said Cartwright. "This fact will be announced as soon as we get home. What I would like to anticipate with you is that the President's disability may be so great that he cannot function as President." He returned the Letter to Hennessy. "If the doctors say he's going to be fine in a few days, we have no problem. But if they say that there's no way of knowing if he is going to be permanently blind, then we're in that gray area of uncertainty."

"A President is disabled," said Hennessy carefully, "when he asserts he is disabled, or when he is unable to communicate whether he is disabled or not. But if he says he is not disabled, then he is not disabled, period."

"Unless he is wrong about his ability to discharge the powers and duties of his office."

"If he's wrong, the burden of proof is not on him—first it's on his Cabinet, and then it's on two-thirds of the Congress."

Cartwright nodded. "Counselor, you need to have available a legal definition of blindness, a medical definition of blindness, and to be able to cite some authorities that show how the inability to see does not affect judgment; some evidence of its noncatastrophic nature would be helpful."

"Are we using the word 'blind'?"

Cartwright pushed a buzzer; Melinda McPhee, the President's secretary, appeared. He asked for a dictionary, put on his glasses. "'Blind: having less than one-tenth of normal vision in the more efficient eye when refractive defects are fully corrected by lenses.'"

"Sounds legal," said Hennessy. "Melinda, what's bugging you?"

She shot him an angry look. "You two, figuring all the angles. Do you know what he's going through? It's the most frightening thing that can happen to a human being. I've never seen him scared before. I'd be a little less scared if you showed some understanding of the agony he must be in."

"Thank you, Melinda," Cartwright said. "It's always good to be reminded of the human considerations. Now would you inform the captain of the medical team that this aircraft leaves for Washington in exactly ten minutes."

"The medics want a meeting with us right away," she replied.

Cartwright rose with a heavy feeling on his chest.

The room atop the jet was filled with doctors, along with the President's aides. Cartwright surveyed them. Melinda, with her notebook; Hennessy trying to look bored, Herb Abelson practically wringing his hands, Smitty glowering, and Jonathan Trumbull, the young presidential speech writer, holding a tape recorder.

The head of the medical team, wearing captain's stripes, opened with the good news. "The President's life is not in danger. Let's begin."

The heart man and the internist reported no complications.

"Mild concussion," diagnosed the brain specialist. "No penetration of the cranium. Hairline fracture of the optic channel; the ophthalmologist will address himself to that."

"Now to the problem area," the captain said. "Dr. Lilith, the patient's eyes."

Lilith looked nervously at the speech writer's recorder. "The President is totally blind. One possible cause is the blockage to the cortex of the synapses leading to the optic nerves. The injury has caused a swelling, which may be temporary; in that case, he could regain his sight in a few days. It's too soon to tell. Frankly, I'd be more optimistic if he'd had some history along these lines and had come out of it after a brief period of sightlessness."

The senior medical man concluded the meeting promptly with assignments to the medical team: four to continue on in their own plane to Harry Bok in Yalta, two to transmit data from Lajes, six to return with the President on *Air Force One.*

Cartwright walked down the corridor to report to the President. The Secret Service agent at the door said he was resting, but the President's voice called out, "Is that you, Lucas? Come in."

The chief of staff sat next to the bed and summarized the way plans were shaping up. "Unfortunately," he felt he had to add, "the eye doctor's report is a question mark."

"Make the assumption," said Ericson, "that I'll be seeing again in two or three days." Cartwright marveled at the natural optimism of Presidents. "Give Nikolayev a chance, so the kooky faction in the Kremlin doesn't get any ideas about taking on China. Lean on Smitty—he'll want to show my X rays on television. When we get back, I want you to keep an eye on Roy Bannerman." Ericson felt that if there were internal trouble, it would come from the Secretary of the Treasury.

IN HIS room at Bethesda Naval Hospital, the President, dressed in sport clothes, listened to the TV news from an easy chair. Melinda McPhee was there to tell him what the screen showed.

"From the CBS News headquarters in Washington," the anchorman reported, "this is the 'CBS Evening News.' Five days after the President of the United States survived the ambush at Yalta, the nation is coming to the realization that it is being led by a blind man. The blindness of the President becomes more ominous with each day. A panel of leading eye specialists met with reporters, and Dr. Perry Lilith gave this pessimistic report."

"Picture of Lilith at the blackboard downstairs," Melinda told the President.

Doctor: "Although there may be marked improvement, it is still too early to tell. We can give no assurance that the President's sight will return."

Back to the anchorman: "For a reaction to the President's disability, first to the Speaker of the House, Republican Mortimer Frelingheusen."

The Speaker, sucking on his pipe, in his office: "Let the man get on his feet again, and see how he can cope. Blindness is a terrible thing, but a lot of blind people lead useful and productive lives. Let's be thankful the President wasn't killed."

Scene switches to Treasury Secretary T. Roy Bannerman, coming out of Bethesda hospital after a brief meeting with the President: "We can't minimize blindness. The presidency is a big job and this is a big drawback. Let's pray it's temporary."

Melinda breathed, "Thanks a heap, old buddy."

She flicked to another network, in the midst of live satellite coverage of Kolkov's state funeral in Moscow: "Western observers have noted that the three chief pallbearers are Georgi Mendeyev, the aged President of the U.S.S.R. and a figurehead; Mihail Voroshilov, the fiery young leader of the party hard-liners; and Foreign Minister Vasily Nikolayev, a moderate. Speculation here in Moscow is that the Politburo will select a troika, perhaps these three, to head the government in a period of transition. . . ."

As she turned the set off, Melinda was ready with the President's News Summary, a forty-page typewritten publication put together each night by a crew of researchers—"the gremlins," they were called, because the daytime staff rarely saw them. The summary had a circulation of only twenty White House staffers, and cost about a hundred thousand dollars a year, but was worth it, for it showed the President how news events were being perceived by the daily press, television, and even the small magazines of opinion.

" 'Summary number one hundred and forty-six,' " she read aloud. One hundred and forty-six days in the presidency, she noted, plus three years in the Illinois governor's mansion, plus four years at the university, drifting with this man from job to job as he had floated to the top. She was pushing forty now, and she had passed up her own chances at marriage. The two of them had experienced a strong mutual attraction soon after she had begun working for him, but she had insisted, and he had agreed, that their relationship be kept on a professional level.

"I'll skip the television rundown, you're ahead of that already," she said. "Here's the press play. 'Sidebar in the *Times* on Vice-President Nichols' activities during tragic week.'"

"He posed for pictures," Ericson said. "I told him to. I want everybody to be reminded of the alternative to me—Arnold Nichols is my secret weapon, our Throttlebottom Vice-President. Melinda, get Cartwright to check on whether Bannerman and the Veep have been spending any time together."

She wrote that down on the margin of the News Summary. His worry about being pushed out of office, she thought, was the insecurity from the blindness. It would pass, if she knew Ericson. Living with changes, using changes to his benefit, playing the breaks, had been his life since she went to work for him.

"Here's one you won't like," Melinda said. "'Constitutional scholars are asking whether a man can be held legally responsible for signing something he demonstrably has not seen, and more specifically, if a blind President's signature is valid on a law.'"

"Hadn't thought of that," said Ericson, hunching a long leg over the arm of his chair. "Get a memo from Hennessy on that. On some documents, the Secretary of State countersigns. There could be a verification statement on each document I sign, by the Secretary of State, saying, 'I read this to him myself.'"

She continued the News Summary, but he cut her off. "What am I doing in the hospital, anyway? They can set up eye-testing equipment in the White House." He picked up the telephone. "Abelson," he said. Then, "Herb? I want to go home. Any medical reason why not?"

"No medical reason, Sven. You wanted people to worry about your being sick, remember? Not just your eyes."

"That's over now," the President said.

THE Vice-President, above all, was determined not to make a mistake. To be too slavish a follower of the President would be a mistake. To veer from the administration line would be a mis-

take. Every interview, every dedication speech, presented new op-
portunities to the Vice-President to commit a blooper. Arnold
Nichols would be careful. Consequently, he knew, he would be
accused of being a middle-road man from a border state. Fine with
him. Now in his late sixties, Nichols would be too old for renomina-
tion if the President ran again. This Vice-President had one chance
at the brass ring; to be there, incorruptible and uncontroversial,
should the President die.

Looking out the bay window of his Massachusetts Avenue
home, Nichols saw Bannerman's limousine swing up the driveway.
The Vice-President never looked forward to these weekly briefings
on economic affairs by the Treasury Secretary, because Bannerman was an impatient pedagogue. But they showed that Nichols
was being kept closely informed, and by T. Roy Bannerman, one of
the three most important investment bankers in the world before
his appointment to head the Treasury.

The regularity of these briefings was a solid cover for whatever
Bannerman wanted to discuss. The Vice-President decided that
today's visit would probably have to do with the division of responsibility in international affairs after the ambush. Under Ericson the National Security Council system had been scrapped. The
President ran international affairs, with the Secretary of State as
a front man; Bannerman ran international economics brilliantly;
and Secretary of Defense Preston Reed was in the process of absorbing covert CIA activities, to centralize security matters.

Abruptly, Bannerman began. "Mr. Vice-President, you and I
have to discuss a matter that nobody else seems willing to face
up to, the President's blindness. Everybody's pretending it's an
ailment that's going to go away in a few days, but it's not."

The Vice-President made soothing sounds, but Bannerman bar-
reled ahead. "I have it on the best authority that the President is
permanently blind."

"What's the best authority?" Nichols' interest quickened.

"The head of New York Hospital. I was chairman of their board
of trustees for years. Their man was brought in for expert advice.
He said that with no previous history of this sort of thing, the

odds are that the President is blind for good. It's malfeasance to act as if we don't know what our responsibility is."

"Look, Roy," the Vice-President said quickly, "if you think the President is permanently disabled and can't discharge his duties, then it's up to you to discuss it with him."

"I know Sven Ericson," said Bannerman. "He'll hang in there no matter what it does to the country."

"You're being unkind," the Vice-President demurred.

"He thinks you're an ass, Arnold," Bannerman continued. "He'll use you as an excuse to hang on."

The Vice-President swallowed.

"But set aside the personal stuff," Bannerman pursued. "Think of Woodrow Wilson in the last year of his life, an invalid, with his wife making the decisions. Or Roosevelt at Yalta, too sick to cope with Stalin. Hell," he nearly shouted, "the President of the United States can't find his way across the room!"

"Please remember my words, Roy," said Nichols. "The words are, 'Tell the President, don't tell me.'"

"Your response is quite proper," Bannerman allowed, "but you will have to call the Cabinet meeting if he won't resign."

"It's not going to come to a confrontation," said Nichols. "When the President realizes how it hampers him to be blind, then we may have to do nothing but applaud his sacrifice."

"Good sense," said Bannerman. "I'll buy that."

"The President needs operational help," Dr. Abelson told the therapist.

"How to move around, how to get dressed," added Melinda.

Hank Fowler nodded. "I understand." He understood, too, the primary cause for concern of the President's aides. Hennessy had said, "You can't come in as a psychologist. You have to be identified publicly as a blind man who has offered to help the President adjust to the physical requirements of not being able to see, even temporarily."

"You needn't introduce me as Doctor," Fowler said mildly. "I'm Hank Fowler. I'm here simply as a man who's been blind for a long time, to teach the President a few tricks of the trade."

Abelson breathed his relief. "They said he was the best in the business," he said to Melinda. "He catches on quick." There was the third-person blunder, talking in the presence of a blind man as if he were not present, and Fowler wondered whether he should correct the President's doctor. He decided to wait.

"The President has certain advantages that you can work with," said Melinda. To Hank, her voice was resonant, warm—unusual in a person whose forte was efficiency. "The Secret Service is constantly with him, and can move him anywhere. The telephone operators, the permanent staff, are right there to get whatever or whomever he wants. The whole government is at his fingertips."

"Uses the phone like a crutch," Dr. Abelson added. "He used to prefer face-to-face meetings."

"How is he taking it?" the therapist asked.

Melinda said, "He's secretive. He's frozen everybody out. He's scared, and he doesn't want us to see it."

"Ericson has never let himself become vulnerable, to anybody or any situation," Abelson said. "Now he's totally vulnerable. He's worried about losing everything. It could do him some good, in a way."

Fowler had the impression that Abelson felt a hint of pleasure at getting his own back from a man whose previous invulnerability had irked him. The woman seemed more serene. "May I touch your face?" he asked her. He reached out and went over her face with his fingertips: high cheekbones, full lips, strong jawline. He thanked her, having done that partly for his own curiosity, mostly to implant a sense of awe at possibly eerie powers of the blind person. A mystique never hurt a psychologist.

"Dr. Abelson, may I see the President now?" said the therapist, rising. "Let me take your arm and let's move out." They left the doctor's basement office in the central White House residence, took an elevator, and went up to the Lincoln Sitting Room, where Abelson announced him to the President.

Fowler said, "Doctor, how about setting up a handshake?"

Abelson moved the psychologist's hand over to the President's,

then guided Fowler to a chair, telling the President, "Hank here is the world's leading expert in helping people who can't see. I'll take off now."

"I understand you bring firsthand experience to your job," Ericson said.

"Let me describe myself, sir." Fowler kept his voice low. "I'm a little guy, square-built, round face. Fifty-two years old, liberal, hair thinning on top, striking black mustache."

"You trim it yourself?"

"Yes, Mr. President. My wife could do it, but I run my own life because it makes me feel cocky, and I need that." His contact made, the therapist said, "This is the famous Lincoln Sitting Room? Could you describe it to me?"

"Sure. This easy chair, where I am, belonged to President Buchanan. To my left is a bookcase. Only thing still here that's Lincoln is the Volk bust, on the desk at my right."

"Put yourself at the center of a clock," said the therapist, "and say I'm twelve o'clock. Where's the desk?"

"Three o'clock."

"The phone?"

"Two in here. One on the desk, say two o'clock, the other at my right hand, toward five o'clock."

"Window?"

"Behind me. Six o'clock."

"Now you want to know how to keep from banging into walls. We have a new gimmick for that." Fowler produced a round, thick object on a watchband and pressed it into the President's hand. "That's a wrist sonar. You heard the expression 'blind as a bat'? Bats don't run into things, because they have a built-in echo device." As the President delightedly strapped the watchband to his wrist, Fowler brought his hand close to the sonar, starting a slight vibration. "It detects obstacles in front of you. Performs the function of a long cane."

"I was worried about having to use a cane," said the President. "That would have made me an object of pity."

"Skillful use of a cane is still best for a blind person, Mr. President. The sonar watch is for you to use until you stop being self-conscious about arousing pity."

The therapist had a few other electronic gadgets to give Ericson a quick boost of morale. For the President's other wrist he produced a watch that told time by touch. "I also have a tape recorder here, size of a pack of cigarettes, and a simple system to bring your hearing speed up to your reading speed," Fowler told him. "If you read fast, you read between four hundred and five hundred words a minute. When people talk fast, they talk at about half that speed. Here is something we do for blinded executives who need to absorb information as quickly as they used to read. I've been taping myself. I'm going to play it back at double rate."

The President said excitedly, "The problem that's been nagging me is how to organize data for a decision. You're showing me that there's more hope than I figured."

Getting into more difficult areas of training, Fowler showed the President how to make a list. On the blank blackboard of his mind a blind man could write, and "see" his own writing. Fowler tried him out on a few numbers and symbols, and was pleased to see he had an apt pupil; not all executives took to this training. "In a couple of months, with your staff getting trained as well, you will actually be able to cope." The therapist felt the time was ripe to slip in a question. "Have trouble when you wake up?"

"What do you mean, Hank?"

"I went blind in my thirties, result of an accident. What bothered me most was waking up in the morning. Not seeing was like not knowing you were up. Started my day in a sweat."

"I'm fine in the morning," said the President.

He'll be a tough one to bring to grips with the reality of being blind, thought Fowler. On this therapy was riding not just the smooth operations of the presidency but the hopes of twenty million handicapped people in America. The President might be euphoric now, with his discovery of electronic aids, but he would soon slip into the inescapable depression of the newly blind.

"You think I can bring this whole thing off, Hank?"

"Look, I'm going to get a cab to the airport, fly home to Atlanta, pack for a month or so here, and come back—all with no help from anybody. Then I'm going to do a job of occupational therapy on you that will make me a hero with every psychologist in the country. I don't know if you are able to discharge the duties of your office, or ever will be, but if we fail, it'll be your fault."

The President stood up and moved over to the desk, Fowler following every motion with his ears. The President's personal physician made known his presence at the door—summoned, Fowler judged, by a button close to the President's hand. "What's the code for your buttons to call people?" the therapist piped up.

The President said, "The top button is Melinda, my secretary; the second is the Secret Service agent at the door; third is Herb Abelson, here; fourth is the White House operator; fifth is Cartwright, my chief of staff. The bottom one is for the man with the black bag, in case of need for a retaliatory nuclear strike. Starts a process that has all kinds of safeguards built in—"

Abelson interrupted. "I'm putting some talking books on the desk—some classics you've been reading, and a new novel."

"It always amazes people," Fowler offered, "when a blind person makes a reference to a current book."

"I'll use that. Herb, what's the latest on Harry Bok?"

"Spoke with him this morning. Not good. No sensation in his legs. Probably he'll never walk again."

The President called the Secret Service agent at the door and made an odd request: "Get me a counterfeit twenty-dollar bill and a red pencil."

The agent answered, "If a counterfeit ten will do, sir, I happen to have one on me. A lot of us carry them for souvenirs."

Ericson took it and the red pencil and wrote a message on the bill. "Can you read it, Herb?"

The doctor read, " 'Help me fight the phonies, Harry! Gratefully, Sven Ericson.' "

Fowler did not yet have the handle on his new patient: now cold, now generous, now persecuted, now confident. Helping him, though, was an opportunity which the therapist was determined not to miss.

"Hiya, Potus. Miss me?"

"Buffie. What are you wearing?"

"Feel and see." She slipped down on the rug, arms across his knees, as he sat in front of the Oval Office fireplace. "They wouldn't let me near you since the ambush. You're really in a cocoon, you know." She gave his legs a hug. It was different being around him when those eyes weren't ricocheting cool glances off you, when they were open and focused on nothing. "I gotta get you some shades, Potus," she told him.

"You think I ought to wear dark glasses?" The question had obviously been in his mind.

"Maybe one of those snazzy one-way mirror outfits motorcycle types wear."

"What do you hear, Buffie, around the press room?" His favorite question, the same question all worried politicians ask.

"They're getting hot for a press conference. They want to see if you've turned into a helpless invalid."

"You haven't mentioned the other time, in the train?"

"I don't even remember another time," she replied. "But that's a hopeful sign, isn't it? You snapped out of it before."

He smoothed the hair away from her forehead, cradled her face in his hands, bent down and gave her a long, tender kiss, then leaned back again. "On the campaign train it was only two days. It's been five days now that I can't see, Buffie. The reason we have to be quiet about the last time is that to reveal it now would leave me open to the charge that I misled the public about my health before the election."

"I see," she said, "and you're worried somebody like me will blab. Ease up! Trust me." She had to tell him. Nobody else would. "You're thinking about losing your grip, and it's making you lose your grip." She got up and went to the door.

"What's got into you?" he asked. She said nothing. "Buffie?" She did not breathe, watching the sightless eyes in the tortured face. "Buffie, you still there?"

She went to him with a sudden rush of feeling that was more than he had ever shown her.

113

WHEN A PRESIDENT begins to prepare for a press conference, the executive branch convulses. Smitty reveled in these moments. He enjoyed flaying the government departments with savage questions because he saw his job as the White House resident conscience. He was fifty—tough, straight, incorruptible, skeptical. The questions his office came up with for the President's briefing book were far nastier and more exhaustive than those ever asked at a press conference.

In his sunny West Wing office, Smitty sipped his coffee before his eleven-a.m. press briefing. He would lead with an announcement that would be welcomed. He would say, "Ladies and gentlemen, on Wednesday, at nine p.m., two weeks to the day since the ambush at Yalta, the President will hold a live televised press conference from the East Room of the White House."

He would spring Hank Fowler on them; the blind therapist would play a few tricks, like tying names to voices, then announce a two-week orientation course for the President and his staff in "aural organization," so that it would be possible to run this country with your eyes closed. If public reaction to the Ericson blindness could be changed from the fear of terrible disability to a game of "How will he overcome this obstacle?" then ugly questions about disability and resignation would be stilled.

Marilee Pinckney was standing in front of Smitty's desk; he motioned for her to sit down.

"What word from Harry Bok?" Smitty asked. "Be good to show the President cares."

"President spoke with him on the telephone. He may be paralyzed from the waist down, but just say that he's recuperating."

At the morning briefing, after Smitty had announced the President's press conference, the first question was, "Will the President wear dark glasses?"

"Of course," Smitty snapped.

"Is he aware of talk among some Cabinet members that he should step aside?"

"Which Cabinet member and what did he say?" Smitty wasn't having any of those phony probes.

"Can he tell light from dark, or does he just see black?"

"Ask him yourself, Wednesday night," said Smitty. He cut the session short and went back to work on the President's briefing book with Marilee. Then he went up to the Lincoln Sitting Room.

"I told them you'd wear dark glasses," he said to the President. "Maybe you'd better get used to wearing them."

Ericson felt in his smoking-jacket pocket for the sunglasses and drew them on. Smitty thought he seemed depressed.

"We're going to have a tough time writing the lead on this one, Smitty." That was rule one of press conferences: Always go with your news lead in mind, or you'd get trapped into providing them with a lead of their own making. Smitty was not going to fall into the President's downcast state.

"Got any good news about your eyes?"

"I can make out that there's a window over there, and I can vaguely tell when shapes move around."

"You mean you're not totally blind?" Smitty let his excitement show through.

"The eye doctor and the lawyers say I am totally blind. Being able to tell light from dark doesn't mean you're not blind."

"Hold on a minute. Have you always been able to tell light from dark since you woke up from the ambush?"

"Sure, I—well, now, let me think. There's some improvement. I'll show you." He got up. "Turn me around a few times." Smitty did so, facing the President toward the wall away from the window. Ericson turned around. "The light comes from there."

"That's our lead for your press conference. 'An improvement.' But the questioning can get personal, like how you shave—"

"White House barber shaves me, same as before." He tensed.

"And how you brush your teeth—"

"Damn!" Ericson covered his lips with his hands, as he did when furious. He tried to compose himself. "You get into the bathroom, and you knock over the toothbrush glass. You feel around the broken glass on the floor and pick up the toothbrush, then try to squeeze toothpaste onto it and you miss and it falls in the sink. . . . Fowler taught me how to brush my teeth!"

Smitty remembered the therapist's advice, so he toughed it out. "You're making me cry, Mr. President. Now, they'll want to know about laws signed when you can't see what you're signing."

"Whenever I sign a bill," said Ericson, "it will be countersigned by the Secretary of State, the Speaker of the House, and a federal judge, under a statement swearing they were present when the bill was read to me. I should call the Speaker to lock that up." Ericson lifted the phone and told the White House operator, "Speaker Mortimer Frelingheusen." To Smitty he said, "Thank God for Mort. He's a Republican, but he's played it straight." In a moment, "Mort? I'm here with Smitty, working over some dirty questions that may come up at the press conference Wednesday."

"You'll get a good rating," the Speaker allowed. "Lot of people want to make sure you're *compos mentis.*"

"I want to thank you for the signature-attesting thing. That'll be a chore, I know. At least a couple hours every week. Maybe you can delegate it after a while."

"No, I'll be glad to listen to them read aloud," said the Speaker, in his New Jersey Middle America monotone. "While I have you on the line, Mr. President, the International Relations Committee and the Defense Committee are concerned about the breaches in the arms control agreement by China-Japan. The Chijaps have been selling nuclear missiles to Zaire and Uganda. If the Africans use them against the Arab-Israeli alliance, we're all in the soup. We could use a statement from you that the administration will consult with Congress on this very soon."

"I want to hear what Secretary Curtice says when he gets back from Moscow at the end of the week, Mort. He advises that Niko-layev seems to be taking charge, and their intelligence system is better than ours when it comes to the Far East. I'll say that we'll consult." With a warm farewell, the President hung up.

"You going to be able to get all this stuff in your head in two days, Mr. President?"

Ericson took off his dark glasses and spun them around. "We'll tape the briefing book and compress it, and I'll run through it tomorrow. Then we'll rehearse walking around the East Room."

THE TELEVIEWING ARRANGEMENT in the press secretary's office takes up most of one wall, playing four networks simultaneously. During press conferences, the speakers are on low volume, since the regular viewer is absent and his office is left empty.

"Ladies and gentlemen, the President of the United States." All four screens showed the press rising as the President walked down the middle aisle of the East Room. All four speakers began murmuring variations of "President Ericson is using his sonar watch to determine the location of the steps." He reached the rostrum, struck a familiar Ericson pose, leaning on the wooden stand with one elbow. The press corps broke out in applause.

He smiled broadly. "Please be seated." As usual he pointed to the senior wire service correspondent, in the front row. "Mr. President," she said, "how do you feel?"

The President shook his head and said, "There's always one question you haven't prepared for." Laughter. Then, soberly, the image on the four screens said, "I've begun to adjust to the shock of not being able to see. I have to absorb information through my ears rather than my eyes, and that takes a little getting used to.

"But I have to tell you how bad I feel about General Secretary Kolkov, who dragged his wounded body over me and saved my life. When I think about him, I don't feel sorry for myself."

The junior wire service reporter asked, "Mr. President, what's the latest on the condition of your eyesight?"

"I have some cautious good news on that," the man in dark glasses on the podium said. "I've begun to make out the difference between light and dark. But at the moment I'm officially blind."

"Don't you think it would be in the best interests of national security, sir, if you stepped aside under the disability provisions of the Twenty-fifth Amendment, until such time as you were fully capable of discharging your duties?"

"No," said the President. There was a pause.

"Could you tell us how you know what you're signing?"

The President went through the procedure of countersignatures.

"Sir, do you think the Vice-President would make a good Acting President—do you have confidence in him?"

117

Nettled, the President took off his glasses for a moment. "I have every confidence in the Vice-President. If I were to die in office or become disabled, he would carry on. But I'm not dead and I'm not disabled. As I understand it, the President is elected by the people and trusted by them to decide on his ability or disability, and I've made that decision. Next?"

A gentleman from *The Christian Science Monitor* said, "Are you concerned, sir, that the sale of nuclear missiles by the Chijaps to the Africans is an abrogation of the arms control agreement?"

The screen showed the President moving into foreign policy with relief. "One reason for my meetings with General Secretary Kolkov was to explore our mutual reaction to the arming of the Fourth World by the Far Eastern powers. A war between the Third World of the Mideast and the Fourth World of Africa and Latin America could spread to the two superpower alliances. The central problem of the 1980s is to avoid that.

"Speaker Frelingheusen has been after me to send the Defense Secretary to the House to testify on the arms sales to, uh, Nigeria. His request will be granted."

The President reached for a glass of water on a table next to the lectern, his hand closing confidently on the glass. Close-up of the glass of water moving to the President's mouth and being returned to the table. Ericson's sonar watch caught the felt cloth, and the glass crashed to the floor. In the silence the camera remained on the broken glass.

"It's the little things that get you down," the President cracked. "Next question." Domestic issues dominated the next ten minutes. After the "Thank you, Mr. President" from the senior wire service reporter, the screens showed a sudden glare and then blackened; an old-fashioned flashbulb had gone off at the President and caused a reaction in the sensitive lenses.

"That came from over there." The President pointed. "Did I pass your test?" The sound picked up the edge of bitterness in his tone as he felt for the step with his foot, walked down off the platform, and made his way—accompanied by the press secretary and two Secret Service agents—out of the East Room.

The sounds of the four-screen set in Smitty's office intermingled: "After a good start, the President's performance in this crucial press conference went downhill." ". . . most glaring error was in confusing the recipient of the nuclear missiles in Africa, certainly not Nigeria, the least militant of the Fourth World nations." ". . . though frankly I cannot blame him for showing a little temper when a photographer broke the rules of the press conference to shoot a flashbulb in his face. The President interpreted that as an insulting test of his truthfulness, after having said that he could tell light from dark." ". . . from an atmosphere of sympathy, an atmosphere of hostility developed."

HENNESSY tore into Cartwright's office after the press conference. Smitty was there, with a depressed Melinda and Fowler.

"They didn't ask one question that wasn't in the briefing book," Smitty insisted. "I edited 'em. Fowler compressed 'em. I heard Ericson rattle them off this afternoon. What got into him?"

Hennessy didn't trust himself to speak. To lose your temper when it served a purpose was one thing; to blow up to no purpose or as a personal indulgence was another.

Cartwright said to Fowler, "He certainly moved in and out of the East Room with authority, thanks to you, Hank."

"My heart sank when the glass broke," the therapist replied.

"To compensate," said the chief of staff, "we had that flashbulb incident. And the Nigerian thing was just a slip of the tongue."

The telephone rang. It was the President. "Reaction here is mixed," Cartwright said. "The reference to Kolkov went over well." Pause. "Mrs. Cartwright watched the press conference at a party which the Bannermans attended. I'll find out what was said." He listened to the President's final comment and hung up. "He'd like to see you in his sitting room," Cartwright told Hennessy.

The special counsel hurried down the colonnade, nodded to Buffie, who passed him silently—that surprised him, she usually had a cheery greeting—and continued on up to the Lincoln Sitting Room.

"You blew it," Hennessy said to the President. "What got into you?" Hennessy knew he would not have been summoned if Ericson did not want a frank assessment.

"What was the worst?"

"You weren't in charge. The real President Ericson never loses his sense of humor, never drops his sense of style. So who do they see? Some blind guy who takes offense, lashes out. Look, you honestly think you're doing the right thing about not quitting?"

"How do I know? Let's give it a month, then we'll see. But we can't say that, because that's a show of weakness. I want to make that decision, I don't want it made for me."

So Ericson must act as if there were no chance of his stepping aside; makes sense, thought Hennessy.

"The presidency is not a job you quit in a hurry, Hennessy. It's instability when you do. Once people get the idea that Presidents they don't think are doing the job should resign, then the four-year term starts crumbling. Unless he is incapacitated for a long time, a President's duty is to stay in office.

"We happen to have a Vice-President who is an amiable jerk. He was not chosen because he would be a good President, but because at the convention I agreed to take Bannerman's choice for a running mate. Operating at twenty percent of capacity, I would be a better President than Nichols operating at one hundred percent of capacity. And I want to be President. I lost my eyesight because I'm President. The office owes me something—"

"No need to rush into an irrevocable decision," Hennessy interrupted. "Coupla weeks, maybe coupla months, we'll see."

The President relaxed, sliding back into his chair.

"Tell me one thing, though," Hennessy said. "How'd you get that photographer to flash that bulb in your face?"

Gleefully, Ericson sailed a slipper in Hennessy's direction, and the President's counsel pretended that it had hit him. After he had said good night, it occurred to Hennessy that they should plot some follow-up to the report Cartwright was to get from his wife about Bannerman's reaction. He came back to find the President on the telephone, looking bleak, saying, "Where could she be? Who saw her after she left here?" The counsel turned away.

THE REASON BUFFIE was unreachable was that she was in the apartment of the President's junior speech writer, Jonathan Trumbull.

She had shown up at his door a couple of hours before and announced, "You've had eyes for me for months, this is your big chance, I want to stay with you tonight." Then the girl's tears, her revelations, the soothing, a first kiss, and now, looking down from the window of Columbia Plaza at Kennedy Center, Jonathan tried to sort it all out, numbering the items as he knew Ericson did.

One, I am twenty-seven years old and this is my first job since graduate school. Two, I am on a collision course with disaster. Three, the President has given me a bird's-eye view of history in the making, just as I had hoped when he remembered a freshman who had taken economics from him and sent for me to be a staff aide. Four, Mr. Cartwright has hinted that I may soon be a special assistant on equal standing with the other speech writers.

He touched the sleeping girl, who drew the covers tighter and moved away. There was this attraction between them, which he and Buffie had felt on *Air Force One*. They were the acknowledged free spirits, who had tasted of Paris, night, and the moon, but it was known that Buffie was the President's special friend.

Yet in unburdening herself before dropping off to sleep, she had burdened Jonathan. "Potus has changed," she had said.

"How has he changed?"

"Possessive. In the old days I was free. You know how all the movies say, 'I want to be needed'? That doesn't do a thing for me. I want to be not needed."

"Now, of course," Jonathan had said, "you're needed more than before. And that upsets you."

"What's driving me up the wall is the guilty feeling I get. Why am I hurting him? What kind of person am I becoming?"

In the morning Jonathan fixed breakfast as she sat on the floor, cross-legged. "You ought to meet Secretary Bannerman," she said with her mouth full. "You'd learn a lot from him."

"Economics isn't my bag." Jonathan shrugged.

"But Bannerman's a good man to know after we all go home."

Jonathan shook his head. The future was four romantic years in the White House, maybe eight. "When you showed up here last night, Buffie, I didn't figure you for a long-range planner."

"The guy has all the money in the world to do good things," she said. "Like start magazines. Or buy book publishers. Look, someday we're gonna be thirty."

"You, maybe." Jonathan laughed. "I'm Peter Pan. But if you say I should get to know Bannerman, fine with me."

Looking out his office window, across East Executive Avenue, T. Roy Bannerman could see the Secretary of Defense leave the East Wing of the White House and cross the street to the Treasury Department. Downstairs, the Treasury Secretary's private elevator was being held in readiness for his fellow Cabinet member.

Bannerman's visitor, Defense Secretary Preston Reed, had been ambassador to the Court of St. James's a few years ago. Bannerman respected Reed—Wall Street lawyer, a foot in nearly every establishment—and he judged Reed to be his equal in intellect, prestige, and savvy; his superior in selflessness, because he had no personal power goals.

He and Reed had known the loci of power long before Ericson's time, and would remain there after Ericson became a memory. Bannerman was accustomed to being derided as a limousine liberal, but he was certain that the country was well served by an aristocracy bred to govern or—if not to govern—at least gently but firmly to guide the governance. Bannerman's power and Reed's clout did not come from money, but from the lifelong assurance that money was not a problem, and from membership in the web of friends and associates around the world who bore the burden of making financial systems and governments work.

A Secret Service agent ushered Reed in. Small, slender, gray, his own man. When Bannerman indicated a chair, Reed shook his head. "Roy, I've been indoors all day. Let's try the park."

Together they left for Lafayette Park, across the street from the White House, and sat on a plain park bench. Good place, Bannerman knew, to be certain they were not being taped.

"I wanted to talk to you," the Treasury Secretary began, "because I want to save this government by constitutional means from a man whose arrogance and pigheadedness will not let him see that he is physically incapable of running it."

The Defense Secretary thought that over. He said, "Roy, suppose you were President, and you went blind. Would you resign?"

"I would step aside without hesitation. And so would you, Preston. The President must always put the country first."

"Moral obligations," intoned the Defense Secretary, "are usually cited by people who don't have a legal leg to stand on. Your legal position is weak, Roy."

"According to the Twenty-fifth Amendment," Bannerman said, "if the President is unable or unwilling to declare himself incapable of discharging his duties, the Vice-President and a simple majority of the Cabinet can make such a declaration to Congress, at which point the Vice-President becomes Acting President. If we get two-thirds of the Congress to agree, within a three-week deadline, then he's out and Nichols remains."

"Close enough," said Reed. "But the amendment deals with the *in*ability of the President to act—not the *dis*ability. The legislative intent was to cover a President who is in a coma, or has been captured by an enemy, or has gone out of his mind."

Bannerman conceded the legal point. "But the remedy of forcing him out against his will would not have been put in the Twenty-fifth Amendment unless there had been a recognition that a sick man is not the best judge of his own inability—the Cabinet is. And in case of disagreement, the Congress is."

"You wouldn't get my vote in the Cabinet on *that* argument."

"What argument would get your vote?"

"The gut of the matter is whether the Far Eastern powers, and the Soviet Union, *think* Ericson is able to discharge his duties. If they assume that this government may not react immediately to a nuclear threat, then our deterrent ceases to be a deterrent."

"You think we're in danger of attack right now?"

"The Defense Intelligence Agency has made this estimate: that the Far Eastern powers think of themselves right now as being in the best position for a strike. A blind Sven Ericson is a man *they think* is incapable of deciding to retaliate in time. Vice-President Nichols at least gives the appearance of capability, and that very *appearance* reduces the risk of war. As Secretary of Defense, I have already urged the President to step down. And in a Cabinet move I would vote accordingly."

That's two of us, Bannerman said to himself.

"There is something else that worries me," the Defense Secretary added. "We have some evidence our friend Nikolayev may have engineered the ambush, to be blamed on the Chinese. If it is true, then the President might be suspicious of a Soviet leader who tried to kill him. We would be better off if both Ericson and Nikolayev were to remove themselves." He looked at his bench mate. "What's the matter, Roy? You look a little sick."

Bannerman felt a genuine sense of shock. "Hits home." Focusing on a vote count, he added, "Curtice is coming back tomorrow. You think we can get him with us?"

"Unlikely," said Reed. "He would be out in a Nichols administration. I wouldn't trust him yet with the Nikolayev-as-assassin possibility. The Secretary of State thinks he now has an inside track to the Soviet leadership."

"Next is Human Resources, Andy Frangipani," Bannerman said. The old Interior, Agriculture, and Commerce departments had been melded into a Department of Natural Resources, and HEW, HUD, Labor, and Transportation were fused into a Department of Human Resources, reducing the Cabinet to State, Defense, Treasury, Justice, Natural, and Human.

"If there is a Cabinet member with a vested interest in voting with the President, it's the Big Flower," Reed observed. Frangipani, former mayor of New York, now headed the health-elderly establishment. Jobs for the handicapped was a favorite cause; blindness in a President was a plus. His institutional and personal rival was Natural Resources Secretary Mike Fong. The Democratic Party had forced Fong on Ericson, partly at Bannerman's behest.

"Figure Fong with us," said Bannerman. "And Attorney General Duparquet will stick with the President down the line."

"That's three to three," said Reed. "We'd have to pull one over. But this whole discussion is academic if the Vice-President uses his veto."

Bannerman nodded. "If I have a majority, I have him."

"Then Curtice is the weak sister."

Reed got up, contemplated the White House—fountains dancing, flag flying on the roof—in the sunset. Continuity. "Curtice might go for a straddle, voting for putting it up to the Congress."

"Preston," Bannerman said, "I have somebody very close to the President, and a strong possibility of a second source. Ericson is suffering fits of depression. We can play to his moods. Avoid a confrontation, have a sensible transition."

"Won't happen. Ericson's a President. He'll hang on like a bulldog. But the intelligence you pick up could make a difference."

Bannerman nodded. Ericson was indeed a President. A less stubborn man would have been better for the country.

Bannerman raised his hand in a farewell. At the corner, he informed his waiting driver that he would not be needed that evening. He had already told his wife that he was planning a clandestine meeting with the President's girl friend and the President's junior speech writer at a dreary Chinese restaurant in Bethesda.

This suborning of loyalty did not give him pleasure. The girl was a cheap opportunist. He was surprised that a man like Ericson would have become so deeply involved with her.

II: THE TWENTY-FIFTH AMENDMENT

Lucas Cartwright was no sooner in the White House car than the mobile phone rang. The operator cautioned him: "This is an insecure communication, sir, the President is calling."

"Read the News Summary yet, Lucas?" The President's voice was worried. "It's about as bad as we thought. Have breakfast with me, Family Dining Room, when you get in."

Less than thirty-six hours after the Wednesday-night press conference, and the reaction storm was breaking. This was Friday.

Mrs. Cartwright—he liked calling his wife Mrs. Cartwright, and

she called him Mr. Cartwright, it was their little code of intimacy—
had reported to him after the dinner party. While Bannerman had
advocated standing by the President, she had learned that he and
unspecified others in the administration were deeply worried about
the President's ability to cope. That Ericson was afraid to hold a
Cabinet meeting. That he was the captive of the staff.

Cartwright slipped on his reading glasses and took a look at the
News Summary:

> TV: Most Democrats interviewed for reactions say the President
> should consider stepping aside temporarily. Most Republicans say
> it's a matter for the Democrats to work out among themselves, tak-
> ing a cue from Speaker Frelingheusen, who told NBC: "When it
> comes to press conferences, I've given a few clinkers myself."

Cartwright skipped to the big-shot columnists. There was an
"inside" report of a division in the White House staff, with Herb
Abelson urging the President to put the nation's needs ahead of
personal ambition. Then, Samuel Zophar's predictable reaction:

> It is no easy thing for a man as energetic, ambitious, and ideal-
> istic as Sven Ericson to step aside. Let the President think it over.
> He will conclude, as a patriot, that the welfare of the country
> comes before other considerations. . . .

Cartwright stopped reading. How must the President feel? Ericson's surface was rough-textured; inside was a gentleness that surprised and delighted men who worked with him; inside that was
core toughness. Whatever was at the center of Ericson, strength or
cold void, the crucible of the White House would render it unal-
loyed before the end. That was what Cartwright liked most, and
sometimes feared most, about working there.

The car stopped at the West Basement entrance. Cartwright
started for his office. In the anteroom, the President's young speech
writer was waiting for him. "Sir, I need to talk to you."

"You know my door is always open, Jonathan," Cartwright said,
"but El Número Uno requires my presence. Would after lunch be

all right?" The young man, obviously distraught, mumbled yes.

A butler was removing the President's plate as Cartwright entered the Family Dining Room. Melinda announced his presence and her own departure. Cartwright sat at the table that had been President Grant's Cabinet table, and ordered hot cereal.

"Nobody else orders oatmeal, Lucas," the President said.

"What about your taste for food, Mr. President? I've heard that when you lose your sight, your other senses become sharper—"

"Malarkey." Ericson sliced the air with his hand. "You're supposed to be able to hear better, or improve your touch or smell or taste. The truth is, you concentrate more. Hank is teaching me how to eat, so I won't act like a slob at a state dinner." He veered suddenly. "Who was the column source on the Abelson thing?"

"That troubled me too," Cartwright said. "Your physician has been looking a little sickly of late, taking your ailment to heart."

"Herb Abelson is the only one around here who wants me to quit. I don't hold it against him. Where is he, anyway?"

"He went home with a cold yesterday."

"It would be good if he stayed home and didn't answer the phone. Abelson worries a lot, and it shows. Now, what poop do you get from your wife? What did Bannerman say?"

Cartwright told him about Bannerman's reaction to the press conference. "Millionaire bastard," said Ericson. "He's going to come at us. Let's war-game this. First they send somebody to see you to appeal to my patriotism."

"Yes. When that doesn't work, another emissary will come, to show how you cannot possibly win in a Cabinet showdown."

"The pressure will mount in the press to 'step aside,'" the President picked up. "Attention is focused on convening a Cabinet meeting without me. I don't like it. Best way to win this fight is to avoid it. Let's block that meeting before it's ever held. What have I got on today?"

"The nine-a.m. national security briefing by the Army Chief of Staff. Appointments with staff members, listed to make the schedule look jammed. Secretary Curtice reports in from Russia at five, when his plane gets in at Andrews."

"Get his plane in a couple of hours earlier," the President directed, "then he meets me and comes out and says how on top of things I am, in time to make the evening news." Ericson shifted the subject. "Who can call the Cabinet meeting to consider the inability of the President?"

"Any member of the Cabinet, or the Vice-President."

"And they're all in town and healthy."

"Regrettably," Cartwright answered. "You'll need a campaign manager."

"The Attorney General's my man. I'll call him first thing."

"That would contribute to let's-have-a-meeting fever."

"Right. There is a packlike quality to the thought and movement in this town. We had it going with us, remember, when we moved hard into foreign affairs. Now it's picking up steam against us."

"But it takes considerable temerity to assemble a team for an assault on the presidency," said Cartwright. "There'll be accusations of usurpation."

"That's the word, Lucas—usurpation." Ericson seemed to perk up. "I won't call the A.G. until we hear a plot's afoot. On second thought, at the right moment get him to call me."

"Grand, that's grand." Cartwright rose and excused himself.

THE White House day crowded in on Cartwright and he was surprised by the appearance of the young speech writer at three o'clock. "You're the only person around here I trust, Mr. Cartwright," Jonathan began. "I think there's going to be an attempt, sir, to drive the President out of office." The writer swallowed.

Very calmly, the President's chief of staff asked, "And what has caused you to think that, Jonathan?"

At that moment the sound of a chopper heralded Secretary of State Curtice's arrival on the lawn; the President wanted Cartwright in their meeting, but it would have to wait.

"Buffie—the photographer—came to my apartment the other night, after the press conference," the speech writer blurted. Haltingly, he recounted his temptation and fall from grace.

"Jonathan, you are carrying on what can only be called a grand tradition. Nobody can protect you from the consequences of that particular liaison."

"I wouldn't take up your time just to tell you I was with the President's girl friend, sir. But, you see, Buffie suggested I meet the Secretary of the Treasury the very next night. How did she know he'd be available so quick unless she had a date with him, and I was to be part of the date from the start?"

"Good deduction," Cartwright said. "You were being set up."

"So we met for dinner, the three of us. Bannerman buttered me up, saying he'd heard of the fine job I'd been doing for President Ericson. Then he asked me how I felt about the President's blindness, and began a pitch on how the true test of loyalty to Ericson was loyalty to the country. He said that a group was banding together to help the President make the right decision about stepping aside, just for a while, until he could cope with the job."

"Did Secretary Bannerman ask you to do anything?"

"To stay in touch through Buffie, and to pass on any poop that indicated the President was falling on his face. He said that there would be a Cabinet meeting to ask the President to step aside, maybe early next week. Said Cabinet members were getting pressure from Natural Resources to move fast."

"Secretary Fong?"

"Guess so. Bannerman pledged me to secrecy, and hinted that I would make my fortune sticking with the President's 'true friends.' Mr. Cartwright, is it possible for the President not to know about me and his girl?"

"I will keep your identity as our informant to myself, Brother Jonathan. The President need not be apprised of the interest you and he share. Go along as you have; your instincts in this are good." Cartwright was convinced that the young man in front of him could be of great value. Not only in what he could learn, but in what he could pass back to the takeover group.

Cartwright gave Jonathan his private telephone numbers, in the office and at home, walked him to the elevator, and bolted for the Oval Office for the meeting with the Secretary of State.

At the door Cartwright paused. How much would he reveal? He

would notify the President of the imminence of the takeover meeting. But what about Buffie? Could she know anything about the condition of Ericson's eyes that the President's chief of staff did not know? Of course not. Cartwright went into the meeting.

THE President and Curtice sat on chairs near the Oval Office fireplace. Ericson seemed to be concentrating profoundly, and his questions about Harry Bok indicated his concern was not perfunctory. But—this was the difference, more than anything—Ericson was not so damnably cocky and detached as before.

Lucas Cartwright looked in. Curtice had been briefed quickly by Melinda McPhee and by a blind therapist on how to operate now with the President. "Here's Lucas," Curtice told the President.

"Come in, Lucas. George says Harry Bok is paralyzed. I want you to see what the Service can do for him in its counterfeit division. A man doesn't need to walk around to look at phony bills."

Curtice wondered if the President knew of the alteration of emphasis concerning the ambush. He would not bring it up if Cartwright did not. That white lie about Kolkov had helped the cause of peace and the alliance between superpowers. Abelson, Bok, Cartwright, and he would have a lifelong bond.

"Give Lucas a quick fill on the aftermath of the ambush," the President said.

"Nikolayev has effective control," the Secretary of State reported. "He tells me the ambush was staged by the Far Eastern powers in an attempt to split the Soviet-American alliance. It would be in the Chijap interest to have the Third World—the Middle Eastern powers, Arabs and Israelis and India—under attack from the Fourth World have-not nations of Africa and Latin America. Within that world strategic situation we have an immediate problem on our borders, as you know: both the Québecois and the Mexicans are aligned against us, leading the Fourth World, along with Nigeria. That makes all the more necessary a solid Soviet-American alliance."

On the way in from the airport, glancing at the newspapers, Curtice had been appalled at the lack of attention given to the dangerous international situation, and the preoccupation with the President's physical difficulties.

"Did the President mention to you the events taking place here at home?" Cartwright said. "The Secretary of the Treasury wants to call a Cabinet meeting to declare the President's inability to function, and to appoint Nichols Acting President. When President Ericson challenges this, Bannerman thinks he can get two-thirds of both houses of Congress to agree that the elected President should be deprived of his office."

"Bannerman is serious?" Curtice asked.

"Maybe," said Cartwright. "He controls the Vice-President and he'll use a cat's-paw to take the lead in the Cabinet."

"I strongly doubt that it will ever come to such a Cabinet meeting," said Curtice, not making any commitments, but leaving the impression that he was loyal to the President. "An abortive coup at such a meeting would make the United States look like a banana republic in the eyes of the world, and might invite some international mischief. Now, should I speak to the newsmen?"

"Yes," said the President. "They're dying to talk to you."

Curtice left the Oval Office with Cartwright.

Cartwright delivered Curtice to Smitty, who walked him into the press briefing room.

Later, in his limousine, Curtice grumbled to an aide, "This city is only interested in who's up, who's down, who's next. If Nikolayev can really pin this thing on the Chinese, the consequences will be enormous. What are they talking about here? Ericson's eyesight!"

"Secretary Fong has asked if he can come over to your house before dinner, sir. He said it was urgent."

Curtice looked sharply at his aide. "I'll go home and get a little sleep first and see him at eight. He can have dinner with us."

The two Cabinet members dined at the Secretary of State's residence and talked for three hours. Mike Fong, former governor of New Mexico, soft sell, low key, was a man most people liked. His argument seemed far more cogent than Curtice had antici-pated: Ericson had lost the ability to govern, the people were los-ing confidence in him. Three and a half years remained in the term, an endless stretch with no real leadership, and the President was too obstinate—or worse, too confused—to step aside temporarily.

Curtice asked if the group that wanted Ericson out had the Vice-President's vote. Mike Fong's answer was that the Vice-President would not veto any action of the majority.

"There's no need to decide tonight," said Fong. "We're going to go ahead with the Cabinet meeting Monday. It's my judgment that a majority will vote for Ericson to step aside."

"Tell Bannerman I'm keeping an open mind," said Curtice.

"Talk it over with the Secretary of Defense," Fong suggested. "Your foreign concerns and Reed's overlap."

After Fong had left, Curtice stood by himself in the balmy spring night. So they were serious. Fong was a good man, wanted to do right. Bannerman was tired of being a power broker and anxious to become the power wielder. Emmett Duparquet was certainly the one Ericson had in mind as his own successor in the next election. Curtice did not quite trust Duparquet, a wealthy Southerner. And when he peeled the onion down to the place where the tears were, Curtice did not trust Ericson, either.

But his appointment as Secretary of State was all Ericson's. How would it look if the first black Secretary of State turned against his President in an unsuccessful grab for power? On the other hand, how would it look for the first black Secretary of State to hang on, like a grateful Uncle Tom, when patriots successfully invoked the Twenty-fifth Amendment and removed a stubborn but physically incapable man from the presidency?

THE White House Mess, two staff dining rooms in the basement of the West Wing, seats about fifty. On Saturdays no tie or jacket is required.

Dr. Herbert Abelson, cold-ridden and irritable, dressed in jeans and an open shirt, slouched into the Mess at noon. The television news the night before spoke of a "fateful weekend at the White House, when so much hung in the balance," and he supposed the President's physician should be around. Waiting for the diet special, he depressed himself by reading stories in the News Summary about a Cabinet revolt and secret studies of the Twenty-fifth Amendment undertaken in the Justice Department.

He picked up the phone near the table and asked the operator for Melinda McPhee. "How's the Chief today?"

"I think he may have your cold. He's sniffling and growling."

He arranged to examine the President at one o'clock.

"Hey, Herb," came a breezy, reedy voice. The sight of Buffie made Abelson's heart sink even lower, she was so fresh and carefree. She sat next to him and said, too low for the waiter to hear, "You look awful." She put her hand on his arm. "I want to see the President. Please tell him that. I think he wants to see me." She took a wedge of cheese off his plate and slipped through the door.

Abelson ate his lunch, signed his chit, and walked upstairs to the anteroom between the Oval Office and the Cabinet Room, Melinda McPhee's domain. She was on the phone, so he went into the Cabinet Room. Hank Fowler was sitting in the President's chair, running his fingers around the buttons under the table.

Abelson had made no sound, but Fowler looked up in his direction immediately. "Caught me," the therapist said. "Who is it?"

"Just your friendly country doctor." Then Abelson decided he'd stop trying to be cheerful. "This place gets on my nerves."

"Help me get the feel of this room."

Abelson motioned to the guard at the door. "Officer, give this man sixty seconds on the Cabinet Room."

"The West Wing was built during the administration of Theodore Roosevelt," the officer began mechanically. "The walkway outside, leading through the French doors to the Rose Garden, was built to accommodate President Franklin Roosevelt's wheelchair. Where you are sitting, sir, is the President's chair, and you really shouldn't sit there." Fowler got up and started moving around the table, touching each chair. "Each Cabinet member has his designated chair," the guard droned on, "with a small brass plaque on the back with his title and the date of his appointment."

"Thank you, Officer," Abelson said. "Can we use this door to the terrace? Hank, you'll like the Rose Garden." They sat on the steps leading down to the formal garden.

"You seem a little low today, Dr. Abelson."

"Grippe, I think." That was silly, trying to fool a professional psychologist. "The fact is, we're a bunch of zombies. Sven Ericson is dead and doesn't know it." Abelson felt his frustrations welling up. "He doesn't know what hit him yet. People around here tell him it's just another challenge he can rise to, but he isn't a whole person anymore."

Fowler nodded. "Good way of putting it."

"But all of us keep propping him up. Do you know why? Cartwright likes White House life, he's happy as a clam at high tide. Hennessy is fascinated with power. Melinda lives for the Chief, thinks he'll come apart if he can't be President. You, too, Hank, you'd like to see a blind man overcome his handicap."

"You?"

"I'm scared. You know what we're playing around with? War, peace, millions of lives. This job may be too big for any one man even when he's in perfect shape. Think of your patient, Hank."

"He's not my patient, he's my student."

"We all pretend you're only teaching him how to feed himself and walk around, but you're a professional shrink. What happens if he's in a depression and an international crisis hits?"

Fowler gave the matter some thought. "It's a fact," he said finally, "that in most cases of sudden blindness, a period of courage and determination is followed by a depression. It will probably happen to Ericson fairly soon. . . . Who's there?"

Melinda was standing behind them. "The President will see the one who can fix a cold."

Abelson went into the Oval Office and stuck a thermometer in the presidential mouth. As he was taking the presidential pulse, he said, "Buffie wants to know why I've been keeping you two apart. So if you want, I'll deliver her to the third floor tonight."

Ericson took the thermometer from under his tongue, said, "Bring her around," and put it back.

Abelson examined the thermometer. "You got ninety-nine and a half. I'll come by every four hours with aspirin."

When Abelson left the Oval Office, Cartwright was waiting

in the corridor and asked him to step down to his corner office.

"Herb," Cartwright said uncomfortably, "I'm going in there now to tell the President that Bannerman is making his move. Secretary Fong has called a Cabinet meeting for ten a.m. on Monday."

"Do they have the votes?"

"Bannerman's one, Fong is two, Reed is three. They need a fourth. Frangipani is solid for us, as is the Attorney General, who will make our case in the Cabinet meeting. Secretary Curtice was with us until this morning, but he has just had a disturbing session with the Secretary of Defense, and he could be wavering."

"How can I help?"

"Your relationship with the President," Cartwright began, "is personal. Mine is professional. There is a personal matter that would be better for you to discuss with him. It has to do with Buffie." Abelson waited. "The young lady," the chief of staff continued, "is a source of concern because she is a potential leak."

The doctor made a face; if Cartwright only knew how discreet Buffie had been. The accident and the previous blindness, the hushing up and the deception when the second, permanent blindness struck—all this was tucked away in one girl's head.

"You don't agree," said Cartwright. "I am informed that Buffie had dinner night before last with Bannerman. The purpose was to recruit another member of the White House staff into the conspiracy to remove the President from office."

Abelson felt his heart constrict. If Buffie worked for Bannerman, then Bannerman knew everything and it was all over. In a way it would be a relief. Would Bannerman give Ericson a chance to resign honorably, or would he insist on disclosing the President's "lack of candor" during the campaign?

"Hennessy'll be here in a moment," the staff chief said. "We're going to break the news to the President about the Cabinet meeting. After that, I'd be grateful if you told him about Buffie."

"No, I got to see Hennessy first. Alone."

"If you wish," Cartwright said coolly. "Use this office. I'll just go and check the news ticker."

When Hennessy came in and saw the jeans-clad Abelson seated

on the couch, he said, "What kind of outfit is that to wear to a fateful weekend?" Then he saw the gray look on Abelson's face and added, "What's your problem? Remember, I'm the lawyer."

"Buffie is working for Bannerman. Tried to recruit one of the staffers to go to work for him the other night. Cartwright doesn't know that Buffie knows about the previous blindness."

"Pull yourself together, Herb," Hennessy said. "We haven't heard from Bannerman yet. If I were he and had Buffie's information, I'd ask for the President's declaration of inability on the grounds that he failed to disclose his potential for blindness before the election. I wouldn't horse around with Cabinet meetings."

"You tell Ericson," Abelson said brokenly. "I haven't got the stomach for it."

"LET me go in alone first," Hennessy said to Cartwright. "Herb doesn't want to be the one to tell him about the girl, so I will. It might be better if it's just him and me."

"Can't it wait? I have an official notification from a Cabinet member that the President might be removed from office."

Hennessy did not feel that it was up to him to widen the circle of those who knew of the previous blindness. That should be Ericson's decision. So he said, "Lucas, the Chief depends on Buffie more than he knows, and in his present state this thing may affect him badly. Are Buffie and Bannerman having an affair?"

"Not to my knowledge. I believe their relationship is one of mutual interest, with him promising her the moon."

"And who's the one she tried to recruit on the staff?"

"I gave my word I wouldn't say."

Hennessy went in to see the President, who was on the couch in the small room off the Oval Office, listening to the News Summary on earphones. Hennessy tapped him on the knee.

"It's me, the intimate adviser. I don't come with good news."

"It's something about Buffie."

"How'd you guess?"

The President smoothed his hair back. "Out with it."

"Cartwright has information that she's in cahoots with Bannerman. She tried to get another White House staffer to leak stuff on you to him."

The President digested that. "Buffie and Bannerman," he said finally. "You suppose it's strictly business?"

"Strictly," Hennessy assured him, "but it's possible that Bannerman knows you were blind during the campaign and we covered it up, and he's waiting to bomb us with this. It's also possible she hasn't told him yet."

"If Buffie's on his team, why shouldn't she tell him?"

Hennessy said, "She's playing both ends against the middle, doing something for him, keeping a secret for us, so she comes out on top no matter who wins."

Ericson sighed. "Oh, Hennessy, that's a hard one to take."

"Don't tell a divorce lawyer about women," Hennessy snapped, hoping to dispel the ravaged look on the President's face. "You'll have to find out if she's blabbed."

Ericson nodded automatically.

"Next, Cartwright is outside, wants to come in now to tell you how your loyal Cabinet is after your hide. He's with us, Sven, and I think we ought to fill him in on the previous blindness."

"No," said the President firmly. "He'll tell his wife, who's a one-woman CIA." Ericson picked up the phone. "Tell Mr. Cartwright to come in," he said to the operator. "Melinda, too." To Hennessy he said, "Let's go into the Oval Office. It's a historic first. The revolt of the Cabinet."

Hennessy steered him to the President's chair behind the President's desk next to the President's flag. Cartwright and Melinda came in and the President said easily, "I hear Buffie has proved to be a security risk."

"We could turn that to our advantage, Mr. President," Cartwright said cheerily, "and pass along misinformation."

"Melinda, I always told you not to trust that girl," Ericson kidded himself, "but you kept insisting she was a great photographer."

"I'm sorry I forced her on you," Melinda said wryly.

Hennessy walked away from the President's desk, seating himself on the couch, observing the tableau. Melinda had probably guessed the big secret long ago, but kept that knowledge to herself. Cartwright did not know the significance of Buffie's defection, only the details; but he was keeping a secret of his own from the President—the fact that Buffie was seeing a particular White House staffer. Hennessy was certain of Buffie's infidelity; he was not telling the President of this deduction because that kind of shock might send a blinded man off the deep end. Tangled web weaving, he thought, among people on the same side.

"At ten thirty this morning," Cartwright stated, "the Secretary of Natural Resources, Michael Fong, telephoned me to say that he intended to call a meeting of the Cabinet to discuss the President's inability to discharge his duties, as set forth in the Twenty-fifth Amendment. You will recollect, Mr. President, that you directed me at our meeting yesterday to inform any member of the Cabinet who made such an approach that no inability existed. I delivered your message to Secretary Fong.

"I also transmitted your message to him that you were sure he was acting out of patriotic concerns, but was profoundly misguided. He then said that he was sending me a copy of a notification of the Cabinet meeting. The letter was delivered to me at one p.m. today, Saturday. The meeting is called for ten a.m., Monday, in the Cabinet Room."

Ericson slowly swiveled his chair. "Be my guest."

"It would be an interesting constitutional question if you insisted on attending," Cartwright went on. "The Attorney General said that he considered the convening of such a meeting to be in accordance with the Twenty-fifth Amendment. But the A.G. also said he thought it would be a power grab, a perversion of the intent of the framers of the amendment."

"You're seeing the A.G. tonight at dinner, Mr. President," Hennessy interjected. "Let him know he's in a real fight."

"Okay, okay." Ericson was irritated. "Everything is crowding in at once. I want to be alone. Send in Fowler."

Melinda led Cartwright and Hennessy out of the Oval Office.

"I never thought the day would come," said Cartwright, "when I couldn't pass on to the President an important message from the director of Central Intelligence." He held up one of the papers he had taken in and out of the President's office.

"What's it say?" asked Hennessy.

"Up to now, the CIA position on the ambush has been that it was probably inspired by the Far Eastern powers, but now the CIA director advises that the possibility exists that Nikolayev engineered a coup. In case a missile comes flying in, it's the sort of thing a President has to have in mind."

Melinda shook her head. "The Boss is right at the edge—all that news today, and that stupid cold. Back off."

"You're wrong," Hennessy said, explaining: "We have to operate as if the Cabinet has stripped him of the presidency and the matter has been put to the Congress. They have three weeks to decide who's President. We'll all be called as witnesses. We're under oath, and the committee counsel says, 'Here is a vital communication from the CIA delivered to the White House at such and such hour. Why was it delayed twenty-four hours? Was it your decision that the President was unable to handle such crucial information?'"

Melinda said in a weary voice to Cartwright, "I'll run you in right after he's finished with Fowler."

"The flower gimmick doesn't work when you've got a cold," the President told Fowler gloomily. Two days before, as part of training in the development of other senses—to help Ericson locate himself in a familiar room—the therapist had ordered a bowl of roses placed on the coffee table near the fireplace. The source of the scent became a landmark for the President.

"Did you find the clock trick useful in orientation?"

"Yeah, that works. As long as nobody forgets to wind it." On the President's desk was a penholder with a small, fast-ticking clock. Across the room, near the hall door, was a freshly installed antique grandfather clock, with a low, slow tick. If Ericson wanted to greet a visitor, he would move toward the right of the source of the slow tick; when he wanted to sign something, he could "hear" his pen. To a stranger the ticking was unnoticeable.

The President had plunged into the training exercises, concentrating on the mental crutches that could get him through the beginning of blindness. But he had offered no opening for introspection, and Fowler was not about to push.

"I've been going around the White House taping sounds you might hear in a normal day," Fowler said. "The slap of envelopes on a table, the air conditioning, the sound of a Secret Service agent walking as compared to that of a secretary—"

"Not today, Hank. Let's just talk." Ericson's breathing was labored. "I haven't discussed it with anyone yet, but I get the feeling everything is closing in."

"It's about time you started into a depression," Fowler reassured him. "I was beginning to think you were some kind of nut."

"What does that mean, Hank?"

"The thing that worried me most at the press conference was your talk about your eyesight improving. I wondered if you were running away from reality."

"I hadn't realized," the President said, "that most people think that being blind is seeing black. I could detect some light the moment I woke up after the ambush. So I called it an improvement, to buy a little time. I was lying, but I wasn't lying to myself."

"It's a shattering time when that realization sinks in."

"It's sunk in," said the President.

"Has it? Here's a test: How long are you going to be blind?"

"I'm no eye doctor." The President's chair made sounds of shifting weight. "How long are *you* going to be blind, Hank?"

"I'm going to be blind the rest of my life." The words hung in the air.

"It's a hell of a thing to get formed in your mouth."

"Well?" said the therapist.

In a firm voice the President said, "I'm going to be blind for the rest of my life."

"And productive, too," added Fowler quickly.

"Answer me this, Hank—what scares you most?"

"Losing my hearing," the therapist replied.

"That was the first thing I thought of after the clock gimmick worked," said Ericson. "This morning I thought I could bring this whole thing off. This afternoon I think I may resign. The feeling I have, it's like a desolation. You say this is a normal reaction, I'll be my old self in no time?"

"I didn't say that," Fowler answered. "I said that after the realization comes the depression. It may last a couple of weeks. Then the blind person makes it back part of the way, or he doesn't. In either case he's never himself again, the way he knew himself to be. His self-image has to change."

"Why can't I sleep at night?"

"You haven't adopted the habit of sleeping to time, you're still sleeping to light."

"Why do I feel so overall lousy?"

"Emotional strain, loss of body tone. You have to work your other senses overtime. It takes something out of you."

"When you went blind, did you have trouble making decisions?"

"My family moved into making all the decisions for me," the therapist said. "I was dependent on them, and they enjoyed it."

"Is that what's happening here? I have a funny feeling Hennessy and Melinda are getting a perverse kick out of it. Furthermore," said Ericson, "if there's one thing a President must have, it's an idea of what comes first. Just a few minutes ago they were informing me about a Cabinet meeting to throw me out of office. I kept telling myself that the most important things to keep in mind were the long-range welfare of the country and the stability of the presidency. But I kept thinking of a girl, and was she ratting on me. She was someone to be young again with, you know. But now she's important, and there's obviously a lack of priority."

Fowler went "Um," to show he was still there. Ericson was beginning to direct the questions at himself, a good sign.

"This particular girl—Buffie, the photographer—happens to have political significance, something she knows and something she's doing. But I'm not even focused on that, I'm worried about her changing toward me. I need her now, and if I let her know I need her, I'll lose her, and if I lose her—"

"You'll have lost all your sex appeal? Your manhood? That's such

141

a predictable reaction, you should be able to set it aside with no trouble." Now Fowler put in the question he felt was central to the situation: "Do you need this job?"

"The job needs me," the President answered too quickly. Evidently he was not prepared to explore how his power needs had become amplified during his sight loss. "Flying blind, I can do a better job than Nichols and Bannerman."

Hank sent in a shaft. "Your words are telling me one thing, but your hostility is telling me something else. What is important is that you know what you are really thinking."

"Hank, enough of my friends have been to psychiatrists, including my ex-wife, whom I don't intend to talk about— The trick is the patient keeps talking until he gets a sudden flash of insight. Is that the pitch? I don't have time for it in this situation. If you have something to tell me about myself that I can use, spit it out."

"They'd throw me out of the union," Fowler said lightly. "So have you decided to chuck the job or not?"

"You crazy, Hank? I only wanted to see what you'd say. But I'm glad we had this talk. See if you can cheer up Herb Abelson." He pushed a button; Melinda came in and asked what he wanted. Ericson said, "Send Marilee Pinckney in."

Marilee, Smitty's deputy, appeared. "Do me a favor," the President said. "Go out and buy an ounce of Ma Griffe perfume. When she's not looking, drop it on Melinda's desk. It's her birthday."

Marilee murmured politely and went off on the errand.

Fowler expressed surprise that Ericson knew which perfume to order.

"It's just a matter of training your olfactory sense, Doctor. And I use an association to remember: Ma Griffe means 'my clutches,' and that's Melinda."

Fowler released his own tension with a laugh.

The telephone made three bleeping noises, and Ericson picked it up. "Yes, Hennessy." After a pause, "Let's do it. You get Herb to deliver Buffie at nine sharp. Tell the A.G. he's to be overheard, starting at nine. And you join the A.G. and me at dinner." Pause. "No, I don't think we should, that's a sucker play." He put the telephone down and told Fowler, "The A.G. and Hennessy have been looking at the law. Seems I have the power to fire any member of the Cabinet between now and the time the meeting takes place. But if I pulled it, there'd be a move to impeach—the American people don't like a shady trick." Fowler could sense the Ericson smile. "Oh, that Hennessy's a bastard."

BUFFIE could hear muffled voices in the dining room, next door to the upstairs family quarters room, where Herb Abelson had taken her and said, "He's having a dinner meeting with the Attorney General and Hennessy. He doesn't know how long it will last; he said for you to stick around."

Now, sitting near the door to the dining room, Buffie could make out the conversation.

Hennessy's voice was booming. "We fire 'em before they meet. Monday morning, Bannerman comes to the White House, and Cartwright slaps an envelope in his hand that says he has been discharged. Bannerman'll scream, but he's got no right to go into that meeting. Does he, Emmett?"

A deep, slightly southern voice said, "There would be no doubt about the ruling. The amendment calls for the 'principal officers of the executive departments.' If a man's been fired five minutes before the meeting, he is out."

"Hennessy, have the envelopes ready," said the President. "I'll tell you what to do when Bannerman and Fong come in Monday."

"Bannerman thinks he has the Secretary of Defense in his pocket," said Hennessy. "He's wrong. The boys in Wall Street are working on him. Unless Bannerman puts counterpressure on Wall Street, Reed will swing over to the President."

"I don't know why you guys are so worried," said Ericson's voice. "Vice-President Nichols has personally assured me that he would veto any attempt to take over unless it were unanimous. Roy Bannerman is in for a big shock if he thinks he's won."

That would be something for Secretary Bannerman to know. Buffie listened next to a lot of legal talk that was hard to follow.

143

Finally she heard the chairs in the dining room scraping the floor. Ericson knocked once and came into the room.

"Hullo, Potus. I left the light off specially for you." She saw his form move to an easy chair. "You know your way around this room," she said. "I'd have stubbed my toe by now."

"When the lights are out, we're even."

"Potus, you worried about losing your job? You mustn't think about that. It wouldn't be for long; you'd be back soon."

"Sure I'm worried. Once you're out, it's all over. Would you stick with me?" There was an edge of sarcasm in his voice. "Where were you the night of the press conference? I needed you then."

"Don't lean on me, Potus. When I'm with you, you know it's because I want to be. There are times when I have to be alone."

"Can I trust you, Buffie?"

"Not completely." She felt defensive, and had plenty to be defensive about, more than he knew. Passing a little poop to Bannerman was a way of getting even or ahead in life, but it was not real betrayal. No, she would never speak about the campaign train incident and the hushing up of his blindness then. She figured Potus would understand.

After a while he said, "The guitar still in the closet?" During the campaign, he had discovered she could pluck at the guitar and had a pretty fair voice.

"You King Saul, me David?" she asked. She went to the closet and took out the guitar.

"You know your Bible." He smiled.

"My Bible movies." She sat cross-legged on the floor. "Gregory Peck was David, strummin' away. Soothed the old king."

"Soothe me," said the President.

The talk of the Bible reminded her of the hymn so many folk singers used as a crowd warm-up. Slowly she began, concentrating on the chords, and singing in her reedy voice:

> "Amazing grace—how sweet the sound—
> That saved a wretch like me!
> I once was lost, but now am found—"

She stopped abruptly, dreading what she had almost done.

"Why'd you stop?"

"Wrong song," she choked.

He touched her hair, felt her wet cheeks. He kissed her gently. "Sing it through."

It was more of a test for her than for him, so she did it sweetly and perfectly, not missing a chord:

> *"I once was lost, but now am found,*
> *Was blind, but now I see."*

She laid her fingers across the strings.

"Everybody knows that one, huh?" He looked thoughtful.

"Just about everybody, Potus." Her voice steadied. "People kind of come together on that song."

Ericson's long arms gripped the arms of the chair the way the statue of Lincoln did in the Memorial. "I ought to know the words to 'Amazing Grace,'" he mused. "Teach it to me, Buffie."

She taught it to him, but afterward asked him why he wanted to dwell on stuff that reminded everybody of blindness.

"You must never run away from it, chum," he said. "If a blind man winces at expressions like 'seeing eye to eye,' he makes people even more fearful. Hennessy looks for plays on 'blind' words, so we all laugh, or groan. Force the fear out in the open. Confront it." He gave her an affectionate hug. "The little leaks can't hurt. Just hold on to that big one and never let it go."

T. Roy Bannerman's Washington home was small but ostentatious, a brick dwelling on Massachusetts Avenue's Embassy Row.

Sunday of the "fateful weekend," the Treasury Secretary spent the morning on the telephone, walking up and down the shaggy white rug of his den, dragging the thirty-foot cord behind him. His White House source—that little opportunist, Ericson's photographer–girl friend—had called after breakfast with three items of intelligence. First, the possibility of dismissals as Fong and Bannerman entered the White House for Monday's Cabinet meeting. Next, the need to shore up Reed at Defense with Wall

Street pressure. Finally, the potential double cross by the Vice-President.

He ticked these off to his wife, who responded, "The Vice-President's the sort who'd go with the last person who spoke to him. But why should he turn down the presidency?"

"He wants to be President, but for more than three weeks," Bannerman replied, "and he doesn't want to go down in history as a would-be usurper that Congress slapped down. I put that non-entity where he is today," Bannerman added, allowing himself a slow burn. "He'd better not double-cross me."

"Do you believe the President?" she asked. That stopped him; maybe Ericson was lying about having a deal with Nichols.

The butler announced Secretary Fong, and Susan Bannerman left. Bannerman wasted no time on amenities. "Mike, we could be fired the minute we walk in there tomorrow morning."

"Won't happen," said Fong. "He'd be inviting impeachment. And we'd be better off. To impeach, you need a simple majority of the House, two-thirds of the Senate. But to declare inability, you need two-thirds in both houses."

Bannerman then told Fong of the need to pressure Reed; Fong was ill at ease, but went along, "since you know how to read Wall Streeters better than I, Roy."

The Treasury Secretary went to the phone, calling one lawyer, one retired banker, the current ambassador to the Court of St. James's in London, and the only living former Defense Secretary. Next Bannerman reached the board chairman of New York Hospital and asked that old fund-raising friend to have his doctors on tap in Washington. Then he tuned in to "Meet the Media." He and Fong watched a panel of newsmen zero in on a pair of constitutional scholars:

QUESTION: What is inability, according to the Constitution?
SCHOLAR I: The framers of the Twenty-fifth Amendment thought it would be a mistake to tie the hands of future Cabinets and Congresses with a specific definition of inability: They left it up to us, so to speak.

"That's good," said Bannerman. "The word 'inability' is what this Cabinet says it is. No precedent."

QUESTION: Well, then, what do *you* think inability means?

SCHOLAR I: I would put a narrow construction on inability. Once we start down the road of "inability to govern," we start saying an unpopular President can be brought down because the people don't like him anymore—and that is certainly not in the spirit of the Constitution. Inability is most specifically a physical ailment that is unarguably disabling—a coma, something that is not in the gray area. When a President insists he is able to perform his duties, only the most overwhelming testimony of medical experts should be used to challenge that assertion.

"You better have a strong medical lineup," Fong said to Bannerman. "Ericson will have his personal physician and the blind psychologist primed to say he's fit as a fiddle."

"Doctors will always disagree," said Bannerman. "This is not a medical decision, it's political—not inability to walk and talk, but an inability to govern. . . ."

QUESTION: Do you agree, Dean McAllister?

SCHOLAR II: I think the opposite. The Cabinet has extraordinary leeway to do what they feel is right, not to act according to the letter of a deliberately vague law, but to do what is right in their judgment. That's what morality is. . . .

"Perfect," said Bannerman. "They'll argue all day, and when you come down to it, it's entirely up to us. Let's turn off that noise and get to work on our strategy for tomorrow."

Fong started to pace the room. "It all hinges on George Curtice, Roy. You run in your doctors, and I make the historical points, but what goes on in that room ain't going to change any votes."

"So the question is—what heat can we put on Curtice?"

Fong nodded. "Reed told you that the CIA now thinks Nikolayev was behind the ambush. If that's true, Curtice is way out on a limb, since he's Nikolayev's buddy. This morning, Reed is

148

telling all this to Curtice, and it's going to scare hell out of him. I'll see him tonight and tell him that his only safe haven is with us."

"Curtice must be made to understand," Bannerman said deliberately, "that if I go down, I'll make it my lifelong occupation to see that he is ruined, that the first black Secretary of State will be remembered as an ignominious failure. And Vice-President Nichols is with us all the way."

As ALWAYS, he came to court early. When Emmett Duparquet practiced criminal law, he liked to sit in the courtroom an hour before anybody else arrived, getting a sense of the scene. In his mind he would people the jury box, cast the empty chairs in the dock and on the bench, and try out his opening argument.

The Attorney General had arrived before the camera crews, and only the radio and pencil press caught him on the way into the West Wing. "I saw the President over the weekend, I spoke to his doctors, I am convinced no inability exists."

In the empty Cabinet Room, Duparquet stood behind his chair, to the right of the Vice-President's chair, across the table from the President's chair, which would be unfilled. The morning summer sun streamed through the French doors; twenty steps away, the President was working in the Oval Office.

The Attorney General walked slowly around the room, forming his defenses. The prosecutors had an edge here that did not exist in the criminal courts, where Duparquet had spent his life first as counsel, then as judge: they did not have to prove their case "beyond a reasonable doubt." They could insist that if enough doubt existed of the President's ability to function, then the Cabinet would be obliged to remove him.

He was not addressing a jury, the tall, silver-haired Floridian reminded himself. Most of the votes had already been decided. Bannerman and Fong, with Reed probable, in favor of removal; he and Frangipani firmly against. The sixth vote was that of the Secretary of State. If Curtice held firm against removal, there could be no majority. If he sought to abstain, the Attorney General would fight against his right to do so, because that would give a three-two majority to the removal forces. The presentation had to be made to one man, George Curtice. "If you think you're going to lose," Lucas Cartwright had told Duparquet, "call a recess before the vote. I may have a handle on Curtice. I wouldn't use it unless I absolutely had to."

In a sense, the appeals judge was present: the Vice-President.

If the Attorney General lost Curtice and the Cabinet, he might still win with the Vice-President's veto.

Duparquet strode out of the Cabinet Room, through the connecting office to the Oval Office, where Ericson sat, coffee in hand, talking to Hennessy.

"Here comes the star quarterback," said Hennessy, "for final instructions from the coach before the big game."

The President did not look well. He had evidently spent a bad night: a gray cast soured his face and he kneaded the knuckles of his large hands.

"Mr. President," said the Attorney General, "we're going to win. I'll bet my job on that. Is there anything you want me to know, beyond all you've told me, before I go in?"

"Don't lose Curtice," Ericson said, "and remember that Bannerman put a lot of heat on Reed. Preston might not have liked that." Duparquet turned to leave.

"General," Ericson called after him, "you're not acting in the interests of one President this morning. You are serving every President who follows. Think of them."

"I will, Mr. President. And that was spoken like a President."

THE other Cabinet members were in the room when the Vice-President arrived. He took his seat, Duparquet and the rest followed. The Vice-President cleared his throat. "It is now ten five a.m., Monday, June 17, and the Cabinet is in session. The meeting was called at the request of Secretary Fong for the purpose of discussing the possible inability of the President to discharge his powers and duties. This is a sad occasion. I would like to go back to the Eisenhower administration's tradition, and begin this Cabinet meeting by asking you to join me in a moment of silent prayer."

Breaking the silence afterward, the Vice-President said, "Secretary Fong, you convened the group, the floor is yours."

Fong said solemnly, "On August 27, 1787, at the Constitutional Convention, John Dickinson of Delaware read the clause about the succession to the presidency upon the 'death, resignation, or disability' of the President to act as President 'until the disability be removed.' He asked, 'What is the extent of the term "disability" and who is to be the judge of it?'

"The first part of that question has never been answered. The second part has been most clearly answered in the Twenty-fifth Amendment: this Cabinet is to be the sole judge. Mr. Attorney General, do you agree with my interpretation of the Constitution?"

"You go ahead and make your case, Mike," Duparquet said.

Bannerman, picking up the argument, said, "I would like to say that the Twenty-fifth Amendment could not be plainer. Ericson could have been a fine President. But tragedy struck, and now he's incapable of making the decision he has to make in the best interests of the country. We have to make that decision for him."

"That's a helluva step to take," said Frangipani, "to strip the presidency from a man the people elected. Especially when he insists he's capable of carrying on."

"Andy," Bannerman said, addressing Frangipani but talking to Curtice and Nichols, "we're not stripping him of his office. We're seeing to it that the other man elected by all the people as his running mate steps into his office until Ericson is well enough to come back. And there is a procedure for him to declare his regained ability. If the Vice-President agrees, he returns without further ado. If the Vice-President doesn't agree, he can go to the Congress, and if one-third—just one-third—agree with Ericson, then he gets his presidency back."

"Let's get to the heart of the matter," Fong said. "Is the President disabled or not? I refer you to page three hundred and nine of the Legislative History, after it states that the Cabinet is best able to decide. 'It is assumed,' it says, 'that such decision would be made only after adequate consultation with medical experts.' The only medical advice we presently have access to rests with a third-string eye doctor at Bethesda Naval Hospital, the President's personal physician, who we all know is in that job because he is the President's buddy, and a therapist without even an M.D. after his name, who was hired to teach the President how to work a cane."

"So what's your idea?" Curtice asked.

"To have the President examined today, now, by a panel of the leading doctors, whom Secretary Bannerman and I have arranged to be in Washington and available."

The Attorney General shook his head in wonderment. "The President is totally blind," he said quietly. "Nobody is suggesting he is not. Do I understand you correctly, Mike? You propose to march in a parade of doctors to say, one after the other, 'Man, is he ever blind! He's *really* blind!' Is that supposed to panic us?"

"You don't understand, Mr. Attorney General," Bannerman said. "Some of the President's close advisers, who want to cling to power at any price, have been spreading the word that Ericson's eyesight is improving. That falsehood ought to be demolished, and your reluctance to subject your client to medical examination shows just how false it is."

"First of all, Mr. Secretary," Duparquet replied, "perhaps I'm old-fashioned, but somehow it strikes me as . . . good taste, as we sit here in the Cabinet Room of the White House, to refer to the President as the President, not as Ericson."

"I stand corrected," Bannerman conceded immediately.

"Second, I consider it a personal affront for you to talk of the President as my client. I am here as a member of the Cabinet, in my own right, not as advocate of another.

"Now then, you can bring every eye doctor in America to swear that the President is blind, and I will ask them each one question: 'Doctor, will you stake your professional reputation on the *im*possibility of this patient's eyes improving?' Then I'll ask: 'Doctor, four weeks after an accident, how certain can you be that a blinded person's eyes will not improve? Ten percent? Forty percent? Sixty percent?' And you want us to throw a President out of office on that kind of fuzzy possibility?"

"He has a point, Roy," said Defense Secretary Reed. "The possibility of improvement is a matter of guesswork. It's today we're thinking about. If he sees again tomorrow, then he can recover the presidency. We're not really in disagreement about eye doctors."

Fong said, "The President's physical health may be fairly good, other than the fact that he is blind. But it's his mental health, the trauma from the shock of the blindness, that makes him incapable. That's what I'm getting at, General."

"And how do you propose to determine his mental incapacity?"

"We have a panel of psychiatrists standing by."

Duparquet rose from his chair, leaned on his knuckles on the Cabinet table. "You would suffer the President of the United States to be examined by a panel of psychiatrists?"

"Gentlemen," said Bannerman, the soul of reason, "in 1919 Woodrow Wilson suffered a severe stroke. His actions were—in the light of present psychiatric knowledge—obviously paranoid. If the Wilson Cabinet had the power that we now have, Wilson would have been examined by competent psychiatrists and he would have been forced to resign."

The Attorney General had no decision to make—Ericson had made it clear to him that he would not set the precedent for psychiatric examination of Presidents who were not actually raving. Duparquet had to show that Ericson's adamant refusal was not unreasonable. Suddenly the Attorney General asked Fong, "Who's your top shrink?"

"Dr. Paul Whitney, president of the American Psychiatric Association, would be considered a logical choice."

"Bring him in," said the Attorney General.

Bannerman looked alarmed, Duparquet noted; their strategy was obviously to turn the psychiatrists away unconsulted, as evidence against an unstable President who would brook no examination. Bannerman had not thought through what an experienced criminal lawyer could do to any psychiatrist's credibility.

Dr. Whitney came in, was seated at the end of the table; the Vice-President swore him to secrecy. After some preliminary discussion of the case, Bannerman followed up: "Doctor, from your experience with patients who have suffered a shock like the loss of sight, what would you say the effect of the ambush at Yalta has been on the President's abilities?"

"I would never attempt to make an individual judgment from afar. Speaking generally, I would say that a traumatic shock like the sudden advent of blindness would have a measurable detrimental effect on the average person's ability to make decisions."

"Would you say, Doctor," Duparquet broke in smoothly, "if a person came through all that absolutely in command of his wits— would you say that would be abnormal?"

"If you take abnormal to mean not the average person's reaction, yes."

"In other words," the Attorney General summed up, "you'd have to be crazy not to be quite upset."

"I understand your point, and it's well taken, sir."

"To move on," Duparquet said, "can a person have manic-depressive or schizophrenic tendencies without being psychotic?"

"Of course. Such words may be used to describe the mental makeup of a patient who has a neurosis. A neurosis is any one of various functional disorders without any visible effect, such as undue anxiety."

"So a report on myself might say that I have this or that neurotic tendency, and incline to depression at times."

"I know what you're getting at, Mr. Attorney General," the psychiatrist said. "I want to point out that in a sensitive situation like this, doctors would avoid using any terminology that might be misunderstood by the general public."

The A.G. continued. "And when a reporter sticks a microphone into the face of a member of the panel and says, 'Is the President neurotic, or not?' the doctor will reply firmly, 'Absolutely not!'"

"Well, you couldn't expect him to say that—"

"On a different subject," Duparquet said, "what's your feeling about psychologists?"

"Qualified psychologists often make excellent therapists."

"Would you say that someone is qualified who has a doctorate in psychology from Harvard Medical School and is a member of the board of directors of the American Psychological Association?"

The psychiatrist nodded. "Dr. Henry Fowler is one of the most brilliant psychologists in the country."

The A.G. decided the moment had come to get the witness out of there. "I want to say how grateful we all are for your willingness to help, sir." He put the knife in gently. "When I was on the bench in Tallahassee, I very much admired the work you did on identity crises, Dr. Whitney. I know my colleague here is proud that it was financed by the Bannerman Foundation."

"It's good of you to remember," said the psychiatrist. "I've always wanted to thank you, Secretary Bannerman, for the assistance your family has been in this field."

"You're very welcome," Bannerman said dryly.

When the psychiatrist had left, Mike Fong said, "You can still muddy up a witness' testimony, General. But you know that the President is sick in the head, or he wouldn't be clinging to power."

"You happen to be wrong, Mike," the A.G. said. "Here is an affidavit from Dr. Fowler, dated this morning, containing his analysis of the mental condition of the President. It states without equivocation that the President is in control of his faculties, and that he is adjusting satisfactorily to one of the most devastating traumas a person can go through."

Frangipani turned to Fong. "Mike, see it my way. The President isn't nuts, and blindness itself is not a sure-thing cause of removal. What you got left? He knocks over a few glasses? He calls Uganda Nigeria or something else? I do that all the time. Let's stay loose. If the President doesn't get better, let's try to talk him into voluntarily stepping out. If worst comes to worst, a month or two from now we meet again. I think a lot of people in the country will agree with me."

"That's a cogent statement, Andy," said Reed. "But I submit that there is only one right thing for us, as a Cabinet, to do. Let me pose the problem from the Defense point of view."

Preston Reed got up, walked to the empty chair at the President's place, and leaned against the back of it. "The most important trust we hold is the survival of the United States. The Second World of the Far East is fomenting trouble between the Third and Fourth worlds, perhaps in the belief that a surrogate war can be fought, drawing in the First World and leaving the Far East with the upper hand.

"Who was behind the Yalta ambush? If the primary target was the Soviet leader and not the American President, then it is possible that the Soviet-American alliance is under great stress, and a war could be imminent." Curtice frowned. The Vice-President swallowed. Bannerman remained impassive and the A.G. emulated him. "At such a time," Reed continued, "our survival would be strongly aided by the appearance of stability and continuity."

"If we *look* paralyzed," Reed drove home, "it is as if we *are* paralyzed. That in itself encourages the more militant elements in the Far East and the U.S.S.R. to take charge. We are then open targets for a nuclear strike. We should send you, the Attorney General, as our messenger to say it is the sense of this Cabinet meeting that the President would serve his country best by resigning. General, don't force us to strike the President down."

They had three votes, thought Duparquet, to our sure two. "Preston," he replied from his chair, "you remember that line of Lincoln's before the Civil War, when he told the Southerners that they did not have an oath registered in heaven to destroy the Union, and that he had taken such an oath to preserve it? If your essential point, Preston, is that the nation not appear to be paralyzed, then why don't we come together and say that we have found the President to be able to carry on, unite behind him, and urge the country to follow our example? You have no oath to overthrow the President; he has an oath to do his duty as he sees it."

"This is leading nowhere," said Bannerman. "Mr. Attorney General, we are not contemplating treason. Secretary Fong, let's move the question."

Fong took up a paper and read, " 'I move that the principal officers of the executive departments, acting under the authority vested in them by the Twenty-fifth Amendment to the Constitution of the United States, declare the present occupant of the office of President of the United States to be unable to discharge the powers and duties of said office, and that the powers and duties of the

President devolve upon the Vice-President as Acting President.'"

"A sadder moment has never taken place in this room," said Andy Frangipani.

The Attorney General turned to Bannerman. "You're out for the brass ring, Bannerman, and God help this country if the likes of you ever seize power."

"I second the motion," was Bannerman's reply.

"The motion has been made and seconded," said Nichols, adding lamely, "Is there any debate?"

Secretary Curtice raised a finger. "Mr. Chairman, I would like to know whether abstentions are in order."

The Vice-President looked at Duparquet and said, "Can the Attorney General give us a ruling on that?"

Get a recess, Duparquet thought; let Cartwright do whatever he could with Curtice now to get him to vote with the President. "A point of information of that importance deserves consultation with the Solicitor General. I can get a solid answer in twenty minutes."

"A twenty-minute recess is granted," said Nichols. "May I suggest that you all remain in the general area of the Cabinet Room."

The Attorney General went to the telephone at the President's seat, asked for the Solicitor General—the man at Justice who handled most of the arguments before the Supreme Court. "Question has come up of abstention. Look in the Legislative History— testimony in the House." The Solicitor General started to tell him he knew the answer, but Duparquet said loudly, "Has to be in fifteen minutes, Charlie," and hung up.

He walked into the West Wing hallway, saw Cartwright, and followed him to his office. "Curtice wants to abstain," he reported. "I'll force him to vote, but he'll vote to remove the President, unless you have a way of turning him around."

"I will drop a ton of bricks on him," said Cartwright sadly.

"Preston Reed is killing us," said Duparquet. "Tell you the truth, he even scared hell out of me."

"Then hit Reed with this," suggested Cartwright. "If Ericson is thrown out, he will go to Congress to get the presidency back. Twenty-one days of debate. If he loses, he goes back every two weeks, declaring his ability. They have to debate and vote again. He could tie the country up in knots."

"Look," said Duparquet, "there's not much time. Clobber Curtice with anything you've got."

"The Legislative History," said Duparquet, after Nichols had reconvened the meeting, "is most specific that each of the executive departments is expected to cast a vote. If the head of that department is not willing or able to vote for any reason, the acting head of the department casts the vote of that department."

Fong said, "I think we might just have a clear majority." He looked to Curtice, who gave a slight nod. Duparquet's heart sank; Cartwright's pressure had not worked. The Secretary of State looked harried but determined.

"Before we vote," said the Defense Secretary, "since there is not much doubt which way the vote is going to go, can't we prevail on the Attorney General to persuade the President to invoke the Twenty-fifth voluntarily, and not insist on being pushed out?"

"President Ericson," the Attorney General replied, "is obligated to resist a wrongful seizure of presidential power."

"You are absolutely certain," said Reed, "that the President intends to push this to a constitutional crisis?"

"You, not he, precipitated this crisis." Duparquet grasped at the straw Cartwright had suggested: "And you have not stopped to consider the national security consequences of your act."

"What do you mean?" asked Reed.

"If the Cabinet should vote to oust the President," said the Attorney General, "President Ericson intends to take this to the Congress to decide the issue. I know the man. He will fight this wrongful seizure as long as there is breath in his body. And don't forget, he will still be President—only the powers and duties of the presidency would be stripped from him. He has told me that he will take that word 'office' literally, and continue to live in the White House and use the Oval Office in his campaign to recover his powers and duties. Then you tell the world, Preston, that the United States is in a stable position."

"You're saying Ericson would conduct a sit-in?" said Reed.

"People who become President," said the A.G., feeling he was getting some traction with Reed, "fight very, very hard. Now let's take the consequences of your action further. Let's say the Congress puts a two-thirds majority together to agree to it. You know what will happen?"

"Tell us," said Bannerman, unruffled.

"Read Paragraph Two of Section Four. It means that if an inability is declared, the President has the right to go back to Congress, again and again—there's no limit on the number of times—and demand they vote on the restoration of his powers."

Bannerman waved his hand impatiently. "He would lose by a greater majority each time. He'd be seen as a fool and a pest."

Frangipani broke in. "He might be seen by a lot of people as the conscience of the presidency, knocking at the door of the Congress every couple of weeks. Be a moving thing."

"No man who put his country before himself would ever do that," said Reed.

"If you don't believe me, ask him," said Duparquet.

"Let's vote," said Bannerman.

"Wait, Roy," Reed said. "What are you getting at, General?"

"Let's put the question of intent to the President himself."

Reed leaned across the President's chair and pushed a button. Melinda McPhee entered, notebook in hand.

"Miss McPhee," said the Attorney General, "take this message to the President. Sir: Would you please write out, in your own hand, any action you intend to take in the event that the Cabinet, the Vice-President, and the Congress declare your inability?" Melinda did not read it back. She turned and left the room.

In a few moments she opened the door and laid the piece of green-tinted stationery firmly in front of the Attorney General. Quite a woman, he permitted himself to think. He watched her shut the door before he picked up the paper.

"It's obviously the President's writing. Here's what he says. 'Mr. Attorney General: If I have to return to the Congress to assert my ability, I would do so, if necessary, again and again.'"

"That is an evil, corrupt thing the President has done," said

159

Reed. "The man is totally devoid of principle." Even as the Defense Secretary began his excoriation of Ericson, Duparquet felt his flicker of hope grow stronger.

At Bannerman's glance, Fong said, "I move the question."

Reed looked at him sharply. "Are you crazy? If the President does what he threatens to do, the nation is paralyzed. That means we're begging for a war. If you bring this to a vote, I'll have to vote against his removal. In terms of war and peace, better one blind Ericson as President than two Presidents."

"Let's vote," Bannerman repeated, glaring at Reed. "I want it on the record that some members of this pusillanimous Cabinet wanted to do their duty."

"The motion has been duly made and seconded," Nichols said wearily. "Roy, you really want to go through with this?" Bannerman, jaw tight, nodded. "Then you will vote in the order of precedence. On the removal of the President, how do you vote? State?"

Curtice looked at Bannerman, shrugged, said, "No."

"Defense?"

Reed said, "No."

"Treasury?"

"The Treasury Secretary votes yes," Bannerman said.

"Justice?"

Duparquet said, "No."

"Natural Resources?"

Fong said, "I see no purpose in my motion anymore. No."

"Human Resources?"

Frangipani boomed, "No!"

"Five to one, the nays have it," said Nichols. "I would like to say that I would have voted no. In my view, the President is able and courageous. The Cabinet and nation should unite behind him."

"Who gets to break the good news?" asked Frangipani.

The Attorney General said, "I think it would be most appropriate for the Vice-President to do that."

"While you're at it," said Preston Reed bitterly, "tell him he'll have my resignation on his desk in an hour."

As the others made their way out, Bannerman and Duparquet

remained behind, seated diagonally across the table. Bannerman looked at Duparquet for a long time. "You're an attractive personality, General, a vote getter. You come from the only southern state that Northerners trust. You're young enough, you could go all the way. But I know what's best for this country."

"I believe you think so. That's what makes you so dangerous." Duparquet got up and left Bannerman sitting there.

III: THAT DAMNED SPEECH

SHE had been in the President's bedroom once before, on a tour with a few White House senior aides, but this was the first time Melinda had been there at seven a.m., seated at the President's bedside, with Ericson propped up by his pillows, sipping his coffee, chortling as she read him the News Summary.

She felt awkward. "Mr. President, why don't you throw on a robe and join me in the dining room?"

"What's the matter, Melinda?"

"You shouldn't be doing business in here if you're not sick."

"You're embarrassed," the President said, amused.

She headed for the door. "I'll be organized on the table."

Ericson entered a moment later, using a cane. First time he had done that, she noted. He hung it on the back of his chair.

"This columnist has it right on the button," Melinda commented, and read, "'President Sven Ericson's political hide was saved by the powerful advocacy of Florida's Emmett Duparquet. As for Attorney General Duparquet, his star is clearly on the rise; the sun-belted savior of the President is now the second most powerful man in the staggering Ericson administration.'"

"Good, good," said Ericson. "Tell Smitty to build the A.G. up."

Melinda mused, "I hate to see anybody become a knight in shining armor. This is the *Ericson* administration."

"You're loyal to a fault, Melinda," the President said. "You smell good, though."

"Thank you for the perfume." She was embarrassed she had not mentioned it before.

"The reason I want to see Duparquet built up is because he's no threat—the way Nichols would be, if he were any good. And for now I want to show what a great team I have."

"Duparquet's ambitious." Melinda was attracted to him in spite of herself, and distrusted him for that.

"Could be the next President. Every Cabinet needs at least one potential President, like Hoover in the Harding Cabinet."

"What is it with you and Hoover?"

"Great President, much misunderstood," said Ericson. "Both he and Wilson wound up broken and hated, the way I will, but history will resuscitate us all."

The summary took them forty-five minutes to complete. The item that concerned him, Melinda knew, was this: "*Times* reports the intelligence community torn in disagreement on who was behind the Yalta ambush—a minority insists that Soviet strong man Nikolayev arranged the assassination himself to seize power."

Melinda left the President and went down to her own office. Then she went out to the Rose Garden with a scissors and cut three flowers for the coffee table in the Oval Office. When she came back, Hennessy was there.

"I hear you had breakfast in bed with the President," he observed. "The times, they are a-changing."

"I'd hate to have a mind like a divorce lawyer."

"Arrange for me to see the President around three. Tell him I heard from an old friend from the campaign. You will see the President's face fall. Tell nobody else, though."

Melinda arranged the roses in a bowl, then went into her office, called two secretaries who worked for her, and plunged into the stack of telegrams and letters that had arrived after the "fateful weekend." Mail was screened routinely across the street in the Executive Office Building computer, with computer-typed replies sent back immediately. Names on the President's "friends" list and VIPs were passed to Melinda for truly personal treatment.

"I understand that you are the only one able to arrange for a table at the Sans Souci." She looked up to see the deeply tanned face of the Attorney General.

"It's after noon now, General." She smiled. "You really ought to plan ahead. For how many?"

"Just the two of us," he said. "I hope you will forgive my brashness, and will accept my invitation."

The "Tallahassee Charmer," they called him. Melinda was more pleased than she would have liked to admit.

At the restaurant, they were seated along the balcony overlooking the pit action. Duparquet surveyed the crowd. "Look down there and you'll see the shimmering waves of power."

"Show me one shimmering wave of power."

"There"—he pointed—"are the director of the FBI and the chief counsel of the Senate Oversight Committee, politely trying to scare hell out of each other. And in the booth over there, the Under Secretary of State is trying to convince somebody that George Curtice really did support Ericson in that meeting."

Melinda wished she had worn a different outfit that day, but who knew she would be invited to lunch by the man she had been thinking about? Mainly because she wanted to stay on the firm ground of political intrigue, she asked him why his strategy was to let George Curtice get away with his role in the meeting.

Duparquet replied, "He'll have a dirty secret, and we'll know it. That'll keep him in line in the next few months."

"Who should get canned?"

"Bannerman and Fong. And Reed's already resigned."

"That's retaliation for their speaking their minds. Will it look good to have a bunch of rubber stamps?"

"Hell with 'em. President can't afford to show weakness, not now, when he's weak."

She leaned back in her chair. "I think I was just hit by a shimmering wave of power."

"I wish I had somebody like you." He did not say for what.

"You might, someday." She chose to take it professionally. "Ericson thinks you'd make a good President."

"He said that?" The Attorney General seemed a little too eager, but then recouped with a flash of honesty. "Melinda, I'm eating out of your hand—did your boss say that?"

She enjoyed giving him the good news. "He said every Cabinet should have a potential President, and you're it for this one."

The captain came with the menu. After they had ordered, the Attorney General asked, "Okay, who's in and who's out?"

"Now we get to the real purpose of the lunch."

"The real purpose of the lunch," he said right back, "is to lay the basis for making a pass at you. Since I hate to be rejected by somebody I respect, I have to stick to business."

"You're in," she said, backing off a bit by adding, "the Cabinet, that is. Cartwright's replacing Reed at Defense."

"Keep going—Bannerman?"

"Out. Cold turkey, tomorrow morning by phone from the President. Hennessy says there will be an investigation on the Hill about the connection between Treasury decisions and the Bannerman real estate empire. Hennessy's playing pretty rough."

Duparquet said sharply, "Man goes for your throat, you clobber him as hard as you can. But if I were President, and went blind, I'd resign."

Melinda did not hide her surprise. "Does the President know that's the way you feel?"

"No. The President's elected to make that decision, not you or me or the Cabinet. And Ericson is mentally competent to do so. I have no difficulty defending him."

"Fong stays in," Melinda continued, as she had been instructed to. Before going to lunch, she had excused herself to wash her hands, and had called the President to see what he wanted told to Duparquet. "He was the author of the motion to declare inability. Keeping him shows that the President is not retaliating."

"Who's in for Bannerman?"

"His deputy—I forget his name—the one we put in under him to represent the President's interests. Hates Bannerman."

"And what was it that Cartwright had on Curtice?"

She looked at him. "What do you want for one lousy lunch, all the inside secrets of the Republic?"

"I'd spring for dinner, for that."

Melinda kept her face in neutral. Cartwright had briefed the

President on Harry Bok's Curtice-instigated memory about Kolkov's heroism, and Ericson had delightedly confided it to Melinda. If Melinda now allowed herself to look knowing, then Duparquet would assume that the President also knew and that would hook what he had been fishing for—that the pressure on Curtice had come directly from the President.

Melinda could not decide whether the Attorney General's banter had a purpose; nor did she know what her response would be if he followed through. She toyed with that throughout lunch. On the way out she turned down his invitation to a ride. "What is it you want me to put in the President's ear, General?"

"Tell him the old Tallahassee Charmer pulled out every stop and couldn't get to first base with you." Duparquet smiled.

She shook hands and walked toward the West Basement entrance of the White House, thinking about her boss and his best new political friend. Ericson, forty-eight, seeming older; Duparquet, fifty-four, seeming more boyish, at once more openly rural and more smoothly urbane. Ericson, introverted, man of thought, deliciously complex, with the ability to convey a genuine warmth when he wanted to; Duparquet, extroverted, man of action, a gambler, a winsome smile, with the ability to project an edge of cruelty in his voice. Both loved the play of power, telling themselves so often that they were idealists underneath the cynicism that they actually became fairly idealistic. She knew one too well, the other not well enough.

Would Duparquet, if blinded as President, really quit? Of course not; the Attorney General was saying that—as Ericson would say it if their roles were reversed—to titillate and intrigue a woman who might be useful one day.

IN A double room on the park side of the Hay-Adams Hotel, facing the White House, Arthur Leigh waited. He knew the difference between hanging around with high hopes and waiting with specific goals.

After the Ericson victory the preceding November, he had not hung around. Ericson had expended Leigh in the campaign, using him to bear the brunt of most angriness. His tacit understanding with Leigh was that a win would merit a bonus, to be determined later. Ericson had shucked Leigh like an old snakeskin.

Seated at the window of the Hay-Adams room, Arthur Leigh read the *Star* and leafed through the *Post.* He had made his presence known to Hennessy, and had stayed put. His paunch hanging over his belt, worn slippers dangling from feet extended across an ottoman, Leigh read about the appointment of Lucas Cartwright as Secretary of Defense, and of the appointment of Hennessy to replace Cartwright as chief of the White House staff. Leigh knew the reason for running a tight, secretive White House staff under Hennessy: the possibility of leakage of the President's previous blindness. Now the year-old episode on the campaign train assumed sinister implications, as evidence that the people had voted for a President while not fully informed of his potential disability. That gave the old manager more leverage.

"The smoking gun," he said aloud.

His wife, accustomed to non sequiturs from her aging husband, looked up. "How long are we staying in Washington, Arthur?"

"Day or so. Maybe another week." The phone rang. "I'll take it," Leigh said. He picked it up and growled, "Yeah?"

"This Leigh?"

"I can see you now, Hennessy, but I haven't got all day."

"Arthur, you haven't another appointment scheduled all week."

"You may be right, but the next one's a beaut."

Hennessy paused. "I can pour you some of Cartwright's leftover bourbon over here in this snazzy office," he said.

Now Leigh, ambling across the park to the White House on a warm afternoon, thinning gray hair disheveled, thought about what he wanted to come away with. This was his last chance at substantial money. If he could get his man appointed highway commissioner in Tennessee, he could expect a sensible decision on an access road to property he held an option on, and then a sale to a developer. The man making the appointment, the patronage man for the Tennessee governor, wanted the word from the White House, so that Ericson would then owe the governor a favor.

Leigh hoped that Hennessy would not mention the episode on the campaign train—that would be amateurish—and he hoped the new staff chief would not take him in to see the President, which would be an embarrassment for Leigh and a mistake for Ericson. One did not see the President on a matter as minor as this.

Leigh gruffed his name to the receptionist inside the West Wing. While he waited, Buffie, in jeans, with a camera in her hand, came in, looked at him levelly, and said, "I heard you were here. You know, Mr. Leigh"—she stepped closer to him, conspiratorially —"we don't talk about that campaign train incident."

"I haven't shot my mouth off," he said, enjoying this. "You?"

"Never told a soul," she said, raising her right hand.

"Who sent you to me just now?"

"Hennessy, of course. I was supposed to soften you up."

Leigh decided she was calculated in her spontaneity.

"After I get your heart all melted," Buffie said, "I'm supposed to take you to Hennessy."

Leigh grinned and followed her down the hall, past the Oval Office, to the corner suite of the chief of staff.

Leigh and Hennessy participated in a forty-minute minuet— campaign recollections, Hennessy's apology for not being able to bring him in to see the President, who was resting.

Then Leigh rose to take his leave. "You may get a call from Tennessee," the politician mentioned on the way out, "checking on a guy named Kerr for highway commissioner. Good guy."

Hennessy nodded noncommittally, as he was supposed to, and walked his visitor to the small elevator.

When Leigh opened the door of the Hay-Adams room, his wife had a message: "Susan Bannerman called. Says why don't we have dinner tonight, just the four of us."

That was fast; Bannerman had somebody in the White House and had not given up the fight. Leigh had to assume first that Bannerman did not know of the President's previous blindness. He guessed further that Bannerman thought Leigh had something on the President. Probably Hennessy had been worried that Leigh was a potential leak. He would know soon enough, through the

Secret Service, that the Bannermans and the Leighs were dining together. No blackmail; just positioning.

"Let's take them up on it," he said to his wife.

THE three black Zil limousines squeezed through the narrow gate in the Kremlin wall and thundered out across Red Square. Vasily Nikolayev, Acting Premier of the Soviet Union, sank low in the back seat of the middle car. He had just been confronted with evidence by the Politburo that Kolkov had not been the hero he was being made out to be. The story of Kolkov saving the American President's life was said to be a Nikolayev fabrication, designed to help him inherit Kolkov's mantle.

"I'm surprised at you, Vasily." The man seated next to him, Slovenski, had been chosen to make the trip to Yalta with Nikolayev because he was accepted as neutral by all factions. "You knew the hospital room had microphones."

Of course Nikolayev knew the Secret Service agent's room was wired. But he had been told that nothing out of the ordinary had been overheard when Bok was visited by Secretary Curtice and the President's man, Cartwright. Still, portions of the tape could not be heard. The Politburo could only entertain suspicions.

A Tupolev supersonic aircraft put the two men in Yalta in under two hours. At the hospital, the KGB had preparations in hand: the American nurse and medical corpsman had both been drugged. Nikolayev and Slovenski, with a recording engineer, were taken to Bok's room, where he was asleep. The sodium pentothal was administered, and Slovenski asked the questions.

"How did General Secretary Kolkov's body get on top of the President's?"

"I dragged him over and put him there."

"And when did you first think up the idea that General Secretary Kolkov saved President Ericson's life?"

"Here in this room. That was what Curtice and Cartwright wanted to hear."

Nikolayev tuned out. Perhaps the situation could still be salvaged; the tape of his conversation with Curtice left room for differing interpretations. Perhaps the Politburo could be convinced of the great advantage in the secret knowledge that the Americans had falsely maintained, that Kolkov saved their President's life. It could be reserved, to play at some critical point.

Nikolayev had a thought. "Ask this final question: Does President Ericson know the truth about Kolkov?"

When put to Bok the question brought an uncertain reply: "I guess Curtice or Cartwright would have told him by now."

"Will you tell the President the truth when you see him?"

"Sure I will. I got no secrets from the President."

Good, Nikolayev thought. It was important that Ericson know that his administration was involved in the fraud.

Next afternoon, in Moscow, Nikolayev looked over a query from an angry U.S. ambassador about suspicious activity at the Yalta hospital the night before. The nurse and medic both insisted they had been drugged. Bok did not remember anything. Nikolayev directed the Foreign Ministry to put a plane at the Americans' disposal in Yalta immediately; he would not permit any such suspicion to poison the diplomatic atmosphere.

"We were planning to give Bok a medal," Nikolayev replied to the ambassador, "but we will put it in the mail."

Bok's back! Harry smiled at the sign carried by a delegation of children of Secret Service men as his wheelchair was moved into the VIP lounge at Andrews Air Force Base for interviews.

"Would you tell us in your own words, Mr. Bok, just what took place during the assault on the President?"

"Everything was happening at once," Harry told the newsmen. "It seemed to me that General Secretary Kolkov was crawling toward the President to protect him. The details are still a blur."

Two days later, Harry got the call to come to the Oval Office.

The President, in dark glasses, seemed strong and cheerful. "I'm alive and kicking, Harry, thanks to you. And thanks to Kolkov, I suppose. Level with me, Harry."

"I threw Kolkov's body on top of you. The idea about his saving your life started with Curtice and Cartwright."

"No chance of it being true, then?"

"Sure there's a chance," Harry backpedaled. "He had his arm out toward you. I won't swear either way."

"Good," the President said. "I noticed the way you handled your airport interview. Fuzzy. Harry, never lie. Remember that. . . . You'll want to talk to Hank Fowler, my blind psychologist, about life in a wheelchair," the President continued. "You'll find it depressing as hell at first, then you snap out of it."

"You've snapped out?"

"Nearly. The hopeless feeling is there, but I can cope. Your new job in counterfeiting can wait. I want you around here. There are only three people I trust—Hennessy and Melinda and you. I can't afford to lose you now." Ericson shifted suddenly. "You think the Russians got you to talk when you didn't know it?"

"Could be."

"You guys want to call a halt?" said Hennessy, rapping on the door. "Mr. President, have you listened to your speedy whiz-bang News Summary?"

"Yes. Read Harry the part about the Bannerman committee," the President directed his new chief of staff.

" 'Two networks led with the announcement of the Committee to Replace the Disabled President,' " Hennessy read, " 'with former Treasury Secretary T. Roy Bannerman as chairman, and a distinguished board of industrialists, bankers, and doctors. Bannerman said it would be nonpartisan and would launch a nationwide membership drive.' "

The President got up. "Let's get some sun." He and Hennessy went out and sat on the colonnade steps. Bok moved his wheelchair to the top of the steps. Melinda joined the three men.

"This is the family," Ericson said. "A divorce lawyer, a spinster, a cripple, and a blind man, and we're running a large part of the world." Ericson's voice was low, "Let me explain first about trusting each other. Trust is always a risk. In this situation, the greater risk is for us to develop gaps in information. Cartwright found out about Buffie making contact with Bannerman; he couldn't put it together with something he didn't know, the incident on the train.

So he waited a couple of days, and the whole presidency could have gone up the flue.

"We four have to share all our information. Hennessy, Melinda knows about me going blind on the campaign train. Melinda, Hennessy knows you are seeing a lot of the Attorney General. Now about trusting other people: don't. Hennessy, find out who Cartwright's contact was that tipped us off about Buffie and Bannerman, but don't tell Lucas about the previous blindness. Melinda, enjoy yourself. I hope you become Duparquet's First Lady someday, but only tell him what I want him to know."

Harry watched Melinda fight against reacting, which made her redden. The President continued. "Harry, have the agents unofficially keep a close watch on the Vice-President and Bannerman. Besides us, the only people who know about the campaign train blindness are Buffie, Leigh, and Herb Abelson. I'll take care of Buffie. You, Hennessy, take care of Leigh. Don't nod, speak up."

"I got it," said Harry.

"I got it, too," said Hennessy. "And I'd just like to say that the Attorney General of the United States is a very lucky man."

"What are we going to do now," Melinda asked, "sit around and tell dirty stories?"

Harry decided Melinda was probably not sore about him or Hennessy knowing about the A.G.—but about the President knowing, and not seeming to care.

After the meeting broke up, the President spoke to Melinda. "I want you to tell the A.G. the truth about Kolkov and the ambush, because he can't sit as my top man on the National Security Council with Cartwright and Curtice without knowing that. But he has no need to know about the previous blindness."

IN THE study of his Georgetown home, Samuel Zophar stared at the blank wall in front of him. Downstairs in the dining room, where he bedazzled the preening transients in power, he decked the walls with signed pictures of the great. Here, at his typewriter, no distractions.

His daughter knocked and looked in. "Man on the phone named Gregor," she said. "Very mysterious, possibly a crackpot."

"He's a Russian," Zophar told his daughter as he picked up the receiver. He listened to a request for a rendezvous and suggested the bar of the Hay-Adams Hotel. Public places were best.

Zophar was early for his appointment. A rumpled man with a sloppily spilling paunch said hello in the lobby. "Leigh," the columnist said cheerily, and invited the politician for a drink. He idly tried a few probes on Leigh, admired the man's noncommittal parries, and finally spotted Gregor, his Soviet contact, across the room. He took leave of Leigh and joined Gregor.

"I have a very big lead," the compact Soviet agent said. "The ambush at Yalta was set up by Vasily Nikolayev and President Ericson. The only target was Kolkov. The American Secret Service agent, Harry Bok, threw Kolkov's dead body over Ericson, as had been arranged, to come up with the story that Kolkov had died a hero, trying to protect Ericson. Ericson was not supposed to be injured."

"The purpose of all this?" Zophar looked contemptuous.

"Kolkov was thinking of a preemptive strike at the Far Eastern powers. Nikolayev wanted to stop him and take his place. But Nikolayev's strength in the Politburo came from Kolkov's men, so Kolkov had to be a dead hero."

"How come Nikolayev is Acting Premier?"

Gregor shook his head vigorously. "Nikolayev is no longer in power. He is in the process of being replaced. The story of the terrible thing the Americans did should come from the Americans. That is why I was told to pass this along to you."

Zophar shrugged. "Have you any hard evidence?"

The Russian shook his head again. "I have control of this tip for three days, then they will use somebody else. I will do some checking to see what can be given to you. How long do you need to get an answer from Ericson?"

"I will not say what I will do or not do. Where is Nikolayev at this moment? Under house arrest?"

"I don't know."

"Give me one detail that is checkable—if your story is true, the White House will know I have it."

Gregor hesitated. Finally he said, "Bok may have talked without knowing it." He gulped the rest of his drink. "Let's meet here tomorrow for breakfast. Nine o'clock. If you cannot show me how you have developed the story, I will be uncommunicative."

From a telephone booth Zophar called the Defense Department and asked for Lucas Cartwright. The former chief of staff, now Secretary of Defense, was in Alaska. With Cartwright absent, James Smith, the press secretary, might be the man.

The press secretary was not there. Trust Smitty to go on that same idiotic trip to Alaska, Zophar fumed, leaving the presidential press office in the hands of some ornament from Vassar. He left word that he would call immediately on Marilee Pinckney.

When he arrived at the White House, Zophar went to the office of the press secretary, occupied by a tall young lady in a prim sweater and skirt. "I have come into possession of some information," he said, "which—if true—could be a source of embarrassment to the President and the nation. I want to verify the facts before rushing into print. Since it is a matter of direct concern to the President, I would prefer to discuss it with him alone."

Marilee Pinckney hesitated. "Can't you just give me a hint?"

"It is a matter that a certain Secret Service agent talked about without realizing it."

"Got it," she said. "I'll be back to you tomorrow."

"Tonight would be better," he pressed.

"No BIG deal," Hennessy assured Marilee Pinckney. "I think I know what Zophar's driving at."

"I was ready to panic and go running to the President. Where is The Man, anyway?"

"In the Lincoln Sitting Room. Jonathan Trumbull is with him; they've been fiddling with a foreign affairs speech."

"I should get back to Zophar tonight," Marilee said.

"When Smitty calls in from the North Slope," Hennessy told her, "don't go into this. Tell Zophar around ten tonight that you reached me, and I said I'd get together with the Secret Service man first thing in the morning." He smiled, feeling sick.

When the door closed behind her, he picked up a phone and said, "Tell Bok I need to see him." Who had leaked to Zophar? Six or seven people knew of the possibility of Harry Bok having talked to the Soviets under truth serum. Anybody who knew of the President's previous blindness would be able to put two and two together from the way Harry had been snatched back. One possibility: that the Russians were leaking what they had learned about the previous blindness from Harry Bok. Another possibility: that Buffie, or Herb Abelson—who was still shaken up— or Leigh, had dropped a hint that reached Zophar.

Melinda and Bok arrived almost simultaneously. "Marilee briefed me," Melinda said. "Just some minor matter about a columnist knowing that Harry blabbed something to the Russians."

"Damn," said Bok, slumping in his wheelchair.

"First we have to find the leak." Hennessy was being suitably calm. "Harry, what's with Buffie?"

"Last night she was with Jonathan Trumbull. No calls to Bannerman lately."

"Abelson?" He didn't like the mopey way the President's physician was acting.

Bok shook his head. "Herb's in Camp Hoover, fishing. He's had no phone calls and no visitors."

"Leigh?" Hennessy was not worried about Leigh. Two days ago a call had come in from Tennessee about a man recommended for highway commissioner, and Hennessy had personally given the order to the governor's office to hire him. The IOU was paid; keeping the secret was Leigh's bread and butter.

"Leigh's been at the Bannerman home within the last couple of days," Bok said. "This afternoon Leigh was in the lobby of the Hay-Adams with columnist Samuel Zophar. Then Leigh went to the home of Vice-President Nichols."

Hennessy closed his eyes. "That bastard Leigh!"

"Don't jump to conclusions," Bok cautioned. "There's a dinner at the Bannermans' tonight. We'll get a report on it."

Melinda said, "Ever since that one-big-happy-family routine the other day, I knew it had to come. You got a scenario, Hennessy?"

"Yup. Preemptive strike. Let's assume our assumption about Leigh and Zophar checks out, and that the VP and Leigh are plotting the succession. We work up a ring-a-ding speech confessing the previous blindness, and go on the air in forty-eight hours. We'll string Zophar along, promise him an exclusive with the President, and let him holler afterward. He'll be sore—let's face it, it's unethical—but it's more important that the President put his case about the previous blindness to the people than that some blowhard commentator get credit for Leigh's leak."

"I like it," Bok said.

Hennessy said he'd talk to them later, and went down to the Mess to eat. After dinner, back in his office, he had a call from Bok.

"Bannerman and Leigh talked about a Nichols administration, with Arthur Leigh as the patronage dispenser. They were always careful to say it would be after the Ericson administration." It appeared Hennessy's hunch was accurate: Leigh was in their camp. Zophar's name had come up as part of the general conversation.

Hennessy called the President. "I need to see you, and I'd like the writer to stick around. I'll see him afterward."

"What's up?"

Hennessy hedged. "I'll be right over."

Jonathan was sitting in an easy chair in the hall when Hennessy reached the Lincoln Sitting Room. "Let me give it to you straight," Hennessy said to Ericson. "Leigh was seen with Zophar this afternoon. Half an hour later, Zophar asked Marilee for an interview with you."

"Um. I thought you said you were taking care of Leigh."

"Evidently he got a better offer."

"Can't be sure," Ericson cautioned. "What did Zophar say?"

"Called it a big story that had to do with something Harry Bok said without knowing it. A bunch of people know how fast we pulled Harry back home. It wouldn't take a lot of imagination for Leigh to figure out that Harry told the Russians about your accident on the campaign train. If you make a speech telling how the pre-

175

vious blindness happened, you'll be ahead of the news curve. If you don't, we'll be apologizing."

"This is the wrong time to rock the boat," the President said. "It could be something else—but no, not if it came from Arthur Leigh."

"Why don't we get our ducks in a row in case we decide to go the speech route?" Hennessy pressed. "Get Jonathan to do a draft, and Hank Fowler can begin to feed it to you in the morning."

"No. That would open it up to two more people, neither one with any particular loyalty to me."

"The kid out there is loyal, Mr. President. Jonathan is the one who told Cartwright about Buffie and Bannerman."

"How does the kid know?"

"He's dating Buffie."

The blood went out of Ericson's face. "Hennessy, that girl has a hold on me. God, you pay for everything."

"You developed an attachment for a woman half your age, Sven," the old friend and former divorce attorney said. "Happens to a lot of guys. But there comes a time when it ends."

Ericson stood up. "Bring Jonathan in. I don't want him to know I know. We'll brief him about the previous blindness. Maybe we can make a case. I just wish, though, that we could be sure we're not overreacting to what we think Zophar has."

WHAT a night! Jonathan marveled, in the White House car that was taking him back to his apartment. First the hours with the President, the intimacy of discussing his dreams; then the block-buster, after Hennessy had come up, about the previous blindness. He shook his head in wonderment at what the President must have been going through the past few weeks. Now it was up to Jonathan to lay out that story in a way to minimize the error in judgment, and accentuate the President's desire to take the American peo-ple into his confidence because he refused to live a lie.

Jonathan put the key in the door of his apartment and noticed it was not double-locked. The lights were on. Buffie was asleep in a chair in front of the television. Jonathan's heart sank. He shook her shoulder until she woke up.

"I was lonely." She stretched. "Mad at me?"

"No." She was adorable in half sleep. "It's just that I have this speech to finish."

"What's it about?"

"Foreign affairs," he half-truthed. "They need it right away. You go in the bedroom and go to sleep. Buzz off."

"Okay." She yawned and got up. She inclined her head respectfully at the bedroom door. "Oh, you're so masterful. You Tarzan, me Jane. You Samson, me Delilah."

Jonathan gave her a sudden, blank look. "Samson. Lost his sight, but it didn't stop him. Kind of reference I need." He went to the telephone and called his researcher.

Now Jonathan had the most important speech of his life to do. He wrote the opening and the peroration, and was hammering out some loose lines for later insert when he heard the telephone ring. The telephone was in the bedroom. He opened the door and was stunned to see Buffie holding the receiver, saying, "Yes, he's here." Buffie smiled and handed it to him. "It's the President."

Jonathan closed his eyes in horror. "Hullo?"

"The President is calling. Would you stand by?"

The President came on the line. "Look, I just spoke with Herb Abelson, who's all upset, so would you put in your draft that I kept this quiet against his better judgment? I want you to know I have every confidence in you. Go to it." He cut off.

Jonathan turned around. "Well, the President didn't send you his best, thank God."

"I hate him so sometimes," she said moodily, wide awake, "because he's so important to me."

"You love him?"

"Of course I love him."

"Then why are you spying on him for Bannerman?"

"There's no future for us. When Ericson talks to me, he's only trying to find out what young people think, or women think. He's a complete user."

"Get some sleep," Jonathan said, but Buffie was not ready.

"Is he gonna spill the big secret?"

"What big secret?"

"He's telling about the time on the train, and you've got to put it together so it will come out innocent."

"You know," he said. "Have you told Bannerman?"

"Course not. What kind of person do you think I am?"

"If Bannerman finds out you knew about it and never told him, you'll be on his blacklist for the rest of your life. These are powerful people. Why do you have to play both ends against the middle?"

She nibbled a fingernail. "I figure if I'm a little loyal to everybody, everybody'll be a little loyal to me."

Strange girl, Jonathan thought, as he went back into the living room to finish the speech. What he could see of the Potomac River was turning from black to gray when the telephone rang again. He moved quickly this time to keep Buffie from grabbing it.

"Mr. Hennessy for you, Mr. Trumbull," the operator said.

Hennessy came on. "Look, we got a problem. Herb Abelson took too many pills and he's dead."

"Suicide? The President's doctor?"

"Maybe, maybe an accident. I'm going to Camp Hoover. If there wasn't any note, there wasn't any suicide. Don't put him in the speech at all, one thing's got nothing to do with the other. I'm calling because we're going to have to go with the speech sooner than the President thinks. Get it to Melinda at eight. Say nothing about Abelson until I get back." He hung up.

"I THOUGHT I told you to have a heart-to-heart with Herb Abelson, Hank," the President said, voice cold.

"You did, sir, and I never got around to it." The consequences of his failure oppressed and frightened the psychologist. "I failed you and I failed Abelson."

A silence, a sigh, then: "What do you think of the speech?" the President asked. Jonathan had read it to them moments before.

"First, about the speech itself. I think it separates naturally into five segments of three minutes each," Fowler said. "You could handle it that way." The therapist was proud of his method of separating a speech, summarizing each segment on a tape that could be received in a small earpiece. It enabled a blind man to appear to speak extemporaneously—from aural notes.

Then Fowler broached the content of the speech. "On your previous blindness, I think you were wrong. I'm not making a moral judgment about whether you should have made public the two-day blindness on the train before the election. I'm thinking medically, as Abelson must have been thinking. You were wrong not to tell your doctors about it after the assassination attempt at Yalta. Concealing relevant medical evidence, perhaps causing the wrong treatment—I can see why it got to Abelson. The time on the train you may have cracked the optic channel—the housing for the optic nerve that goes between the eye and the brain."

"Herb said the X rays didn't show any permanent damage."

"And," Fowler acknowledged, "it could be there wasn't any. But knowing of a previous blindness, an ophthalmologist might have called for a neurosurgeon. A neurosurgeon might have decided to go in and lift the top of the optic canal, to relieve the pressure on the nerve."

"So if I had not decided to keep this quiet," the President said, "I might not be blind today."

"I only raise the possibility now so you'll understand what Abelson was going through."

"Christ," said the President. "He was telling himself that because he listened to me and didn't tell the eye doctor, he'd caused my blindness."

"No doctor would go so far as to say that an alternative treatment would have prevented your blindness."

"Bannerman owns a few doctors who will. Just this morning I said, 'It could be worse,' and sure enough it is."

Fowler looked for a way out. "A lot depends on how your ophthalmologist reacts."

"Uh-huh. Hank, after the speech, I'd appreciate it if you had a talk with the commandant at Bethesda Naval Hospital. Suggest that an operation might have been dangerous in my condition."

"I'll talk to him, Mr. President."

Melinda appeared. "Marilee is here."

"I told Zophar he could see Hennessy around five," Marilee said. "Hennessy can stall him with a promise to get him to see you tomorrow. Speak of the devil, here's our chief of staff now."

"Been a long night." Hennessy stood in the doorway. "I'll come see you in a few minutes about Zophar, good-lookin'."

"There was no note," Hennessy reported to the President. "Either Herb didn't commit suicide, which is the position I'll take, or he mailed a note to his wife maybe, from the post-office box a mile and a half down the road."

"Where, uh . . ."

"In a funeral home near Adas Israel synagogue. Melinda can break the news to his wife."

"Poor Herb," the President said, in a voice Fowler could hardly hear. "We went to school together. Hank, tell Hennessy what you think Herb was depressed about." The psychologist briefed the staff chief on what might have troubled Herb Abelson.

Hennessy moaned, but not about Abelson. "That little eye doctor at Bethesda might wander off the reservation about this."

"Hank will talk to the commandant about that," Ericson said.

When Hennessy had gone, Fowler asked, "How do you feel?"

"Like I'm making a mistake," Ericson replied evenly. "I am doing the right thing, morally, in telling the truth about the previous blindness. But I'm being rushed into it. I don't like jeopardizing everything unless I absolutely have to. But it's important that I hold on to this job."

"For you? For the people?"

"For both." The chair squeaked back and Fowler heard the thump of the President's feet on his desk. "Nichols would be a puppet on a string for Bannerman—and, Hank, Bannerman is not a man of good character. The one nagging item on my conscience goes back to when I bought my nomination by agreeing to Bannerman's choice for a running mate. I cannot let this country suffer for that mistake. So I'll connive, I'll cut a few corners, the way every man who ever worked in this office has had to do. But I'll keep this place out of Bannerman's hands. And I'll be a better President than I would have been with eyes. I'm not as objective as I used to be, and that's good. I'm going to stay, and I'm going to do a hell of a job. You hear that, Hank?" He got out of his chair and walked toward the door leading to his secretary's office.

"Melinda, where is that speech?" Fowler could hear the crack of a head against a door that should not have been closed. The psychologist crossed the room just as the President hit the floor.

"Just a scratch," Hennessy insisted. "The new doctor put some tape on his forehead, and with the TV makeup you'll never see it."

It occurred to Smitty that Hennessy was minimizing everything. The press secretary had arrived at the White House to be hit with the impending Zophar revelation, the previous blindness, and the Abelson suicide, announced publicly as a probable accident. Finally, there had been the news of a speech, to beat the Leigh-to-Zophar leak, which the President might make later that evening.

"According to you, everything is a piece of cake."

"Too much for you, Smitty?"

"Zophar should be in the west lobby now," Smitty said, looking at five p.m. on his watch. "Marilee, bring him in."

"Gentlemen!" Zophar pompously entered the office of the press secretary, waved rather than shook hands. "I would like to see the President on a matter of the utmost gravity."

"That's not impossible," the press secretary said. "We'd be grateful, though, for the chance to check the story. In case your tip turns out to be wrong, it avoids embarrassment."

"I do not deal in tips. My information is solid."

"Sam," Smitty said, "why don't you just tell us as much of the story as you're going to? Then we'll take it from there."

"The Soviets have squeezed some information out of Harry Bok," said Zophar. "Information which, if known at the time of the disability session of the Cabinet, would have resulted in the declaration that the President was disabled."

"Smitty and I will be right back," said Hennessy.

"I hate to bust a man's exclusive," Smitty told Ericson in the Oval Office, "but I think he's got the story. You'd be better off telling the American people your way."

"Hennessy with you?"

"I'm right here. I think you'd be crazy to wait."

"If I had a choice," the President said after some thought, "I wouldn't make the speech now. We're panicking, on the basis of too little information." Pause. "You know why I'm doing it? The reason I was afraid of all along—because the speech is done, I've got it in my head, and I won't easily be able to get up for it again." Another pause. "There's nothing pulling me back from the brink of this, and the momentum is carrying me over. That's not the way I like to make a decision. But set it up, I'll perform. Hank and I will work on it here."

Smitty hurried out to tell Zophar that his story was beaten. Sorry about the exclusive, but the President had previously decided to go on the air.

THE four television sets in the press secretary's office that night carried the same image: the floodlit White House. The voice-overs babbled different versions of the same wonderment.

"This will be the first prepared speech made by President Ericson since the ambush at Yalta six weeks ago. . . ."

"Some say the President has been deeply affected by the death of his personal physician, Dr. Herbert Abelson. There is speculation, too, that this may be the moment President Ericson has decided to step down, under the provisions of the Twenty-fifth Amendment."

". . . and gentlemen, the President of the United States."

The four channels melded into one sound, the voice of Sven Ericson saying, "Good evening, my fellow citizens," in the familiar setting of the Oval Office. "This is the first chance I have had to talk things over with you since the assassination of General Kolkov six weeks ago. Since that tragic day, I have been recuperating from the attack, adjusting to the blindness that it has brought about. And I have been fighting to protect the presidency from an unprecedented seizure of its powers.

"Now, at last, I can come before you to discuss a personal matter, and to reveal a new initiative affecting the future.

"Let me explain how I'm making this speech. This little device in my ear is attached to the tape recorder here on the desk. From time to time, I'll press a button that will play me a recording of my own voice, outlining what I want to say. I'm doing this so that I don't leave anything out that I want to say or you need to hear. So when you see me pause, it's to listen to my notes."

In the press secretary's office, Smitty said, "That's good, he's involving everybody in the business of making the speech."

His deputy shook her head. "Appeals for pity. Not like Ericson."

"First, and briefly, the bad news. Many of you have sent me letters, and recordings of prayers, for which I will always be grateful. But my doctors say that there is no evidence to give me hope that I will regain my sight. Like a million and a half other Americans, I am blind.

"It will be a test of my own character to learn to live with blindness, and a test of the national character for the American people to learn to live with a blind President.

"There was a moment when I may have flunked that test, however, and I want to tell you about it. During the election campaign last year, I made a whistle-stop tour of Ohio on an old-fashioned railroad train. When the train jolted to a stop near Lima, I was thrown against a doorframe and suffered a mild concussion.

"It was announced that I was ill, which was partly true. The whole truth was that for about a day after I banged my head, I could not see. It did not occur to me that I had been temporarily blinded. I thought it was part of the process of being knocked out and seeing stars. Sure enough, in a day or so my eyes were fine.

"In retrospect, I suppose my managers should have put out the fact that I had lost my eyesight for a matter of hours. I've learned my lesson. It's important to face the fact of blindness, to tell the truth about it, and then to triumph over it. And that's why I'm saying to all of you tonight, who may be supporting me in the hope that my eyesight will return—set that hope aside."

The camera showed the President's hand pressing the recorder for his notes. "After the ambush at Yalta, my staff told the Soviets nothing about my loss of sight. Their primary goal was to get the presidential party out of the danger zone and back on American soil as quickly as possible.

"When I had regained consciousness, I realized that I could not see. I may have been wrong not to take my doctors into my confidence regarding last year's concussion. But the previous blindness did not seem that pertinent. My staff and I were concerned with making certain that the nation and the world knew that the President of the United States was well enough to make decisions and, if necessary, to repel any attack.

"In those crucial moments, the nation and I were fortunate to have two great public servants assisting me: George Curtice, the Secretary of State, and Lucas Cartwright, who is now our Secretary of Defense. After consultation with them, I have this afternoon directed that an invitation be extended through normal diplomatic channels to the new Premier of the Soviet Union, Vasily Nikolayev. The government of the United States is prepared to resume negotiations where they were tragically broken off at Yalta. It is our suggestion that these vital talks take place in Washington in the near future, possibly around Labor Day. Let me add this, my fellow Americans: the Ericson administration is ready, willing, *and able* to conduct those negotiations."

Smitty worried. "He's crap shooting. The Russkies haven't responded to the feeler yet—he only made it this afternoon."

Marilee shrugged it off. "No big deal. Nikolayev will come. The President wouldn't take a chance like that."

"Let me come now to a personal word. I had to ask myself a profound question not long ago. Which would be better for the American people—my stepping aside or my going on?

"While I was thinking about this, there was a move to usurp my constitutional authority, making unprecedented use of an untried amendment. I could not allow myself to be pushed out of office—thereby weakening the presidency for all time.

"But now that the crisis is past, I have had to consider it again. Some lines from John Milton, in the epic poem *Samson Agonistes,* were recounted to me. The blinded Samson, in the agony of his imprisonment, cried out for some way to still serve his people:

> *"Now blind, disheartn'd, sham'd, dishonour'd, quell'd,*
> *To what can I be useful, wherein serve*
> *My Nation . . .*

"God answered Samson's cry and gave him back the strength to confront his enemies.

"I'm no Samson bent on destruction. And I don't have the genius of a Milton. But I do know that the American people elect a human being as President. Not a computer, with an infallible memory; not an eagle, with an eagle's eyes. You elect a man, with his faults and weaknesses. The ambush at Yalta cost me my sight, but it may have given me a vision I might never have been graced with otherwise. Now, with God's help, with your help, I will do the job you elected me to do.

"Thank you and good night."

SAMUEL Zophar snapped off the television set. Ericson was turning into a President, he had to grant that. Not every man who was elected President became a President, but Sven Ericson had the requisite character and guile, lion and fox, to qualify. The speech seemed to the columnist to have been crafted with extraordinary care, delivered with halting skill—an example of the powerful use of mass communication in political leadership. But there was something to the Ericson speech that did not meet the ear. What could the columnist do to check those facts he had? First, he could make certain that the Soviets had agreed to send Nikolayev around Labor Day. Next, he could lean on Gregor.

Zophar consulted his address book, dialed the home of a former Secretary of State. The old boy could find out quickly some of what Zophar needed to know; and the ex-Secretary owed the columnist a few. After the call, Zophar telephoned Gregor.

"I need to see you here, right now," he said to the Russian. "Your professional reputation rests on it."

The first of his castings to produce a nibble was from the former Secretary of State. "Samuel, there seems to have been a snafu on the summit invitation. Customarily our man in Moscow sounds out his counterpart on an invitation, to be sure it will be favorably received. That hasn't happened. Either Ericson jumped the gun, or he had a talk with Nikolayev on the hot line. But the director of Central Intelligence doesn't know about any hot-line calls in the past couple of weeks."

Two hours after Ericson's speech, Gregor showed up at Zophar's house. The columnist, in an ominous tone, stated, "It is a lucky thing I didn't trust you. The President has just gone before the world and demonstrated that your information is so much bilge water. Nikolayev is so securely in charge he can afford to leave the Kremlin and come to America."

"At this moment," the Soviet agent said, "Nikolayev is in Lubyanka Prison, being prepared for trial. I have two tapes here. The tape now in the machine is of the hospital room of agent Bok as he is being visited by your Secretary of State and by Lucas Cartwright. You are familiar with their voices?"

"Of course."

"Use the earpiece." Zophar knew that Gregor assumed this room was bugged. He put on the earpiece, grimacing.

Bok: "I dragged him out of the wreck . . . set up a perimeter . . . Chinese face, right between the eyes . . . grenades killed Kolkov. I dragged his body over the President's. . . ."

Curtice: "Might it not have been possible that Kolkov, while still alive, tried to protect the President with his own body?"

Bok: "Dead, I think. Dragged him over—"

Cartwright: "The Secretary . . . is looking for something that might lessen anti-Soviet reaction at home. Like some heroism on the part of Kolkov."

Bok: "Okay. Coulda been that Kolkov crawled over."

That was all. Zophar told Gregor to play the second tape. The drugged voice of the agent corroborated what had been eavesdropped on in the hospital room. The evidence seemed firm.

"How long has Nikolayev been at Lubyanka Prison?"

"Four or five days."

The columnist rose. Gregor gathered up his recorder and left.

Zophar, mounting the stairs to his typewriter, thought of Cartwright. What had motivated that honorable man to engage in this kind of business? "Perhaps it seemed like a good idea at the time," he said aloud.

Bok propelled his wheelchair into Hennessy's office to hear the lawyer say, "You've just been elected to bell the cat."

The agent looked at Melinda McPhee, Hank Fowler, and Hennessy seated around the table, and nodded. Harry had figured he would be the logical candidate to read the Zophar column, and the wire service stories breaking around it, to the President.

"Take the News Summary," Melinda said, handing him the cassette. "As of four this morning, it was a lot of good news."

The President was in the bedroom being shaved, and his radiant good spirits made Harry feel worse. Harry played the News Summary. Then when the barber left, he said, "Now for the bad news. It seems that what we were worried about we shouldn't have been, and what we weren't worried about we should have been."

Ericson's mouth took on a grim I-told-you-so set. "All right, Harry, give it to me straight."

"Today's column by Zophar," Harry said, giving it all too straight. " 'Soviet leader reported ousted. Vasily Nikolayev, who replaced the assassinated Alexei Kolkov as Soviet Premier one month ago, has probably been jailed—because his Politburo colleagues suspect him of conspiring with President Ericson to consolidate his Kremlin power. Tape recordings in the possession of Soviet authorities, which this reporter has heard, show that General Secretary Kolkov did not heroically save President Ericson's life. This was a story concocted after the ambush, by Secretary of State George Curtice and then Chief of Staff Lucas Cartwright, and parroted by Secret Service agent Harry Bok.' "

Bok went through the entire column to the conclusion: " 'We do not yet know if the President's invitation this week to Nikolayev was a desperation maneuver to save the Soviet leader's job, or whether—mind boggling though it is—the Ericson administration does not yet realize that an upheaval is going on in the Kremlin.

What we do know is this: the President, in his praise of his aides in this week's speech, put his seal of approval on the Curtice-Cartwright deceit—and joined in the attempt to mislead the people of both the United States and the Soviet Union.'"

Ericson picked up the phone and called Hennessy. "Tell the director of Central Intelligence that I want to know what the CIA knows about the status of Nikolayev—if he's in jail or in power. If they can't come up with a good idea in an hour, I'm going to pick up the hot line and ask for the man in charge and see who answers. We're not helpless. Get Curtice here for lunch." The President's tone was malevolent. "Just put a freeze on everything. If you can find out where Zophar got his stuff, that would be helpful. He sure didn't get this from Leigh."

Ericson went to the area where his clothes were laid out and proceeded to dress quickly. He reached confidently for each garment, complaining to Bok all the while. "I straighten out the whole previous blindness thing, and then this. Harry, nobody ever told me we plotted with Vasily to cook up a story making Kolkov a hero."

"If you say so, sir."

Buttoning his vest, the President paused. "Maybe it would be better if I had known, and had ratified the action in the national interest. You see," the President thought aloud, "when the story about Kolkov was being cooked up, I was unconscious, half dead. Then, when I was informed, I thought it would be the better part of wisdom to say nothing for the time being."

"But in the press conference you said Kolkov was a big hero."

"I thought it best to back up the battlefield judgment of my top advisers." Ericson liked that better, and Harry watched his expression relax, then harden again. "I wish I hadn't invited Vasily over here in the speech." He pulled on his jacket and checked with his hands to see if his hair was combed.

"What's so bad about inviting him over?"

"Harry, if I knew Nikolayev was finished and I invited him here, it would look like I was gambling on influencing the Kremlin to keep him in power. If I did not know Vasily was out, it'd look

189

like I was the dopiest President since Harding. At this stage, I cannot afford to look stupid."

Harry rolled his wheelchair to the door. "Give me a push." Ericson took the handles and, with Harry giving directions, the President wheeled him to the Oval Office.

"Here we are," Harry remarked. "There's Melinda, looking dependable, and Hennessy, looking all stern."

"You should've told me, Harry," said Hennessy, speaking through Harry to the President. "You can't keep the facts from your lawyer. I didn't know we were only foolin' about Kolkov."

Ericson took his seat behind the old Hoover desk, revolving his chair toward Melinda. "Let's hear from Ma Griffe." The secretary was wearing more perfume than usual, Harry noted.

"The calls are worried," she said. "The A.G. called to register his hope that a clarification would be issued immediately."

"The Hill?"

"Usual jumping up and down," Melinda reported, "but Speaker Frelingheusen telephoned to say he would withhold comment until he sees your statement."

"Here is what we will do," said Ericson. "Melinda, get my Russian translator over to the Situation Room and hook up the videotape for the hot line. Okay, I just want Hennessy now."

Harry wheeled his chair into Melinda's office, next door, via the porch. He listened while she made arrangements for the translator and alerted the White House Communications Agency for the hot-line call. Ericson buzzed; Melinda flicked up the listening switch to hear him say, "Be sure Curtice says nothing to the press until he sees me," and then, looking at Bok, she deliberately failed to lower the intercom switch.

"You didn't need this," they heard Hennessy say to Ericson. "This was avoidable."

"The whole flap could have been avoided, Mark, if you knew what you were doing."

"My fault? I was ten thousand miles away—"

"Not the Kolkov business. The prior blindness. I never had to make the damned speech!" Hennessy was silent, and the Presi-

dent, coldly angry, went on. "Zophar didn't have the prior blindness story. I kept asking you—are you sure he knows? You kept
saying yes. You panicked, and you panicked me."

"Sven, I didn't even know there was a Kolkov story. I figured
you and Harry and Curtice and Cartwright were telling the truth
about him being a big hero. Okay, I blew it," said Hennessy. "You
want Cartwright back?"

"I need Cartwright in the Cabinet. But stop being so sure of
yourself. It's costing me the presidency."

"Have you considered the possibility, Mr. President, sir, that
my erroneous assumption might have been the biggest break you
ever had? Can you imagine where we'd be today if the story had
just broken about you and your buddy Vasily, and we still hadn't
come clean on the first blindness?"

"If I hadn't made the goddamn speech, I wouldn't have made
that mistake about Nikolayev."

"You know why you act so calm in a crisis?" Hennessy's big
voice boomed. "You're calm because you're scared."

Silence. And then the President's voice: "Ah, maybe it was for
the best. I wonder. You think I had to make that speech?"

"You never had to make the goddamn speech. Now let's get to
the Situation Room and put a hot-line call in to whoever. The
translator should be there."

The new version of the hot line—a television telephone in constant satellite contact—would be especially helpful, Melinda and
Harry knew. Seeing Nikolayev was important; a telephone voice
could be imitated.

WHEN Ericson took his place at the table in the Situation
Room, the WHCA corpsman said into his mouthpiece, "The President of the United States is calling the Premier of the Soviet Union."
The American translator repeated the message in Russian. A voice
answered in Russian, and a Russian voice translated: "Your communication is received. Please stand by."

Vasily Nikolayev's Slavic face filled the screen, and Harry, in
relief, whispered to Ericson, "It's Nikolayev," as the Premier said

in Russian, "Mr. President, it is good to talk with you." Nikolayev could speak English, but hot-line protocol required official translation for monitoring by other officials in both capitals.

After the translation, Ericson said, "This is not a military emergency. The purpose of this call is to expedite my public invitation for your visit to this country. It was not possible, for internal reasons, to make a private approach first."

"The Presidium will take your kind invitation under advisement," said the Russian, "and will be pleased when I tell them that your recovery appears to be continuing." Formal, unresponsive.

Ericson became equally formal. "I have taken note of the careful medical attention you so kindly gave my Secret Service aide, Mr. Bok, who has recently returned."

"Agent Bok is considered a hero," said Nikolayev. "He is a worthy product of your marines. Is there any other communication in this emergency channel, Mr. President?" That was a rebuff.

"Thank you and good day," said Ericson, and the corpsman clicked off. To those in the Situation Room, the President ordered, "Hennessy, Bok, McPhee, CIA, stay." The others left. "What do you think?" the President asked the head of the CIA's Soviet desk.

"Let's play it back," the CIA man said. The playback only took a minute.

"Nikolayev is evidently in trouble," said the CIA analyst. "The Politburo, the small body, has always been in charge during transitions. If the much larger Presidium is considering the invitation, then nobody knows who is in charge. Two, his not being able to give an indication about coming over is nothing less than ominous, sir. Three, the way he cut you off at the end was insulting—unless he had no alternative."

"I wanted to give Vasily an opening to tell us something," Ericson said slowly. "He told us that Harry is still considered a hero, which means that they're going to stick with the story that Kolkov was a hero, too, at least for the time being."

"The reference to Bok being a marine seemed gratuitous," the analyst said. "Anything there?"

" 'Tell it to the marines,' " said Ericson. "I used the expression when I was with Vasily. I told him that it came from an ordinary seaman's feeling about dumb marines."

"Then reverse his previous sentence's meaning. He said, 'Agent Bok is considered a hero.' The truth, then, is that Bok is not considered a hero, and neither is Kolkov probably."

"Vasily could be finished," concluded the President. "They know I'm in a bind with my invitation, so they're letting me have a little more rope. They don't confirm the Zophar story, that Nikolayev and his clique are out—they make it possible for me to deny it, and get in deeper."

After a silence, the President added, "I may have to take a bath on this and get it over with. We can't have the Russians thinking they have me lying to the world."

IV: THE SPARKS FLY UPWARD

JONATHAN had not been to work for two days. He had no desire to go back to the White House. He had seen the pictures of the angry picket line, the demonstrations in Lafayette Square, the nose-to-nose buses around the Ellipse keeping that area inaccessible. He had read the tepid reaction to the speech written by him and twisted by the President into a tricky evasion of issues. The next day there were the stories about the deception at Yalta. There had turned out to be a dark side of Ericson he had not perceived: duplicitous in personal matters, deceitful in affairs of state.

Who could he talk this over with? His friends, mostly principled conservatives, had withdrawn their confidence when he went with the centrist Democratic President. The girl he loved was a kind of double agent, luxuriating in duplicity. The old chief of staff, Lucas Cartwright, whom Jonathan always felt offered some solid footing for probity and idealism at the White House, had returned from Alaska, to be savaged in a press conference. Now Jonathan decided to see Cartwright and try to get a piece of truth out of him.

At the Pentagon, Jonathan noticed that the Defense Secretary looked drawn after his media ordeal.

Jonathan came to the point. "I'm running low on heroes, Mr. Cartwright. Why did you cook up that story in Yalta?"

Lucas Cartwright did not flinch. "It was urgent to get the President out of there. We feared that the ambush was just part of an effort to kill him. It was an idea that George Curtice came up with, to trade with Nikolayev for our immediate departure. That white lie may seem like the 'Yalta Deceit' today, but it seemed like a damned good idea at the time."

"That was then. After you got back, did the President know?"

Cartwright hesitated. "It would not be right to discuss with anybody, even you, what I told the President. But remember that President Ericson has been in shock, newly blinded, and under enormous, unbelievable strain. The responsibility for not clarifying the situation is mine and Curtice's."

"If you've made a horrible mistake, shouldn't you resign?"

"That would be my inclination, but I want my loyal derriere firmly planted in that Cabinet seat if another attempt to oust the President is begun."

The telephone interrupted them. "Yes, Hennessy." Cartwright looked surprised. "I have a radio here. Speak to you later." Cartwright told Jonathan, "There appears to be something coming over the air about a group of reporters meeting with Dr. Abelson's widow after the funeral."

He took a transistor radio out of his desk drawer and found an all-news station; the bulletin was on the air: "The grief-stricken widow of the President's physician has released copies of a letter from her late husband, the President's doctor, that came in the mail this morning. Apparently Dr. Abelson wrote the letter in Camp Hoover, a rustic set of cabins some two hours from Washington. Then, in a deep depression, he took the fatal dose of sleeping pills. Here is the text of the letter:

"'Darling Barbara—I can't live with myself. I've always been a coward and now I'm taking a coward's way out. Because I'm a weakling, the President of the United States is blind. Because I'm a weakling, there's a horrible secret in the White House eating at the vitals of our government.

" 'After the accident on the train, when Sven Ericson could not see, I wanted to get an ophthalmologist in for consultation. But Sven said no, and his campaign manager, Leigh, told me I had no right to alarm the people. So I did what no self-respecting doctor would ever do—I went along with my patient on a medical decision. I put politics ahead of medicine.

" 'After the ambush at Yalta, I knew I had to tell the doctors of his previous blindness. But the President leaned on me, and I didn't tell the eye doctor what he needed to know to make a proper diagnosis. If I had, he would surely have called in a neurosurgeon, and maybe Ericson would have had his sight restored.

" 'I failed my country, I failed myself, and I'm sick of failing. I'm going to walk to the mailbox and mail this, come back and take a dozen Seconal. I love you. Good-by. Herb.' "

The transistor prattled on of the scene before the Abelson house, the coming of children and relatives, and then: "Mrs. Abelson is going to face the microphones and cameras now—"

Cartwright turned on the television set in his office. Barbara Abelson's ravaged face came on the screen. The voice-over said she was going to read her husband's suicide note.

"Oh, God," said Jonathan, "it will be on five times today, on the evening newscasts, on tomorrow morning, like Ruby killing Oswald." He realized that he must still be on the President's side, because he was not thinking so much of Abelson, or his widow, as of the devastating impact of the television presentation on the viewing public. He thought he should feel bad about his emotionless outlook. He studied Cartwright's face. The man was more deeply affected than he; Jonathan felt good about that.

"Turn that off," Bannerman told Mike Fong, who switched off the announcer's breathless recap of the performance of Abelson's widow. Bannerman had returned from London furious at the way the Committee to Replace the Disabled President had bungled the attack on Ericson. He had assembled Fong, Vice-President Nichols, and Marty Quinn—the press agent hired to run the committee staff—to a meeting at his home. Fifteen minutes before the Abelson broadcast, Bannerman had taught them something about striking down a President.

"You missed the big one, moral turpitude," he told them, "and made a big fuss over the one that'll never bring him down."

"There are pickets marching around the White House," Nichols pointed out. "That was the committee's doing."

"The Zophar column was a bombshell," said Secretary Fong, "and we followed it up with the telegrams, the marches, the works. Ericson's on the ropes."

Bannerman told himself he could not afford to offend Fong or Nichols, but their stupidity got to him. He explained it slowly, as if to children: "We are not going to win on the battleground of foreign affairs. Not only that. I happen to think Cartwright and Curtice did the right thing to get the President out of danger in a hurry. Let's get off Yalta and get on to the basics right away."

"What are the basics, Mr. Bannerman?" Quinn was malleable; he had been hired to carry out orders.

"He cheated the people in the last election, that's the basic basic," he told them. "We have to go the Twenty-fifth Amendment route again. The only force that can move this Cabinet to do its duty is an infuriated public opinion. And the public will get good and sore when it realizes it's been had. The excuse will be disability, but the real reason will be that he stole the election by failing to disclose his blindness."

They got it. The impact of Barbara Abelson reading her husband's suicide note was excitedly discussed by the others; Bannerman sat silent, his judgment justified, trying to think of a logical way to keep the White House in its state of siege.

"The eye doctor," Bannerman said at last. "Put the heat on him. First we have to have an uproar about the self-sacrifice of Dr. Abelson—whip up the AMA types, all that. Mike, you know my connections in the medical world. Get the eye doctor, have a press conference about how differently he would have treated Ericson if he had known about the previous blindness."

"Military might try to keep him in line," Quinn protested.

"We will guarantee the doctor a future in private practice," Bannerman said. "If there's pressure from the top brass at Bethesda, we can exploit that." How would Ericson have tried to hush up the previous blindness? Perhaps Buffie was the key. Perhaps Arthur Leigh would recall how the cover-up was conducted.

"Mr. Vice-President," Bannerman said formally, "the meeting is about to get down to nitty-gritty and there is no need to hold you here." Nichols took his cue and departed. Bannerman told Quinn to bring Buffie and Leigh to the house in a hurry.

Leigh was first to arrive, pleased with the new notoriety. Mike Fong put it to him: what other details did he have to contribute to the cover-up?

"Ericson sure didn't say so in his speech the other night," Leigh volunteered, "but when the campaign train jolted to a stop, he was in his compartment with a girl, the photographer."

Bannerman's eyes slitted; this meant that Buffie knew about Ericson's previous blindness all along and had said nothing. With possession of that information two weeks ago, he could have turned Ericson out of office. The girl had only passed along tidbits. Perhaps she was a double agent. He would break her and use her.

Bannerman took Leigh away from the others. On the patio, where there was no likelihood of electronic surveillance, looking down the long sweep of lawn, he made the offer abruptly. "Arthur, what do you want in life?"

"I put a President in the White House," Leigh said, "and you can't top that. So it's time I made myself comfortable."

"Done," said Bannerman. "I'll make you a loan, tell you where to invest, and guarantee you against loss. In six months you'll be a wealthy man. We'll pick out the target figure later. Now is the time for you to come forward and tell me what Ericson did to conceal the fact of his previous blindness."

"It could get me in a lot of trouble," Leigh said.

"You will be represented by the best lawyers in the world."

Leigh made up his mind. "Hennessy thought I was going to blab his big secret. So he asked if there was somebody he could appoint back home who would be helpful to me."

"Was the appointment made?"

"Yes, over some local squawks. The heat came from the White House, and the governor couldn't say no."

"What could the appointee have done for you?"

"Highway stuff, zoning, that kind of thing. But nothing was done by the appointee. Or asked for, yet." Only Hennessy had acted corruptly; Leigh had not yet tried to cash in.

Bannerman walked to a low stone bench. Probably Leigh had extorted the appointment from Hennessy, threatening to expose the secret, and now he was offering to turn it around into a bribe offer. Would such a charge stick? Could it be made to reach Ericson himself? Bannerman decided. "Call Zophar, tell him everything. Don't try to absolve yourself totally, everybody knows you're a big boy. How much did you stand to make?"

"Couple million on land alone."

"That's a million and a half after taxes at the most optimistic," Bannerman said. "Let's make the target two million net." He dismissed him: "Today's Wednesday. Arrange the story for Monday morning publication."

Bannerman walked down the patio steps to a telephone in his study and called an aide in New York. He requested an informal FBI rundown on Buffie Masterson and her family within the half hour. He sent the others away before he took the return call. Curiously the girl had never been in trouble. No derogatory information at all; only records of photography and art show prizes.

"Give me the points of leverage," he said to his man, making notes about her family and friends. "Get the line of credit and the bank for the family health-food store in Fond du Lac, and any financial vulnerability." He hung up without saying good-by. He needed the girl's undivided loyalty, which would come from fear of immediate retribution.

"I washed my fayce before I come," Buffie said, in a reference to Shaw's cockney flower girl in strange, luxurious surroundings. She was dressed in a halter and skirt. High heels drew attention to her long legs.

He motioned for her to sit down in the straight chair facing his desk. "You knew about the President's previous blindness." He kept his voice flat, devoid of feeling. "You didn't tell me."

"He knows I knew," she said, as if to herself. She picked up the canvas bag she had laid next to the chair and placed it carefully in her lap, preparing herself for the next development.

"I wonder if you realize how important it was to me, how important to the nation, to know about the previous blindness when the Cabinet was meeting."

He took out some notes and glanced at them. She broke the silence with, "I guess that magazine editor idea is out, huh?"

"You don't seem to understand, Buffie. You double-crossed me. You are going to pay for what you did for as long as you live." Bannerman drew his lips back over his teeth. "I'm going to destroy your life, and the lives of those you love. Do you want to see how it's done?"

"No. I want to go. Can I go?"

"The door's open," he said. She started to rise, hands tightly on her bag. "Fond du Lac, Wisconsin," he mused. "I'm in the banking business, Buffie, and I have a great many associates in that field. Masterson's Health Foods, it says here, has a fifteen-thousand-dollar line of credit, on which it owes some eleven thousand today. Now, overnight, that credit is going to be withdrawn."

She shook her head. "The mean old banker going to foreclose the mortgage on little Nell. That can't happen in this day and age."

He nodded matter-of-factly. "Then there's your sister in Milwaukee. She's on probation after a drug arrest. She's going to be found with her 'stash,' as they call it. The federal facility she will likely be taken to is in Joliet—"

"You win. Stop." Buffie curled forward in her chair, her head pressed to the bag in her lap, and Bannerman watched her body heave with a dry sob. "You sure know how to hurt a girl."

Bannerman hoisted his bulk out of the chair and walked to the window. "Your friend the President is powerless at such a level. He can order the most god-awful atomic strike, but he cannot order a local bank to make a loan, or a local cop not to make an arrest."

"There's got to be something—" She got on her knees. "I'm on my knees, Mr. Bannerman, I'm sorry, I'm sorry—" She began to cry at last, which soon turned to a hysteria.

His slap smashed her halfway across the room. Buffie pulled herself up, breathing deeply, picked up her bag, and gathering some dignity about her, addressed him without tears. "I am terrified, Mr. Bannerman," she said, not sounding terrified at all. "I'll do anything you say. I'm your slave."

As if reluctantly, he nodded. He felt that she meant it.

"EVERY time I go to the front door and pick up the morning paper," said Hennessy, "I get a klong."

Hank Fowler was unfamiliar with the term. "You get a what?"

"The feeling you get," Melinda explained, "when you're out to dinner someplace and you suddenly remember that you invited a dozen guests to your house for an hour before."

"Where's The Man?" Hennessy asked. It was nearly lunchtime, and the President had not appeared in the West Wing.

"Lincoln Sitting Room," she replied. "He's pretty low. Barbara reading that letter really got to him."

"I want to get him off the defensive," Hennessy said. "Book him into an event next week that's controversial but presidential."

Melinda said, "The Attorney General has been nagging us to have the President accompany him to the two hundredth anniversary of some big consitutional deal down in Colonial Williamsburg. Law Day."

"Next week we'll be very pro-Constitution. Hank, could you get him up for a platform speech?" Hennessy asked.

"He'd probably like that," Fowler replied. A voice at his shoulder told him of a call. He went back to his office.

The naval commandant at Bethesda was on the phone. "I can't be responsible, Dr. Fowler. I was following orders." The ophthalmologist, Lilith, was about to "go up the flue," in the commandant's phrase. "He's calling a press conference at the medical association this afternoon. Damn fool thinks he's a celebrity."

Fowler felt the possibility of his own involvement in Ericson's ordeal. "Go on, Admiral—you told him about our talk?"

"Only to impress him that he could expect no White House help when we lowered the boom on him. He got all upset at what he called White House pressure to deny him free speech."

"Admiral, all I asked you to do was to remind him of the medical ethics. Did you think I wanted you to pressure him?"

"I don't know exactly what the President, who is my commander in chief, told you—but the message I got, reading between your lines, was that he wanted this man to be a good sailor."

Fowler hung up before he got the White House into any more trouble. He went out to Melinda and asked her to accompany him to Hennessy's office.

"I got a klong," Fowler said to them, and related his call from the Bethesda Naval Hospital commandant. "I'm frightened."

"Don't be," Hennessy ordered. "It'll be a big deal for one day, and then it'll be forgotten. I'll get our doctors to give Lilith a blast for looking for alibis and making the wrong decisions."

Fowler returned to his office. But when he heard the television on in Melinda's office, he was drawn to the doorway to listen to Dr. Lilith. The ophthalmologist laid out the series of medical deceptions by the President and his staff after the examination in the Azores. Then he referred to Ericson's speech evoking Samson: "... *How well are come upon him his deserts?* I do not suggest that any human being deserves to be blind, but neurosurgery might have made all the difference. The President brought it on himself."

Lilith, his voice now quivering, told of "intense pressure from the White House" to keep quiet; of the admiral passing along warnings of the ruination of his naval career from "the nondoctor who calls himself doctor, Henry Fowler."

Fowler felt dirtied. A little slip, and he was associated with—worse, had become additional evidence of—Ericson's venality.

HENNESSY surveyed the telephone messages laid before him on the long table he had inherited with the office. One was from Duparquet, only a half hour old. He stopped when he saw the one from "Mr. Goodfriend." Mr. Goodfriend was Marty Quinn, the press agent Hennessy had planted on Bannerman's Committee to Replace the Disabled President.

Hennessy had started to call Duparquet when his secretary came in, closed the door, and said, "Couple of FBI gumshoes in the waiting room." Hennessy scowled. Some White House staffer had put his foot in it. He told his secretary to send the FBI men in.

The agents were polite, as usual; one had gray in his hair and did the question asking; the younger took notes.

"Sorry to bother you, sir. How long have you been acquainted with a man named Arthur Leigh?"

"Since the campaign last year."

"When was the last time you saw him?"

Hennessy's lawyer instincts took over. "What's this about?"

"Not at liberty to say, sir, some preliminary checking."

Hennessy touched the "annoy me" button under his desk. His secretary came in. "They're waiting for you, Mr. Hennessy. They say the meeting can't start without you."

"Marie, these gentlemen want the date and time of the visit Arthur Leigh made recently," Hennessy said. "If they like, set up another time to see me Monday."

"There's some urgency involved," the older agent pressed.

"I will not give you rushed answers to important questions. I am familiar with Section 1001 of U.S. Code Eighteen." That was a law, sometimes invoked to cause trouble, that made it a crime to lie to any federal officer—no oath needed. Hennessy was not going into any interview without a witness of his own.

He left his office and, when assured that the FBI men had gone, returned and called the Attorney General. "Emmett, a couple of your boys are over here snooping around—" Hennessy checked his anger, because the President needed Duparquet as never before.

"I called you a little while ago"—Duparquet's voice was formal—"to say that the director of the FBI had assigned some men to an investigation involving Arthur Leigh."

"What's it all about?"

"An allegation of corruption."

That smashed into Hennessy like a torpedo. Someone must have gotten wind of the deal Hennessy had made to take care of Leigh's highway problem. "Am I the target of an investigation?"

"If the matter is considered by the United States Attorney to be worthy of grand jury consideration," Duparquet said evenly, "whoever is the target would be informed."

"As you know, General, I wear two hats, chief of staff and legal counsel to the President. Do you think this might be a good time for the President to appoint someone else to fill the counsel's job?"

"Yes. To avoid any potential conflict of interest."

"I understand." Now came a point it was important to have on the record. "General, please discuss that with the President yourself. It is my intention not to discuss this matter in any way with the President." Hennessy hung up. His stomach was churning and his heart was pounding. He reached for his bottle of antacid.

When Leigh had asked for that highway commissioner appointment, Hennessy had passed the word through the patronage man at the White House to his contact in the Tennessee governor's office. The appointment had been made. It was probably too soon for the highway commissioner to have made a ruling of benefit to Leigh. They could charge that he had ordered the appointment in exchange for Leigh's silence on the previous blindness, but who could substantiate that? So what was the FBI left with? Just the charge that the White House had acceded to the wishes of an old political supporter in the appointment of a friend.

Unless Leigh was the source of the allegation. But what could Leigh gain by getting Hennessy and himself in trouble?

"He could gain a whole lot of money," Hennessy said aloud. If Leigh had sold out to Bannerman, he could bring Hennessy down by charging attempted bribery. Hennessy would countercharge extortion, except that the record would show that he did the favor for Leigh. Hennessy felt the need for a criminal lawyer.

On the intercom, his secretary told him Mr. Goodfriend was calling. "Bannerman's got control of that eye doctor," Marty Quinn reported. "Offered him a deal outside the navy."

"What's with Arthur Leigh?"

"He was at a meeting with Bannerman and Nichols day before

203

yesterday," Quinn reported. "I don't know what they cooked up."

"What they cooked up was me. Look, just in case I have to take off," Hennessy said, "I want you to have another contact here." He gave Quinn Melinda's private number. He thought about Melinda. He pictured her as Beau Geste at Fort Zinderneuf, gallantly propping up dead bodies in the parapets to make attackers think the fort was still defended.

She appeared in his doorway—fine figure, dancer's legs. "The Boss says they're after you. He wants to see you."

"I don't think he should. Not about this. Warn him."

"Emmett told him to cut you off, but he wants to see you."

"What'd you tell him?"

"I told him if he so much as thought twice about not seeing you, I'd break his long white cane."

"I goofed. Again."

She said softly, "We all make mistakes. Oh, Hennessy . . ."

For the next few hours on the telephone, Hennessy went over the matter with an old friend who practiced criminal law in New York. He was having a bourbon by himself when Ericson's cane tapped on the doorjamb and the President appeared.

"Okay," the President sighed, "how do we get out of this one?"

Hennessy explained. "They've got a grand jury impaneled. They've heard Leigh say I bribed him to keep quiet about the blindness, and I'll bet Leigh says I told him you knew all about it. They're going to run me in there Monday and get me to contradict his story. Every time I disagree with Leigh, they'll indict me for perjury. His word against mine—who do you believe?"

"But what if you took the Fifth?"

"No good. An assistant to the President cannot plead self-incrimination. That would be as much as saying Leigh is telling the truth, and it could be the last straw for you."

"Take the Fifth," said Ericson. "This thing is getting out of hand." He shook his head. "I let Herb kill himself, I ruin Harry's chances, I take a sweet guy like Hank and get his reputation smeared. I'm just not going to see you go to jail."

"Sven, I couldn't go through life having taken the Fifth on this and you know it. So I'll testify and I'll tell the grand jury all about the meeting at Bannerman's house, where this was cooked up. I'll force the prosecutors to call Bannerman and Nichols as witnesses and they'll have to perjure themselves till they're blue in the face. It'll be okay."

"Every time you say it'll be okay, I worry. Except for the divorce, and the election, nothing else turned out okay."

"We win the big ones," Hennessy replied. They sat silent for a minute. "Me going might lance the boil in a lot of ways."

"Great. Who'll I trust?"

"Melinda. She'll have a good contact in Bannerman's backyard. A lot depends on whether she can keep Duparquet in line."

"I suppose this is good-by, then."

"Um." Best thing about working for a blind man, Hennessy thought, was he couldn't see your eyes. When he trusted his voice, he said, "You're in my office, I'm not in yours, remember?"

Ericson rose. "Point me toward the center of power."

"I don't want the whole News Summary," Ericson told Melinda. "Just read me the worst." It was past nine, and he was still in bed; he had been doing that all week, ever since that speech.

"Cover of *Time* is the Yalta Deceit," she skimmed, "montage of Cartwright, Curtice, Bok, and Nikolayev in a spiderweb."

"Well, better that than Barbara Abelson."

"She's on the cover of *Newsweek*."

"Hennessy's press conference get a good play?"

"Zophar broke the story Monday morning that he would appear at a grand jury that day, so Hennessy was on the defensive. The headlines were 'Ericson Aide Charged with Bribe Try,' but there was a clip on television last night showing him zapping Bannerman and Nichols as the 'master manipulators' of the whole thing.

"The *Times* says, 'The propriety of the Vice-President's presence at Mr. Bannerman's home while this matter was presumably being discussed is questionable.' And then the needle: 'Whether or not this latest charge turns out to be true, the American public—after a week-long series of shocks about evidence of White House duplicity—is ready to believe the worst about President Ericson's ability to control his staff and his ability to govern. His Cabinet has a responsibility to invoke the Twenty-fifth Amendment. The most rational solution would be for the President to stand aside voluntarily.' "

Ericson put his hands behind his head on the pillow. "What sort of attention is the Attorney General getting?"

"A dandy press," Melinda said, irritated.

"I should be in the office, fighting the good fight. Send in the barber." He held his hand out for a robe, which she gave him. "Can we depend on Duparquet? Is he a good man?"

"He's a fairly good man. I don't know if we can depend on him."

"One of those guys who will defend his integrity, even if it takes him to the White House?"

"Don't be sarcastic—he's done a lot for you." What was she to say? That Emmett was considerate and tender? That she had fixed him dinner at her place last evening, candlelight and wine? "He's ambitious, like you. He has principles, like you. He hasn't been through what you have, though. Nobody's ever hit him hard."

"I want to make it for one term, and then turn it over to somebody I trust," Ericson said slowly. "Could be him. If you haven't told him that already, tell him every five minutes or so. Oh, Melinda, how I wish right now that I could see. I'd be looking at your dark brown, distrusting eyes. But all I can see is Herb's face looking at me, and Barbara's face looking at me."

"Can it," she murmured, motioning the man in the hall to gather up his equipment. "Here's the barber."

As Melinda headed downstairs, shuddering at the blind man's vision of accusing eyes, she saw the men from the General Services Administration removing Hennessy's office files and moving in Smitty's things. Musical chairs to a dirge.

The mail was turning ugly. She called the pollster. "Twenty-eight percent and falling," he said. She hung up and plunged into the plans for the next day in Williamsburg. The President had begun to look forward to it—no formal speech, just some remarks about the Constitution and the rule of law. It would be a relief to get away from the bunker atmosphere of the White House.

Smitty, the new chief of staff, came into her office, elaborately casual, looking over some of the letters. He probably did not know what to do about Ericson's calendar, she figured, and needed her advice, but he didn't want to give up any of his new authority. "The Council of Economic Advisers want to see the Boss."

"He's free this afternoon at five." Melinda was determined to make it hard for the President to mope around. "You could book the economists in this afternoon, and Curtice and the CIA tomorrow before he takes off for Williamsburg."

She realized that she was suddenly running the government of the United States, or at least running that small part of it in control of the President.

ANGELO Frangipani, the Big Flower, parked his Pinto in the space reserved in the Capitol Hill lot for the Speaker of the House. The compact car was his concession to an antipollution lobby, and he liked to say, "I'm the only Cabinet member without a driver, because I need the room in my car." He now walked up the stairs to the office of Mortimer Frelinghuesen. The Secretary of Human Resources was satisfied that if he had a political friend he could trust, it was the Speaker, who supported the Ericson administration on foreign policy, opposed it on domestic affairs, and provided a note of restraint when the "twenty-fivers" were baying.

Andy dropped his white straw fedora on the receptionist's desk, announced himself, and strolled around the ornate old waiting room, thinking about what he wanted to say. The administration of which he was a proud part was on the ropes; the prevailing mood at Human Resources, his agency—which was inclined to like Ericson—was that the President was a political zombie. In such a time, a good politician should count the numbers. Andy knew the numbers in the Cabinet; the Speaker would know the numbers in the House and have a good idea about the Senate.

To the Speaker, a wiry, alert-looking man, Andy came out quickly with, "I don't like what's happening in the country. Nobody sent me to you, Mort, but it can't go on this way."

"Is the President unable to carry out his duties?"

"He could, if they let him," Andy said.

The Speaker nodded. "What is it like with Ericson? Personally, I mean. He can't see, he can't tell where the next blow is coming from. Is he withdrawn? Punchy? Nervous? What?"

"He sleeps too much," Andy replied, "which I do when I don't want to face the day. On the whole, though, he's a scrapper. Mort— never sell him short. He likes that job."

The Speaker shook his head. "He tried to slip past the blindness, and he got trapped on Yalta. He's handled it badly."

"Is that a reason to replace him with Nichols?" said Andy.

"Now we're down to the essentials. If it were up to me, I'd say give the man a chance. On the lack of full disclosure on the previous blindness, he must admit he was wrong. On the Yalta business, he can say his staff did what they thought was best for the country in a tight spot, and he'll back 'em up."

Andy put the question squarely. "If the Cabinet doesn't declare him disabled, will the House impeach him?"

"There are enough votes right now to impeach. But the process takes months. Meanwhile, the country would be paralyzed. That's why I've scotched the impeachment crowd—the House is waiting to see what the Cabinet will do."

The ball was back in Andy's court. "If the Cabinet votes him out and he challenges it in the Congress, will the House sustain the Cabinet?"

"You only need a majority of the House to impeach," the Speaker said unhesitatingly, "but you need two-thirds of the House to sustain a Cabinet removal. If it goes the Cabinet route, the House will *not* have the two-thirds it would need to uphold the Cabinet. Ericson has a forty percent rock-solid support in the House."

Frangipani whistled. "On the other hand, if the Cabinet does not act, then the House will impeach and the Senate convict him?"

"You've always been able to count, Andy."

Andy got up to go. "The alternative to Ericson is Nichols, who's a cat's-paw for Bannerman."

"I don't envy you the choice, Andy. Lesser of evils."

"Forty percent rock solid, huh?" mused Andy. He was hoping he could edge Frelingheusen's prediction over to a commitment, and was not disappointed.

"If it should dip under forty percent," said the Speaker, "I have some IOUs to call that would bring it back. I'd sit 'em in the front row and if I needed 'em, they'd be there. If you want to pass that on to the President, I'd have no objection, but I'd have to deny it if I read it anywhere."

DUPARQUET stepped to the lectern in the Hall of the House of Burgesses at Colonial Williamsburg; the audience was made up of eminent attorneys and jurists. The White House press corps was there, too, spilling along the sides of the narrow room.

The Attorney General would have been happier to be dissociated from the President during a week in which the Justice Department was in the process of indicting his chief aide. But the President was right there, his sightless eyes—he was not wearing dark glasses anymore—in full view.

Duparquet began. "It is an honor to share the platform today with a man whose personal bravery is an inspiration to all Americans—President Sven Ericson." Big applause. "The President will have a few remarks for you later," he said, "which makes me feel like Edward Everett, the man who was the main speaker at Gettysburg." Duparquet launched into his address on the rule of law, which he knew would be interpreted in the light of the investigation of Hennessy and the duplicity of some of his fellow Cabinet members. He concluded with a reference to John Adams and the concept of "a government of laws, not of men."

The handsome, tanned Floridian sat down to applause, and the chairman, a retired justice of the Supreme Court, introduced the President. Every person in the hall watched Ericson rise, make a half left, take five deliberate steps, make a half right, reach out confidently and touch the lectern. Then, before the President could say a word, the visual demonstration began.

Duparquet blanched. At four places in the hall, well-dressed demonstrators, who had blended in with the lawyers, rose and

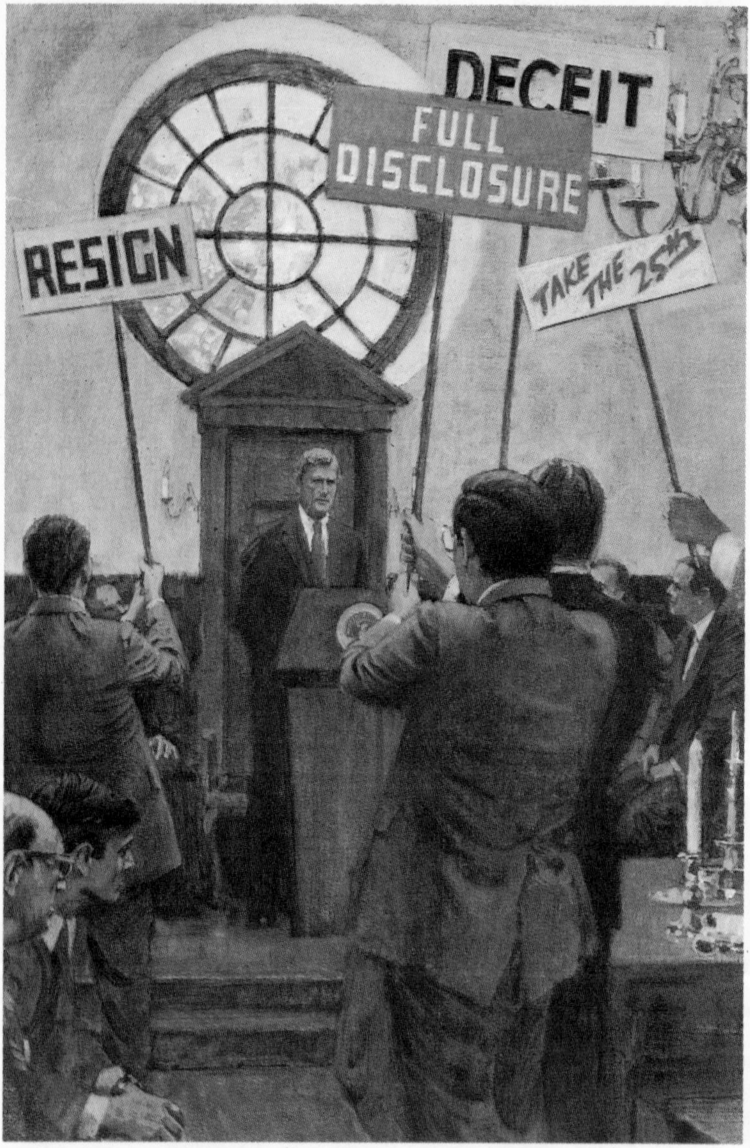
DECEIT
FULL DISCLOSURE
RESIGN
TAKE THE 25th

came forward silently with signs that had been stored under the seats. One sign read RESIGN; the others read DECEIT, TAKE THE 25TH, FULL DISCLOSURE. The audience gasped.

Duparquet was in a quandary; should he tell the President about the signs? That would make the demonstrators' point—that the President was near helpless without staff aid.

"Everybody relax," the President said quietly. "I can tell by the sound of the intake of breath that the demonstration has begun. For those of you who don't have a good angle, the signs read 'Resign,' 'Take the Twenty-fifth,' and similar sentiments. The purpose of a visual demonstration is to show how helpless I am.

"The truth is, I *am* dependent on others for the faculty of sight. This morning Secret Service agents told me that signs were being smuggled into the hall. I told the agents to let the demonstration go forward, because it would be a way for me to demonstrate, too.

"We are met today at the scene of early stirrings of American liberty. In this setting it would be wrong to infringe on anyone's right to free speech.

"I don't have a speech," Ericson continued. "This is a time for soberly reflecting on all the fine and wise things our Attorney General has said about our adherence to the rule of law."

The audience was mesmerized, the demonstrators frozen.

"One episode in history comes to mind. They say that Lord Nelson, in a naval battle, was told by a frightened lieutenant that they were being attacked by a huge armada. Nelson had one blind eye, wore a patch over it. He said to his lieutenant, 'Give me your telescope.' He held it up to his blind eye and pretended to scan the horizon; then he said, 'I see no armada. Sail on.' And they sailed into the Battle of Copenhagen, and won the fight."

He paused. "As I look around this room today, I see no signs to frighten me. I am going to sail on, and this administration is going to persevere."

The President waited for an agent to take his arm, and proceeded off the stage. The place exploded into cheers, the demonstrators put down their signs, the cameramen moved in on them.

"Damn good show," the Attorney General said, hours later, in the cottage assigned to Melinda. "Tell me, though," he said to the President's secretary. "Why do you look so good to me tonight?"

"Happy my boss did well, I guess."

Duparquet wanted her closer to him. He was fifty-four, she was thirty-eight; he could see himself building a new life with this woman. He could talk with her, man to man, make love to her, man to woman, and just be with her, friend to friend. He had never found that combination before. He wondered if he had any competition. The affection between Melinda and Ericson seemed to him avuncular; the President would undoubtedly bless the match.

Melinda walked out on the porch. Duparquet followed her into the starless summer night, and sat with her on the rocking settee. He took her hand and they swung silently for a while.

"You mustn't get euphoric about one good effort by the President," he cautioned her.

"Why can't I enjoy some good news, or a decent reaction?"

"I don't want you to be hurt."

"You mean Hennessy?"

"He will be indicted on Friday for lying to the grand jury."

"That's pretty quick."

"When the chief aide of the President lies to a grand jury, that rates a faster reaction than in ordinary cases."

All she said was, "Does it?" which irritated him, because the principle of all men standing equal before the law had, to some degree, been undercut. The U.S. Attorney, who technically reported to the Attorney General, was an ambitious young man who smelled headlines. He had acted in undue haste, which meant he had a rubber-stamp grand jury. Duparquet was disturbed because the U.S. Attorney was known to be a "Bannerman appointment" in one of the spoils cuts at the convention.

"It would have caused quite a hullabaloo," he went on, "if I had overruled the U.S. Attorney, and the head of the criminal division at Justice, to slow down this case."

"Would have taken a real jerk to stand up against the threat of a hullabaloo," she said evenly, moving back and forth slowly in the darkness, "upholding an individual defendant's rights. Sort of a spoilsport who tries to argue with a lynch mob." That stung him.

"Melinda, he offered Leigh a bribe, with the authority of the President of the United States." He lunged out of the creaking settee and sat on the veranda railing, looking at her in the dark. "Okay. On hard principle, I should have slowed the speed of that prosecution. I should have asked the U.S. Attorney why he had to go the perjury route—there's no doubt Hennessy could have beaten a charge of bribery. And in so doing, I would have been tarred with the brush that's ruining everybody near Ericson—blocking the indictment of his chief aide. Obstructing justice, it would have been called. My career would have ended at that point.

"We might as well have the fundamental issue out," he continued. "One of these days the Cabinet will come together again under the Twenty-fifth. The last time, I was the President's lawyer, because I believed in the case. I made a big point out of this: that the American public made its judgment on Election Day with nothing withheld, in possession of all the facts about Ericson's eyesight. That was a lie."

"He thought you had no need to know. If he had told you, you wouldn't have made such a big deal out of full disclosure. You don't mean you'll double-cross him because he didn't tell you everything. You really think he's in a coma, or crazy?"

"That's not my definition of inability."

"He's just too unpopular, you mean?"

"His blindness is a part of it. His psychological reaction to the pressure is part of it. And the nation's reaction to his physical and psychological condition is part of it. It's a vicious circle, and getting worse. The totality of it is such as to cause, in effect, disability."

"You sound like you're going to vote against him."

"Yes, I am."

The phone rang. "Time for a break," she said.

He heard her talking to a Mr. Goodfriend. In a moment she was back. "You have it neatly set up," she said coldly. "Fong will call the Cabinet together Friday afternoon, a few hours after Hennessy's indictment is handed up." He put his hands on her shoulders and she twisted away. "I'm disappointed in you, Emmett."

"We disagree about the President," he said. "I may be right on some things, you may be right on others. When this is all over—"

"It's over," she said in a rush. "You've had everything Ericson had to offer, and you've had everything I have to offer. Now you're conniving to run the President out of office, turning the country over to the worst kind of people, because you know which way the wind is blowing. You're a politician, Emmett, but you're not a political man."

"And Sven Ericson is?"

"He's becoming one."

"I can't believe that all we have is to be sacrificed because of a political disagreement. Melinda, do you know everything you're turning down?"

She nodded. "I was going to be the First Lady after next."

"There is still that possibility."

"A lot depends on what you do."

She obviously meant what she said; disappointed, frustrated, but not confused, he left the cottage.

AT THE sound of the bolt sliding back, Nikolayev looked from his television set toward the Lubyanka Prison cell door. Slovenski entered the cell. The neutral bureaucrat was usually chosen to bring prisoners good news.

"I have good news," he began.

"The investigation revealed the truth?" said Nikolayev.

"Yes, you conspired with the air force leaders to kill Kolkov and Ericson, and to blame it on the Chinese."

"You call that good news?"

"No, the good news is that you have been named Premier by the Presidium."

In the Zil limousine, the bureaucrat explained the seeming contradictions. "The question that split the Politburo was whether you did the right thing in getting rid of Kolkov. The matter got out of hand, into the Presidium. The decision was that Kolkov was planning a preemptive strike against the Far Eastern powers and that you acted in the interests of the party in eliminating him."

"And the official results of the investigation will say . . . ?"

"Just as you said, the Chinese tried to kill both leaders to drive the two superpowers apart. At the next party congress, if all goes well, you will be elected General Secretary."

Nikolayev sagged inwardly. He was not in power; he was a figurehead.

Slovenski continued. "It is in our interest for President Ericson to remain in power. First, the alternative to him is the banker Bannerman, acting through Nichols. His inclination is to deal separately with the Far Eastern powers, which would cause a division in the U.S.S.R.–U.S. alliance. Second, Ericson invited you to visit Washington, without checking with us first. We could make him look like a fool, or we could make him look very smart. To that extent, his future is in our hands. We can use you to make him beholden to us."

It was beginning to make sense to Nikolayev. The trick would be to get Ericson to ask for his help. The car stopped in front of Nikolayev's apartment in the Kremlin. The Soviet leader walked upstairs and was embraced amid tears by his wife and three children, who had not known if they would ever see him again.

That night, in his darkened living room, he worked out his position. If Ericson could serve out his term, Nikolayev would have three years to wrest control of the party from the Kolkov men.

Step one was to get word to Ericson that he was ready to help if asked. There was always Gregor, the out-of-channels man. He would inform Nikolayev's enemies in the Kremlin what approaches the new Premier was making, but since Nikolayev was supposed to be getting Ericson obligated, that would do no harm. He would send a probe through Gregor to ask Ericson when the simultaneous announcement of the Soviet acceptance of the American invitation would be most propitious.

"I GOT a confession to make, Potus," Buffie said. She was curled in a sitting-room chair, watching the President. She knew she had to get away from Bannerman.

"Don't lay your guilt on me, Buffie. I've got all I can handle."

215

"I been playin' footsie with Bannerman. Nothing serious, I never let on about the campaign train, just little stuff. I wasn't being disloyal to you."

"You were being disloyal, Buffie. But you were also there when I needed you, and they cancel each other out. So relax."

"I can't relax. I'm scared."

"I won't fire you."

"It's not you that scares me. You're a good guy, a friend. But Bannerman scares me plenty. I thought I could kind of play both ends against the middle, but I'm over my head. This is no game, this White House life—people play for keeps. They're mean."

"What's he threatening you with?"

"Everything." She started breathing heavily. "He can ruin my dad's business, and make life hard for my sister."

"Those are just threats, Buffie."

"Potus, believe me, this guy likes to hurt. He slammed me pretty good and I could tell he got a kick out of it—"

"He *hit* you?" asked Ericson, amazed. "Where?"

"In the head, where it doesn't show."

"Okay." The President was businesslike. "What does he want you to do?"

"First he wanted me to give you a message." She grabbed her photographer's case and pulled out the notes. "The best thing for the country is for you to resign. He says you have to think about an ongoing activity worthy of your talents. He says the Institute of International Economic Studies is funded with three million. He says it could be funded with thirty million. You would have the right to name the new board of directors."

"Anything else?"

"He said you could name anything you wanted for me."

"Now, Buffie, I want you to get this straight. Tomorrow morning, that's Thursday, you tell him that I consider his message to be—write down these words—'an arrogant attempt to purchase the presidency.' Add this: 'Any action against you or yours would be prima facie evidence of attempted coercion of me.' Understand, Buffie? That would be evidence of the offer of a bribe."

The phone buzzed on the President's table. "Yes, Melinda. Friday? That's fast. Hennessy— Oh. Sorry about that. See you in the office at eight." He put the phone down and shook his head. "I don't bring people luck anymore."

"Luck changes, Potus."

"Come here, give me your hands."

She knelt next to him and put her hands in his, aware of the skin roughened by working in the photo lab soup. "My hands are my worst part. The rest of my skin is milk white, with a delicious dusting of freckles."

"Who said that?"

"Jonathan."

Ericson laughed. "Are you kids going to move in together?"

"That's old-fashioned 1970s stuff. Jonathan and me, we're going to do it the modern way—marriage contracts and babies and mortgages. Unless Bannerman messes everything up."

"Buffie, I have a blind man's way of telling the truth through your fingers. How else is Bannerman planning to use you?"

"You were with me on the train when you hit your head," she blurted. "I'm supposed to spill that story in time for a clobber-Ericson day on Friday. Leigh must have told him."

"Gives me a venal motive for covering up the accident," Ericson thought aloud. He squeezed her hands. "Tell Bannerman I said that further substantiates the coercion. He'll back off, you'll see."

Potus had become Buffie's new uncle.

MIKE Fong, seated outside the Cabinet Room on the day that had already been dubbed Black Friday by an expectant press, was not so sure that this Cabinet meeting had been a good idea.

The votes of four Cabinet members were needed to remove the President. Fong's was one. Curtice's vote, to expiate his sense of guilt for the Yalta Deceit, was a second. A third possibility was Emmett Duparquet. But where was the fourth? Not Cartwright. Not Zack Parker, the new Treasury Secretary, a forthright Bannerman hater. And Andy Frangipani was an Ericson stalwart.

"Where's the sense in it?" Fong had asked Bannerman.

"Mike, we have to force them to make mistakes," Bannerman had replied. "You have to keep crashing into that door of the Oval Office. The pressure on Ericson has to be enormous."

For ten days, Fong told himself, the Ericson administration had been under a bombardment in the press, in the Congress, and now in the courts, with this morning's indictment of Hennessy. Suicide, scandal, cover-up, international blundering, deceit—the polls showed that the American people were fed up. But Ericson hung in there, politically paralyzed, and stubbornly paralyzing the country. Nichols was no bargain, Fong thought, as the Vice-President appeared in the hallway, but the country could operate.

"Shall we have another go at it?" the Vice-President said, leading the others into the room. After they took their seats, Fong was startled to see, in Treasury's chair, not Zack Parker, Bannerman's replacement, but a tall, pasty-faced man he had not met.

Cartwright immediately said, "The meeting is out of order until the Secretary of the Treasury arrives."

"I'm informed that Secretary Parker has had a severe attack of gastroenteritis," said the Vice-President. "Sitting in his place is the Under Secretary for Monetary Affairs, Albert Hay."

"I suspect foul play," Cartwright said dramatically. "There is going to be a suspicion in the public mind that Secretary Parker's food was tampered with. This is a very fast shuffle."

"It wouldn't kill us to wait till Monday," said Frangipani, "out of respect to Zack Parker."

"I move the question," said Fong.

"Would the Attorney General give us a legal opinion?" Cartwright looked for help.

Duparquet shrugged. "If Mike won't accept a delay, that's it."

"Will you speak for the President, Emmett?" Nichols asked.

"I'll defer to Secretary Cartwright," said Duparquet.

"What are the charges?" Cartwright demanded.

Fong said, "There is only one charge: that the President is unable to fulfill the functions and duties of his office."

"Surely the medical evidence must be newly taken," argued Cartwright.

"We considered the medical evidence from the President's physician last time," said the Vice-President. "It was such a pack of lies that he killed himself over it."

"It ill behooves you to let your mouth water," Cartwright snapped, "at the prospect of seizing the President's powers."

The room tensed. "The Vice-President has the power to veto a decision by this Cabinet," Fong said soothingly, "and so I think it would be a good idea if he rescued himself from further comment. Now, I move the question."

He looked at the Vice-President, who said, "On the vote to remove the President. The Secretary of State."

George Curtice said, "I vote yes."

"The Secretary of Defense."

Cartwright said wearily, "I vote no."

"The Treasury Secretary."

Albert Hay said, "I reached Secretary Parker in the hospital just before the meeting. Treasury votes no."

"I withdraw my charge of foul play," Cartwright said.

"The Attorney General," the Vice-President continued.

"Yes."

"The Secretary of Natural Resources."

"Yes," said Fong to his own motion.

"The Secretary of Human Resources."

"Yes," said Andy Frangipani.

"A vote of yes is a vote to remove the President," said Cartwright, as if perhaps Frangipani did not understand.

"I know," said the Big Flower, with no expression. "The Vice-President is now the Acting President."

Duparquet said to Nichols, "Mr. Acting President, do you choose to exercise your veto?"

"No," said Nichols.

"I would like to propose that we give President Ericson the opportunity to step aside voluntarily," said Cartwright.

They all looked at Fong. "I think that's a compassionate suggestion, Lucas. Why don't you go?"

Cartwright left the Cabinet Room and went toward the Oval

Office. The rest of them sat, saying nothing, for three minutes. Cartwright returned, a note in his hand, looking oddly cheered. "President Ericson has given me this message. 'Yesterday I turned down an offer to purchase the presidency. Now I am turning down your offer to let me resign. I will fight your action in the Congress until the powers of the President are once again in the hands of the person the people elected to that post.'"

Nichols said, "He isn't disputing our right to take this action, is he?"

"No. But if you want the President off the premises, Mr. Acting President, you're going to have to throw him out."

V: THE PRESIDENT

ERICSON leaned back, spinning his desk chair to face the bay window. Maybe he was kidding himself, but he thought he could make out more shades of gray in what had been only black and white images.

The buzzer sounded. It was Melinda. "I don't want to be pushy, but we're all here. Lucas and Smitty and Harry and Hank and me. And the constitutional lawyer you wanted."

"Talk to each other in the Roosevelt Room. I want to think."

Here he was, neither President nor not President. He was a semi-President. What on earth, he wondered, had possessed Andy Frangipani?

Ericson did not relish going into this fight without Hennessy. Lucas Cartwright had turned out to be a stand-up loyalist, but he did not have the zest for a no-quarter battle.

So much to do, if he could hold on. He was the first professional economist to be elected President, the first who understood profoundly the forces that underlay the system that moved the country to prosperity or to hard times. Only Ericson, he told himself—the conservative-sounding Democrat with the first Republican Senate in forty years—only Ericson could effect radical reform in the name of the free economy.

What if I am right? Ericson asked himself. What if I could guide the economy more creatively, more indirectly, making our central achievement the increase of worker productivity—the only way to a steadily rising standard of living?

What if I caved in, and Bannerman and Nichols took us down the path of more tinkering, more blundering, more recessions—wouldn't history condemn me for being the worst kind of coward? He pressed the button for Melinda. She opened the door.

"Let's get to work," he told her.

The others trooped in behind her. "Say hello to Senator Apple," said Cartwright's voice, "your new lawyer." A gnarled old hand grasped Ericson's. Lucas' choice was a pleasant surprise. Apple had retired from the Senate a decade ago to make a pile of money as head of a Washington law firm.

"Mr. President," said the wheezy voice of Senator Apple, "it's been legally done, but I think the Legislative History will show that this despicable action was not the intent of the framers of the Twenty-fifth Amendment. I was the chairman of the Subcommittee on Constitutional Amendments when the Twenty-fifth Amendment was passed."

"You just called me Mr. President," Ericson said. "Am I?"

"You occupy the office of President. However, as soon as a written message is received by the President pro tem of the Senate, and by the Speaker of the House, that the Cabinet has declared you unable to carry out your duties and functions—which should be about now—your powers and duties devolve upon the Vice-President as Acting President."

"So I am President without power."

"Right," Apple said matter-of-factly. "You cannot give an order. But you have residual power."

"What residual power?"

"You still have some control over—well, influence with—your press secretary, your chief of staff."

"How does he get his powers back?" said Lucas Cartwright.

"Step one," said the lawyer, "is to transmit letters to the President pro tem and the Speaker, saying simply, 'Sir: Pursuant to Section Four, Paragraph Two, of the Twenty-fifth Amendment to the Constitution, this is to advise you that no inability exists.'"

Ericson went to his desk, wrote the two letters, and held them out. Smitty, as chief of staff, took them.

"What's step two?" Ericson was moving along.

"The usurpers have four days to challenge your assertion that no inability exists. If they do, Congress shall decide the issue. It would have to be decided within twenty-one days from the moment the issue is joined. If I were they, the minute I delivered the inability letter and put my man in as Acting President, my first act would be to seal your files."

"There's my phone," Melinda said, and left. No phone was ringing. She was—Ericson hoped—going to get his dictabelts out of the safe next to her desk. He felt a flicker of fear. His personal diaries included not only private assessments of men in the administration and the Congress, but worst of all, the dictation during those moments of his deep depression. Hank Fowler had told him that such dictation would be good therapy.

Now Hank was chatting about a Seeing Eye dog which had just been moved into the kennels behind the swimming pool. "I should take a look at him," said Fowler, and left, too.

Smitty went out into the hallway to check the tickers, and returned right away to say, "The letters from the Cabinet were delivered. Now I'll send these."

"I have a chore to do," said Cartwright. Ericson, feeling drained and angry, knew Lucas had to make arrangements for the man with the black bag to switch over to the Acting President and to take up his position in the Vice-President's suite in the Old Executive Office Building, across the street. Let Nichols live with the responsibility of ordering a nuclear strike if the missiles come in, the President thought; it's not one of a President's happier tasks.

There was a rap on the door. "Here's Director Hewitt," Harry Bok said, announcing the head of the Secret Service.

"My duty is to seal the files," Hewitt said. "The Acting President has directed us to slap a seal on everything here in the White House. This is a terrible thing to have to do, Mr. President."

"I quite understand, Rufus."

After Hewitt left, Senator Apple launched into a reminiscence of drawing up the Twenty-fifth Amendment. As the old man rambled on, an insight flooded the President's mind.

Hank Fowler and the dog. When Melinda left the room, Hank must have remembered his copious notes of their conversations, intensely personal and intimate. So he had headed out to the kennels, where—if Ericson was right—he had hidden the cassettes in a doghouse! If a blind psychologist could respond so imaginatively and bravely to crisis, so could a blind President.

Lucas came back, tut-tutting about the way the White House was being battened down.

Ericson asked him, "Who's our nose counter in the House?"

"I shall make discreet inquiries about a floor leader, Mr. President," Cartwright replied. "By the way, I should tell you Frangipani said not to hate him, he was a better friend than you thought, and not to do anything drastic."

Ericson was decisive. "Keep a channel open to Frangipani. He carries weight in the House, and he's a pal of the Speaker's."

"BREAKFAST in this place is a treat," said Jonathan, crunching on an English muffin. Ericson remembered the way the table looked: the flatware gleamed, the linen place mats contrasted with the dark walnut of Grant's Cabinet table, white-gloved waiters hovered over the Sunday brunchers in the Family Dining Room.

Ericson wanted his close aides to have the full Sunday-at-the-White-House treatment, both as reward for loyalty and as incentive to future exertions. Melinda seemed a bit grouchy, but Marilee, the first woman presidential press secretary, was perky.

"Senator Apple has the notes in Buffie's handwriting," said Jonathan, "which he is going to wave on television today. He'll demand an investigation of what he has promised to call 'the most arrogant display of moneyed interests seeking to purchase high office in the history of this nation.'"

"All this is most important," said Lucas, "but the name of the game is One-third Plus One. We need one hundred and forty-six yes votes in the House. Smitty, you are undoubtedly already working on ways to parade individual House members in here to see with their own eyes how undisabled the President is."

"That's twenty-one a day," said Hank. "Twenty-one men times twenty-one days equals around four hundred and thirty-five, the membership of the House."

"Start herding them through here every morning at eight o'clock," Ericson ordered.

"Give them breakfast," Jonathan said, his mouth full.

"And invite their wives," added Melinda.

"And," said Ericson, "nobody knock Speaker Frelingheusen, no matter what he does." He strode out, using the long cane.

Ericson was about to take a chance. Two days before, Marilee had told him that her network boy friend had come to her with a strange probe. A professional Russian source, Gregor something, was anxious to get a message through to the President. Ericson had arranged for the Russian to take a White House tour. Melinda was to be in the ground floor China Room, and would bring Gregor to see somebody "close to the President."

On the second floor of the White House, in the Lincoln Sitting Room, the President received the Soviet agent. Melinda showed him in. Ericson wanted her there to make notes.

"I bear a private message from Premier Nikolayev," the nervous Russian said. "You are understandably interested in some evidence to support the authenticity of the message. I have none. I can only say something about myself that your intelligence agencies have undoubtedly informed you of—that I am the source of the information that was printed in Mr. Zophar's column last week."

Ericson nodded as if that were not news to him. "What is the exact message from the Soviet leader?"

"Premier Nikolayev wants you to know he has returned to his apartment in the Kremlin after a three-week visit to his uncle Felix." Ericson got the reference: Nikolayev had told him about Lubyanka Prison being on Dzerzhinski Square, named after Iron Felix Dzerzhinski of the Soviet secret police.

"Premier Nikolayev is prepared to accept your invitation," Gregor went on, "if you feel such a visit would be personally helpful." To Ericson, the mental picture was of a couple of heavy-weight fighters in the fifteenth round, clinging to each other in a clinch that kept both from collapsing.

"When was the message sent? Try to be precise."

"Probably was given the courier by the Premier Thursday night."

Before the Cabinet meeting of Friday that declared Ericson disabled. If Vasily had used the hot line, at least Curtice's vote might have been turned around. Should the message be answered in a way that returned the matter to official channels, where it would go to the Acting President?

"Take this gentleman for some coffee," Ericson said to Melinda. "I want to consider sending a message back."

When they had left, he puzzled it out. The Russians thought it was in their interest to help Ericson stay in power, because he would then be a weak President, grateful to Nikolayev for the assistance. The Soviet premise was one hundred percent wrong, and Nikolayev knew it. But Nikolayev depended for his own power on the continued false impression within the controlling Kremlin faction that Ericson was dependent upon him. This game of three-dimensional chess enabled Ericson to come to the happy conclusion that it was in America's interest for him to regain presidential power. At least as far as dealing with the Soviets was concerned.

Next question: Would it be helpful to Ericson if Nikolayev now formally accepted Ericson's invitation? Or would such an acceptance bolster Nichols, making it seem as if the Soviets had waited to respond until a new Acting President was in place?

An answer came to him. The heart of the matter was to convince the House of Representatives that Ericson's supposed blunder—of hastily inviting a deposed Soviet Premier, not knowing he was deposed—was no blunder at all. The way to prove that was to insist that the leaks about Nikolayev being ousted were untrue. The Cabinet that threw Ericson out would appear to have made its decision in the poisoned atmosphere of false foreign relations hysteria. But if it ever leaked that Ericson had exchanged messages with the Soviet Premier during the twenty-one-day period when Congress was "deciding the issue," the final vote would surely go against him. Ericson had to reject the Soviet overture in a way that still encouraged Nikolayev to assert his willingness to respond to Ericson's—not Nichols'—invitation.

He sent for Melinda and Gregor. "First point," he began. "I am not responding to any private or public message until I am in a constitutional position to do so. Second, I consider it reprehensible for anyone representing a foreign power to deliberately deceive an American journalist. Your manipulation of Samuel Zophar is repugnant." That should give Nikolayev the signal to hold to the never-happened line, and to show that the American President had invited a Soviet leader who was in power and not in jail. "Finally," said Ericson, "I intend to report this approach to the Acting President and the Secretary of State for the taking of any action they are empowered to take."

Gregor was escorted out, and Ericson dictated a memo to Melinda for Nichols and Curtice. "No rush," Ericson said. "Stick it in the interoffice mail. Or would the regular mail be slower?"

"Nothing is slower than the interoffice mail," Melinda said, in a heartfelt way.

"Incidentally, where's the suitcase with the dictabelts?"

"In a locker at National Airport. I mailed the key to my aunt in Providence."

She took big chances for his sake. How could he tell her he appreciated her? "When you're really teed off at me, Melinda, remind yourself how much I need you."

"I always do."

ERICSON spent his fifth straight morning giving a never-say-die pitch to Congressmen and fielding their questions about the previous blindness, the ambush, and the Yalta Deceit. He felt he was especially effective getting through to the wives.

Afterward he went on a training walk around the Ellipse with his new Seeing Eye dog and Hank Fowler. Then he took a dip in the pool, and had a good laugh when the mutt jumped in after him. He heard the clicking of a camera across the water, and assumed that Buffie was getting pictures.

At the edge of the pool, he asked for a phone and called the pollster. The level of Ericson support had sunk to twenty-five percent. He told the operator to play him the News Summary.

"Topic A, on all four nets, was Nikolayev's personal response to Ericson, accepting his invitation to visit the United States early this fall. Moscow briefers again poured cold water on U.S. press speculation that Nikolayev had ever been deposed or in prison.

"This story tied closely to domestic leads—the historic constitutional confrontation being fought out in the Congress. The Nikolayev response is being used as evidence that Ericson did not blunder in making the invitation.

"In the Hennessy corruption case, bad news for Ericson: the man appointed as highway commissioner in Tennessee at White House insistence turns out to have been convicted, under another name, for fraud ten years ago.

"Other developments: A group called the Committee to Protect the Presidency—made up of young lawyers—charged today that the eye doctor who resigned from the navy yesterday, Dr. Perry Lilith, has been paid off for attacking the President with the offer of a lucrative job at New York Hospital, where the board of trustees is headed by Roy Bannerman. Lilith denies this.

"*The Wall Street Journal* chides Ericson for characterizing as a bribe offer a perfectly legitimate suggestion by former Treasury Secretary Bannerman to pave the way for a productive career after his resignation."

A cheap shot, Ericson admitted, but it had relieved pressure on Buffie. Bannerman had dropped the campaign train sex angle.

Was it worth it? Was he really fighting to defend against the weakening of the presidency, or was that a rationalization? Ericson knew that if he lost in the House, he would not come back to fight again and again. He would resign permanently.

Later, wearing slacks and a sport shirt, the President, with the dog close to him, sat on the steps facing the Rose Garden. He took a deep breath of the sultry garden air.

"Looks like he's got some collie in him."

Ericson tentatively placed the Yankee twang, nasal voice—a White House gardener who sometimes said hello.

"Has he been digging up your flowers?" Ericson asked.

"No, no, he goes his way, I go mine. Never fouls the footpaths, glad to say. Dr. Fowler takes care of the kennel, too."

Ericson smiled at the picture of Hank Fowler guarding his tape cassettes in the doghouse. He pointed over to a flower bed. "What kind of tulips are those?"

After a pause, the gardener said, "I dug out the tulips in late May. Long gone."

The freezing of springtime in his mind's eye was oppressive. The President shot a question at the gardener that he had never asked anyone before: "If you were me, would you quit?" He could safely forecast the answer: Hang in there, Mr. President.

"If I had a work-connected disability," said the gardener, "and the people I put in stuck a knife in my back, I'd chuck it." Ericson did not feel up to replying. "You're wrong to make a pet out of that dog," the gardener added, moving off, "he's a working dog."

A few moments later, Ericson said to the dog, "You know what your name is? Hang in there. You hear?" He abbreviated it, "Hangin'ere."

On the day of the House vote Ericson invited his official family up to the yellow Oval Sitting Room of the residence to watch the proceedings on television. He felt light-headed, fatalistic, as on Election Day the year before. He had done everything he could to persuade, threaten, and cajole every vote that belonged to him.

Melinda sat next to him on a couch, Smitty and Marilee on one facing them. Buffie was taking pictures. Jonathan was fiddling with the TV. "Can't you get that picture better?" the President said, and drew an unembarrassed laugh. Harry watched from his wheelchair. Hank ordered the dog to lie down.

He picked up the phone and said, "Get me Hennessy." The room fell silent. When the operator reached the former chief of staff in New York, the President said, "You watching?"

Hennessy said, "Watching what?"

"There's a soap opera on today. Don't know how it'll come out."

"Don't worry, the good guys always win," Hennessy said.

"I am going to win today," Ericson said, "and you are going to win at your trial."

"Okay, ol' buddy, I'll tune in and root for you. You were good to call, Sven."

Ericson phoned Cartwright on the House floor. "How's your count?" the President asked.

"One thirty-nine plus two."

Five short. "Do your best." He hung up.

The television sound was broadcasting Speaker Frelingheusen's call for the report of the Select Committee on the Disability of the President. The committee chairman, a Republican who had run a thorough series of hearings during the past twenty-one days, rose to say, "Each member, Mr. Speaker, has been provided with the full report of this committee and several memoranda of law concerning Paragraph Two, Section Four, of the Twenty-fifth Amendment, along with the briefs submitted by the President's counsel and the Acting President's counsel." The committee report, voted unanimously, followed:

" 'The President of the United States was removed from office by a duly constituted and properly called meeting of the President's Cabinet,' " the chairman read to a silent House, " 'and the powers and duties of said office devolved upon the Vice-President in accordance with the provisions of Section Four, Paragraph Two, of the Twenty-fifth Amendment. The President, pursuant to the same paragraph, subsequently declared that no inability exists, and the Cabinet has informed both houses of the Congress of its disagreement with the President's judgment. The amendment requires that the Congress decide the issue within twenty-one days.

" 'This committee finds that the decision of the Cabinet was arrived at in proper order and in good faith. The committee also finds that the challenge of the President, and his personal judgment that no inability exists, is also lawfully arrived at. Thus the decision as to whether inability does or does not exist rests with the members of the House and Senate.' "

Frelingheusen's voice was flat. "The clerk will call the roll."

Ericson could hear the Congressmen saying aye or nay, and an occasional present to the question. A yes vote was to support Ericson's demand for reinstatement of presidential powers; one hundred and forty-six (one-third of the membership plus one) was what the commentators called his "magic number."

The clerk's voice droned ominously on. Two-thirds of the way down the roll Lucas Cartwright telephoned. "We're not picking up any new strength, Mr. President. Looks like we've got about a hundred and forty, a hundred and forty-two."

"Frangipani agree?"

"Andy thinks we'll make it, but he can't point to the votes."

"How about some of the men who are passing?" Ericson knew that some Congressmen would vote their consciences only if they had to. If it were clear that Ericson was losing, they would want to be on record as against him.

"Of the eleven who voted present, we have them all down on our list as against you."

"Any chance of reaching them?"

"These men voting present aren't leaving their seats. Most of them are in the front rows."

Ericson was ready for defeat, which he had never been in his life. He was also ready for victory, because he was used to it.

"Zwyorkin." The clerk said the last name.

"No!" shouted Zwyorkin.

The television announcer said, "That's four hundred and thirty Congressmen present and voting, five absent. Ericson has one hundred and forty votes, he's four short. Eleven representatives passed. Here is the clerk's poll of those who have not yet voted."

The clerk called the names. The first voted yes, the next two voted no. Then two yesses. The next man voted yes. A shout went up from Ericson supporters in the House, and a moan sounded in the gallery. To put the seal on the vote, the next five Congressmen also voted yes. Excitedly the television announcer said, "Ericson's got it, he had the votes in reserve!"

Ericson felt his hand being squeezed by Melinda on his left.

Harry Bok's wheelchair squeaked over and the President felt the firm hand on his arm. Jonathan was clapping. Buffie's clicking came closer and he felt her lips brush his cheek.

"Forty-one Presidents of the United States salute you," the President said to the Congress on the television screen. To Melinda he murmured, "Frangipani brought it off."

The gavel was banging, and Speaker Frelingheusen affirmed: "In accordance with Section Four of the Twenty-fifth Amendment to the Constitution, I declare that the powers and duties of the office of the President devolve upon the President."

Seconds later, Cartwright called. "Lucas, you've been one hundred percent true-blue," Ericson said, and felt a surge of admiration for the older man. "Do me a favor. Tell Mike Fong I want his resignation. Tell Emmett Duparquet he's fired."

"Have you forgotten George Curtice?"

"In victory, magnanimity. Tell Andy Frangipani I'd like to see him in the Oval Office." For the first time, Ericson felt the pleasure and the pain of being back in power.

"ANGELO Frangipani," the President said, behind the desk in the Oval Office, rolling the name around in his mouth, "I hate to consider the possibilities of intrigue, with you as kingmaker." He was telling Frangipani that he did not want to hear about any arrangements made with Speaker Frelingheusen, who had obviously delivered those last reluctant votes.

"It turned out they had the votes to impeach you," Frangipani said. "They had a majority of the House, which would have indicted you, and two-thirds of the Senate for a conviction. But they didn't have the two-thirds vote of both Houses required by the Twenty-fifth."

That was it, then; Frangipani had been convinced that if the Cabinet did not act, the Congress would—and the Twenty-fifth Amendment offered more protection to a President.

"You won," said Andy, "but you didn't get a vote of confidence."

"Governing won't be easy this way," Ericson said, opening the door for whatever suggestion Andy had. The President snapped

231

his fingers a couple of times, and his dog came to his side. The animal no longer had to be kept in the kennel, protecting Hank's cassettes. Hank had retrieved his cache, convulsing Ericson with the glum comment, "Damn mutt chewed up two of them."

"What would happen," Frangipani wondered aloud to the dog, "if your master and Nichols were both to quit?"

Frangipani's plan came clear. The third in line to the presidency was the Speaker of the House. "How would the people feel," said Ericson, "about the office changing from one party to another during a President's term?"

"You could maybe shift Democrat to Republican, as long as you didn't shift from a liberal to a conservative," said Andy.

Ericson did not want to take the thought any further at that time. He stood up, extended his hand. "Andy, your blessings come in great disguises."

Frangipani held the President's hand in the two of his own. "Let's go for a ride on your fancy yacht someday. You and me, Bannerman and Fong. Not Nichols. We'll talk."

"I wouldn't want to be party to anything that looked like a deal," Ericson said.

"Lincoln sent a message to his campaign manager at the 1860 convention, 'Make no deals in my name.' And David Davis, the manager, said, 'Hell—we're here, he's not.' Lincoln honored the deals."

"And Davis got on the Supreme Court," Ericson added. "You really want to be a judge?"

"Senator from New York," Andy corrected him. "Which I couldn't do next year if you were dragging the country and the party down. Sue me, I'm selfish."

"I wouldn't sue," said the President softly.

For two days Ericson cut himself off from the News Summary, which he knew was filled with apopletic demands for his resignation after a "vote of no confidence."

Sitting on the steps leading down to the Rose Garden at dusk,

Hank Fowler said to the President, "You're acting funny after your big victory."

Ericson smiled. "You ought to be able to describe my mental attitude with something better than 'acting funny.'"

"You've introverted," said Hank clinically. "After a period of action, you're letting repressed fears catch up with you."

"You wonder why I want to hang on to the presidency?"

"I wonder if you want to anymore. Now that you've defended the office, you'd just as soon chuck it. But you don't want to do anything at a time when you're tired and scared."

Ericson put his hand on his chest. "I always thought the expression 'my heart sunk' was just an expression. But whenever I think of Hennessy behind bars, my heart drops in my chest."

They got up, walked to the Oval Office without a mistake, and Hank went his way. Ericson sat in the dark, the dog at his feet. Melinda buzzed, and said that the Secretary of State was there and wondered if he could see the President.

"George, have dinner with me." Ericson could sense the surprise and delight as Curtice stammered his acceptance.

At dinner, Curtice put the question: "Why haven't you asked for my resignation, Mr. President?"

Ericson's mind framed the honest answer: firing Curtice would alienate blacks, while ostentatiously keeping him bought Ericson some support in that area. Aloud he said, "George, I understood your vote last month, and what you did at Yalta will be remembered kindly by history. And most important, I need you."

"Mr. President, you have just created yourself the most profoundly loyal Secretary of State any President ever had, from here on in." The deep voice picked up. "Next topic: How long is 'from here on in'?"

"Figure at least one whole term, maybe two."

"That's good news," the Secretary said. "Now let's move on Nikolayev. You proved you didn't need him, but he still needs you. Let's get him over here and prop him up."

"I concur," said Ericson. He buzzed for Melinda. "Melinda, the Secretary is going to move forward with the Soviet Union in set-

233

ting the date for Nikolayev's visit. George, you work with her."

Curtice left.

Ericson wanted to get the feel of the White House again. He strapped the walking handle on the dog, felt the animal become an extension of his arm, and they set out. Into the State Dining Room, around the long table, to the mantelpiece. He ran his fingers over the inscription cut in the marble, and read it to the dog: " 'May none but Honest and Wise men rule under This Roof.' John Adams." They continued to the East Room. He felt the dog tense, sensed the Secret Service man directly ahead, said hello and walked around him.

He stopped halfway up the stairs and sat on the landing. Good house, he thought; not a palace, not a museum. Would he weaken it more by staying or by going? Sven Ericson had proven he could not be pushed out; the Twenty-fifth Amendment, with its potential for mischief, would be narrowed by his precedent. And now Andy had skillfully eliminated Ericson's second strongest reason for staying. If Nichols could be removed and if Mort Frelingheusen were the successor, the nation would be well served. He followed the dog up the stairs to the residence, aware that he was going through the decision-making process. A part of the apparatus was missing, he knew: a partner, someone to brag to and lean on. A loner's life had its advantages, but sometimes the blessed privacy wore thin.

The dog took its place at the door to his bedroom, next to the Secret Service man, and Ericson went in, closing the door behind him. Someone moved. His first reaction was annoyance, until a small but very familiar voice said, "It's me, Melinda."

That threw him. After a long pause, Ericson managed to get out, "Long time no see."

"That's the sort of thing Hennessy would say," she whispered.

The double meaning of his own line registered on him. "I used to write all of Hennessy's black humor," he said.

"Are you mad at me?"

"No. A little surprised, that's all." He reached over and touched her familiar face, then brought her forward for a serious kiss.

"You're a lovely woman," he said afterward.

"I feel awkward," she said, "after eight years."

"You needn't."

"What especially killed me was when you found out about Duparquet, it didn't bother you a bit."

In fact, it had, Ericson recalled. "Course not," he said. "I never thought of you like this."

"I suppose I should go."

"No," he said. "Stay with me—from now on." After a pause, "You know, I've been thinking, for years I've only seen what I expected to see, not the woman who was there." Changing mood, he said, "What time is it?"

"Only about eleven."

"Get me Frangipani."

"Back to work." She handed him the receiver when the Secretary came on the line.

"Be at the dock tomorrow night at eight," Ericson said, "for a ride on the fancy yacht. Bring your friends." He handed Melinda the phone. "Tell the navy I want the *Sequoia II* tomorrow night for dinner, four people."

After Melinda had made the arrangements, he said, "Now I want to work this out. When you see an inconsistency, holler. Don't let me get away with anything, and do not let your own prejudices get in our way. Okay?" He felt good that she was there.

THE President was the last to board. Hangin'ere led his master up the gangway. The four men sat together aft, in the open air, making conversation about the dog, until Bannerman abruptly said, "Congratulations on your victory, Mr. President, if you can call a vote of no confidence a victory."

"Good ol' Roy," said Frangipani. "Tell us how you really feel."

Fong cut in. "You won fair and square, Mr. President."

"Let's get down to business," Bannerman said. "Mike told me he and Andy were cooking up a scheme."

"Andy"—disapproval was in Ericson's tone—"you said this would be a smoking of the peace pipe."

"I lied," said Frangipani. "Mike and I have a bomb to drop on both of you. The President will be damned if he'll ever resign if it means that Arnold Nichols becomes President. Right?"

Ericson nodded.

"Here's the solution. You resign, Mr. President, upon receiving the resignation of the Vice-President. The Speaker of the House would then become President."

"Ridiculous," said Bannerman.

"The difficulty," Fong said carefully, "which we recognize, is that it would transfer power in the executive branch from the Democrats to the Republicans."

"No doubt that's a drawback," said Andy. "That's why the President and Vice-President run as a team."

"I don't like it," Ericson said. "Smacks too much of a deal."

"People would stand for a lot," Bannerman said heavily, "to get you out of the White House."

"I have to feed my dog," said the President. "After I do that, we can all have dinner." He went below, to give Fong and Frangipani a chance to work Bannerman over, and to give the double-resignation idea a final review in his own mind.

Fifteen minutes later, Ericson joined the others in the main cabin. After the four had wolfed down their steaks, Bannerman cast the first light of encouragement on the idea. "If you did something like this—and I'm sure Nichols would never stand for it—the successor would have to have a coalition government."

Fong put it forward: "There would have to be some assurance that the new President would appoint a Vice-President from the same party as the resigning President."

Ericson rose. "Nobody can commit the next President to do anything. It would be immoral to ascend to the presidency on the basis of some promise. Let me show you the fo'c'sle, Andy."

The two went up front. "He's nibbling," said Ericson.

"What do you suppose he'll take?" Frangipani said.

"Bannerman wants the vice-presidency for himself, Andy. Look. I cannot even consider it. If you think I am considering it, you're mistaken." Then the President added, "But you've been mistaken before. Go talk to him." It was a pleasure dealing with Andy.

"Come back in ten minutes," said Andy.

"'Make no deals in my name,'" quoted the President, smiling.

Ericson waited while Frangipani dangled the vice-presidency in front of Bannerman. Ericson left it to Andy to get Fong and Bannerman to agree not to ask the next President in advance for such an improper guarantee.

When he came back to the open deck aft, the yacht had arrived at the point in the Potomac opposite George Washington's home, Mount Vernon. The crew lined up for the formal salute, and the tinny tape played "The Star-Spangled Banner." Ericson, saluting, asked his predecessor's forgiveness for what he had decided to do to protect the office the first President had established.

"Andy has made it clear," said Bannerman, after the salute ended, "that nobody can commit the next President to anything. He has given me his promise of 'best efforts.'"

"I have promised nobody anything," said the President firmly, hoping Bannerman would not believe him.

"Of course," Bannerman said impatiently. "I will undertake to get Arnold Nichols into your office tomorrow with his resignation in hand. If I do that, do I have your word that your resignation will be delivered to the Secretary of State within the hour?"

Ericson looked downcast. Solemnly he said, "You have my word. But if anybody approaches Frelingheusen, all bets are off."

"Agreed," said Bannerman.

They sat in silence under the stars as the yacht headed back up the Potomac.

"BANNERMAN's on the phone," Melinda said. "Can I listen in?"

"Take notes," said the President.

"Arnold Nichols is here with me," said Bannerman briskly. "He wishes to speak with you."

"Mr. President?" The Vice-President's voice was strained. "I have written my letter of resignation. I am doing so on the understanding that you will submit your own resignation within one hour after the effective moment of mine."

"Your understanding is correct," Ericson told him. "Come to the Cabinet Room at four o'clock. The Secretary of State will be there. He's the one authorized to receive our resignations."

"I'm convinced it's the best thing for the country." The Vice-President did not sound convinced; Bannerman must have worked him over severely.

As soon as the President hung up, Melinda came in. "I arranged to have the Secretary of State here. And you might want to write your resignation in your own hand."

"Yes." An inch in from the paper's edge he began, "To the Secretary of State: I am sworn to preserve, protect, and defend the Constitution of the United States of America. To make certain that my responsibility is carried out, I hereby resign the office of President." He signed his name, with the date. "How's it look?"

Melinda did not respond right away. After a moment she choked out, "It looks cockeyed."

He tried a couple more times, until she was satisfied.

He arranged for the Chief Justice to come to the Oval Office at four thirty on a matter of some urgency, and to bring his robes. He called the Speaker of the House.

"Mort, I wonder if you'd be available to come by about four thirty today. I need your wife here, too."

Short pause. "We'll be there. Four thirty."

Ericson put down the phone. "Got a Bible?"

"I'll speak to Mrs. Frelingheusen," Melinda said, "and ask her to bring her family Bible. Also to bring her two children."

He nodded, then snapped his fingers. "The oath. It's not the usual federal oath, and the Chief Justice doesn't always know—"

"I have the right one here, typed on a card for him."

"What would I do without you?" Then the meaning of that question struck him. A fear clutched at him of what life would be like without her. "I need you, you know that."

"This is no time to go into that," she said crisply. "The whole government is about to change—"

"It can all wait," he said. "You coming with me, or not?"

"As what?"

239

That stopped him. "As everything," he said, surprised.

"We'll talk about it later."

"I want you to come with me," he said quickly but seriously, "and be my wife."

"I'd like that," she said.

"We get married in a week," he said.

"A month. If we're going to do it, we'll do it right."

"Deal," he said. He pulled her to him.

"We're in the Oval Office," she said after a moment.

"Okay," he said. "Any other last-minute acts?" He leaned back, swiveling his chair and looking out at the brightness, feeling relieved, excited, melancholy, authoritative, knowing that—for a change—this was one of those instances when he had started a chain of events that would march to the conclusion he had intended.

AT FIVE minutes past four the President entered the Cabinet Room. The shaken voice of Secretary of State George Curtice informed him, "Sir, the Vice-President here has just submitted his resignation."

The President smiled and said, "Yes. I brought along my letter, too." He unfolded his letter, put it on the table, took out a pen that he intended to keep, and said, "What time is it?"

"Four seven."

The President wrote the time on the letter, held it out, and Curtice took it from him. Sven Ericson was no longer President of the United States. He felt no different yet.

"George, you go to the Situation Room. I took the liberty of placing a hot-line call for you to Premier Nikolayev, so you can inform him of this action and of the swearing-in of President Frelingheusen. Arnold, please come with me."

They went through to the Oval Office, and in a few moments Melinda ushered in the Speaker of the House. Ericson, in the center of the room, extended his hand. When Speaker Frelingheusen took it, Ericson said, "Good luck, Mr. President.

"A few moments ago," Ericson continued, still holding Frelingheusen's hand, "the Vice-President resigned, and then I resigned. Under the Presidential Succession Act, the office—and the powers and the duties—of the President devolve upon you."

"I was dumbfounded," said President Frelingheusen. "It just wouldn't sink in. Did you ever have an experience like that?"

"Never," said Ericson. They were in the wing chairs next to the fireplace in the Oval Office. It was ten in the morning, and Ericson was to leave by helicopter from the White House lawn at noon. President Frelingheusen, his wife, and kids would move in later that day. "But there was no way of telling you in advance. I didn't have Nichols' resignation in hand."

"Nikolayev," President Frelingheusen said. "You've got him coming in a couple of weeks. I'll keep the appointment."

"Keep George Curtice on at least through the visit," Ericson advised. "Nikolayev's the front for the hard-liners in the Kremlin, who thought I needed him to stay in office. Squeeze Vasily hard on lowering the throw weight. We might not get a chance like this for years, and it may help hold down nuclear development in the Arab-Israeli bloc."

Ericson thought it was probable that Nikolayev would be killed in a plane crash soon, now that his usefulness in dealing with Ericson was ended. "The reason we didn't have this talk before you became President," Ericson said clearly, "was that I wanted to be sure that you took office with no commitments to anybody."

"What of the press speculation about a coalition government?"

"You and I have no understanding on it, unspoken or otherwise. I suppose I have to warn you about one man in my party," said Ericson, as if it were painful. "Roy Bannerman is a man of great power and cunning, and of bad personal character." Ericson knew Frelingheusen set considerable store by personal character.

"Any funny business in the Treasury?"

"Not that I'm aware of, although it might be an idea to look into the relationship between the Treasury, the Export-Import Bank, and the private banks in London. Could be some corruption there." He paused, as if debating whether to go on.

"Bad personal character, you said?"

"He's the sort of man who gets his kicks in slapping around women," Ericson blurted.

"You know that for a fact?"

"An absolute fact, from a woman he abused."

"The SOB."

"Don't be surprised if he comes to you saying he was promised the vice-presidency. He got no promise from me on anything."

"He's finished. What's your assessment of the Big Flower?"

"Be a good Senator. Ready for even more, maybe."

"Um." From the direction of the questioning, Ericson got the feeling that Andy had a good chance of becoming Vice-President.

"Speaking as a civil libertarian," said the new President, "I thought the Attorney General's prosecution of Mark Hennessy was a disgrace. Four days from grand jury appearance to perjury indictment, that's entrapment. Unpardonable."

Ericson shut his eyelids. His successor had worked the syllables "pardon" into the conversation. Frelingheusen was saying that he would do the right thing by Hennessy if he were convicted.

"Your staff is waiting to say good-by," said Frelingheusen.

The two men left the Oval Office for the East Room, where the staff was gathered in a large circle. Ericson took his time, working his way around the circle, saying farewell individually to everyone from Smitty to the White House gardener. When Jonathan Trumbull said his name aloud, Ericson asked, "Where's your girl?"

"She's been following you, taking pictures."

"Is there a place I can stand?" Ericson asked the agent behind him. They took him to a podium in the corner of the room near the piano, and the staff pressed in around him.

"There's a lot of sniffling and snuffling out there," Ericson said in a strong voice. "Let's cut it all out. The first thing is to stop feeling sorry for ourselves. Oh, I'm sorry to miss all the excitement of being at the center. And I'm sorry I didn't have the chance to do my thing on inflation and unemployment, but I'm not about to go riding off into the wilderness. I'm forty-eight years old and I have a whole generation of active life ahead of me—" The room exploded with applause at that, but he stepped on it. "Please, what I want to say is, okay, I'm blind. Not totally blind anymore, and I can see a little better every week, so there's real hope. But blind or not, I'm going to learn to use the skills anybody can learn to lead a full life. After a while, I'll be able to cope with certain jobs as well as anybody.

"That includes political jobs. So I may get active politically in a year or so. Or maybe I'll become the goddamnedest economist you ever saw, or the best teacher in the country. One way or another, you'll hear from me.

"As for my personal life," he went on, "I'll get married again one day. I have the woman in mind, but I've made enough news this week." Affectionate applause. "Let me close on a personal note to a fine group of people whom I like and respect.

"This blindness thing. It changes a man. Sometimes it leaves him in a bog of self-pity. Other times it dredges up some compensating strengths. Any sudden handicap forces you to look at yourself and other people differently. I'm not as detached as I used to be. The cliché is 'compassion.'

"I recall, in church as a kid, an old hymn." Only Buffie would know that now he was stretching a point a little.

> *"Amazing grace—how sweet the sound—*
> *That saved a wretch like me!*
> *I once was lost, but now am found,*
> *Was blind, but now I see.*

"Darkness has a way of concentrating the mind, helping you see what's right."

Ericson had to stop because the force of his own rhetoric unexpectedly affected him. He felt he might well be back in this house once again, as an economic adviser, perhaps, or even more, but not as a long-forgotten visitor.

Accompanied by the new President, he walked slowly down the stairs, out the diplomatic entrance, to the South Lawn, where the sound told him a fair-sized crowd was gathered.

Standing with President Frelingheusen at the beginning of the carpet out on the grass, Ericson took the honor guard's salute. This ceremony was being televised, he knew, and was being watched around the world with the awe, reverence, cynicism, and disbelief that accompany an orderly transition of American power.

When the Marine Band struck up "Hail to the Chief," Ericson came to attention. At its conclusion, he shook the President's hand, embraced the First Lady, took his dog's halter, and began to walk alone out to the chopper, where Hank and Melinda were already aboard. He walked in dignity, never wavering from the center of the red carpet.

Halfway out, he heard somebody start to sing "Amazing Grace." The crowd picked it up—young and old—and the band quickly shifted to it. The dog signaled to Ericson through the halter that he had three more steps to go. He took them, and at the helicopter stairs, he turned to the crowd and the camera and the White House. The impact of everyone singing that music with such genuine affection slammed into him.

Ericson took off his tinted glasses, wiped his eyes, waved once to one side, once to the other, turned, and followed his dog up the steps.

★ ★ ★

At forty-seven, William Safire is a tall, gangling man with a slow smile who has no plans just now for another novel. "In life you have to know who you are," he says. "And I'm a columnist." Twice a week *The New York Times* carries a pithy—often polemical—commentary by Safire, usually on U.S. politics.

Few Washington observers, and certainly few novelists, are more seasoned in the U.S. political arena than Safire. In 1965, already a veteran newsman, TV producer, and president of his own public relations firm, Safire volunteered as an unpaid speech writer in the Nixon campaign for the 1968 Republican nomination. After Nixon's election,

Safire went with him to the White House as a special assistant. Having experienced first victorious euphoria, and later the agony of Watergate, Safire left in 1973 to become a syndicated columnist and to write a memoir, *Before the Fall*, which was published in 1975. Daniel Schorr, in his review of the book, observed that it was "the first real post-Watergate view of Nixon by someone who was both there and innocent."

William Safire

"But," says Safire, "no one really paid any attention to it" (a modest exaggeration), so he decided to write a novel, "because you can *show* rather than *tell* the moral dilemmas." This time attention was paid: the paperback rights alone to *Full Disclosure* were sold for over a million dollars.

He had never written fiction before, so he called up a friend, Herman Wouk, author of *The Caine Mutiny* (and four other Reader's Digest Condensed Books selections), for advice. "Don't read Dostoevski or Tolstoy," Wouk said. "They were both geniuses. Read Trollope."

"So," says Safire, "I sat down and read *Barchester Towers*, and it did help with plotting and developing characters." After writing his first hundred pages he felt he had the hang of it, although "it did seem strange, as an old newspaperman, not to have to check anything." But much of what another novelist might have checked was already in Safire's head, the product of his having lived through a national crisis in the White House.

Does he think, looking back, that being President is enjoyable? No, not for most men, he says. "You have to be a special breed even to run for the office—with a quality of leadership, a whopping ego, and a very thick skin. So this limits the kind of man you get in the White House, and once they get there they like it—most of the time."

Would he want a son of his to go into politics? "Sure, you bet. It's a great way to live fully. It's really bloodless war—like swinging a leaded bat in batting practice. After that, swinging a real bat is child's play."

How about writing? "Well, that's something else again. I really sweat over my columns. It took me a year to write the novel. I don't know a writer who writes easily—that's never child's play."

They called
the little lost dog

Bel Ria

and no life that he touched was
ever the same

A CONDENSATION OF THE NOVEL BY

Sheila Burnford

ILLUSTRATED BY GUY DEEL

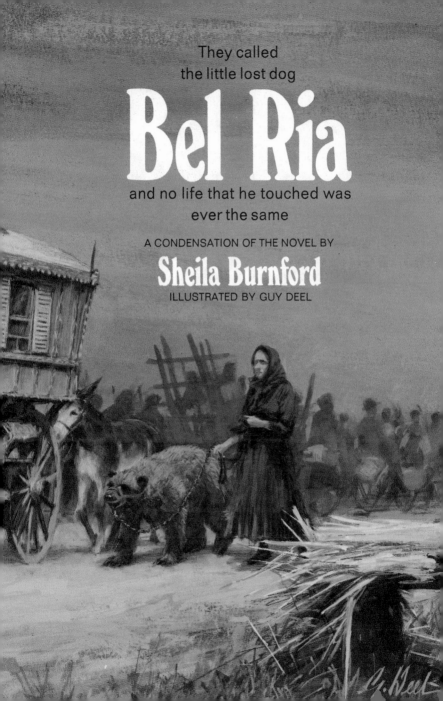

They are all that is left of a
traveling circus act: a small gray dog
and an impish capuchin monkey. When a German
dive-bomber machine-guns away their close-knit
Gypsy life, they set out across war-torn France
and find the only link with their lost world—a
wounded British soldier. For the
indomitable little dog, Bel Ria, their
journey is the beginning of a
heartwarming odyssey. As the war rages
around him he does what he knows best:
amuse and take the minds of men off other
things. To the weary he gives courage;
to the lonely, love and laughter.
Sheila Burnford's touching tale
is a rare and timeless treat.

CHAPTER ONE

ITS flaking red paint almost obscured by dust, an old swaybacked gray horse between the shafts, the caravan stood out even among the bizarre lines of transport that filled the last free roads of France that bright June morning in 1940. Alone it creaked along against the refugee traffic, the endless frieze of handcarts and ancient perambulators, wheelbarrows and farm carts, the weary disillusioned people. All were on the open road, but only the caravan belonged by custom to the open road; only those who lived and had their world by it were true vagrants. A few weeks ago such passersby would have stirred curiosity, but today there was merely a sullen resentment and distrust of strangers who took a road leading back toward the approaching enemy.

Even the little dog that led the caravan was different. There were other dogs on the road, but taking their mood from their owners, they padded along dispiritedly, tails low. This alien dog that passed the other way took vivid form: head and tail held high, it trotted along with cheerful intent, sometimes almost prancing, at a carefully kept distance ahead. It appeared to lead the horse, for the reins lay slack in the hands of an ancient man huddled in shawls on the wide seat, a tiny monkey perched on his shoulder.

Walking at the side, a tall, black-clad granite-faced woman led a shabby bear on a chain, its muzzled head swinging low. A donkey tied to the back of the caravan completed the procession.

Hard pressed by the German spearheads thrusting to close the gap between them and the last escape route in France, an intermittent stream of military traffic and troops moved by on the opposite side of the road, heading for St.-Nazaire, on the Brittany coast. The weary stragglers from the general retreat across France after Dunkirk threaded through the painfully slow civilian congestion with frequent holdups. On the northbound side, only a rare rearguard squadron of light tanks, armored cars, or the occasional army truck being driven back to the wrecking dump at Montoir-de-Bretagne pulled out to pass the caravan, so that almost always it was the civilian traffic opposite that had to give way, and this sometimes engendered outright hostility.

Corporal Donald Sinclair of the Royal Army Service Corps, who through one of the more lunatic entanglements of red tape had orders to drive his empty truck back from the coast to be wrecked at Montoir, was inching along at the heels of the caravan, unable to make his way around it.

It was hot and dusty, the sun beating down from a cloudless sky. At noon there was a long halt while a convoy passed. The black-clad woman took out a goatskin water carrier, which she handed up to the old man; then she drank. The bear, tethered in the shade of a hedge, sank down on its haunches, forepaws extended, begging. She filled a bottle; clasping it like a child, the bear inserted the open end through its muzzle and tilted the contents down its throat. A bucket was set, in turn, before the horse and donkey. Then she filled an enamel bowl, and the dog came running to lap.

A young woman with a child on her hip crossed the road and held up a pitcher, asking for water. The dark face of the elder woman was unresponsive, and the younger woman resorted to sign language. Finally she shouted. The dark woman continued to hold the bowl while her dog lapped. Only when the other spat contemptuously into the bowl did she straighten up, and with eyes blazing she hurled the bowl at the young woman's skirts.

Quick as a flash, the mother picked it up and aimed it at the little dog, who leaped for the driving seat. A stone flew across the road and found a target on the bear's nose. Another stone rattled against the caravan.

Sinclair got out of his truck, prepared to do he knew not what, but he was saved from action by a tank rumbling by. It met the last carrier of the convoy in the middle of the road, and chaos intervened. When the way was cleared, he returned to find the caravan lurched precariously in the ditch, the dog barking, while the woman alternately pushed and hung on to the tilting side. With the aid of a passing dispatch rider and a rifleman, Sinclair got the caravan back on the road.

The woman rummaged in her skirt pocket and extracted a few coins. With a smile of refusal, Sinclair pointed to the water carrier and indicated that he would rather have a drink, but she up-ended the skin, with a wry smile at its emptiness.

They were standing by the driving seat, their heads level with the dog sitting there, his bright, alert eyes under a shaggy topknot going from one face to the other. The doll-sized monkey, now perched on the dog's back, peered ludicrously over the topknot. The woman clicked her fingers. The monkey transferred to her shoulder; the dog jumped down and rose to his hind legs beside her. With the occasional slight motion of her hands she put him through a repertoire of tricks. Accompanied by the tinkling of a bell around his neck, he strutted back and forth, turned three rapid backward somersaults, then finally sat up with one paw raised in salute. The woman's face softened with pride. The dog looked back at her with beaming eyes, his slight body quivering as she tossed him a tidbit, which he caught in midair.

Sinclair applauded. Clearly this display had been his reward. He turned to go. The monkey smacked its lips in a loud kissing noise, then held out an upturned pink paw. The soldier laughed and shook it. "Good-by," he said. "And good luck—*bonne chance, madame.*" But she was hurrying to untie the bear.

She tugged and shouted, but the bear lay unmoving, its eyes sunken. She broke off a branch and raised it threateningly. The bear whimpered and winced, and at this she gave up the struggle. As Sinclair was about to drive off, she ran toward him and pointed to his rifle. Somehow she made him understand: there was no food for it, it was only an added burden, this dancing bear. . . . Sinclair did not hesitate; to his mind this sorry beast would be better out of its misery. It was all over in a second, and the soldier pulled some branches over. The woman shook his hand warmly; then, with a smile, she swung up beside the old man and took the reins. She accorded the soldier a brief nod as he drove past.

The retreating traffic petered out markedly as Sinclair drove on. When he reached Montoir, he handed the truck over to the wrecking crew and was ordered to make his way back to St.-Nazaire for embarkation. "Get there after dusk," the sergeant advised. "It's not a healthy place in daylight."

There was only one truck left at the dump for the eventual transportation of the wrecking crew itself, so Sinclair would have to take his chances of a lift on the road.

At the very moment of leaving the blazing dump at Montoir, ironically, after weeks of bombing and shellfire, Sinclair was wounded; a tin from a burning mobile canteen exploded and tore a jagged path across his ribs, so that every breath he took now was a searing reminder. Someone had covered the wound with a field dressing.

He shouldered his rifle and pack and started off. He had lost a good deal of blood and he was very tired. Dazed and numb, as he walked he thought of his young wife, working in a munitions factory; of his father, a solitary old man in the white cottage that had been home in the long West Highland glen. . . .

A countryman all his life, until he had shed his keeper's tweeds for a uniform in 1939, Sinclair tried to measure his walk now in terms of landmarks on the lonely road that snaked around the loch shore from the cottage to, say, Ballochmyle village. . . . Sick and giddy, he stood at the side of the road, looking in vain for the ruined keep that should be coming into view. Suddenly his knees gave way, the world went into a spin, and he folded gently into a shallow ditch.

He came to and found himself looking into a pair of merry, interested eyes that he recognized immediately, one partly obscured by a few wisps of hair of a familiar topknot. As the dog's head bent closer he heard a faint tinkling. He saw a pair of worn espadrilles, thick black stockings, and a dusty black skirt.

He raised his head and looked around, wincing at the stab of pain. The caravan was drawn up beside the road. Sinclair tried to get to his feet but faltered. The woman was speaking with an incomprehensible urgency as she pointed down the road. She slung his rifle over her shoulder; then, with an arm like steel, she drew him out of the ditch and hurried him up and through the back door of the caravan. He heard the noise of approaching engines and understood her haste. She pushed him onto a narrow bunk at the same time as she scooped bundles of sacks and quilts off an elaborate brass bedstead opposite. She thrust the rifle under the sagging mattress; then, almost before he knew it, Sinclair was stretched out under the bundles. She indicated a tiny ventilation grille at the side, sliding it fractionally open before closing the shutters. Then he felt the light weight of the dog as it stretched across his thighs. The door slammed, and seconds later the caravan swayed into movement. Sinclair gave himself up for the moment to the darkness, the steady *clop-clop* of hoofs, and drifted away.

An alteration in the weight across his thighs roused him, and he heard the tinkle of an alerted head. The caravan halted, and now there were men's voices, harsh and commanding. The caravan must have reached one of the forward German posts. He heard the woman's voice, apparently arguing but not understood by her interrogators, and the sound of heavy boots approaching. As the door was flung open he lay rigid, his breath held. He felt the dog sit up and heard the woman's voice again. Then, extraordinarily, the sound of laughter. The dog jumped down, the boots and voices moved off, and someone closed the door.

Cautiously he put his eye to the tiny strip of light from the ventilation grille. The effect was dramatic, like looking down on a small stage, for he could see only a semicircle of boots and the gray green of German uniforms tucked into them. In the center, now adorned with a small cluster of bells secured to the topknot and around each forepaw, was the little dog. Only a few inches away from Sinclair's eyes were the black skirt and dusty espadrilles of the woman, the toe of one of them raised even as he heard three flute-like notes close to his head. Evidently the old man was providing the music. On the fourth note the toe began to tap, and the dog rose to his hind legs and began to dance. The tune had a lilting rhythm, and in perfect time he pirouetted in a circle, forepaws out and head held high. At the end of each phrase the dog nodded, so that the bells accompanied the last three notes of the repeated phrase. Then he brought the forepaws into action, one at a time, each set of bells in a different pitch from the nodding head.

Not far away, guns rumbled a reminder. Three-quarters of the Western world lay reeling in the bonds of occupation, the wake of smoldering destruction left by these gray-green uniforms. A few short miles would soon end the agony of France, and then all Europe would be overrun—yet for this moment, in this one place, there was nothing but a silvery tinkling and a lilting tune and an audience spellbound before a dog who danced to the bidding of the flute. It was the performance of a virtuoso; the little dog danced as though he lived for it.

So enchanted had Sinclair been that he felt a momentary irritation when the skirt moved and the palm of a hand, occasionally lowered and raised against it, obscured his view, bringing the reality that these concealed signals probably coincided with the movements of head and paws. Yet the dog never appeared to look anywhere but directly ahead. The flute quickened in tempo and the little dancer spun in a small tight circle, the bells sounding wildly; and then, like a clockwork toy running down, slower and slower, down onto his haunches, shaking the bells on each extended forepaw in turn; the paws lowered to the dust, the body following, until, finally, the last shake of bells to the final note of the flute, the head drooped and the dog lay still.

There was a hush, then a round of applause. The woman spoke one soft sibilant, and the dog leaped into life to make a comic bow to the semicircle of boots. The fingers clicked and he came run-

ning. The fingers removed the bells from the paws, then slipped
into a pocket to return with some small reward of food. Two arms
now made a circle, and the dog jumped through it and out of
Sinclair's sight. Next the monkey scuttled into view, holding a tin
cup. Above the guffaws of laughter Sinclair heard the rattle of
coins. The show was over, and as though to affirm this, there was a

burst of mortar fire followed by a crescendo of revving engines.

When the caravan started up again, Sinclair felt it swaying to a right-angled turn. At least they were not traveling away from the coast now; he must get out as soon as possible. He lay still until he reckoned that they must have covered a reasonable distance. Then, summoning every ounce of strength, he pushed aside the covers and retrieved his rifle. He tapped on the half door behind the driving seat. It opened a crack and the woman turned to look back along the potholed road. She gave a grunt of apparent satisfaction, but when Sinclair pushed the door wider, intending to jump, she pressed it back and spoke in an unexpectedly sweet voice. Words that were as incomprehensible as ever, but their message was clear: he must get under cover again. To his insistent repetition of "St.-Nazaire, *St.-Nazaire* . . ." she merely nodded calmly. Then, as though to reassure him, she cracked the whip above the horse's ears and increased the pace.

Presently they turned off the road and creaked to a halt. The woman came through, opened a shutter, and a shaft of sunlight fell on a bright red stain on the soldier's blouse. The dog jumped on the bed and sniffed at it until the woman pushed him aside and undid the buttons, her face concerned. She replaced the field dressing with what looked like a wad of moss, smearing it first with aromatic salve out of a rusty tin, then bound it with a strip torn off the hem of her underskirt. The effect was extraordinarily soothing.

The caravan was on a sandy track under a clump of pines. In an almost leisurely fashion the woman unharnessed the horse; then she helped the old man down and seated him on a folding stool. Next she lighted a small pressure stove, which was soon hissing beneath a blackened billycan. Lastly, accompanied by the dog, with the little monkey around his neck, she walked to the top of a rise and surveyed the land. Satisfied, she turned back and brewed bitter, strong tea, lacing Sinclair's mug from a small medicine bottle rummaged out of the old man's pocket.

The concoction flowed through Sinclair's veins in a heartening molten fire. As he sipped, she took a twig and sketched a map on the sandy ground; here was a back road, too meandering for military traffic, that eventually met up with a secondary road leading into St.-Nazaire. He must set off cross-country for that.

Suddenly the woman said, "*Vive la France!*" Sinclair looked up, startled at this announcement, delivered for the first time in a recognizable language. The dog interpreted by rolling over and over in the sand, then sitting up with a ludicrous imitation of a salute. The doting expression on the dark face was reflected in the intense concentration of the eyes below. She pointed, and the dog jumped up onto the donkey's back. She felt in her pocket, found nothing there, and laid her hand on his head in reward instead.

It was time to go. Unable to express his gratitude in words to this enigmatic, indomitable woman who had taken such a risk for him, Sinclair spoke the one universally accepted word, "Bravo!" and he too patted the dog's head.

The old man suddenly made a grunting imperative noise, holding out the medicine bottle. Only when he saw his offering stowed in the soldier's pocket did he sink again within his shawls. Then Sinclair said good-by and set off.

On the crest of the rise he looked back. The dog, with the monkey astride his back, watched his departure with interest.

CHAPTER TWO

SINCLAIR covered the ground in easy strides, surprisingly refreshed, the pain warmly contained under the moss dressing. It could not be more than ten miles to the coast, and he reckoned on reaching the docks after nightfall, when the rescue ships could steal in under cover of darkness.

He skirted the last field, and as he emerged onto the back road he heard the engine of a Stuka, and saw it sweep toward him below treetop level. As he flung himself down, with a gasp of pain in his ribs, the Stuka screamed over, its machine gun raising spurts of earth. "Bloody lunatic!" shouted Sinclair. There had been nothing in the fields but a scattering of cattle and himself.

He started off again. Presently he was overtaken by an RASC sergeant on an ancient bicycle. Sinclair stepped out beside him.

"Watch out for a daredevil of the skies in a Stuka," he said. "The type that would shoot up a turnip field for the hell of it."

"*Him—*" said the sergeant, disgust flooding his face. "He conquered a couple of Gypsies and a wagon back there."

"In a clump of pines—an old man and a woman—and animals?"

"I wouldn't know about the animals, but there were two bodies all right," said the sergeant. "The wagon was blazing. . . ."

"There was a dog and a monkey," said Sinclair wearily. "It was a little circus act."

"Probably copped it too," said the sergeant, and pedaled off.

Sinclair walked on, but now he was only conscious of an infinite hurt, and the reproachful ache in his mind that if they had not turned off the road for him, they would still be alive—the old flute player and his mischievous little monkey, that rock-strong woman and her shadow the dog. Even the old horse and the patient donkey, all senselessly wiped out.

An hour later, as he turned from wary custom to look back, he saw, less than a hundred yards behind, the furtive figure of a dog slinking along the road. The dog stopped, cowering, and a tiny face with anxious eyes peered over its head.

The dog crept forward, eyes holding in recognition, tail quivering, but Sinclair returned no recognition; there was no place for these animals in his life. Turning abruptly, he continued on without a backward glance, forcing them out of his mind as determinedly as he forced his pace.

In the mellow light of late afternoon he heard the booming of coastal guns. Near St.-Nazaire he saw a lone raider unload a stick of bombs over a field. He crossed the field afterward. The last bomb had scooped a crater deep into the sand of a rabbit warren. The rabbits now lay in a cluster, outwardly unharmed, as though dropped by some retrieving dog.

Sinclair stopped, unable to tear his eyes away. Suddenly the dog appeared, standing utterly still, his head up, as though pulled back by the monkey's paws around his throat. Two pairs of eyes stared at him. It was as though they drew him down to their plight and size, so that he was in proportion to the animals dead and alive of this ruined little world. In a sudden rage at the desecration, he shouted and swore at the dog and the monkey. They must not follow him, they must find some other human association. "Go back!" he yelled. "*Allez!*" He picked up a stone, threw it, deliberately short. The monkey buried its head, but the dog crouched steadfast, its eyes unwavering.

It was useless. Once more he turned, and set off at such a cathartic pace that he reached the outskirts of St.-Nazaire before sunset. Only then did he look back. They were still there. But in the town center he lost them. In the empty cobbled streets he took cover near shuttered houses against the flak and shrapnel. He joined a file of silent men converging on the docks.

The bombardment increased, and Sinclair found his way to the sandbagged emplacement of a wrecked gun. For hours he crouched within the shelter with a dozen or so other men. There was an exchange of experiences over the last hectic weeks, but finally the talk fell away and the group dozed fitfully.

Unable to ease his ribs into a comfortable position, Sinclair remained awake. Taking a packet of cigarettes out of his pocket, he came across the medicine bottle. The swig exploded in his head, then spread its warmth through his veins. He drank to the generosity of the old man and to that fierce-eyed brave woman—and at that moment, almost as though summoned, he felt the wraithlike presence of the dog. A nose touched his hand, and in the red glow of his cigarette he saw the familiar shape of the dog's head and the limpet blur that was the monkey. They had found him, the one tenuous link with their past.

The man beside him flicked a shaded lighter. "Cor," he said. "Look what's here—" and he reached out to the monkey. But the dog whirled with bared teeth as the monkey gibbered fearfully and clung tighter. Another hand proffered a piece of chocolate, but the dog, trembling violently, pressed closer to Sinclair. The monkey grabbed his blouse and with quick nervous decision thrust its head within. Sinclair had never touched a monkey before and felt almost repelled by the dry warmth, but some instinct caused him to cup a hand over its haunches and the little thing burrowed in. He did up the buttons without a thought for the consequences, other than vaguely hoping that the monkey would not sink its teeth in him later. Then Sinclair rested his hand reassuringly on the quivering dog—acknowledging the false premise of his responsibility even as he did so. He should have driven them off.

When the order reached them to move, Sinclair paused, his hand irresolute over the buttons. The monkey was too tiny, too naked a burden to return to the shoulders of a small distraught dog. Even if he did so, it would not be easy to abandon them now that they had made contact. Let someone else make the decision. Let some authority risk its fingers over the dislodgment of the monkey, the sharp teeth of its guardian dog.

The dog kept close to Sinclair's heels. Ahead, men were moving out of cover to the shaded pinprick of light that marked the gangway between the dock and a destroyer. As he awaited his turn to embark he saw that two MPs were stationed on either side of the gangway and were trying to turn back, with well-directed boots, the frantic attempts of another dog, a black collie, to board. He bent down and felt around the neck of the gray blur at his feet. The bell was firmly attached to a metallic thread, but he silenced it by wrenching out the clapper. The next time he looked down, his shadow was no longer there. He shuffled forward and produced his identifying paybook. A gray-faced naval officer inspected it briefly, glanced up at his face, then down at his battle dress. Sinclair looked down too, resigned, expecting to find a telltale paw sticking out, but "Wounded?" asked the officer.

"Not seriously, sir," said Sinclair.

"Report to the medical officer when you board the *Lancastria*," said the officer, his eyes already on the man behind him.

As he stepped onto the gangway, Sinclair could just make out a small form pressed against the canvas sides, only inches away from the boots of one of the MPs, and he marveled at the strategic positioning of this extraordinary little dog. Sure enough, there was a momentary brushing against one leg, and as he stepped off the gangway he felt it again.

The destroyer slipped away from the dock and headed for the

liner that was anchored three miles out. Sinclair had no doubt now that when they transferred to the *Lancastria* his shadow would attach itself to him again.

The *Lancastria's* crew were calm and imperturbable, as though the throngs of weary troops and civilians—women and children among them—were privileged passengers about to set off on a peacetime cruise. Sinclair was directed where to collect a life jacket, where to stow his kit; he was allocated a mattress in number two hold, and finally he was directed to the sick bay.

Now he had to make a decision. A medical officer would obviously take a dim view of the monkey's unhygienic haven, and if he were once listed as wounded, he would be caught up with medical officialdom the moment they landed in England. Was he really going to burden himself with the acceptance of ownership? The smuggling ashore, the concealment? But the dark woman had not hesitated to accept *him* as her responsibility. . . .

Then scrub the sick bay, said Sinclair to himself, suddenly resolute. And scrub the mattress in number two hold as well. The upper deck might be packed, but above was fresh salt air and the velvet June night. He made his way up and found a place beside a sleeping civilian at the end of a row of back-to-back seats; and even before he had wedged himself in, he was aware of a small shape slipping into the narrow tunnel formed at their base. He put a hand down and smiled when he felt the touch of a nose.

He had been handed two thick beef sandwiches soon after boarding. He ate one, then took the meat from the other and passed it behind him, but it remained uneaten on the deck. He pushed a crust inside his blouse, but the monkey seemed to be asleep. Sinclair dozed uneasily.

When he woke at dawn they were still anchored out in the sea roads beyond St.-Nazaire. He felt his chest, but the slight bulge was no longer there. The man beside him opened one eye. "The monkey which is emerged from your vestments is now there," he said in French-accented English, pointing vaguely behind him.

Sinclair looked around, but there was no sign of the monkey or the dog, so he decided to queue up for a mug of tea and another

261

sandwich. On his way he saw the black collie of the night before, leaning possessively against a pack and rifle. A steward told him that he had seen at least a dozen other dogs on board, not to mention several cats. When he heard about the monkey, he produced an apple, some raisins, and a packet of biscuits. "Come back here before we get to the other side," he told Sinclair. "Once they're off the ship most of those animals will be collared by the officials—but there are ways. . . ." He let the words fall significantly.

Sinclair settled on a later rendezvous and made his way back. He had just emerged on deck when, almost simultaneously with the shipboard alarm bells and gunfire, there came the scream of aircraft engines. The liner shuddered convulsively to two nearby explosions, and men flattened on the deck like a pack of cards as the dark shapes passed over and veered toward the coast.

When the all clear rang, Sinclair shoved the fruit and biscuits and a mug of water inside the seat tunnel. His seatmate gazed down with such raised eyebrows that Sinclair felt some explanation about how he had acquired his animal companions was due.

The Frenchman was interested, and in his quaintly pedantic English was able to supply some background to those "peoples of the roads," as he called them. They came from the Basque country to travel the villages of France, as shrouded in antiquity as the Gypsies—possibly of Moorish blood, he thought; always with performing dogs, and selling pegs and withy baskets as a sideline.

As the morning wore on and still the *Lancastria* lay at anchor, a sense of unease began to spread. There were reportedly six thousand passengers aboard. What were they doing, tempting providence by staying here?

As though sensing the unrest, the dog crept out of shelter at last and pressed shivering against Sinclair's knees; woebegone and bedraggled, with tucked-in tail, he was almost unrecognizable as the jaunty little leader of the caravan. Sinclair noticed that almost the entire left flank of the close-curled coat had been singed. The monkey, on the other hand, seemed unscathed. It sat back on its haunches, grimacing between sips of water from the mug. Next it emptied the remaining water over the dog's unflinching head, and then, like a child showing off, it rocked from one foot to the other, gibbering triumphantly as it waved the mug.

The monkey was a diversion, and the troops cheered him on. After a while Sinclair clicked his fingers as he had seen the woman do, and to his surprise the little creature came running, crablike, to offer him the mug. Sinclair dropped in a franc, and the monkey rattled the mug suggestively, then importuned a row of men sitting on a nearby float. Good-humoredly they contributed.

Someone produced a mouth organ and began to play. The monkey jigged and rattled the mug, deftly catching pieces of chocolate or biscuit in the other paw—all of which it brought to Sinclair. The dog began to show a spark of interest; his eyes brightened and his ears crept up. But the interlude was all too short; minutes later the music was drowned out by an alert.

Men flung themselves to the deck again, and monkey and dog fled back into their tunnel. As the aircraft swept screaming toward them, the liner leaped and bucked to the blast of her own guns. Sinclair crouched at the end of the seats. He heard the whistle of approaching bombs, felt the ship shudder violently to each under-water explosion, and hunched himself tightly before the last wailing scream that filled his head to bursting. The bomb dropped down the *Lancastria*'s funnel, exploding with such force that the liner leaped like a mortally wounded animal.

Amid the clang and rattle of falling flak and metal the *Lancastria* listed sharply; it could not be long before she turned turtle. Sinclair reached for his life jacket.

Above the noise a voice through a loudspeaker directed men to remove their clothes and jump, for with the deck already tilting ominously, only the starboard lifeboats could be launched. In minutes the angle had become so steep that men, equipment, and seats avalanched toward the rail. Clinging to the fixed seat as he kicked off his boots, Sinclair waited until the area directly below was cleared; then, as he slithered down, the monkey leaped for his shoulder and clung tightly around his neck. The dog shot past, paws scrabbling without traction until halted by the raised coaming beyond the rail.

The rail was within twenty feet of the water now, the dog desperately balancing on the almost vertical edge. Sinclair scooped him up and jumped. He knew that he must get as far as possible from the sucking vortex that would follow when the ship went down. He was mad to hinder himself with the dog. He released his grip and started swimming, encumbered by the life jacket and breathless with pain. The dog paddled along easily beside him; the monkey's arms were still wrapped around his neck.

A spar of wood to which was still attached part of a cane seat suddenly bobbed up in front of Sinclair; he grabbed it and rested for a moment. The dog tried to get purchase on the wood and raise himself out of the water. He had almost succeeded when the spar rolled over. Choking on the salt water, he bobbed up again, eyes wildly imploring, paws churning ineffectually. Sinclair raised him by the scruff of his neck and rested the forepaws over his own forearm; the dog hung on without struggling.

Sinclair turned to watch the last mortal moments of the *Lancastria*. Her bow already under, men still retreating flylike up the stern, she reared almost three-quarters of her length clear of the surface, then slid slowly to the depths as the waters closed over her in a great swirling emptiness. Heads bobbed up like corks, and in the silence that followed, the shouts of one to another traveled clearly across the water. Sinclair saw fishing boats and launches converge on the area, while farther away to the south he could make out the bow wave of a destroyer heading toward them.

The water was cold, but he felt confident that he would be picked up soon—provided that enemy aircraft had the decency not to shoot up the survivors. And provided that he had the strength to swim out of reach of the oil, he thought more urgently, as he saw the viscid blackness float up and begin to spread.

The grasp of his wood spar was comforting. Sinclair turned away from the oil slick and paddled toward the distant destroyer. Crouched on the life jacket, at the back of his neck, the monkey was burdenless and undemanding. He shifted the dog's paws to the cane seat and pushed on.

A small crate, empty and bouyant, both ends stove in, floated

by. Sinclair caught it, shoving the spar through until the seat jammed against the sides, and the spar rode fairly steadily. He gave the dog a heave, helping him gain the half-submerged seat, where he crouched, shivering. At this the monkey leaped onto the crate top, clear of the water.

The oil when it reached Sinclair spread over in a vile embrace, coating the spar so that his hands slipped off, and for a moment it drifted ahead, its two occupants staring back in anguish. When he caught up with them, the dog tried to scramble up beside the monkey on the crate top, still clear of oil. The crate rocked wildly; somehow the monkey hung on, but the dog slipped and fell into the water. It was as much as Sinclair could do to hold on to the spar. Then, in spite of himself, he bent his elbow under the dog's haunches and helped him slither back onto the cane seat. After many attempts Sinclair undid one of the tapes of his life jacket, passed it under the spar and back, and knotted it securely.

He could see launches and whaleboats zigzagging to and fro as they picked up survivors. But none came his way, although he waved and shouted. Later he was thankful for his apparent invisibility, for the enemy aircraft returned, machine-gunning where the survivors and boats were thickest.

The remaining heads were scattered now, none within earshot, and the silence was oppressive. Sinclair seemed to have drifted farther and farther away from the rescue ships, and as the hours wore on he became increasingly weak. His legs were numb and he knew that he must keep moving them, but all effort to propel his spar toward the distant destroyer had become excruciating.

The monkey seemed to be shrinking, gray and cold; he wondered how long it could survive. It looked so fragile, eyes closed, huddled in its own enwrapping arms. The dog crouched only inches before him, eyes wide and alive, riveted on his, so close as to reflect him within the pupils like twin mirrors.

There were times when Sinclair felt the effort needed to hold on was too much, that it would be simpler just to let go and drift off into oblivion. But always, just as his will was slipping away, he would be jerked back to open his eyes and see himself again in those other intent, summoning ones. Then came an instant of sharp lucidity, and he realized that the moment he no longer saw himself reflected in those eyes, he would no longer see any of the things he held most dear in the world either. He must stay wakeful and cling to the spar, to life—even as these animals clung to their precarious raft, their bodies tensed to balance, to survive.

Once again Sinclair's world was circumscribed to their small one. "All right," he said aloud. "All right, lads, here we go—hold on, everyone, we're *off!*" He kicked his legs until some circulation returned, took a firmer grasp on the oily spar, and swam on.

He was almost unconscious, but his legs were still fractionally moving, his eyes wide open, when the dog began to bark. Suddenly, close above his head, a voice called out, "Cut that life jacket free!" Only then did he rouse into wide-awake panic.

"Grab the dog," Sinclair said, as a pair of arms reached out and hauled him so that he lay half over the coaming of the boat, resting in agony on crunching ribs before he finally slithered over. Someone wiped his mouth and eyes clear of oil, and eased off the cumbersome jacket. The whaleboat was filled with blackened, slumped figures, and from all around came the sounds of retching and coughing from oil-filled stomachs. Suddenly a small blackness detached itself and crawled to Sinclair's side. He clung to it, fiercely protective, and dropped off into unconsciousness at last.

Sıck Berth Attendant Neil MacLean, of HM destroyer *Tertian*, was tending a group of walking wounded on deck when word reached him that the ship's whaleboat had been swung aboard and there was a man hemorrhaging in it. He called for a stretcher and made his way forward. Only two men were left in the whaleboat. MacLean sent the hemorrhage to the ship's doctor, then turned to the other man, the front of his battle dress stained bright recent red. He bent down to take the man's pulse, and his fingers suddenly came in contact with a warm slimy black mass below the hand, so horrible in its unexpectedness that he withdrew his fingers. Part of the black mass split open to red and gleaming white, and a low snarl preceded the snapping together of the white gleam.

"*A'thiaghrna!*" said MacLean, reverting to his native Gaelic.

The man's eyes opened. "Leave the dog be," he whispered.

"I'll leave him all right," said MacLean, with a sour look at the teeth as he investigated the wound. "I need my hands the day."

The man struggled to sit up, but the effort brought an ooze of scarlet froth to his lips.

"Stay where you are," said MacLean sharply, and called for another stretcher. But the soldier suddenly strained up so wildly that he had to hold him down.

The man's words came in such panting distress that MacLean felt certain one lung must have been pierced by a rib fragment. "The animals—where are they?"

"Lying back *resting*," said MacLean as he slid a needle in.

The man's eyes closed, but they shot open again when he was moved to a stretcher on deck. His hand groped to his side, searching. "All right, all right," said MacLean. "Lie still, the dog's there. No one's going to take it away."

As MacLean stood up, a man squatted down beside the stretcher. "It is I," he announced formally, and Sinclair's eyes opened and crinkled in recognition of the French accent.

"You know him?" said MacLean, and the Frenchman nodded. "Keep him from moving, then, until the drug takes effect. Try and keep him warm—and watch out, there's a dog underneath—"

"Yes," said the helper, already busy. "And *le singe*," he added, cocking an eye at a point twenty feet above. MacLean, departing, looked up too; on the superstructure was the tiny huddled figure of a monkey, its eyes fixed on the head of the dog below.

An hour later MacLean returned. The Frenchman had managed to ease off Sinclair's oil-soaked battle dress and had cleaned him up. MacLean looked down on the pale skin, black hair, and dark blue eyes of the West Highlander. The dog lay at the head of the stretcher now, its muzzle on the edge. Sinclair tried to speak, but went into an agonizing spell of coughing. MacLean knelt down and held him until the paroxysm was over.

"I will do his talking," said the Frenchman as MacLean changed the dressing. "He wishes to tell you that he must walk off this ship, for he has these two companions who have come a long way with him. They have no one else apparently. He is obsessed. They are a trust. He must walk off, for if he goes to hospital he will be separated from them, and this is insupportable."

"Och, don't fash yourself, man," said MacLean to Sinclair with cheerful professional mendacity. "No need to worry—you just leave it all to us."

"I have your hand on it?" the soldier whispered, and repeated it in Gaelic. "You'll see to the dog?"

But there was a difference between the professional assurance and the binding promise; MacLean hesitated. The dog lifted its head, and its intense, uncomfortably human eyes watched him. MacLean rose. The dog rose too, still watching. The words were forced out of MacLean, it seemed. "Aye," he said. "I'll see to him, never you fear. You have my hand on it. Now rest. . . ."

When MacLean checked his patient early the next morning, the man was unconscious, his breathing so labored that it hurt even to listen to it. He turned back the blanket and found the monkey curled into a tight ball between the soldier's arm and chest. MacLean's lips pursed with displeasure, but the watching dog growled fiercely when he tried to move it. He decided to leave well alone—let the monkey go ashore on the stretcher undetected; he wished the medical orderlies joy in its discovery. His promise had been for the dog alone. With that in mind, and with practiced skill, he deftly inserted two pills down its throat and dropped a jacket over it. The shores of England loomed out of the mist. He would return for his sleeping bundle in good time. He noted the details in the soldier's paybook.

Two weeks earlier the British Expeditionary Force had been evacuated from the Dunkirk beaches in the most glorious make-shift fleet ever assembled off the coast of England. In the confusion and urgency quite a few fifth columnists and other undesirables had infiltrated with the returning troops.

But by the time *Tertian* docked at Falmouth with the *Lancastria*'s survivors, security had been tightened. The Port Health and Quarantine officials were ready for all four-footed camp followers; an RSPCA van stood waiting, and all suspiciously shaped packs were being examined.

The last of the wounded ashore, Sick Berth Attendant Neil Mac-Lean leaned over *Tertian*'s rail and watched the scene below. He saw a cat removed from a haversack, while several dogs were led off to the van. Something that looked like a white rat peered out of the blanket folds around the neck of one of the walking wounded and was plucked gingerly out despite its owner's protestations that it was British-born and was only coming home like him.

There had been no inspection of the stretcher cases, however; as long as that monkey remained curled in a ball, it would make it safely ashore. He watched the ambulances speeding off with some satisfaction; Sinclair had been in one of the first to go, MacLean having seen to that by marking a priority on his medical tag.

Just then the bo'sun's pipe summoned all hands to clean ship. As MacLean turned to go below, a smacking noise attracted his attention; ten feet overhead, huddled on a life preserver at the bridge rail, was the monkey. MacLean scowled up at it, furious that it had outwitted him. At that moment the quayside siren started wailing, and the monkey fled up the radar stay. MacLean gazed gloomily after, then clattered down to the sick bay.

The doctor had gone ashore with the wounded. MacLean opened the scuttle wide, rolled up his shirt sleeves, and drew the door curtain across. He was safe from interruption until the all clear sounded. From the cupboard under the bunk he drew out a cardboard box. Inside, on an oily blanket, eyes closed, was the dog. The heavy sedative that he had given it would ensure that it remained this way for several more hours—by which time he hoped that he might have some more inspiration as to its future.

He threw the blanket on a pile in the corner by the door, lifted out the limp bundle, and went to work with swabs and surgical spirit and detergent. Toweled dry, the coat was revealed as a closely curled blue gray, the hair singed off in a large area on one flank, and down to a raw burn at the root of the short tail. This he dressed with meticulous care.

The dog had the proportion and fragility of bone that suggested poodle blood; but the hindquarters were exceptionally powerful, and there was an unusual depth of chest. There was the high-domed forehead that MacLean usually associated with present-day overbreeding—and stupidity to go with it—but this dog had an unexpected width between the eyes. The muzzle was short, clean-cut, and pointed. He examined the teeth: shining white, but slightly worn—the dog must be about seven. A parting in the damp hair around the neck caught his attention: close against the skin was a strand of ribbon through which ran a metallic thread. He took it off, finding that it ran through a tiny silver bell with the clapper missing. He wiped the bell off and put it in his pocket.

The all clear went. Scooping up the dog, he wrapped it in a dry towel, then laid it in the oily blanket by the sick-bay door and covered it loosely. Activity returned to the ship.

Now that MacLean was irrevocably embarked on his course, he felt almost exhilarated. Eventually he would ship the dog back to

Sinclair, but that lay in the future. His present plan was based on his guess that they would return to sea the moment the ship was refueled and revictualed. As long as *Tertian* left within the next few hours, everything would be all right; once they were at sea he could count on the sentiment that would arise over such a defenseless stowaway. And fortunately the precedent of animals aboard had already been set: from the captain's bull terrier, Barkis, down to Hyacinthe, the ship's cat, who reigned supreme over the lower decks. And the same maudlin sentiment would go for that damned monkey too, he thought, if it had enough sense to stay out of reach until they sailed. Just so long as he, Neil MacLean, SBA, took care that nothing could be pinned on him in connection with their appearance, he was home free too.

By the time the doctor returned to the sick bay, MacLean had everything shipshape. MacLean asked him about the shore evacuation of the wounded—the RASC corporal, Sinclair, with the lacerated lung? He was pretty far gone, the doctor remembered; they had rushed him off to a local hospital. "Was he anyone you knew?" he asked MacLean absently.

"No, sir," said MacLean. "And now, sir, if you will not be wishing anything further, I will be taking this lot ashore." He gathered up the soiled pile by the door and prepared to depart. His face was white with exhaustion and he suddenly looked very old to the young doctor.

He took the bundle down to the mess which he shared with the petty officers and some of the victualing staff, slinging a hammock there when the destroyer was in port. At sea he slept in the sick bay. The mess was deserted except for Acting Petty Officer Reid. Reid was a closemouthed individual, and MacLean did not trouble to conceal anything from him. MacLean slid the towel-wrapped bundle of dog out on the deck, turned back an edge to reassure himself, then lifted it into his locker. After checking that the ventilation slits at the bottom were not blocked, he locked the door.

"What you got there—Moses?" asked Reid.

"A dog," said MacLean. "See here," he added, rare persuasion in his voice, "you never saw it—neither did I. When we're at sea it

271

appears—something else left behind by the pongos. No one's going to heave a poor wee dog overboard, is he?"

"You might get it as far as Devonport," admitted Reid. "But then what? You'll be up on a charge if you're caught smuggling it ashore. What do you want a dog for anyway?"

"*I* don't want a dog," said MacLean sourly. "I'm doing it for a kinsman. And Devonport's a fair way off yet. I might need a hand—there would be a pint or two in it," he added cautiously.

"Would there be a meal thrown in with the pints, perhaps?"

"Aye," agreed MacLean. "I can count on you, then?"

"Aye, you can that," said Reid, imitating the soft inflection.

Relieved, MacLean went off to scrounge a mug of tea out of the galley.

"Didn't you do some kind of work with animals in civvy street?" asked the assistant cook. "Do you know anything about monkeys?"

"A bit," said MacLean cautiously.

"Then you'd better get up to the foredeck. There's one there and they can't get it down. Chief's in a proper tear about it."

Armed with some nuts, MacLean made his way to the foredeck. The monkey was still clinging to the radar stay. The chief petty officer was directing two ratings to its capture. The monkey looked small and pitiful, its oil-streaked face pinched and furrowed. Mac-Lean had intended to leave it to the crew to find; now he realized that the vital spark that had kept this delicate creature going so miraculously long in nightmare conditions would be extinguished if he did not do something soon.

"Tch, tch, tch," said MacLean, and recognition came into the monkey's eyes. It reached an arm toward him.

MacLean held out his palm with the nuts. The monkey dropped down at once and scuttled to his feet, where it grasped a trouser leg and gazed earnestly up at his face. It put out a hesitant paw, then took a few nuts, stuffing them listlessly into its mouth. The watching group admired this prodigious feat with smiles.

Suddenly the monkey reached for MacLean's hand, swung itself up into the crook of his arm, and clung, shivering, around his neck.

"Now, MacLean," said the chief, "if you'll just double off to the

Harbor Police with it, we'll get on with the job of running this ship—" but the last of his words were drowned by the wail of sirens, and the men scattered to their stations.

"Hang on to it, MacLean," bellowed the chief. "Get it below."

The doctor was still sitting in the sick bay, his feet on the desk, his eyes closed. MacLean coughed gently. "The chief sent me down with one of the *Lancastria's* lot that got left behind, sir."

The doctor opened his eyes and took in the monkey with no change of expression. "What is it, and what's it complaining of?"

"A capuchin monkey, sir, suffering from exposure and possible pneumonia," said MacLean with equal gravity.

The doctor took a stethoscope out of the drawer. "Take a deep breath, capuchin," he said. Then, as the monkey bared its teeth, "*Your* patient, I think, MacLean." He watched with sleepy interest as the patient submitted apathetically to having its eyes swabbed out, drops administered, and crushed tablets poured down its throat. Finally it was cocooned in cotton wool and a towel. "Very professional," the doctor said approvingly. "Now what?"

"The boiler room," said MacLean as he departed.

Three hours later *Tertian* cast off for the open Atlantic, her complement irrevocably increased by two small and very miserable refugees.

CHAPTER FOUR

IN THE circumstances they could not have been more fortunate. *Tertian* was known in the navy as a happy ship; her officers and men had integrated to form the chance medley that makes such a ship, and two more animals were easily assimilated. Besides, she was only fulfilling the role of her familiar alias, "Noah's Ark"—a nickname that had followed inevitably when Lieutenant Commander Andrew Knorr, R.N., had been appointed to her command.

The skipper of Knorr's Ark was the owner of a flaming red beard, as well as the owner of the legendary Barkis, some seventy pounds of solid white bull terrier, who had conformed to life in a destroyer as though he had evolved there.

The new dog had been discovered in the storeroom, most fortuitously by none other than APO Reid. Its presence was duly reported to the captain and entered in the ship's log. Finally SBA MacLean had volunteered to assume responsibility. So, officially at least, one dog had been processed through the proper channels.

Even if he had understood, this knowledge would have been little consolation in his present insensate terror. The crew of *Tertian* were long conditioned to the discomfort and ceaseless sawing movement of a destroyer slicing through the Atlantic swell. Up on the bridge, Barkis relaxed on a bunk in the captain's sea cabin or rolled nonchalantly along the decks, conforming effortlessly to the ship's every movement. Belowdecks, Hyacinthe slept the hours away in her hammock, unmoved by all human disturbance. But to the small newcomer, straining to keep his balance under a fixed table in a small, cramped mess, what was routine to them must have been a heaving nightmare.

He had lived his entire life on the open road. In one flame-seared moment his world had gone, and he had come through the terrors of fire and water to awaken in confinement. Confinement in an unstable steel box filled with the hurrying boots of strangers, his ears assailed by incessant noise, ranging from the bells and wailing pipes to the thunder of guns and the shudder of exploding depth charges.

Above all, it must have been the loneliest of worlds, with only the slightest association of voice and smell between this human who now ordered his life and the soldier from whom stretched back his one link with his lost world. The soldier had shared that world, and the attachment had been deep, however brief. Now there was this stranger, with competent but impersonal hands, a brusque voice, and unsmiling eyes.

A rope collar had been fashioned for him, and he was kept tied up, with only brief forays on the end of a line to where the depth charges were secured over the stern. Here, in an area frequently washed down by following seas, Barkis came to lift his leg, or squat, while his attendant of the moment stood by with a bucket of water. Barkis displayed an overwhelming interest when they met there, but the exuberance of his greeting and the playful buttings of his rock-hard head invariably capsized the small dog's precarious balance and terrified him even more.

He spent the hours in the kneehole of the sick-bay desk or under the mess table, shivering constantly. The endearing topknot had been cut off, his shaggy ears trimmed short, and he had become very thin. He had been trained never to eat anything offered by strangers. Only one familiar hand had slipped tidbits into his mouth, and then always in reward; the same hand that had never touched him save in praise or affection. There had been no bowl set before him, its contents to be eaten alone; always food had meant a shared intimacy, her plate to lick, perhaps a morsel fallen from the old man's fingers, or a handout from the monkey.

MacLean attributed the dog's refusal of food now to a combination of seasickness and changed environment. In charge of an animal experimental laboratory before the war, he had known plenty of sick and miserable animals to refuse food, and almost always they had become reconciled in the end to their lot and had started eating once more. But as the days passed, and his charge continued to exist on tinned milk alone, he was forced to admit that there was a difference between those hunger-striking animals and this abject but adamant little dog who would accept a biscuit, then lay it on the deck untouched; or, if confronted with a bowl, would give the contents a perfunctory sniff, then turn away.

MacLean tried seasick remedies and vitamin pills. He even—and this went very much against his principles—tried feeding by hand, but the dog retched up whatever solids he had been forced to swallow. For the first time in his life MacLean had encountered an animal whose will to resist him was unyielding.

He even consulted the doctor, who announced, "My prescription would be time. Time—and lots of TLC."

"TLC?"

"Tender loving care," said the doctor, who took delight in rousing his dour SBA's invariable reaction to any sentiment. "Patient's name, rank, and number?" he asked.

"It hasn't got a name," said MacLean, stiff with outrage.

"Well, you might start in right there—at least give it a personality, poor little devil." As MacLean departed, the doctor wondered, not for the first time, at the complex nature of this man; how, out of the whole ship's company, one who obviously had no affinity for dogs should have taken over this one was a puzzle.

MacLean was a reticent man. He spent his off-duty time reading or knitting: a loner. He ran the sick bay and dispensary with impersonal efficiency, but he could show the deepest concern toward the wounded or seriously ill. In the six months that he had been on board the doctor could not fault him.

Periodically after shore leave he would return so drunk that only by a miracle had he avoided the defaulters' list. But he had never failed to report for duty on time. "I'm partial to a wee dram. It helps," had been his explanation when the doctor had asked him why he had to drink to such heroic excess.

"Helps what?" the doctor had persisted.

"To pass the time," said MacLean woodenly.

The doctor returned to his job of censoring the crew's letters. Among this week's batch was one that he read twice:

HMS *Tertian*
July 1, 1940

Dear Corporal Sinclair,

It is my sincere hope that you are now well on the road to recovery. I write this line just to tell you that I have your belongings in safekeeping. I found a souvenir among them and enclose it for luck. The clapper was missing, but I have fashioned another.

I would be glad to receive a line from you. There seems little likelihood that I will be able to dispatch the above-mentioned article for some time, as we are kept on the hop just now. But I will see to it that it reaches you in good condition one day, as promised.

Yours sincerely,
Neil MacLean, SBA

It was the first letter of MacLean's that the doctor ever remembered. *Very* interesting, he said to himself. But *why?* He examined a tiny silver bell, neatly cocooned in a pillbox.

MacLean wasted no deep thought in a name. He had been brought up on a farm where each succeeding sheep dog had inherited the name of its predecessor. Thus there was always a Ria if it were a male, and a Meg if it were a bitch. This was therefore a Ria. "I would be obliged if you would be calling the dog Ria to accustom it," he said to Reid and his messmates over tea.

Reid leaned over to pat the dog. "Good dog, *Ria*, but you're nowt but skin and bone, luv." At the concern in this voice the ears pricked slightly and the tail stirred. Reid cleaned his plate with a piece of bread, but his offering was forestalled.

"The dog is fed once a day—by *me*," said MacLean coldly.

So, phoenixlike, and most sadly, arose from the ashes of his former life this new dog, Ria, as unlike that other as it was possible to be. The only hint of his exceptional intelligence might have been remarked in the short time it took him to put meaning to words of a new language, and to interpret the message of ship's bells and pipes. But there was no hint of the vivacious little professional in this bewildered, cowering shadow.

The men of the petty officers' mess tried to give him the reassurance he so obviously needed, to make him one of them, but their attempts wilted under the consistently disapproving glare of one who so forbiddingly kept himself to himself, and made it clear that this extended to his dog as well. In the meantime Ria existed, physically at least, for a fairly adequate diet was being added to the milk in the form of porridge, gravy, and cod-liver oil.

In contrast, shipboard life held the warmest and happiest of worlds for the monkey, who suffered no complexities of devotion, and almost immediately had become a distinct personality, with a name, Louis, and his personal kingdom of number five mess.

Leading Seaman Lessing, who had owned a capuchin monkey in civilian life, had interested himself in Louis from the beginning, when he had been housed, a listless bundle, in a boiler room. Here he had received the best clinical attention from MacLean, but grew daily more apathetic. Lessing had insisted that if the little animal did not have constant contact with a living being, he would pine away, no matter how excellent the treatment.

One day he took matters into his own hands and removed the monkey to number five mess. Wrapping Louis in a woolen scarf, he slept with him, and ate with him on his lap. When watches changed, his opposite number continued this treatment. For days Louis was never out of someone's arms. A seaboot stocking had been neatly tailored to make a pullover; he already owned one pair of knitted shorts, with a second pair on the needles; other devoted hands had netted a small hammock like Hyacinthe's.

Number five mess was an incredibly cramped kingdom, directly above the magazine, much of it taken up with pipes and cables, benches and mess tables, lockers, hatches, even the large round bulk of a gun mounting and ammunition hoists. In it lived some fifty men. Yet Louis thrived, for there was always company. Even when all hands turned out to action stations and Louis was tethered to a table, he was still not alone; there were two men stationed at the ammunition whips leading up from the magazine. He would occupy himself endlessly polishing the table with a prized yellow duster, or swinging in his hammock, slung below the table. At the first explosion of guns or depth charges, however, he hopped into his hammock and covered his head in a woolen scarf.

Tertian had returned to the Biscay coast after Falmouth and ferried back hundreds of troops. Then she was assigned to Atlantic convoy escort duty. The first miles outward bound from Clydeside were an unremitting grind, within range of the German U-boat packs and their long-range Focke-Wulf Condors flying out of Bordeaux. But enemy activity had not yet extended across the Atlantic, and when a convoy reached the fifteenth west meridian it continued alone, or with Canadian-based protection. So *Tertian* turned back with a homeward-bound convoy. Here, before she steamed again into the range of the enemy, there was a blessed interlude when there was time to sleep, to eat a hot meal.

There might even be time then for the off-duty watch in number five mess to bring out a harmonica or a concertina and entertain— and be entertained by—their mascot. The moment any music started, Louis would jump up and down until someone found his enamel mug, then break into a shuffling dance, skillfully catching anything thrown to him; or he would go through an expert routine of gymnastics on a trapeze that had been fashioned for him.

If Louis's gamin qualities were a diversion to tired, tense men, they in turn gave him love and constant company, ingenious toys, his own place at table, where he downed thick cocoa and picked at delicacies heaped upon his plate. If he lacked one thing in his little kingdom, that was his steed and companion, the dog.

MacLean had never intended that dog and monkey should meet, if for no other reason than that the monkey had been from the start totally excluded from the tidy compartment in his mind reserved for the sole responsibility of one small gray dog.

But MacLean had not reckoned on Ria's nose. One day he returned to the sick bay after treating the monkey for a minor skin ailment. He laid his jacket over the chair, then turned to wash his hands. Under the desk, Ria stirred into sudden life as one of the sleeves hung before his nose. He sniffed intently, his tail quivered, and one ear went straight up; somewhere in this steel maze was hidden the other half of his life's act.

A few days later a stoker was admitted to the sick bay, seriously scalded and in great pain. *Tertian* was in mid-Atlantic, and the stoker needed almost constant attention until he could be transferred. For the next week MacLean took what sleep he could on a chair by the sick-bay cot, appearing only briefly in the petty officers' mess, where Reid had undertaken the charge of Ria.

The first evening, spelled off for supper by the doctor, MacLean had gone to the mess to find Reid asleep, Ria wedged in behind him, at his back. "Get down, you," said MacLean sharply, and Ria jumped down at once to the heeling deck.

"Put him back where he was, Doc," said Reid. "When I'm looking out for him, he stays in this bunk." His voice was equable as ever, but there was no mistaking an overtone of finality. MacLean dropped Ria back on the blanket with ill grace.

"A bunk's no place for a dog. It will just encourage bad habits," he said, and returned to the sick bay and his patient.

Perhaps because of the warm security of his contact with

Reid, and the camaraderie that had come his way since the mess was free of MacLean's disapproving eye, Ria's confidence gradually returned. First, and most important, he found his sea legs. Until now he had had to be carried up and down ladders. Reid, after repeatedly placing the dog's paws one after another on the rungs, had persuaded him to scramble up, but the descent was obviously terrifying. Reid stood at the bottom, enticing; the others in the mess encouraged, and Ria crouched at the top, trying to bring himself to make the attempt. Suddenly he launched himself, not down the ladder but into midair, straight at Reid, who fortunately caught him. The watchers stamped their feet and clapped. Ria's delight in his triumph was touching; his tail quivered, and when he was patted he flew up the ladder again.

"Ooplah, my beauty," said Reid, his hands out, and down came Ria again, patently delighted with himself. He had performed, and he had been applauded; but his real reward was his own achievement and Reid's evident pleasure. He soon learned to descend using all four paws, but if exhorted by a cry of "Ooplah" from someone at the bottom, he would always launch into midspace.

The next day Ria climbed the ladder many times, staying at the top to survey the passing world and assay its scents for longer and longer intervals. Many hands reached down to pat him, and his nose investigated each; one in particular filled with such promise that he was emboldened enough to trail its owner's boots. Hesitantly nervous as he set off on his quest, with belly crouched low, he followed the route to the stern, step by wary step, looking back frequently but always urged on by his nose.

His driving need lent him courage as he flitted up and down companionways and along passageways, and then down the final steep ladder, where he crouched, unobserved. There, perched on a man's shoulder, eating a potato, was his monkey.

Lessing, sitting at the far end of the mess with his back to the ladder, thought for a moment that Louis had gone mad when, squeaking and chattering as never before, the monkey suddenly jumped from his shoulder to the deck and scuttled the length of the mess. Lessing saw the cause of the excitement—MacLean's dog, balanced halfway down the ladder, swaying to the ship's roll. Louis leaped for him, yet somehow the dog managed to retain his balance before slithering the rest of the way. As he gained the deck, Louis clasped tightly around his neck, the ship rolled heavily, and they skidded down the slope and finished up under the table, a yipping, chattering tangle of fur.

It was a spectacular first entrance and received the applause it deserved. Ria, his tail quivering like a tuning fork, had come to full, vivid life once more.

Now he made his way to this monkey haven as often as possible. Reid was well aware of what was going on, but as Ria was always punctiliously returned by Lessing after a visit, by unspoken agreement nothing was ever said to MacLean about Ria's double life.

Whenever the bright-eyed, eager little dog came leaping down the ladder, he was greeted with rapturous affection by Louis. Ria was unfailingly patient, even when Louis was at his most mischievous, and would tolerate all liberties, lying still for as long as his tormentor wanted to groom him, jump over or up and down on him, or hang around his neck. However, invariably there came a point when Louis became frustrated over Ria's noncooperation in an act. For, while their performance together had been a way of life, Ria had been conditioned by training and was dependent on commands and signals.

Louis had no such problems, for his performance had been built around what he liked to do naturally. He would perch on Ria's back, leaning forward like a jockey tensed for the start. Chattering in frustration, he would jump up and down to urge his mount on, but Ria could only sit there, with head thrown back and forepaws close together, waiting for the starting signal that never came.

Ria was offered food and invariably it was refused—until the day he arrived during a meal. Louis was guddling around in his own mess tin, and he picked out a morsel that did not seem to meet with his approval, for he lobbed it over to the dog. It was caught and swallowed in a flash, and Ria moved closer, ears cocked expectantly. He was not disappointed. Louis held out another reject and Ria took it gently. When Louis had finished, Ria moved in and polished the mess tin clean. Lessing gave him some of his own dinner, and that disappeared too.

But the day came all too soon when *Tertian* made her rendezvous on the fifteenth west meridian. And there Ria's freedom ended; for, shortly after his patient, the stoker, was transferred to a homebound vessel, MacLean came clattering down the ladder in a mixture of anger and anxiety, haunted every inch of the way in his search from the empty petty officers' mess by thoughts of his charge being swept overboard or fallen down a hatch. It was an infuriating anticlimax to find this domestic idyll: Ria, a look of almost besotted pleasure on his face, being groomed by the monkey in number five mess.

MacLean's relief turned sour. He called twice, but Ria did not stir. He strode over and picked up the dog, but Louis hung on determinedly; as fast as MacLean could disengage one paw, the monkey curled the other fast on the dog's collar. Then, clutching Ria with one hand, Louis made toward this interfering human antagonist the most obscene of his considerable repertoire of obscene gestures. There was a titter of restrained laughter.

"Leave him till the watches change," Lessing suggested. "Louis always lets him go then. I'll bring him back myself."

"The dog has no business to be here, now or anytime. Come, you," said MacLean, scarlet-faced.

"Come on, Doc, be a sport," wheedled the rest of number five mess. "Give them a treat, pore little orphans."

"I'll thank you to get yon brute of a monkey off—*now!*" said MacLean to Lessing.

Lessing's amusement was stopped cold at the venom in the tone. As he pried the furiously protesting Louis loose, he made one last attempt. "But why *not* let them be together when they can? Ria's sort of settled down here with Louis."

"The dog's settled—with *me*," said MacLean. "*I'm* responsible, and I'll not have any daft to-ing and fro-ing all over this ship." He picked up Ria and left.

Reaching the upper deck, MacLean put the dog down and they made their way aft in the darkness. He leaned over the rail, now watching the path of the wake, now watching the small blur that was Ria sniffing the depth charge mountings for traces of Barkis.

The destroyer was tuned to seagoing sounds, the swish of water against the hull, the constant moan of the funnel, but MacLean was deaf to everything except the laughter still ringing in his ears. He bitterly regretted his promise to Sinclair, with the complications of fulfillment, the baffling resistance of the dog.

Back in the sick bay, he filled the basin that bore the label DOG ONLY with water and set it before Ria. He grimly dropped the daily ration of vitamin pills down the dog's throat. Then he removed his shoes and jacket and turned in. Ria lay down by the open door. Two minutes later MacLean was asleep. Two hours later Ria still lay with his head on his paws, his dark eyes wide open and unseeing, as though fixed on some point far beyond the bows of the Ark and the endless expanse of ocean.

CHAPTER FIVE

NEIL MacLean came from a thriving West Highland farm, an undersized asthmatic child in a family of tall strong brothers.

The only manifestation that set this child apart was the marked reluctance of any animal to be near him. As a pungent aroma of friar's balsam from the steaming asthma kettle perpetually enveloped him, his family did not find this surprising. The same explanation prevailed when, as he grew older, he seemed to be able to subdue wild or recalcitrant animals by his presence alone. Altogether the boy could no more tolerate their presence than they could his, for he had only to come into close proximity with an animal and he was seized with the dread wheezing.

He was sent to a specialist who produced a long list of positive allergy tests. Shortly afterward he was sent to the drier climate of inland Morayshire to board with an aunt. The improvement was dramatic; although he was always to remain undersized and thin, he outgrew all allergies. But a residue of his strange power over animals remained, recognized by a local vet who took the boy on to help in school holidays, then later as a full-time assistant.

Neil MacLean became the most efficient handler of animals the vet had ever known, and he encouraged the young man to enter veterinary college. But after two academically successful years he suddenly quit, returned to his assistant's job, and the disappointed vet could get nothing more illuminating out of him other than that "studying was no the life" for him.

He had married eventually, returning from a holiday on the island of Mull with a girl who had red hair, who teased him about his persnicketiness—and who, even while she laughed at him, told him how wonderful he was, so that he became wonderful in his love for her. But two and a half idyllic years later, on a visit home to Mull, she was drowned in her father's fishing boat. The sea kept forever his Margaret and all that had been their life.

After the funeral he had given his notice to the vet; then, stocked up with whiskey, he had returned to their cottage and locked the door. At the end of two weeks, his private wake over, he walked out of the cottage and, his face expressionless as stone, handed the cottage key over to the vet, receiving in return his letter of the highest recommendation to a colleague who was director of the animal laboratory attached to a famous hospital in London.

It was not long before MacLean became the head attendant in charge of the laboratory animals there, and the meticulous conditions in which they lived became a byword among other laboratories. No patient ever received such undivided attention as did the animals in MacLean's care. No animal ever bit his ministering hand, no animal cowered away from him; and no animal ever greeted him with pleasure. His attitude might seem inhuman, but his care was never other than humane.

He volunteered the day after war broke out, and it was typical that, hating the sea, he should go straight to a naval recruiting office. When his veterinary experience was revealed, the medical officer recommended him for training as a sick-berth attendant.

This was the complex, inturned little man to whom fate had sent a small extrovert of a dog; a man who set his highest standards of admiration by the giants of endurance, strength, and self-control. If Neil MacLean could have admired any dog enough to wish it for his own, it would have been one like the fearless, barrel-chested Barkis, not a slight, shivering dog who winced to noise and allowed doll-sized monkeys all liberties.

So Ria, who was only what he was, a dog to amuse, was increasingly bewildered as MacLean strove daily to produce something that approached his idea of what a dog should be.

But the dog's needs were too strong now to be subject to the man's will. With infinite cunning, when he had learned the times that MacLean was occupied with duties, he would slip his collar, then head straight to the haven of number five mess. Invariably he was retrieved, invariably he returned; and no appeal from Lessing or anyone could persuade MacLean to permit the visits.

Louis took an almost human delight in irritating Ria's pursuer, and MacLean, who was usually greeted with vulgar smacking of lips, found himself disliking the monkey with an animosity he had never before felt toward anyone, let alone an animal. His worry over Ria's lack of appetite increased too, for now this disconcerting animal seemed to be living on water alone.

Inevitably came the time when MacLean was confronted with the scene of Ria and Louis sharing a mess tin—worse, the monkey was actually feeding the dog. Mortified, he had said nothing. But his silence was so forceful that for once Ria leaped up the ladder before him and made straight for his proper obscurity under the desk, regardless of the fact that the doctor's feet were there.

He pressed against the friendly legs as though seeking protection. But it was Barkis who was to be his savior of the day. Barkis' claws had to be cut.

"You're wanted on the bridge," said the doctor as MacLean appeared. "Operation Toenails, you lucky chap. I told the captain that you probably had some magical tricks up your sleeve. I did the job last time and it took me nearly a week to recover."

MacLean arrived at the captain's sea cabin, off the bridge, to find there the brawny yeoman signaler and the captain's steward, Smith. The unsuspecting Barkis slept peacefully on the bridge. The captain whistled him in, and he came to the door with his powerful rushing roll, sensed his impending doom, and backed out hastily. "Grab him, Yeoman," shouted the captain, and the signaler leaped in a flying tackle. Barkis rolled over and waved his paws supplicatingly. Nothing would induce him to get to his feet.

Eventually, cooing persuasively, the captain managed to lure the quivering white bulk onto his bunk and thence onto the chart table. "Now!" he said, and like a well-trained team, he, Smith, and the signaler pounced. Barkis fought like a tiger. MacLean got only two claws clipped before the dog fought his way to the floor, where he collapsed on his back again.

MacLean was horrified. Barkis' lack of courage was more than he could stand. "If I might be making a suggestion, sir," he said, "it is that we knock him out with a wee whiff of ether."

The captain sent for the doctor, who agreed, straight-faced and solemn, with MacLean's suggestion. A mask and ether were produced, and, peacefully, Barkis parted with his nails.

Thanking MacLean afterward, the captain asked about Ria—a fine-looking little dog. Intelligent and full of guts too.

MacLean was astonished by this praise from a man he admired above all others. "I had not thought on it, sir," he said, "but, aye, he certainly is a determined wee beast."

Later that afternoon, as MacLean sat at the desk, Ria suddenly came to him and pushed a cold nose into his hand. Pleased, he let his hand lie for a moment on Ria's head. Suddenly he was very conscious of the fragility of the skull. This wee jessie of a dog had endured over eight hours in the water—and heaven knew what else—yet he still had fight in him. "Full of guts," the captain had said—maybe he wasn't far wrong. And intelligent—well, yes, he was no fool. As to fine-looking, if he'd keep his head and ears up the way they were now, he wouldn't be so bad-looking at that.

"You'll do," he said almost grudgingly. "Aye, you'll do."

For the first time in his thirty-eight years of life he had spoken words that were neither commands nor refusals to an animal. Head to one side, ears cocked, Ria's eyes searched the face above as though expecting something further. But at that moment eight bells sounded; time for MacLean's routine inspection of his first-aid packs, stowed on every gun turret throughout the ship; he secured Ria by a length of strong line and left.

He climbed the ladder to A gun and, reaching the platform, found Ria immediately behind him, the collar slipped. Exasperated, he scowled, but Ria, ears at a demure half-mast, gazed studiously into the distance. It was too late to return with him now—and at least he had not made for number five mess. He continued his rounds, the dog close behind, yet never in the way.

They returned to the petty officers' mess. MacLean set the bowl in place, his mouth drawn down as he remembered the intimacy of the monkey's fingers in another dish. Ria gave the contents his usual perfunctory sniff and turned away.

Reid, already eating, watched. "Come on, man," he said in rare irritation. "If you'd stop looking as though you had a mouth full of razor blades, perhaps the dog would eat something—it's enough to put anyone off their grub!"

MacLean looked up, startled. Then suddenly he smiled almost shamefacedly. "Perhaps I am just a thing overanxious."

"And talk about a dog's dinner—who'd want to eat that grisly-looking muck?" Reid ladled some of his own plate into the bowl. "Come on, Mam's little luv, eat up your din-dins," he said, in such a high falsetto that MacLean could not help laughing.

"Go on, eat up," said MacLean, still laughing; and to his astonishment Ria, obviously ravenous, polished the bowl clean.

From then on there was no refusal of meals; a battle had been won. There would have been no doubt in MacLean's mind as to which had triumphed if the point had ever been raised: dogs always came around in the end. Still, it could do no real harm to discipline if the dog continued to eat at the same time as himself, and maybe even have some of his own hot dinner.

THE Atlantic convoys were the very lifelines of England now. The responsibility of protecting them lay mainly with the destroyers, but in the preceding months twenty-two had been sunk and forty-five damaged, almost half their total strength; of those left, many dated back to 1917. But against all odds, sometimes with engines kept going by seeming miracles, with exhausted crews, the convoys kept on coming as that desperate summer of 1940 wore on into autumn gales in the battle for the Atlantic.

Ria had become relaxed now in MacLean's company, attentive and receptive to moods. There were no more problems over food, no humiliating visits to number five mess, no need to tie Ria. He had settled in. Which was just as well, MacLean reflected one morning as he read a letter from Donald Sinclair's wife. Her husband was off the danger list, but he would remain in hospital for some time before being invalided out of the army. "Then, God willing, we can take the dog off your hands."

MacLean put the letter away, his feelings very mixed, and went out on deck into the September sunshine. It had been an eventful last three days. *Tertian* had been diverted from the Clyde on the homeward leg, and on up the west coast of Scotland on a U-boat sighting. The U-boat was trapped and forced to the surface, where she had been promptly scuttled. The crew was picked up by a jubilant *Tertian* and taken to the nearest port, Oban. There she disembarked her captives, and among the congratulatory signals that followed was one delaying her return to the Clyde for twenty-four hours, thus giving both watches some hours ashore.

This was all too familiar ground to MacLean—the land of his forebears, and of Margaret's. The mountainous island of Mull dominated the western horizon, and some twenty miles to the north was the farm where he had been born. Twenty-four hours here would be twenty-four deeply disturbing hours.

It was a Sunday. He sat with his back against the aft super-structure; a few men were sprawled on the deck. But MacLean, not one to be idle, knitted, and as he knitted he read *Gordon, the Hero of Khartoum*, Ria on one side, a mug of tea on the other.

The gentle hills before him were vivid with bracken and heather. A light wind carried the sounds of church bells and bleating sheep and all the tantalizing smells of sun-warmed earth. Suddenly Ria went to the rail, his nose twitching, his eyes searching. He whined, and the distraction irritated MacLean. "Wheesht," he said curtly.

Lessing appeared with Louis, attached to a long line, and settled down to write letters. Louis soon wandered afield, and Ria switched his gaze off the shore to watch him, his tail quivering. Beside him MacLean knitted and read determinedly.

One of Louis's admirers tossed him a biscuit; he caught it and scampered toward Ria. But the line tautened ten feet away, and Louis then tossed the biscuit straight at Ria's mouth. Ria's jaws opened, snapped shut, and the biscuit vanished.

MacLean's patience snapped; he put the book down, seized with revulsion, and *"No!"* he repeated sharply to a second biscuit. But again Ria swallowed. On the third throw MacLean's hand shot out and intercepted the biscuit, putting it into a pocket, where Ria's nose followed. *"Will* you be still," he said, and this time cuffed him lightly. Ria sank his teeth in the hand. He released it immediately, cowering as though ashamed, but his eyes were bright and wary.

MacLean stuffed the hand in his pocket and glanced around, but no one was turned his way. He replaced his bookmark, picked up his mug and knitting, and departed. Ria followed, head held high, walking as though on the tips of his paws.

In the sick bay, MacLean set out cotton wool and antiseptic, and sat down at the desk to dress the oozing punctures. His face was very white. Suddenly he stretched his hand down to Ria's nose. *"Bad!"* he said vehemently, and he cuffed the woolly head again.

Ria's reaction was instantaneous. This time he snarled before he sank his teeth in the hand. Then for a long moment they glared at one another. The man turned away first, his face expressionless as he attended to the wounds. For a full minute Ria remained still as a statue; then he slipped through the door to lie in his usual place outside, his eyes fixed unblinkingly on MacLean.

Through the open scuttle drifted the peaceful sounds and all the sweet headiness of hill and moorland, which suddenly stirred Mac-Lean to such a nostalgia that he laid his head on the desk, sick and dizzy, waiting for the iron band to squeeze his chest.

Ria whined, then came to him. He licked the hand that had struck him, and miraculously MacLean found that he could breathe again. He put his hand on the dog's head, and remembrance now was gentle and kind: a boy riding home on the peat cart, the gorse, and heather-laden summer wind on his face, the sheep high on the hills. . . . He smoothed the ears beneath his fingers, feeling the warmth of the dog's body pressed against his legs. Suddenly the ground was falling away. . . . Perhaps he dozed. . . .

There had been a sheep dog pup, and a child had struck it again and again until it had cringed on the ground; then the child had called it to him, fondled and patted to see the adoration in its eyes, and then he had struck it again, harder this time, until it yelped; then once more the reconciliation. . . .

How long had this gone on? Minutes, hours? He only knew that throughout the summer-laden wind blew steadily, as it did today, filling him with a strange exhilaration and dreadful sorrow; and then had come the fear that he could not breathe—somebody's arms had carried him, then the vapors of friar's balsam steaming from a kettle drifted over all memory. . . .

There was a sound of boots at the far end of the companionway; MacLean jerked awake. He swept everything into the drawer. When Lessing pulled back the curtain, MacLean was sitting tidy and composed, immersed in his book, Ria at his feet.

Lessing was a likable youngster, always dependable. He stood now in the entrance, and looked very awkward and unsure of himself. He was going ashore on the next liberty boat, he said; he thought he'd walk over the hills—would MacLean like to go too?

Still spent within, MacLean lacked his usual defenses; he had rejected all overtures of friendship so consistently that no one ever sought his company. He smiled, his rare transforming smile, and said that there was nothing he would rather do—it was a grand day for the walking; but the doctor was ashore, and he was on duty. He thanked Lessing anyway for thinking of it.

"Let me take Ria, then," Lessing suggested. "It'll do him good to have a run—get out of this tin box for a while."

For a moment MacLean almost reverted to his usual image and told Lessing to mind his own business; then, almost despite himself, he heard his voice saying, "Aye. I'd be glad if you'd take him," and "Off with you, then," to Ria, who bounded after Lessing.

MacLean looked out of the scuttle at the sunlit hills beyond the little port. He had relatives here. His father, or his eldest brother, would take Ria for him, and in time dispatch him back to Sinclair. He called after Lessing, "Hold on a minute!"

The boy's head reappeared around the curtain, and Ria's face followed, his head cocked inquiringly.

"I thought," began MacLean; then, suddenly decisive, he went on, "that this would help," and he made a quick sketch on a note pad. "You'll get out of the town quickly that way, then on up a sheep track until you come to a lochan. . . ."

Three hours later Ria came back, eyes shining, jaunty and confident—a very different dog, as the man who greeted him could not fail to observe. Nor could the dog have failed to sense the difference in the reception from the man.

When the Ark left Oban next morning, steaming down the Firth of Lorne, MacLean was on deck to see the last of his homeland waters. As the black mass of Mull disappeared, some of the lightness of heart that his Margaret had brought returned to him.

Beside him, Ria rose with extended forepaws. He looked up, his eyes merry, and unconsciously MacLean smiled down at him. He suddenly knew that Margaret of all people would have been the one for this dog, that from her extravagance of love and gaiety she would have encouraged all antic nonsense. She had always wanted a dog, but she had understood his aloofness from animals and given way to him. It had been his one denial to her.

"Behave yourself," he said now, but the smile lingered.

CHRISTMAS WAS A freezing, joyless day in mid-Atlantic, with *Tertian* plunging and rearing in mountainous seas, so that there was no dry place on board, and Christmas cheer, perforce, was corned beef and hardtack, for the galley fires had been extinguished. Afterward MacLean put on his heavy-weather gear and went off to check his first-aid caches.

He emerged from the sick bay and, hardly able to stand against the force of the wind, grabbed one of the lifelines that stretched along the deck. But Ria must have slipped out at his heels, for as he turned away from the wind he saw him, paws resisting uselessly against the icy tilt, sliding toward the rails. At the same moment MacLean was aware of a monster wave towering over the port bow. Never knowing afterward how he had done it, he flung himself down, still hanging on to the rope, and grabbed Ria's collar. Somehow he got Ria back inside.

"*A'choin an diabhoil!*" he roared at the shaken, soaking dog, and smacked him resoundingly. This time Ria acknowledged a rightfulness of punishment. With contrite eyes and even a placatory attempt with the end of his tail, he looked very vulnerable. MacLean was totally won over. "You devil of a dog, you," he translated, but softly, and he carried Ria down to Reid to dry him off.

"Stupid animal followed me out," he explained.

"I'll see that he doesn't follow you back up," said Reid.

MacLean left to finish his inspection, and Reid bundled up the shivering dog in a jersey and stowed him on the bunk. Curiously he noticed that Ria did not relax until MacLean returned.

But the subtle change in relationship went unnoticed by anyone else, including MacLean himself, for the transition from him imposing his will to Ria anticipating his wishes had evolved so naturally that he was unaware of it. They remained to the rest of the ship's company the same undemonstrative pair.

"What will you do with him eventually?" the doctor asked MacLean one day.

"Return him to the man who brought him aboard, sir."

The doctor looked up. "It won't be easy, will it—to part with him after all these months?"

There was a long pause. "No, sir," said MacLean at last. "It will not be easy now." The admission was forced out of him.

MacLean had not realized how much of his heart had been given to Ria until *Tertian* returned to Devonport in early March, 1941. He was looking forward to a forty-eight-hour leave and had made plans to spend it walking on Dartmoor with Ria—the first time they would ever have gone off together. When the mail was distributed on their arrival in port, there was a letter for him. Donald Sinclair was out of hospital and returned to his Highland glen. Now at last he could relieve Ria's benefactor of his obligation "so thoughtlessly imposed upon you. Any port that you are in . . . if you could dispatch him from there to Glasgow, someone will pick him up and bring him on to us. . . ." He enclosed a postal order to cover expenses, the train ticket, and the purchase of the obligatory muzzle for "an unaccompanied dog."

Suddenly the world seemed bleak, for within ten minutes of MacLean's confiding this news to Reid, arrangements had slipped inexorably into place: Reid had telephoned his sister, in nearby Plymouth, to ask if she would put Ria on the train to Glasgow.

It all happened so quickly that there was no time to brood. At noon MacLean went ashore with a brushed, trimmed, and bright-eyed Ria. Feeling like a Judas, he handed him over to Reid, who was waiting at the dockyard gates. "Away you go," he said. Ria was very attached to Reid, but now he must have sensed something disastrous; as MacLean turned down a dockside street he whined and struggled to follow.

Reid picked him up to soothe him, but as MacLean rounded the corner he heard a sound that he had never heard before—Ria barking, a high-pitched hysterical bark that was to haunt him for days. He shut out the sound in the nearest pub, drank himself into a state of savage gloom, and barely made it back on board.

They were anchored out in Plymouth Sound. Soon after darkness fell, the sirens had sounded the red alert, which for months had meant nothing more sinister to the town than the approach of an enemy reconnaissance plane or a lone raider. But this night, almost before the first warning notes had ebbed away, the skies were filled with purposeful throbbing, even as the antiaircraft and search-lights came into action. The systematic destruction of the ancient seaport had started.

Tertian was a Devonport ship and many of the men had families onshore. Their own guns joining in the shore barrage, all night long they watched helplessly, jarred by every explosion, seared by every freshly leaping fire. Next morning, those who had homes or relatives there were given shore leave.

Reid found his sister standing aimlessly in front of what had been her house. One side was exposed, the roof was gone, and the kitchen extension at the back lay in an impenetrable heap of rubble. That was where Ria had been when the blitz began, she informed him tearfully; fortunately she herself had been out for supper with the neighbor with whom she was now sheltering.

There was nothing Reid could do. When he returned to *Tertian* to break the news to MacLean, the only consolation he had to offer was that Ria's death must have been instantaneous.

MacLean, standing by the rail, thanked him in an expressionless voice and continued to look at the smoldering city under its pall of smoke. He never spoke of Ria to his shipmates again.

In all too brief a time that day those ashore were recalled. The cruiser *Admiral Hipper* was making a sortie out of Brest, and *Tertian* was to be part of the force sent to intercept.

For days they played cat and mouse, but in the end the prey eluded them, and *Tertian* proceeded on to Gibraltar to refuel.

She passed through the gates of the Mediterranean to become a part of the fleet there, part of the immortal annals of the Tobruk run, Mersa Matrûh, Crete, and the Malta convoys—and she was never to return.

CHAPTER SIX

THE bombardment of Plymouth and Devonport had begun at about nine o'clock at night.

Reid's sister had gone out for supper, and when the first bombs screamed down, Ria was alone in the kitchen. He cowered against the back door; as another bomb began its shrieking pursuit, he bolted under the table. The bomb landed between the next two adjoining houses; the kitchen shuddered to the blast, then settled, sagging.

The deep, quivering silence that followed was intruded upon by a thick acrid smell; then came a crash as the bricks and masonry of the chimney cascaded onto the roof. Slowly, smoothly, the roof blended with the crumbling wall, widening the red gap of sky like a blind pulled back; the floor heaved up and plates slid one by one off the dresser. Human sounds were heard from the street beyond—heavy boots crunching through glass, shouts, sharp orders, whistles. Beyond these noises rose the steady drone of aircraft, the thunder of the dockyard guns, the lighter barking of antiaircraft batteries, the high, whistling crescendo, then the great bass-drum thumping of bombs.

Now the kitchen was light as day, the roof open wide to the flares swaying down from the skies. For a few seconds a hush fell again over the ruined world that had been the kitchen, then the crackle of flames rose just beyond the jagged edges of the roof; and as though summoned by them, the white ghostlike figure of a dog appeared from under the wreckage by the table and drifted across the rubble on the floor, past the door sagging on one hinge, and out into the courtyard. The little ghost cowered, trembling, until the door gave way and crashed down. With that he bolted into the street, his paws scarcely touching the ground.

Now he smelled fear, death, and terrible human excitement, an evil blend that sent him, eyes glazed and wild, skittering across the rubble-strewn streets, shying away from the running boots of wardens and firemen, leaping over obstructions. Galvanized by the flares, the bombs, the salvos from the guns, he ran desperately, aimlessly, through the burning town. Hours later he veered crazily between the tombstones of a churchyard, and there finally collapsed under the solid, sheltering wing of a toppled marble angel.

When the all clear sounded at dawn, the dazed inhabitants of Plymouth emerged to survey their world. The sun came up with its warmth, and the little dog crawled out and licked his bleeding paws. There was no homing urge for the unfamiliar house where Reid had left him, there was no one to search for, no links with anyone or any place; he was derelict, nameless, lost.

He stayed around the churchyard for a while; then the terrifying wail of sirens and fire engines drove him on. He fled down a narrow street, silent and deserted, between rows of small houses, many of them gaping and exposed. The dog sat on the sunny step before the roofless shell of one of these and scratched himself. Across the street a black Labrador scrambled over a mountain of rubble, sniffing and searching. Suddenly it began to dig frantically, whining excitedly as the dust and rubble flew out behind.

The little dog picked his way over the rubble too, and with his nose caught the same message as the Labrador; he started digging beside the large dog. An ARP warden climbed over the wreckage, bent down, and listened; then he shouted, "Hold on. Help's coming." He pulled a whistle from his pocket and blew, until there was an answer of steel-shod boots running, and the siren of a rescue unit. This was too much for the little dog, who tucked his tail between his legs and fled up the street.

He wandered for hours, limping and thirsty, past the great heaving coils from water hydrants, through clouds of smoke, up empty streets where walls trembled above him.

There was only one place he knew, and he returned to it, to his guardian angel in the churchyard.

He was there still when the nightmare started up again soon after dark. Shuddering convulsively, he pressed back into his refuge, until at last the noise and terror drove him out to the streets and the madness of the night before.

The next morning the little dog foraged in garbage cans and the wreckage of shops and houses. He was attracted by the rescue crews working around the clock to free survivors trapped under debris, for apparently the reward of what lay beneath gave much pleasure to man. He often tried to join in digging operations, but always he was driven away by angry voices, sometimes by thrown bricks.

In the afternoon, cowed and slinking now, he wandered to a

residential area on the outskirts of the town, and there, in an orchard adjoining a large garden, he paused, sniffing the air. Then, following some scent or sound, he limped through the garden until he came to a coach house converted to a garage. The windows were blown in and the roof was down, but the walls still stood. To the right of the closed double doors was the original stable door, half open, and the little dog edged in warily to a tangled mass of beams, laths, and slates, his nose working busily.

Where a small inverted V of access to the pile had been formed by two beams he paused, ears cocked, whining excitedly. Now he inserted his head, and like a wraith he infiltrated the tunnel. It widened out after a few yards to a small clearing, the roof formed by a jumble of precariously balanced timbers. An arm protruded from below, and as the dog crawled toward it the fingers opened and closed, as though beckoning. Delighted with his find, he licked the hand, then wagged his tail when a weak, muffled voice responded to his action.

Questing around for a way in, he tried to tunnel down through a mass of plasterboard. As he dug, the vibration loosened part of the delicate construction of beams above, and there was a small avalanche of plaster. The dog yelped as a heavy board pinned one paw; he pulled desperately, and the paw tore free at last. Whimpering, he fell to licking his mangled toes.

The weak voice below whispered for a while, then grew silent, but the hand still moved wearily, as though in search, until at last the fingers found the other paw. He licked the fingers and returned his attention to the injured paw. A glimmer of light high up in the tangled pile slowly faded as darkness fell. The bleeding stanched at last, exhausted with pain and hunger, he laid his head on the other paw, his muzzle resting lightly on the hand. The fingers moved out and up past the matted hair on the crown of his head, then to the sensitive hollow behind his ears. The voice continued, sometimes speaking, sometimes singing.

Gradually the little dog grew weaker. By the evening of the second day there, the hand had gone and the voice was long silent. He could no longer lift his head, and his eyes were sealed with a yellow discharge. He lay without movement, only the occasional flick of one ear betraying the will to live.

On the third morning he raised his head—then suddenly he pushed back on his haunches and broke into a high, wild barking.

ALICE Tremorne had been trapped in the garage at her home, The Cedars, for two nights and days when the dog found her. She had been alone, as Janet Carpenter, her young companion, was away on a holiday and the daily help had left after preparing the evening meal. Restless, and so bored that she had even cleared away the dishes, Mrs. Tremorne suddenly thought of sloe gin. At the start of the war she had put up several bottles. They should have aged pleasantly by now, in the work pit of the garage. She would tell Carpenter to fetch a bottle when she returned. . . .

But the more she thought about the gin, the more she wanted to try it now. Why wait? She would fetch some herself.

Wincing, Mrs. Tremorne rose stiffly to her feet. Then, taking a flashlight, a fur wrap, and her cane, she shuffled down the path to the garage. An elderly woman who never set foot outside without her companion's arm, she hoped she would be able to manipulate the bottles, for her hands as well as her legs were stiff and swollen with arthritis. Anticipating difficulty, she had put two small bottles and a funnel in the string bag over her arm so she could transfer some of the contents in the garage.

When she opened the garage door and shone the light around, she realized that she had forgotten about the boards covering the pit. She would have to remove the ones over the steps. Her knees twinged at the thought. But Mrs. Tremorne somehow managed to lever up enough boards. Puffing and giddy with the effort, she now realized it would be foolhardy to attempt the cement steps of the pit without a handrail. She decided to investigate instead the cupboard in which her bottles of elderberry, ginger, and black currant wines were kept, under the stairs leading to the loft.

Outside the sirens wailed, such a normal evening event that she took no notice. She unlocked the cupboard door, closing it behind her before switching on the light. It was at this precise moment that the antiaircraft defenses ringing the town burst into an excited crackling; and now the dreadful thudding of naval guns joined in, rattling her bottles and sending the suspended light bulb into a crazy dance. Mrs. Tremorne turned off the light and reopened the cupboard door. Suddenly her world was filled with a rushing, screaming noise and her body became strangely weightless; she had been picked up and deposited on the straw on top of her bottles at the bottom of the open pit. At the same time, the roof collapsed, the first beams to fall straddling the pit and supporting the remainder on top. Shaken, her head spinning, Mrs. Tremorne wondered if this were the end. . . .

She came to, some hours later, in thick black silence, conscious of sharp things boring through the straw into her back—the tops of her wine bottles. She lifted her arms, then each leg; everything worked. Apart from an unnerving deafness, she could not find even a scratch; her shoes had been blown off, but she still clutched the flashlight in one hand, the string bag was still over her arm, the bottles intact inside. She struggled to her feet, resting her elbows on the floor at the edge of the pit. She could see chinks of red light in the otherwise impenetrable mass of beams over her. She swept the light around the roof of her prison and saw that even if she had the strength to remove some of the obstruction, the balance was so delicate that she might well bring the whole jumble crashing down. She would have to resign herself to waiting.

She did not know when the all clear sounded at last in the early morning, only that she was very cold and ached in every bone. She shouted and shouted; then, falling silent from sheer exhaustion, she realized that the ARP post at the street corner would probably check the house only. Knowing that Miss Carpenter was away—one of the wardens was her cousin—and finding no evidence of Mrs. Tremorne, they would assume that she had gone out for the evening. But the daily woman would come at nine o'clock, Mrs. Tremorne reassured herself, she would come searching. . . .

But no one came. She moved some bottles to form a straw nest. Sometimes she fell into an exhausted sleep, sometimes she forced herself to stand up in the pit and move her arms and legs. Sometimes she sang. Thirsty, she remembered the sloe gin; transferring some to a small bottle occupied her for a long time, but the result was comforting. The more sips she took, the more it seemed that her hearing was returning; she could even hear occasional traffic from the road beyond the garden. But this only increased her feeling of loneliness and desertion.

In one of these moments, as she clenched and unclenched her fingers against growing stiffness, she heard a soft whining and felt the warm, wet touch of a tongue. She touched a muzzle, ears—a dog had come out of the blackness to her, the only living thing that knew or cared, apparently, that she still existed.

Unfamiliar tears of gratitude welled up in Mrs. Tremorne's eyes. When the pile shifted and an agonized yelp followed, she forgot her own aching bones; she longed only to comfort this warm miraculous link with life. From that moment Mrs. Tremorne determined that if she had to spend another month here, living on gin in total darkness, she would somehow come out of it and see this small creature that had risked its life to come to her.

It was to be another two days before Mrs. Tremorne was found by the devoted Janet Carpenter, who had cut short her holiday to come back when she could receive no satisfaction on the telephone, the lines being down. She had arrived only that morning to find that the daily woman who had promised to look after Mrs. Tremorne had vanished, padlocking her cottage behind her. For a while Miss Carpenter thought Mrs. Tremorne might have vanished with her, to some safer hideout in the country. She knew that her mistress would not have gone out with friends that evening, for the simple reason that she had no friends. But it never occurred to her to think beyond the house.

It was not until she went into the garden that she heard a muffled barking. Puzzled, she traced it to the garage. Plainly there was a dog trapped somewhere in that wreckage; but how to get it out? The cupboard under the stairs hung drunkenly, a pile of broken bottles covered in white dust lying below. On top was a curiously familiar shape: Alice Tremorne's ivory-headed cane. Janet Carpenter turned and ran for the ARP post.

They reached the dog first, a small dog, dusty white save for the red of a mangled forepaw. When the dog was lifted out and laid on the floor, they set to work again.

When they uncovered Mrs. Tremorne, she was stretched out on a bed of straw, her hands folded on her chest under her sable cape. The string of pearls on the massive shelf of her bosom moved up and down with peaceful regularity.

She was taken to hospital, where—almost incredibly for a semi-invalid seventy-six years old—no damage other than a bruising which discolored almost her entire body had been found, and now it was a matter of time and rest only.

The first thing she had asked for was her rescuer, the dog. Miss Carpenter was bidden to find out about this canine hero forthwith. What did it look like? It was just a dog, a small dog, Miss Carpenter said, with a shortish tail and longish ears.

Mrs. Tremorne regarded her with scorn. "It was a miracle," she said. "I held its paw and strength *flowed* out."

The next day Miss Carpenter was able to report that one of the rescue team had taken the dog home, and his wife was looking

Bel Ria

after it; its eyes were open, the wound on the paw was clean, but possibly there were internal injuries or severe shock, for the animal seemed to have lost the will to live—it simply lay in a box without stirring, and was kept going only by the efforts of the woman, with spoonfuls of warm milk laced with precious whiskey.

She must be suitably rewarded, and a vet must be summoned, commanded Mrs. Tremorne. The dog must be installed at The Cedars straightaway. Carpenter must go forth and—here was her alligator bag—set the machinery in motion; a dog basket, the best, to be bought; leads, brushes, bones, and dog delicacies.

If miraculous strength had flowed out of the dog's paw to Alice Tremorne, now the procedure was reversed. By the time Mrs. Tremorne was allowed home to her bed, still stiff and sore, the dog was installed in a basket in her bedroom, his coat brushed to gleaming point, his hair combed to a silken length and tied back from his eyes with a red ribbon. His hocks had been shaved to match the area around the injured paw, over which a baby's bootee was drawn to hold the dressing in place, and several times a day Miss Carpenter, mouth buttoned into a thin line, clipped a leash onto the finest of red leather collars and took her charge for an airing in the garden. Afterward—her lips by then almost invisible—she lifted him into the bed beside Mrs. Tremorne, who then drew her pink silk eiderdown tenderly over.

At first he had hardly stirred, lying with dull, apathetic eyes. When he slept his body twitched convulsively, and Mrs. Tremorne would reach out to pat and talk the reassuring baby talk she had never used before, until he lay quiet again. As the days passed, his tail gradually stirred more and more, his eyes cleared and focused—until one day she awoke to find him stroking her arm with one paw. An indomitable little dog had risen from the ashes.

Now to find a name for him. It seemed to Alice Tremorne that if she tried enough canine names, she might run into one that would sound familiar enough to a dog's ears. Propped up against her pillows, her audience's eyes fixed upon her, she began: Rover, Fido, Blackie, Spot, Kim . . . but none met with any recognition. Then she remembered John Peel and his hounds.

"Yes, I ken John Peel and Ruby too, and Ranter and Rover . . ." No, it wasn't Rover, it was . . . ? She started off again: "*Do ye ken John Peel wi' his coat so gay?*" She sang determinedly, only to get stuck again at Ranter.

She was still at it when Miss Carpenter arrived to take the dog out, and when commanded to make a duet she outran Mrs. Tremorne: "*Ranter and Ringwood and Bellman and True!*"

As Mrs. Tremorne repeated the names, suddenly the dog's ears rose and the round eyes lighted up in seeming recognition. It was Bellman that excited him, but she soon found that the first half of the word had the same effect. "*Bell!*" she said. "Good Bell!" And each time she spoke, the dog's tail wagged furiously. "You see," she said triumphantly. "That's his name—Bell! Time for walkies then, my darling Bell."

In glum silence Carpenter clipped the lead on. Then, almost unheard of, she produced an opinion of her own. "I think Bell's a silly name for a dog. It sounds like a girl, or a chime."

Mrs. Tremorne was not used to mutiny, but she quelled it now with cunning ease. "Neither the feminine nor the dingdong, but *Bel*, who—as I am sure you will remember—was the god of heaven and earth in Babylonian mythology."

Many years' addiction to *The Times* crossword had paid off. Bel he became, the sound of the name near enough to the one to which he had responded for so many years before he became Ria.

Measure for measure Bel returned the love and care lavished on him, and all his natural affection and gaiety, so long denied, returned. He filled out to an attractive, alert healthiness, becoming in the process the closest thing to a poodle to which the united efforts of his mistress and a kennel maid could clip him, the dark shaggy hairs of the outer coat stripping down to a pale, almost lavender gray. The mutilation of his toes left him with a slight limp but did not seem to inconvenience him.

Now that Mrs. Tremorne had an all-engrossing interest, an atmosphere of warmth gradually permeated the normally gloomy house. Miss Carpenter became Janet. Bel loved her, and she enjoyed his company and the interest he brought to her formerly

solitary walks. But undoubtedly the one who received his full devotion was the one whom he had found himself, Mrs. Tremorne.

He seemed to be completely content in his role of companion
to her; a perfect dog, obedient, with faultless manners, even
toward food, for at first he would eat nothing unless she were
eating too. Yet sometimes Mrs. Tremorne felt that it was like living
with a ghostly X, the unknown quantity—who and whatever had
formed his life before he came to her?

There were times when he lay for hours on top of the garden
wall, watching the world that passed below as though waiting to
recognize some familiar form. Mrs. Tremorne gradually discovered
the pattern of his interests: the *clop-clop* of a horse-drawn milk
van or coal cart; servicemen, and sailors in particular.

There were times too when he lay listless and unresponsive,
his eyes infinitely sad and far away. On other occasions he would
sit before her, searching her eyes, straining to get some message
across. "Darling Bel, what are you trying to tell me?" she would
implore, but only a puzzled shadow would flit over his eyes.
However, as the bond between them grew, his need to communicate became stronger.

One day he rose to his hind legs in a bid to keep her attention
longer. She took his forepaws. The wireless was playing Irish jigs,
and she laughed down at him, moving his paws in time to the
music. "Come on, my darling," she said. "Dance with me. . . ." She
moved three stiff, close steps to the right, and then to the left,
and he followed her. "One, two, *three* . . ." Breathless, she let
his paws go, but to her astonishment he circled on, nodding his
head in a quaint little dance. Her reaction was one of admiration
and enchantment—and relief too, for it was as though a barrier
had been broken. Her pleasure was so patent that thereafter he
volunteered this performance from time to time—but only, she
noticed, when the need to communicate became so overwhelming
that he had no other recourse, a unique bestowal of himself.

Because she wanted more than anything else to participate in the
life that ran with hers now, she forced herself to walk more and
more, so that she could go farther afield in the garden and watch

her darling's enjoyment there. Not only did she begin to feel better physically, but she was actually seen at the end of the orchard talking over the fence—about Bel, naturally—to her neighbor.

One afternoon she and Bel had reached the far end of the garden when suddenly he stopped, ears pricked. Then he shot like an arrow down through the hedge, across the orchard beyond, and over the barred gate to the paddock.

Mrs. Tremorne saw the object of his excitement, her neighbor's donkey, the long-retired Fred, who grazed her paddock from time to time. She watched Bel streak across the grass, then slow to a halt, his excitement apparently diminished as he sniffed around. After examining the donkey from every angle, he crouched and sprang onto the shaggy back. Fortunately it was not the first time Fred had felt weight there; fifteen years of children had accustomed him to almost anything. Mrs. Tremorne reveled in the spectacle of Bel, mouth open, tongue lolling as though in laughter, forepaws rigid. Fred moved off, the small rider on his back.

When Mrs. Tremorne called at last, Bel came running, his eyes still alight with excitement. After this, if not bound for the wall, he would trot briskly off in search of Fred.

WITHIN the garden walls, the weeks stretched into months, the war intruding only through the BBC. Plymouth seldom received other than sporadic bombing now, but as the convoys battled against the ever multiplying U-boat packs, such a terrible toll was exacted that rationing became even more stringent.

But it was when Mrs. Tremorne was faced with the prospect of one egg per fortnight and one ounce of butter per week that the full impact of the war was brought home. She turned her attention to the egg problem: they would keep hens. Six chicks were bought; at first they were kept in the kitchen in a box, under the unwavering gaze of Bel. When they slept, he relaxed; when they awoke, their cheepings brought him scurrying. When they were let out, they followed him around as though he were a mother hen, and if he lay down, they climbed all over him. His retinue persisted even when they were grown and had the run of the orchard.

Now Bel's days were full indeed, and by the time a year had passed he was indirectly contributing to the war effort as well; for in a combination of patriotism and the desire to arrest the further stiffening of her fingers in order to groom him, Mrs. Tremorne had learned to knit. Slowly and painfully she knitted for the Naval Comforts Fund, working her way up through scarves and mitts to the ultimate triumph of socks.

If her life had been completely altered by Bel's coming, so was Janet Carpenter's, who seemed ten years younger—almost within five years of her actual thirty-four. Having looked after her elderly parents until they died, she had been untrained for any job and had resigned herself to the gray future of a light-duties companion. But with Mrs. Tremorne occupied and content, she had nerved herself to ask if she might join one of the voluntary services; she now slaved happily two evenings a week in a railway canteen.

Janet proved to be an amusing raconteuse, and brought back a breath of outside life as she regaled Mrs. Tremorne with her encounters over the coffee urns. Mrs. Tremorne, eager to expand her Bel audience, encouraged her to invite lonely or stranded young servicemen and servicewomen back to The Cedars. At Christmas she managed to procure a magnificent turkey and wine, and eight young people sat down to an unforgettable dinner. Afterward one of them produced a penny whistle, another a concertina, and they sang carols. Then, as though to put the final seal of pleasure on this happiest of days, Bel rose to perform his solemn little dance; and as she watched him now, Mrs. Tremorne saw that his eyes sought hers with the same strange intensity of those first weeks. At that moment, with a sudden jealous stab of helplessness, as though she had somehow failed him, she knew without doubt that this was only a part of a presentation; it should go on, but it could not, for something was missing and she could not provide it. Everything else in Bel's life she could provide, but not this release that belonged to someone else.

She did not speak of this to Janet; if she had become such an absurd old woman that she was jealous of a ghost, then it was better to keep it to herself.

CHAPTER SEVEN

I NTO this happy little Eden one day, nearly two years after Bel's arrival, came a stranger. He was in naval uniform, small and slight, with a finely drawn, almost ascetic face. When Janet came to the door, he asked to see Mrs. Tremorne.

"What name?" asked Janet.

"Neil MacLean," he said, then added, "But Mistress Tremorne will not be acquaint with it. I have been trying to trace a dog that was lost in Plymouth in 1941, and I had heard from a nurse at the hospital here that . . ." His voice trailed off.

Janet could feel the blood drain out of her face and a sense of disaster closing in. As she stood staring at MacLean, Mrs. Tremorne's voice floated down the stairs. "If that is the laundry," she said, "tell them that we are missing *two* pillowcases."

Janet found her voice. "It is a Mr. MacLean, wanting to see you about a dog," she called up.

Mrs. Tremorne decided that he must be one of Bel's many garden-wall acquaintances. "Come along up," she said pleasantly.

Upstairs, MacLean followed Alice Tremorne into the small room that she used so that she could watch Bel in the garden or the paddock with field glasses. She hobbled to a chair and sat down, motioning MacLean to sit opposite. "You must be one of Bel's friends?" she said, taking up her knitting.

"I am not acquaint with the name," said MacLean. "As I was telling yon woman at the door, it was about a dog that was thought to have been killed during the blitz in 1941. . . ." He paused, aware of a current of hostility in the room, but there was no change of expression in the pale, wrinkled face. He went on. "I heard in a roundabout way that you acquired a dog then, one that had found you when you were buried under your house—"

"Garage," said Mrs. Tremorne. "It used to be a coach house. . . ."

"Buried under your garage," amended MacLean patiently. "And I thought that it might well have been Ria—"

"Ria?" said Mrs. Tremorne, dropping a stitch.

"That was the name I gave him, for I never knew his real one.

He was brought aboard our destroyer off St.-Nazaire, with one of the survivors from the *Lancastria*. The man was badly wounded, and I kept the dog for him. There was a monkey too. Then I left the dog in Plymouth, and—"

"Monkey?" said Mrs. Tremorne, stalling for time.

He nodded. "It was called Louis."

The room was very still; there was only the clicking of needles. Mrs. Tremorne decided that strategic attack was the best defense. "And what did this dog of yours look like, my man?"

"Ria was not very big," he said. "Dark gray, with a thick coat, and his tail had been docked. He wasn't any breed, mind you, a terrier type, but you couldn't mistake him, for his eyes—very large and bright they were. And he was the cleverest wee beast I ever came across." MacLean stopped, astonished at his loquacity.

"What a wonderful dog he must have been!" said Alice Tremorne with masterly earnestness. "How I wish I could say the same about mine! Like so many of these overbred small poodles nowadays, my darling is very timid and highly strung."

"*Poodle?*" said MacLean.

"Poodle," said Mrs. Tremorne firmly.

"I would like to see him," he said.

"I'm afraid he's not here—he's with friends. What a pity. Now, Mr. MacLean, I am a busy woman. My companion will see you out." She put down her knitting and strained toward the bell. The ball of wool rolled off her lap. As MacLean got to his knees to retrieve it, she looked down and saw a livid scar snaking across his head, the thin hair combed carefully over it. Pity and revulsion stirred simultaneously. And MacLean, his eyes on a level with her swollen ankles, experienced the same reaction.

He stood, the ball of wool in his hand, picked up the knitting, and examined it briefly. "It is the fine sock that you are making," he said. In fact it was a terrible sock, one that would produce blisters on the first foot it encountered.

"There are many of my socks seeing service in the navy," said Mrs. Tremorne. "Scarves and mitts too."

"We are always very grateful for them," he said.

She looked down at his neat navy-blue socks with a critical eye. "Very nicely knitted," she said. "Do they have a double heel?"

"No," said MacLean. "I am not liking the double heel; it is clumsy looking, yon."

"But they last *twice* as long," said Mrs. Tremorne.

"I like single heels," said MacLean coldly.

"They have to be darned," said Mrs. Tremorne. "Double is the *only* way." They glared at one another.

"I never darn," said MacLean with Olympian dignity. "I knit new heels. This is the second pair of heels these have had."

"*You* knitted them?" Mrs. Tremorne said with admiration. "I wish I could turn heels like that—I always get a space there and have to darn it in. Look," she said, "it's starting to form now—"

MacLean hesitated, then, "Here, it's like this," he said, and took up the sock.

Mrs. Tremorne relaxed. Bel was safely in the paddock. According to his inflexible habits, he would not return unless she called him, but she would make sure nevertheless.

Janet, entering the room a few minutes later at the bidding of the bell, expecting she knew not what, found the visitor sitting on a chair drawn up close to Mrs. Tremorne's.

"*Then* pass the slipped stitch over," he was saying.

Mrs. Tremorne looked up. "Ah, Janet, my dear," she said. "Coffee for two, please. Oh, and Janet"—she paused meaningfully—"if that Mr. *Bell* should call, tell him to come back later."

"I'll see that he gets the message," Janet said, almost skipping out the door and down the stairs.

"And now, Mr. MacLean," said Alice Tremorne, "just once again—into the back of the stitch, then . . ." She was playing with fire, she knew; he should go now—but she could not overcome the terrible desire to hear something of Bel's background from this dour, inscrutable little man who had once owned Bel. . . .

While they were having their coffee, MacLean launched into a world of reminiscence about Ria. Mrs. Tremorne listened, and as Bel's life at sea unfolded, so many missing pieces clicked into place; and something else, which she tried to push into the back of her mind, the unconscious laying bare of a man's life and the gradual returning of warmth to it from the coming of the dog. "That Ria—how he affected people. Even me. And so," MacLean ended, "that was why I left him here—I had promised Sinclair—"

Mrs. Tremorne could hardly believe her ears. "You mean to say that after all those months you deliberately *left* him?"

"Aye," he said heavily. "I was not wanting to, but he was not mine; I was only minding him whiles for Sinclair."

Any prickings of conscience Mrs. Tremorne might have had were quenched by this appalling statement. "You, Sinclair—pshaw!" she said. "What about *Ria? His* feelings? You talk about him as though he were a *parcel* to be readdressed—and all to honor some stupid promise! Honor indeed! It was pure heartlessness!" The fact that she was partly defending her own behavior gave a passionate conviction to her words.

MacLean stood up and looked out the window to the orchard beyond, his eye caught by the figure of a donkey ambling in the long grass, a small dog close at its heels.

Mrs. Tremorne had stood up too. "A beautiful view, isn't it?" she said, and handed MacLean his cap. "It has been most interesting meeting you." She managed to smile.

"I was looking at a donkey and a dog in the field over there," he said, and her heart missed a beat.

"What wonderful eyesight you must have," she said smoothly. "That is my neighbor's field."

Now the dog squeezed under the gate and ran up the fence line. As he came closer MacLean saw an impeccable poodle, with squared-off jaws, a shaven tail terminating in a knob of hair, the clipped coat a pale, almost lavender gray.

He turned away from the window. "I am sorry I troubled you, Mistress Tremorne," he said. "I will be going now."

Before she could ring the bell he was halfway down the stairs. He let himself out. And Janet, watching him walk down the path, hurried indoors to rejoice with Mrs. Tremorne.

"Can you see Bel out there?" Mrs. Tremorne asked.

Bel was in the orchard, Janet said. The darling, he must be

waiting for his walkies—she would fetch Mrs. Tremorne's cardigan.

I would not have done it—I would not have lied, Mrs. Tremorne told her conscience fiercely as she made her slow way into the garden, if he had not been so ruthless in his talk of promises.

Bel, untroubled by devious thought, came running now to greet this human who made up his present world, his eyes bright with love. She put out her hand to him, the string bag with her knitting in it dangling from her wrist; he sniffed the hand, the ball of wool, the half-knitted sock—and suddenly he was off like a hound on a trail, up the stairs to the small sitting room, then swift as an arrow down again, and out the open door. Now Bel was throwing himself wildly at the gate, falling back, throwing himself at it again. He could have jumped onto the wall and thence down to the lane below, but it was as though he must go through the gate, follow the reality that had gone through it already.

Janet ran to him, calling, but he took no notice. "Open the gate," said Alice Tremorne steadily. "Quickly—open the gate and let Bel go. . . ." And Janet, standing by the open gate, watched the little gray shadow streak down the road until it vanished.

Half a mile away, MacLean waited for the bus that would take him back to the naval barracks at Devonport, where he was stationed. Before the afternoon's visit he had felt buoyant with excitement; now he felt empty and flat—yet in a curious way expiated and resigned. The bus drew up and he swung himself on board.

"Move along there," said the conductress. "And no dogs allowed, *if* you please." She touched MacLean's shoulder. "Sorry, mate," she said, and smiled down.

Sitting at his feet, looking up at him with the clear, unmistakable eyes, unblinking beneath a ludicrous topknot secured with a red ribbon, was Ria. Together they got off the bus.

MacLean walked the miles back to the naval barracks, looking down every few minutes to reassure himself of the miracle: Ria, cool, contained, and undemonstrative as ever, trotting at his heels. MacLean paused only once as they neared the dockyard gates, and removed the red ribbon.

Exactly three days later, at ten o'clock in the morning, Bel returned to The Cedars. Janet heard him at the garden gate, and ran to let him in. He took the stairs in three bounds, pushed open the bedroom door, and jumped onto Mrs. Tremorne's bed. At that moment she was possibly the happiest woman in England, with Janet a close second.

For the rest of the day Bel followed his usual routine, trotting briskly down the path to the orchard, then on to the paddock, where he sailed through the air to land on the old donkey's dusty brown back. It was as though he had never been absent. The only difference in him was that he no longer wore a ribbon; someone had clipped the long hair on the top of his head.

He was there when Mrs. Tremorne, with Janet, made her way to the orchard. The three had lunch there, and afterward Bel accompanied the old lady up to her room for her afternoon rest.

At four o'clock, after a pleasant tea, Bel went to the door. When Janet took him out, he sat before the gate in silent supplication. Janet looked up at Mrs. Tremorne, who watched from the upstairs window. She seemed almost happy. "Yes, open it," she called down; and then had an inspiration, for she had no idea where to get in touch with MacLean. "Tie on a fresh ribbon before he goes," she said. But the hair was too short and the ribbon had to be tied to his collar. He ran off without a backward glance.

So Ria, arriving back at Devonport barracks three-quarters of an hour later, was able to inform MacLean how and where Bel had spent the afternoon.

Now BEL and Ria merged into Bel Ria, a purposeful little figure often seen trotting along the back roads between Devonport and The Cedars. Communication was soon established between his two owners. One day Mrs. Tremorne tied a label on his collar with an invitation to tea. The deft-fingered MacLean fashioned a small waterproof capsule into which he rolled his acceptance.

At first it was a very formal tea party, with both sides wary. No mention was made of their first meeting, but the specter of a third and rightful owner—rightful to MacLean, but to be fought to the last inch by Mrs. Tremorne—hovered uneasily between them. This

drew them closer. Besides, there was so much that Mrs. Tremorne
wanted to know that only MacLean could unfold.

As MacLean reminisced, Bel Ria sat between them, his eyes
going from one face to the other. When, to MacLean's barely concealed disapproval, the dog's customary saucer of tea and sugar
was handed down, he lapped his tea, then lay quietly down—thus
tactfully omitting his usual sitting-up-to-beg and saluting routine.

After this meeting acquaintance flowered, with Bel Ria as courier
for messages and, as MacLean's talent for fixing things around the
house was revealed, urgent SOSs. On receiving one of these, Mac-
Lean would arrive at The Cedars as soon as he had time off, and
put things right. Soon he took over the grass cutting, for the
gardener could only spare an hour a week now, and the garden
was beginning to look like a wilderness. From there it was a short
step to clearing choked gutters and drains, and putting a coat of
wood preservative on the hen house. At first he would do whatever
he considered had to be done and then depart, refusing to stay for
a meal. It was as though he could not bear to see his undemonstrative Ria behaving again as the pampered Bel.

Bel Ria

Alice Tremorne taxed him with this one day, and he admitted it bluntly. He didn't like dogs—or any animals—made fools of with tricks and the like. She was silent for a moment, her color high, but when she spoke, it was with a new, almost weary tone.

"I don't think it is we who make fools of dogs. I am beginning to think that they make fools of us—they show up our needs and weaknesses." She knew now that MacLean was not the ghostly X of her jealousy. Ria could never have danced for this man.

"Aye," MacLean said at last, the word that she had come to recognize as merely a useful noncommittal. They were standing by the window upstairs, looking across the garden to the roofless shell of the coach house. "Yon needs sorting," he said with a scowl.

"Impossible!" said Mrs. Tremorne. "Carpenters nowadays are charging so much that it would be out of the question."

"Indeed now!" said MacLean, his face brightening.

He left shortly afterward, and as she watched him walk to the gate, her darling Bel following him, she found herself longing that MacLean might be transferred to some remote dog-debarred posting, and his half of Bel Ria restored to her in whole impeccable poodledom once more, his lovely silken topknot unsnipped.

There had been bitter argument over Bel Ria's appearance. Mrs. Tremorne was proud of her grooming talent, but MacLean had wanted a reversal to the shaggy naval look. In the end a compromise had been reached, engineered by the diplomatic Janet. Why not let his coat grow out, but then keep it short to something like Bedlington terrier length? Both had grudgingly accepted this, both had secretly admired the compact result; and both had suffered the same stab of realization when they saw that a few white hairs had grown in to lightly brindle the short, curly coat.

She knew that MacLean had a fortnight's leave coming up, and deep down she had to admit that she would miss this dour little man's unannounced visits, his forthrightness. And so would Janet, she thought; at times nowadays she was positively skittish.

He took her unawares, therefore, on his next appearance, when he put forward the proposal that it might be a very good idea if he were to spend his leave restoring the coach house.

314

Alice Tremorne was delighted. Already she was organizing the details. Janet would turn the yellow bedroom into a bed-sitting-room—Mr. MacLean would be very comfortable there—and it must be a proper financial arrangement with the proper going wage.

When MacLean spoke his voice was cold. There would be no financial arrangement; he would be doing it because he chose to do it. There would be no room in the house. The tack room was still weatherproof; there was water from the pump, and a fireplace to cook by. If Mistress Tremorne would supply a camp bed and a few cooking utensils, that would be all he would be needing.

But Mistress Tremorne would not countenance such a one-sided arrangement. They set to in an argument closely followed by the worried eyes of Bel Ria between them. At the height of it he yawned hugely, stretched, and departed downstairs to Janet.

Unexpectedly Alice Tremorne was seized with laughter. "He's right," she said at last. "We *are* being very boring. I give in! Now will you do me a favor—accept our hospitality for meals?"

MacLean could make concessions too. He accepted gracefully. "It's the grand holiday you will be giving me," he said. "I had nowhere else to go anyway—except perhaps to Scotland, to sort things out with Donald Sinclair. . . ."

The words hung between them.

"That can wait forever as far as I am concerned," Alice Tremorne said flatly. "But the coach house needs sorting out now, before winter."

"Aye," said MacLean, enigmatical as ever. When he left the house with Bel Ria he patted the dog, something Mrs. Tremorne had never seen him do, and nodded cheerfully.

CHAPTER EIGHT

H E CAME with an ecstatically returning Bel Ria, in that portentous autumn of 1943, and settled into the tack room, finding that Janet had determinedly added a carpet, reading light, and even curtains at the windows. As he took off his uniform in exchange for working rig, he shed all worries and the outside world for the little self-contained one of The Cedars, where all the minuscule trivia, the grumblings, the pleasures, were woven into the background of the global tapestry of war. Alice Tremorne's equal indignation with the laundry and Hitler, Janet Carpenter's pleasure in the underwear potential of half a German parachute, even the way a little dog's coat was shorn to the winds of compromise was a part of the fabric of that time.

Bel Ria's reaction to his separate lives brought together virtually under the same roof was one of bewilderment. Although he slept in Alice Tremorne's bedroom, walked with MacLean across the fields in the evening, and sat between them at meals, during the rest of the day he paid frequent restless visits from one to another and seemed unable to relax with either.

Perhaps, his allegiance no longer divided, he felt free to pursue his own ends, for he took to spending more time with the donkey and with Janet—their company undoubtedly restful and undemanding. He spent many more hours too on his garden-wall vigil, his eyes distant, yet his ears flicking to all movement up and down the road.

"It's as though he were watching for someone to come up that road. I used to think it was whoever he belonged to before, but you are here now, and he still waits," said Mrs. Tremorne one morning. She was sitting in a garden chair, listing and dating the intact bottles which MacLean had excavated from the debris. Now he paused in his hammering.

"He would lie like that for hours on board too," he said. "Staring at nothing. Hyacinthe used to curl up beside him whiles, and it seemed he never even noticed she was there."

"Tell me about her, Neil," she said persuasively. "And about Barkis, and the monkey—Luigi, wasn't it?"

"Louis," he said. "Poor wee Louis—" He broke off abruptly. He didn't want to think about the monkey now. Instead he told her about Hyacinthe and her majestic ways. And he told her something of that terrible dawn on their way back from Tobruk, when two Ju-88s swooped out of the rising sun to sink one of their three destroyers and leave *Tertian* lying mortally wounded. Someone had picked up Hyacinthe where she lay in the scuppers with both front legs broken, and dropped her on a stretcher being passed across to *Trumpeter* alongside. She had been taken to hospital in Alexandria with the rest of the survivors, and a surgeon captain had set her legs in plaster. She had made a perfect recovery. "I heard later," said MacLean, "that she came back to England—in a submarine, of all things."

"And Barkis? What happened to him?" asked Mrs. Tremorne.

"The bridge received a direct hit," said MacLean, so tersely that she forbore to ask further questions.

He did not tell her then, or ever, of the ghastly shambles that had been the bridge. Or of any of those sixty-eight shipmates who went with *Tertian*. Nor did he tell her then of Louis.

Neil MacLean sawed and hammered and painted the days away. Now, brown and fit, free for the first time in months of the headaches which had plagued him since they removed the fragment of metal from his head in Alexandria, he did full justice to Mrs. Tremorne's carefully plotted meals.

Neil, as she and Janet called him now, had developed an easy relationship with her, never deferring, often blunt, yet always maintaining a balance of diffidence. Her ruthless determination amused him; his stubborness challenged her. Both loved an argument, for both had hard and fast opinions about almost everything. But disagreement always discomforted Bel Ria, and his nervous yawnings, heralding his imminent departure, were usually enough to make them agree to differ privately. Mrs. Tremorne adopted the diplomatic "Aye." So did Janet, but teasingly.

Janet had blossomed, and her refreshing down-to-earth viewpoint, her often hilarious anecdotes, were the perfect foil to MacLean's taciturnity. He found time to refurbish an old bicycle for her shopping expeditions, and he found too that she made an excellent carpenter's mate, with a good head for heights. Followed up the ladder by the nimble paws of a delighted Bel Ria, they spent many hours working companionably on the roof.

In the evenings Neil and Mrs. Tremorne read or listened to the wireless; sometimes all three sat knitting or sewing, Bel Ria asleep in their contented midst. But Mrs. Tremorne liked it best when she could persuade him to talk about *Tertian*.

One evening he brought over a few photographs. The first was of a fair-headed man by a ship's rail. At his feet was Ria, far sturdier then in his thick coat, but still recognizably her Bel.

"That was the doctor," said MacLean. "None better. He sent me these pictures after I got back here."

The second was of a bearded man in tropical uniform, newly stepped off a gangway, at his heels a massive bull terrier.

"The captain coming aboard at Gibraltar with Barkis," said MacLean. "Himself was the fine gentleman," he added, with such finite simplicity that Alice Tremorne passed swiftly on to the last picture: a tall young seaman with a little monkey wearing a pair of absurd white shorts perched on his shoulder.

"Lessing and Louis in the Mediterranean," said MacLean.

Mrs. Tremorne seemed fascinated by the photograph. "Such a little scrap of a thing to have gone through so much."

"He was a thrawn wee beast," said MacLean with some vehemence. "The men were daft about him, and so was Ria."

"And where is he now?" asked Mrs. Tremorne.

"He went with our Ark." MacLean's face was expressionless.

Mrs. Tremorne had not heard properly. "*Where* did you say?"

MacLean looked across at her. "He went with Lessing and the others," he said gently. "And he's still with them."

"What a happy ending," said Mrs. Tremorne with relief.

"Aye," said MacLean.

He thought of Louis again that night. He had had no affection for the animal, but his end had been such a lonely one, and its defiant rejection had affected him profoundly.

In those desperate moments after *Tertian* had been hit, there was no time to think of Louis. *Tertian* was a sitting target, and the decision was taken to abandon ship, then sink her themselves. Her sister ship, *Trumpeter*, now moving in alongside, was an even more vital target. Every minute counted, and all hands were turned to in searching out the wounded.

One of the last to leave, the coxswain, scrambling over the

wreckage, saw a flicker of movement, and Louis leaped onto the rail ahead. The coxswain grabbed as he passed, but Louis fought free to swarm up a stay, out of reach.

Trumpeter stood off and trained her guns. Close to MacLean, the quartermaster, watching through binoculars, spotted Louis. High on the wireless mast he clung to a stay, his head turned in the direction of *Trumpeter*. The guns thundered.

MacLean was glad now that he had substituted the satisfactory ambiguity to Alice Tremorne. He had not realized until he saw her with the photograph that she had such a vulnerable core. Why burden her with something that had tormented him for weeks afterward when, restless in the long hospital nights, he had tried to equate his obsession over the death of one capuchin monkey with the deaths of so many fine men.

Thinking back, he saw it in perspective for the first time. Loss of life was an accepted gamble that men took when they went to war. But no animal went to war; Louis had been the only alien against that background, caught up in man's lethal affairs.

MacLean knew now that he could never return to the laboratory after the war—there would be too many Louises and Rias and Hyacinthes there to remind him. He slept, absolved, the little ghost of Louis laid to rest at last.

Early in the morning, as though to rid his conscience entirely, he wrote a long letter to Donald Sinclair. He ended it:

. . . so that you must tell me what you would like done, for I am not easy in my mind to bide this way when it is your right. Mind you, I do not speak for Mrs. Tremorne—after all this time she thinks of the dog as hers—and in a way this is so. If it was not for her, this letter would not need to be written. She has been willing enough to let him be with me this half-and-half way, but only because she would do anything for him and it seemed to be his own decision. He is a strange dog.

I will hope to hear from you soon. In the meantime I will try and make him stay here when my leave is up, for finding his own way between D'port and here is too risky with the traffic. And too long, as I am thinking now that he is nearer eleven than ten.

He sealed and stamped the envelope. He would send it now. There was a faint scratch at the door; Bel Ria had arrived. He limped more noticeably than usual on their way to the postbox.

It would rain before afternoon, said Alice Tremorne. Her own aching joints foretold this. She was halfway down the stairs when she made her pronouncement. Near the bottom she stumbled. MacLean took her arm, and to divert her as he helped her to the window seat, he told of his decision to leave Bel Ria at The Cedars when he returned to duty. He felt her arm become rigid.

"Does that mean that—that you are going away—going back to sea?" she said at last, sounding almost fearful.

"No. I'll be at Devonport a while yet, I hope. With the winter coming on, it would seem easier for him." He felt her relax. She sat down, and he saw that she had tears in her eyes. "Mind you," he went on severely, "that doesn't mean any fancy work with the clippers and ribbons—there's plenty to be done yet outside, so I'll be backward and forward to keep an eye on him."

"But perhaps he won't stay once you've gone through that gate," said Mrs. Tremorne worriedly. Then, with sudden cunning, she went on. "Why don't you take Janet to the pictures this afternoon? To get him used to the idea that you *will* come back?"

"Why not? Why not indeed?" he said with sudden recklessness.

Mrs. Tremorne watched them go. Bel Ria made no attempt to follow. "How *nice*," she said as she settled down for a cozy chat with him on her lap. "How nice it would be—I could bring my bedroom downstairs, which would be much easier for us, wouldn't it? And they could have the whole of the upstairs, and then we could all be together! Wouldn't that be lovely, my darling?" Bel Ria regarded her with enthusiastic interest, and after a while she confided another thought. "The coach house would make a wonderful surgery, wouldn't it? I mean if he went back and finished his veterinary degree." Bel Ria stirred his tail agreeably.

He seemed reassured when he saw that Neil's work clothes remained in the tack room on the day of his departure. Janet held Bel Ria at the gate, subdued, as she waved his paw in farewell.

Donald Sinclair's reply was waiting at the barracks:

. . . besides, I have no right—it is between you and Mrs. Tremorne, for the dog has belonged to both of you over these years, and he was with me for less than twenty-four hours. It was a queer time too—if the dog had never found me in that ditch in France, everything would have been different. And his real owner might still be alive. That woman risked everything for me, and in the end the only way I could repay her was to see that her dog was cared for—and that was where you came in.

I hope that one day we will meet and have a good yarn about those days—perhaps next year, when I expect to come south.

Neil handed the letter to Mrs. Tremorne on his next visit.

"So it was a woman," she said, when she had finished reading it. "The one he really belonged to. . . ." She sounded almost sad. "I think I always knew that he never really belonged to either of us; he's just a part of both of us. Look at him"—she glanced across the room to where Bel Ria lay in a patch of sunlight—"you see, he isn't the shaggy Ria of your photographs, or the almost-poodle Bel of mine. He's *Bel Ria* and he became that between us."

MacLean could only nod. Clearly the question of possession had been dispelled. It was never to be revived.

CHAPTER NINE

As THE humans in his life became increasingly possessed by their own intertwining lives, Bel Ria was released to himself; but so gradually did this detachment come about over the following year that it went unremarked. The extended solitude on the wall, the longer withdrawals into sleep in their company, were taken for a natural quietude in his undisputed security.

The impulse to bestow his dance seldom overtook him now, for he was no longer rewarded with Mrs. Tremorne's pleasure, only frustrated by her concern. It seemed to her that he became over-intense when he danced, as though the performance exacted too great an effort, and because of this she tried to avoid it.

Even Neil, returning after a long absence in the spring of 1944, noticed no change other than a muzzle more grayed than he remembered, although that day his mind was occupied with more pressing affairs. He had been posted to a Combined Operations base in Sussex and had come back on an unexpected forty-eight-hour leave. Bel Ria had shadowed him from the moment he had turned in at the gate, but after the first greeting Neil had spied Janet in the garden, and it was she who received all the attention. Within half an hour she and Neil had become engaged. They would marry in December.

Janet had made only one proviso: that Alice Tremorne should always be their responsibility. Neil seemed only surprised that she would bother to mention this. "But I've never thought other than that I'd be taking on the pair of you," he said.

"It won't always be easy," Janet warned. "You don't know what it was like before. Bel Ria can't live forever, and when he's gone she'll be lost for something to lavish her love and attention on. You're *sure* you want to take it on?"

"There will be bairns to take his place one day," he said. "And, yes, I was never surer of anything."

He bent down to pat Bel Ria and then, to Janet's amazement, picked him up and held him in his arms.

"I've never seen you do that before," she commented.

"I was just seeing what it felt like," he said sheepishly.

Everything would go on just the same, they agreed as they walked back to the house, until Neil was demobilized and would finish off his studies for a veterinary degree. In the meantime, as Mrs. Tremorne's bedroom had been moved downstairs, perhaps they could use part of the upstairs as their own quarters.

From the window Alice Tremorne saw them coming, Bel Ria running ahead, the three beings who filled her life. She sat back in her chair with a sigh of content. But a few minutes later she received the news with every appearance of overjoyed astonishment. Not long afterward she had a sudden inspiration for the conversion of the upstairs part of the house. They received this with equal pleasure and surprise.

In June, following D Day, Janet took on a part-time post with the ARP in addition to the railway canteen, so Mrs. Tremorne and

Bel Ria were alone for most of the day now. But they were content and occupied, and each had the other's undivided attention. They had taken up the challenge of cooking. Planting high stools in strategic resting places around the kitchen, Alice Tremorne moved from one to another, talking to her keenly interested taster ensconced on a nearby chair, as she put her full ingenuity into making something delicious out of the nothing of wartime substitutes and those rewarding eggs.

The months slipped by. In August the reentry into Paris was celebrated with *oeufs parisiens;* October brought the occupation of Athens and *oeufs à la grecque.* Her triumph was the wedding feast with one of the hens in aspic.

After this excitement Neil returned to his posting on the south coast, Janet to her jobs, and Bel Ria and Mrs. Tremorne settled down again, avoiding the winter's cold and fuel shortages by moving almost permanently into the warm coziness of the kitchen.

Bel Ria seemed very content with this tranquil existence, becoming reluctant even to desert the warmth of the fire for the wall. Too content altogether, Mrs. Tremorne decided.

"This will never do," she told him briskly one February morning. "We're becoming soft—anyone would think we're getting old," and she began to coax him from the fire for longer and longer periods. Out they went, rain or shine, wind or frost.

"If *I* can do it—*you* can!" she told him as they limped along together in the thin cold sunshine one day. "Smell that," she commanded, poking the rich earth with her cane. And "Fetch!" she exhorted as she whacked at rotting windfalls and fir cones, until suddenly the reluctant exercise turned into an exuberant, rolling, snuffing discovery in the irresistible challenge of spring. Soon Bel Ria was back in charge of his vibrant garden domain.

It was not until the day of Victory in Europe that she was forced to admit that he was slowing up. Out in the garden to share in the jubilation of the long-silenced bells pealing across the countryside, she saw Bel Ria try and fail to make the low jump onto the wall. "Perhaps we're not *quite* as young as we were, my love," she admitted, and she called in two youngsters to move a garden seat close to the wall to make things easier for him. Then she went inside and hung a Union Jack from her bedroom window.

But in truth she herself seemed rejuvenated in this her eightieth year, for there was so much to look forward to. Janet and Neil had their own quarters upstairs now, and it would not be long before he was demobilized. The war at last over, she no longer felt bound to supply His Majesty's navy with knitted comforts, but could ply her needles instead in an endless stream of bootees and bonnets for the child that was on the way. And the assurance that she would be the child's godmother and proxy grandmother all rolled into one gave her carte blanche to order the best in nursery equipment, in the same manner as she had years before ordered the best for a nameless little dog.

There was another, more immediate, excitement to be realized too, the long-awaited visit from Donald Sinclair. Alice Tremorne was alone in the house that day, a day that had become unexpectedly even more momentous. Early in the morning Neil had taken Janet to the hospital, some three weeks earlier than had been anticipated. Mrs. Tremorne hovered between the kitchen and the hall window, unable to settle to anything.

Bel Ria too became increasingly restless, and Mrs. Tremorne watched him settle on the sanctuary of the wall in the early afternoon almost with relief.

He was there when his soldier came walking up the road. Minutes before he came into view Bel Ria half rose, ears pricked, and jumped down off the wall to wait, quivering, on the road.

Donald Sinclair did not recognize him at first; then, as he came nearer, the unmistakable riveting eyes drew him back down the years to that road in France and the dusty, desolate little figure with its rider clinging tightly around its neck. Then the eyes had been filled with entreaty; now they were bright and expectant. Bel Ria waited there, steadily, until the man who was his last link in the human chain that reached back to the open roads of the caravan world picked him up and held him in his arms. He buried his head in the man's jacket, as though seeking once more the reassurance of a bandage torn from familiar clothing.

Sinclair could feel the heart beating beneath his hands. He opened the gate and stood for a long minute, deeply moved; then he walked slowly toward the house.

Alice Tremorne came to the door. After she and Donald Sinclair had introduced themselves, she said, "I think this is an occasion that calls for a little celebration." She led him into the kitchen and directed him to the cupboard with the sloe gin '36.

"My best vintage," she said as she poured two glasses. "I never drink it without thinking of Bel—Bel Ria, I mean; he saved my life, you know, he found me—" She broke off and looked across to where he sat now, with his muzzle laid on the man's knee, whining softly. She had never seen him like this before, so tense that he was almost rigid, his whole being concentrated on Sinclair, excluding her even when she had spoken his name. "There is no need to ask if he recognized you," she said, smiling, for strangely the exclusion did not rankle. She had warmed immediately to this tall gentle-faced Highlander. "Oh, there is so much to tell you, so much to ask. . . . Let's begin at the beginning and go on to the end."

The sloe gin reminded Donald Sinclair of the old man's fire-coursing brew. And he went back to the first encounter with the caravan. He was a natural storyteller, and he re-created in vivid detail the love and excitement, the tragedy and courage of those eventful hours in Bel Ria's life that he had shared.

Mrs. Tremorne spoke only once, when he described the perfection of communication between the dark woman and her dog in the performance on the road. "So that was what he was trying to tell me," she said sadly. "Oh, Bel, if only I had known. . . ."

It was almost dusk when the story ended, and she roused herself to reality. "I wonder what his real name was?" And she told of John Peel's hounds and how Bel had picked out his name.

"I don't think I heard her speak his name once," said Sinclair. "But it was curious that he picked an English word like bell." He drew a box out of his pocket. "It was around his neck," he explained. "I brought it for good luck—for the bairn that's coming."

Mrs. Tremorne opened the box and took out a tiny silver bell on a metallic strip. She shook it, smiling at the clear, sweet tone.

Bel Ria turned as though electrified; then for the first time since Sinclair's arrival he came to her. His tail moved faster and faster, he cocked his head from one side to the other as she tinkled the bell again. She slipped the bell around his neck. He tossed his head, then moved it from side to side in a deliberate rhythmic control that kept the clapper chiming continuously. Enchanted, Mrs. Tremorne clapped her hands in time.

"He had bells around his paws too when he danced," said Sinclair. He clicked his fingers and Bel Ria came running to sit before him, transformed with a jaunty, confident excitement.

He offered his forepaws, one at a time, with a demanding insistence. Donald Sinclair took each one in turn, encircling it with his fingers, smiling down regretfully, but Bel Ria seemed satisfied with the action. He stood stock-still between them for a moment; then, with head erect, he straightened his back in the ritual that had always preceded the tantalizing fragment of the dance bestowed from time to time on Mrs. Tremorne.

Bel Ria took the opening step—and at the same moment the kitchen door burst open before Neil MacLean.

"Janet's fine!" he shouted. "And it's a boy—a fine wee boy!"

He rushed at Mrs. Tremorne and hugged her, so carried away that he almost lifted her off her feet. Then he turned to Donald Sinclair and a flood of Gaelic followed, accompanied by much handshaking and backslapping.

Bel Ria was overtaken by the sense of rejoicing too. He raced around the kitchen like a two-year-old, skidding and barking excitedly, but such was the jubilation that no one heard this most rare demand for notice.

Mrs. Tremorne went to find the hoarded whiskey to wet the new Scot's head. Then, after the initial toast to the new life, they drank a toast to Janet, and to one another.

"And to Bel Ria," said Mrs. Tremorne at last. "For if it were not for you, the three of us would not be celebrating now."

"To Bel Ria," they said, and raised their glasses to him.

After the first commotion had died down, Bel Ria had crept back to sit by Sinclair, pressed close against his leg. Occasionally he shook his head in a bid for inclusion, but the small bell went unheard below the cheerful voices. Then he circled the group, pausing, concentrating intently, as though willing each of them to glance down. He was patted absently, but still the voices rose and fell, denying him. Panting, he returned to sit by the soldier.

"Bel Ria—Bel Ria—" he heard at last, and the hand that lay on his neck set the bell tinkling clearly in the sudden silence.

It was his moment. He had his audience's attention now. He shook his head to set the bell ringing, rose, then straight and steady, eyes fixed ahead, he pirouetted before them.

Mrs. Tremorne had been privileged to these opening movements of his inexplicable little dance. Neil MacLean had never even known about it. Long ago Donald Sinclair had watched it to the conclusion. But now, in the gathering dusk of a silent room, the little dog did not dance for him, or for her. He danced as though he must, for the one who taught him. But her bidding never came, there were no signaling fingers or tapping foot, and he became uncertain in his steps. Panting hard, shaking his head for the reassurance of the bell, he circled slowly and faltered, half lowering himself to the floor, his head turning back as though in search.

Helpless and deeply disturbed, his audience watched. He rose again unsteadily, repeated the circle, and tried a tight spin.

"Oh, no—*no*, Bel," pleaded one. "Let him be," said another; and the third, who alone understood the choreography of this tragic *pas de seul*, looked on silently.

But suddenly Bel Ria seemed to receive confidence. His head went back and his eyes looked forward with a steady eagerness, as though long custom had recalled the closing movements and there was no longer any need for direction.

There was nothing to disquiet now in the certain dignity and perfection of his finale. He circled, slower and slower, his forepaws lowering and his head drooping, once more the perfectly controlled clockwork toy running down. But this time when he sank to the ground in the finale he did not rise again to take his applause and finish his act. It was already over.

Friendly, thoroughly down-to-earth, Sheila Burnford is a grandmother with three grown-up daughters. She was born in the Scottish Highlands, went to school on the Continent, and is now a citizen of Canada—her husband was a pediatrician there.

She lives on the shores of Lake Superior near Thunder Bay, and is an accomplished fisherman and sailor. Her special feeling for animals was reflected in her charming international best seller, *The Incredible Journey*, published in 1961 and made into an immensely successful film by Walt Disney. Next she took two years off to live in an Indian village in the far Canadian north, and wrote a book, *One Woman's Arctic*, describing her experiences there.

Sheila Burnford

Bel Ria, too, is based heavily on personal experience. From Mrs. Burnford's childhood in Provence come vivid memories of Gypsy caravans and the performing animals that often accompanied them. She served as an ambulance driver in World War II and was in Plymouth throughout the blitz on that city. Later she visited St.-Nazaire and met survivors of the ill-fated *Lancastria*. In addition, her husband, who served on destroyers, returned from the island of Crete with a dog of somewhat doubtful parentage.

Animals, Sheila Burnford believes, have an "innate dignity we humans rarely afford them." Her intention in writing *Bel Ria* was to portray a dog that clung indomitably to its own identity while seeming to bend to the whims of its various human owners. She has no time at all for the usual run of sentimental animal stories. "The moment I read that 'Rover thought . . .' I close the book," she says.

Chase the Wind

A CONDENSATION OF THE NOVEL BY

E. V. Thompson

ILLUSTRATED BY ROBERT LAVIN

eir love was haunted by violence and
e beauty of the wild Cornish moors

Josh Retallick's home and heart are in the copper mines of Cornwall, where men like his father struggle in the miner's brutal life of the early nineteenth century. For young Josh, however, the future seems bright: he shows promise as a mining engineer, and he has the love of Miriam Trago, a girl as untamed and natural as the moors she has known since childhood. Josh and Miriam are pledged to one another—until sudden tragedy forces their lives onto separate paths.

Miriam's leads to the Reverend William Thackery, dedicated crusader for the rights of miners, while Josh is drawn to aristocratic Sarah Carlyon, whose father had apprenticed him as a boy. As Josh is caught up in the relentless battle for unionism, he is unaware of an ominous, growing danger.

In this prizewinning novel of social change, a gripping personal saga unfolds against a turbulent background.

CHAPTER ONE

NINETY fathoms below grass, in the darkness at the bottom of the main vertical shaft of Wheal Sharptor copper mine, Joshua Retallick stepped from the ladder onto the ore-strewn floor. The boy took a couple of shaky steps, his legs trembling from the long climb down. Above him, so far up that the clean, star-studded sky could not be seen, was a small, square hole. Through this was hoisted the copper ore that would make one man rich and send fifty more to premature graves.

Josh moved to one side as boots scraped on the wooden rungs overhead. The night shift was coming down. As each man stepped onto the floor he would flex his arms, easing muscles knotted by the fear of falling that made him grip each rung too tightly.

The miners passed into the tunnels that sloped away from the main shaft. Once inside, they paused to light the candles that would give them light to work by and warning of foul air.

Josh followed one of the miners along the tunnel where he knew Ben, his father, was working. At first the tunnel was narrow, with water oozing from the walls. Then, suddenly and dramatically, it opened out into a vault eighty feet wide and thirty high. Here there had been a seam of near-pure copper. Now it was a rock-walled emptiness—the ore long since fed into the belly of a Swansea smelting house and disgorged as gleaming blocks of metal, to be shipped in tall-rigged vessels to a world eager for high-grade Cornish copper.

In the flickering shadows of the candle flames a dirty, sweating figure, stripped to the waist and pushing a laden wheelbarrow, appeared from a small tunnel. Seeing the new arrivals, he rested the wheelbarrow and called back down the tunnel, "Time to wrap it up, Ben. Night shift are here."

The call was taken up by unseen men in other tunnels. "Knock it off! Night men are here!"

Men cramped in unnatural postures gratefully eased their way back from exploratory borings and headed toward the main shaft to begin the long climb to air and home. The young miner who had first signaled the arrival of the relief shift grinned at Josh. "Has Preacher Thackeray given up trying to learn you? Does he think you should be working belowground wi' us now?"

"No." Josh grinned back. "Lessons ended early. There's a meeting of the benefit union at the St. Cleer chapel tonight."

"I wouldn't mention anything about it to your dad. He's not too happy wi' talk about Thackeray's union."

Budge Pearn toweled his body with his rough-spun shirt. At eighteen he was four years older than Josh. His mother had died in childbirth. His father had been killed in a mining accident when Budge was seven years old, and he had been taken into the Retallick household. Now he was married and had a cottage of his own.

"When are you coming up to see my Jenny and the baby?" He pronounced it "bebby." "Little Gwen's right handsome now."

"I know. Jenny brought her down home today. That reminds me. You'd better not be late. Mother gave Jenny some boiling bacon for your supper."

"I'll be up on the moor before your dad sets foot on the ladder. Give my love to your mother." With a cheery wave, he was gone.

FARTHER along the tunnel, Ben Retallick crawled back over a heap of newly dug ore. He was one of the most experienced miners on Wheal Sharptor. But at thirty-five he was reckoned an old man by mining standards. In the 1830s, when a miner had seen his fortieth birthday belowground he was something of a rarity.

Outside, in the wide tunnel, Ben stood upright slowly and saw his son. "Josh! What are you doing down here?"

"My lesson finished early. I thought I'd meet you."

Ben saw Budge Pearn's wheelbarrow, his shovel cast hastily aside, and frowned. It was time the lad learned that a man always emptied his own wheelbarrow. Then he smiled at his thoughts. Budge had plenty of time to learn. With a pretty wife and baby daughter waiting at home, there was more reason to be on the surface than trundling ore down here for three pounds a month.

"Come on, son. Let's go up top and taste some fresh air."

At the ladder there was a great deal of good-natured banter and jostling. Ben stood back. By the end of a shift he had neither the energy of the youngsters nor patience with them.

Another man lacked patience. Moses Trago, broad-shouldered and brutal, elbowed his way to the ladder. Behind him, the quieter John Trago loomed just as large.

The arrival of the two brothers put an end to the miners' good humor, and Ben and Josh shuffled quietly forward with the others.

This was the part of mining that Ben found more difficult with each passing day. From ninety fathoms down there were five hundred and forty ladder rungs to be climbed before a man's head rose from the hole in the ground. Ben used to count them. But no more. These days he gritted his teeth and climbed blindly.

Once on the ladders all talking ceased. A man would regret each mouthful of wasted air when he arrived, lungs roaring for oxygen, at the top of the shaft. Josh was aware of this and he climbed steadily and carefully ahead of his father.

When Josh and Ben were on the fourth ladder, almost fifty feet from the bottom of the shaft, there was a blood-freezing scream high above them. It was a sound Ben had heard many times. His "Ware below!" rang out, and he used the same breath to clamber up to share a rung with Josh. "Swing behind the ladder," he hissed. When the boy obeyed, Ben closed his arms about his son and held him tight against the ladder with arms and knees.

Most times a falling man would mercifully smash his head

against the side of the shaft and know no more. This one was not so fortunate. The scream had died to a low, inhuman sound as he flailed past Josh and his father, but he remained conscious until he crashed onto the floor of the shaft. Josh would remember the sound of it for as long as he lived.

For two full seconds there was silence. It was broken by the clattering of boots as the men on the lower ladders scrambled back down.

"Ben! Ben Retallick!" The cry went up.

"I'm here. Who was it who fell?"

"Budge Pearn."

"Oh my God! His poor maid." Suddenly Ben felt very old. "Wait for me at the fifty-fathom level," he told his son. "There's nothing you can do down there."

Josh swung from behind the ladder and started to climb numbly, not sure whether the lump in his throat would make him cry or be sick. Budge Pearn had been as a big brother to him.

ON THE floor of the shaft, Ben looked at the smashed body and thought of the young, wasted life. "Poor maid!" he repeated. Though only a few weeks past her seventeenth birthday, Jenny Pearn was now a widow with a baby to support. Like Budge she was an orphan, her father having died in an identical accident.

Tom Shovell, the shift captain, swung off the ladder and looked sympathetically at Ben. "We'll do what's necessary here, but I'd be obliged if you would tell Jenny. You—or Jesse." Jesse was Ben's wife. "I needn't tell you how sorry I am. He was well liked."

"There's little comfort in that for poor Jenny."

Ben began the climb once more. At the fifty-fathom level Josh joined him. On the surface, the miners around the top of the shaft murmured their sympathy.

It was quite dark and there was a chill March wind blowing on the moor. Ben and Josh took the path that wound over the shoulder of the tor, toward the cluster of slate and granite cottages huddled in a shallow depression on the east-facing slope. They heard the engine thudding at the Wheal Phoenix in the valley below.

"How . . . how do you think it happened?" Josh asked, speaking for the first time since they had left the shaft.

"I expect Budge was in a hurry. Probably trod on a loose rung. I've seen it happen too often."

He stopped talking as they heard a woman's light footsteps running along the path toward them.

"Ben! Is that you? Oh, thank God you're safe! Thank God!" Jesse Retallick clung to her husband, shaking violently. "They told me there'd been an accident. Was anyone hurt?"

"It was Budge." Ben felt her stiffen in his arms. "He fell from the ladder."

"He's dead, then."

"Yes," said Ben gently. "Jenny hasn't been told yet. I was going to see her, but it might be better if you did."

Jesse was silent for a long time. Then she burst out, "Why? Why did it have to be Budge? They had found so much happiness together. It's that damned mine. Worn ladders, frayed ropes . . ."

"Enough now, Jesse. It gives us our living."

"Try to tell that to Budge—God rest his soul." She sobbed once. A long, uneven breath. But she slipped from Ben's arms when he tried to comfort her. "I'll go to Jenny now. Before she hears the news from someone else." She moved away along the path, and her voice came to them from the darkness. "Ben, I'm not forgetting to thank God it wasn't you."

As she hurried off, her words reminded Ben of the disconcerting, impetuous girl he had married, and he loved her for it.

IN THE kitchen of their small cottage on the outskirts of Henwood village, Josh ladled stew from the pot on the fire into two bowls while Ben eased his boots off. Then they sat, eating in silence. Small but spotless, the kitchen served as dining and living room. In the one other downstairs room were all the "best" possessions.

Suddenly the door banged open and Jesse Retallick bundled Jenny Pearn inside, a thin, pale girl with little Gwen clutched wailing to her. Jesse took her straight through into the best room.

A minute later Jesse was back. "Josh. Upstairs and make yourself a bed on the floor in our room. Jenny will be moving into yours. Ben, take some coals in there for the fireplace. She hasn't started crying yet. When it comes it will be all the worse for the waiting."

Josh left his father filling a bucket with live coals from the kitchen stove, and went upstairs to make his bed in a corner of his parents' bedroom. He was lying there in the darkness when his father finally came into the room carrying a lamp.

Ben saw the glitter of tears on his son's cheeks. He said nothing but walked to the window and looked down the valley. There was light shining from the large windows of the chapel, and he guessed the body of Budge Pearn had arrived there.

Then he heard the sound from downstairs. Starting as a low moan, it quickly swelled until it burst out as a sob. Then Jenny began crying. Painful as it was to listen to, Ben felt a sense of relief. Now, Jenny was someone to comfort, a young girl who had lost her man. Before, she had been unapproachable, locked away.

Ben went downstairs, put on his boots and coat and let himself out of the house. Despite the chill east wind he found a great many villagers gathered in the Henwood chapel. There were inquiries from all sides about Jenny as he strode in the door. The women in the crowd knew that tomorrow, or the next day, it might be their turn. The mines were notorious widow-makers.

Ben was surprised to see the preacher inside the small chapel. The Reverend Wrightwick Roberts rode the North Hill Methodist circuit. Only the larger communities like St. Cleer, where Josh went for his lessons, could support a resident preacher.

The North Hill circuit minister was himself an ex-miner, his shoulders almost as broad as Moses Trago's, but when he spoke his voice was soft. "It's a night for grieving, Ben. The Lord's ways are beyond the understanding of mortals." He looked toward a closed door at the end of the chapel. "Budge is through there. Mary Crabbe is with him."

Mary Crabbe had been taking charge of births and deaths in the district since before Ben was born. Ben nodded his acknowledgment. "It's been a sad day, Wrightwick." He sat on a bench. "You'll see to things? Take the service for him? I'll be paying."

"And what about Theophilus Strike? Won't he give anything?"

Ben managed a faint smile. "That sounds like Preacher Thackeray talking. Theophilus Strike is a mineowner, Wrightwick. He pays wages. Jenny will collect whatever was due to Budge—and a guinea or two besides."

Wrightwick Roberts had frowned at the mention of William Thackeray. The fiery young St. Cleer preacher was fast establishing a reputation as a miners' champion, and the younger men flocked to his sermons on Sundays in the St. Cleer chapel.

"Why do you let Josh stay at Thackeray's school, Ben? He's not a good influence."

Ben shrugged. "His lessons are cheap—and good."

"But Thackeray teaches things you won't find in any schoolbook. He feeds his ideas to young miners. Telling them to band into a union and demand more money is dangerous talk, Ben."

"All I've heard is rumors. None of them from Josh," said Ben, standing up. "But I do know the boy is learning things I would dearly love to have been taught. Josh won't have to go down a mine because he knows nothing else, Wrightwick. And he won't end up in your chapel with Mary Crabbe straightening his broken limbs." Ben stopped and drew a deep breath. "I'll be away now before I say more than I should."

"We've been friends too long for me to take offense," said the preacher. "And I'll walk up with you. I'd like to see Jenny."

BUDGE was buried on a day as gray as the occasion. Wrightwick Roberts sent him on his way to the hereafter with as good a reference as any man could receive, and in the same sermon damned a mine that allowed a man to fall to his death and then failed to send a representative to his funeral.

In all fairness, Theophilus Strike *had* delegated someone—his senior mine captain. But Herman Schmidt could think of better ways to spend an afternoon than listening to a sermon in praise of one of the workers he regarded as little better than animals.

Instead, Schmidt was shut inside his house in the nearby town of Liskeard, already in a state of alcoholic stupor. He spent much less time at the Wheal Sharptor than Theophilus Strike was aware of, but once a week he carried out a full inspection. And from his weekly visit the mine captain was able to compile his reports and direct the operations that kept Wheal Sharptor making profits. Herman Schmidt was a brilliant mine captain, but hated.

"VERY well done, Josh. Your reading is greatly improved."

Josh looked down in embarrassed pleasure. The Reverend William Thackeray was not given to handing out unearned praise to his pupils. Starting these classes had been one of the first tasks he had set himself upon taking up his appointment at the large St. Cleer chapel. A slight, stooping figure, he had accepted many years before that he was no physical match for his fellowmen. So he had chosen words as his weapons. Sent to Cornwall, he saw the appalling rigors of work belowground. It was inevitable that he should become a social reformer. With his power of oratory he quickly earned the enmity of the mineowners and those who held shares in the mines. And he cared little for any of them.

He spoke to Josh again. "Yes, young man, you have it in you to become as educated as anyone in these parts." He suddenly jabbed a long finger an inch from Josh's nose. "But that is only the beginning. *What* are you going to do with that education?"

The question took Josh by surprise. "I don't know, sir—I think I would like to be an engineer."

"An admirable ambition." The menacing finger was lowered, and the preacher glared at the class. "How about the rest of you? You are all the sons of enlightened men. Miners who are determined their sons will be better equipped to earn their living. Does any other student know what he would like to be?"

The hands rose hesitantly and sporadically.

"H'm! We seem beset by uncertainty." He looked around the room at the tousle-headed, ragged boys and sighed. "For all my teaching, I have no doubt most of you will waste your knowledge, using it to count barrowloads of ore."

He shrugged. "At least you won't be cheated by a dishonest mine captain. All right, boys, school is over for today."

THE TRACK FROM the school in St. Cleer wandered aimlessly in the direction of Sharptor, skirting the Caradon mines and dipping to where the great shaft of the Wheal Phoenix yawned deep in the shadowed valley. Josh ignored it and went straight across country, toiling up onto the high, lonely Bodmin Moor.

This was the place he loved above all others. It was a vast landscape of sweeping emptiness, its stunted bushes, bowing to the east, evidence of the prevailing winds of winter. Now the gorse was a tangle of yellow blossom. Here and there a lacework of streams left the turf soft and spongelike. Above it all, blunt-winged buzzards circled in search of prey.

On the moor Josh could think, create his own future. He had told Preacher Thackeray he wanted to be an engineer. In truth, he knew little about mechanical things. He had looked at the steam engines in the Caradon and Phoenix mines and had been impressed with their size and noise, but he knew nothing of their workings. He decided he would find out.

Josh was on the high moor proper now. He paused to watch a buzzard which had strayed into the territory of a pair of crows. While one of them harassed from close range, the second climbed high above, dropping into the battle area with wings closed. The buzzard, sure of its superiority, continued on its course. Only occasionally did it roll onto its back to meet the threat from above with outstretched talons. Then the crows took evasive action.

Josh liked to see the buzzards. They enjoyed a freedom he would dearly love to possess. But there was little time for exploring. In the morning he worked at the mine, dressing the ore at the surface with the women and other children. In the afternoon he attended school at St. Cleer. Most evenings he helped with household chores before settling down to schoolwork. The studying was more difficult since Jenny had come to live with them. Baby Gwen had begun to cut her teeth and she cried a lot.

Josh could see the cottages down the slope. In ten minutes he would be there. But first he had to pass the Tragos' home—and Morwen Trago was sitting astride a boulder at the entrance.

The Tragos were a strange, brooding family, and their house was very much in keeping with their image. It was comprised of gigantic slabs of rock, the back wall buried in the hillside, and the doorway a crevice between the rocks, with a wooden door seven feet high. Here lived Moses Trago and his wife and children, together with his unmarried brother, John. The house had not been built by the Tragos. Superstition had it that it had once been a burial place for the "old men" whose shallow diggings scarred the moor.

Morwen Trago, Moses' eldest son, was almost two years older than Josh. Sliding from the rock, he took up a position straddling the path. Josh approached him warily, stopping ten feet away.

"What do you want, Morwen?"

"What do I want? I live here, Josh Retallick. There's nothing says I can't stand outside my own home."

"Then you'll let me pass?" Josh's face felt taut.

"Of course I will—once I've seen what you have in that bag."

Josh's grip on his canvas schoolbag tightened. "It's only books. They belong to Preacher Thackeray."

"Do they, now? A preacher's books! Religious nonsense, that's what books are."

Morwen was echoing his father's words. They had been accompanied by a stinging cuff on his ear when Morwen had asked whether he could take reading lessons with Preacher Thackeray. That had been when Morwen was working on the surface with Josh. Since then Moses had found work underground for his son.

"Books are only nonsense if you can't read them," Josh retorted. "And they are staying in my bag."

"We'll see about that. . . ." Morwen began to advance toward Josh. He stopped when Josh picked up a broken piece of granite. Morwen weighed his chances of tackling him. Just then a barefoot girl with tangled, long black hair ran between them.

"Stop it, you two! Let him go, Morwen. Ma wouldn't like it if I told her you were bullying."

Miriam Trago was the same age as Josh, but her shrill voice carried the authority that came with being her father's favorite.

With a scornful shrug Morwen said, "Keep your books. Only sissies and preachers read books." He turned and strolled away.

Josh dropped the stone and mumbled, "Thank you, Miriam—though he wouldn't have stopped me."

"I don't care about that. I didn't want to see Morwen's head split open. That's all." With a look almost as scornful as her brother's she too turned away.

"That's not true, Miriam Trago," Josh called after her. "You just don't want people to think you're nice. But you stopped us from fighting because you thought I might get hurt."

Miriam swung around to face him. Then she bent down, took hold of her ragged dress and raised it above her head.

She was wearing nothing beneath it.

Josh's face went scarlet. He turned and fled down the path with her derisive laughter chasing after him. Miriam Trago was as wild and untamed as the moor itself.

CHAPTER TWO

THE wet, cold days gave way to warmer ones as spring advanced into summer. For Josh, the longer days meant more time to spend on the moor. He avoided the Trago home, but often saw Miriam in the distance. She worked a full day shift with her mother on the grading floor at the Wheal Phoenix, but her evenings were spent out on the moor. There she had always felt free.

Although Josh and Miriam would occasionally see each other on the moor, the next encounter between the Retallick and Trago families occurred at a more senior level.

The Sunday evening was warm and pleasant. Ben, Jesse and Josh, a few paces ahead of the shift captain Tom Shovell, Jenny and baby Gwen, were walking slowly homeward from Henwood chapel, making the most of an opportunity to feel sun on their faces. At the edge of the village the Reverend Wrightwick Roberts caught up with them. They spoke together of the new corn laws.

"It's a bad law," said Ben bitterly, "that prevents corn from entering the country and then sends half our own corn elsewhere. Parliament must do something or we'll see the troubles of twenty years ago with us again."

"We don't need any troops in Cornwall," the preacher agreed.

They reached a steep part of the track and, taking the baby from Jenny, Tom tucked the infant into the crook of one arm. He made light work of the gradient, despite the extra pounds that Gwen had put on in recent weeks. In sharp contrast, Jenny was thin to the point of frailness, and her skin had developed a translucence. Grief had changed her into a woman of haunting beauty.

When they arrived at the cottage, Ben, Jesse and Jenny went inside with the baby. Josh stayed outside with the preacher and Tom Shovell. They had not been there for many minutes when a bellow from the moor brought their conversation to an abrupt halt. They turned to see Kate Trago, the wife of Moses, running wildly toward them, her hair streaming behind her, followed by Moses, who lurched with a wide-legged gait.

Kate stumbled and fell in front of the startled group. As Wrightwick Roberts helped her up, they saw that one eye was swollen with an ugly graze beneath it.

Taking the preacher's arm, she pulled him toward the cottage. "Hurry, all of you!" she pleaded. "Moses is mad-drunk. Go inside or he'll kill me—and you!"

The preacher freed his arm. "Take her in, Josh."

"Let me try to reason with him," said Tom. "He'll listen to me."

"He won't listen to anyone in his state. Get everyone into the cottage. Quickly!" the preacher said.

The door banged at his back as he turned to face the drunken miner, steadying himself on the path.

"Out of my way," Moses said. "I want my wife."

Roberts' voice was low and coaxing. "Leave her be, Moses. She's inside talking to Jesse Retallick."

"I don't care who she's talking to. She's a lazy idle slut. No, she's worse than that. She's a thief!" Moses lurched forward, and the preacher winced at the gin fumes the drunken miner belched into his face.

"You know what she did? Do you want to know what that bloody woman did?" He screwed his mouth up. "She took money from my pocket. That's what. Took it when she thought I was asleep."

"I expect she had need of it." The preacher's voice was calm.

The miner's unshaven upper lip curled in a sneer. "I'll tell you what she has need of. I don't have to go to chapel to learn how to run my life. I'll do it my way. So will she!"

He lunged toward the door, but Wrightwick Roberts was too quick for him. He stooped, put his shoulder beneath the other man's armpit and heaved. Moses Trago took eight or nine uncontrolled backward paces before crashing to the ground.

Sheer rage sobered him momentarily. "I'll kill you for that!"

He came up with unexpected speed, but someone else was faster. The door behind the preacher was jerked open, and he was thrust aside as Ben Retallick took the headlong rush of Moses Trago and closed his arms around the drunken miner.

Moses was no stranger to fighting. He staggered about until both men fell heavily to the ground. Ben's grip slackened for an instant. It was enough. Flinging his wide shoulders back, Moses broke the encircling grip and scrambled to his feet.

Ben was still on his knees when Moses' boot took him on the shoulder and knocked him down again. Then Moses moved quickly around him, kicking him in the ribs, aiming for his head. One of his wilder kicks missed completely, and Ben was quick enough to grasp the foot and with a twist send his opponent sprawling. As Moses began to rise, Ben's rock-hard fist struck his temple and dropped him backward, prostrate.

"Now there's as fine a punch as ever I have seen," said Wrightwick Roberts. "It would have felled a bullock."

"It needed to." Ben rubbed his knuckles.

It took four bucketfuls of water, flung unceremoniously over his face, to make Moses Trago stir. He twitched, shuddered, rolled from side to side, then sat up, groaning, head between his hands.

"You may think you are suffering now, Moses," the preacher told him. "One day you'll have to answer to the Lord for your misdeeds. This drubbing will be as a gentle tap on the hand compared with what will happen to you then."

Moses' reply was an oath accompanied by another groan. He got to his feet, swaying and glaring.

"You'll live to regret this day, Ben Retallick," he said. "So will you, Preacher." He raised his voice to be sure it carried into the house. "You tell that woman of mine if she dares show her face inside my home I'll break every bone in her body."

He turned and staggered away toward the high moor.

"You'd best be careful of him, Ben," said Tom Shovell from the doorway. "Moses is a dangerous man."

"Tom is right. You keep clear of him." Kate Trago came from the house, peering painfully through her one good eye.

"He'll be all right when he sobers up," declared Ben. "We were boys together, Kate. I know Moses Trago as well as any man."

"No!" Kate shook her head. "Moses is not the man you once knew. In the last few years he's changed. Oh, I know he's always been rough, but now he's turned sour inside. He envies you more than anyone else, Ben. You've got all the things that Moses hasn't. Respect. A house. I know it sounds stupid, but he hates you for being part of something he's scorned all his life."

She stopped abruptly. "I've said far too much. Take heed of it and I'll have thanked you for helping me. I must go now."

"You can't go yet!" Ben protested. "Moses will kill you."

"He won't." She shook her head. "He'll go home, stumble onto his bed and sleep until morn. Then he'll get up and go to the mine. That's all there is in his life. Drink, sleep and work. But he won't hurt me anymore." There was the gleam of a tear in her eye. "Besides, I'm his wife. I've got to go to him."

She went on her way without looking back.

THREE days after the fight Miriam Trago waylaid Josh as he walked home from the St. Cleer chapel school. She stepped out from the tall ferns into his path when he was on the high, flat moor, hidden from the cottages on the other side of the tor.

"Hello." It was a casual greeting.

"Hello." Josh's reply was more cautious. His small feud with Morwen had exploded into something far more serious now that their fathers were involved.

But Miriam had not sought him out to extend the feud. "Have

346

you been to the chapel school?" It was an unnecessary question. They both knew it. "What do you learn there?"

"Oh, lots of things. Reading. Writing. Sums."

"I wish I could learn to read and write."

"Why don't you ask your dad to let you go?"

She shook her head. "I did ask him. He says there's no need for such fancy ways for girls." The mention of Moses Trago brought about a long, uncomfortable silence.

"My dad's not all bad, you know," she said at last.

As she spoke she looked down at her bare feet. They had long been a subject of disapproval among the women of Henwood. But Miriam enjoyed feeling the springy turf beneath her toes. "He doesn't hit me often. When he does he's always sorry afterward."

Josh said nothing. He was anxious to avoid a clash.

"He works hard. Even your dad says he's a good worker."

"So he might be. But he gets very quarrelsome when he's been drinking."

Her head came up and her eyes met his. "He doesn't mean anything by it." Then the challenge subsided. She touched the corner of a book that protruded from his bag. "What's this?"

"It's a writing book."

"Show me. I want to see what your writing looks like. Please!"

Josh hesitated. Despite Miriam's apparent interest he was still wary of her. "All right." He extracted the book from his bag and opened it to disclose handwriting that was small but not very neat.

She was impressed. "Did you write it all? What does it say?"

He nodded, absurdly pleased. "There's lots more. Almost a whole book full." He began to read: "*He saith unto him the third time, Simon, son of Jonas, lovest thou me? . . .*" Josh read two pages before closing the book. "That was from the Bible."

"It was beautiful!" Miriam's expression was full of wonder. For the first time he noticed that she had very dark eyes, fringed by the longest eyelashes he had ever seen.

"Could you write my name—Miriam?"

Josh nodded. "Yes." He rummaged in the bag and came out with a scrap of paper. "I need something to rest this on."

347

"I know just the thing; it's in a secret place. Nobody but me knows of it." She took his hand and, full of excitement, pulled him after her as she left the path and plunged into the ferns.

When they reached an apparently impenetrable barrier of gorse, she released his hand and dropped to her knees. "Follow me."

She disappeared into a low, dark tunnel that twisted and turned through the evergreens for twenty feet before coming out into sparkling sunlight. Thick bushes were all around, but in the center, a large flat rock and two others, leaning against one another, formed a small triangular cave. When Josh stood up, he could see the whole of the Phoenix valley through the tops of the gorse bushes, but it would have been impossible for anyone to see him and Miriam from below.

"Here, rest the paper on this rock."

She sat cross-legged on the granite, her skirt tucked between her legs, her callused knees as brown as a gypsy's. Josh unslung his bag and, taking out a book, placed it on the rock. Then he smoothed out a piece of paper and laid it on the book. He knelt and with a thick-leaded pencil carefully wrote and called aloud the letters. "M-I-R-I-A-M. Miriam. There you are!"

She had been watching him, hardly daring to breathe. Now she took the paper as though it were a magic formula for all the riches of the world. "This really is my name? It says Miriam?"

"Yes."

Her reaction was most satisfactory. "Can I keep it?"

"Of course you can. It's of no use to me."

"This is the first time I've ever seen my name written down. I'll keep it forever and always."

"I'll teach you to write it yourself, if you like."

She gripped his arm. "Oh, please!"

He first had to show her how to hold the pencil; then how to form the letters, with his hand clenched over hers. It took a long time and the result was far from satisfactory, although Josh insisted it was fine.

"No." Miriam clutched the paper with Josh's effort on it. "This is much better. But I'll do it properly, if you'll learn me."

"I don't know," said Josh uncertainly.

"I'll show you a badger's burrow."

Josh wavered. Sensing a weak spot, Miriam prized it open. "The badgers have babies."

Josh's resolution crumbled. "All right. I'll teach you. But I want to see the badgers first."

"Come on, then." Miriam was elated. Her whole being ached with wanting to learn the things Josh was learning.

He followed her through the gorse tunnel and they headed across the moor. Miriam took a direct course, deviating only once to avoid a bog. A little farther on they dropped into a deep gully.

"We must go quietly now." She laid a hand on his arm and Josh edged forward. He had never seen a badger, but in the tales of his schoolmates the badger was as strong as a ram, bold as a fox, and armed with claws the length of a boy's fingers.

"Here, sit by me and don't say a word," Miriam whispered as she pulled him down onto a grassy bank.

"Where are they?" It came out as a hoarse whisper.

"Shhh! Over there." She pointed to a mound of earth twelve feet away, from which a sprawling thornbush grew. "See the paths?"

Now Josh could make out four well-worn tracks leading into the bush. "Where are the badgers?" he said softly.

"They'll be out soon."

They sat in silence. The evening was warm and peaceful, and Josh even found it pleasant being arm to arm with Miriam. There was a nice smell to her, a scent of fern and heather.

Suddenly she clutched him. "There! Did you hear that?"

"No. What am I listening for?"

"That thumping noise in the ground. It's the badgers. That means they'll be coming out now."

Soon from under the bush a long head, marked with black and white stripes, came into view. The badger raised its nose and sniffed, then advanced cautiously, bringing its long-haired gray-brown body into view. It was larger than Josh had imagined. As large as a medium-sized dog. Suddenly it was gone.

"It saw us!" he exclaimed, bitterly disappointed.

"Shhh! He didn't see you. He always does this to make sure it's safe for the babies. They'll all come out now."

She had hardly finished speaking when the male lumbered straight out from the bush, closely followed by two cubs. The female, more cautious, brought up the rear.

Josh held his breath as the badgers moved along their path and into a nearby forest of ferns. As he leaned sideways to follow their progress, a stone turned beneath his hand and bounced down the small embankment. With a startled squeak the female badger sent the cubs in headlong flight back to the burrow, and the male quartered the ground after them, emitting excited grunts and squeaks. He paused to raise a reproachful nose in Josh's direction. Then he too was gone. "I'm sorry," said Josh sheepishly.

Miriam jumped down to the floor of the gully. "It doesn't matter. I've seen them lots of times." She looked at him suspiciously. "But I showed them to you like I promised. You'll still learn me to read and write?"

Josh nodded. "Yes. Meet me on my way home from the chapel and I'll give you a lesson. Not every day, though."

They finally settled for three days a week, and Josh set the strap of his bag back on his shoulder. "Are you coming?"

Miriam shook her head. "There's a full moon tonight, and I want to watch it from up there." She pointed to the great rock mass of Sharp Tor rising above the moor. "Why don't you come with me?"

"No, I must get back for supper. Mother will be wondering where I am."

"If you come up Sharp Tor with me, I'll let you kiss me."

"I don't want to." He turned his back and walked away.

"You will one day, Josh Retallick. You will one day!" Her voice mocked him as he set off across the moor.

NOBODY had noticed how late Josh was. The house was full of people, among them most of the miners from Ben Retallick's shift, including Tom Shovell and Nehemeziah Lancellis, the mine hostler who shared the stables of the horses he tended.

It was Wrightwick Roberts' booming voice that met Josh's ears.

"I am not happy about this trip into Bodmin. To go to a public hanging is shameful enough. With it taking place on Fair Day, there will be all manner of sinful things to entice our young men."

"But it's a double hanging of miners," argued one of the men. "They're from the Kit Hill mine. Some of us know them."

"There's nothing to be proud of in knowing convicted murderers," retorted Roberts.

"From what I hear, others were more to blame than them for the killing," said Jesse Retallick from the kitchen doorway. "A militiaman, wasn't it?"

There was a growl of assent from the miners.

"There can be little excuse for killing a man, Jesse," said Roberts. "A man's life is sacred."

"And so is a man's family!" Jesse retorted, hands planted firmly on her hips. "Didn't the shareholders lock the men out? Then wouldn't give them the money they were due? It's not surprising the miners got angry. But even then the shareholders wouldn't stand up to them like men. They called in the militia."

"These are things you don't understand, Jesse," said Roberts. "The men wanted a charter. They spoke of uniting all the miners in the district. It's dangerous talk, Jesse."

"I may not understand about charters and uniting the miners, Wrightwick Roberts. I do know how a man would feel if he saw his family starving, and him knowing the shareholders owed him money!" Red-faced, Jesse angrily slammed the kitchen door.

Ben Retallick chuckled. "I could have told you it wasn't wise to tell Jesse she didn't understand, when she feels so strongly."

The preacher ran a handkerchief around the inside of his collar, then held up a big hand for silence. "All right, men. Now we've decided to go to Bodmin, we'll get down to details. Nehemeziah, how many wagons will we have?"

THE day of the execution dawned bright and clear. The sun rose on loaded wagons being pulled by toiling horses up the steep track from the Sharptor mine. Chapel-going miners and their families had possession of the front half of the convoy, while the last two wagons were filled with the younger men—including Morwen Trago—among whom bottles of gin were already being passed.

Josh found himself sitting close to Miriam. But this was a different Miriam from the one he met on the moor for her lessons. True, she still wore no shoes, but her hair had been brushed back tidily and the dress she had on was made from new calico. As always, however, she kept up a steady stream of chatter. The embarrassed Josh said little in reply. But when someone called that Bodmin could be seen up ahead, he knelt beside her, looking between the straddled legs of the driver on his high seat. The hoofs of the horses struck sparks from the teeth-rattling cobbles as the wagoner held them back down the steep approach to the town.

The slanting rays of the morning sun woke a million window-panes, and the streets were at times so narrow that the upstairs of the houses leaned toward each other. The mine wagons trundled down a lane to a churned-up field, three-parts full of wagons, and the young men quickly moved off in a rowdy bunch, eager to sample the delights of the town. The Reverend Wrightwick Roberts watched them go with a sad heart.

"Now, Josh, what are you going to do? Will you come with us?" Jesse Retallick asked.

"No." Josh saw the disapproving look his mother was giving the barefoot Miriam. "I'll walk about and see what's going on."

"Mind you behave yourself. Have you still got your shilling?"

He held it out toward her, grinning happily.

"Good. Don't lose it. And be back here at six o'clock."

Soon Josh and Miriam found themselves among stalls and shops that displayed everything imaginable, from shoes to saddles and sweets to horses. Josh spent a farthing on some sweets. They wandered along in bulge-cheeked silence until they found themselves before a great iron-studded gate, set into the gray wall of the prison. Here were the gallows, on a raised platform, and two oiled and prestretched ropes with noosed ends hung from the crossbeam. The officer in charge of the guard paced about, shouting to clear a passage between the gate and the gallows.

As nothing else seemed to be happening, Josh and Miriam

walked about Bodmin and returned shortly before noon. The crowd had swelled to fill the vast space in front of the prison and overflowed halfway up the slope of the opposite hill.

At five minutes to twelve the prison gates swung open. Led by a single drummer, two columns of soldiers in bright red coats and white crossbelts marched slowly from the dusty courtyard within.

Shuffling between the lines of soldiers were the two wretched miners, heavily manacled and chained to each other. There was a murmur of anger from the crowd, and the soldiers fingered their guns uneasily as the condemned men were prodded onto the platform. The hangman, his head hooded, stepped forward.

"Brothers!" boomed the voice of Wrightwick Roberts. "Brothers! Join me in a prayer for these two sinners who are nearing the judgment of the Lord. Let us appeal for His mercy."

There was a rippling movement through the crowd as all of the women and most of the men dropped to their knees. The voice of Wrightwick Roberts rang out. "Lord, we thank thee for this opportunity to ask your forgiveness. . . ."

"Why is Preacher Roberts thanking God?" Miriam asked in a hoarse whisper. "Aren't they going to hang them after all?"

"Of course they are going to hang them."

Miriam fell silent. Preacher Roberts' prayer was long, and when he had finished, he ordered the crowd to stand and sing a hymn.

As the words rose from ten thousand throats, the officer of the guard found it difficult to contain his impatience. He saw the hangman standing beside the condemned men, his hands clasped in front of him as though he were in chapel.

When the third verse began, the officer spoke to a sergeant, who roused the hangman and persuaded him to place the nooses about the necks of the two men. This caused the singing to falter.

The officer stepped forward. His voice was nerve-tight. "Silence!" he called. "Silence in the name of the Queen."

The noise from the crowd subsided quickly.

"It is my duty to see that the sentence of death passed upon Thomas Arthur Sleedon and William Joseph Darling is carried out in accordance with the laws of this realm. They have been found guilty of the murder of Henry Talbot, a militiaman. Before the sentence is carried out they may speak their last words. May God rest their souls."

"And may He rot yours and the souls of all those who oppress the miners of this county."

An astonished Josh recognized the voice of his teacher, William Thackeray. The small man stood in the midst of a group of stamping and shouting miners less than twenty yards from the gallows.

There was a murmur of agreement from the crowd, but William Thackeray had more to say. "The militia is supposed to uphold the law—not carry out the orders of the shareholders who keep miners poor. The wrong men are on the scaffold!" he shouted. "It should be the shareholders! The mineowners!"

"Yes! Take them down! Release them!" The crowd swayed forward toward the gallows' platform.

The officer shouted an order, and the soldiers brought muskets to their shoulders. At the same time the hangman gripped a large wooden lever set into one of the uprights.

Above the hullabaloo a woman's voice could be heard screaming, "Thomas! Oh, God! Thomas!" One of the condemned men, a look of anguish on his face, took a step forward—and trod into eternity. The trapdoor dropped down on oiled hinges, and both men fell until the ropes jerked them to a fatal halt.

There was a sudden hush. Josh became aware that Miriam was clutching his arm, her fingernails biting into his wrist.

"It was horrible! Horrible!" She began sobbing.

Josh tried to comfort her, but too much was happening about them. The crowd was angry. As the soldiers cut down the two dead men, a stone landed with a thud on the platform. It was followed by another—and another.

Some soldiers carried the two bodies toward the prison gate, and the remaining soldiers formed a tight line facing the crowd and retreated step by step. As they neared the gate, those on the extreme ends of the line came under attack from the young miners. The officer snapped out an order, and the line of soldiers halted. Half of them dropped to one knee, muskets pointed at their tormentors. The officer raised his sword. It fell, a flash of silver in the sun, and the muskets spoke.

At the last moment the soldiers raised their weapons and the musket balls sped harmlessly overhead. But the crowd was thrown into panic. Thousands fled. Holding Miriam's hand, Josh ran, not stopping until they reached the safety of the narrow streets.

His feeling of relief was almost immediately replaced by a sense of foolishness. No soldiers were pursuing them. There had been no second volley. But Miriam's tearstained face was real enough.

"Come on," said Josh harshly, because of the discovery that he was still holding her hand. "It's all over. I'll buy you some more sweets—and we'll go in to watch the dancing bear."

They saw the bear, an unhappy, degraded animal, and they bought more sweets. By late afternoon Miriam had succeeded in pushing thoughts of the hanging to the back of her mind.

As it was a holiday, the town's inns were open all day. Drunken men, and not a few women, became commonplace. Those unfortunate enough to fall in some alley were quickly relieved of their valuables by gangs of young villains.

But trouble of a different kind caught up with Miriam and Josh. When a fight erupted in the town's main street, they hurried down a narrow alleyway in an attempt to bypass the area. There they saw a thickset man, straddle-legged, close to the wall of a house. Josh's instinct was to hurry past, but the man turned and blocked their way. It was Herman Schmidt, the Sharptor mine captain.

"Well, well! What have we here?" The thick accent was in no way helped by the alcohol he had drunk. He staggered forward.

"What you want?" He was talking to Miriam. "You looking for a man? All right, Cornish whore. How much you charge, eh?"

Josh edged backward and tried to pull Miriam with him, but Schmidt grabbed her arm. "You hear me? How much?"

"One guinea."

Josh looked at Miriam in amazement.

"A guinea! What you take me for?" Schmidt snorted. Then he stooped to look at her. "You are young. You have a room?"

She nodded.

"Then I give you half a guinea."

"A guinea."

"Half a guinea!" the mine captain roared. "No woman is worth a whole guinea. Not even a German virgin."

"Miriam, come away."

She waved her free hand behind her, signaling Josh to go.

"What are you doing here, boy?" Schmidt peered at Josh, trying to focus bloodshot eyes. "Don't I know you?" He shook his head heavily. "I should know you. But go away. Run off."

Josh stood his ground. The mine captain pulled a coin from his pocket. "Here. Is this a half-guinea?"

Miriam snatched it from him. "Yes."

"Come, then. Where do you live?"

Josh caught Miriam's hand, thoroughly alarmed. "Don't go with him, Miriam. He'll hurt you. Don't go."

Herman Schmidt said angrily, "When I give an order it is meant to be obeyed." The back of his heavy hand swung, knocking Josh off-balance. Josh thought he heard Miriam scream as his head struck the wall. Then everything went black.

When he opened his eyes, Miriam and Schmidt were gone. He felt sick. He scoured the alleyways in the vicinity, but there was no sign of them. Soon the shadows began to grow long. Despondently he made his way back to the field where the wagons stood, and clambered onto the one they had come in.

Gradually more Henwood villagers arrived. He saw his mother and father. Jesse, seeing her son was safe, waved cheerily. Suddenly Miriam was there, scrambling into the wagon. She was bubbling over with happiness, as if nothing had happened.

"Oh, Josh! You don't know how glad I am to see you. When you fell, I thought Schmidt had killed you. As soon as I could I came back to look for you, but you'd gone. Where have you been?"

Her words poured out. "See! I've been shopping. I bought a comb for my ma. Some tobacco for Dad. A new cap for Morwen. Ribbon for me . . ." She paused. "And I've bought this for you."

She held something out. It was a pocketknife, bone-handled, with two blades that folded into it. He was tempted.

"I don't want it."

Miriam's eyes opened wide. "You don't think . . . ? You don't believe I went with that—that *animal?*"

A couple of women looked around at the vehemence of her words. Miriam lowered her voice. "I wasn't going to let him get away with the things he said to me. I took his money—and it was a whole guinea, not a half-guinea. When I found a house with the door open, I took him inside and told him to go upstairs and wait for me in the bedroom. I suppose he's still there."

She smiled, expecting Josh to smile in return. But Josh's thoughts were in a turmoil. "Taking his money was stealing. You should have come away with me when I wanted you to."

"It was *not* stealing. He deserved to pay for hitting you. Anyway, he had hold of my arm. I couldn't have got away. If I'd struggled, he would have hit me too."

The wagon had filled up fast, and now the driver climbed up onto the seat. With his "Hups!" and "Heave-hos," the horses strained into their harness to begin the climb away from the town.

In the crowded, swaying wagon, Josh sat with his arms wrapped around his drawn-up knees, thoroughly miserable. What bothered him most was that Miriam had been immediately aware of what Schmidt was talking about. He stole a look at her in the dark and thought he saw tears. "Miriam, I'm sorry. I don't think you did anything wrong—and the knife is a lovely present."

She sniffed noisily, then wiped her eyes. Without a word the pocketknife was placed in his hand.

He squeezed her hand awkwardly. "I wasn't much help, was I?"

"That wasn't your fault," she said indignantly. "He hit you."

There was silence between them for a few minutes, and a song was started in the next wagon. Ahead of them a miner had jumped down and was leading the way with a lantern.

The singing gradually died away, and only the soft clumping of the horses' hoofs and the squeak and creak of the wagons broke the silence. Her head drooped to rest on his shoulder. He felt very grown up and protective toward this disturbing girl who slumbered quietly beside him.

Chase the Wind

CHAPTER THREE

William Thackeray rode back to St. Cleer in an excited mood. He knew his words had stirred the huge crowd. The thought that he had been partly responsible for the act which had sent the condemned men to the gallows never crossed his mind. He knew they had attended the meeting he had called at Kit Hill when their troubles first started. But Preacher Thackeray was to be found wherever the Cornish miners had trouble, urging them to join together to improve their lot in life.

Thackeray's preaching was not directed against the shareholders alone. He censured the government for their shortsighted agricultural policies which sent food prices soaring. The scarcity of corn had been growing steadily worse throughout England. It had not been helped by laws which prevented corn from being imported, in a misguided attempt to protect the farmers' interests. Thackeray also pointed a stern finger at farmers who took advantage of the laws to withhold corn from the markets, raising prices to a level that miners found impossible to afford.

The preacher was halfway to St. Cleer when he overtook a group of men traveling in the same direction as himself.

"Is that Preacher Thackeray?" one of them called.

"Unless I'm mistaken that's John Kittow of Caradon. What do you want with me?"

The small group of miners closed about him, and John Kittow lowered his voice. "We'd like a word with you, Preacher. Somewhere quiet."

"I'll meet you anytime, John. Won't it do here?"

"No, Preacher. Better if 'tis said where there's light to see who's listening and walls to stop them as shouldn't be."

"Then you'd better make it the chapel."

"Tomorrow night? After the late shift comes up?"

"That's all right with me, John." His horse danced sideways, and Thackeray yanked it to a halt. "But what's it about?"

"Corn, Preacher. That's it in one word. Corn!"

358

HERMAN SCHMIDT DID NOT put in an appearance at the Sharptor mine the next day, and word went around that the mine captain had been arrested and kept in Bodmin's lockup overnight. He had gotten a message to the Sharptor mineowner, and Theophilus Strike had gone to Bodmin and managed to smooth over what could have been a very serious situation. Schmidt had been arrested on a charge of entering a dwelling with intent to commit a felony. There was also a charge of assaulting a constable.

For what remained of that summer, Herman Schmidt was a quieter, more reasonable man. Nevertheless, it was some weeks before Josh was able to see the mine captain without a sinking feeling in his stomach. He need not have worried. Herman Schmidt could remember nothing of the events that had led to his arrest.

THE lights were burning well into the night in the St. Cleer Methodist church for the meeting between Preacher William Thackeray and the miners of Caradon led by John Kittow. Only selected miners were allowed into the chapel. Others who called were told at the door by two burly Caradon men to conduct their business on a more convenient occasion. Nobody questioned it. Far better to accept whatever the preacher was doing.

The miners of Caradon had determined to do more than talk about their problems. They had already formulated a rough plan of action. They were having this meeting to work out the details.

CALLINGTON market was smaller than many others in the county. But trade was usually brisk, and lately it had become a collection center for farm produce. From here it would be hauled to Cotehele quay and shipped downriver to the port of Plymouth.

On this particular day the observant onlooker might have noticed an unusually high proportion of miners. All morning the farm wagons trundled into Callington with produce and livestock. The corn market was at the very center of the town, outside a stone-built granary. Here miner, countryman and town dweller crowded around the auctioneer as he called loudly for bids.

The responses came quickly and eagerly. "Sixty-five shillings!

Seventy, seventy-five." At eighty shillings for a quarter, all but the most determined dropped out, including combines who had pooled their cash. When the price reached one hundred and five, only the merchants remained—none of them from Cornwall.

Then a voice, deep and very Cornish, came from the back of the crowd. "Eighty shillings, and I'll take the lot."

The auctioneer smiled. "I'm sorry, sir, you're a little late. The bidding has reached one hundred and five shillings."

"You heard eighty shillings, and that's all you'll be getting. I'll take the lot." John Kittow pushed his way to the front.

"You can't do this! I've been bid one hundred and five shillings. I am honor bound to sell at the best price."

"There's nothing honorable in keeping food from those who need it. Nor in robbing those who can pay more. Eighty shillings is a fair price for a quarter, and that's what it will be sold for."

The auctioneer protested once more, and John Kittow pushed him from his perch into the midst of the miners. Terrified, he was passed to the rear over the heads of the cheering men.

"Now!" John Kittow put up his hands for silence. "We're selling corn to whoever wants it. No bidding—first come, first served. Is it agreed that eighty shillings a quarter is a fair price?"

There was a majority shout of assent, but one man called out, "The farmers have made enough profit from corn. Sell it at sixty shillings. Forty, even!"

"None of that talk! There's been work put into the growing of it. A man is entitled to his living. Eighty shillings is what it will be sold for. Come on, now! What are you waiting for?"

Word of what was happening went quickly through the market, and crowds thronged to the sale. Corn had been missing from the area for so long that some young children had never known the taste of it. A few farmers protested at the unorthodox sale, but when the crowd turned on them they withdrew, angry and sullen.

The immediate stocks did not last the hour, but then the shout went up that there was plenty more corn in the granary. In ten minutes the doors had been battered down and bags of corn were passed out to enable the sale to continue.

The whole affair was conducted in an efficient manner, proving that the hours of discussion in the St. Cleer chapel had not been wasted. The miners worked in threes—one man measuring corn, the second taking the money from the customer and placing it into the canvas bag held by the third.

At one stage John Kittow saw an old woman, wrinkled face anxious beneath her frayed widow's shawl, watching the proceedings. "Is it corn you're wanting, mother?" he asked. "Come over here with me and we'll see that you get it without waiting."

"Ah, will I now?" The woman's voice was as old as her face. "And what d'you think I'll be paying you with?"

John Kittow asked, "You'll be a widow, then, mother?"

"These twenty years," she replied. "And he went the same way that you'll go. With his lungs full of dust from the mine."

"We'll all go when the time comes," he said. "But there'll be no miner's widow leaving today without corn for her belly." He spoke to a man who looked up as he was filling a half-empty sack. "Some corn for a miner's widow. As much as she can carry away."

He drew some coins from his pocket and threw them into the money bag. "If any more widows, or others in need, come for corn, give it to them. Pay it from your own pockets. You'll get it back from the mine fund. But make sure the money goes into the bag. I'll have no one saying there has been any dishonesty here today."

When the last bushel had been sold, the money was brought to Kittow and he passed it on to the farmers. They admitted that it tallied with the amount of corn delivered at the miners' price. The miners of Caradon then withdrew from the town as peacefully as they had arrived.

The military was called out and a troop of soldiers rode into Callington the next day, but there was little they could, or would, do. Though the price was not what the farmers had expected, they still had made a good profit. The regiment's colonel had no wish to blow up a rural incident into a people's uprising.

The remainder of that summer went quickly. For Josh it had been a season he hoped might never end, but the long, happy evenings on the moor with Miriam grew shorter. Almost before they realized it, the wind was rattling leafless branches, and the horses working the mine-pump capstans blew steam from wide nostrils as they trudged in circles on their long road to nowhere.

"I⊤'s hard to believe that Christmas is only two weeks away." Jesse Retallick beat up the mixture for a pudding. "It'll be baby Gwen's first Christmas. It's such a pity her father isn't alive to see her face when she gets her presents."

"I believe Budge *will* see her face," said Jenny quietly. Tom Shovell was a religious man and he had been a constant visitor to the house. His simple faith had helped restore her peace of mind. The deep sense of loss was still there, but it was now possible to talk about Budge without her dissolving into tears.

Jesse turned to Josh, who was reading in a corner by the fire. "With Christmas over, life will be very different for you, young man." Her manner was jocular, but she felt sadness deep inside. The year 1839 would see great changes in the household. Thanks to Josh's education, Theophilus Strike had offered him the chance to become a mine engineer. He would be away on an apprenticeship for close on three years at Harvey's foundry and engineering works at Hayle. There he would learn how to build and look after the type of engine Theophilus Strike planned to install in the Sharptor mine—an engine to drain the wet, deeper shafts.

Strike had costed the whole operation carefully. As the Hayle foundry was to build the engine, Josh would be involved with it from the beginning. His presence on the mine later would avoid the necessity of calling an engineer from Hayle when something went wrong. Eventually, Josh's apprenticeship would save the mineowner a great deal of money.

He had not, of course, told Josh about this when he called him, with his father, for an interview. Instead, he had offered him the chance of three years at Hayle in return for an undertaking by Josh to work at the Sharptor mine for ten years. To his astonishment and Ben Retallick's dismay Josh had refused this offer. For him it was a desperate gamble. Josh wanted to be an engineer more than anything else in the world, but ten years was a long time to be tied to one employer. Five years' tied employment with a reasonable salary constituted his terms of acceptance.

Strike's astonishment had momentarily turned to anger. He knew there was not another boy at Sharptor with Josh's education, and without an engineer he believed it could be disastrous to buy an engine. And so he agreed to Josh's terms.

When Josh and Ben left Strike's office, the miner regarded his son with incredulous respect. "I never thought I'd live to see the day when a son of mine would call his own tune to a mineowner! Josh, if cheek is what matters, you'll go far in this world."

"It wasn't cheek," Josh said, hiding his elation. "I know what I will be worth to Theophilus Strike. He knows it too."

It was true. Josh and Preacher Thackeray had spent a whole evening discussing the matter, and the preacher had proved his case with simple mathematics. Thus Josh had attended the interview armed with the same facts as the mineowner.

Now he looked affectionately at his mother as she busied herself with the pudding. "Don't let's talk about my going away."

"And why not? It's something to be pleased about. Be thankful your father doesn't want his son to follow him down the mine. There's many who can't wait to get their children belowground. Moses Trago never wasted any time with his Morwen."

The mention of Moses reminded Jesse of something that had been on her mind for days. In a quiet way she had found out about the schooling Josh was giving to Miriam and she approved of it. Miriam Trago had more about her than most girls of her age. If she could escape from the influence of her family, then Jesse wished the girl luck. "I haven't seen that Trago girl lately. What's she doing for Christmas?"

Josh looked surprised at the question. "I don't know. Probably nothing. They don't keep Christmas. Moses Trago says it's just another day. Except that he doesn't work."

"Then it's time she learned different. Tell her that she's welcome here for Christmas Day. That's if you'd like to have her?"

Astonishment and pleasure wrestled for supremacy on Josh's face. "Can I tell her now?" He slammed his book shut.

363

"At this time of night? You're not going up to that Trago place?"

"No, she won't be there, but I know where to find her."

"Well, be back before your father returns from the meeting."

It was dark on the hillside and a chill hung in the air, but Josh was too happy to notice. He crawled along the tunnel to the hideout. There was a glimmer of light ahead, and he called softly, "Miriam! It's me." He rose and advanced into the space between the rocks. A candle was tucked into a small recess so that it was well sheltered from the wind. Beside it were jammed a couple of books, and behind them was a pile of papers filled with Miriam's untidy writing. Her eyes looked darker in the candlelight.

"Josh! What are you doing here? Is something wrong?"

"No, nothing's wrong." He held it back as long as he could. "I just wondered . . . how you would like to spend Christmas Day at the cottage. Have dinner with us and everything."

Her expression made the journey in the dark worthwhile. "Honest? Who said I could come? Your mother?"

He nodded.

Josh had become used to Miriam's impetuosity by now, and after submitting to the first onslaught of violent hugging, he broke free.

"Then that's all settled. I'll go back and tell Mother."

"Can't you stay for a while and help me? There are lots of long words in this book. I don't understand them."

"No. Dad will be home from the chapel meeting soon." He shivered. "It's freezing cold up here. I don't know how you can learn anything in this weather."

"Where else can I go?" She carefully placed her books in a tin box she had managed to acquire and tucked it well back into a crevice between the rocks. Then she snuffed out the candle and crawled through the gorse tunnel behind Josh. Once out on the moor she took his hand in a perfectly natural gesture.

"I've always wanted to have a *real* Christmas. What's it like?"

He told her. Of the holly wreaths decorating the pictures. The small presents and the large meals. He tried to put into words the atmosphere of Christmas. She listened in silence until they arrived at the track that led to the Trago home.

"Are you sure I won't be in the way?" She frowned. "If it's a family thing, I mean?"

"Of course you won't. You've been invited. Jenny and the baby will be there. Tom Shovell too. Besides, I want you to come."

"All right, then." She was happy again.

"I've got to go now. I'll see you tomorrow—same time?"

"Yes." She leaned forward and kissed him on the lips. For all the clumsy inexperience of it, he walked home without feeling the cold, as tall as any man.

On Christmas Eve, just before dusk, the Sharptor mine ceased working. The men came to the surface to be greeted by Theophilus Strike, who handed each man a large fat goose, freshly killed, and a half-guinea.

The next morning Josh rose before first light to begin building up the fire. Usually this was the time when the presents would be opened, but today they were waiting until Miriam arrived.

"I hope she won't be too late," said Jesse as she began frying breakfast. "I can't wait to see the baby's face when she gets her presents."

Josh walked to the window and caught a glimpse of color in the mist that he knew was Miriam's best dress. "Here she is," he cried, and stepped outside. But she wasn't there. Puzzled, he walked to the gate and again caught the glimpse of color. "Miriam!"

She came out from behind a gorse thicket where she had been hiding.

"What are you doing? We've been waiting for you. We can't open any presents until you're there."

Miriam shrugged her shoulders. "I haven't seen you for a couple of days. I thought your mother might have forgotten she invited me. Or your dad might have said I couldn't come."

"What would he say that for? Hurry up! Everyone's waiting."

"Just a minute." Miriam bent down behind the bushes and picked up a pile of badly wrapped parcels.

"What are they?"

Her chin went up. "They're presents. Everyone gives presents at Christmas." She did not add that it was a custom unknown in the Trago household.

Now Miriam allowed some of her excitement to shake itself loose. Only her mother knew that she would be spending the day with the Retallicks, and the secret was safe with her.

Jesse stood in the cottage doorway watching Miriam and Josh coming along the path. "Stop there!" she said suddenly, her words jolting them to an immediate halt at the door.

"It's bad luck to enter the house with bare feet at Christmas," Jesse went on. She had been straight-faced until now, but seeing Miriam's dismay she smiled. "So we'll just have to do something about that. Here, child." She picked up a parcel from a chair just inside the doorway and handed it to Miriam. "A very happy Christmas to you. . . . And don't stand there gawking," she said to Josh. "Take her parcels while she looks at her present."

Speechless, Josh did as he was told while Miriam carefully opened the wrappings. Inside was a pair of shiny black shoes, made of soft leather. Miriam's eyes said everything.

Hurriedly she placed the shoes on the ground and slipped her feet into them. They were a good fit, and Jesse nodded her head in satisfaction. "I didn't think they would be too far off."

"They're beautiful!" said Miriam. "Thank you, Mrs. Retallick."

"Now come on into the kitchen and have some breakfast, child, before we let all the warm air out of the house."

Miriam smiled happily at Josh as she was ushered inside.

After breakfast they adjourned to the best room. It was time for the presents to be opened. Miriam had some anxious moments, fearing that the gifts she had brought might not be acceptable. But the remainder of Herman Schmidt's guinea had been well used. There was a leather purse for Mrs. Retallick, and Jesse was delighted. The gifts for Josh's father, Jenny and the baby were equally well received. For Josh there was a bright neckerchief.

Then Josh brought out his present for Miriam, and she knew by the silence of the others that it was something special. It felt like a book—a thick book.

It was. When the wrappings were taken off, Miriam held a

beautiful leather-bound Bible in her hands. She opened the cover. Inside was written: "To Miriam Trago from Josh Retallick."

"Thank you, Josh," sounded totally inadequate, but it was all she was able to say.

"You won't find better reading. . . . Talking about the Good Book, it's time to be thinking of chapel," said Ben Retallick, rising. There was general movement in the room, and Miriam felt uncertain about what was expected of her, but Jesse came to her rescue.

"We'll let them go off to chapel. You can help me with dinner." To the others she said, "And don't you let Wrightwick Roberts ramble on until everyone has a spoiled meal waiting at home."

Josh knew his mother had planned things this way. By the time he and the others returned from chapel she would have thoroughly assessed Miriam's character. The thought of it kept him fidgeting all through a service which seemed to go on forever. But finally it was over, and they said their last "Happy Christmas!"

As Ben and Josh, Jenny, and Tom Shovell filed into the house, Jesse was smiling, and Josh knew that whatever she had been looking for in their guest she had found.

The meal Jesse served, for the one day when the menu was not controlled by economy, was gigantic—she had saved up during the whole year for it—with the stuffed goose as the centerpiece. Afterward they sat around talking and playing word games—except for Ben, who snored gently in his chair by the fire most of the afternoon.

All too soon, however, Tom Shovell put on his coat, and it was time for Miriam to go home too. At the door her reluctance to leave was so apparent that Jesse's heart went out to her and she hugged her close. "I'm sorry you have to go, my dear. It's been lovely having you. Mind you come here often to see us. I shall be very hurt if you don't."

Miriam kissed her impulsively, and with everyone's "Good night" ringing in her ears she set off with Josh into the darkness. Once out of the light of the cottage she took Josh's arm and hugged it to her. "Oh, Josh!" she said. "It's been such a wonderful day. The best in my whole life!"

Miriam's Christmas with the Retallicks was supposed to have been a secret, but she was not clever enough to keep it from the remainder of her family for long and she suffered cruelly when her father found out.

It was Kate Trago who brought the news to the Retallicks. She knocked on their door on New Year's Eve at the height of a rainstorm, but would not enter. Jesse had to drag her inside.

"Sit down by the fire and get warm," Jesse said. "Now tell me what's happened."

Josh was studying in the best room. Hearing voices, he came through to the kitchen.

"It was Moses," Kate was saying. "He found out Miriam had spent Christmas in this house and there was a terrible scene."

"Oh! And who told him she was here?"

"He found the shoes you gave her. I tried to stop her saying anything about them, but she was too worked up to listen. All she kept doing was shouting for him to give them back to her. Then it came out. She said she'd spent Christmas Day here. It was the best day of her life, she told him. And the more he laid into her the more she shouted defiance at him."

Josh's face had gone the color of chalk. "Did he beat her bad?"

"I don't know!" Kate Trago was close to tears. "When I tried to pull him away, he knocked me down. If it hadn't been for our Morwen, I think Moses would have killed her."

"Morwen stopped his father?" Jesse knew the boy was big for his age. Even so, he was no match for Moses.

"Yes." Kate Trago began trembling violently. "While they fought, Miriam was able to get out. I haven't seen her since."

"When did this happen?" Jesse asked.

Kate Trago looked shamefaced. "Night before last."

"*What!* And you haven't looked for her before this? The poor girl could be dying somewhere."

"I know—but I was so sure she would be here."

"Josh, have you seen Miriam?"

"No. But I think I know where to find her." He was already putting on his boots.

369

Kate Trago stood up. "I must go. I've left the younger ones alone up there. Take care of her, when you find her—and tell her it's all right to come home. Moses won't touch her again. He's sorry for what he did. He wouldn't say it to anyone, but I know it."

"We won't argue about that now." Jesse's lips drew tight.

Josh banged out of the house and into the bitterly cold night. He dreaded what he might find at the hideout.

At the entrance to the narrow gorse tunnel he paused and listened. He thought he could hear sound from within, and when he came into the clearing he recognized it as shallow, rasping breathing. He had heard it once before, when his grandfather was fighting a losing battle with death.

Josh fumbled with numb fingers for the candle. Finally it cast its flickering light. Miriam was slumped with her back against the rock, sheltered from the wind. Her left eye was puffed up like an apple, and a bloody graze extended across her forehead.

He dropped to one knee beside her and, putting a hand gently beneath her chin, lifted her head. Weakly she tried to jerk away from him, and the movement caused her to groan. He could see now that both her eyes were swollen and tight closed. She must have been lying here, completely blind, for two days and nights.

"Miriam! Can you hear? It's me. Josh. It's all right now. I'll get you out of here."

When he tried to lift her, however, he touched one of her ribs, and she cried out in pain as it grated beneath his fingers. The next few minutes were a nightmare. But by dragging, pushing and heaving, he finally succeeded in getting her out onto the moor. Then, during a swaying pause for breath, he heard people crashing through the undergrowth toward him. Thinking that one of them might be Moses Trago, Josh lowered Miriam quietly to the ground. Whoever it was began to move away, up the slope.

"It must have been Josh," a man said.

Josh recognized his father's soft voice. "Dad! Over here."

Within seconds Ben and Tom Shovell loomed out of the darkness in front of him. "Have you found the girl?"

"Yes, but she's hurt badly."

"All right, Ben. Gently now. I have her." And the big shift captain cradled Miriam in his arms as though she were a baby.

Miriam was laid up in Jesse and Ben's bedroom for three weeks, while Josh slept in the kitchen downstairs. At first the doctor from the Caradon mine was a daily visitor. He strapped her ribs—two of them were broken—and worked on her face. He feared her nose was also broken, but when the swelling around her eyes began to go down he was pleased to acknowledge that he had been wrong.

On the fifth day Miriam could see from one eye, and she progressed steadily thereafter. Kate Trago was a frequent visitor. She always came after dark and would sit next to her daughter's bed, saying scarcely a word and wringing her hands nervously.

When Miriam was able to sit up in a chair for an hour each day, she received a visitor who caused great consternation in the Retallick house. He too came after dark, but the fact that he knocked at the door and waited quietly was unusual.

Josh opened the door—and promptly slammed it shut. Turning to his father in alarm, he said, "It's Moses."

Ben leaped from his chair, and Jesse reached for a heavy poker. Moses knocked again. Ben motioned for Josh to move back and opened the door himself.

Moses stood before him, his hat in his hands. "I've come to take Miriam home."

"Then you've had a wasted journey." Ben controlled his anger.

Jesse was less reticent. "You take one step into this house, Moses Trago, and you'll feel this poker across your head. That girl has suffered enough at your hands."

"I haven't come here to quarrel, Mrs. Retallick. What has happened is done. It can't be forgotten. All the same, Miriam is my daughter and I want her home." He fought to control himself.

Then a voice from the stairs made them all look up. "Mrs. Retallick, please let him come in." Miriam's face was still discolored and she clung to the handrail unsteadily.

A look passed between Jesse and Ben, then Ben stood back from the door. "You can go up to see her. But father or not, she'll not leave this house until she's well."

Moses stepped inside, his shoulders filling the doorway, and he went upstairs to the room where Miriam slept.

Downstairs the only sound for a long time was the crackling of wood on the fire. Suddenly Josh said fiercely, "He's not taking her with him."

"Don't go climbing fences until they are built," said Ben.

They heard Moses Trago come out of the bedroom and clump heavily down the stairs. He looked from one to the other.

"She says she'll be coming home when she's well," he said. "Until then I'd be obliged if you'd have her here. I'll pay for her keep. And for the doctor. Here are two guineas."

"We'll take one guinea for the doctor," retorted Jesse. "Whatever else we do is because we're fond of the girl."

Moses Trago flushed angrily. "Then give this guinea to the boy," he said. "I hear he found her."

Josh stood up, his heart pounding. "I did that for Miriam. Not for your money. Buy her some new shoes with it to make up for those you burned."

He felt his mother's eyes on him. Kate Trago had not told her that during the fight in the Trago home Moses had thrown Miriam's shoes onto the fire. Miriam had told Josh and had been more upset about it than she was for her injuries.

Moses looked at him from beneath shaggy brows. "I've already promised Miriam some new shoes. I've also told her she can have schooling from that preacher at St. Cleer. When she's well enough, her mother will come for her." He nodded, then left.

"The cheek of the man!" Jesse all but exploded.

"Hush, now," said Ben. "Moses Trago cannot change. Keeping his temper tonight cost him much. Give him credit for that."

MIRIAM returned home one week before Josh was due to begin his apprenticeship at Hayle. Both departures hit Jesse hard. She had become very fond of the girl. Her quick wit and an ever-ready willingness to learn had endeared her to the whole household.

With Miriam out of the house, it was time to stitch and iron and generally prepare Josh for a stay in a town which, although hardly fifty miles distant, was as remote to Jesse as the Highlands of Scotland.

Josh himself put off thinking about it until the last minute. He had finished his schooling, and as a parting gift the Reverend Thackeray gave him an old wood-and-leather chest to carry his belongings. He also gave him some words of advice.

"While you're away you'll be learning new things and meeting new people," he said. "Never let them make you forget where you come from, or the men who remain here—working and dying in wretched conditions. And if you hear anyone at Hayle talking about a union of miners, listen to him. I'm convinced that's where the future of the miner lies." He held out his hand. "Good-by and good luck, Josh. May God be with you."

His next farewell was with Miriam. He had not looked forward to it. "I'll write and tell you all about Hayle as soon as I arrive," he declared as they stood on the path between their two homes.

"And I'll write straight back."

"Well . . . I'll say good-by, then." He held her briefly and kissed her cheek. "Take care of yourself, Miriam."

"And you, Josh. I shall miss you terribly."

He realized that he was going to miss her more than anyone else at Sharptor. He would have liked to tell her so but did not know how to begin. He turned and walked away. Looking back, he saw her standing on the path, a teeth-chattering little figure waving bravely until he was out of sight.

That left only his family the following morning. Jesse fussed about him as he sat on the seat of the ore wagon beside Nehemeziah. "You be good, mind. No fighting—and write often."

"Yes, Mother."

The aged hostler flicked the reins and the wagon creaked away. Josh waved until the huddled group of his parents, Jenny, the baby and Tom Shovell disappeared from view around a curve.

Josh and Nehemeziah were on the first wagon of the day to leave the mine for Moorswater. This was the inland terminal of the canal linking the mining area with the port of Looe. From Looe, Josh would travel on to his new home by sea.

CHAPTER FOUR

It was dawn when the small cargo ship rode the tide into Hayle harbor. Josh stood on deck, his trunk beside him, shivering in the cold mist which drifted across the Hayle River. On the far bank were the ugly stone buildings of the works that was to be his home for the next three years. Smoke from the foundry and smelting chimneys belched forth thick and dirty, darkening the mist.

With the help of a longboat, the ship edged in to the jetty. A steward handled Josh's trunk, and Josh hurried down the gangway. Then, struggling with the trunk, he set off along the busy quayside.

Before he had gone twenty yards, a boy of about his own age appeared alongside him. "You Joshua Retallick?" he asked. Although Josh did not recognize the accent, it was pure cockney. "Yes."

"Tom Fiddler's the name. I've been sent to meet you." He grinned, his manner friendly. Each taking one of the handles of the trunk, they let it swing at arm's length between them as they walked off the quay and followed a muddy path between piles of rough ore, rusting girders and new-cast boiler parts to a huge granite-block building that was Harvey's foundry.

When they passed an opening as wide and tall as a miner's cottage, the heat and roar from within sent Josh staggering. "You'll soon get used to that," said his companion. "But at first you'll be gasping for breath whenever they open a furnace door near you."

They soon entered the single-story dormitory, and Tom pointed out Josh's bed and locker. After Josh had changed into working clothes, Tom took him to meet the works manager.

William Carlyon was a tall, hook-nosed, no-nonsense man. He dismissed Tom with a peremptory wave of his hand and leaned back in his chair. "So this is the young man we must turn into an engineer. All in three short years!" He sniffed derisively. "That is scarcely enough time to teach you to work an engine, let alone build or repair one." He stood up abruptly and walked to the door, beckoning Josh to follow him. "But we'll make a start."

An hour later Josh was helping a toothless old ex-miner shovel coal into the greedy furnaces and bring them up to a heat that would boil iron. For a week Josh carried out this task, returning to the dormitory at the end of each working day sweating and coal-grimy. The other apprentices were friendly, but they all worked a long day in different sections of the foundry, and there was little opportunity to get to know them quickly. In the evenings they spent hours writing notes or studying plans of engines.

It would be a while before he would get down to actual engineering. At the end of his week as a stoker he would be helping to load the ore into the furnaces. Then he would learn how to handle the molten metal that poured like a brew from hell into the waiting molds. Boilers, pipes, beams and tramway lines, all were made at Harvey's Hayle foundry.

The apprentices worked a six-day week. The seventh day was theirs to do with as they wished, provided they did not miss the two-hour service held in Hayle Methodist chapel in the morning or tea at the works manager's house in the afternoon.

On Josh's first Sunday, he and the other apprentices, washed and wearing their best clothes, assembled outside the Carlyon house to escort the family to chapel. William and Molly Carlyon had two daughters, Sarah and Mary. Sarah was Josh's age, but Mary was only six, spoiled by family and apprentices alike.

Josh took an immediate liking to Mary and she to him. All the way to the chapel she chattered. By the time they got there she had elicited details of his home, parents and a great deal more.

Inside the chapel, Josh sat behind the Carlyon girls. He could not help noticing the whiteness of their necks and the golden hair drawn back in identical plaits. Paradoxically it made him think of Miriam's brown skin and untidy black hair. Homesickness rose in him, and he wondered what she was doing at that moment. He decided to write home after the service and enclose a note for her.

SUNDAY afternoon tea in the Carlyon house, at the huge table with its white cloth and silver cutlery, was one part of his new life Josh would gladly have forgone. It would have been less of an ordeal had he been seated with the other boys. But as the newest apprentice he was placed between Mrs. Carlyon and Sarah.

Mrs. Carlyon quickly established that his father worked in one of the smaller mines and Josh would be tied to the same mine for some years after his apprenticeship. After that she lost a certain amount of interest. Not so Sarah.

To the Cornish of the far west, Bodmin Moor was vague and mysterious, shrouded in the mists of legend. Sarah was curious to know more about it. When he began talking to her about the moor, Josh temporarily forgot his shyness. By the time he had finished he found that everyone was listening.

"You know your moor well, Josh," said William Carlyon. "Take the same interest in engineering, and Mr. Strike won't be sorry he sent you to Hayle." He stood up. "Now it is time to send you all back to your dormitory to prepare for tomorrow. We look forward to your company next Sunday."

Josh's life settled into a pattern that varied only in the work he was doing. Gradually he began to enjoy his Sundays with the Carlyons. If Mrs. Carlyon was not happy because Sarah spent most of the time talking only to Josh, she never mentioned it.

As the mild winter gave way to spring, Josh looked forward to Easter for two reasons. One was that after the weekend he would at last begin to learn about steam engines. The second was that there would be a four-day holiday, and he was going home, traveling with no less a personage than Francis Trevithick, son of the great Cornish engineer and inventor, Richard Trevithick.

Richard had married into the Harvey family, and his son, Francis, had learned his skills with them. Josh had met him at the Carlyon house, and it was there Francis made his offer to take the boy as far as Launceston in his own coach. After that Josh would have to walk the last few miles to Sharptor.

At a minute past six o'clock in the Good Friday dawn, Francis Trevithick's carriage swung up to the works gate and Josh climbed inside. "Enjoy the ride while you can," Trevithick told him as the coach swayed in rhythm with the horses' gait. "There's little enough good road. Now tell me what you've learned here."

Josh started to say that he had not been at Harvey's many months, but Trevithick waved this aside. "Nonsense! You will have learned quite a lot, I am sure. How do you bank a furnace to get the maximum heat from it? And what do you do to keep it at the highest possible temperature using the minimum of coal? Then what about molding—you've done some of that, haven't you?"

Josh gave Trevithick his answers—briefly at first, but the engineer demanded more detail, probing Josh's knowledge. "What are you going to do when you leave Hayle?" he asked finally.

Josh told him about Theophilus Strike and the Sharptor mine.

"This mine of yours—it's still being pumped by horsepower?" Trevithick spat the question out. "What depth has it reached? How many men are working it?"

Josh told him.

"Then why does Strike operate in such a primitive fashion?" Trevithick snorted. "What provision is there for a man-hoist?"

Josh confessed that he had heard no mention of any—adding that he was determined to do something about it eventually.

"Good for you. How long does it take a man to reach the surface from a deep shaft? Twenty minutes? Half an hour? By that time he is thoroughly exhausted. If his hand slips, he doesn't have the strength to save himself. If he survives to crawl out of his hole, the cold air will tear at his lungs like a steel rasp. My God, boy! Our miners deserve better than that. Look here." He produced paper and pencil. "I'll show you how an ordinary pumping engine can also be used to bring men to the surface. My father designed it. It's the simplest principle imaginable. Persuade mineowners to provide a lift for their men, and you are halfway toward forcing them to accept that they are employing human beings."

Josh took possession of each drawing as Trevithick discarded it. He thought of Budge Pearn. Had there been a man-hoist in Sharptor mine, Jenny would not be a widow today.

"Preacher Thackeray is always saying the very same thing."

"Preacher Thackeray?" Trevithick frowned. "I've heard of him. He's the man who wants all miners to unite. That's dangerous talk, young Retallick. Help to make the miners' lot an easier one by all means. That is Christian charity. But don't try to put ideas into a man's head that he is the equal of his employer. Put power into irresponsible hands and there is but one outcome. The sort of bloodbath that swept France not many years past. But politics holds no interest for me. Nor you, if you have sense. Now do you understand the principle of the lift?"

Josh asked a few more questions. Trevithick answered him and drew quick diagrams, cursing as the coach bumped and jolted.

"It is far too bumpy for drawing," he said finally. "Somewhere I have a detailed set of plans that my father once drew up. I will send them to you at Hayle. Tell me instead what you know of the principles of a steam engine."

And so the hours and the miles sped by until they arrived at Launceston. As Josh left the coach and said good-by, the engineer patted him encouragingly on the shoulder.

When the coach was well on its way, Josh turned onto a track leading across the moor. It was a clear day, and he could see the Sharptor ridge from three miles off. Before he had gone another half mile an excited, panting Miriam was running to meet him.

"Josh! Let me look at you. You have grown taller and broader. You have—don't laugh."

Josh hugged her, still laughing. He had not realized how much he had missed her. There were changes in her too. "What's been going on? Your hair! You've had it cut." It had been brushed so much it shone. "And that's a new dress! I must have been gone much longer than I realized. You're not the same Miriam."

"Josh Retallick!" She looked at him for a moment, then laughed. "William said I must tidy myself if I wanted him to teach me."

It came as a shock to realize she was talking of Preacher Thackeray. She was going to his school in St. Cleer regularly. All the same, Josh had been taught by Thackeray for years without ever using his Christian name. Miriam prattled on. "Jenny washed my hair and cut it for me. And my dad bought these shoes."

She saw his face and stopped. "What's the matter, Josh? Don't you like me as I am now?"

"I—I don't know. You've grown up so much."

"I thought you wanted me to grow up," she said quietly.

"Yes." Josh felt awkward. "It's just a bit of a surprise."

She took his hand and spoke, looking down at the ground. "It's a special sort of surprise, Josh—and only for you."

It was better then, walking home across the moor, clasped hands swinging between them. By the time they reached the cottage it was as though he had never been away, except that there was more to talk about. His mother fussed about him excessively, and his father said very little after his initial handshake. Ben looked well satisfied, though.

The weekend went all too quickly. Josh spent most of the time around the house with his family, or on the moor with Miriam.

She walked as far as St. Cleer with him on his return. From there he was traveling by coach to Truro. The trip was a present from his father; however, the money he had saved was only sufficient for Josh to travel on the outside of the coach, and he would have a seventeen-mile walk from Truro to the works.

They arrived at St. Cleer just as the coachman's horn called for boarding. There were things Josh had wanted to say to Miriam. Now there was neither the time nor, of a sudden, the words.

"Don't you want to go, Josh?" Miriam was studying his face.

"It's not that I don't want to go. It's . . ." He shrugged helplessly.

"Is it because of me?"

He nodded. "Yes."

"Then you've no need to worry, Josh. I will be counting the days until you are back. But quickly now; the coach is leaving."

As the coachman cracked his whip, Josh snatched a kiss and jumped aboard. He waved until the horses' trot became a canter and St. Cleer and Miriam receded over the brow of the hill.

THERE was little time for brooding in the days and weeks that followed. William Carlyon was determined that the engineers trained at Harvey's should match the engines for which they would be responsible. Also, when he heard why Trevithick had sent the plans for the man-hoists to Josh, he not only saw that Josh received the fullest possible training as an engineer but that he was fully

379

conversant with all the latest developments in man-hoist design.

Josh was a born engineer. His letters to Miriam and his family were full of his new skills and interests. Even in the company of the Carlyon family he could speak of little else, and this did not always please Sarah.

One midsummer Sunday as they were returning from chapel, he was in the middle of extolling the virtues of Harvey's latest engine when Sarah suddenly stopped and stamped her foot. "I'm sick of engines! I'm surrounded by the smell of engines, bits of engines and men who work with engines. I *hate* engines!"

With that she lifted her chin and flounced off, leaving a stunned Josh staring after her.

It was with some trepidation that he went to tea at the Carlyons'. Sarah behaved as though nothing had happened, but he was still very careful not to talk about engines. Soon the conversation turned to horse riding. The Carlyon girls had owned ponies for years, and for her recent birthday Sarah had been given a full-blooded hunter, Hector, a beautiful, spirited horse.

"Have you ever ridden?" she asked Josh.

"No. Except bareback on the cart horses at the mine."

"Wouldn't you like to learn to ride properly?"

"Yes. But I could never find the time."

"Of course you could." Sarah had him firmly on the hook. "Papa, Josh says he would love to learn to ride but doesn't have time. He could ride Pedlar on Sundays, couldn't he?" Pedlar was the pony which had been succeeded by her new hunter.

"If Josh can fit it in with his studies, I have no objections."

"Now, then. Can we start at once?"

"I can't wear these boots on a horse," protested Josh.

"Papa, you never wear your riding boots anymore. Can Josh borrow them?"

William Carlyon grinned at him. "It's no use," he said. "Sarah has decided that you are to have a riding lesson. I would never hear the last of it if I spoiled her plans. Come along."

Josh followed him upstairs, to return after a time wearing tall, shiny riding boots. Sarah had changed into a dark brown riding habit, and at the stables Josh saddled the horses under her instruction. Soon they were jogging across open country.

Drawing in beside him, Sarah said, "Why did you tell me you couldn't ride? You are doing splendidly."

"It's like riding the mine horses," he replied, "except that there's something to hold on to and somewhere for your feet."

"Come on, then!" cried Sarah. "I'll race you up that hill." She dug in her heels, and the hunter bounded ahead.

Josh followed suit, and it was now that he learned the difference between sitting a slow-jogging pony and one that is galloping. One moment his face was buried in the horse's coarse mane. The next, his head was jerked back and all he could see was sky. Fortunately the pony found it almost as uncomfortable to have such an uncontrolled weight on its back. It slowed, so that Josh was able to bring it back under control and take it to the top of the hill.

Sarah had dismounted and was waiting, flushed from the gallop. Her golden hair had fallen about her shoulders. "I won! Why didn't you give Pedlar his head? He enjoys a good run."

"He didn't enjoy it today," declared Josh, swinging gratefully to the ground. "I wasn't doing any of the things he is used to."

Sarah laughed. "You'll learn. I'll show you on the way back. But look over there. Isn't that worth coming up here to see?"

She pointed north to where the farmland sloped toward St. Ives Bay. A few red-sailed fishing boats leaned away from the wind in the sea beyond, and near the horizon, two packets crowded on full sail. "It's beautiful here, isn't it?" she said.

"Yes. But you have to see the moor to know what beauty is."

"I've seen it," said Sarah. "We went to Barnstaple once and crossed over it. It's a bleak, dreary place."

"It isn't! Get away from the road and you'll find the rivers and tors and valleys. They're alive with more animal and plant life than you will ever have seen in one place before."

Sarah caught his expression. "And have you discovered all these birds and animals and plants by yourself?"

He cleared his throat before answering. "Sometimes by myself. Sometimes with Miriam."

Sarah stroked Hector's nose. "Who's Miriam?"

He tried to describe her but was aware that his word picture was a mere sketch of the wild moorland girl. He did not know whether the fault lay in his telling, or because it was impossible to describe Miriam without having the moor near.

Sarah flicked the reins back over Hector's head. "I think we ought to go home now," she said, swinging up to the saddle before Josh could help her. On the return journey she showed him how to hold himself and move with the pony; yet there was a reserve between them that had not been present before.

Back in the stable, he thanked her for the lesson. "Will we be able to go again next Sunday?" he asked.

Some of her sparkle returned. "All right. We'll make it a regular Sunday treat. We can go out early, before breakfast. That's the time I enjoy it the best." So riding became part of Josh's routine. He liked both the ride and Sarah's company.

WHEN his first year ended, Josh spent a short Christmas interlude with his family and Miriam. However, his mind was constantly slipping away to tackle some technical problem. Miriam accepted his preoccupation proudly. She believed that Josh would one day be a brilliant mine engineer.

It was the summer of 1840 when something happened which might well have altered Josh's whole career. He was working with William Carlyon in Harvey's foundry yard when a horseman clattered through the gate. The rider was in almost as much of a lather as the horse. With a sense of foreboding, Josh recognized Nehemeziah Lancellis, Mr. Strike's gnarled little hostler.

"Josh, boy! I've brought bad news for 'ee. Best get home."

"What's happened?"

" 'Tis Ben. . . . He was working on a tunnel off the main shaft. New man set off a bad explosion. . . . Roof's down with Ben and three more neath it. Schmidt won't have rescue work. He's back on the drink. . . . Best get there and sort it out, Josh."

"I'll go now, Nehemeziah. I'll take your horse."

"No! He'm clapped, Josh! Wouldn't last half a mile."

"Josh!" Sarah had run from the house and heard the news. "Take Hector. He's the fastest horse you'll find."

"Can I?" Josh turned to William Carlyon.

"Of course! It's Sarah's horse to do with as she wishes."

Josh hurried away to throw off his working clothes and put on his riding gear. By the time he was back in the yard, Sarah was leading the big horse, fully saddled, from the stable.

He mounted, a competent rider now. Then, to a chorus of good wishes, he clattered out of the yard, soon allowing the big horse to stretch out into a mile-consuming gallop.

CHAPTER FIVE

HERMAN Schmidt, red-faced and angry, stood at the entrance to the collapsed tunnel at Sharptor, facing a sullen crowd of miners.

"Go back to work, all of you. There is nothing to be done, I say. The roof has collapsed. The men inside are dead."

Tom Shovell stepped forward. "With all due respect, Captain, that isn't our way. Ben and the others may well be dead, but we'll see that they have a decent burial. We owe them that."

"Them you owe nothing! Me you owe everything!" Schmidt shouted. "And I say you work—you hear? Work! If anyone tries to go into this tunnel, he is no longer employed at the Sharptor mine."

Tom's face paled. "No, Captain Schmidt. We will dig out the tunnel until we find those men. Dead or alive."

There was a sudden commotion in the crowd as Wrightwick Roberts pushed to the front. "What is this, a meeting? Hold your meetings later. What we need now are men with picks and strong arms. Come on. Give me something to dig with."

"They must go back to work," Schmidt repeated.

"They'll go back when they've brought out Ben Retallick and the others," said Roberts. "Come on, Tom. In we go."

With a nod the shift captain fell in behind the preacher. Schmidt moved to block their path and was sent reeling by Roberts. Before he had recovered his balance the entrance to the tunnel was crowded with miners, and candles were being passed forward.

A hundred feet in, the preacher and Tom Shovell came to a tumbled barrier of rock that completely blocked the passage. "This doesn't look good," said Roberts.

Tom Shovell looked crestfallen. "The man on the powder was a new man from the Kit Hill workings. He told me he was used to black-powder blasting." He nodded, indicating the fallen rock, sending a shower of wax to the floor from the candle attached to his helmet. "But this isn't the work of an experienced man."

"We'd better get at it," said the preacher. Lighting other candles from the one he held, he placed them on rough ledges hacked into the walls. "There'll not be room for more than one man to work here. I'll have first turn and you pass back the rocks I get out."

"We'll need a bit of shoring up," Tom said. Then he called over his shoulder, "Pass the word back along the tunnel. Fetch in some timber and saws."

Roberts strained at a huge block of granite. When it was reluctantly prized free, a trickle of smaller rocks showered into the place it had occupied. These were soon cleared, and the preacher climbed into the hole.

Gradually he disappeared from view into the tunnel he was making. The shift captain moved candles forward with him. As the preacher advanced, his progress slowed. With his great strength he was able to work loose large chunks of rock, but then, since there was room for only one man inside the tunnel, he had to manhandle them back to the beginning of the fall himself. Miraculously, the answer to this problem presented itself.

Roberts had advanced only six yards when John and Moses Trago arrived. Moses called in, "Come on out and give these weaklings here a hand, Preacher. I'll take a spell in there."

Wrightwick Roberts, his fingers torn and bleeding from the rough granite, submitted gratefully and backed out into the comparative spaciousness of the undamaged tunnel. Moses scrambled in and started working as though his own life depended upon it.

By the time Josh finally brought the frothing, sweat-darkened Hector to a halt at the entrance to the mine, the amount of rock being brought out was more than during a normal working day.

While the horse was led away to the stables, Josh hurried down the ladder and along the tunnel. When he reached the place where the fall began, he stripped off his jacket and shirt and crawled into the hole, working his way forward to where Tom Shovell, Preacher Roberts and John Trago were backing up Moses.

Tom Shovell was scarcely recognizable beneath layers of dust. "Things are looking bad, Josh."

"So they told me outside. I'd rather dig than think about it. I'm going up to take over ahead for a while."

"What are you doing back there?" Moses Trago shouted. "Having a bloody tea party? Take this rock from me before I lose it."

"Josh Retallick has just arrived," called Tom as he wrestled with a hundred-pound rock. "He's coming up to take over."

"Tell him to stay back there and save his breath for heaving stones. There's more than enough of them here."

The tunnel had progressed another ten yards before Moses stopped suddenly and called on the men to listen. The call went back until all was quiet. Then they heard the sound of metal upon rock, as though a pickaxe were being used—ahead of them!

Moses Trago began attacking the fallen rock with renewed vigor. "It's them!" he growled. Soon the chinking sound became clearer. Then there was a cascade of shale and stones. When the dust cleared, the excited rescuers saw the drawn face of a man peering at them from the underground tomb.

"Thank God! Thank God!" The face began to contort, and it looked as though the man would burst into tears.

"Thank Him later, if you must." Moses Trago slithered into the open tunnel beside the man. "Where are the others?"

The rescued miner pointed behind him.

A few yards farther on they came upon a second fall. Protruding from beneath this pile of rock a man lay, face down, the lower part of his body hidden by rocks. It was Ben Retallick.

He looked dead, but as Josh dropped to his knees beside him, a flickering candle in his hand, he stirred with a groan. "Aaagh! Who's that?"

"It's all right, Dad. Don't try to move. We'll soon have you out."

"Josh! What are you doing here? Aaagh!" The cry of pain came with a shifting of stones amid the fall.

Wrightwick Roberts crouched alongside Josh. "Where does it hurt most, Ben?"

"It's the weight on my legs." Ben gritted his teeth. "I think my right leg is broken. But you get on with what you have to do. John Maddiver took the full force of the fall, with his brother. I think one of them is lying across my feet."

There was the sound of voices from the rescue tunnel and Tom Shovell stumbled forward, followed by a tall, thin man whom Josh recognized as the Wheal Phoenix mine doctor.

"We'll have him out in a few seconds," called Moses. "Preacher, give us some of your strength on this rock. You'd best call on your Lord to help us too. Josh, pull out your father as soon as he's free."

Moses and Tom Shovell stood shoulder to shoulder with Wrightwick Roberts. They strained together, muscles cracking, until slowly the thick slab of granite began to rise, inch by agonizing inch. At last, assisted by the doctor, Josh pulled his father clear.

As the slab was lowered again, Josh saw the fingers of a man protruding from beneath it, where his father's legs had been.

While the doctor examined Ben's swollen and discolored leg, Josh began to thank Moses. "I don't need your thanks," said the big miner churlishly. "I owed the Retallicks a debt for what you once did for my Miriam. That debt is now paid. The Trago family owes nothing to anybody."

After hearing the doctor's opinion that the fracture was a simple one, Josh left his father and made his way to the surface. Arriving there, he was blinded by the light and almost bowled over as his mother flung herself at him.

"Josh, what's going on in there? Have they found him?"

His eyes were more accustomed to the light now, and Josh saw Miriam and Jenny standing beside him. Disentangling himself, he said, "Dad's all right." His mother sagged with relief. "He's got a broken leg. But it's a simple break."

"How about the other two who were with your father?" asked one of the miners in the crowd.

"There's little chance of them being alive," replied Josh, remembering the fingers beneath the rock. "But Moses and the others are still digging."

A woman began crying loudly.

"The price of being a miner's wife," said Miriam bitterly. "Her husband gone, a family to support, and within the month she'll have to be out of her cottage. That's the system her husband gave his life for."

Josh looked at her in surprise. She was learning more than mathematics and English at the St. Cleer school. It could have been the Reverend Thackeray himself talking.

Twenty minutes later Ben Retallick was carried from the shaft and Moses came with him. He singled out Mary Crabbe, on the edge of the crowd. "There's work for you, Mary."

"Both of them?" Her seared old face was devoid of emotion.

"Yes. Both of them. Dead because the Wheal Sharptor employs second-rate men to do its blasting."

He said this deliberately loudly as Theophilus Strike came through the crowd. The mineowner heard, but chose to ignore the remark. He made his way to Ben. "I'm pleased to see you safe. Herman Schmidt told me you were dead."

"And so he'd be, if left to that German," put in Moses.

There were shouts of agreement from the crowd. Strike flushed and turned to Tom Shovell. "Captain Schmidt came to me with some story of a roof fall. Four men killed and you refusing to obey orders, he said. What is it all about?"

"There's one of his dead men," said the shift captain, pointing to Ben. "Captain Schmidt wanted us to abandon any rescue attempt. He said there was nothing to be done."

"There seem to be a few matters that need clearing up," said Strike. He turned to Josh. "And what are you doing here?"

"I was brought word of what had happened and came at once."

Strike took in his scuffed riding boots. "Then you'd better get back there and not waste good learning time," he snapped.

"My horse will be ready to ride in the morning."

"*Your* horse, eh? I'm paying for you to become an engineer,

387

Retallick. Not to learn how to be a gentleman and own horses."

"It's not my own horse and I've learned to ride on Sundays, when there are no studies," said Josh defiantly.

Strike raised his eyebrows. "Young man, go home now and take your mother with you. I want to speak to your father. And to you too, Tom Shovell. The rest begone or you will be prosecuted for trespass."

"Pig!" hissed Miriam as they went off. But Jesse's heart was light within her. Ben was alive, his injury far less serious than she dared hope. And her son was with her.

Ben came home carried by Tom Shovell and escorted by a crowd of off-duty miners. "Every one of them grinning like a sheep," commented the astonished Jesse. It was with very good reason.

"Come along, Jesse," said Ben, his face all smiles despite his injury. "Don't be slow opening the door when your husband is carried home by the new mine captain."

"You, Tom?" His face betrayed the answer, and Jesse hugged him. "Oh, I'm so glad! But what happened to Captain Schmidt?"

"He won't be back. Seems he reeked of alcohol when he barged in on Theophilus Strike. He said a few things that one doesn't say to a mineowner. Josh, take note!"

"That's wonderful news. Sharptor will be a happier mine now."

"But that's not all, lad," said one of the men. "Ask your father who is to take Tom's place—when his leg has mended."

"Ben! You've been made shift captain?" cried Jesse.

Ben nodded, then had to ward off his wife as she hugged him next. "Steady now, Jesse. Remember my leg."

"It's a pity it took two deaths to make Theophilus Strike see sense," said Miriam. She turned and went into the kitchen.

"My God!" said Ben quietly. "Every time I look at that girl I see Jesse as she was when she was young. There's spirit there."

"Too much for my liking," said Tom. "I think a woman should be gentler altogether." His gaze followed Jenny Pearn as she followed Miriam into the kitchen.

There were times later that evening when Josh too wished that Miriam were a more conventional girl with a less defiant mind.

The talk over the meal moved to Josh's ride from Hayle. He had to tell them about Sarah Carlyon and his riding lessons. Miriam asked a number of questions, but it was not until he was walking her home that she pursued the subject of Sarah.

"Why did she pick you for lessons?" she asked.

Josh shrugged. "I don't know. It just happened."

"Is Sarah very beautiful?" asked Miriam, after a silence.

"Well . . . she's quite pretty, I suppose."

"More beautiful than me, Josh?"

"No." He was able to say it with complete honesty.

"Have you ever kissed her?"

"Of course not! She means nothing to me, Miriam."

"That's all right, then." Suddenly she turned and threw her arms about him. As Josh drew her close, she responded with a passionate kiss that made him feel as though his whole being were on fire. But, as quickly as it had begun, Miriam was pushing him away. "No, Josh. Please. Don't let it be like that with me."

He let his arms fall to his sides. "I'm sorry."

"Don't feel sorry. I want you to need me. But please try to wait a while longer. It won't be too long, will it?"

"Only until I come home and start earning."

She kissed him again. "I must go. . . . Josh, I love you. I love you so much I could burst with it."

"I love you too, Miriam." It sounded strange now that he had finally put his thoughts into words.

On the way home to the cottage, Josh heard Moses and Morwen going up the path to the moorland cave house, both singing drunkenly. He wished his apprenticeship were over so that he could marry Miriam and take her away to be with him.

BACK at Hayle, the weeks and months went by. Lost in sheer hard work, summer slipped into autumn. By November, Josh was sufficiently well trained to go with a team of Harvey's engineers to install some machinery in a local tin mine. It was the best possible experience for him.

The work had just been completed when winter came. Not a

man or woman alive in Cornwall could remember one like it. Hayle harbor lay silent, jammed with ships unable to move because of the blinding storms. The snow hid the toll roads, the fields and tors. For Josh it meant a great disappointment. He could not travel home to spend Christmas at Sharptor.

Nor was there any way of informing Ben and Jesse that he would not be coming. They knew it in their hearts, though, that travel through the snow was quite impossible. Only Miriam nursed the hope that some miracle would allow Josh to make the journey.

"Perhaps it is just up here on the moor that the snow is so bad," she said on Christmas Eve. She was wearing a new dress, pinched in at the waist to show off her slim, developing figure.

"No, it's the same all over the county," said Ben from the rocking chair close to the fire. "Not even a sea gull could get home in weather like this."

"I wonder what sort of Christmas Josh will have at Hayle?" put in Jenny as she lifted a large, steaming kettle from the fire.

"Oh, he'll do well enough," said Ben. "William Carlyon and his family will see to that. I think they've taken quite a fancy to our Josh. Theophilus Strike was talking to me about it the other day. He said that Josh was regarded as one of the most promising engineers they've ever had at Hayle."

Jenny came across the room and put a comforting arm about Miriam. "Never mind. I'm quite sure Josh will be home soon."

"It's all right for you," said Miriam. "Tom Shovell will be here for his Christmas meal." But then she managed a smile. Jenny was a very gentle, loving girl. Nobody was happier than Miriam at the romance between the mine captain and the young widow.

All the same, Miriam did not enjoy her Christmas. Not only was there the disappointment of not having Josh, there was also the misery of jealousy. For at Hayle, Josh was spending Christmas with a girl Miriam knew instinctively was in love with him.

THE year 1841 sped along as though it were in a hurry to get somewhere, and the Wheal Sharptor's engine became an exciting reality for Josh. By late summer it was being assembled—the boiler, the massive beam and numerous pipes, gears and wheels. Elsewhere it was rare for a mine engineer to be involved in the manufacture of his own engine, and in this Josh was lucky.

Finally all that could be done at Hayle was complete and the equipment loaded onto a ship to be carried around the coast to Looe and then by canal to Moorswater. There Josh would accompany the engine on the difficult overland journey to Sharptor.

Suddenly the years of studying were over. It was a strange feeling. For almost three years Hayle had been everything to him—home, work and recreation. Leaving it would be a wrench.

His parting with the Carlyons was difficult. He had become genuinely fond of the family. Especially, he had to admit, of Sarah. His feelings for her were not as tempestuous as those he had for Miriam; they were gentle, affectionate.

When Mrs. Carlyon had hugged him and given him a motherly kiss, she said, "Surely you are not going without saying good-by to the horses? Sarah, take Josh down to the stables. You have both had many happy hours riding together."

Josh walked with Sarah in silence to the stables. He opened the door and they went inside, into the warm and familiar smell.

"Good-by, Hector, old chap," said Josh, patting the horse's neck as the big animal nuzzled his ear. "I'm going to miss you."

"Will you miss me too, Josh?" It was an unhappy little plea.

"I'll miss you a lot, Sarah. You've been very very kind to me while I've been here."

She turned away, and he knew she was crying.

"Sarah! Don't." He touched her shoulders and she turned into him, letting the sobs come noisily.

"Please don't cry." He held her close as she clung to him. Then he was kissing her, and she was responding with a hunger that made his body react as once before. With Miriam.

He tried to move away, but she clung to him in desperation. "Don't go, Josh. Don't leave me."

"I must, Sarah. My apprenticeship is over. You know that."

"I only know I can't face life here without you," Sarah cried.

"You mustn't talk like that," he said gently. "Your family have been very good to me, Sarah. If I thought I was repaying them by making you unhappy, I would be very upset."

She pulled away from him and looked down at the ground. "I'm making a fool of myself, aren't I?"

"No, of course not."

She nodded her head violently. "Yes, I am." She fumbled in her sleeve for a handkerchief and blew her nose. "I'm all right now," she said thickly.

"That's good." He put out a hand to take her arm. "We'd better go. The men will be waiting for me."

"You go. I want to stay here for a while."

He hesitated. This was harder than he had ever imagined it would be. "All right. Good-by, Sarah."

"Good-by. . . . Josh?" He stopped and turned at the door. "Will you write to me? Tell me how you are getting on?"

"Of course I will."

"I'd like that. Good-by, Josh. Think of me sometimes."

When he went outside, the men were in the wagon. Harvey's was supplying a team of four men to install the engine, traveling with all the tools they would need. As soon as he climbed on board, the driver whipped up the horses and they trundled off.

They arrived at Sharptor the following day. After a brief reunion with his family—Miriam was at work at the Wheal Phoenix—Josh hurried away to Looe, leaving his team to inspect the newly constructed enginehouse. He meant to ensure that sufficient care was taken with the engine on its way up the canal.

The boiler looked huge sitting on the jetty alongside the ship that had carried it. But the massive thirty-ton beam was the most difficult item to handle. Josh expressed doubts about carrying it up the canal, but the canal company had a barge which had been built for this very purpose. The Wheal Caradon had used it two years before, when they had expanded their workings.

Josh thought that if the Wheal Caradon had needed a special barge for their beam, they would probably have a wagon capable of handling the heavy equipment too. When the beam had been secured aboard the barge, Josh rode off to inquire.

THE PINCH-FACED Captain Frisby had responsibility for the largest copper-mining complex in east Cornwall. "The Wheal Sharptor, eh?" he said. "How far are you expanding? I'm not lending equipment to another mine that might put us out of business."

Josh looked around at the highly industrialized Caradon complex, its numerous chimneys and air of bustle and industry. Wheal Sharptor was not in the same class, and Josh said as much.

"That may be the way it is now," said the Caradon captain, "but who knows what may happen next year?"

Josh felt the anger boiling up within him. It was unheard-of for one mine to refuse to help another when it would cost nothing. "I don't think Sharptor will ever be a big mine," he repeated, "but one day you might need another engineer. You'll always be able to call on me."

"If ever I need another engineer, I won't send for a boy," retorted the captain. But he looked at Josh with interest. "Where did you pick up your engineering? Loafing in some boilerhouse?"

"No, I learned it properly at Harvey's of Hayle. The engine on its way up from Looe is one that I helped build," replied Josh.

"Is that offer of yours a promise?" asked the captain.

"If you need help, I'm sure Tom Shovell will be happy for me to come."

"H'm! Well, I may hold you to your promise. You can take the wagon. But you'll have to provide your own horses. I'm not wearing out my horses for the Wheal Sharptor."

Josh was quite happy with that arrangement. Nehemeziah and his stableboys were able to muster seventeen pairs of horses, and with the impressive team jangling their brass-embellished harnesses, the heavy wagon was hauled away from the mine with such ease that it might have been a pony cart.

At Moorswater the engine was transferred from barge to wagon, and Josh began the slow return to Sharptor. It was midnight before he arrived, but the family had waited up with his supper. Only Miriam was not with them. He commented on that while he was eating.

"Miriam doesn't spend much time at Sharptor these days," explained his mother. "She puts in a full day's work at the Wheal Phoenix. Then she goes to St. Cleer to do her schooling."

"Miriam's staying away in order to save us from any unpleasantness," said Ben, "that's all."

"I don't understand. What unpleasantness?"

Jenny rose from her seat. "It's my fault, Josh. Do you remember how Moses Trago used to be when he'd been drinking?"

Josh nodded.

"Now he's far worse. It's as though the drink has drowned the normal part of his mind." Jenny shuddered. "He came to the house when your mother was in the kitchen and must have thought I was here alone. He started mauling me. Your mother had to threaten him with the meat cleaver before he'd go."

"But that's not all of it," put in Jesse. "He began coming to the door to ask for Miriam. It meant nothing to him whether she was here or not. It was an excuse to leer at Jenny."

"And now Miriam's staying away so that he'll have no excuse for coming here?"

"Yes. I'm sorry, Josh," said Jenny.

The following morning, however, when Josh let himself out of the cottage into the hill mist, Miriam's silent figure darted forward and the next moment he was embracing her.

"I'd almost given you up for lost," he said, holding her at arm's length to look at her. "Where have you been?"

"I expect your mother told you what happened, Josh. I'm not going to bring trouble on them again. Where are you going now? Can I walk with you?"

"I'm going to the Sharptor mine. We're beginning to put the engine together. It's a fine engine, Miriam."

"I'm quite sure it is if you've helped to build it." She clung to his arm as they swung along the path. They halted a short distance from the mine. "Will you see me tonight, Josh?"

"I'll do my best. It will be difficult for a couple of days, though. The men from Harvey's want to see the engine working by Saturday so they can return home." He smiled at her. "But I'm home for good, Miriam. We have a lifetime ahead of us."

"I know. I'm so happy I could burst. I won't wait around tonight. I'll go straight on to my lessons after work. You must talk with William; he is always asking about you."

It still sounded strange to hear her call the Reverend Thackeray William. "Give him my regards," he said. "I must go now."

"Bye, Josh."

He kissed her quickly, then strode away to the mine.

CHAPTER SIX

As JOSH had anticipated, building the engine kept him working at a frenzied pace. The machine was scheduled for completion at the end of the week. Several days would pass before the long plungers would extend to the bottom of the shaft and link up with the water pump. But on Saturday the boiler would be filled, the fire started and the shiny piston rod would set the great beam rocking.

By four o'clock Theophilus Strike and some of his friends were inside the boiler room, watching the new pressure gauge register. Outside, at the windows, were the families of every man who worked on the mine, together with those who were off duty. Ben Retallick and Jesse were well to the front. Jenny Pearn had stayed at home with young Gwen, who was recovering from a bad bout of measles.

The steam pressure reached working level. Black smoke spewed forth from the tall stone chimney and chased the wind up the slope. The water began rattling in the pipes. Then, as the needle hovered halfway across the dial of the gauge, the Hayle engineer decided it was time. "All right, Josh. Open them now."

Josh twisted the steam valve, and with oiled precision the piston rose slowly from its casing, pushing the beam with it. At the end of its stroke it returned with equal slowness and a faint sigh of escaping steam.

Theophilus Strike was impressed. "It's incredibly silent," he said. "I thought it would make a din you could hear for miles."

"You'll hear enough from it when it's driving the pumping rods into the shaft," answered the Hayle engineer. "But she'll never be a noisy engine. You may thank your own engineer for that. He supervised the building of it well, Mr. Strike."

From outside the enginehouse came shouts and cheers as the horse-operated water pump became history and steam took over.

JENNY Pearn set the kettle on the fire in the kitchen. Behind her she heard the latch on the outside door click shut. "Jesse?" she called. "How was Josh's engine? Oh my God!"

Standing swaying inside the room was Moses Trago, his face black with underground dirt and streaked with sweat.

Jenny put her left hand to her throat. The other felt behind her for the doorframe. Slowly she moved along the wall. She knew she had to get away.

Moses' eyes followed her. He took two lurching steps into the room and made a drunken gesture with his hand. "Come here!"

Jenny did not move.

Moses lumbered heavily toward her. Now he was close enough for her to know the strong animal smell that reached out from his body and the gin on his breath.

"Please, Moses, no," Jenny begged. "My babe. Don't—"

He grabbed her dress at the shoulder. She struggled to break free, but his grip held and the fabric parted. Pulling her roughly toward him, Moses closed a hand bruisingly around her flesh.

BEFORE long the heat in the engine room had become oppressive and almost everyone had left. Only Josh and Tom remained, chatting, when one of the village boys came panting up to the door.

"Captain Shovell! Captain Shovell! Ben Retallick says will you get down to his place. Quick as you can."

"What's happened?"

"I don't know, but he looked terrible fierce. I could hear someone crying inside the house."

Josh and Tom Shovell set off at a run.

There were half a dozen or so men at the cottage, among them Wrightwick Roberts. They stopped talking when Tom and Josh entered. Josh heard a moaning sound coming from the bedroom.

"Who's upstairs? What's happened?"

"It's Jenny," said Ben, his eyes on Tom. "Moses Trago was here while we were all up at the Wheal Sharptor."

The mine captain's hands closed into fists. "Evil!" he muttered. "Evil follows Moses like a shadow."

"Is Jenny hurt bad?" Josh's throat felt dry.

"That's something only your mother and Jenny will know," answered his father. "It looks bad. We found her lying unconscious on the floor with most of her clothes ripped from her."

Tom Shovell's fists twitched again. "We're wasting time. Let's get out and find him."

"Yes," Ben said reluctantly. "It's something that must be done."

"There can be no other way," said Wrightwick Roberts softly.

"I'll come with you," Josh cried.

"No. I want you to stay here, Josh," his father said. "Moses might come back." He swung away and left the house, the other men following. Tom Shovell walked like a man in a bad dream.

"Ben!" Jesse was calling from the bedroom.

"He's gone out with the others."

"To find Moses? Oh, God!" She came down the stairs. "Hasn't there been tragedy enough for one day? Josh, go and stop them."

"Dad said I was to stay here. And he's right."

"Right? There will be no right done this day." She stood in front of him, pleading. "Josh, don't think I'm worried for Moses Trago. He's forfeited all claim to human sympathy. But if your father and the others do what they have in mind, they'll spill his evil onto all of us. Please go and stop them. I beg you!"

His mother's passionate outburst confused him. But his father's words had left no room for argument. "I want you to stay here," he had said. If he left the house now and Moses did return, Josh could only blame himself. He could not go.

By DUSK there was no sign of Ben Retallick or the other men. Josh went out and looked up the hillside, but there was nothing except a train of pack mules coming down the slope from a new mining venture high on the moor. Beyond the rocky heights of

Sharptor a dark cloud was building and thunder rumbled. He went back inside, where Jesse busied herself in the kitchen.

It had been dark an hour before there was the scraping of boots on stone. Josh hurriedly unlocked the door, and the men entered grim-faced. "There'll be no need to lock the door against Moses Trago again," one miner said.

"So you found him," Jesse said flatly. "You found him and you were judge and jury—and God Himself."

"It wasn't like that." Wrightwick Roberts' big fingers tangled and untangled themselves jerkily. "He fell, Jesse. It was an accident. We had him cornered at the top of the old shaft and called on him to give himself up. He was throwing rocks at us. As he stooped for one at the edge, he slipped and fell down the shaft."

"Did you actually see this with your own eyes, Wrightwick Roberts? Or did one of you who was closer to Moses say that's what happened and you all agreed it must be so?"

There was an uncomfortable silence during which Jesse looked at each man in turn, hoping that one would meet her gaze.

"Tom, you'd better go upstairs to that poor girl. I only hope there were no witnesses to this night's work."

Again the men looked uncomfortable, and Jesse gasped, "Someone did see you! Who was it?"

"There was no other to see what happened." This from Wrightwick Roberts. "Although the Trago girl was following us shortly before. But it really was an accident."

Josh reached for his coat and bolted through the door. He could imagine Miriam following the men hunting her father, hoping to find him first and warn him, then witnessing his death.

The storm was almost overhead now. Between the rumbles of thunder, the lightning picked out the bushes and rocks of the moor and gave them long, trembling shadows. Gusts of wind ripped through the undergrowth. Finally Josh reached his destination. On hands and knees he crawled through the gorse tunnel into the hideout. It was silent inside, and he thought he had guessed wrong. Then a sustained web of lightning broke up the sky and he saw her, crouching in a corner.

"Miriam!" He dropped down beside her. "I'm so sorry."

He had expected that she would cling to him; but she showed no emotion. Her body was rigid. Only her lips moved.

"They killed him, cornered him like a dog in a sheep pen."

His hands went out to her shoulders. "They didn't mean to do it, Miriam. He slipped."

"No!" She spat the word out. "They killed him. I saw it."

"They wanted to take him back. He had to be caught after what he did." Josh tried to draw her to him, but she remained stiff for another minute. Then suddenly, without any warning, she brought her mouth up to his. Fierce and demanding.

It took him by surprise, but he responded immediately and eagerly. She slipped sideways to lie on the grass, and he went down with her. Her hands slipped inside his jacket and began plucking his shirt loose from his trousers, clutching, clawing at his back. Then he was rolling onto her, and she was straining to receive him.

LATER he stood up slowly, feeling rain pound against him. She lay where he had left her, not moving.

Josh was uneasy. Something was not right. "Here, take my jacket. You're getting soaked."

He reached out a hand to her, but she flinched back.

"What's the matter? Did I hurt you? I'm sorry, but you wanted it to happen as much as I did, didn't you?"

She ignored the jacket. "Did I, Josh? Are you quite sure? If I tell Morwen and Uncle John you forced me, held me down and took me, will they believe you—or me? Will they get the men out to hunt you? Perhaps they'll drive you to the top of some mine shaft. They'll give you a choice, Josh. Face their flailing sticks— or back into the hole in the ground."

"Miriam, you don't know what you're saying. We're going to be married."

"No!" Thunder rumbled away in the background. Wearily she shrugged herself into her limp dress. "How can I marry you? Your father killed mine."

Josh attempted to deny it, but she screamed, "He did! He murdered him." Her voice broke. "It's finished between us, Josh."

He took hold of her, but she slipped beneath his arms. Before he could stop her she had gone, into the gorse tunnel.

"Miriam—come back!" As he stumbled after her, a flash of lightning blinded him, and the wind threw the words in his teeth.

MOSES TRAGO was buried at St. Cleer with only his family present. The Reverend William Thackeray took the service. When it came to an end, he put a comforting arm about Miriam's shoulders and led her away from the graveside. Her mother and John Trago followed, but the scowling Morwen turned and walked off without a backward glance.

Josh had known about the funeral. And though he desperately wanted to speak to Miriam, he knew better than to attend. He was still bewildered and unable to think straight about himself. For a couple of days after the night of the storm his unhappiness had been mingled with fear. However, there had been no knock at the door, no crowd of angry miners eager to avenge the seduction of a young girl. Now only the uncertainty remained.

He tried to intercept Miriam up on the moor, on her way home from work at the Wheal Phoenix, but she never came. When he inquired, he found she had not been to work since the death of her father. Then he decided to wait near the Tragos' rock home.

Josh was watching the path from the cover of an ivy-clad rock when he heard a sound in the undergrowth and turned to face Morwen Trago.

"What are you spying on us for, Josh Retallick? Haven't you and your lot done enough?"

"I came up here to see Miriam," said Josh.

"Then you'll have a long wait, because Miriam isn't here."

"What do you mean? Where is she? I must see her."

"Must? Who do you think you are? Just because you've been away to learn about engines and come home riding a horse with a saddle, you needn't think everyone will jump to do your bidding. Leave Miriam alone. She doesn't want to see you again."

"You're lying, Morwen. She'd never say that."

"No Retallick calls me a liar. I've told you to leave Miriam alone. This should help you remember it." Morwen's booted foot lashed out, but Josh managed to twist his body away from the steel-rimmed heel before closing and grappling with him. Wrestling and gouging, they rolled down the slope to land with a breath-shaking thud on the hard-packed path. Few blows were struck on either side. It was a mauling, wrestling fight, until the hands of a man stronger than either of them prized them apart.

It was John Trago. "Hasn't there been enough fighting between our families? Is it to be carried on by the sons now?"

Morwen began to struggle, but John shook his nephew until his teeth rattled. "Stop it, I say!"

Morwen ceased his struggles, and John released him. "Now, what's this all about?" The big man's voice was surprisingly soft.

"I caught him snooping around," said a surly Morwen.

"I was trying to see Miriam."

"You won't find her here anymore," said John. "She's at St. Cleer, at Preacher Thackeray's house."

"Thank you. That's all I wanted to know." Josh had turned to go when John's call stopped him.

"Josh! You must leave her be, now. She's getting married."

Shock and disbelief hit Josh with a near-physical blow. "Married? It isn't possible! Who ... ?"

"She's marrying Preacher Thackeray this coming week."

Josh's mouth hung open. William Thackeray had been his friend. He had taught Josh not only how to read and write, but even how to think. Furthermore, he knew of Josh's love for Miriam. He could not marry her. It would be a complete betrayal.

"Don't try to see her, Josh," John Trago went on. "It would only distress her. This is a good marriage for Miriam. A chance to get away from the past and lead a normal life. If you think anything at all of her, don't ruin that chance."

But Josh hardly heard the rest of John Trago's words. He stumbled away along the path, his mind in a turmoil. He walked aimlessly. When he did become aware of things around him, he saw the rock hideout just ahead. He crawled gratefully into its shelter and sat looking at the spot where he had lain with Miriam on that stormy night less than a week before.

Something metallic gleamed in a crevice between the rocks. It was a tin box. Lifting it down, he prized off the lid and found a full record of the relationship between himself and Miriam. Not only were there all the letters he had sent to her while he was at Hayle but also the pages of arithmetic he had taught her. Finally, on a scrap of paper, he saw a faded word: "Miriam." She had been happy that day, delighted at seeing her name in writing for the first time. "I'll keep it forever," she had said. It seemed that her forever had come to an end.

Josh left then, but not to go home. He set off in the opposite direction—to St. Cleer to see the Reverend William Thackeray.

At the gate to the stone cottage behind the chapel, Josh hesitated. Coming across the moor, he had rehearsed what he would say. He would tell the preacher that for Miriam to marry anyone but himself would be a dreadful mistake. They, Miriam and Josh, loved each other and always had. He had thought of saying that they had already given themselves to each other but decided to keep that as a last, desperate bid to prevent the marriage.

While he hesitated, William Thackeray came out of the cottage. Closing the door, he walked down the path toward his former pupil. "Josh! How wonderful to see you. How are you?"

Josh ignored the preacher's outstretched hand. "I want to speak to you about Miriam," he blurted out, feeling awkward and adolescent, a pupil with the master.

"Yes, I know, Josh. Miriam and I are to be married."

Josh couldn't understand how the preacher was able to maintain such composure. "She was going to marry me," he said.

"I know. That is why I am glad you have come to see me, Josh. I would have been unhappy that someone we both care for had come between us. Miriam feels the same way."

"Where is she now?"

"I'm sorry. That is something I am not willing to tell you."

"I only want to hear her tell me herself that everything is over between us. I'll believe it then."

"You will have to accept it from me, Josh. Miriam is going to be my wife."

The preacher's reasonable tone made Josh angry. "She can't marry you! Ask her about—" The words stuck in his throat.

"She has told me all I want to hear, and we will be married on Sunday. I think we really won't achieve anything pursuing this conversation." Thackeray moved off toward the chapel. "I'm sorry, Josh. I'll pray for your peace of mind."

Angry and ashamed at the tears that stung his eyes, Josh turned away. Thackeray had won, but he would not allow this man who had once been his friend to witness his humiliation.

However, someone else witnessed his defeat. From her room upstairs in the preacher's home Miriam watched Josh walk away, hunched in his unhappiness. And it was his misery she shared, not William Thackeray's victory.

THERE were two weddings that month. In the chapel at St. Cleer, William Thackeray was married to Miriam Trago, while in the little whitewashed chapel at Henwood, Jenny Pearn became Mrs. Tom Shovell. Josh went to neither wedding. He made the excuse to Jenny that there were last-minute adjustments to be made to the pumps at the mine. He could not have sat through the service without torturing himself with thoughts of the other wedding.

There *was* something Josh was working on in the mine. The pumps were operated by a series of huge wooden rods, moved up and down by a rocking beam. They extended to the bottom of the shaft, and rose and fell extremely slowly. Inspired by the plans given to him by Francis Trevithick, Josh was using this slow speed to provide a means of raising men to the surface.

The idea was simple. The length of the engine's stroke was some twelve feet, and Josh had bolted blocks of wood to the rods at a distance of twelve feet apart. At the same intervals up the shaft he had built platforms into the wooden framework. It would be a simple matter for a man to step onto a block and ride up for twelve feet. Then he would step off and wait for the next stroke of the pump to ride up the next twelve feet in the same manner.

Josh did not have to wait long for the mineowner's reaction. One afternoon Theophilus Strike arrived to inspect the new machine. "So now we have become a modern mine," he said to Tom Shovell as Josh set the engine in motion. "How is the pump working?"

"Why not go down and see for yourself, Mr. Strike? I've built a new idea into the pumping system. It means that the men will be able to come up from the levels without using the ladders."

"What the devil do you mean?" Strike blazed, looking at Josh, who had made the suggestion. "Your job was to put in the engine and pumping system, not install some fool idea of your own."

"It's not exactly my idea," said Josh. "It was Richard Trevithick's. His son gave me the drawings."

"Francis Trevithick?" There was an immediate change of attitude. The Cornish engineering family was a highly respected one. "When did he come to Sharptor?"

"He didn't. I met him at Hayle."

"And how much did this idea cost?"

"Virtually nothing. We made use of materials already to hand."

The mineowner looked searchingly at Josh. "All right," he said finally. "Take me down to the fifty-fathom level and I'll see for myself how it works. Give me a helmet, someone."

Josh led the way, stepping onto the block as it came up to its maximum height. The descent was easy. The platforms were sufficiently large, and the low speed of the engine eliminated much of the danger. The primitive lift was certainly lacking in safety measures, but it was better than a wet ladder for a tired man.

When his tour of inspection was over, Strike returned aboveground. It was obvious he had enjoyed the experience.

"You have done well, Josh. Thanks, no doubt, to Trevithick's plans. I only hope your lift is not going to make my miners soft."

"At the end of a shift a man is already tired," said Josh. "Anyone who has seen them gasping for breath after the climb would never think it soft to find another way to get them up."

"Joshua Retallick, I like your initiative, and I will agree to allow the men to use this man-lift, as you call it, but I do not need to be lectured on the lot of the miner. On the Wheal Sharptor a man is paid a fair wage for a day's work. No one is forcing him to stay."

"I think Josh was only trying to explain that we'll be able to use our older, more experienced men at the deeper levels now we have the man-lift," put in Tom Shovell hastily. "We haven't been able to use them before because the climb back up was too much."

"I am fully aware of what he was saying," replied the mineowner. "I hope he is equally certain of my meaning."

"You'll have to watch that tongue of yours," said Tom when the mineowner had gone beyond hearing.

"I only spoke the truth," protested Josh.

"Strike doesn't want to know about that. While you've been away, your friend the preacher at St. Cleer has been out and about complaining of the miners' conditions. Wherever he goes there's trouble. Strike knows you were schooled by him and it bothers him. Learn to choose your words when he's near."

"He needn't worry about my association with Preacher Thackeray," said Josh bitterly. "He's no friend of mine."

CHAPTER SEVEN

CLOSE as the weddings of Miriam and Jenny had been, the births of their respective babies in the summer of 1842 were closer. Both children were born in the dark of the same night—hoping, some said, that the absence of light might hide their secrets.

Miriam's son was born after twelve hours of painful labor. She writhed on the bed in the cottage behind the chapel, biting back the screams that each pain drew from her and the name of the child's father that was on her tongue. Not until the pain had almost sapped her strength did the baby finally make his way into the world, adding his cries to the gasps of his mother.

Jenny had an easier time, if such events are measured in terms of physical pain. When Mary Crabbe arrived to perform the duties of midwife, the birth was well under way. But the baby, also a boy, was stillborn.

There was sympathy for Jenny, but little for Miriam. That her child was also conceived out of wedlock was unanimously agreed.

Most of the gossips had it that William Thackeray was the father, but there were knowing looks in Josh's direction. For his part he gave no sign that he knew their opinions, or cared.

The engine at the mine was running well, and word of the man-lift was spreading. It was not long before Captain Frisby, from the Wheal Caradon, sent a messenger asking Josh to call and see him.

Josh went after work that same day. The Caradon captain came immediately to the point. "Tell me about this man-lift of yours. How much would it cost to put one into the Caradon?"

Josh grinned. "It would cost next to nothing. But since when has the Wheal Caradon been so concerned about its men?" It was well known that for all its great size and high production the Wheal Caradon miners were among the worst paid in the country.

"You sound like a union man," said Captain Frisby angrily. "But I didn't bring you here to quarrel. I'm asking you to do this job for me. When can you start?"

"I can't," said Josh. "But send a couple of your carpenters across to the Sharptor tomorrow and I'll show them what to do."

"Will you inspect it when it's done?"

"Yes, I'll do that, but what's wrong with your own engineer?"

"Caradon hasn't got a proper engineer at the moment," Frisby admitted. "You could have the job if you wanted it. I'll pay you half as much again as you are getting now."

Josh smiled. "Sorry, Captain. I appreciate your offer, but Sharptor suits me for the time being. Pay half as much again to all your men, and engineers would be banging on your door."

"Yes, and so would the shareholders. Perhaps it is just as well you won't come to work for me. I have no shortage of men to preach about fair pay for the miners and their union."

Captain Frisby was not the only one to become increasingly aware of union talk. It was something that had been discussed for years wherever miners gathered. Preacher Thackeray, for one, was dedicated to unionism. He was an eloquent speaker, and when he spoke men listened. Even Josh had attended one of his open-air meetings. The reason he did not attend any more was that Miriam occasionally delivered a speech, and though it had been more than a year since her marriage, Josh did not feel able to face her.

Time had brought changes for the whole Trago family. Soon after Miriam's wedding John Trago had come down the hill to the Retallick cottage. Although every inch a Trago, he lacked the menace that had always traveled with his older brother.

"Come on in," said Jesse. "Though I can't think of a Trago who's crossed this doorstep without bringing trouble."

"I hope all that is past, Jesse," said the big man uneasily. "That's what I've come to speak to you and Ben about." He cleared his throat. "I wanted to tell you that I hold no grudge against you, Ben, or your family. No more does Kate. We neither of us believe the death of Moses was deliberate."

It was Ben's turn to look ill at ease.

John Trago cleared his throat once more. "I'm going to marry Kate and look after her and the children. I'll try to give them a bit more of life than they've had up to now."

"You have my good wishes, John," said Ben.

"There's something more. I think the children should be brought up to feel they are just like everyone else. Not some strange beings who live in a cave on the moor. There's a house to rent in Henwood that I've been promised. That's a start. But I want Kate and the children to live without people pointing at them, whispering that they're the family of Moses Trago, the man who raped Jenny."

Ben nodded. "That makes good sense. How can I help?"

"You're a respected man in the village. If you put it about that you have no argument with us, everyone else will do the same."

"We'll do that willingly," Jesse said. "But what about Morwen?"

"Morwen's gone," John said. "He thinks a soldier's life has more to offer him than being down a mine. I can't say that he's wrong." He edged to the door. "I'm very obliged to you. Kate will be too."

By the year 1843 the copper mines were going through a boom such as they had never known. But the boom was not indicative of the country as a whole. Corn was again short; nobody knew why. And in Cornwall a slump in the market for tin had the tin miners wandering the county in search of work. A few mines—and the

Caradon was one—saw the plight of the tinners as something from which to gain advantage. Captain Frisby took the tinners on at low wages and then cut back the pay of his own men. It aroused great anger among the established miners, but they dared do little. As Thackeray was quick to tell them, if there had been a union of miners, such a situation would never have arisen.

Another result of the slump in tin mining was that the demand for mine engines dropped and the Cornish engine works had to search out new customers.

Josh was working in the enginehouse of the Sharptor mine when a voice from the doorway said, "I'm pleased to see you haven't forgotten everything you learned at Harvey's, Josh."

Swinging around, he saw William Carlyon standing in the doorway. Then Sarah pushed past her father and threw her arms about Josh's neck. He was unable to ward her off, because his hands were black with grease. There was nothing to do but enjoy her embrace until she finally released him.

"What are you doing here?" Josh spoke to Mr. Carlyon, but his eyes were on Sarah. She had grown taller, and with her long blond ringlets tied behind her neck she was strikingly beautiful.

William Carlyon smiled. "I have to go to Bristol on business. I thought it a good opportunity to give the family a holiday. Mary and Mrs. Carlyon are with your mother at the cottage."

As they talked, Josh rubbed his hands with a piece of rag.

"I rode all the way here on Hector," said Sarah. "And Mary rode partway on the pony you used to ride at Hayle. The rest of the time she was in the coach with Mama. I changed into this new dress at your cottage. Do you like it? It's from London."

"It's beautiful," he said. "Far too good for an enginehouse."

"That's what I told her," said William Carlyon. "I would like to meet your father and Captain Shovell," he went on. "One of the men said they were at the explosives store. Where will I find that?"

Josh started to lead the way, but William Carlyon stopped him. "No, just point me in the right direction. You see that Sarah gets back to the cottage. It's all right. We spent last evening with Theophilus Strike. I told him we should be robbing him of his

409

engineer for as long as we were here. And he made no objection."

Josh sent one of the miners to guide Mr. Carlyon to the explosives store. Then, after giving instructions to his engineman, he set off with Sarah.

"Are you pleased to see me, Josh?" Sarah looked up at him provocatively.

"If you're fishing for compliments, then the answer is yes. You're even more beautiful than I remembered."

The Josh she had known at Hayle would not have been bold enough to pay her such a compliment. Sarah looked again at Josh and saw the new confidence in him. "You've changed."

"Is that good or bad?" His smile was a challenge.

"I'm not sure. For you it is probably good. For me . . . ?" She shrugged and there was a moment of silence. Then she smiled.

"Come on, Josh. If I don't get you home soon, my sister will come
looking for you. She's talked of nothing but seeing you for days."

When they arrived at the cottage, Mary ran out and flung herself at Josh, and Mrs. Carlyon made predictable remarks about his
having "filled out." But she had a speculative look in her eyes when
she watched Sarah and Josh together. It was a relief when Sarah
asked if he would like to go for a ride. Soon he was leading the
way on Mary's pony along the path to the high moor, while Sarah
followed on Hector.

Once above the ridge, they rode knee to knee through the
bracken. Sarah gave Josh a warm smile. "This is just like old times.
You don't know how I have missed you, Josh. Have you done much
riding since you left Hayle?"

He looked at her sharply. Did she really understand so little about life in a mining community? "I'm a workingman now, Sarah. I have little time to ride and no horse to use if I wanted to."

"I am sure Mr. Strike would lend you one of his horses."

"He pays me for doing a job. I don't think he would take kindly to a request from me to borrow one of his horses for my pleasure."

"I am sure he would," replied Sarah. "But it's far too lovely a day to have an argument. I'll race you to that circle of stones."

The circle of stones was a mile away, and Sarah arrived a hundred yards ahead of Josh. "Phew! I'd forgotten a lot of things about riding," he said, laughing. "One of them is that unless you're in practice it leaves you as blown as the horse." He dismounted and started to help Sarah to the ground.

She rested her hands on his shoulders and jumped down lightly. But when she landed she did not remove her hands. Josh looked down at her and she came to him, arms meeting about his neck. As they kissed, her ardor matched his own. Then she rested her head on his chest. "Oh, Josh! I have missed you terribly."

"I think you really mean it."

"You know very well I do." She stooped and thoughtfully picked up a raven's feather from the ground, black and glossy. "What about that girl, Miriam? Do you still see her?"

"No. She married a preacher. Preacher Thackeray."

"Preacher Thackeray!" Sarah was happy again. "Mr. Strike was telling Papa about him. He said he's a troublemaker."

"Theophilus Strike is an employer. He's bound to oppose Thackeray, who preaches for a union of all the miners."

"Don't tell me you agree with him?" she said, half bantering.

"Of course I agree with him, Sarah. I'm a miner."

"No. You aren't like those creatures we saw coming out of a shaft on our way here. They were filthy, horribly coarse men."

Josh was about to argue further, but he had no wish to spoil Sarah's day by explaining the facts of mining life to her. She was far too happy. She was also very lovely. He helped her back into her saddle and then he too remounted.

"One day I'll take you down a mine," he promised. "Then you'll see how difficult it is for a man to keep clean when he's working."

"I'll keep you to that, Josh Retallick."

At that moment a fox broke from a gorse thicket not twenty yards ahead of them. With a yell Josh kicked the ribs of his startled pony and gave chase. Sarah was slower to start, but Hector quickly overtook Josh's mount. The chase ended when the fox scrambled up a bank where the horses could not follow.

Sarah thoroughly enjoyed the gallop. When they arrived back at the cottage, she gave a dramatic version of the pursuit.

Mary pouted. "If I had been there, I'd have caught it," she said to impress Josh. "I can ride as well as Sarah. You come and watch me when I go riding at home."

"I wish I could," replied Josh.

"You'll get that chance sooner than you expect," said William Carlyon. "I managed to pick up some business from Theophilus Strike last night. He said that if Tom Shovell thought it a good idea, the Wheal Sharptor should have an engine for hoisting ore to the surface. He also said he wants you to come to Hayle to supervise the making of it, Josh."

While William Carlyon was talking, Jesse Retallick had been watching Sarah's face light up. Jesse was both pleased and saddened. Her son might not yet be aware of it, but she knew she was going to lose him to this girl.

Josh traveled to Hayle early the following month. Harvey's foundry had not changed, but life was very different for him there now. He was a guest in the works manager's home, with ample spare time. He discussed engines with Harvey's designers, and although he lacked years, his ideas were taken seriously.

But the time Josh spent at Hayle was not devoted entirely to work. He and Sarah had their favorite shingle beach which they would often visit, riding out along the cliffs above St. Ives Bay. One evening he accompanied Sarah and her sister to a Beethoven concert, given in the chapel by a touring orchestra. Josh found himself in a new land. He had discovered music.

"Isn't it beautiful?" Sarah whispered, and he nodded, not daring to speak. When the music ended he applauded in numb amazement, returning to earth only as they left the chapel and went outside to the world of belching chimneys.

"What is the matter, Josh?" Sarah asked. "Didn't you enjoy the concert? You're looking very unhappy."

"I enjoyed it very much. If I look sad, it must be because I was thinking I might never attend another."

"Why not? We have concerts at Hayle several times a year."

"But I'm not working at Hayle," he reminded her.

"You could be," Sarah declared pointedly.

"Yes, Josh, come and work here," said Mary excitedly. "If you don't, we will have to come all the way to Sharptor to see you and Sarah if you get—"

"*Mary!*"

The young girl bit back her words and looked fearfully at Josh. To Mary's relief—and Sarah's embarrassment—he laughed. The thought of marriage to Sarah had been with him as a vague, shapeless idea ever since her visit to Sharptor. He did not love her—certainly not in the tempestuous way he had loved Miriam. But he was very fond of her. And he was lonely.

Looking back on it later, Josh knew that if it had not been for Mary's words he would never have made his decision. He would have been unable to summon up the courage had he not been aware that Sarah had discussed it—if only with her young sister.

"I want you to go home by yourself, Mary," he said gently. "I'm taking Sarah for a walk by the river."

"Mama said I was to come with you or people would talk."

"That was at the concert, silly! Go on home," Sarah said.

"It's all right, Mary. I'll explain to your mother."

Mary watched as Josh and Sarah turned off toward the river. Then she ran home as fast as she could.

Josh avoided Sarah's eyes as they walked on, hand in hand. "We come from very different backgrounds, you and I," he began. "And there are things that must be made clear before I can say what's on my mind."

"Josh! You know yourself Papa is always talking of his mining background. He's very proud of it."

"Yes, but you've been brought up to expect things a miner could never give you."

"You keep talking of miners, Josh. You're an engineer."

"True. But I live and work in a mining community. There would be no large house, no horse, no concerts like tonight."

"Concerts are not essential. I disagree about a horse. It would cost little to feed Hector if there were grazing available."

"There are other things too. I spend hours at the mine, and you would have no one to talk to. You would probably be unhappy."

They stopped at the water's edge and Sarah turned to him, the moon at her back, her face in shadow. "Josh, either you don't know me as well as I thought, or you are trying to argue yourself out of something. I am sorry if Mary made you feel that you had to say something." Her voice broke. "Now shall we go?"

"No." He believed she must hear his heart pounding. "What I am trying to say is . . . Sarah, will you marry me?"

"You mean it, Josh? You really mean it?"

"Yes, Sarah. I mean it."

"Oh yes, Josh! Yes! Yes! Yes!"

She clung to him, and he could feel tears running warm and wet down her cheeks. "I thought you'd decided you didn't want to marry me. I was trying to be brave and sensible about it, but I was so unhappy inside." She kissed him hungrily. "Josh, I love you so very very much. And I'll make you a good wife. I can cook and sew and housekeep—and I'll get rid of Hector."

"No, you won't. We'll find some way to keep him. I won't have anyone saying you lowered yourself to marry me."

Sarah laughed through her tears. "Oh, Josh, you are funny!"

The Carlyon family were sitting in the parlor when Josh walked in with Sarah. There was an air of expectancy in the room. Sarah seated herself on the sofa beside her mother and looked at her hands, clasped tightly in her lap.

"Sit down, Josh." William Carlyon pointed to the armchair that faced his own.

"I'd rather stand, if you don't mind. There's something I would like to say—I mean, to ask."

Instantly Mrs. Carlyon was on her feet, ushering Sarah and the vigorously protesting Mary from the room.

Josh continued to stand, and cleared his throat twice before William Carlyon said, "For goodness' sake sit down, Josh. You want to marry Sarah. There, I've said it for you. Let's talk about it."

Josh moved across the room and perched on the armchair.

"That's better. Now, you've already asked Sarah, of course?" Josh nodded. "Yes."

"There's no need to ask what she said. I'm surprised she hasn't proposed to you long before this. Do you have any idea where you might live?"

Josh said he had not.

"Don't think I'm interfering, Josh. But Sarah is used to a little more material comfort than you can provide at the moment."

"I'm aware of that. I said so to Sarah."

"When I was at Sharptor, I noticed a derelict house a couple of hundred yards up the hill. Had a couple of cleared fields behind it. Do you know where I mean?"

"Yes. We call it the idle farm. It's never been lived in during my lifetime. I think it belongs to Theophilus Strike."

"Couldn't be better. Josh, I'll buy that derelict farm for you and Sarah as a wedding present, and give you a houseful of furniture. You can get your miners together to put the house in order."

When Josh protested, William Carlyon cut him short. "The house and land will be cheap, Josh. But it does mean that Sarah will be able to keep that horse of hers. And it will give me great pleasure to make you a gift of your first home." He beamed. "Now, that's settled. Get everyone back while I bring out the brandy. This calls for a celebration."

JOSH returned home to Sharptor to break the news to his family.

His parents were delighted. "She'll make you a good wife," Jesse said. "A daughter I'll be proud to welcome."

Theophilus Strike was happy to sell the old farm to William Carlyon at a fair price. For his own contribution, he undertook to supply the building materials necessary for its renovation.

Later that weekend Josh inspected the farmhouse with his father. It was larger than Josh had expected, with four good rooms downstairs and five up.

"It's going to be a major job," said Ben when the tour was over. "You've got little more than the shell of a house to work on. But the walls are as stout as you'll find anywhere."

Josh smiled ruefully. "But there is so much to do and I'll be away for weeks supervising the finishing of the new engine. I can't see it ever being ready to live in."

"Nonsense! The first thing needed is a roof to keep the weather out. We'll have that done by the time you come home."

Ben was better than his word. When Josh brought the new engine around the edge of the hill, he saw the once idle house standing proud and tall with new roof, doors and windows. The men from the mine had completed everything but the plastering inside. By working really hard at it Josh could have the house finished and be married to Sarah in little more than a month.

AT ABOUT this time Josh became involved in an incident at the Wheal Caradon. Captain Frisby had continued to take on destitute tin miners, and now, even though the disgruntled copper miners were bearing the brunt of any tasks requiring special knowledge of copper mining, he cut their wages further to correspond with those paid to the ex-tinners. The anger of the copper miners exploded. They downed tools and a noisy crowd assembled in front of Frisby's office, demanding that the decision be reversed.

Preacher Thackeray heard of the troubles and hurried to the mine, seizing the opportunity to call a meeting of the men. Standing on a rock so he could be seen by everyone, he sympathized with the copper miners and applauded their actions. He also praised their courage. "Your stand here today against greed and injustice will be felt in every mine in Cornwall," he said. "Remember, it's your very livelihood you're fighting for—the future not only of yourselves but of your families."

"Tell that to the tinners!" called a voice from the crowd.

"While there are tinners and copper men you'll never achieve anything," replied the preacher. "No stranger should come here and take away another man's livelihood by selling himself cheap; but you're all miners, and the day you accept that and unite you'll have won a great victory."

The roar of approval was interrupted by a question from one of the miners, John Kittow, the man who had masterminded the sale of corn in Callington market some years before. "That's all very well, Preacher. But this talk of union is tomorrow talk. We've had our pay cut today. What do we do?"

"You do what you please," shouted an ex-tinner. "We're going on shift."

"There'll be no work done tonight," called a Caradon man. "Not unless a tinner wants his head busted."

"Please, no fighting!" Thackeray turned to the incoming men. "This is your chance to show a united front. Call off your shift."

"They can't do anything else," shouted one of the copper men. "They won't get past us."

There was uncertainty among the tinners, and Thackeray seized upon it. "I'm pleading with you," he repeated. "Turn around and go home. I'll speak to Captain Frisby."

There was an earnest conversation among the night shift, and a general nodding of heads. "All right," said their spokesman grudgingly. "But we'll be back tomorrow."

From his office Captain Frisby had watched them leave, and anger boiled up inside him. When Thackeray came to negotiate, Frisby turned the key in the lock and refused to open the door.

"Captain Frisby," Thackeray called, "let me in and we'll talk this matter over sensibly—"

"There's nothing to be said."

For a few minutes more Thackeray tried to persuade the mine captain to change his mind, but eventually he went back to the men. "Give him time to cool off," he said. "If you can stop the morning shift from working, he'll know you mean business."

"Preacher Thackeray!" John Kittow spat on the ground. "I don't like all this talk. All we want is to go back to work for the pay we were getting before today. If you have our interests at heart, I suggest you warn the miners not to come to work until our pay is back to what it was. If they don't listen, they'll be in big trouble."

"And that's your answer to Frisby? To cause trouble? Give him an excuse to call in the militia?"

"No, Preacher. I'm on my way now to ask someone to come and talk to Captain Frisby for us." He turned to the other miners. "You stay here. I'm going to find Josh Retallick."

Thackeray's surprise was apparent at the mention of Josh's name, but then he nodded thoughtfully. "Yes. Captain Frisby might listen to Josh. But it's a lot to ask of a young man."

As Thackeray rode home he felt he had suffered a bitter defeat. His was a personal crusade; yet he had allowed the initiative to slip from his hands and pass to another man.

Josh was in the kitchen of the Retallick cottage when John Kittow arrived. Josh had never spoken to the man and he was puzzled when Kittow said he would like to speak to him. "It's to ask a favor of you," the miner added.

"A favor? Something to do with engineering?"

"No. There's trouble at the Wheal Caradon. Bad trouble." John Kittow went on to tell him about the events that had followed Captain Frisby's wage cut.

"Why, the old skinflint!" Jesse Retallick was outraged.

Ben waved his wife into silence. "Theophilus Strike won't like you getting mixed up in the Caradon's troubles, Josh."

"It isn't on Strike's time," retorted Josh. To Kittow he said, "How can I help? Preacher Thackeray is more persuasive."

"The preacher might be more used to talking," Kittow agreed, "but Captain Frisby knows you. You've been brought up in mining and you've done a great deal of learning besides."

There was silence. At last Josh said, "All right, I'll come."

It was quite dark by the time they arrived at the Wheal Caradon, but few miners had gone home. They sat around bonfires near the main shaft. The shadowy faces in the firelight were those of worried men. Behind them the beam of the big pumping engine rocked slowly on its axle. Josh with his engineer's mind noted that behind the steady thump of the engine there was another, less usual, noise. The packing on the huge piston was disintegrating.

"I'll go over to see Frisby on my own," he said to John Kittow. He headed toward the mine captain's office and knocked heavily on the door. "It's Josh Retallick," he called. "Can I speak to you?"

"If you come from that preacher, you're wasting your time."

"Preacher Thackeray is capable of talking for himself," Josh said sharply. "Your miners asked me to speak to you. Out of regard for yourself and them, I agreed."

There was no reply, and Josh was about to turn away when a key grated in the lock and the door swung open. Josh took a seat to face the mine captain across a large desk in the lamplit room.

Captain Frisby was defiant. "I am prepared to talk to you. But I'll not be dictated to by that rabble outside."

"Captain, that 'rabble' has built the Wheal Caradon into one of the largest copper mines in Cornwall. They can just as easily destroy it."

"What do you mean 'destroy it'? They won't get away with smashing equipment on this mine."

"Nobody will have to touch a thing," said Josh. "The piston packing is going on the pumping engine. I give it twenty-four hours before it breaks down completely. You haven't got an engineer at the mine, have you?"

"The enginemen can carry out simple repairs like that."

"You've cut the enginemen's wages," said Josh. "They're keeping the engines running, but I can't see them doing repairs."

Captain Frisby licked his lips. A mere forty-eight hours without pumping would be sufficient to flood the new level and stop it from being worked for a very long time.

"All right. Tell the enginemen their pay stays the same."

"I'm sorry," said Josh. "But the enginemen must go along with the miners now. And I don't suppose you'll find it easy to get another job after this."

The mine captain's head snapped up. "Me? The shareholders won't dismiss me for doing what I'm paid for."

"How do you see your job, Captain Frisby?"

"The same as every mine captain. To run my mine, bring up the maximum ore and make a good profit."

"How much have your profits risen since last year?"

"They haven't," admitted Captain Frisby. "But a lot of man-hours have gone into opening up the new level."

"The Wheal Sharptor also has gone deeper to open a new level. Yet our profit is running fifty percent above last year."

"It's a small mine. You can't compare it with the Caradon."

"Then take the Wheal Phoenix. Their profit is way up."

"Luck!" argued Frisby. "They drove into a rich lode."

"No, Captain. There's never been such a boom in copper. Every mine in the county is riding high. When your shareholders see their dividends at the end of this year, they'll ask questions."

Josh had put his finger on the real reason for the pay cutting. It was Frisby's last desperate attempt to bring profits up.

"It's the men," Captain Frisby mumbled. "They're lazy. If I paid them what they're worth, their families would all go hungry."

"You're wrong." Josh stood up and paced back and forth. "You must face the fact that your methods have failed. Pay low wages and you get second-rate work. You still have a few good miners left. Pay them well and let them set the standard."

Josh expected Frisby to argue, but he stayed silent. Encouraged, Josh went on. "There are a few months to go before the dividend is called. Give your miners some encouragement. There's a good chance that your profit will be up enough to satisfy all but the greediest shareholder."

Josh could see the uncertainty on Captain Frisby's face. It was time to take his greatest gamble. "Well, I've said all I have to say. I'll be going now."

"Wait!" The cry was one of sheer desperation. "If I agree to do the things you've mentioned, the men will think they've beaten me. I wouldn't be able to hold up my head on the mine."

Josh said, "That won't happen if you tell the men you made the decision to cut their wages because the Caradon is the only mine not to have a rise in profits. Tell them if they are prepared to raise production, you will keep their wages at the present level—get them working with you instead of against you." He had a sudden thought. "Who are your shift captains?"

Captain Frisby looked away. "They've all left."

Josh shook his head incredulously. "Do you know John Kittow?"

"Yes. He's one of the men out there, isn't he?"

"He's a good sound miner," said Josh. "I've heard others say so. Make him your senior shift captain. Explain to him. Tell him you've reconsidered the situation. He'll do the rest."

It took the captain a full minute to make up his mind. He nodded. "All right. Tell Kittow to come and see me now."

CHAPTER EIGHT

As Josh's wedding date neared, the house on the hill occupied most of his spare time. There were still fire grates to be built, doors to be hung and a hundred small improvements to be carried out.

Sometimes he would go up to the house when it was too dark to work and just sit at the window. Watching the night advance over the Devon hills, he tried to identify the pinpoints of light that speckled the countryside. On the horizon a rash of lights marked the great city of Plymouth. Josh had never been there.

He wondered what it would be like living here with Sarah. There were times when he had grave doubts about their future, but he had heard such fears were natural enough.

One evening early in March he was upstairs painting one of the bedrooms when he heard the kitchen door open. It did not surprise him. His mother was a frequent visitor. Then he heard a sound he could not place, low and gurgling. The stairs creaked, and seconds later Miriam appeared on the landing, her young son in her arms. Josh, in complete surprise, dropped the paintbrush.

"Wh-what are you doing here?" he whispered.

"I'm sorry. I came to Henwood to visit my mother. . . . I'd heard about your house and I wanted to see it. But I didn't think you'd be here now." The words came tumbling out, tripping over each other. In her arms the baby gurgled away, completely unconcerned. Miriam turned quickly, as though to run down the stairs.

422

"No, don't go! I mean . . . you can look around if you like."

"I'd rather not, Josh. Not with you here."

"I'll go if it makes you feel any easier."

"Don't be silly!" Her laugh was softer, less uninhibited than he remembered. "It's your house." She watched him move through the open doorway. "You're looking well," she said.

"Am I?" He felt awkward and tongue-tied.

She walked slowly down the stairs and he followed. Stopping in the kitchen, she ran her finger over the dust on top of the new range. "This is a fine stove, Josh. Sarah will be able to cook some grand meals on it. . . . I always wondered whether you might marry her one day."

"That's funny. She always thought I'd marry you. So did I."

He saw the anguish on her face. "Josh, don't talk about such things now. Please! Oh, I shouldn't have come. I'm sorry."

The baby tugged at his white woolen bonnet, pulling it off and dropping it to the floor. Josh retrieved it. Tiny fingers reached out, and he handed it back.

"What do you call him?" The baby had his finger in his grasp now. He was chubby, his eyes as blue as Josh's own.

"Daniel."

"Hello, Daniel." He jigged his finger up and down.

Miriam pulled the baby away. "Don't, Josh. Don't!"

He beat her to the door and put his back against it. "Why not Miriam? Why mustn't I play with him?"

"Don't make me say it, Josh. Please." The tears stood out from her eyes, and she crumpled down onto a window seat. "Oh, God! Why did I come here?"

Josh moved toward her. Seeing her cry like this threatened to tear him apart. "I shouldn't have pushed you into that."

She was shaking and it alarmed the baby.

"Here. Let me take him." Dropping to one knee, he took Daniel from her and laid him on the floor on a pile of cloth that had been used to protect some newly delivered furniture. Miriam fumbled in her sleeve for a handkerchief.

"William has been very good to me—to us, Josh. He's a kind man who still talks well of you. He has wanted to invite you to our meetings. But I dreaded seeing you again, face to face."

She raised her eyes to meet his, and all the emotions he could see there were his own. Suddenly he was holding her. His mouth crushed hers and her arms were about him.

As abruptly as it had begun they drew apart, both shocked with the force of their feelings. "I'm sorry," he said lamely.

"It was as much my fault as yours." She picked up the baby and gave Josh a gentle look. "Now I don't need to ask myself what I might do if I were to meet you," she said. "I have my answer."

"Don't go yet," he said. "Stay a while longer."

"No, Josh. I'm married. You too have your future to think of."

"What future? I can't marry Sarah. Not now—"

"Shhh! You felt sorry for me, that's all. Of course you'll marry Sarah and be very happy in this lovely house. But I'm glad you've seen Daniel. It has worried me."

"You just can't walk out of my life, Miriam—not again."

She smiled. "You know I must, for everyone's sake. Be happy, Josh. I'll pray for that." She opened the door and was gone.

THE wedding was proclaimed the event of the year in Hayle. The chapel, decorated with hundreds of flowers, was packed with family and guests. Included in their ranks were Theophilus Strike, Tom Shovell and Jenny from Sharptor, and Wrightwick Roberts was there to help the Hayle preacher with the service.

The ceremony was simple and moving. When it was over, Josh and Sarah returned in a gaily decorated pony trap to the Carlyon house. There the presents were on view, among them a silver dish from Francis Trevithick. During the reception Josh was asked many questions about his man-lift by ex-Harvey apprentices who were complete strangers to him.

"It is wonderful to have a famous husband," teased Sarah.

Afterward Sarah and Josh traveled to Sharptor by coach—alone. Jesse Retallick protested that it was unnecessary extravagance to use two coaches when they were all going to the same place, but William Carlyon stayed firm.

When the newlyweds arrived at their new home, a fire was burning in the parlor and there were fresh spring flowers everywhere, all provided by the wives of the Sharptor miners. This was a traditional homecoming, their way of welcoming Sarah.

Much later that night Josh lay in bed, thinking about the future. Beside him Sarah was curled up, asleep. They had made love for the first time, but it was not a wildly passionate union. Josh realized then that for Sarah this would always be more a wifely duty than an abandoned pouring out of emotion.

But this lack was the only fault Josh could possibly have found with Sarah. She was a promising cook, a good housekeeper, and she genuinely loved him.

"You've got a fine wife, Josh," said Ben one evening as he and Josh walked down the hill. "Mind you take good care of her."

Josh confirmed that he would.

"Have you seen anything of Miriam since you've been wed?"

Josh answered quite truthfully that he had not.

"From all accounts she's leading her husband a merry dance. You were wise to break with her when you did."

"In what way is she leading Preacher Thackeray a dance?"

"By making him look a fool. Talking to meetings of miners. Trying to tell grown men about the benefits of this miners' union."

Josh laughed. "I think he's well pleased with her. He believes not only in the equality of men—but women as well."

"Then he's more of a fool than I took him for."

"WHAT are you thinking about?" Sarah asked.

It was a sultry late-summer night and the bedroom was filled with soft silver moonlight.

Josh pulled her toward him. "I can't sleep. That's all."

She snuggled closer. "Something's bothering you. Is it anything to do with that man who called this evening?"

"John Kittow? Not entirely. The miners at Kit Hill are having trouble. He wants me to go to a meeting tomorrow night."

She rose on one elbow. "You're not going?"

"I told him I would."

"Theophilus Strike won't like it."

"Sarah, this is none of Theophilus Strike's business."

"And the Kit Hill miners are none of *your* business."

It was their first serious argument. They lay side by side in silence for a long time before Josh heard a strangled sob.

"Sarah, please don't cry."

"Oh, Josh! I'm so miserable!"

He turned and put his arms about her, soothing her until she stopped crying.

"I'm sorry, Josh. That was silly of me." And when he was about to protest she said, "No! You must do what you feel you should do. I have no right to object."

"You're my wife, Sarah. You have every right. I wish that you were interested enough to want to know what it's all about."

"I don't want to know. I wouldn't understand it. You know what you're doing, and I accept that, so please don't be angry."

THE Kit Hill men's grievance was with the store run by the mine, which had a stranglehold on the miners' families. It was the only place a new worker could obtain credit. His tools came from there, as well as the essential furniture to set up a home. The cost was higher than elsewhere, but few men had any choice.

Occasionally mine-store owners became greedy, especially if they thought some of the miners' money was escaping them, and increased their prices. This was the problem at Kit Hill.

When Josh and John Kittow arrived for the meeting, there must have been a hundred and fifty men standing in uneasy groups. Kittow and Josh picked their way toward a heap of mine waste that would serve as a platform. Josh looked about them and said, "John, who called the meeting?"

"A miner named Harry Reeve. I can't see him here."

"Well, if he can't bother to turn up, I see no sense in staying."

"Give him a few minutes," pleaded Kittow. "Something must have happened to keep him away."

Suddenly a red-faced man, perspiration tracking down his face, pushed past them, climbed up onto the heap of mine waste and turned to the crowd. "Quiet, please! Shut up and listen to me! Harry Reeve won't be coming tonight. He's been arrested."

There was a stunned silence.

"Not only Harry Reeve. Four others also."

The crowd erupted with angry calls of "Why? Why?"

"I'll tell you why," shouted the sweating man. "The shareholders thought they'd put a stop to this meeting by arresting Harry and the others for incitement to riot. They're in the Callington lockup."

There was a roar from the assembly as a second man scrambled up onto the rubble. "We'll show them what a riot is," he shouted. "We'll go and get Harry out."

The first man tried to bring order. "No, wait! Someone went to fetch Preacher Thackeray. He'll know what to do."

"We already know what to do," shouted the second man.

Josh pushed his way roughly through the miners and joined the other two men on the mound. He was big enough to gain their attention. "Wait!" he called. "If you go to Callington and break into the lockup, no court in the county will find Harry Reeve and the others not guilty."

There were catcalls and shouts. But above the hubbub someone yelled, "It's Joshua Retallick. Let him speak."

Now he had their full attention. "The worst thing you could possibly do is use violence. There are other ways of achieving your ends. But you must decide here and now what you want. Then make sure every last man in the Kit Hill mine is with you."

"That's the soundest advice I've heard at any meeting. You're absolutely right, Josh." It was William Thackeray. He had arrived unnoticed, his neat little gig making no sound on the soft grass. But it was not the preacher who caused Josh to become suddenly tongue-tied. It was Miriam, seated beside him.

Miriam was just as surprised to see Josh, but she managed a faint smile. With her long hair blown by the wind and her face flushed with excitement she still had all the wild beauty of the young girl Josh had explored the moor with. Not a man at the meeting could fail to be stirred by her presence.

William Thackeray handed his wife from the gig and pushed

his way to the front of the crowd, with Miriam following. This type of gathering was his natural environment.

To the crowd he cried, "You've heard what Josh Retallick said. I endorse his every word. Is there any man who has other ideas? You! The bearded man at the front. What do you suggest?"

The bearded miner, unhappy at being singled out, spoke hesitantly. "I say we march on Callington and release Harry Reeve."

William Thackeray turned to Miriam in a way that was familiar to any miner who had attended their meetings. "He suggests that this band of good men—let's say two hundred miners—march on Callington. What do you think would happen?"

Miriam looked out over the crowd. "They are fine men. Each one capable of holding his own in any fistfight." Her voice rang clear, so that no one missed her words. But some of the miners were puzzled. The preacher's wife seemed to be contradicting him. Then Miriam reached down inside her dress and pulled out a small linen bag attached to a drawstring about her neck.

"Yes, you are brave men," she said. "Any man who earns his living belowground has courage."

She held up the linen bag. "Yet this small bag would hold enough musket shot to kill any one of you!"

The men were looking puzzled again, but Miriam did not leave them in suspense for long. "You wonder what this has to do with you? Then I'll tell you. At this very moment a full company of soldiers—more than a hundred disciplined troops—are riding posthaste from Bodmin barracks to Callington. *Every single one of those soldiers carries this much musket shot!*"

Concealing the bag again, Miriam struck a pose with hands on hips. "Do you take the Callington magistrate for a fool? He knew what you would do when he arrested the leading Kit Hill unionists. There was a horseman on his way to Bodmin for soldiers before the ink was dry on the warrant for Harry Reeve's arrest!"

"Then what can we do?" called one of the miners.

This was a cue William Thackeray had been waiting for. "That must be for you to decide," he declared. "But first, how many Kit Hill miners are *not* at this meeting?"

"Not more than fifty," replied one miner.

"I suggest you make certain those fifty join with you to stop all work in the Kit Hill mine."

This provoked noisy mutterings. "What do you say, Retallick?" one man shouted.

Josh had been standing at the rear of the group on the mound. Now he stepped forward, avoiding Miriam's gaze. "I say do as Preacher Thackeray suggests. Get the others with you. Tell the captain you'll allow the enginemen to go in for one week only. By the end of that time the prices in the mine store should have been lowered and Harry Reeve and the others released. If they haven't been, tell him the enginemen will shut off the pumps and allow the mine to flood."

Josh's words received noisy approval. Suddenly John Kittow was pushing his way to the front. "I'd like a word with the men," he said, and Josh helped him up onto the pile of stones.

John Kittow came straight to the point. "We've been through trouble ourselves at the Wheal Caradon. Because we know what it means to have support at a time like this, we held a meeting last night. It was agreed by our men that they would each give a shilling a week to help during the time you're not working."

There was cheering and shouting from the Kit Hill men.

"Not only that—listen now!" Kittow went on. "The Wheal Phoenix men have told me they'll each give sixpence a week."

"We've done it! We've done it!" William Thackeray was pumping Kittow's hand and literally dancing up and down. "A union of miners has become a reality in Cornwall!"

His elation was almost matched by that of the miners. With the threat of starvation removed, they knew they could win their fight. Josh, though still uncomfortable in Miriam's presence, found himself caught up in the infectious enthusiasm.

"Come, Josh!" Thackeray said. "We will celebrate our success with a glass of wine. You must come home with us."

And Miriam managed a "Please, Josh."

"Of course he'll come. He's been absent from our circle of friends for far too long."

At the preacher's house, Thackeray put the gig away while Josh followed Miriam into the parlor. She lit a lamp, and after a heavy silence she said, "It's nice to see you here, Josh. William has missed your friendship. We both have."

"Friendship might be difficult in the circumstances."

"No, Josh. There are many things William doesn't know—and needn't know. But even if he did, I feel sure he'd forgive us. As a preacher he's well aware of the weaknesses of men and women."

"What about Daniel?"

Miriam drew in a deep breath. "Daniel is part of William's family. He loves him very much." She bit her lip. "Josh, let's not make tonight unhappy. I really am pleased to have you here."

William Thackeray had entered the room quietly. He saw the look on Miriam's face as she spoke to Josh, but he said nothing. Going straight to a cupboard, he took out three glasses and filled them. Handing the glasses around, he raised his in a salute.

"To the union. To the miners' fund and to a better understanding between all Christian men, whatever their lot in life. May they all be as God made them—equal!"

"I'd like to propose another toast," said Josh gravely. "To the freedom of the men who were arrested today for trying to exercise that equality."

THAT very night the Kit Hill mine store was burned to the ground, the flames lighting the skyline atop the hill.

The incident sealed the fate of the five men held in custody. There had been hopes that they would be brought before the magistrate on some trifling charge. But after the fire they were sent in custody to Bodmin jail to await trial, charged with conspiracy to destroy property. It was generally recognized that they had little chance of an acquittal now.

A FEW days after the Kit Hill fire Theophilus Strike sent for Josh. When he entered the office, Strike's voice fairly thundered. "Joshua! What's this nonsense about you being involved with the criminals who burned down the Kit Hill store?"

431

"I know nothing about the burning down of the Kit Hill store," Josh replied, meeting the mineowner's eyes.

"Joshua, I have it from a very reliable source that you were at the meeting that preceded the burning."

"Then your reliable source will have told you I warned the miners against taking any unlawful action."

"So you don't deny attending this meeting?"

"I don't deny it, Mr. Strike. I'm of the opinion the Kit Hill miners have a just grievance."

Strike looked at him in amazement. "You have the brass to stand there and admit that you support men who burn a building to the ground? I've a good mind to dismiss you here and now. Anyone who condones violence among miners is dangerous to have around."

Josh refused to be cowed. "I've never condoned violence or supported the destruction of property. I'm in sympathy with the miners because they have a just grievance. Perhaps if I quote some prices charged at the Kit Hill store, you'll understand." He began with the prices of foodstuffs. They were roughly twice the normal. Then he mentioned candles, and the tools a miner needed belowground. Some were almost four times the fair price.

Strike was shaken, but he was an owner, not a miner. "Even if the Kit Hill miners were being robbed, what business is it of yours? You're an engineer, not a miner."

Taking a deep breath, Josh put into words what he had hardly been able to channel into conscious thought before. "I'm an engineer now, Mr. Strike. I have you to thank for that. But long before I was an engineer I was a miner's son. There were evenings when I went to the top of the shaft to wait for my father to come up from shift, and he wouldn't even see me. He'd crawl from the shaft and collapse on his belly, sucking in air with such a noise I feared his lungs might burst. No son should see his father crawling like a wounded animal from a hole in the ground.

"I worked hard at Hayle, Mr. Strike. I was determined to master engineering. It was a way of making sure my sons would never see me lying on the ground at the top of a mine shaft. That's why

I built the man-lift. . . . But it doesn't end there. I've seen what life is like outside a mine. I've ridden in a coach. I've been to a concert and heard music I never knew existed. I'm realistic enough to know that every miner can't become a gentleman overnight. But there must be more for him than bed, drink and work.

"Maybe that's why I went to that meeting. Perhaps I wanted to tell them something of what I've just told you."

Strike was looking at him in a strange way. "You're a humanitarian. I fear you'll find it unrewarding."

His anger had completely gone. "I'll be perfectly honest with you. I called you in with the express intention of dismissing you. I had no thought of giving you a hearing. Now I have, and though I must doubt your cause, I can respect your sincerity."

Josh began to thank the mineowner, but Strike cut him short with an impatient gesture. "Don't thank me, Joshua. In all probability I would be helping you more if I gave you an ultimatum: forget your ideas or lose your post here. But I believe you have to work out your own destiny—and God help you!"

THE Kit Hill miners kept the mine idle for a full week. Then, at an extraordinary meeting of the shareholders, it was reported that the enginemen were ready to join the miners.

The shareholders hurriedly arrived at a solution whereby the blame for the men's grievances was placed on the mine captain. It was grossly unfair, since he had only been carrying out their instructions. Nevertheless, with their scapegoat dismissed, a settlement was reached and the miners resumed work.

But there was to be no happy ending for Harry Reeve and those arrested with him. When the miners demanded their release, they were told it was out of the shareholders' hands.

Preacher Thackeray attended the miners' trial. Late on the second day Josh saw him riding across the moor, direct from Bodmin.

"The court found them guilty, Josh."

It came as no surprise. The whole countryside had been expecting it. "And the sentence?" Josh asked.

"Fourteen years' transportation!"

Josh winced. Except in very rare cases such a punishment meant banishment for life. A man was shipped abroad, usually to Australia, to work as a convict for the duration of his sentence. Upon its expiration he was free to work for his fare home. If he could find someone to pay him more than a subsistence wage, it would still take him years to save the fare.

The preacher shook his head sorrowfully. "The men accepted the sentence," he said. "They had known all along what might happen to them because of their beliefs. But one day we'll win, Josh. We *must* win. . . . And each tiny victory, no matter how small, is a step closer to that goal."

Josh turned away. Must the price of victory always be paid in imprisoned men and starving children?

Sarah was in the kitchen when he got home, and the exaggerated clatter indicated that she was not in the best of moods. Nevertheless, he told her the outcome of the trial.

"Well! What did you expect?" she snapped. Her dislike of unionism had hardened since a visit to Hayle two weeks before. "You were a fool to get yourself involved. Mother thinks so too."

Josh paused. "What has your mother got to do with it?"

Sarah flushed. "Isn't it natural for a girl to talk over her problems with her mother?"

"I hadn't realized I was a problem."

"You know very well what I mean, Josh. It worries me to see you mixed up with something like this."

"It worried Theophilus Strike too. But at least he tried to understand my feelings about the union. That's more than you'll do."

"I have more important things to occupy my mind."

"What sort of things? Whether to wear the blue dress rather than the pink one to Launceston market?" It was spiteful and he knew it, but it was out before he could bite it back.

Sarah placed the pan she was holding carefully in the cupboard and dried her hands before answering him.

"No. The sort of thing that is occupying my mind at the moment is whether I will bear you a son or a daughter."

"You—you're pregnant? Why didn't you say something before?"

"You've been so involved with this silly union business that I was scarcely able to gain your attention long enough to tell you anything. Anyway, I wasn't absolutely certain. That's why I went home. Dr. Scott examined me and told me for sure."

"Why did you see the doctor? Is something wrong?"

His concern brought a smile from Sarah. "Of course not. It's usual for a woman who is having a baby to see a doctor."

"But Mary Crabbe delivers just about every baby in the district. Jenny didn't see a doctor when she was expecting."

"Well, I'm not Jenny," said Sarah sharply. She looked suddenly unhappy. "You haven't even said you are pleased!"

"Of course I'm pleased." He took her into his arms and kissed her gently. "And I think you're very clever. . . ."

CHAPTER NINE

In mid-December of that year of 1844 Josh should have been leaving with Sarah to spend Christmas at Hayle, but an abnormally wet winter was causing concern in the Wheal Sharptor. The great engine was pumping at twice its normal speed yet barely managing to hold its own against the water. Josh felt he could not leave the mine. The baby wasn't due for nearly five months, so in spite of Sarah's sulking he decided to stay on for a while longer.

Theophilus Strike's light carriage was taking Sarah to the Carlyons. Josh loaded her cases and fussed about her, settling her into her seat. "Now you take care," he said, "and keep well wrapped. I'll be with you on Christmas Eve."

"I wish you were coming with me," cried Sarah, clinging to him.

"So do I," said Josh honestly. "But it won't be long. In the meantime you'll be surrounded by your family."

The day after Sarah left, the wind changed direction and the temperature dropped rapidly. Snow began to fall at dusk and gradually put a covering on the sodden ground. Then the wind and snow vied in their efforts to outdo each other.

The battle raged for five days before a brief truce was called on Christmas Eve. From the bedroom window of the house Josh looked down on a pure white, featureless world. There was neither track nor hedge showing, and the wind had mounded snow over the few cottages within view. He had never known such weather. There would be no Christmas at Hayle for him.

THE Christmas Josh shared with his parents was happy, like so many others, except that he could not help feeling guilty about not being with his wife. It was not until the new year that a gentle thaw set in and he was even able to send a letter off to Sarah with the coach from St. Cleer. He hoped she would be coming home soon, for the house felt big and empty without her.

The snow melted and a strong drying wind blew in from the east and still she did not return. He was beginning to get anxious when a letter arrived at last from Hayle.

Sarah's Christmas had been spoiled because Josh was not there, and she chided him for not having come with her before the snows. Finally she stated that her unhappiness had brought her so low her mother refused to allow her to travel until she recovered.

The tone of the letter so alarmed Josh that he set off on Hector that weekend. It came as an anticlimax to arrive and find nobody there. The shift foreman let him into the Carlyon house and told him the family had gone out to visit friends.

It was dusk before the Carlyons' small coach rumbled in through the works gate and Sarah alighted, laughing gaily with her mother and sister, Mary. She did not look ill. When she saw Josh, there was a confused silence before she flung herself at him.

"Josh! What are you doing here?"

"I came because of your letter telling me how ill you were."

Sarah looked embarrassed, but her mother came to her rescue. "And so she has been ill. Today is the first day she has been anything like her old self."

Sarah squeezed his arm. "It's lovely to see you, Josh."

"I'm very relieved to see you looking well," he replied. "I've been imagining all sorts of things as I rode here."

William Carlyon had been driving the coach, and after handing it over to a hostler he came into the house and shook Josh's hand warmly. "It's good to have you here, my boy. I've been surrounded by these women since before Christmas. Let me get you a drink. What'll you have?"

Josh said he would have a brandy. William Carlyon went to the drinks cupboard and poured it. Eagerly Mary handed it to him.

"Will you be able to stay with us for long?" she asked.

Josh shook his head. "Until Sunday only."

There was an immediate outcry from Sarah. "Why, Josh? Surely the mine can spare you for a few days?"

Josh put down his brandy. "I thought you would want to come back with me. If you are feeling well enough."

Mrs. Carlyon threw up her hands in horror. "It would be madness. The poor girl has been so ill."

Since his arrival Josh had been nursing a suspicion that Sarah's mother was trying to arrange things so Sarah should have the baby at Hayle. "The journey would be worse for her next week," he said. "Even more so the week after."

"Why not let her have the baby here, Josh?"

He had been right. Now it was out in the open.

"It would be much, much better from Sarah's point of view." Mrs. Carlyon waxed enthusiastic. "Dr. Scott would be on hand. He knows Sarah and he's very good at delivering babies."

"We have doctors at Sharptor too."

"Mine doctors," Mrs. Carlyon snorted. "I wouldn't trust one of them to deliver a litter of pigs."

William Carlyon stood up. "Josh is right, Molly. Sarah's place is with her husband. We shouldn't interfere." He held up a hand to silence his wife. "I know she hasn't been too well, but there's nothing wrong with her now."

"Well! I'm only trying to do my best for Sarah. If that's going to be considered interference, there's nothing more to be said! Come along, Mary."

She swept out of the room, followed by her younger daughter.

"I think that could be termed a royal exit," commented William Carlyon. "Now, if you'll excuse me, I need to check with the foreman that everything is well in the foundry."

437

Sarah and Josh were silent for a few minutes after he left. "Don't you want to come home, Sarah?" Josh said at last.

She looked down at her hands, and tears filled her eyes, "Of course I do, but I'm scared, Josh."

"Scared! Of what?"

She shrugged helplessly. "Of everything. Of spending so much time on my own. Of the moor. Most of all of having the baby."

"Don't you want the baby?"

"Yes! It's just . . . Oh, Josh. I don't know anyone at Sharptor. I feel as though I am a complete stranger."

"But, Sarah, you've only lived there for a short while. And the folk are concerned about you. There isn't one of them who hasn't asked after you since news got around about the baby. Why, they've even asked as far off as St. Cleer."

Sarah looked up at him steadily. "You mean Miriam?"

"Yes."

"Do you wish you had married her instead of me?"

"Is that what you believe?"

"I don't know what to believe. I only know that I get knotted up inside when you are off somewhere with that preacher, because I think you might be talking to her and comparing us."

He was relieved when she dropped her gaze. "Sarah, I married you because I wanted to. Nobody forced me to do it. I was—and am—very proud to have you for my wife. I've known Miriam all my life. I couldn't forget her if I wanted to. But you are my wife and Miriam is married to my friend. Need I say more?"

"No. I'm sorry." She rose from her chair. "Poor Josh. I've given you a bad time, haven't I? We'll return to Sharptor and I'll be a dutiful wife." She managed a smile. "And I do love you."

THEY went back to Sharptor on Sunday. The next months were very happy ones for both of them. It snowed sporadically until the end of February, and it was pleasant to sit indoors in front of a crackling log fire. The house at Sharptor became a home.

There was no shortage of work at the mine. The main pump needed an overhaul, and Josh, with his assistants, completed it quickly. His latest man-lift was a proper cage with improved gearing, which meant that the men could be brought up to grass in record time. In an emergency it could prove invaluable.

Josh showed the plans to Theophilus Strike one afternoon, and the mineowner was enthusiastic. "You must patent it," he said.

Josh protested that it would have to be proved first. But Strike insisted. "It will work. Anyone can see that. And it will be copied. If you won't patent it, I'll do it for you."

He was as good as his word. A month after the system was installed and had had its trial run, a mine-engineering company in the North of England was negotiating with Josh to build a similar system, with Josh to receive a fair percentage of the profits.

Then, early in March, his brief period of contentment came to an end. Josh arrived home one night to find Sarah lying back in the rocking chair in the kitchen, pale and frightened.

"Thank God you are here, Josh!" She rolled her head from side to side, a spasm of pain gripping her. "The baby. I think it's coming. Oh, Josh, help me. Help me! Please!"

Josh grasped her forearms until the pain passed. "Don't move, Sarah. I'll go and find the doctor."

"No!" she screamed. "Don't leave me!" Her voice rose in a cry of animal anguish.

Josh was in a quandary. The baby was not due for another seven weeks. Something was seriously wrong. Yet if he left Sarah alone even for a short while she might become hysterical.

Then he heard a sound from the track that went past the house. He opened the door and in the gloom made out the shape of a cart.

"Hey! Stop!" He ran from the house, waving his arms, and the cart creaked to a halt. It was being driven by a farm lad.

"I need your help," said Josh. "My wife is in the house and our baby is coming." He dug into his pocket and came out with a silver coin. "Look! Here's a shilling. Go down to the mine and tell them that Sarah Retallick up at Idle Farm needs help quickly."

The boy snatched the coin and whipped up his horse.

Josh rushed back inside. He found Sarah struggling to her feet. "I thought you had gone. Oh, God, Josh! Help me."

He held her tight until the latest spasm passed. Then he guided her gently upstairs to their bedroom and helped her into the special nightdress she had set aside for this occasion.

"I'm just going down to put water on the stove. That's what they did when young Gwen was born."

"Don't be long, Josh. Don't leave me alone."

He hurried downstairs, threw logs on the fire and put pots and kettles on the stove. Every few seconds he looked through the window, expecting help to arrive. Then an agonized scream sent him rushing upstairs again.

"It's coming! It's coming! I can feel it."

Sarah was not exaggerating. Her frenzied thrashing had caused her nightdress to work up, and there, just emerging from her body, was the dark head of a baby. There was no time for nervousness now. Josh took hold of the baby's head as Sarah screamed in agony. He was never sure whether it was his doing or whether nature supplied the twist that turned its shoulders. But suddenly the baby had arrived—a tiny, damp, bloody object.

Sarah lay back on the bed, sucking in great gulps of air, and Josh was wondering what to do with the motionless baby when he heard the door open downstairs. "Josh! Sarah!" his mother called.

"Come quickly. The baby's here."

Jesse Retallick ran up the stairs and saw Josh crouched, holding the baby. "Has it cried yet?" she asked.

"No." Josh looked startled.

Throwing off her cloak, Jesse took the baby and, hanging it head downward by its ankles, slapped it on the backside.

She put a finger inside its mouth, checking that the throat was clear. Then she smacked it again. The third slap brought forth a cry, like the feeble mewing of a kitten.

Jesse looked worried. "Tom's trying to find Mary Crabbe," she said. "And your father's gone for the mine doctor at the Phoenix."

Poor Sarah, exhausted by the pain and effort, opened her eyes. "Josh. What is it, a boy? Have I given you a son?"

"It's a boy," said Jesse.

"I'm glad," Sarah murmured wearily. "Can I hold him?"

440

"Not yet, my love." Jesse turned to Josh. "Get me some of that hot water I saw on the stove. And some towels."

Josh, pleased to have someone else give the orders, ran up and down the stairs, carrying hot water and towels up, and empty pots down to be refilled and heated. After one such trip he returned to discover that Jesse had severed the umbilical cord and placed the baby in the small crib, which was not yet completed.

"I want a hot-water bottle for the baby," Jesse said quickly.

Ben Retallick came into the kitchen as Josh was filling an earthenware bottle from the large kettle. "It's a boy," said Josh. "I delivered it. Where's the doctor?"

"He was too drunk. Are Sarah and the baby all right?"

"I don't think Mother is very happy with either of them." Taking the bottle, he went up the stairs ahead of his father.

In the bedroom, Jesse was kneading Sarah's stomach as though it were a pile of dough, and without pausing, she looked questioningly at Ben. "The doctor wasn't available," he said, going across to the crib. "Is our grandson all right?"

Jesse took the hot-water bottle from Josh, wrapped it up well and pushed it down beside the still infant. She whispered, "The baby has come much too soon. It's a weakling. But I'm more worried about Sarah. The afterbirth has got to come away, and she's desperately tired. Oh, if only Mary Crabbe was here!"

In spite of all Jesse's efforts the baby died soon after. Nor had she any more success with Sarah's afterbirth.

"Josh," Jesse called, "come up and sit with Sarah. Keep her forehead cool. She's in a fever."

Sarah's appearance shocked him. She was gaunt and haggard. As he bathed her forehead, he tried not to let his gaze wander to the sheet-draped crib in which lay the body of their child.

It was nearly dawn before he heard Mary Crabbe's wheezing approach up the stairs. She stood in the doorway, her hair uncombed, gazing about her and breathing laboriously.

"Get out!" she snapped at Josh. "And take that with you." She pointed to the crib. "It's ill luck to have death in the room."

Josh gently moved the crib out of the room and went downstairs. In the kitchen, Ben told him he had sent a rider to Hayle to tell the Carlyons of the night's happenings.

He and Josh were talking quietly when Jesse hurried in for another pot of water. "It's all right!" she announced. "Mary Crabbe's done it. The afterbirth has come away."

The relief in the room was enormous.

Ben cleared his throat. "I'm sorry about the baby, Josh. Seems he came into the world too soon."

"Or too late!"

They had not heard Mary Crabbe come down the stairs. She stood in the doorway, hair awry, as solid as a toad. "There are few eldest sons in these parts who weren't begotten in the fern of the moor." She cackled. "There's more love to be found there."

The two men looked at each other, but Mary Crabbe had not finished. "And there will be precious little love to be found in this house. Shame, yes. And more. But you'll find out soon enough!" Pulling her dirty shawl about her shoulders, she shuffled out of the house, talking to herself as she walked away to the village.

"I think her mind has finally gone," said Ben sadly. "She's so old she doesn't know what she is saying half the time. Forget her words, Josh, and remember only her deeds."

"Yes." Josh nodded his head. He looked pale and shaken. Then, turning abruptly, he said, "I'm going up to Sarah."

Sarah was quite still. Josh felt her forehead. It was cool now.

"I'm sorry, Josh." Her lips hardly moved.

"Shhh! You've done nothing to be sorry about. You're a very brave girl and I'm proud of you."

A tear tracked rapidly down her face. "No. It wasn't meant to be, Josh. It should have been Miriam here bearing your child. I've always known that. She belongs to the moor as you do."

"Now what kind of talk is this?" Jesse had come in, and she began gathering soiled bedding. She brushed back a wisp of fair hair from Sarah's face, then took Josh's arm. "Leave her, Josh. She's had a bad time and needs sleep. Go off somewhere and rest yourself. It's been a hard night for you too. I'll look after Sarah."

442

He walked alone on the moor for three hours. Mary Crabbe's words had disturbed him greatly, but Sarah's had upset him more. He could not put them out of his mind.

It was dark when the coach carrying Sarah's mother rolled into the yard of the old farmhouse. Seconds later she swept up the stairs to the bedroom where Sarah still lay in an exhausted sleep. With only the briefest of nods to Jesse, she went directly to the bedside. Tight-lipped, she shook her head in a gesture of displeasure at what she saw, and walked from the room.

Josh was in the kitchen when Jesse and Mrs. Carlyon entered. "A fine mess you've made of looking after my daughter. . . ." Mrs. Carlyon launched straight into the attack. "'We have doctors at Sharptor too,' you said. What of your doctors now?"

"Mrs. Carlyon," Josh said, "the baby was so early that nobody was ready. I did my best. It wasn't enough."

"And what about Sarah? She is a very sick girl."

"Sarah is an exhausted woman," he replied. "Don't upset her."

"Upset my own daughter!" Mrs. Carlyon bristled. "I came here with a reckless coachman, bounced about until I'm covered in bruises, and now I'm told I mustn't upset my own daughter!"

"Sarah is your daughter. But she's also my wife. My father sent to tell you what was happening because he thought you had a right to know. If I thought you were going to add to Sarah's distress, I'd put you back in your carriage this minute."

Mrs. Carlyon appeared to be actually swelling with rage.

"That's enough, Josh," Jesse said. "Go and fetch some logs for the fire while I make Mrs. Carlyon a cup of tea. Go on, now!"

He went reluctantly. Later Jesse made him promise to hold his tongue and not quarrel with Sarah's mother. But that night, as Josh made himself up a bed in another room, he had the uncomfortable feeling that he was an interloper in his own home.

Waking in the morning light, Josh heard the murmur of voices from the bedroom along the corridor. Flinging back the bedclothes, he hurried to Sarah's room. She was propped up against pillows, her eyes dark hollows. Her mother was sitting beside her.

"Hello, love." He kissed Sarah and took her hand. "How are you feeling this morning?"

"Much better, thank you."

"I'll go and freshen myself up." Mrs. Carlyon had not thawed from the previous evening.

"No. Don't go!" Sarah cried. Without warning she burst into tears. Josh's arms went about her, but he could not stop her sobbing. Determinedly, Mrs. Carlyon eased her from his arms and laid her back against the pillows. "Leave us now. She's upset."

Bewildered, Josh left and readied himself for work. He could still hear her crying as he went out.

He worried about her all day. That evening he rushed straight home and up to the bedroom, where he was greatly relieved to see Sarah sitting up. But as soon as he spoke to her she began weeping uncontrollably once more.

This state of affairs continued for days. Nothing he said could prevent Sarah from crying whenever he entered the room. He tried talking to her, telling her that losing the baby was not her fault. But she would not listen. Once when he dropped to one knee beside the bed and kissed her, she flung her head violently to one side. "No, Josh! No! I don't want to have another dead baby. Please, no more. . . ." He tried holding her and saying nothing, but the crying sounded even louder in the silence. Always in the background was the tight-lipped presence of Mrs. Carlyon.

Sarah left her bed to ride in the Carlyon coach to the baby's funeral. Josh hoped with the simple ceremony behind them she would begin to improve. But nothing changed, and after a week he had a guilty feeling of relief when Mrs. Carlyon announced she was taking Sarah home to Hayle for a long period of convalescence.

"What do you mean by 'a long period'?" he asked.

"I mean for just as long as it takes her to become a healthy, happy young woman again. I'm worried about her state of mind."

"Yes. All right. Sarah will be better with someone to talk to. Up here there is nobody but Jenny of her own age. And having me around doesn't seem to be helping."

But Josh was deeply unhappy. During their brief time together he had learned to love Sarah. It was a quieter, less devouring love than the one he had shared with Miriam, but he accepted that there were degrees of love. Now the girl who had come to his house as a bride was leaving it, with only a tiny tombstone in the village graveyard to record her stay.

WITH Sarah gone, Josh lost all purpose in life. For the first few weeks he leaned heavily on his family and friends. He visited Jenny and Tom Shovell and spent hours playing with young Gwen. He called on people he had scarcely spoken to for years. He sent off three letters in the first fortnight after Sarah left and received replies to none of them.

Then, suddenly, Josh's mood changed. He began spending his evenings at the Cheesewring Inn in Henwood village, where he could better forget the lonely house on the tor and the girl who was no longer there.

One night in early summer Josh roared his good-bys from the inn doorway and lurched out into the village street. For a long swaying minute he allowed his eyes to become accustomed to the gloom. Then a soft voice at his elbow said, "Hello, Josh."

"Who's that? Miriam! What are you doing here?"

"I've come to see you. But I'm not going to talk to you outside this place. Let's walk."

He shook her hand from his arm. "Leave me alone. I can get home on my own."

"Come on, now. Don't cause a scene and embarrass me."

"I wouldn't want to embarrass the reverend's lady." He straightened his shoulders and stepped forward determinedly, making almost twenty yards before hooking his toe into the mud scraper beside a door and dropping to one knee.

"Damn!" he muttered as Miriam got him back onto his feet. "Why are you here?" he demanded. "Where's William?"

"He's at home, looking after Daniel. My mother isn't well. I'm staying with her until tomorrow. No, don't pull away."

Josh allowed himself to be guided along the track, uphill from the village. He was all right, he told himself; but his legs seemed to be in more of a hurry than his body. "Why aren't you with your mother, instead of fussing with me?"

"Because I brought you a letter from St. Cleer."

"A letter? Where is it? What are you doing with it?"

"It arrived on today's coach from Hayle. I said I would bring it with me. I thought it might be one you were waiting for."

"I am, Miriam. It's the first one since—since Sarah went away." He was thinking more clearly now, the slur gone from his words.

"Yes, I thought that might be the case."

Not until they were inside the house and Miriam had doused him with water from the kitchen pump to sober him up did she hand him the letter. Tearing it open, he read quickly, then handed it back. "It's from Sarah's sister," he said. "Read it."

Miriam read, "Dear Josh, I hope you are not too lonely living by yourself in that big house. How is Hector? Sarah is a lot better now, but I have not been able to talk to her properly because the doctor said she must be kept very quiet. I saw her sitting by her bedroom window yesterday and I waved. I wish you could come to stay with us, but Mama says that would upset Sarah too much. I don't know why. I am very sorry about the baby because I wanted to be an aunt. I must end now. Lots of love, Mary."

"Oh! I thought the letter came from Sarah or I wouldn't have made such a fuss about it."

"I'm glad you did. It's the first news I've had since she left."

Miriam turned and smoothed her dress. "Well, I must go, or I'll be getting myself gossiped about in Henwood."

"Thank you for the letter, Miriam. And for helping me."

"I hate to see a good man destroying himself. You have your problems, Josh, and I might be partly to blame for them. But you won't find any answers inside an inn."

"Where do you suggest I start looking for the answers—Hayle?"

"That's up to you, Josh."

"Hayle is out of the question at the moment. Sarah bursts into tears at the sight of me."

"Sarah's being looked after. But what about you? Will you cease being Josh the engineer and become Josh the Sharptor drunk?"

"No, Miriam," he said. "From now on I'll manage without the aid of the Cheesewring Inn."

She started out the kitchen door, then stopped. "If you're still feeling the same way tomorrow evening, perhaps you'll walk me back to St. Cleer. Have supper with William and me."

"Yes," he said. "I'd like that."

THE next evening William Thackeray stood at the window of his study and watched the arrival of his wife and Josh with a frown. But minutes later his smile was as welcoming as any loving husband whose wife has been away.

"It's nice to have you home again," he said, kissing her. "Josh! How good to see you." William Thackeray grasped Josh's hand in both his own. "I can't tell you how sorry I am about the baby and poor Sarah. I heard she was very ill."

"Yes." Josh sighed. "She's with her parents at Hayle."

"An unhappy time for you." He gave Josh a calculating look.

"He's been on his own for too long," said Miriam. "I thought it was time he had a good meal." She smiled at the two men. "I'll go and find Daniel. Then I'll start the cooking."

Thackeray invited Josh into the parlor. "We've a lot to talk about," he said. "Have you heard about the miners' benefit scheme? Sixpence a week collected from each miner guarantees him ten shillings a week if he's home because of an injury received in the mine. Think of the peace of mind . . ."

When Miriam called them to the kitchen, the discussion of the union halted. Daniel ate with them, and provided the topic for conversation until the meal was over.

Daniel was a bright, attractive child now in his third year. In his presence Josh became unusually tongue-tied, wanting the boy to talk to him, yet not sure of his ability to reply. At last Miriam led Daniel away to bed, ignoring his vigorous protests.

"That young man has a strong will," commented Josh.

"I suspect it's an inheritance from his mother," replied Thackeray. "She's one in a million. She teaches in my school, corrects my sermons and can hold her own in a union meeting. She's the perfect wife for a minister." Josh did his best to agree with him. Thackeray rubbed his hands. "Now, we've been discussing the benefit scheme," he went on. "What do you think of it?"

"I can't see anyone raising objections," Josh replied. "Theophilus Strike is antiunion, but even he will see that this is for the good of every miner. And it won't cost him a penny."

But Theophilus Strike did not see it that way when Josh put it to him later. "We don't need such a scheme in the Wheal Sharptor!" he declared. "Our accident rate is lower than any mine in the county. Who thought of it, that St. Cleer preacher?"

"As a matter of fact he did."

"I thought as much. That preacher wants to become a power in this part of the county. Unionism is his way of doing it. To me it's no more than a personal annoyance; but others will stop at nothing to stamp it out, and someone will suffer. This preacher is far too slippery for it to be him. Make sure it isn't you."

"Then you agree to the men contributing to a benefit fund?"

"No, Joshua. But I won't stop them. And I'll not have any preacher coming here to tell me how to run my mine."

"I don't think it will come to that, Mr. Strike."

"Think! Boy, you stop thinking when you walk away from an engine. Now, be damned to your unionism. Find your father and tell him I want to inspect the new deep level."

Strike walked out of the office, leaving Josh looking after him. Josh had argued for the preacher, but he knew how dangerous Thackeray could be. Soon after Harry Reeve and the other Kit Hill leaders were transported there had been an ugly rumor that the preacher had arranged their arrests. It was said he was jealous of the stature they were gaining in the eyes of the men.

But Josh shrugged it off. Thackeray had done a great deal for the union. To doubt him would be totally unworthy.

It was as much a result of this guilty feeling as for any other reason that Josh rode Hector over to St. Cleer that evening. He found the preacher in his study, and was welcomed warmly.

"It's always a pleasure to see you, Josh," he said. "Let me make some tea. I'm alone for an hour or so. Miriam is taking a class for girls this evening. By the way, there's a letter here for you. It came on today's coach. Miriam asked me to take it over to Sharptor tomorrow." He began searching through his desk. Finally he held an envelope up in triumph. "Here we are!"

Josh took the letter and to his delight recognized Sarah's handwriting, though it was more irregular than usual. Tearing it open, he began to read excitedly. Gradually his expression changed from delight to surprise, then to dismay.

The preacher was watching him closely. "Is it bad news?"

Instead of speaking, Josh handed the letter to Thackeray.

"My dear Josh," it began. "I cannot tell you how much it upsets me to write so, but I feel it is the only honest thing to do. You know I was never really happy at Sharptor. Mother has said many times it would have been better had we never married, and I now realize it is true. I have brought only unhappiness to you. I was not even capable of giving you a child. My tears threaten to wash away every word that I write, but it must be said. I do not want to see you ever again, Josh. Whatever you decide to do with your life, I wish you the happiness and success I know you can achieve. God bless you. Sarah."

"You can't take any notice of this letter, Josh," William said. "The very writing shows that the poor girl is sick. She must have worked herself up into a terrible state to have written this."

Josh looked at the preacher with unseeing eyes. "I knew she wasn't happy at Sharptor. But that would have changed. Now . . ." Punching a fist into the palm of his hand, he spun on his heel.

"Where are you going?"

"To Hayle."

Josh's unheralded appearance on Hector at Harvey's foundry brought a variety of reactions from the Carlyon family, ranging from Mary's unreserved pleasure to open hostility from Mrs. Carlyon. Sarah was not downstairs, and her mother angrily made it clear she had no intention of allowing Josh to go up to her.

"I should never have allowed her to send that foolish letter!"

"It was a letter from your daughter to her husband," Josh said, with equal anger. "She had every right to send it."

"What's all this?" William Carlyon came into the room and shook his son-in-law's hand warmly. "What sort of greeting is this for a man who looks as though he's ridden through the night?"

"I don't care if he's ridden for a week. Sarah is not well enough to see him," Mrs. Carlyon persisted.

At that moment the door from the hall opened and Sarah came in. She looked quite normal and healthy until she saw Josh. Then she froze, her hand flying to her mouth. There was something in her eyes that disturbed him greatly. It was a lost, unreal look.

"Sarah!" As he moved toward her she shrank back. "Sarah, I won't hurt you. I've just come to see you."

She looked around, seeking some way of escape, her face twitching as though she were in physical pain.

"There, you see? You're terrifying the girl." Mrs. Carlyon could hardly keep the triumph from her voice.

"Sarah, it's me. Josh."

Sarah cringed back until she was touching the wall. Then she edged sideways toward the door.

"Sarah, Josh wouldn't hurt you," Mr. Carlyon told her.

Everyone was talking to her, looking at her. Their words beat in upon her like waves in a storm, pounding her brain.

Her hand touched the door handle. She turned it—and was gone. Josh rushed to follow her, but Mrs. Carlyon barred his way.

"Leave her! Haven't you done enough?"

"All right! All right," said Josh wearily. "You've proved your point. But when am I going to be able to talk to her?"

"When I, and the doctor, say so," replied Mrs. Carlyon. "Not one minute before."

Josh felt tired and sick. Whatever anyone said, there could be no arguing with the look on Sarah's face when she saw him. "If you'll make sure she's all right, I'll return to Sharptor now."

"Nonsense," said his father-in-law. "You must stay for a meal."

Josh shook his head. "Thank you, but no. I—"

"Sarah isn't in her room. Mama! Papa! Sarah isn't here." The cry came from Mary, who had gone to look for her sister.

Mrs. Carlyon ran from the room, and Josh heard doors being opened and slammed shut as she searched upstairs. Then she returned, sheer hatred on her face as she looked at Josh. "Sarah isn't up there anywhere," she said. "If anything has happened to that girl, it will be your fault."

"That's enough, Molly," said her husband. "I'm sure Sarah's quite safe. Probably in the garden."

It was Josh who noticed that Hector was not where he had left him, near the front gate to the Carlyon house. And in the street outside Harvey's they spoke to an old man who had seen a girl with flowing golden hair galloping a horse out of Hayle along the St. Ives road.

Josh and William Carlyon were quickly mounted on horses. "Have you any idea where she might be heading?" Mr. Carlyon flung over his shoulder as they sped along the open road. "Was there a place you were both fond of?"

"Only one along this road," Josh shouted, "and I pray to God she hasn't gone there."

But his fears were soon realized. They found Hector with trailing rein and heaving sides at the top of a narrow track that clung to the jagged cliffs above St. Ives Bay. Below was a familiar tiny patch of shingle.

Twice on the way down Josh slipped. He saved himself by clinging to the coarse grass growing in the crevices of rock.

There was nothing to be seen at the bottom of the cliff. Only the water at high tide, lapping at the ragged black rocks.

As more men arrived from Hayle, the search extended for miles along the coast. But it was not until after midday, when the tide had ebbed, that a man standing on the cliffs cried out that he could see something caught in the rocks.

A fishing boat from St. Ives, one of half a dozen called to join the search, went close in while Josh and Mr. Carlyon watched helplessly from shore. They saw the boat swing broadside to the rocks, the men at the oars straining to hold it off. One of the young men left his oar and plunged over the side. Twice he dived down. Then he surfaced, dragging something behind him.

Sarah Retallick had been found.

"IT WASN'T your fault, Josh. She didn't know what she was doing." In spite of his own deep grief William Carlyon was far kinder than his wife. There would be nights when Josh would wake in a cold sweat hearing her screaming "Murderer!" at him.

"Whether it was my fault today or sometime in the past I'll never know," said Josh. He was mounted on Hector and ready to return to Sharptor. He was desperately weary, but he could not bear to stay at Hayle for a moment longer. Sarah would be buried in the little Hayle cemetery, and Josh did not want to be there. He wanted to keep his own memories of the beautiful girl with long fair hair who had shared a brief part of his life.

"Good-by, Mr. Carlyon," he said. "I'm sorry to have brought such unhappiness to your family. I grieve for Sarah too."

Josh reined the horse around and rode away to the east.

CHAPTER TEN

AFTER Sarah's death Josh threw himself into his work with vigor. He constructed a pump to force clean air into the newest shaft, and set about making modifications on his man-lift. The royalties from it were beginning to come in regularly.

There were problems that summer. A reversion to the corn policy of a few years before meant that the bulk of the coming harvest would be sent from Cornwall to the towns of the southeast and the industrial centers of the Midlands. Again the miners protested, and Josh entered wholeheartedly into their cause.

All through that hot summer of 1845, Josh, William Thackeray and Miriam traveled around Cornwall addressing meetings. The Miners' Union was now an accomplished fact. One evening on the sands at Par, three thousand miners turned up to hear Josh and Thackeray spell out what the corn policy would mean to them.

"Well, Josh," said the preacher as they set their horses toward home afterward, "I think Parliament has done our task for us. The Cornish miners are united as never before. If we can keep them together, we'll be able to improve their lot a hundredfold."

"If the militia interfere," said Josh, "someone will get hurt."

"Don't be so parochial," said William Thackeray. "Think of the cause as a whole. If the militia are called in and miners are hurt—or killed—public sympathy will swing to our side."

"Tell that to the families of those who die," retorted Josh.

Thackeray looked at Josh in exasperation. "There are times when I find it difficult to understand you. We're taking part in a revolution. In revolutions men get hurt."

"It sounds as though we're fighting for different causes," said Josh. "You're dreaming of some great movement of the future. A power—to influence Parliament. I believe in unionism because I want to see the lot of the miner made easier and safer."

"Admirable sentiments, Josh. But limiting to progress."

Josh smiled. "Had anyone told you a few years ago that three thousand miners would attend one of your meetings, you'd have been delirious with joy. Now you talk of limited progress."

The preacher shrugged. "When you have three hundred, you dream of three thousand. When that's achieved, you look for thirty thousand." He kicked his horse into a canter. "Miriam has a rabbit pie waiting for us. Tomorrow will take care of itself."

The subject came up again during the meal. Miriam was well aware of her huband's ambitions, and it was to him she spoke. "What happens on the day you have your thirty thousand miners gathered? How long do you think you could lead them?"

"I'm sorry, Miriam. I don't understand."

"Calling meetings and discussing ways of improving the living standards of the miner is all right. It's part of a minister's work. But march at the head of thirty thousand men and I think there will be a very different reaction."

"I have no plans to march anywhere. My plan is for the miners to blockade the ports peaceably, to prevent grain from being taken away before every Cornish miner is provided for."

"And do you think you're going to appear at the ports of Corn-

453

wall and take everyone by surprise? It's too late for that. There's been so much talk. Rumor has it in Bristol that the Somerset militia are being mustered for service in Cornwall."

"Then I hope they have the sense not to interfere with any peaceable action taken by the miners," said her husband. "That would certainly precipitate violence."

"It would never come to that," said Miriam. "The army will arrive first and arrest the leaders. That means you and Josh."

"I fail to understand you, Miriam!" He got up from the table angrily. "What do you want me to do? Drop out of the movement because there might be trouble?"

"No." Miriam was calm. "I am merely saying that you should restrict your public remarks to miners' welfare. Anything else should be discussed with a few leaders in private."

For a moment Thackeray looked as though he had been struck dumb. Then he banged his fist on the table. "She's right, Josh! If we carry on the way we are, there can be only one end. But if I preach moderation, what grounds could they possibly have for arresting me? We're going to do some serious planning."

But the change was not easily made. At public union meetings the men expected scathing attacks on the iniquitous corn policy. Instead, they heard of the safety measures provided in mines as a result of union representation. Questions about the corn laws were carefully sidestepped. But on most nights the chapel at St. Cleer was occupied by leaders, and messengers galloped the roads of Cornwall with instructions for a master plan.

That plan soon became clear. One farmer brought the first creaking wagonload of corn down the steep lane to Boscastle harbor. He found the way blocked by two hundred grim-faced miners. There was no violence and little argument. But so impressed was the farmer that he promptly turned around and sold his wagonload in Camelford market, contrary to the orders of Parliament. The same thing happened to the next farmer. And the next.

The news was hailed throughout the county as a miners' victory. The more naïve among them awaited changes in the law. However, Parliament had other ideas. The militia arrived and were garrisoned throughout the county. But by far the most ominous threat came when the 32nd Foot—Cornwall's own regular regiment—returned from overseas duty and garrisoned at Bodmin.

One of the soldiers with the 32nd was Morwen Trago. And he soon arrived at Preacher Thackeray's gate in St. Cleer.

Miriam was overjoyed to see him. Army life suited him; he looked very smart in his red coat with the white crossbelts. William Thackeray stayed in the background while they reminisced, intruding only to keep Morwen's tankard filled. When the conversation showed signs of flagging, the small preacher joined in.

"You've led an interesting life since you left the mine, Morwen. You'll find things much quieter in Cornwall."

"Don't you believe it!" The ale had caused his cheeks to glow fiery red. "They don't pay soldiers to sit on their backsides, Preacher. They've got us down here for a reason."

"A reason for the army here in Cornwall?"

"We've been told this outcry against the corn laws is just an excuse to start a revolution, to overthrow Queen and Parliament. But they'll have a surprise when they start."

"I'm quite sure they will." Preacher Thackeray leaned back in his chair and looked at the half-drunken soldier. "But I doubt whether your regiment could defeat the whole of the county."

"It isn't only our regiment." Morwen waved his tankard unsteadily. "There's militia from Wales and Devon. Then there's the navy. The miners are trying to stop corn from leaving the ports, aren't they? At the first sign of trouble the men-of-war come in."

"Men-of-war, eh?" Preacher Thackeray mused. Morwen, he saw, was now staring and glassy-eyed. "I think I'd better help our guest up to the spare bedroom," he said to Miriam.

When William returned downstairs, he began pacing the floor of the parlor. "So Parliament is expecting trouble? Sending marines, militia and a regular regiment against us." He looked at Miriam. "One thing is clear. Morwen's not aware of my involvement or he wouldn't have said so much. It must already be accepted my interest is purely in the welfare of the miner."

Now THE MILITARY authorities ordered the farmers to inform the nearest magistrate when corn was ready for delivery. A party of militiamen would then accompany the corn-laden wagons to one of many large barns hired for the purpose throughout the county. A guard was placed on the barn until all the corn for that area was gathered in. Then, under escort, it was taken to the nearest port. The idea worked so effectively that the county authorities told Parliament the matter was fully under control.

The miners saw themselves defeated, and they began preparing for a more violent form of protest.

Josh was appalled. "There is absolutely no excuse for the use of force now," he told the miners' representatives. "Most families have corn. While it may not be as much as they normally use, properly husbanded it will last the winter."

Had Preacher Thackeray sided with Josh they might have turned the tide. But there were times when Preacher Thackeray felt jealous at the respect the engineer commanded. He voted against Josh's moderate policy.

Perhaps there were other reasons too for the cooling-off in their relationship. Before Morwen Trago had left the preacher's house he had walked with Thackeray in the garden. They spoke of many things, of the troubles in the country and the changes that had occurred in the mining industry. When Thackeray mentioned Josh's inventions, Morwen expressed misgivings about the preacher becoming too friendly with the Sharptor engineer. It was not wise, he said, in view of Miriam and Josh's attachment in the past. Then he dropped his bombshell. He had heard some of his officers talking, he said. Josh's name had been mentioned in connection with leadership of the union.

William said nothing, but Morwen's concern nourished seeds that were already planted in his mind.

LATE in August, Jenny Shovell gave birth to a son. News that she was in labor came to the Retallick house shortly after dusk. Jesse threw a shawl about her shoulders, and Josh went along to the Shovells' house with her.

Some of the women from the village were already there, as were a number of Sharptor miners, all talking in the kitchen when old Mary Crabbe came in. Respectfully the men stepped back to allow her through. She had almost reached the door that led to the stairs when she stopped. It was as though someone had called her. Turning, her wild dark eyes came to rest on Josh.

"Out of this house, Josh Retallick," she shrieked. "I'll deliver no baby beneath the same roof as you. Or the curse on you will be laid on the child."

There was a horrified silence. Tom Shovell looked apprehensively from the woman to Josh and back again.

"It's all right, Tom. I'm going," said Josh.

"Ignore the old fool, Josh," said a young miner. "It's the full moon. You know what she's like at such times."

"There's a grown moon," cackled Mary. "But before there's another you'll have reason to know how crazy Mary Crabbe is."

"Oh, come on, Mary!" said one of the shift captains. "Josh has had his troubles. Give the boy some luck now."

"If I thought it would do any good I would," said the old crone. "But if you mind the business of others you must expect to inherit their troubles. That's all I have to say."

With that she shuffled from the room. Josh left the house at once. He was superstitious enough to believe Mary a true witch. And he could not recall one forecast she had made that had not come true.

THE following day a worried Jesse Retallick spoke to Josh about Mary Crabbe's words. "It's this stupid union business." She made a gesture of resignation. "I don't know what will become of you, Josh. Why don't you marry? You could have the choice of any girl in the county. You've got a good job and that fine house."

"I don't want the house. I'd rather stay here. And the last thing I want is to marry another girl and take her there."

While they were talking, Ben had appeared to be sleeping in his chair. Now, suddenly, he stood up and crossed to the window. "I thought I could hear something. It seems the soldiers aren't content to stay in their barracks. See, they've come looking for trouble."

457

Josh hurried to join his father. He saw about sixty soldiers marching up the road from Henwood village. Keeping time to the steady, monotonous beat of a lone drummer, they headed south toward the Phoenix and Caradon mines. Along the way they had collected a motley following of jeering and catcalling boys.

"Let's walk up to Wheal Sharptor," Ben said. "I won't rest easy until I see the soldiers clear of the mine."

But the soldiers appeared to have no designs on the Sharptor mine. As Josh and his father climbed the hill, they saw the men turn down the track to the Phoenix mine.

"The fools!" exclaimed Josh. "What do they think they're doing? If some of the Phoenix militants are still aboveground, there'll be trouble."

"We'd best go down and see if we can stop it," said Ben.

"No. You stay up here and make sure none of the Sharptor miners interfere. I'll go to the Phoenix."

Josh set off at a run, but the soldiers reached the mine before him. The officer allowed them to break ranks, and they stood around, looking arrogant in their smart uniforms. One of the boys sorting ore hurried to fetch the mine captain. When he arrived, he left no doubt as to who was in charge of the Wheal Phoenix.

"What do you want here? And tell your men to stay clear of the machinery. Apart from the danger, the crusher they're leaning against cost a lot of money."

"I came here for water for my men and a place where they could rest and eat a meal," said the officer.

"Water they're welcome to." The mine captain called one of the boys to fetch two buckets of water. He spoke to the officer. "As for a rest and meal, this is a working mine; I'll not have my boys distracted while your soldiers lounge about eating."

"That's hardly a sociable attitude. We're your county's own regiment. We even have a man from your village in our ranks."

"I've already seen Morwen Trago. He's welcome anytime, but not in a soldier's uniform."

"Then I think we'll go to the mine on the hill." He nodded up at Sharptor. "Perhaps we'll receive more civility there."

"Don't waste your time," said Josh, stepping forward. "Soldiers would be as much in the way at Wheal Sharptor as here."

"Oh?" The officer's eyes glittered angrily. "Are the men of the Phoenix spokesmen for every mine in Cornwall?"

"I'm not from the Wheal Phoenix. My name is Retallick. I'm the engineer at Sharptor."

"Retallick? I've heard that name before."

"It's likely. Retallick's a common enough Cornish name."

"Well, I've no wish to put a strain on the hospitality of such generous hosts," said the officer. "Fall the men in, Sergeant." He half bowed. "Good-by, gentlemen." Looking directly at Josh, he said, "I feel quite sure we'll met again, Mr. Retallick."

Striding to the head of the column, he rapped out a command, and to the beat of the drummer they marched downhill.

"I think we convinced them they aren't needed hereabouts," said the mine captain.

"No doubt," replied Josh. He made his way up the hill to Sharptor. It seemed to him that the scene was being set for violence.

It came on a beautiful hot day in late September. Josh was cleaning his hands in the tub outside the enginehouse when a convoy of laden coal wagons creaked into the mine, returning from the canal head at Moorswater.

"Them from Wheal Caradon has got themselves a parcel of trouble," called old Nehemeziah Lancellis as he climbed stiffly down from the lead wagon.

Josh was instantly concerned. "What's happened?"

Nehemeziah spat into the dust. "Whole lot of 'em downed shovels. Gone to Looe to stop a corn boat leaving. Damn fools."

"That's ridiculous!" Josh was alarmed. "They know the soldiers are at Looe. They'd as soon shoot a miner as a rabbit."

"Don't know about such things," said old Nehemeziah. "But I was to tell you where they'm heading. Spoiling for a fight too."

"Is Preacher Thackeray with them?"

"Him?" Nehemeziah laughed derisively. "He's the spoon that does the stirring, not the pot that sits on the fire."

Josh's mind was racing. The men were on foot. It might be

possible to take a horse and head them off. "Do you know what time they left?"

"I got news of it an hour ago. They'd be well on the way now."

The chances of preventing the miners from reaching the port were very slim indeed, but Josh would try.

He was not the only one worried about the Caradon miners. A mile out from Looe, riding Hector along the brown tidal waters of the Looe River, he caught up with John Kittow. The Caradon miners' leader was bounding along on a packhorse that had seen better days. When Josh reined in beside him, all he seemed able to say was, "Fools! The bloody fools!"

"What are their plans?" asked Josh.

"Plans? They're going to keep the corn from being loaded onto a ship. I doubt if they've thought beyond that."

"Weren't you able to stop them? They usually listen to you."

"They might have listened to me, but I was over to Callington to hire a couple of blacksmiths. When I got back, it was to a mine without miners. How did you find out about it?"

Josh explained. "I hope we can avoid bloodshed."

Rounding a bend down the hill into Looe town, they were greeted by the roar of a large crowd of angry men. The sounds came from the wharf just beyond the arched bridge. On the bridge itself were farmers' wagons, escorted by mounted soldiers wearing the blue jackets and plumed helmets of Dragoon Guards.

Josh kneed Hector forward. The scene at the dockside was even worse than he had feared. The Caradon men had gathered support along the way, and there must have been six or seven hundred miners packed in a mob on the open jetty.

Fifty wagons of corn were drawn up at the water's edge, white-faced farmers fingering the reins of their horses uncertainly. Between the wagons and the angry miners a line of red-coated foot soldiers stood with guns held ready. A few miners were arguing with an officer whom Josh recognized as the one who had led his men into the Wheal Phoenix. Josh spurred his horse forward.

A magistrate was proclaiming the Riot Act to the miners, declaring them officially a "riotous assembly." This was sufficient in a court to justify any violence that might be used against them. Even so, it might still be possible to avert bloodshed.

Then, in the midst of the heated argument, the officer grabbed the shirtfront of one of the miners. The miner struck out wildly, and two others rained blows upon the officer.

This was sufficient for the sergeant with the platoon. At a hoarse command every second man in the line dropped to one knee, rifles aimed at the crowd. Before a horrified Josh could do or say anything, a volley of shots rang out. When the acrid smoke cleared, half a dozen miners lay on the ground.

There were shouts and screams as the crowd began to push away from the red-coated soldiers, only to find their retreat barred by the mounted dragoons, who had advanced from the bridge and now bore down upon them with drawn sabers.

Josh rode at the foot soldiers, calling on them not to fire again. He was too late. Another volley was ordered and more miners slumped to the ground. Josh was caught in the charge of the dragoons. Frightened by the noise, Hector reared, crashing down against one of the horses. The animal slipped on the smooth cobblestones and fell to the ground, carrying its rider with it.

Then Josh was in the middle of the hacking sabers. A blade slashed his back, and a burning pain seared through his shoulder. Hector stumbled and Josh was thrown to the ground. He clambered to his feet, and there in front of him, not fifteen feet away, was the officer in charge of the foot soldiers. Bloodied and bruised, he pointed at Josh and ordered, "Get him! Get that man!"

All was utter confusion, with foot soldiers, horse soldiers and miners running over the wide jetty. Josh saw an opening and ran for it. Close behind a gun roared, and he felt a hard blow in the left arm. He spun about and clutched it just above the elbow. Hot blood oozed between his fingers. Then, miraculously, John Kittow appeared, still mounted and with Hector's reins in his hand. "Quick, Josh!" he called. "Hurry!"

Josh pulled himself into the saddle and clattered after the Caradon miner through a narrow passageway, then galloped past shuttered shops to the bridge and out of the town.

They rode hard for another mile before John Kittow pulled his horse in alongside Josh. By now the fire in Josh's back was burning fiercely and his arm throbbed alarmingly.

"My God, Josh! You're a bloody mess. Get off down by the canal. I'll need water to clean you up."

Josh swung from Hector's back when they got there, staggering as his feet touched the ground. The miner stripped Josh's shirt from him and began swabbing his wounds with his neckerchief. His arm was quickly cleaned. The musket ball had gone straight through, without touching bone. His back was a different matter, laid open from the left shoulder to the right side of his waist.

"I don't like the looks of this, Josh. You must see a doctor as quickly as we can reach one."

"It better be a doctor well away from here," said Josh, gritting

his teeth against the pain of the tidal salt water. "That officer brought his men around the mines. I told him my name, and he said he'd heard of me. I doubt very much if my wound was the result of a chance shot."

"No. I'd swear it was Morwen Trago who fired. And if they know you, they'll come for you at Sharptor."

"We'll worry about that when we get there. Can you bind my back, John?"

Kittow took off his own shirt and began tearing it into strips. "I'll do what I can, but it won't last, Josh." He laid strips of cloth along the saber cut, then bound the remainder of the shirt around Josh's body to hold it in place. "That will have to do for now. Can you get back on your horse?"

Josh nodded, with more assurance than he felt, and they set off once more, following the line of the canal toward Moorswater.

By the time they reached there, Josh was reeling in the saddle.

"You're in no fit state to ride further, Josh."

"I'll be all right in a few minutes." He rested both hands on the horse's neck, trying to ignore the pain.

Another three miles put them on the moor west of St. Cleer. "We'll make those rocks up ahead," said John Kittow. "I'll leave you there and find a doctor."

"Go into St. Cleer," gasped Josh. "Tell Preacher Thackeray."

At the rocks, John lowered him to the ground only half conscious, and left him with Hector's reins twisted about his wrist. "I'll be back in half an hour," he promised.

It was a clear night with a full moon on the horizon when John Kittow rode off. Sometime later Josh was wakened from an exhausted sleep. Looking up, he saw the moon high in the sky. John had been gone far too long. Something was wrong.

Then he heard the sound which had disturbed him. It was the jingle of harness. Painfully he rose to his feet and held Hector's head still, relying on the rocks to hide him as horsemen passed not twenty yards away. They were troopers, searching for him.

When they had disappeared, Josh mounted Hector. The effort caused the blood to flow once more from the wound in his back. He urged the horse away from the track, heading for Sharptor and the cottage of his parents. As he picked his way down the last hillside close to the cottage, Hector slipped, dislodging a stone. Josh heard an exclamation from someone in the shadows.

"Who's there?" The soldiers had been expecting him.

Josh pulled Hector about in a tight turn. Behind him he heard the dragoons mount hurriedly. Then horses were crashing through the bracken after him. He coaxed Hector into a canter, the movement jarring his wounds unmercifully. He could not keep going like this for long. His only chance lay in outwitting them.

Crouching low, he put Hector into a gallop in an effort to gain some distance. Then, pulling the horse to a halt, he jumped awkwardly from the saddle. Slapping its haunches, he called, "Go, Hector! Give them a run, boy."

The big horse galloped off, leaving Josh in the tall ferns.

The dragoons were well spread out as one by one they passed the place where Josh was hiding. When the last of them had pounded into the distance, he stood up. He knew where he must go. He had not been there for some years, but he had no trouble finding it. The tunnel through the gorse was slightly overgrown, and a needle-loaded branch seared the wound in his back. He almost fainted, but made it to the rock hideout and collapsed.

Josh was right in assuming something had gone seriously wrong with John Kittow. The miner was a reliable shift captain, but sadly he did not have a quick, inquiring mind. Otherwise, he might have wondered about the number of horses tethered near the preacher's house. As it was, he simply hurried to the door, banged upon it, and when it was opened by a pale, wide-eyed Miriam, he blurted out, "Where's Preacher Thackeray? I must see him. Josh is badly hurt."

The uniformed figure of Miriam's brother, Morwen Trago, stepped into the light behind her. Two dragoons rushed from the shadows, and John Kittow was a prisoner. They dragged him into the house and pushed him into a chair in the kitchen. Miriam was bundled into the passageway outside. Triumphantly Morwen said, "So my shot didn't go astray. Where is Josh now?"

John Kittow glared at him and said nothing.

"Don't be stupid, Kittow," said Morwen. "It won't be well received at your trial if it comes out that you protected him."

"My trial for what? All Josh and I did was try to stop the miners causing trouble."

"That's a likely story." Morwen grinned. "You and Retallick were leading them. Inciting them to violence."

"You're a liar, Morwen Trago. A true son of your father. Where's Preacher Thackeray? He'll know I'm telling the truth."

"I doubt whether my brother-in-law will know anything of the sort," replied Morwen smugly. "He was here when everything was happening. Now he's gone to do what he can to comfort the miners you and Retallick misled into such a stupid venture."

He signaled to the dragoons. "Take him away."

JOSH SLEPT FITFULLY through the night. Twice he heard horses trotting along the path beyond the gorse passage. But the soldiers would find nothing in the darkness.

When next he woke, the sun was high. It took him a few minutes to place where he was, to be aware of the sounds about him—the distant steady thump of the Sharptor mine engine; farther away, the noises of the Wheal Phoenix. It was a normal moorland day, but Josh sensed his life would never be the same again. He felt stiff, and during his exhausted sleep he had moved, causing his back to bleed extensively. He was much weaker than he wanted to believe.

He tried to get to his feet. Using the rocks as support, he shuffled a few steps to look out through a small aperture over the needle-spined gorse. There he saw red-coated soldiers beating through the undergrowth. They were working up the slope, away from his position; that was hopeful. But he could not risk leaving the hide-out during daylight. He sank back on the dry earth, feeling tired and desperate.

He was still there when Miriam found him soon after sunset. Word had come back to St. Cleer that he had been chased in the darkness above the Retallick cottage, that the soldiers had taken his horse a mile away. Immediately Miriam had known where he was.

When she saw him lying so still, her first thought was that he was dead. But when she dropped to her knees and touched his face, his eyelids flickered and he tried to speak.

"Shhh!" Miriam whispered, lighting a candle stub and pushing it well back into a crevice in the rocks. "Keep your voice very low. I've got food and some bandages. Are you badly hurt?"

"I don't know. But how . . . ?"

"John Kittow told us last night before they took him away."

"Took him away? He did nothing wrong. We went to Looe to try to stop the miners."

"They're saying you led the rioting. That John Kittow was with you. He's to appear before the magistrate tomorrow."

"But William knows the truth of it. He knows I've always been against violence. John felt the same way."

466

Miriam's expression changed. "You mustn't expect William to say anything, Josh. For or against you."

"But he must, Miriam! He knows John and I are innocent. He knows the arguments I put forward at meetings. He can tell them."

"And admit that he's one of the union leaders, Josh? No, expect nothing from William and you're not likely to be disappointed." There was bitterness in her voice. "Besides, I don't think he'll be in Cornwall much longer. He's been called to London. The Church authorities want to know about his activities here. He intends leaving as the leader of a successful campaign. There's already news that Parliament has stopped the export of corn from Cornwall and other country districts."

Josh sagged visibly. "Then the miners were right."

"No!" Miriam was having difficulty in separating the strips of cloth from his wound where the blood had dried through them. "There wouldn't have been time for news of the fight at Looe to get to London. Parliament made their decision before the miners marched on Looe. If the men had been a little more patient, there wouldn't be seven of them lying dead."

Miriam had water with her and some herbal balm. She dressed his wounds as best she could, then gave him the food she had brought. He ate greedily. When he had finished, she said, "What are we going to do with you now, Josh?"

"You mustn't become any more involved. Think of yourself and young Daniel. How were you able to get away today?"

"My mother isn't well. I've come to Henwood to visit her."

"All the same, I'd rather you weren't mixed up in this."

"I'm already involved." She looked down at him. "William has always known how close we were as children. But in recent months he seems to have become strangely jealous. Then again, he resented the way the miners looked to you. He's a very ambitious man—I believe he saw you as a threat to his ambitions. And when Morwen came to see us they talked together a great deal. Once Morwen even came to the house with his officer, but they stopped talking whenever I got close to them."

She watched him unhappily. "I believe William has a lot to do with you being hunted now, Josh. He'll do nothing to help you."

"But how could he have known I'd go to Looe?"

"I don't know—unless he sent someone to tell you about the miners. Anyone who knows you could guess what your actions would be. Once there, Morwen and his officer could pick you out."

"No, Miriam. I don't believe anyone would do that."

"*You* wouldn't do it, Josh. But William would." She stood up. "I'm going now. You'll be safe here tonight. I'll return tomorrow with more food. No, don't argue. I want to."

Josh spent a miserable night. Around midnight the wind rose and within an hour it began to rain, a skin-soaking drizzle. When Miriam came early next morning, she found him cold and shivering, crouching like some sick animal. She had set out from her mother's house with some hot broth in a covered bowl. It was no more than lukewarm when she fed it between his chattering teeth, but it was sufficient to stop his shivering.

"Uncle John is going to send word to your father at the mine this morning, telling him not to worry. But we must get you beneath a roof and have a doctor look at your wounds. I know one place where you'll be safe. In your own house. The soldiers have already searched it, and they're not guarding it. Isn't there a hay-loft above the stables?"

Josh nodded.

"Then that's the place. It isn't far if we go straight across the moor. You've got to make the effort now, Josh."

The crawl through the tunnel was not too difficult. Once outside, Miriam helped him to his feet. They staggered for a few yards before he fell, dragging her down with him.

"I'm sorry," he gasped. "I don't think I can make it."

"Of course you can. You've *got* to do it. The soldiers will find you here if you stay."

Painfully he regained his feet. This time he covered twice the distance before tripping. After what seemed an eternity they arrived at the wall behind the old farmyard. Miriam helped Josh over and pushed him up the ladder to the loft step by step. With a groan he dropped gratefully into the sweet hay.

"We've done it, Josh. I told you we would."

That night she brought a drunken mine doctor from the North Hill district, who dressed the wound and drew the edges together with rough stitches. Then he cleaned the bullet hole in Josh's arm with a swab and an iron rod, and Josh fainted.

But the crude methods marked a turning point. On the third day after the doctor's visit, Miriam was pleased to see Josh on his feet as she came up the ladder into the hayloft. "You're looking like your old self today," she said.

"I'm beginning to feel like the Josh you once knew," he replied.

Suddenly there was a sound in the yard. They froze. Footsteps approached the door of the stable.

"We know you're up there, Josh Retallick." It was Morwen Trago. "Come down or I'll take great delight in coming up and shooting you again."

Miriam's eyes showed disbelief, then terror. "He must have followed me!" she whispered. "Let me speak to him—"

"No!" Holding her arm to prevent her from going, he called, "Morwen! You know I'm here alone?"

There was a brief silence. "If you say so," Morwen answered.

"I do say so and I have no wish to see my property torn apart."

"Then come down."

"There must be some other way, Josh," Miriam whispered.

"No. I'm going now. Stay until we're well clear." He kissed her quickly, then walked to the ladder. "I'm coming."

Josh's captors handled him roughly as they tied his hands behind his back and pushed him out of the stable. Fortunately he managed to keep most of their blows from his back.

He was a sorry sight as they marched him past the Retallick cottage. Seeing him from the window, Jesse screamed and ran outside. The soldiers pushed her back, but Ben's booming voice stopped them. "That's our son. If you hope to get out of mining country with your lives, you'll let his mother speak to him."

Tom Shovell and some of the off-duty miners had come, drawn by the commotion. They formed up behind the shift captain, and the soldiers realized the truth in Ben Retallick's words.

"Make it brief," said Morwen surlily.

"Josh, what have they done to you?"

"Don't fuss over me. Everything is going to be all right. I'm not guilty of anything. As anyone who was at Looe knows."

"That's what John Kittow told the magistrate," replied Jesse. "But he was sent to Bodmin jail to await trial."

"Then the truth must wait to come out at the trial," said Josh. "I must go now. Please don't worry."

CHAPTER ELEVEN

BODMIN jail was comparatively modern, having not yet acquired the smell of decay found in most prisons of the realm. Here was only the smell of man—his sweat, his filth and his fear.

In a large communal cell Josh was reunited with John Kittow and the nine other miners who had been arrested on that violent, late-summer day.

"I'm not going to say I'm pleased to see you," said John Kittow, leading Josh into a corner of the huge cage. "As each day went by my hopes rose that you'd made good your escape. How are your wounds? And what's been happening to you?"

Josh told the Caradon shift captain of his adventures since the Looe battle. And he told him he had heard that William Thackeray might be responsible for the misfortune that had befallen them.

"Now you mention it," mused Kittow, "the miner who told me the men were on their way to Looe said something about having sent Nehemeziah on to tell you. He could well have been acting on Preacher Thackeray's orders. But why would Thackeray do such a thing?"

Josh shrugged and said nothing.

"Well, don't worry, Josh. Our miners won't allow us to rot away. They'll force Thackeray to take some action."

"You're fooling yourself if you believe that, John. The judge must make an example of us. It wouldn't do for miners to believe they can take the law into their own hands. No, John. Preacher Thackeray has won."

470

That night an evil-smelling, greasy meal was distributed. The food was every bit as unpalatable as it looked, but all that Josh spurned was grabbed and gobbled up by other inmates of the common cell.

The following day Josh was brought a meal of beef and vegetables. When he expressed surprise, he was informed by the jailer that Theophilus Strike had arranged for him to have food brought in from outside. There was enough for Josh to share with John Kittow. A doctor also arrived, who changed the dressings on Josh's wounds and said they were doing nicely.

Furthermore, that same day a roly-poly little man was escorted into the cell and introduced himself as Reuben Button, a solicitor engaged by Strike to examine Josh's defense.

Button oozed confidence from every pore. "Now," he said, seating himself on a stool the warder had brought for him. "Tell me exactly what happened. From the very beginning."

Josh told him. At the end of his story the solicitor frowned. "You're quite sure you're leaving nothing out?"

"I've told you everything," replied Josh. "Apart from knocking the dragoon from his horse—and that was hardly a premeditated act—I did nothing. My sole object in going to Looe was to stop the miners from doing something stupid."

"Why then were the soldiers so anxious to apprehend you?"

"There are two possible explanations. The first is Morwen Trago. We were boys together, and he has no fondness for me or my family. He was the soldier who put a bullet through my arm."

"I see." The solicitor was busily writing. "And the other reason?"

"The officer in charge of the soldiers brought them to the Wheal Phoenix recently. While there, I warned him to keep away from the Wheal Sharptor. He asked for my name and I told him."

"Well! Well! Bad blood between yourself and the officer."

There were many more questions before Mr. Button folded his papers and tucked them away. "Of course this was a riotous assembly," he said. "That is most serious. However, we have an interesting defense. Very interesting. Now I have another little matter to attend to."

He waved a scented handkerchief in front of his nose. "Mr. Strike—whom I must say I have found to be a very generous man—wishes that you be made as comfortable as is possible prior to your trial. He has authorized me to obtain a private cell."

"I'm much obliged to him," said Josh. "Would it be asking too much for John Kittow to enjoy the privilege with me?"

"Provided little extra expense is involved, I see no problem."

Mr. Button was as good as his word, and before nightfall Josh and John were lodged in a cell on the first floor of the jail.

The days passed with very little to disturb the monotony, apart from the visits of either Mr. Button or the solicitor engaged by the union to defend John Kittow and the other miners. Josh's wounds healed satisfactorily. Then they were all told that an additional charge was to be brought against them, that of being party to a conspiracy contrary to the Treasonable and Seditious Practices Act. It was on such a charge that the Kit Hill miners had been convicted and transported when the mine store was burned down.

One day Jesse and Ben Retallick came to the jail to see their son. Jesse looked old with grief, all her fire drained from her. Even Ben, a man by any standards, did little more than twiddle his hat between his fingers during the uncomfortable visit.

In sharp contrast, Theophilus Strike was later escorted to the cell by the governor of the prison. After satisfying himself that Josh was as comfortable as could reasonably be expected, Strike turned his attention to Josh's arrest and impending trial.

"The whole thing is preposterous," he fumed. "I've warned you about meddling in the affairs of miners, but that doesn't make you a criminal. You're an engineer, and I need you at the mine."

After Strike had gone, Josh realized nothing had changed. But he felt better for the visit.

On the day before the trial at Bodmin assizes, Josh had two very special visitors—Miriam and Daniel.

Josh was appalled. "You should never have come. It's not right for Daniel to be in such surroundings."

"I feel the same about you," she replied with a forced smile.

For a long time they spoke of nothing in particular. Then John

472

Kittow asked to be taken out for exercise, a privilege arranged for by Theophilus Strike.

When the Caradon mine leader had gone, Josh asked, "Does William know you're here?"

Miriam shook her head. "No, but it would make little difference if he did. We've been going separate ways since your arrest."

"You mean you've left him?"

"No, we're still living under the same roof, but that's all."

"Miriam, I won't have you ruining your life on my account."

"You're not the sole reason for things being the way they are, Josh. William knew I wasn't in love with him when we married, but I liked and respected him. That respect has gone now, and without it I find our relationship impossible."

"I'm sorry." It was totally inadequate.

"You needn't be. I've accepted it, and William has many other things to occupy his mind. There are meetings full of talk about the defense of union members who are facing trial for their ideals. I'm more convinced than ever that William plotted with Morwen to have you involved in the disturbances at Looe."

"Is it possible to get any proof?"

"No. Unless either William or Morwen admit to it. They are hardly likely to do that. What do you think will happen at the trial, Josh?"

He shrugged. "My solicitor says we have a strong case. I hope he's right. I understand the prosecution will be asking for the death penalty if we're found guilty of all charges."

He saw the look of horror on her face and hurriedly added, "But he's quite sure we needn't fear that."

"I should hope not! You're innocent. Neither you nor John had anything to do with what happened!"

She clung to him then and Josh kissed her hungrily. The fire was still there between them, but a cell was no place for romance. "Miriam, please go now. And whatever happens, take care of yourself and Daniel."

Tears were commonplace in Bodmin jail and the jailer avoided looking at Miriam as he let her and Daniel out of the cell.

IT WAS A DULL, sullen November day when Josh, John Kittow and the nine other miners were taken to the assize court for trial. They were all squeezed into a long prisoners' dock with steel spikes adorning the rail around it. Before them was the raised bench and the deep-red padded chair reserved for the judge.

To one side of them the jurors formed a double line on their hard benches. Between the judge's bench and the prisoners were the tables reserved for the barristers, solicitors and clerks. And at the rear, the public gallery was packed to overflowing with miners and families of the accused men.

A door behind the bench opened and a black-gowned usher appeared. "Silence for His Lordship Judge Denman."

The occupants of the courtroom rose. A bulbous-nosed man with flowing wig and red robes swept in and took his chair.

"Be seated!"

The prisoners were prodded to their feet as the clerk began calling out their names.

"You stand charged that on the twenty-fourth day of September you did, in the borough of Looe, in the county of Cornwall, riotously and unlawfully assemble. . . .

"You are further charged that on divers dates you did treasonably and seditiously conspire against the State. . . ."

The dull voice droned on, detailing statute and section against which they were alleged to have offended. When he had finished, he called upon each of them to say whether he was guilty or not guilty.

One after another the men declared their innocence. On the first occasion the reply brought a small cheer from the gallery. The judge announced sternly that unless the public refrained from voicing their feelings he would have the court cleared.

Now the prisoners were allowed to be seated and the case against them began.

"It is," the prosecuting barrister declared, "quite simple and straightforward. Prior to this unhappily eventful day the miners had been stirred up by men like the defendants Retallick and Kittow, and misled into forming unconstitutional alliances, such as the Miners' Union. They disagreed with Parliament's policy on the sale of corn, and they deliberately set out to use force in order to change it. This disgraceful day at Looe was not a thing decided upon a few hours before the event. It was part of a well-thought-out plan. Gathered together were men from mines throughout east and central Cornwall. They knew exactly where to go, proof beyond any reasonable doubt of a treasonable conspiracy to achieve their selfish and dangerous aims.

"Although undeniably guilty, the men standing before you in this court were—with two exceptions—simple miners. The two exceptions are Joshua Retallick and John Kittow, who were important members of the mining community. And, mounted and in clear view of the others, these two led that cowardly, unlawful mob. This is briefly the case for the prosecution. Now I will call witnesses who will prove it beyond any shadow of a doubt."

First came the magistrate, pompous and eager, to tell how, disregarding the insults hurled at him by "hundreds of miners bent upon mischief" he completed the reading of the Riot Act.

Mr. Button, seated beside the barrister defending Josh, leaned over and whispered something. The barrister stood up.

"Magistrate Phipps, I am quite sure you behaved with commendable courage. Indeed, would I not be right in saying that you assessed the situation in a calm and brave manner?"

The surprised magistrate beamed. "I did my best, sir."

"Then no doubt you were aware of the composition of the crowd. Were they afoot or mounted?"

"Why, they were all afoot, of course."

"And yet the prosecution has informed the court that my client, Mr. Retallick, and Mr. Kittow were both mounted. Am I correct in assuming that neither man was present when you read out the Riot Act? They were not members of this riotous assembly?"

"We-ell . . . They might have been at the back."

"But you did not see them?"

The magistrate was forced to agree that he did not.

Then the counsel for the Miners' Union tried to make the magistrate say that the miners were behaving in an orderly manner. His argument was remarkably lacking in conviction.

Next came the evidence of the soldiers. They spoke of being ordered to fire into the crowd to save their officer, of defending themselves. Their evidence was well rehearsed. Nobody, unless he had been at the scene, would have doubted them.

The dragoons' evidence was far more damning. When they arrived, Josh and John Kittow were part of the crowd. One dragoon told of being attacked by Josh and falling beneath the feet of the horses. It was, he insisted, a deliberate attack.

"Surely not," argued the barrister representing Josh. "Was my client armed?"

The dragoon grudgingly admitted he did not believe so.

"Yet you had a saber drawn and were prepared to use it upon my client?" The eyebrows of the barrister were a statement in themselves. "And you are telling us that Joshua Retallick—un-armed—*attacked* you? Attacked a soldier with a saber clear of its sheath, a saber raised and ready for use?"

"Yes, sir. He had his arm raised to strike me."

"I submit it was far more likely his arm was raised to protect himself from the blow of an upraised saber."

"No, sir. It was a deliberate attack on me."

"If such an assertion were true, it would make my client a fool. I will be proving later that he is far from that."

Then it was the turn of Morwen Trago. He swore that Josh had been with the miners at the time they entered Looe, urging them to attack the soldiers. He had seen him strike down one dragoon, and when Josh had been about to attack another, he, Morwen Trago, had fired at him, wounding him in the arm.

"Is it true," asked Josh's barrister in cross-examination, "that you knew Joshua Retallick as a boy?"

"Yes. We lived close to each other on the moor."

"And did you like him?"

Morwen shrugged. "I neither liked nor disliked him."

"No? You must have a remarkable talent for forgiveness, Morwen Trago. Is it not true you believe Joshua Retallick's father to be responsible for the death of your own father?"

"He *was* responsible."

"Surely not. Didn't your father rape a girl who lived with the Retallicks? When pursued, I believe he slipped and fell into a disused mine shaft and was killed?"

"No! He didn't fall. He was pushed."

"There is proof of this allegation, of course? Your father's—er—murderers were tried and found guilty?"

"No, but that's what happened."

"That may be what you choose to believe. It has not been corroborated. Be that as it may, do you still claim that you have no hatred for anyone who bears the name Retallick?"

Morwen Trago said nothing.

"Certain silences," said the barrister, "shout louder than words. But I put it to you that you did *not* see my client arrive with the miners. What is more, if you told the truth about what you saw on this fateful day, not only would Joshua Retallick be acquitted, but he would leave this court with the praises of the learned judge ringing in his ears for attempting to prevent the bloodshed that took place."

"No! That's not true!"

But Morwen Trago's cries were drowned by the stamping feet and howls of support from the public gallery. This time there was no silencing the crowd. At this stage the judge adjourned the proceedings for the day.

On the return journey to the jail the accused miners were optimistic, convinced that the mood of those in the public gallery represented the view of the jury. But the next day, when the defense presented its side, it soon became apparent to Josh that there were few sympathetic witnesses.

Of those in the dock only Josh was called to tell his story. He told how he and John Kittow had ridden into Looe in a vain attempt to head off the miners. He testified that except for the scuffle including the officer he had not seen the miners use violence. Yes, he admitted, he had knocked a dragoon from his horse. But the fault lay with the horses rather than with their riders.

His manner was quiet and straightforward enough to impress the jury. Then the prosecuting barrister began to cross-examine him.

"Joshua Retallick, you have told the court you rode to Looe in great haste when you learned of the miners' action. Is it not true you set off knowing that you would be able to influence them?"

"I hoped they might listen to me."

"No doubt they had listened to you in the past when you addressed their meetings?"

"I addressed very few meetings."

"Is it not true that the miners regard you as a leader of this union movement?"

"It is a miners' union and I have spoken to them."

"Thank you. I think we agree. You are a leader of this so-called union. Now, let us pass on to what you have told the court. You say you went to Looe in a vain attempt to prevent the miners from doing something which you now agree was stupid?"

"Yes."

"But when you discovered they intended carrying out their unlawful plan of seizing the corn wagons, you decided to join them."

"No."

"Further. When you saw the dragoons moving in to quell this riot, you personally led an assault on them."

"No. I have said what happened."

"If the jury and I choose not to believe your version of the day's happenings, Mr. Retallick, I trust you will forgive us."

With this the prosecuting counsel sat down.

Then came the character witnesses to speak on behalf of the miners. Shift captains in the main. But there were two shareholders from the Caradon mine to speak for John Kittow. They praised his diligence and spoke of him as a man of integrity.

Of the witnesses who appeared for Josh, the first was Theophilus Strike. In his usual forthright manner the mineowner called the charges preposterous. "Joshua Retallick," he said, "is a brilliant engineer. His contribution to mine safety is recognized far beyond the borders of his own county. He has patented a mine lift that will revolutionize safety standards."

Strike went on to say that he had never heard Josh preach or practice violence, that his interest in the Miners' Union was a humanitarian one. The mineowner had in fact discussed it with him. He was perfectly satisfied that Josh was concerned with the well-being of the miners and nothing more.

The next witness was William Carlyon. He smiled sympathetically in Josh's direction as he took the stand. He too spoke of Josh as a brilliant engineer with a great future.

"I believe your relationship with the prisoner is a close one?"

"Yes." William Carlyon's voice was pitched low. "He was my daughter's husband."

"Was?"

"My daughter died as the result of childbirth last spring. The baby died also."

The statement brought Josh sympathetic glances from the jury.

"So, Joshua Retallick had recently lost both his wife and his child. It left him a lonely man, I would imagine. To overcome such desolation most intelligent men would probably devote themselves to something that would occupy both their time and thoughts. A cause. Perhaps a miners' union?"

"I would say that was highly probable."

"Do you think he would become involved to such an extent that he would advocate violence, Mr. Carlyon?"

"No. Josh is not a violent man."

"That is what I too believe. Thank you, Mr. Carlyon."

The prosecuting barrister asked William Carlyon a few questions, but he failed to overturn his evidence. Then it was time for the prosecution to conclude its case. The prosecuting barrister addressed the court.

"My lord. Gentlemen of the jury. You have listened to the evidence in a case of the utmost seriousness. A case that involves a section of the community placing themselves above the law. Attempting to impose their will upon others. This is a crime aimed at the very structure upon which our way of life depends, the upholding of law. You have heard the evidence of honest men. They have told you how these men in the dock, with others, marched upon Looe. They knew soldiers would be there. They knew they would have to fight to have their way. Because of their actions one soldier died and others were injured.

"From his own lips you heard Joshua Retallick admit he was in the habit of addressing union meetings of these miners. Retallick did not admit he was responsible for conspiring that the miners march to Looe. We could not expect him to do that. But I am sure that you, the members of the jury, will recognize the truth. His companion Kittow is perhaps more misguided than evil, but he is as guilty as Retallick. You will—you must—find him and all the other prisoners guilty as charged."

In a heavy silence the counsel for the prosecution sat down.

The miners' defense barrister made a long, repetitious speech that had the jurors fidgeting on the hard benches and said nothing new. Then it was the turn of Josh's counsel.

"My lord. I have no intention of taking up much of your time. Allow me only to remind you of the facts that have emerged.

"There was a disorder at Looe on the twenty-fourth of September of this year. That is beyond dispute. But the magistrate who read the Riot Act, a cool, calm citizen, did not see Joshua Retallick. Of course he didn't. Joshua Retallick was not there!

"Ah, you might say, but the soldiers saw him! All I dispute is *when* they saw him. I am not suggesting they are lying. Simply confused. They were excited, perhaps fearful—and who can blame them? They were greatly outnumbered. But what a pity they did not allow Joshua Retallick to talk to the crowd.

"He had gone to Looe in a vain attempt to prevent the miners from behaving foolishly. It was an action in keeping with his character. His concern for the miner was well known. His employer came here to inform this court that Joshua Retallick was no criminal, but a man and an engineer held in high esteem. William Carlyon also confirmed Joshua Retallick's standing in the world of engineering. This is the man you are asked to judge now. A brilliant engineer. A man who cares for the miner. No stranger to personal tragedy. Is it feasible that he would act in a manner so completely out of character, as the prosecution would have you believe? Gentlemen of the jury, I ask that justice be done. That you allow Joshua Retallick to leave this court as a free man."

The deep silence that followed his speech was broken by the judge. "Thank you, gentlemen. If you've finished, I will sum up the case for the jury."

He went through the case in a somewhat haphazard manner, leaving out portions he felt disinclined to emphasize. When he finished, the prisoners were prodded to their feet, the judge rose and bowed and the jurors filed off to their room.

The jury stayed out for an hour, during which time the prisoners were kept in the cells beneath the assize court building. Then they were hustled back to the courtroom as the jurors returned.

"Gentlemen of the jury. Have you reached a verdict?"

"We have," replied the foreman.

"And how do you find the prisoners?"

"On the charge of riotously assembling, we find the prisoners Retallick and Kittow not guilty. All the others guilty."

Gasps came from the public gallery. The judge frowned.

"And on the charge of being parties to a treasonable and seditious conspiracy?"

"We find all the prisoners guilty."

This time there was no denying the shouts of "No! No!" from the public gallery.

"Silence!" The judge looked at the men in the dock. "I shall deal first of all with those of you found guilty of being part of a riotous assembly." He read out the names of the miners. "This is a most serious crime. One which cannot be tolerated in any civilized country. You are all grown men and fully responsible for your acts. In light of this I sentence you to transportation for a period of seven years."

There were groans and cries from their relatives.

"Now I come to the other charge on which you have been found guilty. Conspiring to commit treason. Such actions are aimed at the very foundations of the land. Allowed to go unchecked they can have only one outcome. In France we have seen it happen. Those men I have just named will serve a further fourteen years' sentence of transportation, to run concurrently with their previous sentence."

This provoked more cries from the public gallery.

"Take the men I have sentenced down," ordered the judge.

When all was quiet again, he looked at Josh Retallick and John Kittow and his lips drew to a tight, thin line.

"Kittow. You are, I feel, a man who has allowed himself to be led by his companion. Nevertheless, I cannot overlook your part in this grave offense. I therefore sentence you to be transported for a period of fourteen years."

John Kittow swayed in the dock and Josh gripped his arm in sympathy. He had no illusions now as to his own fate.

"Joshua Retallick, I can find little to say in your favor. You have been found guilty of a crime which a man of your intelligence could conceivably have carried through to its logical conclusion—the overthrow of organized government. Such an offense carries with it the death penalty. I will tell you quite openly that it was my intention to pass such a sentence upon you. But the evidence of William Carlyon moved me. He suggested that personal tragedy may have impaired your judgment. For this reason alone I will exercise mercy. Joshua Retallick, I sentence you to be transported for life."

"That's not justice! You're sentencing an innocent man!"

Josh recognized Miriam's voice before pandemonium broke loose. He was taken down to the cells as soldiers, ushers and constables moved in upon the screaming crowd in the gallery.

OUTSIDE the court building Theophilus Strike, himself angry at what he considered to be a gross miscarriage of justice, watched the more vociferous objectors to the verdict being hurled into the street. When two soldiers appeared carrying Miriam between them, Strike stepped forward to her rescue. Not stopping to argue, the soldiers released Miriam and hurried back inside.

"Young lady! Aren't you the Trago girl who married Preacher Thackeray?" Strike asked.

Miriam's anger had boiled away. Dispirited, she managed a yes.

"I thought I recognized you in the courtroom." He took her arm and led her away along the street. Any resentment she might have had toward him was dispelled by his next words. "I refuse to believe I see defeat in your face. No child of Moses Trago could possibly have heard of the word. Do you have a carriage?"

Miriam shook her head.

"Good! I have one at the inn along here. I'll give you a ride home, and on the way you can tell me why you are so sure of Josh's innocence."

WILLIAM Thackeray was writing a letter in his study when the carriage drew up outside the chapel cottage. He watched in amazement as Theophilus Strike stepped from it and handed Miriam out. The mineowner chatted seriously to her for a few minutes before climbing back inside the coach.

When Miriam entered the house, her husband demanded to know why she had come in a carriage with the mineowner.

"He brought me back from Bodmin assizes. That's where all Josh's friends have been today—together with those of his enemies with the courage to so declare themselves."

"And who won the day? Josh—or his 'enemies'?"

"He was sentenced to transportation for life."

"How tragic. Poor Josh did much for the miners."

"Then why weren't you in court? You could have helped him."

"I would have been pleased to help had it been possible. But who would have taken my word against all those witnesses who actually *saw* what went on?"

"You would never have gone into that courtroom. You would have been far too worried that the conspiracy of you, Morwen and his officer to involve Josh might come out."

"What an incredible suggestion, my dear. But in view of your distraught state I'll ignore it."

"Ignore it if you wish. I doubt if Mr. Strike will."

"Strike? You told him of your wild imaginings?"

It was the first time she had ever seen genuine fear on his face.

"Far more than that, William. I gave him facts. I told him of the meetings between you and Morwen. Gave him the date the officer came here with him to meet you."

Now she called on a calculated bluff. "And I told him of the conversation I overheard between you and the officer."

Miriam saw the anger on William's face. Without warning his arm swung in a wide arc and he struck her across the face.

"You Judas harlot! This is the thanks I get for taking you into my home and giving you my name. Don't you think I knew what had gone on between you and Josh before? Oh yes, I knew—but I forgave you. Now you would give up all you have here—all that's decent—for someone who would be best forgotten."

"I gave up all that was decent years ago, William Thackeray." She fingered the side of her face where he had struck. "I'll be leaving your house in the morning. Daniel will go with me. And I'd rather you didn't make things difficult, William. If I were to write a detailed letter to the Church authorities, you wouldn't remain in the Church one day more. Now, if you'll stand aside, I have things to do upstairs."

BUT Miriam still had one last distressing meeting with her husband before the break became final.

It was after he returned from London and his long-awaited appearance before the Church authorities. It had been a stormy and unsatisfactory meeting for Thackeray, and it showed in the way he slouched in the saddle riding into Henwood village.

Miriam opened her mother's door to him and stepped outside.

Thackeray did his best to project his old authority. "I've come for you and Daniel, Miriam."

"Then you've had a wasted journey, William."

"You're my wife, Miriam—and Daniel is my son. If necessary, I'll seek recourse to the courts."

"No, you wouldn't. You fear what I might say in a courtroom."

"I fear nothing that might be said here in Cornwall. It would not follow us to London, and that's where I've been ordered."

"What I have to say would follow you to the grave, William. So don't make me say it."

"Miriam, forget what's gone. Let's try again. I have to return to London, but we can work for others there just as we did here."

"Did we? No, William. I *thought* that was what we were doing, but it was all to build your reputation. The price of it was far too high. I don't want to see you again—ever."

"But what will you do? And Daniel—you must consider him."

"I have. I'll work on the mine for him. And he'll get a better education from me than most other boys around here."

"I beg you, Miriam. Don't let it end like this."

"Go away!" The words were torn from her as her husband's composure disintegrated before her eyes. She despised him, but she was sorry for him also. Turning, she fled into the house.

THE prisoners sentenced for the Looe riots were taken in chains directly from the court to the prison hulk *Captivity,* anchored off the naval dockyard at Devonport, where they would be held until a transport was available to take them to Australia.

The ship was the battered shell of an old man-of-war. When the prisoners were still fifty yards from the dark shape, the downwind stench was enough to make a man puke. Their boat bumped against the side of the hulk, and the sentenced miners made their way up a slippery gangway in the darkness. Josh was parted from John Kittow so quickly that he did not have time to say good-by before they were thrust into separate holds.

He never saw John Kittow again. Three months later the former shift captain died in a typhoid outbreak on the foul hulk.

Josh and the others were pushed down a steep ladder into a stinking hold. All around were the sounds of men, moaning, snoring and coughing. The hatch cover was slammed shut and the miners were left to grope their way forward in the blackness. They finally found a small space, and by easing out other prisoners they made room to sit down.

Sleep was out of the question. They were part of a walking nightmare. There was filth everywhere. Convicts lay chained together like wild beasts. Red-eyed and unshaven, they put gruff questions to the newcomers, resentful of their recent freedom. They asked about the world of which they were no longer part, the half-real world that belonged to another lifetime.

For five ghastly weeks Josh was on the *Captivity*. Many times he feared for his sanity. He learned to fight like the worst of his fellow prisoners for the abominable food that was lowered to them twice daily, and to endure abject degradation.

One day the hatch cover was removed and a jailer called his name. The warder made Josh climb halfway up the ladder before he would come down to loose the chain attaching him to the others. Then, with only the chains about his ankles, Josh awkwardly climbed the rest of the way and shuffled after the jailer to the hulk overseer's office.

The overseer looked at Josh. "Your name Joshua Retallick?"

"Yes."

The man sniffed. "You're not my idea of a brilliant engineer."

Josh's hopes took a sudden climb. There must be some word from outside. "I was an engineer once," he said.

"There'd better be no 'was' about it," said the overseer. "I've a letter here from a Mr. Carlyon which says you're to be sent to Australia. Going on a regular immigrant ship with a warder on his way to Botany Bay with his family. Seems they've found copper in Australia and need someone out there to install some engines. It's all here, together with a release order signed by a minister of the Queen. There's another letter, from a Mr. Strike, promising to pay all expenses incurred in your transfer. Why he bothers himself with a convict I don't know."

Again he sniffed his disapproval. "Your ship is lying at Falmouth. You'll get out of those stinking rags and be taken there under escort. But remember, you'll still be a prisoner."

It was unbelievable. Josh could not accept the truth of it—even when he stood on a jetty, the *Captivity* behind him.

The two warders traveling with him said very little along the way. They set off by coach and in the early afternoon of the next day arrived at Falmouth. There they boarded a sailing vessel larger than any Josh had seen. He was escorted to a windowless cabin down in the bowels of the ship and handed over to his jailer for the long journey to Australia.

Samuel Evans was very different from the jailers on the hulk.

He was a family man and spoke to Josh as one man to another.

"Hello, Joshua. I can do nothing about the fact that you're a convicted prisoner. While we're in harbor you'll be locked in this cabin. Once at sea you'll be free to wander about the ship. However, the captain has made me responsible for your good behavior. Do I have your word you'll not attempt to escape?"

"You have it—and my deep gratitude," said Josh.

"Good, then it's settled. Mr. Carlyon brought some clothes for you. We should sail on the morning tide. You're fortunate to have good and wealthy friends, Joshua."

When the warder left, Josh sat down on the narrow bunk. He felt like weeping. The dreadful nightmare of the hulk was over.

The next day a fairly strong northeaster blew from the land. In no time the vessel was well out into the Channel.

After the evening meal, Evans took Josh on a tour of the ship. Then, aware that Josh would want to savor his freedom, the warder left him alone on deck. From now until they arrived at their destination, Josh would be treated as a free man.

The deck was deserted and dark, with only a few lanterns swinging in tiny islands of light around each gangway. Josh made his way to the stern. Along the scarcely discernible Cornwall coast he could see the lights of cottages. Loneliness welled up inside him. He thought of his parents in the cottage on the slopes of Sharp Tor. And Miriam. . . .

He shivered. It was cold. He could have gone below but wanted to stay here with his thoughts.

A figure came up to stand close to him. Josh half turned but could make out only a pale shadow that was a face.

"Josh, is that you?"

He could not believe it. "Miriam?"

"Oh, Josh!" She was in his arms, holding him as though the wind might tear him away from her.

Now he was certain the whole thing was a dream. "What are you doing here?" he asked. "William! Is he with you?"

"No, Josh. William is in London. And don't let's mention him after tonight."

"And Daniel?"

"He's here on the ship with me—with us. Come down to my cabin and see him. I have a lovely cabin, Josh. Theophilus Strike got it for me."

"Strike? What has he to do with you being here?"

She laughed. "I'll tell you the whole story when we get below."

Her cabin was very comfortable. It had two bunks, on the smaller of which Daniel lay sleeping. Miriam took off her cloak and began to explain her presence on the ship.

"I was at your trial," she began.

"I know. I heard you." Josh smiled.

"Mr. Strike heard me too. I was thrown out onto the street by the soldiers, and he came to my rescue. He'd recognized me as Morwen's sister, he said, and had heard I was Preacher Thackeray's wife. In view of this he couldn't understand why I should be shouting your innocence in court. I told him what I believed had happened—that William and Morwen had arranged for you to become involved at Looe. He said he would cause inquiries to be made. Then he took me home to St. Cleer in his coach.

"William saw me alighting from the coach and demanded to know what I was doing with Theophilus Strike. I told him exactly what I had told Mr. Strike."

"Wasn't that a foolish thing to do?"

Miriam shrugged. "I was so angry it didn't matter. But William struck me. It was the first and last time. The next morning I took Daniel with me to Henwood to stay with my mother."

"But that doesn't explain how you came to be here."

"Patience, Josh. Theophilus Strike wasn't able to obtain any further evidence and asked your father to tell me. Incidentally, both your father and mother know I'm here with you."

"And they approve?"

"I think they were deeply shocked at first, but the day before I left Henwood your mother came to see me. She asked me to give you the love and blessing of both of them. She said she'd be happy knowing you would have me to look after you."

"Poor Mother. But . . ."

"I know—the story of why I'm here. Two weeks ago Mr. Strike came down to the village to speak to me again. He wanted to know what I intended doing with my future. He asked me many very personal questions. Then he told me the great news. He said William Carlyon had received an order for mine engines from a man who had discovered copper ore in Australia. It was a rich find, and many men in London were prepared to back the scheme. Parliament too were very interested. They thought it would help open up the country to settlers. And the man not only wanted the engines but also a good engineer. Mr. Strike journeyed to London. When he returned, he had a letter which said you could go to Australia and work the engines, providing your fare was paid in advance, which he did immediately. I think he must have some very important friends."

"Thank you. That explains why I am here! But I'm still no wiser about you being here too."

"Well," said Miriam, "among the questions that Mr. Strike asked me was why I was so concerned about you. I told him."

"You told him what?"

"I told him I loved you. That I'd always loved you and that I only married William because in some horribly confused way it seemed that I was being loyal to my father.

"He asked me if I believed it possible for you and me to make a new life together if we had the opportunity. I said yes. That was all. He arranged for me to come as a passenger on this ship."

"If I live to be a thousand, I'll never be able to repay Theophilus Strike for all he's done for me," said Josh. He looked at Miriam. "You know I love you too, don't you?"

Her answer was to cling to him fiercely. "We can start our new lives from now. I have a lot of money here for you. Mr. Strike said it's royalties on the patent of one of your inventions."

"He's a good man," said Josh. He suddenly held Miriam away from him. "But what about Daniel? What will you tell him?"

"What is there to tell him, Josh? He's still little more than a baby. *You* are his father. You've known that all along. I told Theophilus Strike about that too."

She looked at him with tears of happiness on her face. "My passage was booked on this ship in the name of Mrs. Retallick. We have our son, Daniel Retallick, with us and are heading to a new life together."

"You mustn't forget I'm still a convict, Miriam."

She waved his words aside. "Only in name. When we get there, you'll find that Theophilus Strike has sorted everything out for you. You'll start work as an engineer. In a short time everybody will have forgotten you were ever a convict."

She took down a small tin box from a shelf by her bunk. Opening it, she removed a piece of crumpled paper which she smoothed out and gave to him.

"Do you remember the day you wrote this for me?"

Written on the paper in a childish handwriting was a single word: "Miriam."

He nodded. "I remember. You made me write it so you could copy it. Then you persuaded me to teach you to read and write."

"Write it again, Josh." Not understanding, he took the paper and a pencil from her and carefully wrote "Miriam" beneath the name he had written many years before. When he had finished, she took the paper and looked at it with as much pleasure as she had shown on that moorland day when they were children.

"That's beautiful. But now," she said, "you have something far more important to teach me. You have to teach me how to live, to be a complete person again. Will you do that, Josh?"

"I can only teach you the things I know myself, Miriam." He trembled a little as he drew her, soft and yielding, to him.

"We'll both have to learn about them together."

Ernest V. Thompson
*Prizewinning
Historical Novelist*

It is not surprising that the author of *Chase
the Wind* lives near Bodmin Moor, the setting of this, his first novel. What is surprising
is that a man who writes with such feeling of
the Cornwall copper mines and the families
who have worked them for centuries is a
comparative newcomer to the area—a resident of scarcely six years.

Thompson was born in London in 1931 and was evacuated to Oxford-
shire during the blitz of World War II. At fifteen he joined the Royal
Navy as a telegraphist and was off on a tour of duty that would take him
to the Aegean Sea, the Arctic and the Far East. After his naval service
ended in 1956, he had an active life as policeman and security officer in
such far-flung posts as Bristol, Hong Kong and Rhodesia. He was also
beginning to write short stories, which appeared in magazines, starting
with the Bristol *Police Review* and even finding publication in South
Africa and the Republic of Ireland.

In 1970 Thompson, with his wife, returned to England to embark on
a full-time writing career. They bought a seventeen-year-old motorcycle
and ended up in Cornwall, where they "met a lot of grand people and
went grandly broke," he recalls. He worked as a sweeper in a local factory and later as a house detective in a London hotel. Then Ernest and
Celia Thompson returned to Cornwall and settled down in a derelict
mine cottage at Henwood village. Thompson found a job with the
Ministry of Defence in Plymouth Dockyard, and started writing.

The story began to grow as his research took him to old mine shafts,
deserted engine houses, libraries, and the local parish registry, where he
found the names for some of his characters. The resulting manuscript,
Chase the Wind, won first prize over more than two hundred entries in a
historical-novel competition sponsored by American and British publishers (Coward, McCann & Geoghegan in New York; Macmillan and Pan
Books in London).

Now, still in his forties, E. V. Thompson has a lot of living behind him
and what may very well be a promising career ahead.

The FAN

A CONDENSATION OF THE NOVEL BY

BOB RANDALL

ILLUSTRATED BY DARRELL SWEET

A young man

worships

an aging star

and his

letters to her

are

adoring

until . . .

Best Wishes
Sally Ross

Sally Ross is a glamorous star, adored by her public—especially by Douglas Breen, who calls himself her "greatest fan."

Douglas wants to protect her. From what? Only he knows. As a shadowy terror assumes shape and purpose, it is clear that "the fan" will do anything to serve his beloved. *Anything*.

Told entirely through brief letters, this remarkable story builds to a shattering climax.

The Cast

SALLY ROSS .... Broadway and
Hollywood star

BELLE GOLDMAN .... Sally's secretary

JAKE BURMAN .... Sally's ex-husband,
a producer at
Continental Studios

STAN JOHNSTON .... A police detective

DAVID .... A young man

BRET LAIRD .... Sally's agent

JO AND SYLVAN COLTON .... Friends of Sally's

LILYAN PETERS .... Ex-movie star, friend of Sally's

EDITH PATERSONN .... Sally's next-door neighbor

BESS ASHER .... Belle Goldman's sister

and

DOUGLAS BREEN .... The fan

BRET LAIRD LTD.

25 EAST 57 STREET

Jan. 25, '76

Dear Sal,

The script arrived from Dino De Laurentiis. It's interesting, but frankly I don't see it as a star vehicle. I'm sending it on to you anyway. Will you please return my calls? Much as I love chatting with Belle and hearing all about her voluminous family, I still need to know how you feel about the *Tatters* contract. Also, *Who's Who in the Theatre* arrived, noticeably missing your birth year. You been talking to the Gabors lately?

Bret

Selton, Marks & Landau, Realtors
1231 AVENUE OF THE AMERICAS

January 26, 1976

Dear Miss Ross:

We've had several complaints now from other shareholders in The Bradford about the noise coming from your apartment in the early hours of the morning. We do understand the need for a star such as yourself to unwind at unconventional hours, but for the sake of your neighbors, could you try to do it more quietly?

Thank you.

Charles Stern

January 26th, 1976

Dear Miss Ross:

I don't know if you remember me, but I'm the young man who last wrote you several weeks ago, to congratulate you on your new show, *So I Bit Him,* soon to go into rehearsals. I know it will be another hit, as only you can give Broadway. I was wondering whether you had any new photographs taken recently. If so, I would love one for my collection.

Your greatest fan,
Douglas Breen
780 West 71st Street
New York City

Jo Colton

Jan. 27. The morning aft.

Dear Sal,

Just a bread and butter note to tell you that Sylvan and I had a wonderful time the other night, at least as much as we can remember of it. You really will be the death of us.

Jo

P.S. Are you or are you not coming out to Shelter Island for your birthday? And are you bringing someone?

2/1

Dear Jo,

Sal asked me to let you know she can't make it. Too much to do in town. And between you and me, I think this is one birthday she'd just as soon skip. It's the big five-o, near as I can figure out.

But ask her again, will you? She could use a few days off. I'll get her to bring someone really kicky—female, a hell of a lot of laughs—me. I could also use a few days off. Tell Sylvan I can still beat the pants off him at backgammon.

Belle

P.S. Jake wrote Sal that he'd love to hear from you two. He's at Continental Studios now. Did you know he got married again a few weeks ago? Sal took it pretty well, but if you ask me, she's still got a case on him herself.

Feb. 9, 1976

Dear Sal:

Yesterday, while I was hiding out from all this southern California sunshine, I dug out our old marriage certificate. I thought I'd have it bronzed and send it to you for your birthday. Then I saw your birth date on it.

Welcome to the fifties, baby.

Do yourself a favor, huh? I know how you react to birthdays. Don't do a number on this one.

There's a chance I may fly in at the end of the month for a couple of days. If I do, I'll bring Heidi with me. You'll like her, Sal. She's a sweet kid.

Now I've got to get back out into that sunshine. Don't they ever shut it off?

Love,
Jake

SALLY ROSS

Thursday the 12th.

Dear Jake,

You rat. I will not be anywhere remotely near fifty. I will be forty-six. And I ought to know. After all, I've been forty-six several times now and I recognize it. So I don't care what the marriage certificate says. Incidentally, my darling, what are you doing holding on to that old thing? We had it revoked years ago, you know.

I still love you, as always.

Dolores Gray told me she had lunch with you and your new

499

missus the other day in old L.A. Dolores said she's quite a knock-out, despite the teeny hint of cross-eyedness. Excuse the bitchiness but ex-wives are allowed, especially when ex-husbands marry girls young enough to be my sister. (Heidi? Her name is really Heidi? Does she have braids? How is she on milking goats?)

Listen, if you bronze the certificate will you at least have the decency to ink out my age first? For old times' sake?

Your Gal Sal

February 17th, 1976

Dear Miss Ross:

I couldn't possibly let your birthday go by without wishing you an Oscar-Tony-Emmy-winning day! You are the greatest star in the firmament and your birthday should be a national holiday with schools let out and cheering in the streets!

Not to sound self-interested, but I haven't received that photograph yet. And I've cleared the most perfect spot for it in my apartment. If you could send it, it would really make my day. Again, congratulations, congratulations!

Your greatest fan,
Douglas Breen
780 West 71st Street
New York City

Sal:

Hors d'oeuvres are in the oven. Just turn it to 250 for about twenty minutes. You do know how to turn the oven on, don't you? It never occurred to me to ask.

Also, don't forget, the car comes to get you at nine thirty for "The Mike Douglas Show" in Philly, so kick the gang out early. And hold it down, will you? You got neighbors. I won't be in tomorrow till eleven, so don't forget to set the alarm like you always do.

Listen, at midnight go into the bathroom and look in the stall

500

shower. A little present from your secretary. Don't be embarrassed, it only cost an arm and a leg. Happy forty-sixth. (Now, there's a real present!)

Belle

2/20

Dear Penthouse C,

Look, I'm sorry for the words we had in the elevator yesterday, but you really got my goat. I've been Sally Ross's secretary for six years and believe me, she's not at all what you said. So let's bury the hatchet, okay? Next time Sally lets off steam with a few friends, come on over and join the party instead of ratting to the cops. You'll like her.

So—friends?

Belle Goldman

EDITH PATERSONN · 941 FIFTH AVENUE

Feb. 21

Dear Miss Goldman,

Thank you so much for your very kind invitation to join in Miss Ross's bacchanals, but my husband and I prefer revels of a quieter nature. Especially at three in the morning.

Mrs. Patersonn
(Penthouse C)

Dear Mrs. Patersonn,

Drop dead.

Mrs. Belle Goldman

SALLY ROSS

Belle,

Had to leave for an interview at the crack of dawn. Please, please try to remember to get my stationery from Tiffany's. I'll be reduced to writing on toilet paper soon. (Also, there's a surprise in the package for you.)

The pictures arrived. Please autograph them and get them out. And before I forget, what possessed you to tell the gargoyle next door to drop dead. Honestly, Belle, at your age?

Sal

Sal:

What do you mean at my age? My age is your age minus two, in case you forgot.

I sent off the pictures, I told Bret you'd call him sometime before dawn, I got the laundry, and I'm off to the Bronx now to get off my feet. See you in the morning. By the way, your stationery is on the kitchen counter. Thanks a lot for mine. I'll be the only woman in the A & P with a grocery list written on Tiffany paper. (Hold on to your money, will you? Stop buying me expensive things I don't need.) Incidentally, I told her to drop dead because I'm too much of a lady to tell her what I really meant.

Belle

February 25th, 1976

Dear Miss Ross,

Or might I call you Sally?

The picture arrived and it's gorgeous! You always look fantastic in white! I took it with me to the record shop where I work, and at lunchtime I went directly to a frame store and selected a simple Lucite frame to house it. It looks fabulous on my dresser. Just the touch this place needed!

Your greatest fan,
Douglas Breen
780 West 71st Street
New York City

SALLY ROSS

Thursday the 26th.

Dear Jake,

This letter comes to you from the crankiest old lady the world has seen since Mrs. Macbeth. I started off this morning by snapping at Belle like a fishwife over nothing at all. Well, not precisely nothing at all. She started a war with her highness next door and I'm caught square in the middle. Know anyone who wants a penthouse cheap?

Then, having spat my venom at Belle, I went over to the Algonquin to meet Gideon Riggs, the choreographer for *So I Bit Him*. Just a little get-acquainted lunch. Nothing could possibly go wrong, right? Wrong. Mr. Riggs, it turns out, is all of one foot tall, give or take an inch. I'm sure they found him under a toadstool. And lucky me, he was desperate to tell me about a routine he'd already worked out in his miniature head. I am to do an entire number comprised of—are you sitting?—cartwheels and splits. I explained to the munchkin that I don't do cartwheels and splits these days. He explained to me that there was nothing to it. Inside of two days he'd have me looking like an Olympic gymnast. Good lord, are we going to have fun in rehearsals!

Oh, Jake, I'm so old. I look like what's left in Grant's Tomb. Don't you just love it when I feel sorry for myself? Well, why not? Gretel, or whatever her name is, has you and all I've got is eight percent of the gross of *So I Bit Him*. Can you believe they tried to get me for six?

Well, it's time to apologize to Belle again. It's the third time she's been at the refrigerator in the last five minutes.

I love you but it sure doesn't solve my problems.

Your Gal Sal

Dear Doug,

Surprised to hear from me? I know I haven't written in a while, but old friends are allowed to be lazy, aren't they? The reason for this letter is first to say hi and second to tell you that Ginnie and I will be in New York on the third for two days.

Listen, old buddy, I don't like to be pushy, but Ginnie would get an enormous kick out of meeting Sally Ross, and so would your buddy here. Since you're her best friend and a big wheel at the company she records for—got the message?

I promise not to embarrass you in front of her. I won't even mention those great old days in Camp Kawanaloonah. So, what do you say? Is it a date?

Phil

March 1st, 1976

Dear Phil,

Bad timing. Much as Sally would love to meet you, and I'd love to spend some time recalling those grand old days of yore, no can do. I've simply got to get her away for a few days to rest up before rehearsals of *So I Bit Him* start. That's her new blockbuster, you know. I've read the script and it's sensational! We plan to leave tomorrow night so, unfortunately, we'll be gone! Luck is no lady tonight!

But Sally insisted I pass along her latest photograph. Hope you have a good time in the Big Apple.

Your friend,
Douglas Breen

March 1st, 1976

Dear Sally,

Something really awful happened the other morning!

I was late for work and had to dash. Well, to make an endless story short, I forgot to unplug my toaster, which is the old-fashioned kind, and I had a small fire. Luckily only a few odds and ends were ruined, but alas and alack, your photograph was among them!

I know how expensive those "glossies" are, but I'd give my eye-teeth for a replacement. Is there any chance? I'd gladly reimburse you for the cost.

> Your greatest fan,
> Douglas Breen
> 780 West 71st Street
> New York City

CONTINENTAL CS STUDIOS

Mar. 2, 1976

Dear Sal:

Knock it off. You're as gorgeous as you ever were, and you know it. No joke, baby. Like the man says, you're not getting older. Just better.

As for me, I'm in the doghouse at the moment. We had Bob and Lola Redford to dinner last night and Heidi was a little overawed by them. Maybe that's why she didn't say a word for a solid hour. Not one syllable.

When they left I mentioned it to her but it must have come out a recrimination because pretty soon she was off upstairs doing some big-time sulking. I was never much good in the tact department, was I? But you wouldn't have sulked. Remember the night we had Lord and Lady Savile to dinner and you made her laugh so hard she got the hiccups and we had to put a bag over her head?

505

Well, you go apologize to Belle and I'll go apologize to Heidi and everybody'll be friends again. And stop feeling sorry for yourself. You've got everything a woman could want, including all my love.

Jake

3/5

Dear Mr. Breen,

Miss Ross wanted me to tell you how sorry she was about your fire. Luckily nothing more important than her picture burned up. Enclosed find another. Any member of Miss Ross's fan club is entitled to seconds.

Belle Goldman
Secretary to Miss Ross

SALLY ROSS

Saturday the 6th.

Dear Jake,

Nice try. You always were the best liar in L.A., and that's no mean accomplishment. But your letter could have been written by Disney for all the truth there was in it. Facts are facts, darling, and fifty is fifty.

Jake, what you wrote about that first little cloud over your honeymoon cottage has started me thinking about our own honeymoon. You're absolutely right. I wouldn't have sulked. I would have sent you to the hospital with a concussion. So count your blessings.

No woman talks in front of Robert Redford. Not if she has one drop of estrogen in her body.

Love from Lady Methuselah.

Sal

Dear Ms. Goldman,

I couldn't possibly allow your very snide letter to go unanswered. You may feel that because you have the good fortune to be Sally Ross's secretary, that allows you to be offhand with people, but it certainly does not.

For your information, I am not a member of anyone's "fan club." Not even someone as stellar as Sally. I am not one of those silly "little" people, as you so smugly insinuated.

Moreover, your reference to Sally's picture as unimportant is, I think, a breach of loyalty. Anyone as wonderful as Sally is entitled to only the purest devotion from her employees. Or would it be fair turnabout to say "servants"?

> Douglas Breen
> 780 West 71st Street
> New York City

3/10

Dear Mr. Breen,

Are you for real? Listen, I hear Ethel Merman loves to send out pictures. Bother her for a while and give us a rest.

> Belle Goldman

March 13th, 1976

Dear Sally,

The last thing I would want to do is trouble you. But the enclosed letter I received from your secretary must not go unattended, for your sake. What, I fear, is this person doing to your reputation? I'm quite sure you know nothing about it. The fact is this: I merely requested a picture of you as I have done many times in the past. Suddenly, to be faced with this kind of vituperation, this unnecessary rudeness, is most alarming.

The Fan

I fear your secretary needs a sharp talking to and a firm reprimand. Doesn't she know that the relationship between a star, such as yourself, and a true fan, such as myself, is sacrosanct?

Again, I deeply regret involving you and would not have done so were there any other way.

> Your greatest fan,
> Douglas Breen
> 780 West 71st Street
> New York City

Sal:

You split the seam in the seat of your black pants suit. Again. If you're looking for your snack tonight, try the vegetable crisper. I'm taking all the Sara Lee home with me. We're beginning to spend a little too much money on needles and thread around here. Incidentally, you're on "The Late Show" tonight. The one where you and Peter Lawford out-cute each other. Oh, I took your advice and I didn't answer the creep. Only one thing. What does sacrosanct mean? See you in the morning.

Also, try not to leave your shoes right in front of the front door, huh? Some of us who don't focus so well at nine in the morning could live without an obstacle course.

> Belle

SALLY ROSS

Belle,

Got in at dawn's early, so if you fall over my shoes please land quietly. First rehearsal at twelve. Get me up by ten thirty even if you have to set fire to the bed. I'll need at least an hour to pull myself together for my grand entrance.

Ha ha on you. You forgot the Nestle's chocolate bits in the pantry.

> Fatso

March 20th, 1976

Dear Sally,

Just a note to inquire as to whether you had that "little talk" with your secretary yet. Sally, I know what a loving person you are, but sometimes it is a mistake to be too soft with subordinates. An example in question. At the record shop where I work (temporarily, I assure you, for I do have my "plans") there is a young girl recently hired. Sally, believe me when I tell you she is not the brightest person in the world. It adds painfully to my already busy day to have to explain things to her endlessly. Yesterday, she asked our manager (an ogre) if she might extend her lunch hour to have her hair done. Well, she arrived back at the shop after three! I was harassed beyond belief, having to do not only my own work, but hers as well! And when I brought this sad state of affairs to her attention, she was rude into the bargain!

You see what a mistake it is to be too human when dealing with people whose only interest is themselves. Have that talk with your secretary. You owe it to yourself.

Sally, I'd dearly love to pick up a bit of "insider's knowledge." From my collection of *Photoplay* magazines, I understand that you and Peter Lawford were once an "item." Is it true or mere studio hogwash?

Please let me know. Love from

> Your greatest fan,
> Douglas Breen
> 780 West 71st Street
> New York City

· BELLE · GOLDMAN ·

Dear Sal,

Good work, you found me. But I am hiding in the back of the cupboard because I have four billion calories in me and I am for the guests Friday night, not for you. Belle said if you eat me, the

509

next part you will be offered is the lead in the life story of the Goodyear blimp.

She says you should eat my friend, the carrot. It's in the vegetable crisper. She also said she will break both your thumbs if I'm not here in the morning.

Sara Lee

P.S. How do you like the stationery? I figured if you could use the good stuff to leave me notes, I could do the same.

SALLY ROSS

Dear Belle,

Welcome to the refrigerator. I am a grapefruit. You may eat me. I am also the exact shape of your rear end, so watch who you leave notes to. In case you haven't passed a mirror recently, you ain't no Audrey Hepburn yourself.

Madame Arbuckle

March 22nd, 1976

Dear Sally,

Well, just time for a few lines before I catch my bus to the record "shoppe."

Life is so tedious at the moment.

That girl at the shop continues to be a thorn in my side. Yesterday she told the manager I was looking up her skirt when she climbed up to get records from the top shelf. I promise you, it's simply not true! It's a case of what she'd like me to do, if you ask me.

I know she finds me attractive. No, Sally, I'm not being self-congratulatory. I have been told all my life that I'm unusually good-looking. I have bright blue eyes, a clear complexion, and a good body. She, on the other hand, has none of these attributes! So she can just forget any smarmy ideas she may have conjured up concerning her and me.

Must run now. Will write tomorrow and that's a promise!

Love,
Douglas
780 West 71st Street
New York City

P.S. I'm awaiting the "scoop" about you and Peter Lawford!

• B E L L E • G O L D M A N •

3/25

Dear Bess,

How do you like the stationery? A gift from Sal. You know how much it cost? A buck a letter. Honest, Sis, I saw the bill.

Thanks for the pictures of the kids. Greg's getting to be quite a guy. Tell him if he smokes pot again his old aunt'll come out there and pin his ears back.

You want to read something nutty? I'm enclosing a letter from one of Sal's fans, the one I wrote you about. Now he's telling her how good-looking he is. Maybe we ought to ask him for a picture. Well, it takes all kinds.

Love to your gang,
Belle

CONTINENTAL CS STUDIOS

Mar. 25, 1976

Dear Sal:

I've got a few minutes between conferences to write to my favorite ex. Everything is fine at home these days. Heidi's taking a class in gourmet cookery, so call your broker to buy Alka-Seltzer.

I've been trying to peddle Franklin the idea of doing a remake of *Camille,* but every time I mention it he just sits there and nods at me like I'm out of my mind. Maybe he's right.

Listen, get the show on fast and we'll buy the film rights. Then you come out here and do the movie and we'll have ourselves a time. I could use one about now. Between Franklin's nodding and Heidi's cooking, my ulcer's back in town.

You're young, you're beautiful, you're terrific. But, then, what do I know? I'm the idiot who wants to do *Camille.*

> Love,
> Jake

March 26th, 1976

Dear Sally,

Forgive me for not writing but the last few days have been murder!

Well, I finally had it out with the new girl at the shop. The straw that broke the proverbial camel's back came the other day when I asked her to get down an album for a customer and she told me to get it myself! What nerve. I immediately stormed up to our manager and laid the whole mess in his lap. Now, here's the shocking part. He told me to leave her alone! That's right, he completely took her side, although I've been working at the shop for six months and she's brand-new!

Sally, I don't like to conjecture but does it sound like he and she are more than employer-employee, if you know what I mean? It would certainly explain a lot of things.

How wondrous to be a star and above the niggling pettiness of shopgirls. Though, of course, your life is not without problems. Speaking of which, what did your secretary say when you informed her of the proper behavior toward your correspondents? I hope she was properly contrite, but these menials do have their way of turning everything around so they end up blameless, don't they?

Now, you really must take time to drop me a line. I'm still dying to know about you and Peter Lawford. You can tell me, Sally. I wouldn't betray a confidence from you for all the "tea in China." After all, I do love you, you know.

As always,
Douglas
780 West 71st Street
New York City

SALLY ROSS

Monday the 29th

Darling Jake,

It's a marvelous idea and if Franklin doesn't see it he's out of his mind. Don't you dare say another self-effacing word about yourself to me. I was there when you pulled Paramount out of the pits, remember?

Are you or are you not drinking milk before meals like you're supposed to, dummy?

But enough about you. On to my favorite topic, me. Today we started blocking out "My Time," a kind of "Don't Rain on My Parade" number. In it, I'm transformed from a dowdy housefrau into a liberated creature complete with feather boa. Lord, Jake, why do costume designers always want to bury me in feathers? Do I look like a chicken?

So, what has that midget Riggs (or as we kids call him, Tinker Bell) got up his size-two sleeve for the number? (I finally convinced him that cartwheels and splits are inappropriate for a hundred-and-two-year-old woman.) I spin. That's right, he wants me to come on spinning and continue spinning all the way downstage. I ask you, Jake, would you want to see some old bag in feathers spin around like a demented parrot?

I'm glad all is beautiful between you and Snow White again. Just be nice, Jake, and don't let your bossy side take over. It ain't your best side, you know.

Your Gal Sal

March 29th, 1976

Dear Sally,

What an incorrigible correspondent you are!

Just kidding, Sally. You are, as always, the dearest, sweetest, most heavenly creature in the world. But Sally, ages have gone by since I asked about you and Peter Lawford, and still no reply! I do need word from you in my hour of travail. Things at the shop are worse than ever. That girl should be slapped silly. She has taken to saying cruel and untrue things about me behind my back!

All I can say is, she'd better watch her tongue because life has a way of bringing its own comeuppances to those who have nothing better to do than slander their betters.

But enough of me. I read in the *Post* that *So I Bit Him* looks like a hit. Of course it will be. Doesn't it have the greatest, the most resplendent star in the world in it? Despite the fact that she is far from a dutiful correspondent (still kidding). But I would love to hear from you. Take a moment out. For Me.

> The one who
> adores you,
> Douglas
> 780 West 71st Street
> New York City

March 30th, 1976

Dear Sally,

Still no letter from you!

Things at the shop are far from satisfactory. If you only knew how much a line from you would mean to me. Soon, dear Sally. Things are not well.

> Love,
> Douglas
> 780 West 71st Street
> New York City

4/4

Dear Mr. Breen,

I'm sorry but Miss Ross's schedule at the moment does not permit her to answer fan mail in person.

Belle Goldman

April 7th, 1976

Dear Sally,

Again the intervention of your secretary!

Clearly your little talk with her did no good and a threat of dismissal would be more appropriate.

She flouts me with snide references to fan clubs and fan letters. Yes, I am certainly your greatest fan, but I am much more than that. I am a friend. Someone you can turn to in times of distress. Someone who will always be there for you, in any way you want me.

I mean that, Sally. I can be the closest friend you ever had. Your confidant. And yes, if you so desired, even your lover. It has taken me a long time to say this but it is true. And believe me, I can make you very, very happy. Both in body and in mind.

Explain to that woman who works for you that she is not to treat me in such an offhand way. Who knows, someday I might be her employer as well!

More love than
I can say,
Douglas
780 West 71st Street
New York City

• BELLE • GOLDMAN •

4/10

Dear Mr. Breen,

All right, enough's enough. I haven't bothered Miss Ross with your latest letters, but now you're getting out of hand. The postal authorities frown on your kind of offer. So just suppose you quit writing.

Belle Goldman

April 12th, 1976

Dear Sally,

Now I understand all too clearly why I haven't heard from you. Your secretary as much as admitted that she's been destroying my letters to you!

Sally, it is clear that she wants no one to get close to you, lest her position be endangered. But *why?* Have you checked your jewelry lately? Perhaps a visit to your bank might not be altogether unrevealing. I know the thought of embezzlement is distasteful, but clearly the woman is not to be trusted.

I worry for you, my darling. When I think of you, at the mercy of that conniving woman, I shudder! We must turn our minds to what can be done to protect you from her.

I understand that you might be frightened to dismiss her, fearing retaliation. If I were with you, could you find the courage? No one will hurt you while I'm near, you know.

I dare not send this letter to your home, in case SHE gets her hands on it. Instead, I will send it to the theater. I will not sign my last name nor my address. You know where you can reach me—the same address you sent your photograph to.

We must talk, Sally. We can devise a plan of action if we work together. *Love conquers all.*

Douglas

CONTINENTAL CS STUDIOS

April 12, 1976

Dear Sal:

I took a poll at the commissary over lunch. Jack Slattery and Dustin Hoffman voted yes, they'd love to see you spinning around in feathers. Sidney Lumet and Chuck Wilton said they'd rather see you spinning without the feathers. And Joan Blondell said she'd just love to see you. So be a good girl and do what you're told.

Love,
Jake

LILYAN PETERS

April 12

Dear Sal—

Had dinner tonight with Carol and Joe and Harvey Korman after the taping of their show, and the talk came round to you. Everyone wished you were there to keep us laughing. Carol's cut her hair again, Joe looks gorgeous all gray, and Harvey flirted with me, bless his heart. The grapevine is saying nasty things about your new show, but if anybody can turn dross into gold, you can. Just remember all the tricks you stole from me.

Joe asked if I'd like to do a guest shot on their show, but I don't know. I can't do comedy, my singing and dancing are abysmal, so what would I do? Just stand there and let everyone marvel that I don't look worse than I do? I think I'll pass.

Well, dear, good luck with the show and drop me a line when you get a chance.

Love,
Lil

SALLY ROSS

Wednesday the 14th.

Dear Lil,

Don't be a dope—do the show. Joe won't let you look bad. You've still got the old studio aura and that's what they'll tune in to see. Just wear a lot of sequins and stick out your front.

Whaddya mean tricks I stole from you? May I remind you it was yours truly who got you through that musical number in *Stepping Out?* There's no gratitude in this world.

Do the guest spot. Give Carol and Joe my love and keep a little for yourself.

Sal

April 14th, 1976

Dear Sally,

Things are worse than I feared!

I decided not to mail the letter, but to bring it to the theater personally on my lunch hour and, in that way, to make absolutely sure it did not go astray.

I went to the stage entrance and let myself in. A wondrous digression! Standing there in the darkened backstage area, I heard that dulcet, thrilling voice I've come to know and love. Yours! Sally, you cannot know how much it meant to me to realize we were but a few feet apart. It was our first shared moment—our first rendezvous, if you will. I was thrilled.

Then it happened.

A woman, middle-aged, gray of hair, in a blue-and-white checked suit of nondescript style, came in the stage door and curtly brushed by me. She went up to a man seated at a desk and he addressed her as *Belle!*

Yes, it was her. *That* woman! And then it happened, Sally. He

handed to her mail intended for your eyes alone! Do you understand the full implications of that? Whatever her game, whatever
her plan of action against you, she is not in it alone! There are
others assisting and abetting her!

I left the theater quickly, shaken to the core. Sally, my dear, I
dare not send my letters to you, lest they find out the extent of
our knowledge of their nefarious activities. No place is safe—
neither the theater nor your residence.

But Sally, I will continue to write. Somehow you must know
that my thoughts "wend your way," although for the moment I
must hold these letters in trust for you. Soon enough, my Sally, I
will find a way to get them to you. And to defend you against
those who would do you harm.

I love you. Trust me. *I will be near.*

Douglas

SALLY ROSS

Sunday the 18th.

Angel Jake,

Well, Nirvana is here. A day off. And what better way to spend
it than writing to you.

Also, darling, I need advice. I considered Dear Abby, but then I
remembered there you are, sitting behind your desk at Continental
with nothing better to do than listen to the problems of your own
Auntie Mame, so here goes. I'll make a scenario of it, so you'll feel
at home. Fade in. Gorgeous star, early forties (Listen, it's my
scenario!), sneaks out of rehearsals and across the street to a little
coffee shop because five more minutes with our infant composer
and I really would look my age.

Close-up of radiant but tired actress sitting in the coffee shop
over a little bouillon. Camera pans from actress to back booth.
Close-up of absolutely beautiful young man, giving actress the
sweetest smile you ever saw. Oh, Jake, talk about your blue eyes.
Talk about your nonexistent waistline. Talk about your two dots

519

for a nose! Medium shot. Breathtaking young man and stunning slightly older woman are sitting at the same table, chatting amiably. Young man is so interested in, so sympathetic with stunning ever-so-slightly older woman it could break your heart.

Now, unfortunately, we cut to stunning actress galloping across the street, with suitable regality, back to Mr. Mozart. But, darling, the plot thickens. Fade in on same coffee shop, next day, after rehearsal. Ravishing barely forty-year-old actress, costume designer and a few gypsies have decided to go to Joe Allen's and say nasty things about Riggs. As we pass the coffee shop, who should be there, two little dots pressed up against the glass, but the breathtaking young man! He waves and smiles, I go inside to ask him if he'd like to join us. He says—HE'D RATHER HAVE ME TO HIMSELF! Thirty-six-year-old actress goes into swoon and sends the others off alone.

Vaseline on the camera lens for the next scene—it's so romantic. We sit over coffee and I pour out my heart to him. I complain about Riggs's fetish for gymnastics, I complain about Hollywood, I complain about people who complain, everything. And all the while those gorgeous blue eyes stare and sympathize and practically eat me up. Finally I get to feeling so young I pass puberty going the wrong way.

What's happening to me, Jake? I was never the kind to have entanglements with young men, was I? But there's something so sweetly strange about him. I know nothing about him, really. (Who has a chance to talk with me around?) But he smiles as if he has a secret—a beautiful secret.

Oh, Jake, has it really come to this? Getting crushes on young men in coffee shops? I don't care. I've felt so rotten lately, so used up, and now, for the last few days at least, I've felt so good. So hopeful. Is that wrong?

Of course Belle thinks the whole thing is ludicrous, but Belle can afford to be normal. She lost her husband the fair way, to disease. I lost mine to show business. (Not your career, darling. Mine. I know what a fool I was.)

So, does the screen goddess stand a chance with the blue-eyed young prince? How does it work with you and Bopeep? But of course, older men are allowed to fall in love with younger women.

I told him I'd see him there tomorrow.

Should I? Oh please say yes, Jake. Say whatever you need to get by is aces with me. And be just a little jealous, darling, in a vestigial way, for my sake.

Love,
Y.G.S.

April 18th, 1976

Dear Sally,

I have begun.

Soon, my darling, all will be revealed to you and you will know that you are not alone and at the mercy of foes. You have me, Sally, and all is in *capable* hands!

If I could but tell you how capable these loving hands are, and to what extent they have gone in the past to protect those I love, and to what extent they would go in the future to protect you! I am not a person who is easily manipulated, as those who have tried it have learned. An example in point:

A certain tradesman who shall remain nameless once accused me of petty filchery in his place of business. Sally, I am no thief. It was clearly a case of the *pot* calling the *kettle* black, as this nameless person was notorious for selling inferior merchandise at exorbitant prices! This vendor approached my parents with his vile lies and they were unmoved by all my protestations of innocence. Some people are fortunate enough to have trusting and loving parents. Alas, such was not the case for me. My father, a taciturn and thoughtless man, paid off the tradesman and the entire "situation" was soon forgotten by everyone. Except me.

Two months later, as fate would have it, the man's shop was afflicted by fire and much of his overpriced merchandise damaged beyond salvage. I hope you understand my meaning, Sally. If only I could send you this letter, how it would help you in your hour of need!

But on to "lighter" news. I went in search of a proper box to house these epistles, to keep them safe. (Think how tragic it might have been were the letters of the Brownings lost to the world!) I found what I was looking for in, of all places, The Godiva Chocolate Shoppe! It's in dark green velvet with leaves and flowers adorning the top, and it houses two pounds of chocolates. Would that I could save these morsels for you, but by the time it is safe to give them to you, who knows what state they might be in? So last night I sat before my television set emptying the box. There goes my diet!

Meanwhile, on the home front, all goes badly. Friday, the trollop and I had a scene right in front of several customers. The profanities that issued forth from her wretched mouth! Something must be done on that subject, too. But you must not worry about my problems. Know only that you are safe and I am with you. Closer than you think.

Douglas

Breen *&* 10 GREENWICH DRIVE

April 20.

Dear Douglas,

Last night Mr. Rafferty called your father to discuss your behavior at the store. Douglas, when your father asked Mr. Rafferty to give you that job, it was as a personal favor. You gave us your word that you would *try* this time. Yet Mr. Rafferty told your father he would have to let you go if there was one more outburst of any kind. It hurt me deeply to hear what you called that young woman at the store. That kind of language was never permitted in our home.

Douglas, you are not taking your future seriously. You're twenty-five now and should be thinking about a career and marriage. Your father and I do not want to be disappointed in you. Please make sure we're not.

Mother

4/20

Dear Bess,

Glad to hear Lennie's sciatica is better. Went to Sid's grave Sunday. I don't know what I'm paying for—they're not keeping it up the way they ought to. It's hard to believe it's been eleven years now since Sid died. It seems like yesterday.

Feeling funny lately—listless and nervous. My doctor says there's nothing wrong with me but I don't know. I'm cranky as hell and my imagination is working overtime. The other night I thought someone was following me. Maybe that would be the best thing that could happen to me. It sure worked for Sal. She's still seeing that kid, you know. I finally got a glimpse of him at the theater where he was waiting for her. I gotta admit if I was twenty years younger I could go for him myself.

All right, enough already. I've got to get my subway home now. Love to your gang,

Belle

CONTINENTAL CS STUDIOS

Apr. 20, 1976

Dear Sal:

Of course see him. If he makes you happy, I don't care if he's fourteen years old and wears Clearasil. For once in your life, Sal, do what feels good and not what looks good.

What do you mean, a *little* jealous? I'm a lot jealous. Nobody could completely stop loving you, don't you know that? That's why you're a star, not because of your singing.

Franklin just buzzed. Time for another round.

Love,
Jake

SALLY ROSS

Thursday the 22nd.

Dear Jake,

And precisely what is wrong with my singing?

Thank you, darling, for your letter and your endless understanding. You always did give me more than I had any right to.

Now, to business. His name is David. He says he's twenty-nine, but I think he's stretching it, and he's there every night after rehearsals waiting to walk me home. (Yes, he carries my script.) God, Jake, it's so flattering and young and marvelous. Yes, and foolish, I know. But then if I was sensible I'd still be Sally Flaherty with the rhinoid nose from God-forbid Yonkers. What am I talking about? Even in the crib, I recall looking between the slats and recoiling at the lace curtains on the windows. By the time I was five I had saved half the money for my nose job.

And I'll tell you something. If I'm going crazy, I like it. It's a lot more fun than being very serious about which slipcover material to choose.

Love to Heidi. See? I called her Heidi.

Y.G.S.

Breen *&* 10 GREENWICH DRIVE

April 22.

Dear Douglas,

Just two days ago I wrote asking you to straighten yourself out and to take your responsibilities seriously. Obviously my advice went unattended. Mr. Rafferty just called to tell us he had been forced to let you go.

Douglas, I don't know what to say to you. I had hoped that after all the troubles you've caused us, you would finally be ready to make us proud of you. I see that's not the way it's going to be.

Your father is furious with you, and I am more disappointed than I can say.

Your father insists that he will not help you out this time. You must live within your means whether that be unemployment or a part-time job until you learn how to get along with people.

Douglas, I have only one more thought on the subject. Do you remember the psychiatrist we sent you to after that trouble in college? Do you feel it would help to see someone now? Clearly something must be done to break this pattern of yours.

Mother

April 22nd, 1976

Dear Sally,

Break out the champagne! Call the columnists! I am a free man again! Yes, Sally, I finally bid a not-so-fond "adieu" to the record shop, its manager and his little strumpet!!! It was just too much. Her insults, his lax attitude, the whole "kit and kaboodle." And so I simply quit. On the spot.

The cause of this, my final scene, is as follows: After lunch I returned to the shop to find that a shipment of new albums was in the process of being set out in the bins. Knowing full well that our "friend," the girl we love to hate, lacked the necessary "gray matter" to place the albums where they belonged, I hurried to check. Of course, I was right. Jacques Brel under pop males, Simon and Garfunkel re-releases under new groups, and on and on. It was a shambles! Naturally I brought this sad state of affairs to our manager's attention. Quietly. Discreetly. But who had tiptoed up behind me and was listening, vulturelike, to my protestations? None other than the perpetrator. And that despicable urchin actually accused me of having moved the albums around in the bins, just to make her look bad!

CAN YOU BELIEVE IT?!

It was then that our manager made his mistake. Plainly, and in full view of dozens of witnesses, he implied that he, too, suspected me of switching the albums! I was livid! Outraged! I handed in my resignation, effective *immediately!* Sally, I have worked my fingers to the bone for that shop—and to be paid back in such a high-handed way! Well, they'll have to manage without you-know-who from now on. I've had it!

My darling, thoughtlessly, I have wandered on about my *own* problems. Please forgive me, but if you only knew what has been done already on your behalf! Suffice it to know that I am nearer than you think, and soon, very soon, my plan will go into effect!!!

Then, my own dazzling glamorous star, we will be free to express our love, both spiritually and *physically*.

Douglas

SALLY ROSS

Sunday the 25th.

Dear Jake,

The last two days have been—how shall I put it?—Armageddon. But this is not about to be one of my usual letters of Complaint. I shall merely throw my head back and laugh at it all. And that's how they'll find me, laughing, when they come to cart me off to that little sanatarium in the East Sixties where all the best psychotics go.

My darling Belle has taken the most infuriating dislike to David and uses every excuse to drop little hints that his mother is calling. I had no idea she could be so mean. Years with me, no doubt. But it's so unreasonable. I know he hasn't taken to her, but he's just a boy. If only Belle would put herself out a little instead of the endless snide remarks. She says he's rude to her but when I ask how, Belle says it's not what he says it's the way he says it. Now, I ask you, is that an answer? Why is she, of all people, adding to my problems? He needs to be built up, not put down.

Oh, Jake, why is life never simple? Why can't prince charmings come in the right size and shape and age? And why did we ever divorce? Whatever I said, I take it back. Your marriage to Heidi is revoked. You are to get on the next plane and get back here. Tomorrow morning, when I wake up, I'll see your face on the pillow next to mine, your socks will be on the floor like always, and I'll never be old or lonely again.

Enough. I'll have myself in tears soon, and everybody knows armored tanks don't cry. I do love you, though a lot of good it does me. Be especially nice to my replacement, will you? After all, it serves me right. I never would sign a run-of-the-play contract.

Y.G.S.

• BELLE • GOLDMAN •

4/27

Dear Bess,

Got the scarf—it's a beauty. You got the talent in the family, all right. Thanks a million for knitting it.

Things around here have been moving at a swift pace. Straight down. I wrote you about Sal's little friend? What a schlemiel he is! The other morning he comes into the kitchen when I'm making Sal coffee and he starts in. A touch of cinnamon in her coffee, like in Paris. Just a suggestion, mind you. Or what about anisette! For crying out loud, I'm trying to get the damn water to boil, and Donnie Osmond is giving with the cook's tour! Also, he goes through her papers. I caught him. He said it was all so interesting he couldn't resist. Nasty little snoop. Bess, I hope I never get to the point where all I want is a man, any man. Thank God for Sid. Once you've had a winner, you're not interested in also-rans.

Speaking of creeps, something weird happened the other night. I got followed home from the subway. It was dark and I couldn't see him, but he stayed behind me for a couple of blocks. Boy, the things this city is coming to. I swear if Sid hadn't bought the house right after we were married, I'd sell it and move to Jersey like everybody else. But I've got my memories here.

Well, time to hit the subway. Love to your gang,

Belle

ST. BERNADETTE'S HOSPITAL
678 East 198th St., Bronx, N.Y. 10062

April 27

Dear Chuck,

Here I sit in the middle of the emergency room remembering your advice to do my residency at some nice suburban country club hospital instead of this ghetto sideshow. All I can say is cripes, were you right. Let's hope it'll all pay off and some day I'll join you in private practice and the sixty percent bracket. I just took care of a knifing that practically made me puke. Some guy attacked a woman on the subway and really did a job on her. He carved her face up so bad half of her jawbone was exposed.

Okay, I'm going to try for a nap now. See ya.

Jeff

SALLY ROSS

Weds. the 28

Dear Jake,

I tried and tried to call you. The most horrible thing has happened. Belle was attacked and nearly killed last night. She was on her way home to that jungle she lives in, when she was mugged on the subway platform. I've tried to get her to move in with me but no, she had to live in that house of hers. Now she's in the hospital with Lord knows what injuries and she still isn't conscious. Her doctor wouldn't tell me a thing. It seems you have to be next of kin to get any information in these stinking hospitals. All he said was that she's sedated. But thank God, she'll be all right. He swore to me she would.

Why would anyone do it? What could she have had on her? A few dollars? Whatever he got, I hope he spends it on an overdose.

528

Jake, please call me immediately, whatever the time here or there. With Belle gone, there's no one else to turn to. I don't even know where David is. I waited for him after rehearsal but he never showed up. It's just as well. I'm in such a state, you're the only person I could talk to.

Sal

SALLY ROSS

Thursday the 29th.

Dear Jake,

Where are you, anyway? No one can reach you. Leave a number, for heaven's sake, don't just run off.

They still won't let me see Belle. I called Paul Gross. He's a trustee at Mt. Sinai and he got on the phone and found out what happened. She was attacked with a knife and cut up pretty badly. Her doctor swears she will be all right. I've spent the last day and a half in the hospital, just sitting, waiting for some word. Thank heaven for David. The poor thing doesn't know what to say to ease things for me, but at least he's here now.

This afternoon, when her doctor assured me for the millionth time I wouldn't be allowed to see her, I went back to rehearsal. What a business. That old saw about smiling when you're sad left out the real point—that it kills you to do it. Sometimes I think my real feelings are buried under so many years of being tough and laughing on the outside that I'll never get back to them. I swear to you, Jake, I sat there in that hospital, a few yards away from my best friend, who's lying there mugged, and when people started staring at me, it actually occurred to me to wonder if my makeup was on! What kind of monster could do that?

I feel so guilty. I've been so rotten to Belle lately and now I can't even get in to see her and tell her I love her and I'm sorry.

I'm sorry. I'm just going a little crazy. Please call.

Sal

Jo Colton

Dear Sal,

Sylvan and I are so worried about you, after our phone conversation last night. Sal, there isn't anything you can do there. Wouldn't it be better to come out to the island and stay with us for a few days? I don't like the idea of your being alone now.

Jo

Western Union   Telegram

04/29/76 1388

```
MS SALLY ROSS
941 FIFTH AVENUE
NEW YORK NY

ARRIVING IN NEW YORK SATURDAY AFTERNOON AND
WILL GO DIRECTLY TO HOSPITAL. THANK YOU BUT
PLAN TO STAY AT BELLE'S HOUSE. THANK YOU FOR
EVERYTHING. BESS ASHER
```

April 30th, 1976

Manager, Water's Edge Inn
Sag Harbor

Dear Sir:

I should like to reserve your finest suite from the evening of May the twenty-ninth through May the thirty-first, 1976.

We require your best accommodations—a separate sitting room, dressing room and, of course, a private and luxurious bath.

We will require on arrival a tray of canapés and a bottle of champagne, properly chilled. Imported, please.

I enclose my check for one hundred dollars as a deposit.

Please see to it that everything is as it should be. You see, my guest for the weekend is none other than the international star, Sally Ross, and wherever Sally and I choose to vacation soon gets the close scrutiny of the very best class of persons.

Sincerely yours,
Douglas Breen
780 West 71st Street
New York City

April 30th, 1976

ARNO Florist
Sag Harbor

Dear Sir:
I shall be a guest at the Water's Edge Inn commencing the twenty-ninth of May, 1976.

My companion and I will be arriving approximately at midnight. I would like delivered in advance of that hour several bouquets of your finest floral creations.

Red roses, I think. Long stemmed. A dozen.

Violets. Several small and artful bunches, in crystal vases.

A single spray of orchids, placed on the bed table. Pink, or perhaps white. I leave this up to your expertise.

I enclose thirty-five dollars by check as deposit for above.

Sincerely yours,
Douglas Breen
780 West 71st Street
New York City

April 30th, 1976

Dear Sally,
Now you know. And any thoughts you may have had about my sincerity must be gone, washed away by my "tidal wave of love."

My darling. My star. My mate.

It was all so simple! Those purveyors of popular entertainments would have one believe that a violent act is ugly and brutal. Such is simply not the case! It is beautiful—almost balletic—and it has a sensuousness of its own, not unlike the act of love. I want to share it all with you.

I arrived at your address at approximately four in the afternoon. And a sumptuous afternoon it was! The sunshine dappled the pavements as it "fluttered" through the trees in Central Park. Across the street, your apartment house, majestic and old-world, stood like an old friend welcoming me.

I sat on a bench in front of the park and waited, fondling the knife in my pocket, knowing that it was the instrument by which I was to prove my love, my adoration of you.

As I sat there, an old man made his way up the avenue, pushing one of those carts that sell hot dogs. Several children ran up to him, and I wondered whether someday it would be our children, dashing to satisfy their cravings. Of course I understand that it would be extremely difficult for you to juxtapose motherhood and your career, and I leave the choice completely up to you. I would, of course, be delighted at the prospect of fathering another "little Sally" but never at the risk of interfering with your career. We must be sensible, Sally. You owe your public a great deal. For surely they have "put you where you are," and they do love you. Love of that sort brings its own responsibilities, and we must not be selfish. For we are not ordinary people, free to live our lives with no thought to others. We are, whether it be fortunate or ill, in the "limelight."

But I digress.

It was about five o'clock when that woman rounded the corner and went into your building, laden with packages. I recall wondering whether some of those packages were intended for herself rather than you, bought with what was no doubt stolen money or forged charge plates. As she stopped to speak to the doorman, there was something about the way they leaned into each other, something clandestine. I made a mental note to study him at another time. We cannot be too careful.

Several minutes after six, she came out and turned east at the corner. I followed at a safe distance. On Lexington Avenue she went into the subway. I did likewise. And when the train came, I entered the same car at its opposite end. Heaven was on our side, Sally, for the car was filled, making it easier for me to view the woman without her noticing.

But oh, the people! The stench of those poor pitiable denizens of this world, scurrying home to their little cells. Thank the Lord above, Sally, you have never known this kind of life. I thank God that I am soon to be rid of it forever. At that moment, I truly felt something akin to the pity that certain religious figures are supposed to have felt for the masses. I wished them well. I really did. We have so much and they so little.

By now the train was hurtling into the Bronx. That woman sat dozing, her head occasionally nodding. For a moment I almost felt sorry for her, too. But then I remembered the peril she placed you in and all sorrow vanished.

The train pulled out of the Crotona Park station and the woman shook off her drowsiness and got up.

At the next station, she got out.

As did I.

With the knife in my jacket pocket, my hand tight around it, I followed. Heaven was still on our side, Sally. The woman chose to exit by a staircase at the far end of the platform. Alone. She pushed through a revolving metal gate into a small vestibule. I pushed through behind her.

I called her name and as she turned, my knife sliced through the air and into her face. I do not know how many times I struck her. I only know I viewed this happening as if through a dreamlike mist. A ballet of right against wrong. Surely the valiant warriors of the Crusades knew this exhilaration!

When it was over, the calm and peace that follow an act of love descended on me. I fear nothing now. I shall mail this to your home. If I do not hear from you, I will know that my instincts about your doorman are correct and I shall know what to do.

Douglas

SALLY ROSS

Saturday the 1st.

Dear Jake,

Thank you, darling, for sitting up half the night with me on the phone. You're always there for me when I need you. I hope Heidi understood. (Whyever did you take her on a *camping* trip? Now you're hiking up and down mountains?)

I saw Belle this afternoon. Jake, half her face is wrapped in bandages and she's so pale! When I first saw her, I almost cried. But then, as I sat there, she started to smile. She even called me names when I did cry. There never was anyone like her.

Or you. What have I ever done to deserve both of you?

All my love,
Sal

May 1st, 1976

Dearest Sally,

I have had a dream, and you must know who it was about. You!

In it, I came across you sunbathing on a stretch of white and deserted beach. You lay there, your face lifted to the blazing sun, those perfect and world-adored features beneath a coating of some protective balm, the scent of which assailed my nostrils. You wore a modest bathing suit of white and blue stripes and as I stood above you gazing down at your voluptuous womanhood, you opened your eyes and looked up at me.

You held your arms up to me, beckoning me closer, your moist lips parted for my kiss.

And I gave it to you, my dearest! There on those white sands, the waves at our feet, I left a trail of kisses on your goddess body. You told me that there had never been anyone but me and never could be. And I knew that all I had done and all I might do to hold and protect you was but the beginning. That here was the love that we have waited for, alone and harmed, in an alien world.

That is how it is for us, Sally. Belle Goldman was only the first to feel the wrath of your protector. Fair warning to anyone who dares stand between me and my adored Sally.

Douglas

CONTINENTAL **CS** STUDIOS

May 3, 1976

Dear Sal:

There's no one in the world I'd rather sit up half the night with than you. I just wish it could be for laughs and not because of poor Belle. Give her all my love, will you?

And stop wondering what you've done to deserve us. It's simple. You loved us.

Jake

SALLY ROSS

Monday the 3rd.

Dear Jake,

Either Belle will be entered in the *Guinness Book of Records* under recuperative powers or I'm getting used to seeing her in that hospital bed, because this morning she looked absolutely marvelous! She's even tougher than I am.

Did I write that her sister is here from St. Louis? She looks so much like Belle, and we carried on like we'd known each other for years. Even in that dreadful place, the three of us had a wonderful time. It was like a sorority pajama party.

David. Jake, I don't know about David. Sometimes I think he's a godsend and sometimes I think he's a third nostril. We left the hospital the other night and I was so tired I could have crawled into bed with Belle. What did he want to do? Go out to Joe's and have "a few laughs." I gave in, just for one drink. Stephen and Carol Schwartz were there, and we sat with them. Jake, they're about his age and yet they behaved like grown-ups, why couldn't he? He went on and on about Paris in the spring and the boring Tuileries and the incredibly tedious Petit Palais. It was two in the morning when I finally got him out of there. I know beggars can't be all that finicky, but I still wish he were you.

Must run now and take away the dry cleaning or I'll have nothing to wear. I see how much I need Belle. Everything is out of place, the mail is piling up (I only open envelopes from Continental) and the phone is driving me crazy. Tons of love and gratitude.

Y.G.S.

May 4th, 1976

Dear Sally,

Each morning I rush down to the mailbox, jumping the stairs two at a time in my excitement. But still no letter has come!

I did expect that after my "action of love" you would have written. I am not asking for thanks. True love is given freely. But I did expect some indication that you were pleased. I know we must be clever. Now there are police to contend with, as well as the others who were in league with your secretary. But surely you could find some means of posting a letter without being observed.

Sally, if you are holding off writing because of my last letter, I can only say I am sorry if it offended you. I believe that when two people are in love, as we are, their bodies become sacred tools for expressing that most divine of all things, the act of love. So please, do not be affronted at my directness. It was not for lack of respect, but for love of you that I wrote.

And please, my love, answer me quickly. I am beginning to fear another interloper. If such is the case, do not be afraid. I know how to deal with your enemies.

Douglas

536

SALLY ROSS

Wednesday the 5th.

Dear Jake,

So much news. Belle is practically her old self again, and she's absolutely furious at having to be in the hospital. She remembers very little of what happened. Just hearing someone call out, turning and being hit. It's a blessing. The police think that Belle might know more than she's saying, but is afraid to tell. They don't know our Belle. The last thing she was afraid of was a caterpillar that crawled onto her baby blanket. You should see her laugh now. She puckers out the side of her mouth and goes hoo-hoo so she won't move the stitches. Yesterday she threw a glass of water at me when I told her a joke.

Now, as to the rest of my so-called life. This afternoon Edgar assembled the company for an announcement. A week from Monday, ready or not, *So I Bit Him* starts previewing! We were stunned. I mean, we're not even sure how it ends yet!

Jake, in the second act of this little nuclear device, my husband leaves me, my son leaves me, even my best friend takes a walk, and how does our writer resolve it? I simply stand center stage, stick out my brave little chin and say, "They'll be back!" Then I go into a reprise of "My Turn," proving beyond a shadow of a doubt that I am one of the meanest shrews of this century!

Now on to my last topic of complaint. David has it in his pretty little head that I'm going to take him on a cruise or something. Poor darling needs to get away. I explained that I'm in rehearsals for a play that, heaven forbid, starts previews in a week and, moreover, I wouldn't leave Belle alone now. But he'll have none of it. I don't know what to do. I know this little fling won't amount to a row of beans, but I do care for him.

Well, I must get to this apartment. There's clothing, unopened mail and dishes all over the place. I love you. Don't go on any more camping trips and drink your milk.

Y.G.S.

ST. BERNADETTE'S HOSPITAL
678 East 198th St., Bronx, N.Y. 10062

5/5

Dear Bess,

Thanks a million for flying in. It helped a lot to have you here. And just think, we finally got together and you did all the talking. Isn't Sal something? I knew you two would hit it off. She's here all the time, kidding me, hollering at me, sticking up for the moron nurses and that shmendrick in white.

Meanwhile, I'm getting the star treatment, except for the food. I'd give my right arm for a hot pastrami on rye with mustard and my other arm to be able to eat it. Have one for me, will you, and tell Greg I'm sorry not to be able to take him to Sal's opening-night party. I'll take him to the closing night instead.

Love to your gang,

Belle

CONTINENTAL STUDIOS

May 7, 1976

Dear Sal:

I know what you're going through with David, baby, because I'm going through the same thing with Heidi. She still hasn't warmed up to any of my friends, and she sits around the house just waiting for me. Has it occurred to you how funny it is that we both ended up with people so much younger than ourselves? Sometimes, late at night, I sit in front of the fire and try to remember what split us up. The thing is, I don't know. It sure wasn't that we didn't love each other enough. Tell you what, I'll turn around, you kick me, then you turn around and I'll kick you.

I've got to figure out some way to get Heidi out of the house and off my back. I do love her. She's a wonderful girl. But maybe that's it. She's a girl, not a woman.

Take care of Belle and yourself.

Jake

SALLY ROSS

Monday the 10th.

Dear Jake,

Your letter arrived this morning. It's the only one in the mounting pile that I opened. Now, without being asked for it, I shall launch into one of my famous advice to the lovelorn columns.

I just don't understand it. I was always the hothead, you were the patient one. Now you sound all huffy and self-righteous. She's not even thirty yet. What do you expect? Being a wife to a man as important as you are is no easy task, believe me. If she feels out of place with your friends, she is. Your friends are all cocktail party monsters, and she's a young goat-milking girl from the mountains. Patience, my darling. Soon she'll discover her credit cards and spend her days scurrying in and out of Tiffany's and not care when you come home. So enjoy her vulnerability and humanness while she's got them. Besides, you do have a few minor flaws yourself. Like taking a woman by the elbow on the street but always walking a step in front of her, so she has to sidestep like a geisha. Or staring at a person as if you're listening for five minutes and then saying "What? I missed that."

Belle just called from the hospital. She thinks she remembers that just before she was attacked she heard someone call her name. I told her to call the police right away and tell them, but I don't understand. How could anyone who knew her do that to her, and risk getting caught for a few dollars? I think I'll head back to the hospital. Belle sounded upset. The house and mail can wait.

I love you and I wish you would keep your temper.

Y.G.S.

May 10, 1976

Dear Mr. Stern:

You are aware that my husband and I have been dissatisfied for some time with The Bradford because of our proximity to Miss Ross. Well, last night, or should I say early this morning, a difficult situation became intolerable.

At approximately two o'clock this morning, Miss Ross started to scream, not her usual lighthearted revels, but true screaming. Several of the residents, including my husband, rushed into the hallway and pounded on the door, to see if she was all right. The next sound we heard had to be the breaking of every dish and glass in her apartment. And more obscenities. At which point, she came to the door and told us all to go away. We went back into our apartments and tried to salvage what little sleep was left.

This morning several of the shareholders got together informally at my apartment. The point is this: If Miss Ross cannot be convinced to curb her late-night noisemaking, we are quite prepared to take legal action against her. I will call you on Thursday when my husband and I return from the country. I hope by then you can assure us of some meaningful progress.

Sincerely yours,
Mrs. Edith Patersonn

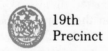 19th
Precinct

Stan—

Caplan wants you over at 941 Fifth Avenue, the Ross penthouse, as soon as you get in. Give Anderson whatever you've got left on the Williams case, as he'll be taking it over.

Willy

TO THE ENTIRE CAST AND CREW OF *SO I BIT HIM*

DUE TO ILLNESS, SALLY ROSS WILL BE UNABLE TO ATTEND REHEARS-
ALS FOR THE NEXT FEW DAYS. THE NEW OPENING FOR PREVIEWS IS
MAY 22. CHECK THE REHEARSAL SCHEDULE BELOW FOR YOUR CALLS.

LILYAN PETERS

May 11th, 1976

Dear Sal,

I called Belle at the hospital this afternoon and she told me
what happened. What a nightmare! I know the police are doing
everything they can, but wouldn't you feel safer out of New York
now? Forget the show; your safety comes first. Why don't you
fly out here and stay with me until the police catch him? You
shouldn't be alone now, Sal. I spoke to Jake and he thinks it's a
good idea, too.

Lil

SALLY ROSS

Tuesday the 11th.

Dear Jake,

Thank you for what you said on the phone this morning, but
you were wrong. I *am* responsible for what happened to Belle.
You said it was crazy to feel this way and maybe I am going a
little crazy. When I opened those letters and read them, I started
to scream. Oh my God, Jake, I should have known! Belle made a
joke of his letters, but I should have known that Belle never sees
danger until it's upon her. Now those letters are long since gone,
and all we know is his first name. Douglas. Belle has tried and tried
to remember his last name but she can't. We called her sister in
St. Louis. Belle sent her one of the letters, but she threw it away
and can't remember his name either. The only thing we do know

is that he works in a record store, but where? There are thousands of record stores in Manhattan alone.

In his letters he said that I knew where to write to him. What is he talking about? I don't even know who he is!

Paul Gross—my friend who's the trustee at Mt. Sinai—came over last night when I couldn't sleep again. I told him what the letters said as closely as I could remember. The police have them now. Paul said he sounds paranoid and that sometimes paranoids get sidetracked onto other delusions and never return. But could we ever be sure?!

Oh, Jake, I'm falling apart. I can't sleep or think of anything but my poor darling Belle.

No, darling, don't fly in. You have business you must attend to and I'm not alone. David is here and my detective is really more of a psychiatrist anyway. His name is Stan Johnston and he has two kids, and God love him, he even knows how to make me smile. But call me every night, please?

So much love,
Sal

"Destiny is written in the stars"

May 12th. 12:55 p.m.

Dear Miss Ross:

Lilyan Peters came to see me this morning about you. I am an astrologer and have aided the police in several investigations in the past. In order to be of service, I must first know the exact time, day and date of your birth. Miss Peters told me you are an Aquarian. In general, the next few weeks are ones of peace and contemplation for Aquarians, but I will need more specific information to be of greater help.

Most sincerely yours,
Marna Todd

May 12th, 1976

Dear Sally,

Still no reply from you.

What am I to think? Terrible thoughts have "crept" into my mind. Doubts about you, my love, my star. But even as these thoughts assailed me, I knew they had to be groundless. So I set out to disprove them once and for all. I knew that to go too near to your apartment might prove dangerous to us. But in the park not far from your residence is a "grassy knoll" from which one has an unobstructed view of the front entrance of your building. I was particularly attentive to the doorman with whom your ex-secretary had her clandestine exchange, but in three days, Sally, at the moment of mail delivery, that man was only there once! Other doormen were in evidence on the second and third days of my scrutiny! Therefore, my letters must have reached you!

Why then have you not replied to them?

A word, Sally, is all that I ask. No, I do not ask, I demand it. In the name of love. I have been so mistreated and maligned by persons I trusted in the past, it has not been easy for me to place my trust, newly washed clean with hope and love, in you. Only you can alleviate the doubts that torture my mind. I await your letter in much the same state that a drowning man awaits a breath of cool perfumed air.

Douglas

ST. BERNADETTE'S HOSPITAL
678 East 198th St., Bronx, N.Y. 10062

5/12

Dear Bess,

I've got a splitting headache right now, thanks to your call and Sal's visit. I wish you'd both calm down. He's not after me, and anyway I'm not a patient in this place anymore, I'm a prisoner. My room is kept locked, and if I set foot outside, some nurse moves up and hustles me back in here. So stop calling me every second. You're driving me nuts. And you're a pleasure compared to Sal. I'm supposed to stay calm so I can get well, but how am I supposed to be calm when Sal keeps crying that it's all her fault? It's nobody's fault, or if it is, it's mine. I was the one who answered his letters. I wish Sal would stop beating herself up over it. Today she said when this whole thing is over she's taking me on a spree all over Europe. Can you see that? Maybe we'll pick ourselves up a couple of gigolos in Rome and go on a toot. Believe me, I could use one. The one effect this tsurus has had on me is to show me you gotta live while you've got the chance. I'd sure like to see Paris. I already know how to say yes in French, so I'm halfway there, right?

Love to your gang,

Belle

19th
Precinct

Stan—

Burns called to tell you nothing on record stores in Manhattan and the girls are half through Brooklyn. Bronx is next. Caplan wants to know what's happening.

Willy

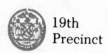

19th
Precinct

Willy,

Tell Caplan what's happening is that yesterday was my eleventh anniversary which I didn't get to go home for and my wife is stinking mad at me and we're working as fast as we can but nothing's happening, okay?

Stan

SALLY ROSS

Thursday the 13th

Dear Jake,

This morning another letter arrived from him. You know I'm not allowed to open my mail until Stan has seen it. Well, he didn't want me to read it and I didn't fight him. Just seeing the envelope gave me the shudders. But he said it was good news and gave them more to work with. He was almost gleeful. Oh, darling, wouldn't it be wonderful if this was it? I'm much calmer now, thanks mostly to Stan and Belle. She continues to get better every day, and I'm going back to rehearsals tomorrow. So you see, the old bag isn't quite the sissy she seemed.

I love you like always,

Y.G.S.

May 16th, 1976

Dear Sally,

Confusion reigns.

Not having heard from you, I knew I had to do something, so I sat down and made my plans, logically, coolly. I realize now that you are being watched far too closely to permit you to run the risk of communicating with me. I must be more patient. I must not give in to petulance or doubt or rash decisions, and I have not, my darling. Your well-being is in the hands of someone whose love makes him an "Einstein."

I knew that to watch your "comings and goings" from my previous perch atop the grassy knoll in the park might prove a mistake. (If my letters are being intercepted, wouldn't your guards place onlookers there?) So I took the Fifth Avenue bus at Seventy-ninth Street. As it moved downtown, past your dwelling, I carefully scrutinized all those on the street, on benches in front of the park, in parked cars. This proved to be no easy task. To be thorough in my examination required no less than six trips.

It was, to put it mildly, exhausting and expensive. But I did learn the following. One young man in jeans and a jacket that purported to be leather, but even from a distance was obviously vinyl, was seen by me on each and every trip! My worst suspicions have been confirmed! We are being watched. Do not be afraid, my darling. I will be near, of that you can be sure. But as in other perplexing situations, he wins who does not move too quickly. I shall mail this letter and then plan carefully and calmly. I pray that you, too, are calm.

Douglas

May 16th, 1976

Dear Sally,

A second epistle on the selfsame day!

But necessary, my darling, to tell you what is afoot. After mailing this afternoon's letter, I am sorry to say that no solution presented itself. Only one need gnawed at me—to see you. To assure myself that you are well, and to assuage these yearnings to hold and touch and make magnificent love to you.

So I ventured forth, this time to the vicinity of the theater, rather than your residence. And happy circumstance! Across the street from the theater, I saw a small coffee shop from which I could gain a perfect vantage point. I quickly went in and, not knowing how long my vigil might take, ordered a large meal. Surely the sight of someone lingering over an early dinner would arouse no suspicion.

Luck was to be on my side today, for hardly had three-quarters of an hour gone by when the stage door opened and various persons exited onto the street. From their apparel, I took them to be performers. And then, all my prayers were answered! Wearing a red velour pullover, black slacks that hugged your voluptuous body, and a black scarf tied around your hair, you appeared! My heart leapt! And broke. To be so close, my darling, and not to be able to run to you! The pain of love, as the poets have said. I know all too well their meaning.

546

But you were not alone. A man in a gray suit stood with you. He hailed a taxi and you both got in. Who is he, Sally? I pray he is a mere friend. If not, I will know what to do.

All the love that the sonnets of Shakespeare contain,

Douglas

SALLY ROSS

Monday the 17th.

Dear Jake,

Well, your gal Sal is back again. No more hysterics, no more acting like a jackass. It's glorious to be back in harness and, extraordinary as it seems, everybody worked miracles on the show in my absence. It's much tighter now.

Last night you asked about David and I hedged. It was too embarrassing to tell you on the phone, darling, and what with my playing the final scene from Camille all over the place lately, I forgot to write you about him. So here goes.

David, it turns out, is not precisely almost thirty years old. David is—heaven help me—twenty. Two-oh. Nineteen plus one. I could die. Jake, how can you tell a man's age these days with all the vitamins they shove in them? And not only is he just this side of puberty, but he still goes to school! (I'm going to be sick, I know it.) Granted, he goes to school at the Sorbonne, but he goes to school nevertheless. He's a history scholar and had to go back to Paris for the summer session. So on Thursday I drove my little friend to Kennedy and watched as he toddled onto a 747 for Paris. Then went home and hid under the covers.

I am that portion of a horse that passes through the stable door last.

If you write Belle, please don't mention anything about David. I don't want her to know just yet. She'd open her stitches yelling at me. I love you. Be well, my darling, and make a million so you can retire to a hilltop with Heidi.

Y.G.S.

Jo Colton

May 17.

Dear Sal,

Well, Sylvan just returned from town with our tickets. In seven days, we'll be clicking our tourist Brownies in front of the Kremlin. I still feel disloyal leaving the day before your previews start and with this cloud hanging over you, and we would never do so if you hadn't shrieked like a banshee at me. You have the key to the house. Please use it. There's firewood in the basement and food in the freezer. Will bring you something extravagant from Moscow.

All our love,
Jo and Sylvan

SALLY ROSS

Thursday the 20th.

Dear Jake,

It's almost over, my darling! This morning Belle's sister called from St. Louis. She remembered his name! It's Douglas Green. Stan almost leapt for joy. One more day before previews start. To think, we will have him put away before then!

Oh my Jakila, it's July Fourth, Bastille Day and V-E Day all rolled into one! Love, love, love,

Y.G.S.

SALLY ROSS

Friday the 21st.

Dear Jake,

This morning two letters arrived from him. Stan read them and said he's sure he's on the verge of showing himself. Lord, I hope so. Still haven't read the letters, which is just as well.

Incidentally, I was a touch optimistic yesterday. There are 23
D. Greens/Greenes in Manhattan, 20 in Brooklyn, 19 in the Bronx,
21 in Queens, and heaven knows how many on Long Island. As
Belle would say, I need this?

Y.G.S.

Western Union   Telegram

05/22/76 1253

```
MS SALLY ROSS, DLR BACKSTAGE
MOROSCO THEATRE 217 WEST 45TH ST
NEW YORK NY

JUST REMEMBER WHAT YOU STOLE FROM ME. LIL
```

Western Union   Telegram

05/22/76 1251

```
MISS SALLY ROSS, DLR BACKSTAGE
MOROSCO THEATRE 217 WEST 45TH STREET
NEW YORK NY

TONIGHT I HAD PRUNE JUICE, CREAM OF MUSHROOM
SOUP, PUREED PEAS AND TEA. SO WHAT ARE YOU
DOING? BELLE
```

Western Union   Telegram

05/22/76 245P

```
SALLY ROSS, DLR BACKSTAGE
MOROSCO THEATRE 217 WEST 45 ST
NEW YORK NY

SHAKE THOSE FEATHERS, BABY. JAKE
```

May 22nd, 1976

Dear Sally,

Would that this letter might contain nothing but advice on your first preview of *So I Bit Him*. Would that I could merely ramble on about that unflattering garb in the first act or that tawdry soliloquy that opens the second act. Yes, Sally, I was there. Alas, such advice will have to come later. For now, I am overcome with what I witnessed after the show. But I will relate all that happened in the order in which it occurred.

During the first act I sat gazing at my own "true love" and carefully made notes mentally—which lines worked, which did not, which performers lacked the necessary "presence." All that I might draw attention to to aid you in your newest endeavor. It was during the intermission, however, that all "hell broke loose."

I saw that man. The selfsame man you left rehearsal with mere days ago. He was standing at the rear of the orchestra, imbibing an orange drink with a woman and another man. As I moved closer, another couple joined the conversation. And the man to whom I have alluded was introduced as "Detective Johnson." Detective! My heart nearly burst through my suit! Surely it was just as I'd imagined. You are being hounded by the police!

How I sat through the second act I'll never know. Somehow, despite the presence of this man, I knew I had to get close enough to give you some sign, some small indication that I was at hand. So when the final curtain fell, I walked slowly out of the theater to the stage entrance. A small crowd was already forming, awaiting their chance to see you. It was easy to fall in with them, to pretend to be one of those tawdry little people.

My plan was ingenious. Inside my program I had written a message to you. I would merely ask for your autograph, and as you signed you would see the message. Finally, the door opened and you stepped through, on the arm of that man!

At first I thought he was restraining you, but you signed several autographs without his interference. I stepped back in the crowd, too frightened to carry out my task. Then it happened. You started to move off, but as you did, you took his arm again! And I heard you utter the words that made me go cold. You said to him, "You're coming to the party with me and that's that!"

Could those be the words of a victim to her persecutor? And the smile with which you entreated him! I stood riveted to the spot, watching you and this policeman disappear together.

Sally, what am I to think? Was it mere charade? Were you using your unique God-given acting ability to "pull the wool over his eyes?" I must know. I must know now.

I shall mail this letter immediately and shall expect a reply posthaste. It may be dangerous to get in touch with me, but you must find a way. As your future husband, I order it.

Douglas

P.S. My message was simply, "I love you. Do not be afraid."

SALLY ROSS

Sunday the 23rd

Dear Lil,

Thanks for the telegram, but I guess I didn't steal quite enough from you. The first preview was a disaster! Besides looking a hundred and ten, I apparently performed that way.

Tell me, Lil, how does retirement work? I'm thinking about going into that line.

Love,
Sal

May 23rd, 1976

Dear Sally,

I cannot endure this waiting, the black horrible thoughts that "worm" their way into my mind! And still no answer from you!

You must write quickly. Not only to put my mind at ease. There is another consideration. It was meant to be a surprise, but now I see I must tell you.

Sally, I know how exhausting preparing a show can be. So I arranged a respite for you. At considerable cost, I have reserved a splendid suite at a fashionable resort. It was my plan to take you there Saturday night, after your performance.

So you see, you must write to me *immediately. Immediately.*

If I do not hear from you, what recourse can I have but to think that you have been using me to rid yourself of those you wished gone, with no real concern for me?

Do not do that to me, Sally. Please.

Douglas

19th
Precinct

Stan—
Burns' office called. *David* Green of 1231 Ocean Drive, Rockaway, works for a distributor of Motown records.

Willy

SALLY ROSS

Monday the 24th.

Dear Jake,

Well, the next time you see me if I look like someone's great-grandmother, don't be surprised. I just had ten years added to my age from sheer fright.

A few days ago Stan told me not to leave the apartment without him. That didn't sit too well, I can tell you. I was sure this meant that the mugger was coming after *me*, but Stan assures me he's not. His letters are still filled with adoration, still pleading with me to write him. God, if only I knew *where* to write him, this nightmare would be over. Stan said it was only a matter of procedures, regulations, et cetera. I didn't buy any of it and Stan finally told me the truth. The man has been hanging around, trying to get a look at me. But not, Stan swears, to harm me. Just to look. Okay, so this morning I was sitting around, waiting for Stan to get here and the worst happened. I ran out of cigarettes. Now, Jake, you know my powers of self-control. I fixated somewhere at the four-year-old level. So, moron that I am, I thought I would take a quick trot around the corner and pick up a pack.

Well, darling, I got what was coming to me. In spades. As I came out of the grocery store, puffing away and thinking how brave I was, I saw him. A young man standing at the corner and pretending not to look at me but staring all the same. I clutched. By the time I'd puffed my way back to Fifth, I was practically in tears. Thank God, the first sight I saw was Stan, just going into the house. I ran to him, shrieking that the man was following me. And then I turned around and there he was, pretending he was going to cross the street! Now Stan takes me by the arm and leads me directly to the man! Every movie I ever saw was running full speed in my head. Stan was handing me over to the enemy. They were in it together. But when the sounds of my pulse pounding in my ears stopped sufficiently so that I could hear, I found out that the young man following me was a plainclothes policeman. It seems I've been watched by the police for days. Well, talk about your relief, your embarrassment. And then, talk about your lectures! He should give up police work and become a director.

All right, I've used your shoulder enough for one day and I'm already hideously late for rehearsal. Stan says he's going to carry me there in his coat pocket. Oh, would that he could!

Love from an ever so slightly shaking ex tobacco addict,
                                                                      Y.G.S.

                                                                      May 25th, 1976
Dear Sally,
    Two more days and still no answer. I am at my "wit's end" with you, Sally. Even in this, my moment of anguish, I do not want to think of you as anything but the Sally I've come to love. True, I now see another side of you, but surely it is not a "black"

side. Merely the childlike self-absorbed side of a woman who is used to being treated as if she were the only one who mattered. And generally speaking, that is true. But in this instance, Sally, I matter too. If I am to be your life mate, you must treat me with the care and concern with which I treat you. The rest of the world may like or "lump" it, but my feelings must be of utmost importance to you. Otherwise, how are we to have a fulfilled life together? If you've got it in your head that I would be satisfied basking in your shadow, you've got another think coming. But enough, for the moment. I feel myself getting angry with you, and I do not wish to be angry with the woman I love.

I expect your letter and full apology in the morning.

> With disappointment,
> Douglas

May 26th, 1976

Dear Sally,

After a sleepless night of soul-searching I now am forced to send you this, my ultimatum. If I do not hear from you within twenty-four hours, I wash my hands of you. You may think that, as a star, it is your due to treat those who care for you with utter lack of concern. But there is more than one kind of star. I am another and as such demand the treatment due me. One more day, Sally. That is all you have. And if you miss this opportunity, you will never hear from me again.

One day.

> Douglas

May 27th, 1976

Dear Sally,

You have lost.

Very well, it is on your head. I now believe the unthinkable. You used me for your own ends. You lied and schemed and took advantage of my innocent love for you. You truly are the "bitch"

I could not bring myself to believe you were. A self-centered, egomaniacal, ruthless "bitch."

Well, you shall have no more of my attention or my time. You are on your own now, and I'm sorry to say you deserve whatever happens to you. Pipers will be paid and you have run up quite a "bill" with yours.

When I think that two nights from now was to have been the beginning of our mutual ecstasy, the awakening of our love.

What a fool I've been.

What a stupid, naïve fool.

But even fools wake up, given enough provocation.

You must be taught a lesson—of that there can be no doubt. I do not know whether to let life catch up with you or whether to take it into my own very capable hands. As you doubtless know, I am *very good* at teaching lessons. If you don't believe me, ask Belle Goldman. She will tell you how I deal with those who would hurt me.

Douglas

CONTINENTAL **CS** STUDIOS

May 27, 1976

Dear Sal:

Okay, that's it. I'll be in New York on the 29th, soon as I tie up some loose ends here. I don't want to hear another word about it. Baby, who was the one who took care of me when I had infectious hepatitis? The name was Sal. Who was it who held my hand when Twentieth fired me? A kid named Sal. Who taught me what loving was all about? Sal.

Don't deny me my chance to act the big shot, will you? Even Heidi thinks I should go. Besides, a chance to get away from Franklin doesn't come up every day.

Love
Jake

ST. BERNADETTE'S HOSPITAL
678 East 198th St., Bronx, N.Y. 10062

5/27

Dear Bess,

Well, congratulate me. The shmendrick in white just dropped by to tell me they're letting me go home in a couple of days. It's going to be some relief to get out of here. Sal wants me to come stay with her, but much as I love her, I'm only comfortable in my own place. I tried to tell her that but it took her detective-in-waiting to convince her it wouldn't be a good idea to have me around the place. I asked him why and he hedged.

These damn bandages have got to stay on for another month, the shmendrick says. I must be some sight under all the gauze. Seems I'm going to need a little plastic surgery somewhere down the pike. Well, I was no beauty before. Maybe now's my chance. Love to your gang,

Belle

May 27th, 1976

Dear Bitch,

Are you worrying? I hope so, because believe me, you have a great deal to worry about.

Wouldn't it be too, too dreadful if that renowned face of yours met the same fate as that of your ex-secretary?

Delicious.

Absolutely delicious.

What makes it even more divine is that there's nothing you can do about it. Should you go to the police, you will have to incriminate yourself in the aforementioned assault.

Delicious. Absolutely delicious.

A former friend

May 27th, 1976

Dear Sally,

Hello again! I do hope you appreciate all the time and expense you are putting me through. But then, noblesse oblige. Sally, a word of warning. Gossip has it that a certain "gift" has been sent you. My advice is to open all packages *very carefully*, if you know what I mean. I surely wouldn't want anything to happen to you, now would I?

A former friend

 19th
Precinct

Stan—

Burns called to say they've drawn a blank on D. Greens and all record stores in the metropolitan area. What next?

Willy

SALLY ROSS

Thursday the 27th

Dear Jake,

Let me try to explain to you calmly and rationally why I don't want you here. First, your place is with Heidi, not me. Second, I am not alone. I have policemen constantly underfoot and Belle and all my friends.

Now here's the real reason. All my life, Jake, I've manipulated people into taking supporting roles in my life. You know it's true. If I'd ever let you share top billing in our marriage we'd still be together. I'm fifty years old now and my life is not what I wanted it to be. And that's clearly the reason. I know old dogs aren't supposed to change, but I must, if I'm to get any satisfaction from the years ahead. So I'm starting now. I adore you for wanting to come, but I can't fall back into my old pattern. All it gets you is

557

a big French rococo penthouse in which you live all alone. Please help me, Jake. I need, just once in my life, not to be selfish.

Today Stan and I took Belle home. She'll have a nurse staying with her, named, and could I make this up, Miss Priddy Ketchum. You know, I've never been to Belle's house before. The darling has plastered the place with pictures of me, her husband, who was truly funny-looking in a virile male way, and her family.

We get a letter from the mugger almost every day now, and Stan says it's the best sign possible. I still refuse to read them (not that I'd be allowed to anyway). I'm getting a wee bit of a case on Stan. He's like a burly, younger you, but without the space between the front teeth. Love, love and more love,

Y.G.S.

CONTINENTAL CS STUDIOS

May 29, 1976

Dear Sal:

You've never understood that you give as much as you take. All right, I won't come. But if you change your mind, don't keep it to yourself.

Love,
Jake

P.S. If your life isn't what you want it to be, it's because the world is full of idiots. Like me.

May 29th, 1976

Dear Sally:

I just realized a simply awful faux pas I unwittingly committed! And I'm so, so regretful. I didn't send you an opening-night present. Now, what to get you? "Hmmm."

They're doing wonderful things these days with guns. Or perhaps poison would be more appropriate. But let me think. What would really be appropriate for such as you?

I have it! Just the thing. Gorgeous! By the time you receive this letter, you will already have received my "gift."

I hope you liked it. Ciao for now.

A former friend

SALLY ROSS

Sunday the 30th.

Oh, Jake,

It's all so loathsome. So degenerate. I don't know if I can hold out until it's over. But of course you don't know what I'm talking about. Yesterday afternoon when I went into my dressing room, oh God, Jake, someone had ripped and hacked the place to pieces! Everything in shreds! Not someone. It was Him. Jake, the police have been lying to me all the time. His letters haven't been filled with love at all. He's after me now. Stan tried to deny it, but he couldn't. He says this is exactly what they want—that I'm constantly watched and if he gets near they'll catch him. But why didn't they catch him yesterday?! Honestly, Jake, it's like he's some kind of devil. If only we knew where he lived! He still thinks I do. Oh, Jake, I'm frightened. Truly, truly frightened.

Sal

 19th Precinct

Willy,

Arrange twenty-four-hour surveillance on the Morosco. Get Bridges up to the Goldman house in the Bronx. Find out where Stan is and have him call me.

Caplan

May 30th, 1976

Dear Sally:

Well, was it everything you had hoped for? I only wish I had been able to be there when you found your "gift," but you know what a heavy schedule I'm on these days. So much to do. So very many social obligations. It's all too too tiring. But fear not, Sally, I can always find time for you. And I do have another gift in mind. Of a more lasting nature. The kind one only gets once in a lifetime. Can you guess what it is? That's right. I am going to kill you.

Now, how shall we arrange it? You don't take the subway, and you have that cute policeman with you. "Hmmmm."

I will find a way. You know I will. There's nothing you can do to stop me. By now you must have surmised that I am no ordinary person and so it will be in no ordinary way.

A former friend

May 30th, 1976

Dear Phil,

Best to you and Ginnie, and am still smarting for not having seen you two way back when. Next trip we'll definitely get together and set the town on its ear.

Phil, I've got a little problem. Sally's doing a TV special in a few weeks, where she plays an assortment of roles. You know the type of show. Sketches, songs, dances. The problem is this. In one sequence she portrays a German spy in the Second World War, for which she needs a Luger pistol. Well, believe it or not, we are having one hell of a time finding one. But this morning I remembered you used to have a Luger. So, the favor is, have you still got it, is it in working condition (she's supposed to fire a few blanks) and can we borrow it? I'd sure appreciate it. Tell you what. You loan us the gun and the next time you and Ginnie come to town, Sally and I will make sure you have a time to tell your grandchildren about, okay?

Your friend,
Douglas Breen

May 31st, 1976

Dear Sally:

Well, it's all been too too tiring. What has? Why, deciding how to kill you, my dear. I want you to know all I'm going through for you so that you truly appreciate my efforts. Today I dashed out and did some comparison shopping on your behalf. Have you any idea of the price of a rifle with telescopic lens? My dear, they must think they're selling pure gold! But then everything is so high these days, isn't it? I saw a darling pistol, however, which was within my price range. Then I got to thinking, I'd have to get awfully close for it to do any serious damage to you, and there's still that policeman to deal with.

A word of warning. If you're thinking of telling the police where to find me, may I remind you of a few things. I would not hesitate for a moment to let the world know that your secretary's "accident" was your idea. I was merely your tool. I understand that before one loses consciousness in the gas chamber the odor of cyanide causes one to choke to death on one's own vomit. And frequently, one jolt of electricity in the electric chair is not enough to kill, merely to cause agony.

At least, I will be merciful.

Then, too, I might change my mind, mightn't I?

But then again, I might not.

What a quandary.

A former friend

June 2, 76

Dear Doug,

Sorry but when Ginnie and I got married my mother went on a rampage and cleaned out my room and threw away *all* my guns. Wish I could have helped you out. I don't understand why it's so hard to find a Luger in New York of all places. Have they tried Buy-Lines? Good luck with the show. You really are getting to be a big shot, aren't you?

Phil

SALLY ROSS

Wednesday the 2nd.

Dear Jake,

Thank you, darling. I know what I'm putting you through with my constant calls, but the sound of your voice is the only thing that helps. That and the pills the doctor gave me, and I suppose I'm overusing both.

Jake, I think about us so much now, about what we had together and what we didn't. There's something I want to confess to you, darling. Something I couldn't bring myself to say on the phone.

I always knew about you and that girl from Paramount. I knew when it began, when you and she would meet for lunch. I knew you were with her on that weekend in San Francisco. Do you remember what I did when you returned from that weekend? Remember the presents and how sweet and caring I was? It wasn't because I was afraid of losing you. I knew you loved me and not her. It was to hurt you, Jake. To make you agonize with guilt.

Forgive me, Jake. I know why you turned to her. Because I had robbed you of your dignity, your manhood and your self-esteem. The only fair thing I ever did was to let you go. I was fair in that, wasn't I? And now you have a new life—one that will give you everything I was too crippled to give, and I'm so happy for you.

These pills are really something. I can barely read what I'm writing. But I've got to wipe our slate clean just in case. No, I'm not being hysterical about the mugger. I now know what he plans to do. You see, today when Stan was out of the room, I took one of the letters from his jacket and read it. He's going to kill me. And I don't think anybody can stop him. The funny thing is, I don't know how I feel about it anymore. I've been afraid for so long, I'm getting numbed to it. Is life so dear that I should fight for it or would it be better to let it go, like I let you go?

I wish I could sleep. I wish I could walk out on the show. If this is ever over and I'm still alive, I'm going to do something. I don't know what, but I've got to do something to make the years that are left better. Who knows, perhaps I could even understand why Sally Flaherty needed everything and ended up with nothing. I'm sorry, darling. I'm being self-pitying and ugly.

I love you.

Sal

June 4th, 1976

Dear Detective Johnson:

Although we've never met, I hope you'll pardon my presumption in writing to you, care of Sally. You see, I am the man who had that little "set-to" with Belle Goldman, a fact for which I now feel more than a little regret. There are, however, so many mitigating circumstances of which you know nothing. Things are frequently not what they seem to a casual outsider, I assure you.

That brings me to the reason for this note. I wish to end this "cloud" which hangs over me. And so I am now willing to reveal to you and you alone the full facts and hidden meanings behind the aforementioned "set-to."

I will not, of course, set them down in this letter, lest "certain well-known personages" are precognizant of what I have to say. No, these facts will have to be given person-to-person.

Now, I am not such a fool that I would tell you where to meet me. That would indeed be foolhardy! Therefore, I make the following request. On the northwest corner of Eighth Avenue and Forty-eighth Street is a public telephone booth, the number of which I jotted down this morning. My suggestion is that you appear there at three o'clock next Tuesday afternoon and take possession of the booth. I will call you at precisely three twenty and tell you all that you wish to know—all those hidden aspects of which you know nothing.

Until next Tuesday at three, I remain, yours truly,

The Man You Have
Been Searching For

June 4th, 1976

Dear Phil,

Don't worry about it. As it turns out, Sally's crazed producer decided to have the German sketch updated to America in the fifties. I got a gun two days ago.

Your friend,
Douglas Breen
780 West 71st Street
New York City

CONTINENTAL CS STUDIOS

June 5, 1976

Dear Sal:

It kills me to see you torture yourself. I was the one to blame, not you. Never you, Sal.

I didn't have an affair with that girl. I just let you think so. You had just agreed to do another picture and leave me for two months. That's why I did it. To make you stay.

Our marriage went bad for only one reason. I wasn't good enough for you. But I did love you, Sal, and I still do. That'll never change. Please forgive me if you can.

Jake

· BELLE · GOLDMAN ·

6/7

Dear Bess,

Well, the shmendrick says I'm coming along fine, but he doesn't want me to go under the knife before the fall. They're going to fix me up with some kind of partial face mask for the summer. What a life. Did I write you I have a cop here during the days now? It's getting to be quite a bingo parlor. Me, Ketchum, my cop,

564

Sal, her cop, what a group. But at least there's a chance it may be over soon. The nut's going to talk to Sal's cop on the telephone tomorrow. Probably to repeat all that junk about Sal helping to plan his attack on me. This guy's so nutty he even gives crazy a bad name. Well, for once I'm glad he's nutty because maybe he'll buy what the cops are planning. They're going to try to convince him they believe him and that if he testifies against Sal, they'll let him off. I hope Sal's cop is a good talker.

Meanwhile, Sal is in terrible shape. She refuses to postpone that stinking show, keeps talking about always letting people down and that's why all this is happening. She won't lay off the pills, and she won't listen to reason. I don't understand it but it's breaking my heart.

All right, so now I'm upset enough for one day. I'll sign off and play pisha paysha with Ketchum. At least it keeps her shut up for a while. Love to your gang,

Belle

19th
Precinct

Rivera—

Caplan wants you to cover for Stan at the Ross penthouse. 941 Fifth. Stan should be back to relieve you in a couple of days. His leg is stiff but it was just a flesh wound.

Willy

SALLY ROSS

Wednesday the 9th.

Dear Jake,

Everyone close to me is in peril. First Belle, now Stan. How could he shoot him in that telephone booth and still get away? He's not human, Jake. He couldn't be. I'm not allowed to leave the apartment now to see Belle or to go to rehearsals. But it won't make any difference. I'm going to die. I know it.

Don't let Belle stay alone in New York. Make her move to California and don't mind her complaining. It's just the way she is. She doesn't mean anything by it.

I want to sleep. I'll write you every day until it's over.

Sal

P.S. There's nothing to forgive. It wasn't your fault, darling. It was mine.

June 9th, 1976

Dear Sally,

I see in today's paper that Gretchen Wyler is playing your role in previews of *So I Bit Him.* Whyever? Are you too frightened to pursue your own all-important career?

I'm sorry to have killed your little detective. He was always with you, you see, and I had to show you that nothing can stop me.

It was so simple. I merely hid on a low rooftop and awaited him. Why are they keeping it out of the papers? Isn't the public entitled to know everything about their sacred cow, you?

Last night I dreamt of us. We dwelt in a mansion of many rooms, sun and flower filled, bursting with joy. You gave yourself to me several times in that dream and the ecstasy surpassed my wildest desires. And then you told me you forgave my every action and that you understood they were necessitated by my love for you.

You see, strange as it seems, I do still regard you with vestiges of love, although I know you to be the kind of woman no one should love.

You must return to the show. Gretchen is marvelous, of course, but can you deny the world that special magic that is yours alone? Can you be that selfish? Of course you can. I forget to whom I am speaking. Soon, Sally. I shall kill you soon.

I tire of this charade.

Douglas

SALLY ROSS

Thursday

Dear Jake,

I have a nurse now. I don't know what's happening to me. The pills, I suppose. She only gives me one at a time but they don't work. When I finally drift off to sleep, it's worse than when I can't. Before my mother died she used to stare out of the hospital window, hour after hour, as I stare out of my window now. The city is so beautiful. Do you remember how beautiful it was in the forties? I was beautiful then, too, wasn't I? And you, so sweet and shy and strong.

One pill at a time and no liquor. She makes me tea. Can you imagine that? It's funny, isn't it? I'm not frightened anymore. It's a blessing not to be frightened. I've always been frightened, did you know that? When I was little, sometimes the fear was so great I'd hide for hours. But I'm not frightened now.

Sal

June 10th, 1976

Dear Sally,

Another dream of you as you once were. We were walking, hand in hand, and you stroked my face and told me you loved me. And the light that shone from your eyes! I can't bear what has happened to us! I can't bear hating the only person I've ever loved! Is it possible I've misjudged you? Is it possible you wanted to write but knew that would lead my enemies to me? I am plagued with doubts. If only I could see you, speak with you, hear the utterances I yearn to hear from your own lips. If I have been wrong, what can I do? How would you ever forgive me? Sally, I want, more than life itself, to love you again.

Douglas

CONTINENTAL **CS** STUDIOS

June 11, 1976

Dear Sal:

I've never been good at expressing how I feel, but now I've got to try. I'm afraid for you, honey. Not only because of that man, but because of something in you. Something that was always there but is exploding out of all proportion.

It's a way you have of hiding, of covering up what you really feel. As if you think the real Sally Flaherty needs to be hidden away for fear that if people saw her they'd run. It's why you always checked yourself from the outside. And probably why you became Sally Ross in the first place. Sal, I swear to you there's nothing in you that needs to be hidden away. You don't deserve any punishment, honey. You've never done anything to earn it. Please, Sal, please go easier on yourself. And please don't take so many pills. It's making it all worse. I love you.

Jake

SALLY ROSS

Friday

Dear Jake,

No sleep again. I wandered through the apartment in the middle of the night and by accident woke up the policewoman who stays with me now. She came charging out of her room with a gun. With a gun, Jake! It's all so funny.

I'm not staying here anymore. I don't care what happens. I'm going away. I know they won't let me, so I'll have to leave at night when she's asleep. I know where I want to be and what I want to see before I die. I love you. Good-by.

Sal

June 11th, 1976

Dear Sally,

What can I do? After what I did to that detective, I know they won't permit you to leave your apartment to talk to me. I can't get your number, for it's unlisted. I must talk to you. Please, please, Sally, call me. You know my address. I can't give you my phone number, lest they read this letter, but you can look it up. Please call, Sally. Guilt hounds me at every turn. Despite everything I've done and said, I love you. I won't harm you. I never would have. The fact that you have not told the police where to find me leads me to think you do care for me, for surely it cannot be only fear that keeps you silent. I'd die for you, Sally. If you don't forgive me, I will die for you.

Douglas

SALLY ROSS

Saturday

Dear Jake,

She caught me last night. But not tonight. I have three pills I didn't take. I'll crush them and put them in her dinner. I only hope he doesn't kill me before I get there.

You always made me so happy.

Sal

Western Union　　　　　　　　**Telegram**

06/12/76 1384

MR. JAKE BURMAN, DLR
CONTINENTAL STUDIOS
LOS ANGELES, CAL.

SAL HAS DISAPPEARED. DO YOU KNOW WHERE SHE IS?
COULDN'T REACH YOU. I'M SICK WITH WORRY.
PLEASE CALL QUICKLY. BELLE

Jo Colton

Sunday

Dear Jake,

It's done, and now I'm alone—finally, mercifully alone. And so peaceful, my darling.

I walked up and down beside the ocean this afternoon. It's so utterly beautiful, Jake. That's why I wanted to be here. To see the ocean and the sky. Just to have seen it, to have experienced the incredible grandeur of the world is enough. Could there be anything more beautiful?

I've come to understand so many things in the past few weeks. It's as though I've come through a long dark passageway into the blessed light. It really doesn't matter what happens now. Because I've seen the ocean and the sky. There were sandpipers on the beach. Their lives are so short and yet still glorious. You see, it doesn't matter how long life lasts. The point is just to glimpse it, if only for a moment.

I love you. I've always loved you. I always will love you. You, Belle, the ocean and the sky. What a rich life I've had!

And if it's over, well then, it's over. If he kills me today, know that my last thoughts were of you.

Sal

June 15th, 1976

Dear Sally,

It's hopeless, isn't it? I have murdered more than a man. I have murdered our life together and the only love I have ever known.

I know now that there is no way out for us. Life without you is meaningless. By the time you read this letter I will be dead.

I die willingly for the torment I have caused you. I die happily because my death proves that I loved you as few men have ever loved. I die joyously for I have known the joy of your love. I beg your forgiveness for all I have done to pain you.

570

I wish you a life filled with joy, for that, and that alone, is what you deserve. You are a God to me.

Good-by, my Sally, my dearest, my love.

Douglas

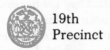

Stan—

I sent the photographs of the charred body to Harris, as well as photostats of the letter to Sally Ross that was near the body. Caplan says now that the Ross case is wrapped up he wants you back on Williams.

Willy

· B E L L E · G O L D M A N ·

6/18

Dear Bess,

I'm sitting here in Sal's apartment having my second gin and tonic (all right, my third), Sal's in the tub singing and I'm so happy I could bust. I intend to get so roaring drunk that her majesty next door will move to Connecticut!

Look, I deserve it. I've had a couple of days that would put a Mack truck in its grave. Until Jake finally called to tell us where Sal was, I thought I'd drop dead from fear. I thought *he* had her. Then when we found out he killed himself, oh, Bess, I never in my life knew what relief was until that moment. But what a way to do it! He poured gasoline all over himself like one of those crazy monks. All I can say is thank God it's over.

My poor Sal. What she's been through! When we got to Shelter Island, she was sitting there in the Coltons' house, staring at the ocean, just waiting. For him, I guess. When we told her he was dead she just looked at us. First at Stan, then at me. For a minute

571

I got scared that she really had flipped out, but then, thank God, she started to cry. All the way back to the city I held her in my arms and she cried—to tell you the truth, so did I—while Stan sat up front beaming like a moron. I like that one. He's my date for opening night. (Don't get excited—he's married.) Tomorrow Sal goes back into rehearsals. They say the show's in pretty good shape now and the opening's been set for week after next.

Oh, look who just came in the room fresh from her bath with a piece of Sara Lee in her hand. Hold on, I gotta go smack her.

Hello again. Tonight we're staying home and watching TV, although certain ex-movie queens think they're going out to kick up their heels. I'll kill her. Wait, I take it back. That's not funny. Love to your gang,

Belle

SALLY ROSS

Tuesday the 29th.

Dear Jake,

Well, the opening is finally here. An hour and a half away. Do you realize this is the first letter I've written you in weeks! I wasn't kidding when I said I was swearing off letters. But tonight the circuits are busy and I think I already owe the telephone company my first month's percentage. Oh darling, I still can't believe it's over, and that he's dead instead of me. It's so wonderful to be normal again. I'm so gloriously happy! Belle is screaming that we've got to go. I'll finish this letter after the opening-night party—even if I can't see straight. Have I mentioned I love you?

June 29th, 1976

Dear Sally,

You will never read this letter, my darling. I am writing it so the world will know a love such as ours existed.

No, my darling, I am far from dead. That charred body was

not mine. It was the body of a sacrificial "lamb," a carefully selected lost soul whose acquaintance I had made. I regretted having
to end his life, but what could I do? How else could I assure those
around you that there was no further need for them? How else
could I ensure your return to the show? For both were necessary.

I shall not mail this letter. It will be found in my pocket after
you and I share that most intimate of love acts, death. I shall be
sitting in the first row at your opening tonight. The gun I carry
will unite us for all eternity. You will die as you have lived, in the
glory and glow of starlight, and I will die in the reflection of that
glow. It is mere hours away now, Sally. Mere hours before nothing
can part us ever again.

Sally, my own, my treasure, my beloved.

Douglas

Epilogue

The following letters arrived at Sally Ross's apartment the day
after her death.

ARNO FLORIST
Sag Harbor

June 27, 1976

Dear Miss Ross:

I have been trying to contact Mr. Douglas Breen of 780 West
71st Street, New York City, without success in regard to his bill.
Mr. Breen sent me a check for thirty-five dollars on account for
flowers delivered to the Water's Edge Inn on May 29th. The
manager of the inn told me you were to be Mr. Breen's companion
for the weekend. The flowers were delivered but there is $25.35
due. I would appreciate payment as soon as possible.

Sincerely yours,
Morton Fry

CONTINENTAL **CS** STUDIOS

June 29, 1976

Sal:

By the time you get this letter, I'll be somewhere over the Grand Canyon, facing east. Look for me after the show Wednesday night. Baby, now that you've proven whatever it was you had to prove, you can't stop me from coming. It's for *my* sake now. Heidi and I have decided to call it quits. She's a nice girl, but I don't think I can settle for a nice girl. Not when I'm still used to a great one. I've got so much to say to you, Sal. I couldn't even start on the phone or I would've broken down and cried, which is why this letter. Look for me, darling. Wednesday night.

Jake

Actor, Playwright, Author—A Man of Parts

Bob Randall, the creator of Sally Ross and her "greatest fan," has had strong ties to the theater for years. After graduation from New York University in 1958 he joined the American Savoyards, a Gilbert and Sullivan operetta company, as understudy to the actor who played comedy leads. This actor proved to be remarkably robust, even appearing onstage in a wheelchair after breaking his leg. In three years Randall never made it out of the chorus. By that time a stage career had begun to lose its appeal. He was planning to be married and didn't think his fifteen-dollar-a-week salary would support a family. He had also decided to earn his living as a writer.

There followed a stint in advertising as a copywriter and, later, a creative director. However, Randall's weekends were devoted to teaching himself to write. It took a scant ten years, during which he literally filled cupboards with his work—at first songs and nightclub skits, most of which never sold. One of his revues closed after two days and was called "interminable" by a *New York Times* drama critic. Finally Randall got an idea for a play in which a man and a woman meet and fall in love while apartment hunting. A year later *6 Rms Riv Vu* was drawing full houses on Broadway. After that he wrote another hit play, *The Magic Show*, and he says, "I've been a writer ever since."

Bob Randall

The most difficult part of the craft, according to Bob, was learning to expose his feelings. He explains that his fiction, like that of many authors, is rooted firmly in life, and his characters represent aspects of his own personality.

Even Douglas Breen, the fan? "Yes," says Randall without hesitation. "Douglas is my rage, my anger, my loneliness. Sally is an extension of my need to be the focal point. I think I also have her ability to love a friend with such devotion. And I have Belle's impatience with people who injure themselves."

The Fan is Randall's first novel, and now that he has his toe in the water, he's planning three more. He'll also be masterminding a TV series about career girls, which he has sold to CBS.

Bob Randall expects to be busy for the next ten years. Today he makes his home in an elegant Manhattan duplex, where his children, Julia and Edward, love to slide down the banisters.

ACKNOWLEDGMENT

Page 3: toy horse-drawn pumper, c. 1874, courtesy of the
SmithKline Corporation.